Jilly Cooper is a journa
The author of many
including *Riders*, *Rivals*,
Jealous, *Appassionata*,
Gloucestershire with
greyhound, Feather, and five cats. She was appointed
OBE in the 2004 Queen's Birthday Honours List for
her contribution to literature.

Visit the author's website at www.jillycooper.co.uk

'Cooper skilfully weaves her vast cast of characters' stories into a seamless whole and punctuates it all with extremely funny jokes, her customary kindness, even to the initially unloveable and the verve and zippiness that are her trademark ... Most remarkably of all, she gets better and better with age ... When I got my hands on a copy of *Wicked!*, it quickly became clear that I would have to put my life on hold for the rest of the week, and I did, ignoring deadlines, leaving children unfed, until I'd galloped through each of its 800-odd pages (which frequently involved staying up half the night, gripped)' India Knight, *Waterstones Books Quarterly*

'First-class reading pleasure' Rachel Johnson, *Tatler*

'Unbeatable beach reading' *The Week*

'Lots of high jinks and general naughtiness ... it's vintage Cooper' Rachel Cooke, *Observer*

'A hugely enjoyable romp with teenage hormones, teacher lust and toy boys galore' Richard and Judy in the *Daily Express*

'Perfect escapist entertainment' Ian Rankin writing for *The Guardian Review*

'Completely lovely and full of hilariously beautiful people. I always hate finishing her books' Marina Hyde, *Guardian*

''Cooper has tremendous fun with this clash of the classes' Toby Clements, *Daily Telegraph*

'The perfect beach companion' Wendy Holden, *Daily Mail*

'Hilarious and daring' Joanna Briscoe, *Guardian*

www.**books**at**transworld**.co.uk

Also by Jilly Cooper

FICTION	Pandora
	The Rutshire Chronicles:
	Riders
	Rivals
	Polo
	The Man Who Made Husbands Jealous
	Appassionata
	Score!
NON-FICTION	Animals in War
	Class
	How to Survive Christmas
	Hotfoot to Zabriskie Point (with Patrick Lichfield)
	Intelligent and Loyal
	Jolly Marsupial
	Jolly Super
	Jolly Superlative
	Jolly Super Too
	Super Cooper
	Super Jilly
	Super Men and Super Women
	The Common Years
	Turn Right at the Spotted Dog
	Work and Wedlock
	Angels Rush In
	Araminta's Wedding
CHILDREN'S BOOKS	Little Mabel
	Little Mabel's Great Escape
	Little Mabel Saves the Day
	Little Mabel Wins
ROMANCE	Bella
	Emily
	Harriet
	Imogen
	Lisa & Co
	Octavia
	Prudence
ANTHOLOGIES	The British in Love
	Violets and Vinegar

WICKED!

JILLY COOPER

CORGI BOOKS

TRANSWORLD PUBLISHERS
61-63 Uxbridge Road, London W5 5SA,
a division of The Random House Group Ltd
www.booksattransworld.co.uk

WICKED!
A CORGI BOOK: 9780552156035

PRINTING HISTORY
Bantam edition published 2006
Corgi edition published 2007

Copyright © Jilly Cooper 2006

Jilly Cooper has asserted her right under the Copyright, Designs and
Patents Act 1988 to be identified as the author of this work.

This book is a work of fiction and, except in the case of historical fact,
any resemblance to actual persons, living or dead, is purely coincidental.

The author and publishers are grateful for permission to quote
from 'Three Little Birds', Words and Music by Bob Marley.
© Copyright 1977 Blue Mountain Music Limited. Used by
permission of Music Sales Limited. All Rights Reserved.
International Copyright Secured.

A CIP catalogue record for this book
is available from the British Library

This book is sold subject to the condition that it shall not,
by way of trade or otherwise, be lent, re-sold, hired out,
or otherwise circulated without the publisher's prior
consent in any form of binding or cover other than that
in which it is published and without a similar condition,
including this condition, being imposed on the
subsequent purchaser.

Addresses for Random House Group Ltd companies outside
the UK can be found at: www.randomhouse.co.uk
The Random House Group Ltd Reg. No. 954009

The Random House Group Ltd makes every effort to ensure that the
papers used in its books are made from trees that have been
legally sourced from well-managed and credibly certified
forests. Our paper procurement policy can be found at:
www.randomhouse.co.uk/paper.htm

Typeset in 10/12pt New Baskerville by
Falcon Oast Graphic Art Ltd.

Printed and bound in Germany by
GGP Media GmbH, Poessneck

Every effort has been made to obtain the necessary permissions
with reference to copyright material, both illustrative and quoted.
We apologize for any omissions in this respect and will be pleased
to make the appropriate acknowledgements in any future edition.

This book is dedicated with love and admiration to two great headmistresses, Virginia Frayer and Katherine Eckersley, and also in loving memory of the Angel School, Islington, and Village High School, Derby

CAST OF CHARACTERS

ADELE
Single mother who teaches geography at Larkminster Comprehensive (otherwise known as Larks).

PARIS ALVASTON
Larks pupil and icon. Founder member of the notorious Wolf Pack.

ANATOLE
Bagley Hall pupil and beguiling son of the Russian Minister of Affaires.

RUFUS ANDERSON
Brilliant and eccentric head of geography at Bagley Hall. Henpecked father of two, liable to leave coursework on trains.

SHEENA ANDERSON
Rufus's concupiscent careerist wife – the main reason Rufus hasn't been given a house at Bagley Hall.

MRS AXFORD
Chief caterer at Bagley Hall.

MISS BASKET
A menopausal misfit who teaches geography at Larks.

BEA FROM THE BEEB
A researcher at the Teaching Awards.

DORA BELVEDON	Bagley Hall new girl. Determined to support her pony and her chocolate Labrador by flogging school scandal to the tabloids.
DICKY BELVEDON	Dora's equally resourceful twin brother who runs his own school shop at Bagley Hall selling booze and fags.
LADY BELVEDON (ANTHEA)	Dicky and Dora's young, very pretty, very spoilt mother. A Violet Elizabeth Bottox, drastically impoverished by widow-hood, and determined to hunt for a rich new husband, unobserved by her beady son and daughter.
JUPITER BELVEDON	Dora and Dicky's machiavellian eldest brother, chairman of the governors at Bagley Hall, Tory MP for Larkminster, and tipped to take over the party leadership.
HANNA BELVEDON	Jupiter's lovely and loving wife, a painter.
SOPHY BELVEDON	An English teacher of splendid proportions and great charm. Ian and Patience Cartwright's daughter, and wife of Jupiter Belvedon's younger brother, Alizarin.

DULCIE BELVEDON	Adorable and self-willed daughter of Sophy and Alizarin.
SIR HUGO BETTS	Governor of Larks who sleeps through most meetings.
JAMES BENSON	An extremely smooth private doctor.
THE BISHOP OF LARKMINSTER	A governor of Bagley Hall.
GORDON BLENCHLEY	The unsavoury care manager of Oaktree Court, Paris Alvaston's children's home.
HENGIST BRETT-TAYLOR	Hugely charismatic head-master of Bagley Hall.
SALLY BRETT-TAYLOR	Hengist's wife, classic beauty and jolly good sort, hugely contributory towards Hengist's success.
ORIANA BRETT-TAYLOR	Hengist and Sally's daughter, a much admired BBC foreign correspondent.
WALLY BRISTOW	Stalwart site manager at Larks.
GENERAL BROADSTAIRS	Lord Lieutenant of Larkshire and governor of Bagley Hall.
'BOFFIN' BROOKS	The cleverest boy at Bagley Hall, a humourless prig.
SIR GORDON BROOKS	Boffin's father, a thrusting captain of industry.

ALEX BRUCE	Deputy head of Bagley Hall, nicknamed Mr Fussy.
POPPET BRUCE	His dreadful wife, who teaches RE. An acronymphomaniac, determined to impose total political correctness on Bagley Hall.
CHARISMA BRUCE	Alex and Poppet's severely gifted daughter.
MARIA CAMBOLA	Larks's splendidly flamboyant head of music.
RUPERT CAMPBELL-BLACK	Former showjumping champion and Tory Minister for Sport. Now leading owner/trainer, and director of Venturer, the local ITV station. Despite being as bloody-minded as he is beautiful, Rupert is still Nirvana for most women.
TAGGIE CAMPBELL-BLACK	His adored wife – an angel.
XAVIER CAMPBELL-BLACK	Bagley Hall pupil and Rupert and Taggie's adopted Colombian son, who has hit moody adolescence head-on.
BIANCA CAMPBELL-BLACK	Xavier's ravishingly pretty, sunny-natured younger sister, also adopted and Colombian.

IAN CARTWRIGHT	Former commanding officer of a tank regiment, now bursar at Bagley Hall.
PATIENCE CARTWRIGHT	Ian's loyal wife – a trooper who teaches riding and runs the stables at Bagley.
MRS CHALFORD	Head of history at Larks. A self-important bossy boots who likes to be referred to as 'Chally'.
TARQUIN COURTNEY	Charismatic captain of rugger at Bagley Hall.
ALISON COX	Sally Brett-Taylor's housekeeper, known as 'Coxie'.
JANNA CURTIS	Larks's very young, Yorkshire-born headmistress.
P.C. CUTHBERT	A zero-tolerant police constable, determined to impose order on Larks.
DANIJELA	Larks pupil from Bosnia.
DANNY	Larks pupil from Ireland.
EMLYN DAVIES	A former Welsh rugby international, known as Attila the Hunk, who teaches history at Bagley Hall and coaches the rugger fifteens to serial victory.
DEBBIE	Ace cook at Larks.
ARTIE DEVERELL	Head of modern languages at Bagley Hall.

ASHTON DOUGLAS	The sinister, lisping Chief Executive Officer of S and C Services, the private company brought in by the Government to supervise education in Larkshire.
ENID	Lachrymose librarian at Larks.
PRIMROSE DUDDON	Earnest, noble-browed, ample-breasted form prefect at Bagley Hall.
VICKY FAIRCHILD	Two-faced but both of them extremely pretty. Cures truancy at Larks overnight when Janna Curtis appoints her as head of drama.
JASON FENTON	Larks's deputy head of drama, known as Goldilocks.
PIERS FLEMING	Wayward head of English at Bagley Hall.
JOHNNIE FOWLER	Good-looking Larks hell-raiser; BNP supporter; persistent truant.
LANDO FRANCE-LYNCH	Master of the Bagley Beagles, whose sparse intellect is compensated for by dazzling all-round athletic and equestrian ability.
DAISY FRANCE-LYNCH	His sweet mother, a painter, wife of Ricky France-Lynch, former England polo captain.

FREDDIE	A waiter at La Perdrix d'Or restaurant.
CHIEF INSPECTOR TIMOTHY GABLECROSS	A wise, kind and extremely clever policeman.
MAGS GABLECROSS	The wise, kind wife of the Chief Inspector, part-time modern languages teacher at Larks.
GLORIA	PE teacher at Larks not given to hiding her physical lights under bushels.
THEO GRAHAM	Head of classics at Bagley Hall, an outwardly crusty old bachelor with a heart of gold. Takes out his hearing aid on Speech Day.
GILLIAN GRIMSTON	Head of Searston Abbey, an extremely successful Larkminster grant-maintained school for girls.
LILY HAMILTON	Aunt of Jupiter, Dicky and Dora Belvedon. A merry, very youthful octogenarian and Janna Curtis's next-door neighbour in the village of Wilmington.
DAME HERMIONE HAREFIELD	World famous diva, seriously tiresome, brings out the Crippen in all.
WADE HARGREAVES	An unexpectedly humane Ofsted Inspector.
DENZIL HARPER	Head of PE at Bagley Hall.

UNCLE HARLEY	Jamaican drugs dealer, lives on and off with Feral Jackson's mother.
SIR DAVID 'HATCHET' HAWKLEY	Headmaster of Fleetley, illustrious classical scholar. Later Lord Hawkley.
LADY HAWKLEY (HELEN)	A nervy beauty. Having numbered Rupert Campbell-Black and Roberto Rannaldini among her former husbands, Helen hopes marriage to David Hawkley means calmer waters.
ROD HYDE	An awful autocrat, head-master of St James's, a highly successful Larkminster grant-maintained school, known as St Jimmy's.
'SKUNK' ILLINGWORTH	Deputy head of science at Larks.
'FERAL' JACKSON	Larks's leading truant, Paris Alvaston's best friend and founder member of the Wolf Pack. Afro-Caribbean, beautiful beyond belief, seriously dyslexic, and a natural athlete.
NANCY JACKSON	Feral's mother, a heroin addict.
JESSAMY	A teaching assistant at Larks.

JESSICA   Hengist Brett-Taylor's stunning second secretary, a typomaniac.

JOAN JOHNSON   Head of science at Bagley Hall, also in charge of Boudicca, the only girls' house. Nicknamed 'No-Joke Joan' because of a total lack of humour.

MRS KAMANI   Long-suffering owner of Larks's nearest newsagent's.

KATA   Larks pupil and wistful asylum-seeker from Kosovo.

AYSHA KHAN   One of Larks's few achievers. Destined for an arranged marriage in Pakistan.

RASCHID KHAN   Aysha's bullying father.

MRS KHAN   Aysha's bullied but surprisingly brave mother.

RUSSELL LAMBERT   Ponderous chairman both of Larks's governors and Larkminster planning committee.

LANCE   An understandably terrified newly qualified Larks history teacher.

AMBER LLOYD-FOXE   Minxy founder member of the 'Bagley Babes', otherwise known as the 'Three Disgraces'.

BILLY LLOYD-FOXE	Amber's father, an ex-Olympic showjumper, now a presenter for the BBC.
JANEY LLOYD-FOXE	His unprincipled journalist wife.
JUNIOR LLOYD-FOXE	Amber's merry, racing-mad twin brother.
LYDIA	Another understandably terrified newly qualified Larks English teacher.
LUBEMIR	Albanian asylum-seeker and safe-breaker, which makes him an extremely useful partner-in-crime to Cosmo Rannaldini.
MR MATES	Larks science master, almost as old as Archimedes.
KITTEN MEADOWS	Larks pupil and sassy, hell-cat girlfriend of Johnnie Fowler.
JOE MEAKIN	Under-master in Alex Bruce's house at Bagley Hall.
ROWAN MERTON	School secretary at Larks.
MRS MILLS	A jolly member of Ofsted.
MISS MISERDEN	Old biddy endlessly complaining about Larks misbehaviour.
TEDDY MURRAY	Randal Stancombe's foreman.
NADINE	Paris Alvaston's social worker.

MARTIN 'MONSTER' NORMAN	Larks pupil. Overweight bully and coward.
'STORMIN'' NORMAN	Larks parent governor and Monster's mother, given to storming into Larks and punching anyone who crosses her ewe lamb.
MISS PAINSWICK	Hengist Brett-Taylor's besotted and ferociously efficient secretary.
CINDY PAYNE	Deceptively cosy New Labour county councillor in charge of education.
KYLIE ROSE PECK	Sweet-natured Larks pupil and member of the Wolf Pack. So eternally up the duff, she'll soon qualify for a free tower block.
CHANTAL PECK	Kylie Rose's mother and also a parent governor at Larks.
CAMERON PECK	Kylie Rose's baby son.
GANYMEDE	Another baby son of Kylie Rose.
COLIN 'COL' PETERS	Editor of the *Larkminster Gazette*. A big, nasty toad in a small pond.
PHIL PIERCE	Head of science at Larks, loved by the children and a great supporter of Janna Curtis.

MIKE PITTS	Larks's deputy head, furious the head's job has been given to Janna Curtis.
COSMO RANNALDINI	Dame Hermione's son and Bagley Hall warlord, with a pop group called the Cosmonaughties and the same lethal sex appeal as his father, the great conductor Roberto Rannaldini.
DESMOND REYNOLDS	Smooth Larkminster estate agent known as 'Des Res'.
ROCKY	Larks pupil and ungentle giant until the Ritalin kicks in.
BIFFO RUDGE	Head of maths at Bagley Hall, ex-rowing Blue, who frequently rides his bike into the River Fleet while coaching the school eight.
ROBBIE RUSHTON	Larks's incurably lazy, left-wing head of geography.
CARA SHARPE	Larks's fearsome head of English and drama.
'SATAN' SIMMONS	Larks bully and best friend of Monster Norman.
SMART	Stalwart Bagley Hall rugger player.
PEARL SMITH	Another Larks hell-cat, member of the Wolf Pack.
MISS SPICER	An unfazed member of Ofsted.

SAM SPINK	Bossy-boots union representative at Larks.
SOLLY THE UNDERTAKER	Governor at Larks.
RANDAL STANCOMBE	Handsome Randal, definitely Mr Dicey rather than Mr Darcy, a wildly successful property developer. One of his private estates of desirable residences, Cavendish Plaza, sits uncomfortably close to Larks.
JADE STANCOMBE	Randal's daughter, sharp-clawed glamourpuss and Bagley Babe.
MISS SWEET	Beleaguered under-matron at Boudicca, reluctantly put in charge of Bagley's sex education.
CRISPIN THOMAS	Incurably greedy deputy director of S and C Services.
TRAFFORD	An unspeakably scrofulous but highly successful artist.
GRANT TYLER	An electronics giant.
MISS UGLOW	Larks RE teacher.
PETE WAINWRIGHT	Genial under-manager at Larkminster Rovers, the local second division football club.
BERTIE WALLACE	Raffish co-owner of Gafellyn Castle in Wales.

RUTH WALTON	A ravishing adventuress, voted on to Bagley Hall's board of governors to ensure full houses at meetings.
MILLY WALTON	The third Bagley Babe, charming and emollient but overshadowed by her gorgeous mother.
THE HON. JACK WATERLANE	Bagley Hall thicko, captain of the Chinless Wanderers.
LORD WATERLANE	Jack's father, who shares his son's fondness for rough trade.
STEWART 'STEW' WILBY	Powerful and visionary headmaster of Redfords, Janna Curtis's former school in the West Riding. Also Janna's former lover.
SPOTTY WILKINS	Bagley Hall pupil.
DAFYDD WILLIAMS	Sometime builder and piss artist.
'GRAFFI' WILLIAMS	Dafydd's son, and captivating, conniving fifth member of the Wolf Pack. Nicknamed 'Graffi' for his skill at spraying luminous paint on buildings.
BRIGADIER CHRISTIAN WOODFORD	A delightful octogenarian, hugely interested in matters military and his beautiful neighbour, Lily Hamilton.
MISS WORMLEY	English mistress at Bagley Hall – poor thing.

THE ANIMALS

CADBURY   Dora Belvedon's chocolate Labrador.

LOOFAH   Dora Belvedon's delinquent pony.

PARTNER   Janna Curtis's ginger and white mongrel.

NORTHCLIFFE   Patience Cartwright's golden retriever.

ELAINE   Hengist Brett-Taylor's white greyhound.

GENERAL   Lily Hamilton's white and black Persian cat.

VERLAINE AND RIMBAUD   Artie Deverell's Jack Russells.

BOGOTÁ   Xavier Campbell-Black's black Labrador.

HINDSIGHT   Theo Graham's marmalade cat.

FAST   One of Rupert Campbell-Black's horses. Aptly named.

PENSCOMBE PETERKIN   Another of Rupert Campbell-Black's star horses.

BELUGA

An extremely kind horse who teaches Paris Alvaston to ride.

PLOVER

Patience Cartwright's grey mare, doted on by Beluga.

1

Larkminster, county town of Larkshire, has long been considered the most precious jewel in the Cotswolds' crown. Throughout the year, its streets are paved with tourists, admiring the glorious pale gold twelfth-century cathedral, the Queen Anne courthouse and the ancient castle, whose battlements descend into the River Fleet as it idles its way round the town.

Larkminster, famous for its splendid beeches and limes and designated England's Town of Trees at the Millennium, was anticipating further fame because its newly elected Conservative MP, Jupiter Belvedon, was hotly tipped to take over the Tory party and oust Tony Blair at the next election.

In his Larkminster constituency, the machiavellian Jupiter was frustrated by a hung Labour and Lib-Dem county council who always voted tactically to keep out the Tories. But in January 2001, to the county council's horror, central government decided to take the running of Larkshire's schools away from the local education authority, who they felt was mismanaging its finances and not adhering sufficiently to the national curriculum. They then handed this task to a private company called S and C Services, the 'S' and the 'C' standing for 'Support' and 'Challenge'.

Larkminster itself boasted a famous public school, Bagley Hall, some five miles outside the town; a choir school attached to the cathedral; two excellent state schools: Searston Abbey and St James's, known as St Jimmy's; and a perfectly frightful sink school, Larkminster Comprehensive, which was situated on the edge of the town's black spot, the notorious Shakespeare Estate.

Like many outwardly serene and elegant West Country towns, Larkminster was greatly exercised by the increase in violent crime, for which it believed the Shakespeare Estate and Larkminster Comprehensive, or 'Larks' as it was known, were entirely responsible.

Randal Stancombe, a Rich List property developer and a hugely influential local player with a manicured finger in every pie, was particularly concerned. Cavendish Plaza, one of his private estates of desirable residences newly built above the flood plain of the River Fleet, was constantly troubled by Larks delinquents mugging, nicking car radios and knocking fairies off Rolls-Royces on their way to school. Randal Stancombe was putting increasing pressure on the police and the county council to clean up the area.

Larkminster Comp had for some years been a candidate for closure. It was at the bottom of the league tables and could only muster five hundred children rattling around in a building large enough for twelve hundred. Taxpayers' money should not be squandered heating empty schools.

Reading the graffiti on the wall, and not liking the prospect of bullying interference from a private company like S and C Services, the then headmaster, Ted Mitchell, had immediately resigned in February 2001. Larks Comp should have been shut down then, but the county council and S and C Services, nervous of the local uproar, the petitions, the poster campaigns, the marches on County Hall and even Westminster and the inevitable loss of seats that occur whenever a school is threatened with closure, dodged the issue.

They should have handed the job to Larks's deputy

head, Mike Pitts, a seedy alcoholic who would have killed off the place in a few months. Instead they decided to give Larks a last chance and in April advertised in *The Times Educational Supplement* for a new head. This was why on a hot sunny day in early May, Janna Curtis, head of English at Redfords Comprehensive in West Yorkshire, caught the Intercity from Leeds to Larkminster.

On any journey, Janna overloaded herself with work which she truly intended to do. Aware that Year Eleven would be taking their first English exam in less than three weeks, she should have reread her GCSE revision notes. She should also have checked the English department's activities for the rest of term. Even more important, she should have tackled the pile of information about Larks Comp and the area that she had downloaded from the internet.

But after registering that Larks was underachieving disastrously and those 'right-wing bastards' Randal Stancombe and S and C Services were putting the boot in, she was sidetracked by a *Daily Mail* abandoned by a passenger getting off at Birmingham. Despite her horror at its right-wing views, she soon became engrossed in a story about Posh and Becks, followed by Lynda Lee-Potter's much too enthusiastic comments about 'another right-wing bastard': Rupert Campbell-Black.

The train was stiflingly hot. Even if she'd had the money, Janna would never have done anything so revoltingly elitist as travel first class, but she wished air conditioning extended into standard class as well, so she didn't go scarlet before her interview. She was gagging for a large vodka and tonic to steady her nerves, but, on no breakfast, she'd become garrulous. Not that she was going to get the job; they'd think her much too young and inexperienced and she wasn't even sure she wanted it.

Gazing at a cloud of pink and white apple blossom

clashing with bilious yellow fields of rape as the train trundled through Worcestershire, Janna reflected that the past three years at Redfords had been the most thrilling of her life. The cheers must have been heard in Westminster the day she and the other staff were told their school had finally struggled out of special measures (the euphemism for a dangerously failing school).

The fight to save Redfords had been unrelenting, but who minded working until midnight, week in, week out, when you were in love with the headmaster, Stew Wilby, who had made you head of English before you were thirty and who frequently put down his magic wand to shag you on the office carpet?

In the end Stew couldn't bring himself to leave his wife, Beth, and had retreated into a marriage far more intact than he had made out. People were beginning to gossip and the warmth of the reference Stew had sent to the governing board at Larks – which he had showed her yesterday: 'I shall be devastated to lose an out-standing teacher, but I cannot stand in Janna Curtis's way' – gave Janna the feeling that he might be relieved to see the back of her.

'Staying with Beth, staying with Beth,' mocked the wheels as the train rattled over the border into the wooded valleys of Larkshire. In her positive moments, all Janna wanted was to escape as far as possible from Stew into a challenge that would give her no time to mourn. Larkminster Comp seemed the answer.

She was met at the station by Phil Pierce, Larks's head of science. Bony-faced, bespectacled, mousy-haired, he wore a creased sand-coloured suit, obviously dragged out of a back drawer in honour of the heat wave and jazzed up by a blue silk tie covered in leaping red frogs.

Phil didn't drive Janna to Larks via the Shakespeare Estate to bump over litter-strewn roads and breathe in the stench of bins dustmen were too scared to empty.

Instead he took her on the longer scenic route where she could enjoy the River Fleet sparkling, the white cherry blossom in the Town of Trees dancing against ominously rain-filled navy-blue clouds and the lichen blazing like little suns on the ancient buildings.

'How beautiful,' sighed Janna, then bristled with disapproval as she noticed, hanging overhead like birds of prey, a number of huge cranes bearing the name of Randal Stancombe.

'That capitalist monster's doing a lot of work,' she stormed, 'and I didn't realize that fascist bast— I mean fiend was MP here,' as she caught sight of posters of pale, patrician Jupiter Belvedon in the window of the Conservative Club. 'I bet he's in league with S and C Services,' she added furiously. 'Private companies only take over education to make a fat profit.'

'Representatives of S and C Services will certainly be at your interview later,' said Phil Pierce gently, 'so perhaps . . .'

'I'd better button my lip,' sighed Janna, 'and my clothes,' she added, doing up the buttons of the crocus-yellow dress she had bought from Jigsaw after school yesterday.

Looking at the terrace houses painted in neat pastels, their front gardens bright with wallflowers and forget-me-nots, Janna wondered if Larkminster might be too smug, rich and middle class.

As if reading her thoughts, Phil Pierce said: 'This may seem a prosperous county, but there's a very high level of socio-economic deprivation. Eighty per cent of our children are on free school dinners. Many have special educational needs.'

'I hope you receive sufficient funding.'

'Does anyone?' sighed Phil. 'This is Larks.'

Janna was agreeably charmed by the tawny, romantically rambling Victorian building perched on the side of a hill, its turrets and battlements swathed in pink clematis and amethyst wisteria, its parkland crowded with rare trees and with cow parsley and wild garlic advancing in waves on wildly daisied lawns.

Phil kicked off by giving her a quick tour of the school, which was conveniently empty of challenging children because it was polling day at the local elections.

All one needed for outside, reflected Janna, were a pair of secateurs and a mowing machine. The windows could also be mended and unboarded, the graffiti painted over and the chains, taps and locks replaced in the lavatories. The corridors and classroom walls were also badly lacking in posters, paintings and written work by the children. Redfords, her school in Yorkshire, was like walking into a rainbow.

She was disappointed that there were no children around, so no one could watch her taking a lesson. This had always secured her jobs in the past. Instead she was given post to deal with, to show off her management skills, and made a good impression by immediately tackling anything involving media and parents. She was also handed two budgets and quickly identified why one was good, the other bad.

She was aware of being beadily scrutinized by the school secretary, Rowan Merton, who was conventionally pretty: lovely skin, grey eyes, dark brown bob; but who simultaneously radiated smugness and disapproval, like the cat who'd got the cream and found it off.

Still too nervous to eat, Janna refused the quick bite of lunch offered her by Phil Pierce. She was then whisked away to an off-site interview because the governors were equally nervous of the Larks deputy head, Mike Pitts, who, livid he hadn't been offered the job, was likely to grow nasty when sobering up after lunch.

Only as Janna was leaving the Larks building did the heavens open, so she didn't appreciate in how many places rain normally poured in through the roof.

2

Janna was interviewed round the corner, past a row of boarded-up shops, in a pub called the Ghost and Castle, which was of the same tawny, turreted architecture as the school. The landlord was clearly a joker. A skeleton propped up the public bar, which was adorned with etchings of ghosts draped in sheets terrorizing maidens or old men in nightcaps. Rooms off were entitled Spook-Easy and Spirits Bar. The plat du jour chalked up on a blackboard was Ghoulash at £4.50.

Janna giggled and wondered how many Larks pupils were regulars here. At least they could mug up for GCSE in the Macbeth room, whose blood-red walls were decorated with lurid oils of Banquo's ghost, Duncan's murder and a sleepwalking Lady Macbeth. Here Larks's governors, a semi-circle of the Great and the Good, mostly councillors and educationalists, awaited her.

Think before you speak and remember eye contact at all times, Janna told herself as, beaming at everyone, she swivelled round like a searchlight.

The chairman of the governors, Russell Lambert, had tiny eyes, sticking-out ears, a long nose like King Babar and loved the sound of his pompous, very put-on voice. A big elephant in a small watering hole, thought Janna.

Like most good teachers, she of necessity picked up names quickly. As Russell Lambert introduced her, she clocked first Brett Scott, a board member of Larkminster Rovers, who had an appropriately roving eye and looked game for a great night on the tiles, and secondly Crispin Thomas, deputy educational director of S and C Services, who did not.

Crispin, a petulant, pig-faced blond, had a snuffling voice, and from his tan and the spare tyre billowing over the waistband of his off-white suit, had recently returned from a self-indulgent holiday.

Under a painting of the Weird Sisters and infinitely more terrifying, like a crow who'd been made over by Trinny and Susannah, quivered a woman with black, straight hair and a twitching scarlet mouth. Appropriately named Cara Sharpe, she was a teacher governor, supposed to present the concerns of the staff to the governing body.

And I bet she sneaks to both sides, thought Janna.

'Cara is our immensely effective head of English and drama,' said Russell sycophantically.

So she won't welcome any interference on the English front from me, Janna surmised, squaring her little shoulders. At the end of the row, the vice-chairman, Sir Hugo Betts, who resembled a camel on Prozac, fought sleep.

Russell Lambert made no bones about the state of the school: 'Larks is at rock bottom.'

'Then it can only go up,' said Janna cheerfully.

Her audience knew from her impressive CV that she had been a crucial part of the high-flying team that had turned around disastrously failing Redfords. But then she had been led by a charismatic head, Stew Wilby. If she took on Larks, she would be on her own.

She also seemed terrifyingly young. She had lots of dark freckles and wild, rippling dark red hair, a big mouth (which she seldom kept shut), merry onyx-brown eyes and a snub nose. She was not beautiful –

her jaw was too square – but she had a face of great sweetness, humour and friendliness. She was small, about five feet one, and after the drenching of rain, her crocus-yellow dress clung enticingly to a very pretty figure. A teardrop of mascara on her cheekbone gave a look of Pierrot.

Phil Pierce, who was very taken, asked her how she would deal with an underachieving teacher.

'I'd immediately involve the head of department,' replied Janna in her soft Yorkshire accent, 'and tact-fully find out what's wrong. Is it discipline? Are the children trampling all over him? Is it poor teaching? Academically has he got what it takes, or is he present-ing material wrongly? And then, gently, because if he's underachieving he'll have no confidence, try and work it through. After this,' she went on, 'he would either succeed or fail. If the latter, he's not right for teaching, because the education of children is all that matters.'

The semi-circle – except for scowling Cara Sharpe, Rowan Merton, who was taking the minutes, and Sir Hugo Betts, who was asleep – smiled approvingly.

'What are your weaknesses?' snuffled Crispin Thomas from S and C.

Janna laughed. 'Short legs and an even shorter fuse. But my strengths are that I adore children and I thrive on hard work. Are the parents involved here?'

'Well, we get the odd troublemaker,' said Russell heartily, failing to add that a large proportion of Larks parents were too out of it from drugs to register. 'The children can be challenging.'

'I don't mind challenging children,' said Janna. 'You couldn't find more sad and demoralized kids than the ones at Redfords, but in a few months—'

'Yes, we read about that in the *Guardian*,' interrupted Crispin rudely.

Janna bit her lip; they didn't seem interested in her past.

'I want to give every child and teacher the chance to

31

shine and for them to leave my school with their confidence boosted to enable them to survive and enjoy the world.'

She paused hopefully. A loud snore rent the air followed by an even more thunderous rumble from her own tummy, which woke Sir Hugo with a start.

'What, what, what?' He groped for his flies.

Janna caught Phil Pierce's eye and burst out laughing, so everyone else laughed except Cara and Rowan.

Janna had expected the board to get in touch in a week or so, but Russell Lambert, at a nod from Crispin Thomas, asked her to wait in an ante-room entitled Your Favourite Haunt. Phil Pierce brought her a cup of tea and some egg sandwiches, at which she was still too nervous to do more than nibble. Phil was such a sweet man; she'd love working with him.

Breathing in dark purple lilac, she gazed out of the window at buildings darkened to the colour of toffee by the rain and trees as various in their greenness as kids in any school. Beyond lay the deep blue undulation of the Malvern Hills. Surely she could find fulfilment and happiness here?

She was summoned back by Rowan, looking beadier than ever.

'We've decided not to waste your time asking you to come for a second interview,' announced Russell Lambert.

Janna's face fell.

'It was good of you all to see me,' she muttered. 'I know I look young . . .'

'We'd like to offer you the job,' said Russell.

Janna burst into tears, her mascara mingling with her freckles as she babbled, 'That's wicked! Fantastic! Are you sure? I'm going to be a head, such an honour, I promise to justify your faith, that's really wicked.'

The half-circle smiled indulgently.

'Can I buy you all a drink to celebrate?' stammered Janna, reaching for her briefcase. 'On me, I mean.'

'Should be on us,' said the director of Larkminster Rovers. 'What'll you have, love?'

'Not if she's going to catch the fast train home,' said Russell, looking at his watch, 'and Crispin and I have to talk salaries and technicalities with . . . may I call you Janna?'

Half an hour later on the Ghost and Castle steps, Janna was still thanking them.

'I'd like to walk to the station,' she confessed. 'I want to drink in my new town. Doesn't matter if I get the later train. I'm so excited, I'll float home.'

But as she hadn't yet signed the contract, Russell, not risking Janna anywhere near the Shakespeare Estate, steered her towards his very clean Rover. Despite the stifling heat of the day, he pulled on thick brown leather driving gloves as though he didn't want to leave fingerprints on anything. As he settled in the driving seat, she noticed how his spreading thighs filled his grey flannel trousers.

As they passed the offices of the *Larkminster Gazette*, a billboard announced Randal Stancombe's latest plans for the area.

'That greedy fat cat's got a stranglehold on everything,' spat Janna.

'Wearing my other hat,' reproved Russell, 'as chair of the local planning committee, I can assure you Randal is a very good friend indeed to Larkminster, not least because of the thousands of people he employs.'

Feeling he'd been squashing, he then suggested Janna might like to ring her parents with news of her job.

'Mum passed away at Christmas.' Janna paused. 'She would have been right proud. I wish I could text her in heaven. We came from a very poor family; Mum scrubbed floors to pay for my school uniform, but she loved books and always encouraged us to read. She used to take me to see the Brontës' house in Haworth. I read English because of her.'

'And your father?'

'Dad was a steelworker. He used to take me to Headingly and Old Trafford. Then he left home; he couldn't cope with Mum being ill.' Her voice faltered. She wasn't going to add that her father had been violent and had drunk the family penniless.

She wished she could ring Stew but he'd be taking a staff meeting. Yorkshire was so full of painful memories; she'd be glad to get down south and make a fresh start.

Nothing, however, had prepared her for the anguish of leaving Redfords. Parents and children, who'd thought she'd be with them for ever, seemed equally devastated.

'Why are you living us?' wrote one eleven-year-old. 'I don't want you to live.'

'Are your new children better than us?' wrote another. 'Please change your mind.'

Almost harder to bear was the despair of the older pupils, including some of the roughest, toughest boys, whom she was abandoning in the middle of their GCSE course.

'How will we ever understand *Much Ado* without you? We're going to miss you, miss.'

They all gave her good-luck presents and cards they could ill afford and Janna couldn't look them in the eye and tell them the truth: 'I'm leaving because your headmaster broke my heart and now it's breaking twice.'

Then Stew had done the sweetest thing: he'd had framed a group photograph of the entire school, which every teacher and child had signed. Janna cried every time she looked at it.

Some teachers were very sad she was leaving and wished her well. Others, jealous of her closeness to Stew, expressed their incredulity at her getting the job.

'You'd better cut your hair, you'll never have time to wash that mane every morning. And do buy some sensible clothes.'

34

'And you'll have to curb that temper and you won't be able to swan into meetings twenty minutes late if you're taking them.'

Waylaid by a sobbing child, Janna would forget about time.

There had also been the hell of seeing Stew interview and appoint her successor: a willowy brunette with large, serious, hazel eyes behind her spectacles – the bloody cow – and everyone getting excited about a Christmas production of *Oliver!* of which Janna would be no part.

Stew had taken her out for a discreet farewell dinner and, because she was moving to the country, given her a little Staffordshire cow as a leaving present.

'I'm so proud of you, Janny. You've probably got eighteen months to try and turn round that school. Don't lose your rag and antagonize people unnecessarily and go easy on the "boogers", "bluddies" and "basstards", they just show off your Yorkshire accent.' Then, pinching her cheek when she looked sulky: 'I don't want anything to wreck your lovely, generous, spontaneous nature.'

'Yeah, yeah. "The only failure is not to have tried",' Janna quoted one of Redfords's mantras back at him.

After a second bottle they had both cried and Stew had quoted: '"So, we'll go no more a-roving",' but when he got to the bit about the sword outwearing its sheath and the heart wearing out the breast, Janna remembered how they'd worn out the carpet in his office.

I've given him my Bridget Jones years, she thought bitterly. Sometimes she wondered why she loved him so much: his hair was thinning, his body thickening and, apart from the penetrating dark brown eyes, his square face lacked beauty, but whenever he spoke, everyone listened and his powers of persuasion were infinite.

'Little Jannie, I cannot believe you're going to be a headmistress.' His fingers edged over her breast.

'We can still meet. Can I come home this evening?'

'No,' snapped Janna. 'I'm a head, but no longer a mistress.'

Janna, however, was never cast down for long. At half-term, she had come south and found herself a minute but adorable eighteenth-century house called Jubilee Cottage. Like a child's drawing, it had a path spilling over with catmint and lavender leading up to a gabled porch with 'Jubilate' engraved above the door and mullioned windows on either side. It was the last house in the small village of Wilmington, which had a pub, a shop and a watercress-choked stream dawdling along the edge of the High Street.

Janna could easily afford the mortgage on her splendid new salary. She couldn't believe she'd be earning so much.

Wilmington thankfully was three miles from Larkminster Comp. However much you loved kids, it was a mistake to live over your school. When she grew tired of telling her children they were all stars, she could escape home, wander on her own lawn in bare feet and gaze up at her own stars.

All the same, missing Stew, it was terribly easy to go through a bottle of wine of an evening.

'I shall buy a new car and get a dog,' vowed Janna.

...

3

From the middle of August, Janna was in and out of
her new school familiarizing herself with everything,
palling up with Wally Bristow, the site manager, who
like most site managers was the fountain of all wisdom.

Wally had short, slicked-back brown hair and wise
grey eyes in a round, smiling face as dependable and
reassuring as a digestive biscuit. Living but three
minutes from Larks, he was always on call except on
Thursday evening, when he and a team of bell-ringers
rehearsed for Sunday's service in St Mary's Church
next door, or on Saturday afternoons when
Larkminster Rovers played at home. He was in-
ordinately proud of a good-looking son, Ben, who'd
risen to sergeant in the Royal Engineers.

Janna's heart swelled when she saw Wally had
repainted the board outside the school in dark blue
gloss and written in gold letters: 'LARKMINSTER
COMPREHENSIVE SCHOOL. Head Teacher: Janna
Curtis'.

'Oh Wally, I've got to make every child feel they're
the greatest and discover each one's special talents.'

'Smokin', spittin', swearin', runnin' away, fightin'
and urinatin' in phone boxes,' intoned Wally. 'As we
can't fill the places, we get all the dropouts that get
sacked or rejected by other schools.'

Wally showed her Smokers', a steep, grassy bank

down which the children vanished so they could smoke, do drugs, drink and even shag unobserved by the staffroom.

'I don't want to frighten you, Janna,' he went on as they lunched on cans of lager and Marks and Spencer's prawn sandwiches, 'but the kids are running wild. Most of them only come in to trash the place and play football. The rest are off havin' babies or appearin' in court. They're demoralized by the staff, who are either off sick from "stress" ' – Wally gave a snort of disbelief – 'old dinosaurs hanging on for retirement, or commies who grumble at everything and threaten strike action if you keep them a minute late.'

Wally also warned her of tricky teachers: Mike Pitts, the deputy head, who taught maths, did the timetable and who was always burning joss sticks and scented candles to disguise the drink fumes; and Cara Sharpe, who'd glared at Janna at her interview.

'Everyone hates Cara, but humours her. She wanted Mike as head, and her to get deputy head to look good on her CV. She and Mike are thick as thieves. Don't trust them. Cara's a bitch to the kids.'

'Not any more she won't be. Where are the playing fields?'

'Don't have any: they were sold off by the council. The rest of the land is on too much of a slope and you can't swing a gerbil in the playground.'

The playground was indeed awful: a square of tarmac surrounded by broken rusty railings with no basketball nets and two overhanging sycamores, whose leaves, curling and covered in sinister black spots, provided the only shade.

Everything had deteriorated since Janna's interview in May. A lower-angled sun revealed damp patches and peeling plaster in every classroom. The once lovely garden and parkland were choked with thistles and nettles. Pale phlox and red-hot pokers were broken or bent double by bindweed which seemed to symbolize the red tape threatening to strangle Janna's hopes. An in-tray of forms to be filled in nearly hit the ceiling.

The GCSE results out in late August had dropped to four per cent of the pupils gaining A–C grades in five subjects. Only these gave Larks points in the league tables, and only Cara Sharpe and Phil Pierce, the gentle head of science who'd met Janna at the station, had got most of their children through.

'Phil's a good bloke,' said Wally, 'firm, but very fair. He's always online to answer pupils' homework questions. The kids love him.'

'Why's he still here?' asked Janna gloomily.

'He's very loyal. Trouble with kids here, they leave at sixteen so they don't have to come back and face the music of terrible GCSE results.'

'Where do they go on to?'

'The dole queue or the nick.'

Janna kicked off by tackling her office, which was full of the presence of Mike Pitts, who'd done her job for the spring and summer terms and who clearly hadn't wanted people to follow his movements. The door had a security lock and a heavy dark blind pulled down over the big window hiding a view over the playground to houses, the River Fleet and grey-green woods beyond.

Janna insisted a doubtful Wally remove both lock and blind.

'I want to be accessible to both children and staff.'

Shaking his head, Wally got out his screwdriver.

'It really ain't surprising [he sang in a rich baritone],
That we're rising, rising, rising,
Soon we'll reach Division One.
Premier, Wembley, here we come.'

'What's that song?' demanded Janna.

'Larkminster Rovers's battle hymn. We got to the second division last season. Now we've got to stay there.'

'Larks is going up the league tables too [sang Janna],
Soon we'll reach Division One.
Premier, Wembley, here we come.'

Wally nearly dropped his screwdriver as her sweet
soaring voice rattled the window panes.

Having scraped scented candle wax off the furniture
and scrubbed the room from top to toe, Janna and
Wally painted her office white, hung cherry-red
curtains and laid rush matting on the floor.

'I need a settee and a couple of armchairs so people
can relax when they come in here.'

'The kids'll trash them, the settee'll be an incitement
to rape or teachers grumbling and those white walls
won't last a minute,' sighed Wally.

'Then we'll cover them with pictures.'

Up went *Desiderata* and *Hold the Dream* embroidered
by Janna's Auntie Glad, followed by big photographs of
Wharfedale, Fountains Abbey and Stew's photograph
of all the children and teachers at Redfords waving
goodbye in front of a square grey school building.

On a side table Janna put Stew's Staffordshire cow
and a big bunch of Michaelmas daisies and late roses
rescued from Larks's flower beds.

'My goodness, you have been working hard,' mocked
Rowan Merton when she looked in a week before term
started.

As a working wife and mother with photographs of
her husband and two little girls all over her office, on
the door of which was printed 'Assistant to the Head',
Rowan prided herself on juggling. She had wound
Mike Pitts round her little finger and clearly didn't
fancy extending herself for a woman – particularly one
in a denim mini, with a smudged face and her red curls
in a ponytail.

'Have you flown in to rescue us?' she mocked. 'Like
Red Adair in a skirt?'

'No, I've come to show you how to save yourselves,' retorted Janna tartly, then, remembering Stew's advice about not antagonizing people, added, 'How are Scarlet and Meagan? They must have loved having you to themselves in the holidays.'

Rowan relented fractionally and said they had, then launched into a list of staff requests for broken chairs, desks, leaking windows and computers to be mended.

'And Mrs Sharpe wants a blind. The sun casts such a glare, no one can read the whiteboard in the afternoon.'

Cara Sharpe's own glare, Janna would have thought, would see off any competition.

'And my anglepoise lamp collapses without the aid of two bulldog clips and the angle being wedged open by the last *Education Year Book*,' went on Rowan. 'If Wally could sort all those things out before term begins?'

'Wally's flat out,' snapped Janna.

Rowan glanced round the office. 'Yes, I can see. Nice settee. We have to watch the budget now S and C hold the purse strings.'

Slowly, Janna familiarized herself with classrooms, halls, gym and labyrinthine adjoining corridors in the main building, which was known as School House. Fifty yards away, the annexe, known as Appletree because it had been built on the site of an old orchard, housed the labs, music, design and technology and food technology departments.

Then she pored over the children's personal files, counting the asylum-seekers, Indians, Pakistanis and Afro-Caribbeans – far fewer than at Redfords. She had also noticed lots of BNPs and swastikas amongst the graffiti: she would have to watch out for racist bullying. She was now frantically trying to memorize the names before term began.

'The ones you have to watch are those going into

41

Year Nine and particularly the Wolf Pack,' said Wally as he carried in a mini-fridge for milk, butter and orange juice, and put jam, marmalade, coffee, tea bags, lots of biscuits, two packs of Mars and Twix bars and a tin of Quality Street in the cupboard. 'These won't last a minute.'

'Oh, shut up,' said Janna, who was gazing down at a photograph of a beautiful black boy with long dark eyelashes and a smile of utter innocence.

Wally glanced over her shoulder. 'He's Wolf Pack. Feral Jackson. Comes into school to play football and start fights. Very druggy background; mother's an addict, off her face all day. Feral went inside at the beginning of the holidays for mugging some women shoppers. His brother Joey was shot to death last year. Uncle Harley, his mum's boyfriend, is a mega pusher. That's Feral's best mate, Paris Alvaston.'

Janna looked at the boy's ghostly face, the wonderful bone structure, the watchful pale grey eyes of a merle collie.

'Paris has been in different care homes since he was two,' added Wally. 'Goes AWOL from time to time on trains all over the country searching for his mother. Advertised for a home in the local paper last year, but there were no takers. Shame really.'

'That's terrible.' Janna reached out and switched on the kettle. 'Poor boy.'

'Looks too spooky. Teachers say he's very clever, writes wonderful stories one day, then just puts his name at the top of the paper the next. Everything goes inside. He and Feral are joined at the very narrow hip. Give them a detention and they jump out of the window, climb down the wisteria and run away.

'That's Griffith Williams, known as "Graffi".' Wally pointed to a thickset boy with black curls and wicked sliding dark eyes. 'Graffi was a Welshman, Graffi was a thief . . . But he's a good laugh. Don't stand anywhere near him or he'll graffiti you. That's Pearl Smith: she's

42

got a temper on her, scratch the eyes out of any girl who tries to get off with her boys, particularly Feral. She's trouble. Cuts herself. Got arms like ladders.'

'Well, she's not wearing make-up and having hair that colour in my school,' said Janna firmly as she broke open a packet and dropped tea bags into two mugs. 'That one's pretty.'

'Kylie Rose. Already had one kid at twelve – wanted something to love. Time she spends on her back, she'll have another any minute. Anything to avoid SATs. Those five make up the Wolf Pack.'

'Feral, Paris, Graffi, Pearl and Kylie Rose,' intoned Janna as she poured boiling water over the tea bags and added milk and two sugars for Wally, who carried on with her lesson.

'There are three more you want to watch from Year Nine. One's Rocky; he's autistic. Attention Deficit Disorder they call it these days,' he added scornfully. 'Nice kid, but violent if he don't get his Ritalin. More serious are "Satan" Simmons – a racist bully, excluded last term for carrying a gun, overturned on appeal because his father's a councillor – and "Monster" Norman. Monster's mixed race' – Wally stirred his tea thoughtfully – 'in that his dad, who keeps walking out, is a quarter black, which Monster denies, which makes him even more of a racist bully. He's also a great snivelling toad, really spiteful, but his mother's a governor, so you can't touch him.'

Janna put her hand over the names: Freddie 'Feral' Jackson, such a beautiful face; Paris Alvaston: no one could forget him either, he looked so hauntingly sad; Griffith 'Graffi' Williams; Pearl; Kylie Rose; 'Satan' Simmons; Rocky; 'Monster' Norman.'

'What's that?' she demanded, noticing a switch inside the well of her desk.

'Your panic button,' said Wally, then, when Janna looked mutinous: 'You don't know what you're up against. Most of our kids come from the Shakespeare

Estate. Their parents are crazy people who respect no one. From the beginning of term you're wearing a radio mike, and if there's any trouble, you summon back-up. Someone's always on call on the internal radio link.'

'I'm not bothering with any of that junk. This is going to be a happy school.'

Before the teachers came back, Wally also gave her a sneak preview of the staffroom.

'Why do they need a security lock?' she asked as Wally punched out the code to enter.

'To keep out violent kids and parents.'

'And me too, presumably. God, it's awful! Who'd want to break in here?'

Walls the luminous olive green of a child about to be sick were not enhanced by brown and yellow check curtains. Mock leather chairs in the dingiest browns and beiges huddled dispiritedly round low tables. Staff pigeonholes overflowed, clearly untackled since last term. Three potted plants had baked to death on the window sill. A Hoover, weak from underwork, was slumped against an ancient television set. Health and safety laws and union posters promising significant reductions in workload shared the noticeboard with details of half-price Calvin Klein button-fly boxers and Winnie-the-Pooh character socks. Also pinned up was a letter from Cotchester University announcing that a former pupil Marilyn Finch had attained a second in maths.

'For those who remember Marilyn,' Mike Pitts had scribbled across the bottom, 'all our efforts were worthwhile.'

'Only graduate Larks ever had,' volunteered Wally. 'Pittsy taught her.'

'I'm going to have to tackle him on the timetable,' sighed Janna. 'It's covered with drink rings and Year Seven A and Year Eight B are having English with the same teacher in the same classroom at the same time on Tuesday morning – and it gets worse. God, look at that.'

On the breakfast bar, untouched since the end-of-term party, sink and draining board were crowded with dirty wine glasses, moth-filled cups and orange-juice cartons. Scrumpy, beer and vegetable-juice cans littered the floor.

Debbie the cleaner, said Wally disapprovingly, would blitz the place before the first staff meeting tomorrow.

'None of this lot can wash up a cup.'

'We'd better buy them a dishwasher.'

'They'd never load it.'

To the right of the door, imperilling entry, hung a dartboard with two scarlet-feathered darts plunged deep into the bull's eye. Last year's Christmas decorations had been chucked into a far corner between a ping-pong table with one leg supported by a German dictionary and a billiard table with a badly ripped cloth.

'Don't matter,' said Wally philosophically. 'Table's mostly used for late-night nooky.'

'Anyone I know?' asked Janna, who'd moved to examine a big picture frame, which contained cigarette-card-sized photographs of all the staff in order of seniority. Heading these were the Dinosaurs who'd been at Larks for ever. To memorize them, Janna had made an acronym – P.U.B.I.C. – out of the first letters of their names. 'P' for Pitts, 'U' for Uglow (Miss) who taught RE, 'B' for Basket (Miss) who taught geography, 'I' for Illingworth (Mr) who taught science and 'C' for Chalford (Mrs) who taught history.

'That's one I haven't memorized,' mused Janna, 'with the piled-up dark hair and operatic make-up. She must be Miss Cambola, head of music.'

Wally, however, had noticed that into Janna's photograph on the far top left someone had plunged the missing red-feathered dart between the eyes. Hastily

Wally whipped it out. Fortunately, Janna had been distracted by the photograph of a good-looking blond man, affectedly cupping his face between long fingers.

'He's not bad.'

'Jason Fenton. Kids call him Goldilocks. Cara Sharpe's toyboy, so hands off. He wanted her job as head of drama and English, and believes in constantly switching schools to jack up his status and his salary. Claims you go stale if you stay more than a year, which upsets the Dinosaurs, who've been here for ever.'

'And him?' Janna pointed to a black-eyed, black-browed, bearded man with dishevelled black hair.

'Robbie Rushton, chief leftie, rabble-rouser and has-bin. Spends his time plotting and telling you what you can't do. Longs for a strike so he can appear on TV again. He and Jason both have the hots for Gloria, deputy head of PE.' Wally pointed to a pouting strawberry blonde. 'Gloria prefers Jason because he's posher and washes more. "Soon we'll reach Division One. Premier, Wembley, here we come,"' sang Wally.

Who the hell had plunged that dart into Janna's photograph, he wondered? She was such a sweet kid. He was determined to protect her.

'"P" for Pitts, "U" for Uglow, "B" for Basket, "I" for Illingworth, "C" for Chalford,' intoned Janna.

4

On 3 September, all the staff came into school for a full day to prepare work and classrooms for the children, whose first day of term was the fourth. New staff were also initiated into school practice: which included what coloured exercise books to use, pupil data files, playground rotas, policy towards parents and bullying, and what was laughingly known as the golden rules of behaviour management.

Janna had decided to break the ice and tradition by scheduling her first staff meeting at five o'clock, rather than first thing. Desperate for it to go well, she had not only memorized names and achievements until her head was bursting, but also ordered in three large quiches and a couple of crates of red and white to jolly things along.

Her day running up to the meeting was frantic: coping with endless requests and demands (mostly, it seemed, not to teach the Wolf Pack), and having a most unpleasant spat with Mike Pitts, who hadn't taken kindly to criticism of his timetable.

'Then do it yourself.'

'No,' countered Janna bravely, 'it's your job to put it right.'

She had fared little better with Sam Spink, the union rep, who had very short hair shaved at the back, a large bottom and an even larger sense of her own importance. Her straining brown leggings stopped at mid-calf leaving a hairy gap above her Winnie-the-Pooh character socks, which seemed to give out signals that she was not all work and no play, and clearly regarded herself as a bit of a card. She proceeded to lecture Janna at great length about not prolonging the school day by a second. Remembering yet again Stew's instruction about not antagonizing colleagues unnecessarily, Janna just managed to keep her temper.

She then had to welcome two newly qualified teachers – NQTs or Not Quite Togethers, as they were known – pretty, plump, earnest Lydia who taught English, and pale Lance, teaching history. They were so full of hope and trepidation that Janna couldn't bear them to be bludgeoned by the weary cynicism of the other staff and spent longer than she should discussing Thomas Hardy country and the battlefields, where they had respectively spent their holidays in order to glean fascinating information to relay to their classes. Thus she was still talking and in jeans and a T-shirt when Rowan Merton put her sleek dark bob round the door:

'Two minutes to kick-off, headmistress.'

'Why didn't you warn me?' screamed Janna.

'You insisted on not being bothered.'

Janna only had time to sling on a denim jacket and slap on some blusher – God, she looked tired – before belting down the corridor. Across reception, at her instructions, Wally had strung a brightly coloured banner saying: 'Welcome back all Larks teachers and children'.

'So demeaning to refer to the students as children,' grumbled Sam Spink.

The meeting was held in the non-smoking staffroom. Outside, a muttering band of lefties, headed by the black-eyed, wild-haired Robbie Rushton, drew feverishly on last fags. Inside, Debbie the cleaner had pulled a blinder. The place was gleaming. Janna made

48

a mental note to buy Debbie a box of chocolates. Gallant Wally had, in addition, attacked the immediate garden and a smell of mown grass and newly turned earth drifting in through the window gave an illusion of spring and fresh starts.

The Dinosaurs had clearly been emailed by a furious Mike Pitts. Having bagged most of the dingy chairs and chuntering disapprovingly about 'heads in jeans squandering the budget on drink', they were getting stuck into the red. Mike Pitts ostentatiously asked for a mineral water. Skunk Illingworth, who taught science, stank of BO and wore socks, sandals and shorts, had just cut himself a huge slice of quiche and filled up a pint mug with white.

'She's going to have the students out of uniform and calling us by our Christian names in a trice,' he grumbled.

Heart thumping, Janna glanced round at the sea of faces: appraising, hostile, suspicious, waiting for some-one to make a move. Thank God, Phil Pierce, who'd befriended her at her interview, rushed straight over, kissing her on both cheeks and apologizing profusely for not being in touch.

Like most teachers, he looked fifteen years younger after the summer break. His kind eyes were clear, his hair bleached, his bony face dark tanned. He and his wife had just come back from Kenya, he said. He'd popped in earlier, but Rowan had stressed that Janna was tied up. He hoped she was OK. Then he intro-duced Miss Cambola of the large bosom, piled-up hair and stage make-up, and Janna scored immediate brownie points by remembering she taught music, was a fine mezzo and sang with the Larkminster Operatic Society.

'You must join us,' said Miss Cambola. 'Wally tells me you have a beautiful voice. We're doing *Don Giovanni* in November and have yet to cast Zerlina.'

'I'm afraid I won't have time,' said Janna wistfully.

'Well anyway, come to supper. Have you met Mags Gablecross? She teaches French part-time.'

'And has a wedding in the offing,' said Janna, shaking hands with a sweet-faced woman in her fifties.

'You are well briefed.' Mags smiled. 'Your predecessor hardly recognized his staff.'

'Oh, thank you,' stammered Janna, 'and your husband's the great detective.'

'He'd like you to say so. He said to call him if you get any hassle.' Margaret popped the Chief Inspector's card into Janna's jacket pocket. 'You must come to supper and meet him.'

Vastly cheered, Janna worked the room, enquiring after new babies, congratulating on engagements and new houses, expressing sorrow over deaths and hearing endless complaints about the new Year Nine and the Wolf Pack.

She was aware of Mike Pitts skulking in a corner not meeting her eyes and Cara Sharpe also avoiding her. In a scarlet dress, which clung to her rapacious, elongated body and matched her drooping vermilion mouth, Cara looked far more attractive than she had at Janna's interview. Her ebony hair seemed softer and curlier, but her face was still as hard as the earth in those poor dead potted plants.

She was also busy upstaging other teachers over their GCSE results. 'How did Mitzi do in geography?' she called across to Miss Basket: one of the Dinosaurs who had buck teeth, a pale, wispy fringe and a twitching face shiny enough to check one's make-up in, and who promptly stepped back into the Christmas decorations with a loud crunch, replying that Mitzi had only got a D.

'You amaze me, she's so easy to teach,' mocked Cara. 'She got A stars in drama, English and English lit. for me.'

Bitch, thought Janna and promptly told a crestfallen Miss Basket, 'You did brilliantly with those asylum-seekers, getting C grades in such a short time.'

50

Miss Basket blushed with passionate gratitude. Cara looked furious. Then Janna spoilt it by congratulating Basket on a new grandson.

'I never married,' squawked Basket.

Everyone suppressed smiles except Cara Sharpe, who laughed openly before turning glittering eyes on Lydia, the NQT who was the most junior member of her department:

'You've got Year Nine E tomorrow, Lydia, you'll find them a doddle.'

Janna swung round in horror. Year Nine E included the Wolf Pack, Monster and Satan, not to mention autistic, often violent Rocky. They'd eat poor Lydia for the breakfast their parents probably wouldn't provide.

'You must look out for Paris Alvaston,' Janna advised Lydia as Wally topped up their glasses. 'I hear he writes wonderful stories.'

'With respect,' sneered Cara, 'Paris is a no-hoper, like all the Wolf Pack. You have to tell them five times to do anything, they're always late or don't come in at all, and never do their homework. Paris, arrogant little beast, does what he pleases and the others follow suit.'

'Not a doddle then, as you promised Lydia,' flared up Janna, quite forgetting about keeping her trap shut. 'That's a very negative attitude.'

'I'm entirely on Cara's side. The Wolf Pack are beyond control.' A tall man with blond curls and smooth golden-brown skin had joined the group. 'Pearl's a hell-cat and Kylie Rose a nympho. If I'm going to teach them, I want a chastity belt and CCTV in the classroom.'

This must be Jason Fenton, alias Goldilocks. He was certainly pretty, his regular features marred only by rather bulging blue eyes, as though the transformation from frog into Prince Charming had not been absolute.

'We mustn't let past behaviour dictate the future,' Janna said firmly. 'The Wolf Pack are clearly forceful characters.'

'You can't make a difference with that lot,' drawled Jason, 'they're too damaged.'

The room had gone quiet, quivering collectively with expectation.

'If you feel like that,' said Janna furiously, 'you shouldn't be teaching here.'

'I couldn't agree more.' Jason smiled into her eyes. 'I've been trying to see you all day to hand in my notice.' Over the gasps of amazement he added: 'But Rowan Merton wouldn't let me cross your threshold,' and, shoving an envelope into Janna's hand, he turned towards the door.

A striking strawberry blonde in a non-existent skirt and a clinging pink vest glued to her worked-out body, whom Janna recognized as Gloria, the deputy head of PE, gave a wail: 'When are you going, Jase?'

'If one resigns on the first day of term, one can be over the hills and far way by half-term.'

'And *where* are you going?' hissed an incensed, wrong-footed Cara.

'To Bagley Hall as head of drama,' said Jason, filling up his glass on the way out.

'That's an independent,' thundered Sam Spink.

'I know,' murmured Jason. 'Adequate funding, nineteen weeks' holiday, a decent salary and no Wolf Pack: need I say more? Here's to me,' and, draining his glass, he was gone.

Over a thunderous murmur of chat, Janna had to pull herself and the meeting together. Clapping her hands for quiet, assuring everyone she wouldn't keep them long, she then had to express great regret that Larks had had to bid farewell to ten teachers she had never met. There were broad grins when she described a former ICT master as a 'tower of strength', when he'd evidently jumped half the female staff and impregnated two supply teachers, and laughter when she expressed deep regret at the death of some former head, who'd only emigrated with his wife to Tasmania.

'Mike Pitts wouldn't have slipped up like that,' muttered Skunk Illingworth, the science Dinosaur, refilling his pint mug.

'I will get to know you all soon,' apologized Janna. She took a deep breath and looked round. Somehow she must rally them. Then Jason returned. Seeing him grinning superciliously and lounging against the wall, Janna's resolve was stiffened and she kicked off by attacking her staff for their atrocious GCSE results.

'We must start from this moment to improve. If we can get our children to behave, then we can teach them, and they will behave if they're interested.' She smiled at Lydia in the front row.

'They will also behave if this is a happy school and they have fun here as well as learning. We must give them and the school back its pride so they'll stop trashing and graffitiing the place.

'Wally has worked so hard restoring the building over the holidays. Debbie has worked so hard cleaning up in here. Frankly, it was a tip.' Out of the corner of her eye, she saw Wally clutching his head. 'In turn,' she went on, 'I'd like you all to work hard transforming your classrooms. We want examples of good work on the walls and the corridors and colour and excitement everywhere.' Then, beaming at the furious faces: 'And will you all start smiling around the place, particularly at the children, making them feel valued and welcome.'

Only Phil Pierce, Lydia and Lance, Mags Gablecross and Miss Cambola, the busty music mistress, smiled back.

As Janna took a fortifying slug of white, she heard a loud cough to her left and, glancing round, saw Sam Spink tapping the glass of her watch.

'You were saying?' snapped Janna.

Marching over, Sam said in a stage whisper that could be heard in the gods at Covent Garden: 'People have been in school since eight-thirty, nearly nine hours, working flat out to get everything shipshape. Many colleagues need to collect kids from child-minders, others have long journeys home and want to be alert for their students tomorrow. I'm sure you're aware that anything over eight hours is unacceptable. Any minute they'll walk out of their own accord.'

'OK,' muttered Janna, turning to her now utterly captive audience, 'we'll call it a day. I'm afraid it's been a very long one. Thank you all for coming. I look forward to working with you,' then she hissed at Sam Spink, 'and I'll personally string you up by your Winnie-the-Pooh character socks if you ever cheek me in public like that again,' before stalking out.

'Remember always to smile around the school,' Cara Sharpe called after her.

'Never thanked me for taking Year Ten to Anglesey in July,' repeated Skunk as he petulantly emptied bottles, then glasses into his mug.

Phil and Wally were kind and complimentary, but Janna knew she'd blown it.

'This place needs shaking up,' said Phil. 'Would you like to come home for a bite of supper?'

'Oh, I'd love to,' said Janna longingly, 'but I've got so much to do.'

She still hadn't written her speech for assembly and her in-tray, to quote Larkminster Rovers's battle hymn, was 'rising, rising, rising'.

She was also jolted to realize that in the old days, before she'd become part of the high-flying team at Redfords, she'd have probably been out hassling senior management like Sam Spink: was poacher turning keeper?

The full moon, like a newly washed plate, followed her home – perhaps she *should* buy the staffroom a dishwasher. Jubilee Cottage was cold, smelt musty and didn't look welcoming because she still hadn't unpacked her stuff or put up any pictures. Most of them, admittedly, were adorning her office at Larks.

Poor little cottage, she must give it some TLC along with five hundred disturbed children and at least twenty-eight bolshie staff.

A large vodka and tonic followed by Pot Noodles wasn't a good idea either. She'd promptly thrown up the lot. Then she washed her hair. Nagged to present a more respectable image by her fellow teachers at Redfords, she had had her red curls lopped to the shoulders, then defiantly invested in a pink suit decorated with darker pink roses which should jazz up tomorrow's proceedings.

As heads covered up to ten miles a day policing their schools, she had also bought a pair of dark pink shoes with tiny heels. She laid everything out on a chair. By the time she'd showered and put on a nightie, it was half past twelve.

She fell to her knees. 'Oh please, dear God, help me to save my school.'

If you banged your head on the pillow and recited something last thing, you were supposed to remember it in the morning.

'Feral Jackson, Paris Alvaston, Graffi Williams, Pearl Smith, Kylie Rose Peck . . .' The faces of the Wolf Pack swam before her eyes throughout the night.

Then she overslept and didn't get to school until eight-fifteen.

At the bottom of the drive, in anticipation of a new term, were already gathering lawyers' assistants waiting to hand out leaflets encouraging disgruntled parents to sue the school, pushers lurking with offers of drugs or steroids, and expelled pupils hanging around to duff up pupils they'd been chucked out for terrorizing.

On her desk, Janna found a pile of good-luck cards, but nothing from Stew, not even a phone message. She was also outraged to receive a card on which Tory blue flowers – bluebells, flax and forget-me-nots – were intertwined and exquisitely painted by someone called Hanna Belvedon. Inside was a handwritten note from

Jupiter Belvedon, presumably the artist's husband and Larkminster's Conservative MP, welcoming Janna to Larkshire and hoping she'd ring him if she needed help. As if she'd accept help from a rotten Tory.

Out of the window she could see pupils straggling up the drive, smoking, arguing, fighting. Several posters and the welcome-back sign had already been ripped down. There was a crash as a brick flew through a window in reception.

Two minutes before assembly was due to start, Rowan Merton bustled in quivering with excitement:

'You might like to open this before kick-off.'

It was a beautifully wrapped and pink-ribboned bottle of champagne. Darling Stew had remembered. Turning towards the window, so Rowan couldn't look over her shoulder, Janna opened the little white envelope and was almost winded with disappointment as she read: 'Dear Miss Curtis, This is to wish you great luck, I hope you'll lunch with me one day soon. Yours ever, Hengist Brett-Taylor'.

'Who the hell's Hengist Brett-Taylor?'

Rowan was so impressed, she forgot for a moment to be hostile.

'Don't you know? He's head of Bagley Hall.' Then, when Janna looked blank: 'Our local independent school – frightfully posh. He was on *Question Time* last Thursday making mincemeat of poor Estelle Morris. Livens up any programme.'

'Not Ghengist Khan,' whispered Janna in horror, 'that fascist pig?'

'Well, I don't approve of Hengist's politics,' said Rowan shirtily, 'but he's drop-dead gorgeous.'

'He's an arrogant bastard,' who, now Janna remembered, had just poached Jason Fenton, another arrogant bastard. They'd suit each other. She was about to drop the bottle of champagne in the bin, when the bell went, so she put it in the fridge. She might well need it later.

Applying another layer of pale pink lipstick, she defiantly drenched herself in Diorissimo, buttoned up her suit to flaunt her small waist, and jumped at the sound of a wolf whistle.

'You look absolutely gorgeous,' sighed Phil Pierce, who'd come to collect her, 'roses, roses all the way. The kids are going to love you.'

Hearing the overwhelming din of children pouring down the corridor into the main hall, Janna started to shake. The task ahead seemed utterly awesome.

5

Dora, the eleven-year-old sister of Larkminster's Tory MP, Jupiter Belvedon, had heard that the young headmistress starting at Larks, the local sink school, was an absolute cracker. Dora thought this most unlikely. Schoolmistresses in her experience were such old boots that anything without two heads and a squint was described as 'attractive'.

Dora had therefore risen at seven to ride her skewbald pony Loofah along the River Fleet and into Larkminster to check Janna out. Dora also needed to think. She was very exercised because she was starting boarding at a new school, Bagley Hall, in a week's time. Dora's mother, Anthea, kept saying Bagley Hall was like Chewton Glen or the Ritz, but to Dora it was prison – particularly as she'd be separated from Loofah and Cadbury, her chocolate Labrador, who bounded ahead of them putting up duck. Dora was worried about both Loofah and Cadbury. Her sweet father, who'd been dotty about animals, would have looked after them, but alas, he'd died recently and her mother regarded both animals as a tie and a needless expense.

Dora sighed and helped herself to blackberries in the hedgerows. Loofah was much too small for her. He'd need lifts soon to stop her feet scraping the ground. He also bucked, sat down and bit people, but she loved him far too much to sell him. Life was very hard when you had so many animal dependants. Dora edged a KitKat out of her jodhpur pocket to share with the two of them. Her mother, Anthea, was always warning Dora she'd get spots and never attract a boyfriend.

Who wanted soppy boyfriends? thought Dora scornfully.

Dora had thick, flaxen plaits and even thicker curly blonde eyelashes, which seemed designed to stop the peak of her hard hat falling over her turned-up nose. Her big eyes were the same drained turquoise as the sky on the horizon. Slender, small for her age, she was redeemed from over-prettiness by a determined chin and a mouth frequently pursed in disapproval.

And Dora had much to disapprove of. Her beautiful mother, Anthea, in appearance all dewy-eyed softness, was in reality catting around with loads of boyfriends, including an awful old judge and a rose-grower – both married – and playing the disconsolate, impoverished widow for all she was worth. Fed up with the school run and anxious to enjoy an unbridled sex life, Anthea clearly wanted Dora out of the way, locked up at Bagley Hall.

The sole plus for Dora was that for several years she had been augmenting her income by leaking stories to the press. Her mother's romantic attachments had provided excellent copy.

Bagley Hall should prove even more remunerative. Hengist Brett-Taylor, the head, whom her mother fancied almost as much as Rupert Campbell-Black, was never out of the news. Her twin brother Dicky, who'd been boarding since he was eight and was so pretty he was the toast of the rugby fifteen, had torrid tales of the antics of the pupils.

But alas, her chilly eldest brother, Jupiter, as well as being MP for Larkshire, was chairman of the governors at Bagley Hall and, petrified of sleaze, had already given Dora a stern lecture about keeping her Max Clifford tendencies in check: 'If I hear you've been tipping off the press about anyone at Bagley or in the family, particularly me, there'll be big trouble.'

Jupiter was a beast, reflected Dora, appropriating the family home and all the money when her father died, so Dora, Dicky and their mother Anthea were now crammed into tiny Foxglove Cottage in Bagley village.

Ancient trees stroked the bleached fields with long shadows as Dora reached the outskirts of Larkminster. As she crossed the bridge, the cathedral clock struck eight. Ahead, she could see the beautiful golden houses of the Close, the market and the thriving bustling town. Trotting past St Jimmy's, the highly successful boys' school, entering the Shakespeare Estate, Dora was overtaken by an Interflora van heading nervously towards Larks Comp.

No one drove through the Shakespeare Estate by choice because of the glass and needles all over the roads. Screaming and shouting could be heard issuing from broken, boarded-up windows. Discarded fridges and burnt-out cars littered the gardens. An ashen druggie mumbled in the gutter. A gang of youths, hanging round a motorbike, hurled abuse at Dora as she passed.

Dora didn't care. She called off Cadbury who was taunting a snarling pit bull on a very short lead and looked up enviously at the satellite dishes clustered like black convolvulus on the houses. Her mother was too mean to install Sky in Foxglove Cottage.

Next door to the Shakespeare Estate, as a complete contrast, was a private estate called Cavendish Plaza, which was protected by huge electric gates, security guards and a great abstract in the forecourt, sculpted by Dora's gallery-owning father's most awful artist, Colin Casey Andrews, which was enough to frighten off any burglar, thought Dora sourly.

Cavendish Plaza was one of the brainchildren of developer Randal Stancombe, who was slapping houses, shops and supermarkets all over Larkshire and whom her mother also thought was frightfully attractive, but whose hot, devouring, knowing dark eyes made Dora's flesh crawl.

Cavendish Plaza had its own shops and access to the High Street on the other side. Dora, riding on, came to a chip shop with boarded-up windows and a pub called the Ghost and Castle, then stiffened with interest as she saw the notorious Wolf Pack slouching out of the newsagent's, loaded up with goodies. Feral Jackson was breaking the cellophane round a chicken tikka sandwich.

Everyone knew Feral. Although not yet fourteen, he was already five feet nine with snake hips, three-foot-wide shoulders and a middle finger permanently jabbing the air. He'd been up before Dora's mother at the Juvenile Court in the summer for mugging.

'And gave me such a disgustingly undressing look when we remanded him in custody,' her mother had complained.

In the end Feral had been sent for a month to a Young Offenders' Institute, and if he recognized her as her mother's daughter he'd probably knife her as well. Dora shot off down a side road.

Janna's arrival at Larks was, in fact, causing universal excitement.

Rod Hyde, head of St Jimmy's, picked up a magnifying glass to look at a photograph of Janna in the *Larkminster Gazette*. She had nice breasts and an air of confidence that would soon disappear. Pride comes before a fall. Rod Hyde was full of such little homilies. 'Good schools are like good parents,' he was always saying, 'caring and demanding.'

Rod Hyde was very bald but shaved his remaining hair. He had a firm muscular figure, a ginger beard, and believed in exercise and cold baths. St Jimmy's' results had been staggeringly good this year and they were edging nearer Bagley Hall in the league tables.

As a local super head, Rod Hyde was certain his friends, who ran S and C Services, would soon send him into Larks on a rescue mission. He would much enjoy giving Janna Curtis guidance.

Randal Stancombe, property developer, finished working out in his rooftop gymnasium. Before having a shower, he picked up his binoculars and looked down with pride on Cavendish Plaza, his beautiful private estate with its mature trees, still-emerald green lawns and swimming pools, where topless tenants were taking advantage of the Indian summer.

Randal's hands, however, clenched on his binoculars as he turned them towards Larks Comp. He could see all those ruffians straggling in, scrapping, stopping to light fags or worse. Randal's tenants were constantly complaining about stolen cars and streets paved with chewing gum.

Janna Curtis looked pretty tasty in her photograph in the *Gazette*, decided Randal. She might make bold statements about turning the school round, but this Lark had two broken wings. S and C Services were bound to keep her so short of money, she'd soon be desperate for sponsorship. Interesting to see how long she'd take to approach him. Randal loved having power over women.

Randal's daughter Jade, a very attractive young lady, rising fourteen years of age, was starting her third year at Bagley Hall and dating a fellow pupil, Cosmo Rannaldini, the son of Dame Hermione Harefield, the globally famous diva. One forked out school fees mainly for the contacts. Randal would soon ask Dame Hermione to open his hypermall outside Birmingham.

Over at Bagley Hall, Hengist Brett-Taylor, who'd just spent five weeks in Umbria to avoid the middle classes and those with new money, was drafting a speech for the new pupils' parents.

'May I first issue a very warm welcome to all of you here tonight,' he wrote. 'But also point out what will rapidly become clear to you as the years roll by: that the headmaster of Bagley Hall is rather like the figurehead on an old wooden sailing ship. It is vaguely decorative and there is a clear understanding that one really ought to have one if one is to be seen doing the proper thing, but it is of course of absolutely no practical use whatsoever and does nothing.'

Hengist's glow at nearing the top of the country's league tables in both A and GCSE levels was slightly dimmed by having to face several more massive hurdles at the start of term. In addition, he had to address the first staff meeting, the first assembly, the drinks party or 'shout-in' for new staff, not to mention keynote speeches to new pupils and sixth-formers and finally the first sermon in chapel on Sunday week.

The problem was to avoid repeating oneself or descending into platitudes, which was why Francis Bacon's essays, full of invigorating epigrams, was open on his desk. Hengist, who was terrified of boredom, was simultaneously drinking black coffee, listening to Brahms' Symphony No. 2 on Radio 3, watching a video of Bagley's first fifteen's recent tour of South Africa and fondly admiring a white greyhound fast asleep on her back on the window seat.

Thank God all the holiday activities – sport and foreign trips – had passed without mishap. 'Toff school goes berserk in convent on rugger tour' could leave a huge clear-up job at the beginning of term.

Hengist gazed out at a sea of green playing fields broken only by the white rugger posts and a little wood, Badger's Retreat, in the distance, to which he kept adding young trees.

The Brahms had finished. Bagley's first fifteen had reached half-time. Picking up the *Larkminster Gazette*, Hengist looked at Janna's picture and shook his head:

'Poor, poor little lamb to the slaughter.'

The Bishop of Larkminster, on his knees in his bed-room in the Bishop's Palace overlooking the River Fleet, was praying without much hope that Janna Curtis, only a child herself, would be able to tame those dreadfully disturbed children who came from such appalling backgrounds. Next moment, he jumped out of skin still pink from his bath as a football parted the magnolia grandiflora and crashed against a pane of his Queen Anne window.

Creaking to his feet and bustling to the window, the Bishop caught a glimpse of white teeth like the crescent moon in a wicked laughing black face as, having retrieved his ball, the invader dropped back into the road. Here his companion, with a can of blue paint, was changing the 'u' in 'Please Shut the Gate' to an 'i'.

'Little buggers,' thundered the Bishop.

The Wolf Pack had no intention of going into school. The grass was too long to play football. So they played in the street. Fists were shaking and windows banged in fury as their ball shed the petals of a yellow rose, then snapped off the head of a tiger lily, before knocking down a row of milk bottles like ninepins.

Feral had finished his chicken sandwich but was still hungry, as he and Paris argued the merits of Arsenal and Liverpool. They once had a fight over whether Thierry Henry was a better player than Michael Owen that had gone on for three days. Feral and Graffi were careful not to mention programmes they had watched last night in front of Paris. Viewing in Paris's children's home was strictly limited. The television was switched off at nine and monitored for sex and violence, which meant no *Big Brother*, *EastEnders*, or *The Bill*.

Pearl Smith, in a vile mood, was kicking a Coke tin. One of the few pupils at Larks who looked good in the hard crimson of the school uniform, she wore a skimpy crop top in that colour instead of the regulation sweat-shirt. Her arm throbbed where she'd cut herself last night, after her mother's boyfriend had pushed her across the room for pinching her new baby sister.

Graffi, who'd appropriated another can of paint, was writing 'Stancombe is an asshole' on an outside wall of Cavendish Plaza.

'Very limited vocabulary,' mocked Paris, opening a stolen bar of Crunchie.

'Fuck off, professor,' replied Graffi. 'Teach me some new words then.'

Feral, meanwhile, had opened a nicked *Larkminster Gazette* and was studying Janna's picture.

'Don't look much,' snarled Pearl. 'Crap 'air, crap figure.'

'Oh, I don't know,' said Graffi, to wind her up.

Next moment, Kylie Rose, the fifth member of the Wolf Pack, carrying a pregnancy kit stolen from the High Street, joined them.

'I only got Mum to babysit Cameron by promising I'd go into school,' she told the others, then, peering at the *Gazette*, 'A-a-a-a-h. Janna says she's looking forward to meeting us. Isn't she pretty?'

'Let's go and take the piss,' said Feral, handing the paper to Paris. 'Wally might have mowed the grass.'

Feral could do anything with a football and now, see-ing Dora Belvedon approaching, drove it between the conker-brown legs of her pony, Loofah, who reared up. Only Dora's excellent seat kept her in the saddle. Enraged, she rode straight at the Wolf Pack. As he leapt out of the way, Feral slashed at Loofah's reins with a knife, adding in a hoarse deep voice: 'Fuck off, you snotty little slag.'

Next moment Cadbury, the Labrador, came storm-ing to the rescue, barking furiously. Feral, who was terrified of dogs, bolted, followed by the others. Only Paris, who protected and looked after Robin, the old fox terrier who lived at his children's home, stood his ground with hand outstretched, until Cadbury wagged his tail and licked the Crunchie crumbs off his fingers.

He had the palest face Dora had ever seen.

'Don't you dare suck up to my dog,' she yelled.

'Fuck off, you stuck-up bitch,' hissed Paris.

His face stayed with Dora. Apart from the curled lip and gelled, spiky hair, he looked like the ghost on the inn sign of the Ghost and Castle.

6

Assembly at Larks was held in the main hall. On the walls in between doorways leading to classrooms hung bad portraits of former heads: bearded gentlemen in wing collars or wearing cravats with their hair brushed forward. There were also boards listing head boys and more recent heads. How cross Mike Pitts, skulking at the back, must have felt not to have made it up there.

Moth-eaten bottle-green velvet curtains flanked the platform, whose only props included a lectern, a few chairs and, to the right, a grand piano. Behind, having remarkably escaped the school vandals, soared a stained-glass window depicting a languid Archangel Michael with his flaming sword raised to kebab an inoffensive little dragon.

The dragon et moi, thought Janna, unless I catch this mob by the throat. The butterflies in her tummy had grown into blindly crashing pterodactyls as she stood in the wings, trying to concentrate on Phil Pierce's flattering introduction. Although there were only three hundred children after the register had been taken, there seemed an awful lot of them. Above her, chewing gum and surreptitiously chatting into their mobiles, Years Ten and Eleven hung over the balcony rail. In the body of the hall stood Years Eight and Nine, who'd struggled to their feet when prodded by their various form tutors, who ringed them with arms folded like riot police anticipating trouble.

With a thud of relief, Janna thought how attractive the children looked with their bright, curious faces: brown, black, yellow, pink, white, deathly pale, a few tanned, but now tinged with glowing ruby, emerald, violet, sapphire and amber by the light streaming through the stained glass. Both Wally and Phil crossed fingers behind their backs as she bounded up onto the platform, wearing an orange builder's hat.

'Good morning, everyone.' She beamed round at her astonished audience. 'I couldn't decide whether to wear this or a bullet-proof vest, but you all look so friendly, I needn't have worried, so let's kick off with one of your favourite songs.'

Crossing the platform she sat down at the piano and strummed out the introduction to the Larkminster Rovers battle hymn, then, with her sweet, pure voice ringing round the hall, launched into the first verse.

As she reached the second, Miss Cambola, head of music, ran up the platform steps and, in a rich mezzo, splendid bosom heaving, joined in: ' "Europe ain't seen nuffink yet." '

After a stunned silence, everyone else joined in, roaring out the chorus to loud whistling, cheering and stamping of feet.

How at ease she is with the kids, thought Wally as he uncrossed his fingers. And how bonny she looked in her rose suit, with her flaming red curls and her freckles breaking through her make-up.

After a second encore, Janna shut the piano, bowed, then whipped off her hat and held it out to a smiling Phil Pierce, who dropped in a pound coin to roars of laughter.

Janna turned to her audience. 'I'm so pleased to be here.'

'We're not,' shouted a voice from the gallery.

Janna laughed: 'Give me time.'

'She is very pretty,' whispered Kylie Rose, 'and nice.'

'She's ancient,' snarled Pearl.

'I was going through your personal files last night,' continued Janna, 'and discovered some truly excellent work.'

She then praised several children who'd done well in exams and in class.

'I particularly want to commend Aysha Khan's progress in science, and Paris Alvaston's essays, and Graffi Williams's artwork.'

'You can see it on walls all over the town,' shouted a wag.

'I want us to build on these wonderful successes, "rising, rising" like Larkminster Rovers till we get to the top. I'm determined to find what each one of you is good at. Everyone's a star at something. Never be afraid to ask for help or to pop into my office to tell me your problems. I and the other teachers are here to help.'

Seeing Cara Sharpe turn green like the witch in *Snow White* and raising her eyebrows to heaven, Janna took a deep breath:

'I'd like to tell you a story about some begonias, which are kinds of bulbs I planted in pots on the window ledge in my classroom at my last school. I planted seven. They were red, yellow, orange, pink, crimson, cream and white.'

'Oh, get on,' yelled a bruiser Janna recognized as Satan Simmons.

'These bulbs grew very fast on my window ledge,' she went on, 'except one little white one, which didn't put out a single shoot. I was sure it was dead. Days passed and all the others bloomed in wonderful colours, red, yellow, orange, pink, crimson and cream.'

'Cream ain't a colour,' shouted Pearl.

'OK, OK,' went on Janna. 'But as Christmas approached, all the six had finished flowering. I was about to store them for next year and chuck the little white one in the bin, when suddenly it put out leaves and grew and grew until it flowered just at Christmas, when there were no flowers around. And it gave more pleasure than any of the other begonias. So if you're a late developer, don't worry, your time will come.'

Now she'd got their attention, she went on: 'You're all good at something – there are all sorts of exciting new GCSEs. Have you thought of taking one in child development? All you need do is study a little brother or sister.'

'Christ, no,' sneered Pearl, lighting a fag.

Janna's eyes flashed.

'And you're good at smoking, Pearl Smith,' she yelled in sudden outrage. 'You're only thirteen; how dare you ruin your lungs?'

Pearl dropped her cigarette, staggered that Janna knew her name and age.

'I want to see you in my office immediately after assembly,' said Janna ominously. 'You're Pearl's head of year, aren't you, Mrs Sharpe? Please see that she's there.'

Cara Sharpe was hopping. So was Pearl when she reached Janna's office. Her breath was coming in great gasps lifting her little crimson crop top even higher above her groin-level mini.

She seemed to be deliberately breaking every school rule. Her hair drawn back into a cascade of ringlets was dyed more colours than the begonias. Studs gleamed from her belly button, nose and ears, from which, in addition, hung big gold loops. A silver cross nestled in her cleavage. A cat tattoo crawled under a gold ankle bracelet. More alarmingly, scars laddered her arms where she'd cut herself.

Yet with her wide-apart stick legs above killer heels, her sharp nose and chin, her shiny dark eyes, which kept glancing sideways at Janna, and her savage perkiness, she resembled nothing so much as a robin.

'How d'you know my name?'

'Because I care about you,' said Janna gently.

'Don't know me.'

'I want to very, very much.'

Pearl looked sullenly up at the photograph of smiling, waving Redfords pupils. 'Your last school?'

Janna nodded.

'Where is it?'

'Yorkshire.'

'Never been there. Miss Basket, our crap geography teacher, has never been to London.'

Janna suppressed a smile.

'We were the worst school in Yorkshire, right at the bottom,' she said.

'Like us.'

Janna went to the fridge. 'Would you like a Coke?'

'OK. Mrs Sharpe's a bitch.'

'In what way?'

'Blames it on us that she didn't get your job. If our SATs had been better, she would have. She never says anyfing nice when she marks our stuff.'

'How's your new baby sister?' asked Janna.

'Mum wanted to put her in my room – screams all night – and expects me to babysit so she can go out with her toyboy. I said no fucking way. I used to live with my boxer dad, but he's inside for burglary to feed his habit.'

A depressing smell of unflavoured mince was drifting up from the kitchens. I must do something about the food, thought Janna.

'I had a sister who trashed my room,' she said, 'but we get on now. I've heard you're very bright.'

'Paris is the clever one,' said Pearl. 'If he wasn't so cool, he'd get bullied for being a boffin.'

They were interrupted by screams and yells; next minute, Kylie rushed in in high excitement. 'Quickly, miss. Feral and Monster are killing each other in classroom G.'

Not yet wired up, with no thought of summoning back-up or enlisting help from other staff, Janna hurtled down the corridor.

'Christ, she's fast,' gasped Pearl as she and Kylie Rose panted after her.

Half Year Nine E was standing on desks, cheering on the protagonists; occasionally they got so heated, they started punching each other. Graffi was grinning broadly and offering two to one on Feral winning. Paris lounged against the wall pretending to be reading *David Copperfield*, but watching and waiting to jump to Feral's aid.

Young Lydia, suffering a baptism of fire in her first lesson, cringed in a corner, a book called *Dealing with Disruptive Students in the Classroom* sticking out of her pocket.

Janna promptly pummelled and shoved the audience out of the classroom, but they rushed round outside and continued to peer in through the window, applauding and egging on their heroes.

'C'mon, Feral.'

'C'mon, Monster.'

Monster was as huge as a sea lion; Feral, lithe as a panther, prowled round, taunting him, hitting Monster in the eye, which started bleeding, then skipping out of the way as Monster tried to punch him in the stomach. Now they were locked, throwing blows, Feral wincing as he was crushed by Monster's brute strength. Noticing Feral's hand stealing down his jeans, followed by a flash of silver, Janna dived between them.

'Stop it,' she screamed over escalating shrieks and yells. Next moment Feral's knife was thrust in her face, halting within an inch of her nose.

'Pack it in, Feral,' repeated Janna, 'and you too, Monster.'

Chivalry was not in Feral's code, but he admired guts. The rest of the class crept back in through window or door.

'You have a very sexy mouth, Feral,' observed Janna. 'If occasionally you raised it at both corners, and showed your beautiful teeth in a smile rather than an animal snarl, you could look very attractive. And please give me that knife.'

Feral put down his knife and started to laugh, so everyone else did too.

'She's OK,' muttered Pearl.

'I said she was nice,' said Kylie.

'You're wasted on Larks, miss,' observed Graffi, 'you should be refereeing Man U or Arsenal.'

Janna turned to a quivering, ashen Lydia. 'All right, love?'

'F-f-fine.' Then, with hero-worship in her eyes: 'You're the bravest person I've ever met.'

Phil Pierce and Mike Pitts, who were waiting in the passage, were not of the same opinion.

'You stupid fool,' said Phil. 'You could have been killed. Why in hell didn't you call for back-up?'

'I forgot my radio mike,' said Janna, jolted by his rage.

'Well, for God's sake, don't forget it again. This school is not the place for suicide missions.'

Back in her office, Janna was greeted by a smug Rowan.

'I've been trying and trying to page you. Both the Bishop of Larkminster and Mrs Kamani from the corner shop have been on the phone complaining about the Wolf Pack playing football and shoplifting. Evidently Pearl raised her skirt and distracted Mrs Kamani's young son while the boys helped themselves. Next time she's going to press charges.'

It was after six-thirty. People had been banging on Janna's door all day, wanting a piece of her or to give her a piece of their minds. News of her breaking up a fight had whizzed round the building, opinion dividing sharply as to whether she had been incredibly brave or glory-mongering.

Crispin Thomas, ringing from S and C Services, no doubt tipped off by Mike Pitts or Cara, was in the latter camp.

'Feral could have been up on a murder charge and the school brought into disrepute because of your thoughtless irresponsibility,' he snuffled in his asthmatic, pig-like voice. 'And what's this about singing football songs in assembly?'

Janna decided to call it a day and go home.

'Thank you,' she said to Rowan as she took Hengist Brett-Taylor's bottle of champagne out of the fridge, 'you've been a great support.'

Rowan, who knew she hadn't, had the grace to blush.

In reception, Wally was mending windows.

'You did triffic,' he told her. 'Don't listen to the others. Mike Pitts downloaded all his assemblies off the internet. The kids loved you. Just promise to wear that radio mike.'

'It bulks out my skirt at the back,' grumbled Janna.

'Better be wired up than washed up, when you're doing so good,' said Wally.

Maybe, but every poster she'd put up in reception had been ripped down. As she went towards the car park, she discovered someone spraying a large penis in dark browns, purples and pinks on a newly painted wall.

The artist was poised to bolt when Janna called out:

'I don't know how many penises you've seen in your short life, Graffi Williams, but normally the glans is longer. Those testicles, in my experience, are too big, although the wrinkling of the scrotal sac is masterly.'

As Graffi's jaw and his spray can crashed to the ground, Janna went on:

'I've got a spare wall in my lounge at my new cottage. I've been wondering how to decorate it. Would you have a moment to pop over at the weekend and give me some ideas for a mural? I'll pay you, but I'd rather you didn't do cocks. There are enough of them crowing in the farm across the fields. Bring Paris, if you like. I'll clear it with the children's home.'

7

After the dark, frenzied intensity of her day, Janna was astonished by the tranquil beauty of the evening. Beyond the hedgerows, slate-blue with sloes and festooned with scarlet skeins of bryony, newly harvested fields rose in platinum-blond sweeps to woods so lush and glossy from endless rain that they appeared to have spent the summer in some expensive greenhouse.

Janna was trying to decide if the orange-gold sheen on the trees was the first fires of autumn or gilding by the setting sun when she plunged like a train into one of Larkshire's dark tunnels: hawthorn, hazel, blackthorn and elder, rising thickly from high banks and impenetrably intertwined overhead by traveller's joy. Down and down she went, until she emerged blinking into the village of Wilmington, passing the duck pond and the village green bordered with pale gold cottages, swerving to avoid a mallard and his wife ambling down the High Street in the direction of the Dog and Duck.

Jubilee Cottage was the last house on the right. As she parked her new pea-green Polo in the street, because the garage was still filled with unpacked boxes, Janna thought she had never been so tired. She'd survived, but the prospect of tomorrow terrified her. Getting out, she caught sight of her neighbour deadheading roses in the mothy dusk, who called out:

'How did you get on? I've been reading about you in

the *Gazette*. Come and have a drink, if you're not too tired. I'd have asked you earlier, but I've been away. My name's Lily Hamilton.'

Lily must be well into her seventies, thought Janna, but she was still very beautiful, with gentian-blue eyes, luxuriant grey hair drawn into a bun and a poker-straight back.

'What a lovely garden,' sighed Janna, admiring white geraniums, phlox and roses luminous in the dusk. 'Mine's a tip.'

'You've been far too busy. I always think one tackles gardens the second year. I'm afraid it's like the Harrods' depository,' she went on, leading Janna into a drawing room crammed with furniture, suggesting departure from a much larger house. Pictures covered every inch of wall. Over the fireplace hung a very explicit nude, with far more rings and studs piercing her voluptuous body than Pearl Smith. Dominating the room was a lovely pale pink and green silk striped sofa, whose arms had been ripped to shreds. The culprit, a vast fluffy black and white cat whom Lily introduced as the General, was stretched out unrepentantly in one corner. In the other lay an even larger stuffed badger. Seeing Janna's frown of disapproval, Lily explained the badger was already stuffed when she acquired him.

'He was in an auction, looking so sad and unloved, I got him for fifteen shillings.'

Wondering if Lily was a bit dotty, Janna waved Hengist's bottle of champagne. 'Why don't we drink this?'

'Tepid champagne is a crime against nature,' observed Lily. 'Let's cool it in the deep freeze and first drink this stuff, which is much less nice.' She filled Janna's glass with white.

Parked between cat and badger, Janna admitted the day had been rough.

'The older staff are so antagonistic, and they're not giving any lead to the younger teachers.'

Then she explained who'd sent her the champagne, which deteriorated into a rant against independent schools and 'fascist bastards' like Hengist Brett-Taylor in particular.

'All those facilities wasted on a few spoilt kids, whose rich parents are too selfish to look after them and just pack them off into the upper-class care of a boarding school.'

'I don't think children in care jet home to Moscow or New York at the weekend,' said Lily. 'Or race up to London. And I promise you, Hengist is a charmer. I'm sure you'd like him if you met him. He doesn't take himself at all seriously, he's awfully good-looking, and he's worked wonders with Bagley. They were a pack of tearaways five years ago. Now they're near the top of the league tables.'

'Perhaps he could give me a few tips,' said Janna sarcastically. 'Although it can't be difficult with all that money and tiny classes and vast playing fields for the kids to let off steam. How d'you know him?'

'My nephew Dicky's a pupil, Dora his twin sister starts this term and Rupert Campbell-Black's children go there as well.'

Which sent Janna into more shivering shock-horror:

'Rupert Campbell-Black's the most arrogant, spoilt, foxhunting, right-wing bastard.'

'But again, decidedly attractive,' laughed Lily, topping up Janna's glass. 'He does have – even more than Hengist – alarming charm.'

The General heaved himself onto Janna's knee, purring and kneading.

'I must get a cat,' sighed Janna, rubbing him behind his pink ears.

'Do,' said Lily, 'then we can catsit for each other. Why did you take on Larks?'

After a second glass on an empty stomach, Janna found herself telling Lily all about Stew.

'He swore he was going to leave Beth, his wife, and

marry me. He just had to see his son graduate, then it was his daughter's wedding, then Beth's hysterectomy, then it was going to be the moment Redfords came out of special measures.

'But the afternoon we found out, he immediately rang up Beth: "Darling, we've done it, put a bottle of bubbly on ice," and booked a table at the Box Tree. They went out to celebrate with the deputy head and his wife. I realized then he'd never leave her.'

'You poor child.' Lily patted her hand. 'For many married people, particularly men, adultery is merely an amusing hobby.'

'He really was a bastard,' mused Janna.

'But a left-wing one this time,' observed Lily.

Janna burst out laughing:

'I was so desperate to get away from the situation, and so longing to be a head, it rather blinded me to Larks's imperfections. Shall we tackle that bottle of bubbly now? And you can tell me why Hengist Brett-Taylor is so attractive and also about Wilmington.'

'Very much "Miss Marple" territory,' said Lily.

'Who's the handsome old gentleman who lives five doors down?'

'That's the Brigadier, Brigadier Christian Woodford. He always salutes my General' – Lily nodded at the cat on Janna's knee – 'when they meet in the street. His wife died recently; nearly bankrupted himself paying her medical bills. She needed twenty-four-hour nursing at home. I don't know if he'll be able to afford to stay.

'He had a terrific war. He's very well read and knows a huge amount about natural history, particularly wild flowers.'

'Like you do,' said Janna, looking at the autumn squills and meadow cranesbill in a vase on top of the bookshelf and the wild-flower books in the shelves. Glancing up at a watercolour of meadowsweet and willowherb, she added, 'I recognize that artist.'

'Hanna Belvedon, married to my nephew Jupiter.'

Then at Janna's raised eyebrows, 'Our local MP.'

'Your nephew? But he's another sneering—'

'Right-wing bastard. Here I entirely agree with you,' smiled Lily and then confided that it was Jupiter who had chucked her out of her lovely house in Limesbridge when Raymond, his father and Lily's brother, had died last year. 'He needed the rent money to boost his political campaign.'

'I told you he was a bastard,' said Janna indignantly.

'I shouldn't have sneaked,' sighed Lily, 'but I do think you should have lunch with Hengist. He's got an awfully nice wife and a daughter about your age. You must meet some young people. We're rather a geriatric bunch in Wilmington.'

'I love Wilmington,' protested Janna. 'It's the sweetest village in the world.'

'What fun you've come to live here. Are you desperately tired or shall we have some scrambled eggs?'

Dew soaked Janna's legs. The planets Saturn and, appropriately, Jupiter were rising, glowing green and contained by mist like lights from the angels' electric toothbrushes, as she tottered home after midnight.

What a darling Lily was. After the death of her sweet mother, Janna had plunged into work, and never properly mourned her loss. How wonderful if Lily could become a friend.

Tripping over a boot rack, Janna fell on top of a large bunch of pink and orange lilies wilting in the porch.

'Good luck,' said the card, 'missing you terribly, all love, Stew'.

8

Janna was woken by raging hangover and torrential rain and things went from bad to worse. She found Wally sweeping up more glass from two broken windows. Two door handles had been broken off in the lavatories. The walls in reception had been attacked with a hammer and rain poured in through the roof into the main hall and several classrooms.

Adele, who taught geography and had two children and no husband, rang in sick, so there was no one to take her classes. Another teacher, who hadn't turned up yesterday, wrote saying she'd taken a job in Canada. Ten of the children, believed to be truanting, had evidently gone elsewhere. This hardly put Janna in carnival mood to welcome the new intake of Year Seven: eleven-year-olds fresh from their primary schools.

Leaving Mags Gablecross, who had a free period, to show them round and explain their timetables, Janna took refuge in an empty classroom to fine-tune what she was going to say to their parents. The cleaners had piled the chairs on the tables to show they had swept the floor. Next moment, a tall, handsome hellraiser from Year Nine, known to be a staunch BNP supporter, staggered in with glazed eyes.

'Good morning, Johnnie Fowler,' called out Janna, proud she'd remembered his name.

Johnnie immediately grabbed a chair and hurled it at her. Just missing her head, it crashed into the whiteboard.

Radio mike forgotten, Janna fled into the corridor, slap into Phil Pierce. She collapsed against his dark blue shirt.

'Help,' she yelped.

For a moment his arms closed around her and she snuggled into him, heart hammering, breath coming in great gasps, then they both pulled away.

'Johnnie Fowler hurled a chair at me.'

Phil went straight into the classroom, slowly calming Johnnie and sending him back to his own classroom.

'He was coming down from crack.'

'He ought to be excluded or at least suspended,' raged Janna.

'If he goes home, it won't do any good. He'll be out on the street thieving. He mugged an old lady last term. Mother's on her own and can't control him, poor woman.'

Janna felt ashamed. Phil was such a good guy, who had a true empathy with the kids. She was horrified how much she'd enjoyed having his arms round her.

Janna then addressed the new Year Seven parents, who were touched, assuming her frightful shakes were due to nerves at meeting them rather than hangover or Johnnie Fowler.

'Your children will always have a special place in my heart,' she told them, 'because I'm starting at Larks at the same time as they are. We'll go up the school together, and I will learn as much from them as I hope they will from me. I will do everything to make them really enjoy learning. Any problems, please come to me and I hope to welcome you all at parents' meetings.'

She smiled round. The Year Seven parents smiled back. Most of them had been disasters at school and had been phobic about crossing the threshold. Largely from the Shakespeare Estate, they looked like children themselves. If they'd had these kids in their early teens, they need only be in their mid twenties now, which made Janna feel dreadfully old.

As she finished speaking, Mags Gablecross brought in a little girl with huge slanting dark eyes and straight black hair. She was adorable, but sobbing. Mags explained that she came from Paris Alvaston's children's home and had just arrived from Kosovo. Her mother had died in a shootout. Her father was missing, believed killed, in the war. She didn't speak any English and was called Kata.

'Now, which of you is grown-up and kind enough to look after Kata?' Janna asked the children.

Every hand went up.

Afterwards, having just managed to keep down two Alka-Seltzer and feeling incapable of tackling not one, but now two buckling in-trays, Janna informed Rowan Merton she was going to sit in on some classes. Armed with her radio mike, Janna went onto the corridors, fantasizing she was June in *The Bill* or, more likely, a sapper moving from minefield to minefield. She was aware of children roaring past her, swearing, fighting, chatting on their mobiles, drifting in late.

Out of a window, she noticed rabble-rousing Robbie Rushton and Gloria the gymnast creeping in through a side door. They should have been taking geography and PE. No wonder the kids were running wild.

A nice change, however, was Miss Uglow's RE class. 'Ugly', who refused to teach anything but the Bible, was held in equal proportions of terror, respect and love by her pupils.

'Jesus clothed the naked, fed the hungry, and educated the ignorant,' she was telling an enraptured Year Eight, 'which is what I'm doing now.'

Janna smiled and moved on. Rounding the corner, she went slap into Mike Pitts. Obviously tipped off by beady Rowan, he was spluttering to Miss

Basket, the menopausal misfit who taught geography.

'As a dedicated professional for twenty-five years, I'm not having some chit of a young woman sitting in on my lessons.' Catching sight of Janna, he turned an even deeper shade of magenta.

Miss Basket melted into the Ladies. Janna followed Mike into his office.

'Could we have a word?'

Mike glanced at the clock. 'I'm teaching in five minutes.'

Clearly a bit of a handsome dandy, judging by past cartoons of him as a cricketer and footballer on the walls, Mike looked dreadful now: his puffy face as bloodshot as his eyes; snowfalls of scurf on the shoulders of his blazer. Joss sticks glowed on his desk. His hands shook as he fussily shoved papers into a blue folder.

Poor man, thought Janna, I usurped him.

'We ought to try and get to know each other,' she stammered. Then, on wild impulse: 'Would you like to come to supper on Sunday?'

'My wife and I prefer to forget school at the weekend.'

Janna flushed. 'Well, perhaps a drink during the week?'

'Quite frankly, I'm too drained. I find if one has fulfilled one's professional commitments, socializing at the end of a working day is not on the agenda. Now, if you'll excuse me.'

Bastard, thought Janna. Feeling the parched earth of a drooping jasmine on the window ledge, she instinctively picked up the green watering can beside it.

'Don't,' yelled Mike, adding hastily, 'I like to look after my own plants. Women overwater.'

That's gin in that watering can, thought Janna, catching a whiff.

Mike glared at her, daring her to confront him.

'We have to work together . . .' Her voice trailed off. 'I must go.'

'I'll come with you,' insisted Janna.

In his classroom, they found a sweet-faced Indian girl in a pale blue sari: a teaching assistant who helped the slower pupils, particularly the foreign ones with poor English, by explaining questions to them and showing them how to write the answers. She was now laying out worksheets and consulting an algebra textbook, and told Janna she had been at Larks for four terms. She loved the job because it was so rewarding seeing understanding dawning on the children's faces and how the slow ones blossomed if you took time to explain things.

'I'd like to start an after-school maths club.'

'Wonderful idea. Come and see me.'

'We must get on,' interrupted Mike, 'the students will be here in a minute.' Tetchily, he handed the Indian girl a page of squares and triangles. 'Can you get me some marker pens and photostat this?'

'She's great,' said Janna as the girl left the room. 'What's her name?'

'I've no idea.'

And Janna flipped. 'This is disgraceful. She's the only black teacher in the school, she's been here a year and you don't know her name.'

'She's only a teaching assistant.'

'Working her butt off for you and the kids. You ought to know everyone in your department and what they're up to, and in the school, you're deputy head, for God's sake.'

'I will not be spoken to like that.'

Both jumped at a knock on the door. It was Rowan Merton, dying to find out what was going on.

'Phone for you, Janna.'

'I'm busy.'

'It's Russell Lambert, our chair of governors. Says it's urgent.'

Bitterly regretting her outburst of temper and aware

she had made an even more implacable enemy, Janna ran back to her office.

Russell, whom Janna could still only think of as Babar, king of the elephants, head of the Tusk Force, was at his most portentous.

'Good morning, Janna, bad news I'm afraid. Harry Fitzgerald, head of a school in the north of the county, has had a coronary. Ashton Douglas, head of S and C, has just phoned. They want Phil Pierce to take over as head immediately.'

'Can't they take Mike Pitts and his joss sticks?' wailed Janna unguardedly.

'You'll need your deputy head,' reproved Russell. 'You'd be very weak on the maths front if Mike goes.'

'I'll never survive without you,' Janna moaned later to Phil, who had the grace to look sheepish.

'I'm sorry, Janna, I hate to let you down, but I can't resist the chance to be a head.'

He didn't add that Janna had been disturbing his sleep recently: she was so brave but so vulnerable. He loved his wife; safer if he took himself out of harm's way.

'Anyway, Harry Fitzgerald will probably pull through and I'll be back in a few weeks.'

'I'm only cross because Skunk Illingworth will have to be promoted to head of science. He'll be so up himself. When are you going?'

'Tomorrow.'

Crispin Thomas from S and C Services rang later.

'You're providing a bloody sight more challenge than support, swiping my best teacher,' stormed Janna.

Crispin laughed fatly. 'We know, we know. We're going to send Rod Hyde, the super head from St Jimmy's, round to give you a hand next week.'

Outside, rain was still tipping down; the awful playground was filling up with puddles.

'I don't need Rod Hyde. I was hired to run this joint.

Our playground needs a makeover for a start,' and Janna hung up because of more screams and yells coming from the direction of the history block.

Running into the classroom, Nine E again, she found tin soldiers and a model battlefield scattered all over the floor. Next moment, a display of shrapnel and shell splinters, the collection of Lance, the newly qualified teacher, went flying. Lance and his teaching assistant were cringing in a corner and the appalling Monster Norman, no doubt feeling he had lost face after his fight with Feral yesterday, had taken centre stage as he menaced a terrified sobbing Asian girl.

'Teacher's pet, teacher's pet,' he hissed. 'Paki swot, Paki swot.'

His victim was Aysha Khan, who'd made such progress after two terms that Janna had singled her out in assembly.

The children, diverted by fights – this was their theatre – had formed a four-deep circle round the participants.

'Black rubbish, black shit,' taunted Monster, then spat in Aysha's face.

'Stop that,' shouted Janna, pushing her way through the crowd, too enraged to be frightened.

Monster, who she noticed had a shadow of moustache on his sweating upper lip, had a lit cigarette in his hand.

'Go home, fucking Paki bitch,' he yelled and was about to burn her arm when Janna dragged his hand away, grabbing the cigarette, stamping on it and turning on him.

'How dare you!'

'Go on,' mocked Monster, 'touch me, hit me, you try it. I'll get you fired, you'll never work again, you sad bitch.'

'You loathsome thug.' Caution had deserted Janna once more. 'Get out of here, you revolting bully.'

'Go on, miss, 'it 'im,' yelled Pearl.

'My mum's a governor.' Monster's evil, sallow, pasty face was disintegrating like goat's cheese in liquid as he gathered saliva in his mouth.

'I don't care. Out, out!'

'Well done, miss,' cheered the children as Monster, already on his mobile to his mother, pummelled his way out of the classroom.

'Are you all right, miss?' asked Kylie Rose. 'Shall I get you a cup of tea?'

In the doorway, Wally was shaking his head again. 'When will you learn, Janna?'

A hovering Jason 'Goldilocks' Fenton was also highly amused.

'Wherever you go, there's a rumpus. So exciting. I might not hand in my notice after all.'

Janna turned on him furiously too. 'Out,' she yelled.

She was picking up toy soldiers and sorting out a mortified Lance – 'I wanted to defend you, but I couldn't somehow. Not sure I'm cut out to be a teacher' – when there was a further rumpus in the corridor.

'Where's Miss Fucking Curtis?' bellowed a voice and Monster Norman's mother, predictably nicknamed 'Stormin'', square, massive and enraged, with a whiskery jaw thrust out, came barging in.

'Why are you always picking on my Martin?'

She raised her fist. Janna got out her mobile.

'If we can't discuss this, Mrs Norman, I'm calling the police. Your Martin was sadistically bullying another pupil.'

Only Wally seizing Mrs Norman's arm stopped her punching Janna in the face.

To Janna's horror, the following day, two governors (Russell Lambert and Cara Sharpe), Crispin Thomas from S and C and Mike Pitts (as deputy head), overturned Monster's exclusion, mostly on Cara's testimony.

'Martin's a sweet, caring boy,' she cooed, 'I've never had any trouble with him.'

'Nor have I,' agreed Mike, who was wearing a purple shirt to match his nose as he helped himself to another extra strong mint.

'He abused Aysha in the most revolting and racist way,' raged Janna. 'He terrorizes half his classmates. We'll never get a happy school with kids like him around.'

'Don't forget you incur a hefty five-thousand-pound fine every time you permanently exclude a pupil,' snuffled fat Crispin, accepting a mint. 'It's not as though you're oversubscribed or rolling in money. You really must be more restrained in your attitude. I'm getting complaints from all over and you've only been here three days. Calling Martin a "loathsome thug" is hardly the way to address challenging behaviour.'

Monster was suspended for three days.

The children were devastated when they heard of Phil Pierce's defection. Their favourite teacher had become just another rat leaving a sinking ship.

9

On Saturday morning, Janna sneaked into Larks to tackle her towering in-tray unobserved by Rowan Merton. Following Stew's maxim that if anything's important, people will write a second time, she chucked ninety-five per cent of her 'bin-tray' into six black dustbin bags. Perhaps Mike Pitts had a 'gin-tray' – he'd locked his office, so she couldn't check his watering can.

Yesterday afternoon, Miss Cambola had flung open the staffroom door and, rattling the teeth of the Dinosaurs and nearly bringing down the whole crumbling building, sang at the top of her voice: 'Thank God it's Friday.'

She had also written on the back of a postcard of Caruso: 'Congratulations! You have survived a whole week and done well, Regards, Maria Cambola', reducing Janna to tears of gratitude.

Having fired off thirty emails, mostly thanking people who'd sent her good-luck cards, Janna made the decision to hold a prospective-parents' evening at the end of the month. This would give her the clout and everyone the incentive to smarten up the school, painting as many classrooms as possible and papering walls and corridors with some decent kids' work, even if she had to write and draw it herself. Full of excitement, she first wrote copy for an ad in the *Larkminster*

Gazette, inviting prospective parents to the event, then secondly, a glowing report of Larks's progress and plans for the future. These she delivered to the Gazette on the way home.

Earlier in the week, she had rung Mr Blenchley, the care manager of Oaktree Court, Paris's children's home, who sounded bullying and humourless and who had a thick clogged voice like leftover lumpy porridge not going down the plughole.

Little Kata from Kosovo was adjusting to the regime, he said, and it was all right for Paris to come to tea with Graffi:

'But as the lad pleases himself, I doubt he'll show up.'

It was one of those mellow, hazy afternoons only September can produce. Midges jived idly with thistle-down. The field at the end of the village was being ploughed up, two men in yellow tractors sailing back and forth over the Venetian-red earth and waving at Janna as she sat in the garden worrying about her first governors' meeting on Monday. There was so much that needed tackling: permission to fire three-quarters of the staff for a start.

A flock of red admirals was guzzling sweetness from the long purple stems of a buddleia bush, but ignoring the honeysuckle next door – like pupils flocking to St Jimmy's and Searston Abbey rather than Larks, she thought sadly. She was just wondering how to galvanize the staff at Monday's morning briefing when the doorbell rang.

To her delight and amazement, it was Graffi, bringing both Paris and Feral. As they swarmed in, laughing and larky as the players in *Hamlet*, Janna suspected they had been enjoying a spliff or two on the way.

'How grand to see you. No Kylie and Pearl?'

'Kylie's minding baby Cameron,' said Graffi, 'giving her mum a day off. Pearl's got a hairdressing job. Don't think she'd have got here on those heels, anyway.'

'Did you walk all the way?' asked Janna, and then thought: How stupid, how else could they have afforded to come?

Taking Graffi by the arm, she led them down the hall into the kitchen, newly painted buttercup yellow and brightened by good-luck cards and framed children's drawings.

'Are you starving? I was planning to give you "high tea", as we call it in Yorkshire, a bit later,' she asked, getting out dark green mugs and a big bottle of Coke.

Opening a jumbo bag of crisps with her teeth, then bending down to pull out a blue bowl into which to decant them, she found all three boys staring at her. Barefoot, wearing tight jeans and a clinging blue-striped matelot jersey, with her wild russet curls escaping from a tartan toggle, she didn't look remotely like a headmistress.

'I don't bother to dress up much at weekends,' she stammered.

'Nice Aga.' Graffi patted its dark blue flanks. 'My mum's ambition's to have one.'

'It was already there when I moved in,' said Janna hastily.

She loved the Aga, but felt, like the burglar alarm, it was rather too middle-class.

'Why don't you explore?'

As she put knives, forks and willow-patterned plates on a tray, the boys careered round the house, opening doors and cupboards, picking up and examining ornaments.

'It's fucking tiny,' said Paris, who was accustomed to Oaktree Court, a great house once belonging to the very rich, now ironically inhabited by children who had nothing.

'This bed's fucking large,' agreed Graffi and Feral, who were used to sharing with several brothers and sisters and sometimes a drunken father or fleeing mother, when they discovered Janna's attic bedroom.

Hung with blue gingham curtains, the four-poster only left room for triangular shelves slotted into one corner, a television, fitted cupboards and a dressing table which Janna had to perch on the bottom of the bed to use.

'Fink there's a bloke in her life?' asked Feral.

'Hope not,' said Graffi, breathing in scent bottles.

'Wouldn't mind giving her one,' said Feral.

'Oh, shut up, you're incorrigible,' snapped Paris, who was examining the books, mostly classics, on either side of the bed.

'Whatever that means. This bed's fucking comfortable,' said a bouncing Feral. Then, glancing sideways at Stew's photograph, which, after Monday's flowers, was on show again: 'That must be her father.'

Joyous as otters, they bounded downstairs (emptying the crisp bowl en route) out into the garden, fascinated by reddening apples, French beans hanging from wigwams, potatoes and carrots actually growing in the ground.

'What the hell's that?'

'It's a marrer,' said Graffi. 'My nan used to stuff them.'

Holding it against his groin, Feral indulged in a few pelvic thrusts. 'Looks as though it orta do the stuffing.'

While Paris stopped to stroke Lily's cat, the General, who was tightroping along the fence, Graffi and Feral began kicking a football round the lawn. Watching their antics from the kitchen, Janna thought how perfectly they complemented each other. Paris, ghostly pale, seemed lit by moonlight, Feral by the sun. Feral was so arrogant, like George Eliot's cock, who thought the sun had risen to hear him crow. It wasn't just the lift of his jaw, or the swing of his hips, or the lean elongated body that made a red T-shirt, cheap fake leather jacket and black jeans look a million dollars. He'd make a fortune as a model. The long brown eyes curling up at the corner, with thick lashes creating a natural eyeliner, were haughty too; even the huge white smile said, 'I'm superior.'

But, despite this hauteur, like a feral cat he constantly glanced round checking for danger. Made edgy by the alien territory of the countryside, he shot inside when a dozy brown and white cow put her nose over the fence, and ran upstairs to watch football.

Physically, Graffi was a mixture of the two and, with his stocky build, olive skin and wicked dark eyes, needed only a black beret on his unruly dark curls, a smock and an easel to be having *déjeuner sur l'herbe* with naked beauties.

Janna took him into the low-beamed living room, which was painted cream with a pale coral sofa and chairs. Set into one wall was a stone fireplace filled with apple logs. The second wall was mostly a west-facing window overlooking fields and woods. Against the third was an upright piano and floor-to-ceiling shelves for Janna's books, music and CDs. The empty fourth awaited Graffi's genius.

Blown away that Janna trusted him, Graffi borrowed paper and pencil and started sketching. How would she like a view of the cathedral, houses in the Close, softened by lots of trees, a few cows paddling in the river to 'scare Feral away', people walking their dogs on the towpath?

'That sounds champion, as long as you don't graffiti the buildings.'

'Make it look more lived in. Nice place this. My da's a builder, does a lot of work for Randal Stancombe. If you want anything done, he could hide it.' Then, going back to the wall: 'It'll take a few Saturdays.'

'That's fine. You could come Sundays as well.'

'Nah, I'm busy Sundays. Going to look at them cows.' And he wandered off to kick a ball on the lawn with Feral.

Chests of books were lying round, so Paris took them

out and put them onto the shelves, his face growing paler as he kept stopping to read. Janna helped him, pointing out favourites: *Rebecca, Middlemarch, Wuthering Heights,* giving him spare copies of Byron, *Le Grand Meaulnes* and *The Catcher in the Rye.*

Paris found the cottage blissfully quiet after Oaktree Court, where someone was always sobbing, screaming and fighting, and wardens or social workers were always asking questions or needling him: 'Get your long nose out of that book. Come on, open up, open up.'

'How long have you loved reading?' asked Janna.

'Since I was about nine. Head teacher of my school in Nottingham put me in charge of the library, so I could borrow all the books I wanted. I saved up to buy a torch and read under the bedclothes all night. That torch lit up my life.'

Children in care are usually attention-seekers, or, like Paris, internalize everything. Looking at the cool, deadpan face, its only colour the eyes bloodshot from reading, few people realized the raging emotional torrents beneath the layers of ice.

Paris had been two when his mother dumped him on the door of a children's home in Alvaston, outside Derby. He had been clinging onto a glass ball containing the Eiffel Tower in a snow storm – still his most treasured possession. On his royal-blue knitted jumper was pinned a note: 'Please look after my son. His name is Paris.'

No one had ever found his mother. Early adoption was delayed, hoping she'd come forward. Afterwards, there was no one to sign the papers.

Every so often, when the moon was full, longing for his mother overwhelmed him, and he went searching for her on trains round the country. When he was twelve, he had suffered the humiliation of putting his photograph in the local paper advertising for a family. The photograph, taken in the fluorescent light of the children's home, made him look like a death's head. Paris for once had dropped his guard and written the accompanying copy, which Nadine his social worker had rejigged: 'Paris is a healthy twelve-year-old, who has been in care for a number of years. He has a few behaviour problems and needs firm handling,' which, translated, meant trouble with a capital 'T'.

Paris, affecting a total lack of interest, had hung around waiting for the post, expecting Cameron Diaz or Posh and Becks to roll up in a big car and whisk him off to love and luxury. But there had been no takers.

Feral and Graffi had carried him during this humiliation. He, in turn, had carried Feral when his older brother Joey dissed the head of a rival gang, who took him outside and shot him dead. Feral's mother, Nancy, had emerged briefly from a drug-induced stupor to achieve fleeting fame bewailing the loss on television. But as it was only black killing black, the public and police soon forgot and moved on to another tragedy. Nancy turned back to her drugs.

Feral was dyslexic and, ashamed he wrote and read so poorly, truanted persistently. Paris, who was very clever, translated for him and explained questions.

'He's my one-to-one teaching assistant,' boasted Feral.

Out of eighteen homes and eleven schools, Paris's three years at Larks and Oaktree Court had been his longest placement. Terrified of being dragged away to a new care home in another part of the country, he tried not to complain or rock the boat.

'I've got two copies of *The Moonstone*, so here's one for you,' said Janna, 'and here's Lily coming up the path.'

Lily was in high fettle. She had just won a hundred pounds on the three o'clock and been making elder-flower wine. Feral and Graffi came scuttling down the stairs for new diversion.

'Boys, this is my friend Lily Hamilton who lives next

door, and Lily, these are my friends, Graffi, who's paint-ing me a mural, Paris, who's sorting out my bookshelves, and Feral, who's an ace footballer.'

'Really?' said Lily. 'My nephew Dicky is besotted with Man U; I confess a fondness for Arsenal.'

'That's cool, man,' said Feral approvingly.

'I'm about to watch them on Sky,' said Lily. 'Would you like to come and have a look and test this summer's elderflower wine?'

Needing no more encouragement, Feral and Graffi bounded after her.

10

Paris preferred to stay with the books and Janna. With her sweet face and rippling red hair, she was like those beautiful women in pre-Raphaelite paintings. He tried not to stare. As she handed her books and their hands touched occasionally, she told him about her parents' evening.

'I want the place to look so good, people will really want to send their children to Larks.'

Paris said nothing. Oh God, she thought, he has no parents, I'm a tactless cow. Changing the subject hurriedly, she said she was planning a project on the lark.

'In literature, art, music and real life. I don't know if larks are singing at the moment, but we could take a tape recorder into the fields. I'm going to call the project "Larks Ascending" to symbolize our climb out of special measures.'

' "To hear the lark begin his flight, And singing startle the dull night," ' murmured Paris, handing her a tattered copy of *Anna Karenina*.

' "From his watch-tower in the skies, Till the dappled dawn doth rise," ' carried on Janna, clapping her hands. 'Fantastic, exactly the kind of stuff we need. Will you copy it out for me and perhaps write a poem about a lark yourself?'

Larks were always having to move on because of tractors ploughing and harrowing, and people sowing seed and spraying pesticides and fertilizers, thought Paris bitterly, just like him moving from home to home.

Whoops and yells from next door indicated that Arsenal must have scored.

'Tell me about Graffi,' said Janna as she slotted *Northanger Abbey* between *Emma* and *Persuasion*.

'His dad earns good when he's in work. Nice bloke but the money seems to evaporate in the betting shop or the pub. Graffi's got two elder brothers and a sister; then, after him, his mother had a Downs Syndrome baby, and all the attention goes on her. Graffi gets the shit kicked out of him by the elder kids, but his mother – when she works in the pub evenings and Sundays – expects Graffi, because he's easy-going, to look after his sister. Graffi loves her to bits but he gets jealous and worries she'll be bullied when she goes to primary school next year.'

'Where does he live – on the Shakespeare Estate?'

'Hamlet Street. Feral's Macbeth, Kylie's Dogberry, Pearl's Othello – which figures: she's dead jealous. Monster Norman's Iago, which figures too.'

'Is it really rough?'

'If you want respect, the only way is to act tough and deal drugs,' said Paris. 'Randal Stancombe's sniffing round the place, wants to offer it a leisure centre.'

'So young people have somewhere to go in the evening to keep them off the streets,' volunteered Graffi, returning at half-time.

'I like the streets,' grumbled Feral. 'I don't want no youth club woofter teaching me no ballroom dancing.'

'More walls to draw on,' said Graffi. 'I like that lady next door. She's got terrific pictures on her wall, that nude over the mantelpiece looks straight out of a porn mag. That elderflower wine's not bad neiver; she said it didn't matter as we wasn't driving.'

Out of the corner of her eye, Janna saw Feral pick up a very pretty pink and white paperweight, put it in his pocket, then put it back again.

'What d'you want to be in life, Feral?' she asked.

Feral gave her his huge, charming, dodgy smile.

'Twenty-one, man.'

'I beg your pardon?'

'If you live on the Shakespeare Estate, it's an achievement to stay alive to the weekend,' explained Graffi. 'I've done this drawing of Lily's cat.'

'That's so good.' Janna took it to the light. 'You must give it to Lily. When you get back from the second half, I'll have your tea ready.'

While Paris became immersed in *The Catcher in the Rye*, Janna produced a real Yorkshire tea, with lardy cake, dripping toast, jam roly poly, crumpets and very strong tea out of a big brown pot.

As a returning Feral and Graffi helped her carry it to the table outside, Feral looked up at the kitchen beam. 'What's that long thick black thing called?' he asked.

'Feral Jackson,' quipped Graffi.

'Fuck off, man,' said Feral, who was in a good mood. Arsenal had won resoundingly.

The sinking sun was turning the stubble a soft mushroom pink. Housemartins and swallows gathered on the telegraph wires; rooks were jangling in the beeches; a purple and silver air balloon drifted up the valley, like a bauble escaped from a Christmas tree. As the boys sat down on a rickety old garden bench and devoured everything, helicopters kept chugging overhead.

'Is there an air show on or something?'

'Naaah,' sneered Graffi, 'it's toff kids being taken back to Bagley Hall.'

With only a slight stab of guilt, Janna realized none of her emails had been to thank Hengist Brett-Taylor for his bottle of champagne.

'That dark blue one' – Graffi pointed towards the sky – 'belongs to Rupert Campbell-Black, who my dad hero-worships because Rupert's given him so many winners. And that's Randy Scandal,' he added as

Rupert's helicopter was followed five minutes later by one in dark crimson bearing Randal Stancombe's name in gold letters and his logo of a little gold house.

'Randal's got a hot daughter called Jade,' said Feral. 'I wouldn't mind giving her one, wiping the smug smile off her face.'

Paris shivered. Oaktree Court was a grand old building set back from the main road on the way to St Jimmy's and Searston Abbey. Randal Stancombe's henchmen had been spotted in the grounds. Converted, it would make splendid luxury flats in the catchment area of the two schools, and once again Paris's security would be blown.

Seeing the shiver, and how inadequately Paris was dressed in his thin nylon tracksuit and trainers with the soles coming off, Janna suggested they went inside.

'It's nice here,' said Graffi.

'Nadine, your social worker, rang me yesterday,' Janna told Paris.

'Nosy old bitch,' said Paris flatly.

'She spoke well of you,' laughed Janna. 'She said you told the other children fantastic stories at bedtime. Why don't you write them down?'

'Did once. Cara Sharpe said they were crap.'

'That's only her opinion,' said Graffi. 'She's head of drama as well as English but I don't fink she's read a play since she left uni.'

'I told her I wanted to be an actor and she pissed herself.' Paris gave a cackle. 'She said: "With an accent like yours, you've got to be joking."'

For a second, Janna gasped in terror.

'That was extraordinary. That was Cara's laugh and voice exactly.'

'Paris can do anyone,' said Feral.

'Do Mike Pitts,' said Graffi, wiping his hands on his jeans and picking up his pen to draw Janna.

Paris pursed his lips: '"If it weren't for my professional commitment, I'd have left teaching yearsh ago and been earning a million a year running I-Shee-I."'

Janna gave a scream of laughter. Once again the imitation was perfect. Paris had even caught Mike's drunken slur.

Then he did Rowan: '"Ay'm so busy juggling my job, my husband and my two little girls, I forget to have 'me' time."' Paris looked up from under his lashes like Rowan did.

'You're brilliant,' cried Janna, 'you *must* become an actor.'

'"Moost I really? Thut's lovely, in fuct it's chumpion,"' said Paris.

'That's me,' giggled Janna. 'I thought I'd lost my accent a bit down here.'

Paris smiled – and Janna felt truly weak at the knees. He was like some Arctic Prince who'd strayed southwards and might melt any moment in the autumn sunset.

I will do anything to make his life better, she told herself.

They were reserved but not shy, these boys. Although only thirteen or fourteen, they were old before their time, hardened and aged by poverty, loss, lack of security and the contempt of others. But at the same time, they were all hunky: muscular from the fight to survive, and sure of their sexuality.

Overwhelmed with longing for both a lover and a child of her own, Janna was aware that Feral, Graffi and Paris fell halfway between the two. Suddenly she knew she had to send them home.

'We must decide a fee for the mural,' she told Graffi.

'Five grand a day,' Graffi grinned, looking round for the picture he had drawn of her, but Paris had already whipped it.

Janna gave Paris a carrier bag for his books and, for all of them, a big bag of Cox's apples from the tree at the bottom of the garden. But running upstairs for a cardigan, glancing out of her bedroom window, she saw them chucking the apples at each other. Paris, with his long nose still in *The Catcher in the Rye*, stretched out a hand to take a perfect catch as they sauntered up the lane.

Back in the kitchen, the laptop she'd been working on had been opened. Then she gave a gasp of horrified amusement.

To the words: 'Get rid of three-quarters of the teachers, I wish', someone had added, 'Why not start with Cara Sharpe, Mike Pitts, Skunk Illingworth, Chalford (you ain't met her yet), Sam Spink, Robbie Rushton and Hot Flush Basket for a start.' Janna's sentiments exactly.

She ought to work, but she was so pleased to be interrupted by a call from Lily saying she'd enjoyed the wine-tasting as much as Feral and Graffi: 'What delightful boys. Feral's going to help me make sloe gin and Graffi did an excellent drawing of General, caught the angle of his whiskers exactly. If I hadn't fallen out with him, I'd show it to my nephew Jupiter, who's a dealer when he's not being an MP. Feral gave me a spliff.'

'Lily,' said Janna shocked.

'I haven't had one since another nephew, Jonathan, got married. Come and have a drink.'

Janna slept fitfully. Outside her window, Mars blazed golden and angry, a ginger tom cat seeing off a fierce dog. I've got to fight and win, she thought.

11

With Mars in the ascendant, the battle raged on at Larks. On Monday, a physics supply teacher was so unnerved by her first encounter with Year Nine E that she fled down the drive with singed eyebrows and blackened fringe and was never seen again.

'Who was she covering for?' demanded Janna.

Rowan glanced up at the timetable: 'Sam Spink. She's gone to the TUC conference.'

'She never asked me.'

'She cleared it with Mike Pitts last term. There was a memo' – Rowan looked disapprovingly at Janna's dramatically diminished in-tray – 'but it seems to have been chucked away.'

'How long's she gone for?'

'All week. Sam's awfully conscientious. She feels it's crucial to exchange views and keep up with modern legislation.'

'You bet she does, when it involves swilling brandy Alexanders all night in the Metropole.'

Returning from a shouting match in Mike's office, Janna caught Robbie Rushton and Gloria the gymnast sneaking in at midday, claiming that the boat on which they'd been sailing had run aground.

'So will you if you skive any more,' yelled Janna.

A day of hassle left her drained and defensive.

Remembering the support the governors at Redfords had given Stew when the going got tough, she looked forward to pouring out her grievances to her own governors, who'd been so friendly at her interview and who were, after all, responsible for Larks's appalling state.

The meeting was held after school in A18, classroom of Robbie Rushton, who, for once in a hundred years, made a point of working late, so Debbie the cleaner had to sweep and arrange chairs and glasses of water around his martyred presence.

'Robbie's so conscientious,' cooed Cara to arriving governors, as he finally took himself and a huge pile of marking away.

Classroom A18 was one of the worst. Damp patches on the ceiling resembled the map of India and Bangladesh. A rattle of drips was filling up two buckets. Year Eleven, ironically, were studying the story of water: irrigation, the rain cycle, domestic canals and wells. Year Ten, on the other hand, were learning about earthquakes, photographs and diagrams of which also covered the peeling walls. It wasn't long before Janna wished the floorboards would split open and swallow her up.

Mike Pitts wasn't present, but his spies were. Rowan Merton, wafting Anaïs Anaïs, had changed into a clean white shirt and was taking the minutes. Cara, as a teacher governor, having saved Monster Norman from being expelled last week, was thick as thieves and parked next to his mother, Stormin' Norman, also a parent governor.

Bring me my bully-proof vest, muttered Janna.

Kylie Rose's mother, Chantal, another parent governor, held up the whole proceedings by saying: 'Can we discuss this?' at every new item and making eyes at snuffling Crispin Thomas, whom she didn't realize was gay and who looked fatter than ever.

Crispin was accompanied by his boss, Ashton

Douglas, S and C Services' Director of Education, an infinitely more formidable adversary who utterly unnerved Janna. His handsome, regular features were somehow blurred like soap left too long in the bath. An air of vulnerability (created by a lisp and soft light brown curls flopping from a middle parting) was belied by the coldest green eyes she had ever seen. Languid as a Beardsley aesthete, Ashton wore a mauve silk shirt, a beautifully cut grey suit and reeked of sweet, cloying scent.

He was now murmuring to Sir Hugo Betts, the camel on Prozac. Sir Hugo was disappointed Janna didn't look nearly as bonny as at her interview, so there would be even less to keep him awake.

Russell Lambert as chairman droned on and on, loving the sound of his own voice and expressing sadness that Brett Scott, the jolly director of Larkminster Rovers, had resigned, not having appreciated the extent of a governor's workload. He had been replaced by a local undertaker, called Solly, who at least can bury us, thought Janna.

She longed to weigh in on the atrocious state of the school, but in a subtle shift of emphasis, she was now held responsible for all Larks's evils. Five other pupils had gone out of county to other schools. Attendance was down by sixty-seven.

'What plans do you have to impwove the situation?' asked Ashton Douglas silkily.

Janna told them about her prospective-parents' evening.

'Hope it's not an *EastEnders* night,' warned Chantal Peck.

Russell then expressed the governors' horror at the disastrous league-table results, with commendable exceptions – they all nodded deferentially at Cara Sharpe. What was Janna intending to do about that?

'I need a massive increase in funding,' said Janna, 'and must smarten up the school. Take this classroom.

If you're into virtual reality, we can re-create the monsoon season every time it rains. If we don't mend the roof, we'll need an ark. And moving to Australia' – she tore a peeling strip of paper off the walls – 'we can re-create the eucalyptus.'

No one smiled.

'No, it isn't funny,' agreed Janna. 'We also need hundreds more textbooks; we need to replace four computers. We need an IT technician.

'On the non-teaching side, we need a part-time gardener to sweep up the leaves, which will soon be cascading down from the trees – the only proud thing in this place. Above all we need a decent cook' – both Cara and Rowan Merton were frantically making notes – 'to give the children a really nourishing hot meal in the middle of the day. Dinners here are the only food many of them can rely on, but they're so disgusting, most of the kids won't eat them.'

'Mrs Molly does her best with limited resources,' protested Cara.

'There was a blood-stained plaster in the shepherd's pie on Friday.'

'The shepherd must have cut himself shearing,' murmured Solly the undertaker with a ghostly chuckle.

'And most of all' – Janna plunged in feet first – 'we need some more teachers. Ten of them, including my head of history, Mrs Chalford, whom I've never even met, are off with stress. The only way to attract new talent is to pay them better.'

But no more money was forthcoming.

S and C Services, Ashton Douglas reminded her smoothly, had been brought in by the Government because the local education authority couldn't balance the books. Janna must learn, like everyone else, to economize.

'We must have more money.' Janna banged the table with her little fist. 'You're a private company. You're not in this for love but to make a fat profit, that's why

107

you don't want to give any extra to me. But it's so defeatist to let us self-destruct.'

There was a horrified pause and a flicker of amused malice in Ashton Douglas's cold green eyes.

'Your job, my dear, is to sort out the mess.'

'I've been here a week. If I'm going to sort out this "mess" I need your support. I lost my best teacher last week.' She daren't in front of Cara and Rowan say that Mike Pitts was useless. 'The junior staff are utterly demoralized. The children—'

Clearing his throat, Ashton Douglas cut right across her.

'With wespect, we shouldn't be discussing teaching matters in fwont of Mrs Sharpe. If you need funding, I suggest you look for sponsors in the town: Wandal Stancombe, or Gwant Tyler, our local IT giant. Get the local community on side.'

'Why not mobilize your parents?' suggested Crispin Thomas, smiling at Stormin' Norman and Chantal. 'Last year Searston Abbey and St Jimmy's raised fifteen and twenty thousand pounds respectively.'

'They've got hundreds of middle-class parents who aren't struggling to pay any school fees,' raged Janna. 'Of course they chip in. We don't have middle-class parents at Larks.'

'Ay take exception to that,' bridled Chantal Peck.

'That uncalled-for wemark should be struck from the minutes,' said Ashton. 'If you attwacted more pupils, we could allow you more money. So concentrate on your prospective-parents' meeting. Wod Hyde will also be here to advise you next week.' Then, at Janna's look of outrage: 'You'll find him a bweath of fwesh air.'

'An image that conjures up icy winds blasting in from Siberia,' snapped Janna, 'blowing everything that matters out of the window. I don't want Rod Hyde telling me what to do. I just need more money.

'The children need some treats,' she pleaded. 'They have such bleak lives. We should offer them rewards: a fun day out to look forward to and in recognition of good behaviour.'

'What did you have in mind?' asked Crispin sarcastically.

'The London Eye perhaps, or Tate Modern. A lot of them have never been to the seaside or inside the cathedral or a museum.'

'You'd trust them in a museum?' said Cara incredulously.

'Once they realized we did, they'd start behaving better.'

'Which brings me to behaviour management,' said Russell Lambert. 'We notice you've introduced a new system of mentors.'

'It worked very well at Redfords,' said Janna defensively. 'Means any kid can go to a mentor if they're being bullied or have a problem. I had ten of the more responsible members of Year Eleven photographed last Thursday. Their pictures are now up in the corridors.'

'A needless expense.' Ashton smiled thinly. 'Surely they could have brought photogwaphs from home.'

'It made it more of an honour,' said Janna. 'They look really good.'

There was a knock on the door. It was Kylie Rose, come to collect her mother Chantal and bearing Cameron, a sweet jolly baby who'd inherited his mother's blond, blue-eyed beauty. His charm was lost on Crispin Thomas, however, when his besotted grandmother thrust him into the deputy educational director's arms, particularly when Cameron threw up on Crispin's cream suit.

'Come and see the mentors' photographs,' said Janna hastily, leading everyone off to admire the display, only to find the photographs had already been adorned with moustaches and squints, with the names crossed out and replaced by 'Wanker' and worse.

Janna promptly lost her rag again and shouted at

109

anyone within range. She was just calming down when kind Kylie Rose tugged her sleeve.

'You're easily the best teacher in the school, miss.'

'Am I?' Janna was marginally mollified.

'Easily the best at shouting,' said Kylie Rose.

The governors smirked.

'Phone for you,' called Rowan from Janna's office.

'I'm busy.'

'Says he's an old friend from Redfords.'

Janna shot into the office.

'I tried the cottage,' announced Stew. 'Somehow I knew you'd be still working.'

'Oh Stew.' How lovely to hear the broad, warm, measured Yorkshire accent.

'How are you getting on, love?'

'Horribly. It's hell.' Janna kicked her door shut. 'I hate most of the staff. They gang up. There aren't enough of them. The only nice guy's been hijacked to head up another school. The deputy head's a total lush.'

'What about the kids?'

'Animals, most of them.'

'That's not like you, Janna. What about your PA? She sounded friendly enough on the phone.'

'Worst of the lot. She sneers, sneaks and pumps up my in-tray to demoralize me.' Swinging round, Janna went scarlet; Rowan who must have quietly opened the door was standing outraged in the doorway. 'I've got to go, Stew, ring me later at home.'

But Stew didn't ring back. Why had she moaned so much?

Laugh and the world laughs with you, weep and you weep alone, her mother had always told her. If only she were still alive.

The fall-out was awful. Cara, backed up by Rowan, was straight on to Mike Pitts and the rest of the staff, reporting everything that had been said.

110

No one would meet Janna's eye the next day. Molly the cook walked out. Even Wally, her dear friend, looked at her reproachfully, until she explained that she wanted to get in some gardening help, to free him for more important tasks.

That same morning, however, Debbie the cleaner, who'd been blown away by the big box of chocolates Janna had given her for blitzing the staffroom, came blushing into the head's office. As she got on so well with Molly's other assistants, how would Janna feel if they took over school dinners on a month's trial?

'Profoundly relieved,' replied Janna. 'Oh, Debbie, thank you, that's the best bit of news I've had for ages. Start today.'

'You deserve some luck,' said Debbie. 'Lots of us think you're 'uman.'

Ironically, Janna was saved by the greatest tragedy. Towards the end of the day, which was 11 September, she was trying to explain Arthur Miller to a sullen group of fifteen-year-olds, who seemed only interested that he'd been married to Marilyn Monroe, when Rowan rushed in to say the World Trade Center had been hit.

Mike Pitts and Cara thought the school should carry on as normal. Janna insisted that this was history and the children must see it.

In no time, Wally had rigged up the big screen attached to a television in the main hall. The excited pupils lugged chairs in from the dining room to watch the terrible events unfold. At first, these were like so many Hollywood films, it was hard for them to understand it was the real thing. But they were soon screaming, sobbing and sometimes cheering. Janna stood to the side of the screen, explaining what was happening.

The Wolf Pack, when they first saw people leaping out of the flaming tower windows, exchanged glances, because they were always escaping that way, but here

111

there was no wisteria to aid their descent, and horror gripped them too.

When it was time to go home, she called for a minute's silence to pray for America and the suffering of its people, thanking God for the courage of the emergency services and hoping as many people as possible had escaped to safety.

Next day at assembly she gave everyone an update on the tragedy and who was responsible, and when fights broke out between the Muslim children and the Hindus and the Christians, she tried to impress on them that ordinary people weren't to blame. She asked the senior classes to write poems about the tragedy. Paris's was marvellous.

As the days passed, a huge mutual interest developed as the children learnt about the courage of the firemen and the brave search-and-rescue dogs. Some of the children said their parents thought Bin Laden was a hero, and more frightful fights ensued.

Cara and Mike Pitts, however, were constantly on the telephone, stirring up trouble. When it was crucial to raise Larks's position in the league tables, why was Janna wasting the entire school's afternoon watching television?

'It's called global citizenship,' protested Janna when Ashton Douglas carpeted her.

'Wod Hyde will be with you tomorrow,' said Ashton nastily. 'He'll sort you out.'

12

Janna had always felt that one of the cruellest humiliations was when heads of very successful establishments known as 'beacon schools' were posted in to sort out failing schools, 'yanking them up by the hair' as the Education Secretary so charmingly put it.

Janna's russet curls were well and truly yanked by the smug and self-regarding Rod Hyde who, as head of St Jimmy's, had been forced to redesign his writing paper to accommodate all the awards and accolades his school had received.

Arriving at Larks, Rod immediately showed how well he got on with Janna's staff, joshing Mike Pitts, Skunk Illingworth and Robbie Rushton, kissing Cara on both hollowed cheeks and warmly quizzing Sam Spink about her week at the TUC conference.

'I'm sure you found it very empowering. You must debrief me over a few jars.'

Janna ground her teeth.

Known as Jesus Christ Superhead, Rod showed off his spare figure and muscular freckled arms by wearing short-sleeved shirts tucked into belted trousers. On colder days, he wore a rust-coloured cardigan to match his ginger beard.

A control freak, Rod received an emotional charge from acting as a 'critical friend', rolling up at Larks, telling Janna what was wrong with her and her school, attacking both her management skills and her teaching.

Janna, on the rare occasions she had time to teach, delivered the national curriculum as if it had been freed from its chains. When, on Rod's first day, Lydia rang in sick at the prospect of teaching *Macbeth* to Year Nine E, Janna took over, refusing to be fazed when Rod parked himself at the back, busily making notes on his clipboard.

It happened to be the day when Rocky, the huge curly-haired autistic boy kept comparatively calm by Ritalin, was in one of his more eccentric moods. Wandering in, he took one look at Rod and shut himself in the store cupboard at the back of the classroom.

'The Macbeths were a glamorous career couple,' Janna was saying, 'like Tony and Cherie Blair or Bill and Hillary Clinton. We tend to think of them as middle-aged and childless, but probably they were young, young enough to have kids who might inherit the throne, which may have been why Macbeth told Lady Macbeth to "bring forth men children only".'

The class then had a spirited discussion on the right age to have children. Kylie Rose said 'twelve'. They then moved on to Macduff being ripped untimely from his mother's womb.

'That's a cop-out, miss,' volunteered Paris.

'I think Shakespeare meant that Macduff's mum had a Caesarean,' explained Janna, 'but you're right, Paris, it is a cop-out.'

How difficult not to be touched when she saw his pale face flood with colour.

'You must also remember Macbeth was a mighty warrior, a fantastic killing machine.'

'Like Russell Crowe in *Gladiator*,' said Pearl.

'Or Arnie in *Terminator*,' said a sepulchral voice from the cupboard.

The class giggled.

'Exactly, Rocky,' called out Janna. 'Macbeth was on a

fantastic high having routed the terrorists who were trying to overthrow Duncan, the King of Scotland, who
was also his wife's cousin. Mighty Macbeth had been
on a killing spree that was hugely applauded. Like
scoring a hat trick for Arsenal or Liverpool. The world
was at his feet.

'Now tell me, what did Macbeth have in common
with Stalin, Hitler and Saddam Hussein?'

'They all had moustaches,' shouted Pearl.

'Like Baldie Hyde,' called out the sepulchral voice
from the cupboard.

More giggling as the class stared round at Rod.

'They all deteriorated into tyrants and mass
murderers,' said Janna quickly. 'Now, for homework,
you've got two choices, one of which may appeal more
to the girls, particularly you, Pearl. If you were a
costume designer and in charge of make-up, how
would you kit out the Weird Sisters?'

'I'd put them in baggy, raggy, gypsy-style costumes,'
said Pearl, 'wiv red and purple hair, blackened-out
teeth and cruel scarlet mouths.'

'Like Cara Sharpe,' intoned Rocky from his hideout.

'That's enough,' said Janna firmly. 'The other choice
is to imagine you're a war correspondent like John
Simpson or Kate Adie, and write a script telling the
viewers at home about Macbeth's first victory, bringing
in the routing of the rebels, the Norwegian support
and the butchering of the treacherous Thane of
Cawdor, ripping him open or unseaming him "from
the navel to the chaps". If you've got time, you could
list questions for an interview with Macbeth or Banquo
and add Macbeth's possible answers.'

Year Nine E were gratifyingly enraptured and
groaned when the bell went. Throughout the lesson,
however, Janna had kept seeing Rod Hyde's tongue,
green as a wild garlic leaf, as he pointedly yawned.
Afterwards he couldn't wait to tick her off.

'You're far too familiar, and if you digress all the

115

time, you'll never get them through their exams.'

'They're not taking GCSEs for nearly three years. I want them to enjoy Shakespeare.'

'And you talk too much,' Rod consulted his clipboard, as they walked back to her office. 'Try to be a listening head rather than a talking one. Don't take this personally,' he added when Janna looked mutinous, 'it's for your own good.

'And you must stop blowing your top. I know we redheads are volatile' – he crinkled his small eyes – 'but you lose dignity every time you raise your voice to students and colleagues. Ashton tells me you displayed unedifying aggression at the governors' meeting. Has it occurred to you that you're the reason so many of your staff are off with stress?'

Janna dug her nails into her palms and counted to ten. Next moment, she and Rod were sent flying by a yelling gang from Year Ten, stampeding like buffaloes towards the playground.

'Don't run,' howled Janna.

'Don't run,' said Rod quietly.

Infuriatingly the gang mumbled, 'Sorry, sir,' and shambled off.

'You must instil discipline here.' Rod shut her office door behind them. 'Coloured hair, beaded necklaces, particularly for boys, rings in the navel or the tongue, and shaved heads must all go.'

Ten days ago, Janna would have agreed with him, but he was irritating her so much, she said she liked children expressing themselves.

'And you should cut down that wisteria, which seems the accepted escape route for most of your hooligans.'

'That wisteria's older than me or even you, and much more beautiful.'

'Dear Janna' – Rod pursed his red lips – 'you're not helping yourself. Caring Cara Sharpe also tells me' – he turned back to his clipboard – 'you've been working here until eleven at night. Terribly unfair to

116

Wally, who has to lock up after you. He does have a life.'

'Wally's never complained,' stammered Janna.

'He's too nice,' said Rod pompously. 'Start thinking of other people. You wouldn't have to work so late if you organized your day better. Now stop sulking and turn on that coffee machine.'

Somehow, Janna managed not to rip him from navel to chaps with her paper knife, but she cried herself to sleep that night. Were the children and staff really acting up and demoralized because she was such a bitch?

For his next visit, Rod called a breakfast meeting at 8.00 a.m.

'You provide the croissants. I'll provide the pearls of wisdom.'

He'd been jogging and dripped with sweat when he arrived. Janna had to watch him getting butter, marmalade and crumbs all over his red beard as he poured scorn on Larks's place in the league tables.

'It'd help if you and Searston Abbey didn't cream off all the best pupils,' snarled Janna. 'Think how disadvantaged our kids are. Most of them have no quiet room at home to do their homework and no one able to help them. Unemployment's at an all-time high on the Shakespeare Estate, so the kids, as well as helping out with the shopping, have to take evening and weekend jobs to make ends meet. Poor little Graffi fell asleep at his desk this morning.'

'Probably been doing drugs all night,' said Rod dismissively. 'You must get your parents on side. Ours were in school all weekend, installing benches in the playground – that's one reason our results are spectacular. We'll be catching up with Bagley Hall in a year or two and then Hengist B-T will have to look to his laurels. No parent will want to fork out twenty-odd thousand a year only to get thrashed by a maintained school.'

'What's Hengist like?' Janna was annoyed to find herself asking.

'Terminally frivolous and arrogant,' snapped Rod. 'Typical public-school Hooray Henry, far too big for his green wellies.'

As Janna bent down to retrieve a pen, Rod suppressed an urge to pull down her panties and smack her freckled bottom. Sheila, his 'superb wife' of twenty-seven years, an ex-nurse, who called him 'head teacher' in bed, didn't excite him quite enough. One day Janna Curtis would express gratitude for the way he'd imposed discipline on her and her school.

'I shall be spending one to one and a half days a week with you from now on,' he announced.

'How d'you find the time?' asked Janna sulkily.

'I delegate. Ask a busy person.'

On the following day, Rod rolled up in a big black hat, which he left in Janna's office. Later in the morning, passing Year Nine E's history lesson, he found Paris wearing it and doing a dazzling imitation of Rod addressing the troops:

' "As part of our caring and supportive ethos . . ." '

Rod was outraged and snatched back his hat.

'Others make allowances for you, Paris Alvaston, because of your unfortunate circumstances, and you abuse it,' he shouted. 'I shall speak with Mr Blenchley.'

'Mr Blenchley'll make Paris's life hell,' protested Janna.

The Wolf Pack, who also thought Rod's remarks were below the belt, started pelting him with textbooks and pencil boxes and banging their desk lids when he tried to shut them up.

Nor was Rod's impression of Larks improved later in the day, when Graffi caught him whispering to Cara Sharpe just inside the huge stationery cupboard and locked them both in.

Only after an hour did Rowan hear banging and let them out.

Rod had gone maroon with fury. 'How dare you?' he bellowed at Graffi, who was now wearing the hat.

'You and Mrs Sharpe was saying horrible things about Miss,' said Graffi and, jumping out of the window, slithered down the wisteria and ran laughing down the drive.

'This school deserves to be closed down,' exploded Rod.

Janna, meanwhile, was working on her Larks Ascending project for her prospective-parents' evening.

'We need to put everything about larks, how high up they sing, how they nest on the ground, how because of modern farming, they're getting fewer and fewer.'

'Like Larks's pupils,' said Feral.

Janna and Paris raided the dictionary of quotations for poems about larks. Cambola searched for music. Graffi did a wonderful drawing of Rod Hyde as Edward Lear's Old Man with bird droppings on his head and with owls, larks, hens and wrens nesting in his beard. Graffi also helped Janna cover the corridor walls with pictures by the children and torn-out paintings by Old Masters. They tried not to laugh when Mike Pitts wandered in after a lunchtime session at the Ghost and Castle and remarked:

'That Modigliani's not a bad painter. What class is he in?'

Janna knew she ought to sack Mike for drinking, but who would back her up? She ought to sack him for perfidy too. When she came back unexpectedly from a meeting, she found him whispering into her telephone. Seeing her, he flushed even redder and hung up.

Janna had immediately pressed redial, and an answering voice had said, 'Ashton Douglas.'

Janna was so thrown, she revealed who she was and instantly received a bollocking for her treatment of Rod Hyde.

'As part of his caring, supportive ethos, Wod gives of his valuable time and you put up disgusting paintings of him on the wall and treat him with twuculence and disrespect.'

'He's a bloody clipboard junkie who upsets the kids.'

'Your school is spiralling out of control,' said Ashton coldly.

'Ashton to Ashton, dust to dust,' screamed Janna, slamming down the telephone. When it rang again, she was, for once, able to snatch it up before a suspicious Rowan.

'Janna Curtis,' she snapped.

'This is Hengist Brett-Taylor.' The deep lazy voice was laced with laughter. 'I wonder if you'd like to have lunch this week.'

Janna was about to refuse when she saw Monster Norman's mother charging up the corridor, and abandoning her open-door policy, kicked it shut and leant against it.

'Yes, please.'

'How about Wednesday?'

She had a finance meeting at four-thirty, so she could escape early.

'That's OK.'

'I thought we'd go to La Perdrix d'Or in Cathedral Street. Shall I pick you up?'

'No, I'll meet you there.'

'At one o'clock, then. I really look forward to it.'

13

Janna looked forward to lunch with Hengist less and less. She had her prospective-parents' evening the following day and shouldn't be skiving. Nor should she be fraternizing with the enemy with Rowan clocking her every move, particularly when Janna came in in her rose-festooned pink suit, with her newly washed russet curls bouncing around her shoulders.

But, by the time a German teacher and a lab assistant had given in their notice, the boys' lavatories had blocked yet again and Satan Simmons had been carted off to hospital after an encounter with a broken bottle, Janna was ready for a large drink.

Only when she had driven past the Ghost and Castle did she pull in to tart up, not helped by her trembling hands zigzagging her eyeliner, spilling base on her pink satin camisole top and drenching her in so much of Stew's Chanel No 5, big-headed bloody Brett-Taylor would be bound to construe it as a come-on. In an attempt to look school-marmish, she groped furiously for a hairband in the glove compartment, and scraped back as many of her curls as possible. Then she jumped as, in the driving mirror, she caught sight of Rowan, Gloria the gymnast and perfidious Jason Fenton sloping off for an early lunch, no doubt to bitch about her. It was debatable who blushed most when they recognized her car storming off.

121

Janna grew increasingly flustered because she was late and Cathedral Street long, punctuated with cherry trees and composed of seemingly identical eighteenth-century shopfronts and she'd forgotten the French name of the restaurant – something like Pederast's Door. She was scuttling up and down, when Hengist, who'd been looking out, pulled her in from the street.

'You are absolutely sweet to make it.'

And Janna gasped because he was a good foot taller than she was and undeniably gorgeous-looking, with thick springy dark hair, unflecked by grey, brushed back and curling over the collar. In addition, he had heavy-lidded, amused eyes, the very dark green of rain-soaked cedars, an unlined face still brown from the summer, a nose with several dents in it, a square jaw with a cleft chin and a wonderfully smooth smiling mouth, framing even white teeth, most of them capped after the bashing they had received on the rugger field.

He was conventionally dressed in a longish tweed jacket, dark-yellow cords, an olive-green shirt and an MCC tie, but as his lemon aftershave mingled amorously with Chanel No 5 on the warm windless autumn air, he seemed utterly in the heroic mould. Casting Hector or Horatius who kept the bridge for a Hollywood epic, you would look no further. Beneath the languid amiability, he exuded huge energy, and after the Hydes and Skunks, who'd been her fare for the last month, he seemed like a god.

Janna bristled instinctively:

'I've got a finance meeting; I haven't got long.'

'Then the sooner you have a large drink the better.'

Hengist ordered her (without asking) a glass of champagne and, picking up his glass of red and the biography of Cardinal Mazarin that he'd left on the bar, he led her through a packed restaurant to what was clearly the best table, overlooking the water meadows and the river.

'The view's breathtaking, but you must sit with your back to it, because it's so good for my street cred to be seen with you and it means that all the fat cats lunching here will think: how pretty she is, and pour money into your school.'

'I wish,' sighed Janna.

'I've brought you a present,' said Hengist.

In a blue box tied with crimson ribbon was a long silver spoon.

'I know you feel you're supping or lunching with the devil,' he said, laughing at her. 'I've read all about your views in the *TES* and the *Guardian* – "upper-class care" indeed – but I promise I won't bite except my food, which is excellent here. Thank you, Freddie.' He smiled at the spiky-haired young waiter who'd brought over Janna's champagne and the menu.

'Now get that inside you,' he went on. 'You'll need it to endure the appalling Russell Lambert and the even more appalling Crispin and Ashton. What a coven of fairies you've surrounded yourself with.'

'I don't want to discuss my governors,' said Janna primly and untruthfully.

'I've cracked the governor problem,' confided Hengist. 'We have two meetings a year. One over dinner at Boodle's, my club in London, which they all adore. Then, in early November, they all come down to Bagley for dinner and the night. Sally, my wife, is a fantastic cook. Wonderful smells drift into the boardroom throughout the meeting, so they're desperate to get through it and onto pre-dinner drinks. Then they push off first thing in the morning.

'But my pièce de résistance has been to get the most ravishing mother onto the board, a divorcee called Mrs Walton, so we always get full attendance and all the governors are so busy looking at her boobs, they OK everything.'

Janna tried and failed to look disapproving.

'Sally and I call her the governing body, but she'd be

123

wasted on Ashton or Crispin,' said Hengist idly. 'You'd do better with Brad Pitt.'

'Or Jason Fenton,' snapped Janna.

'Oh dear, I'd forgotten him.'

'Self-satisfied little narcissist. I passed him bunking off with two other teachers today when they thought I'd left for lunch. He'd have been admiring himself in the shop windows if they weren't all boarded up round Larks. I'm over the moon you've taken him off my hands.'

'At least I've done something right.'

Hengist looked so delighted, Janna burst out laughing.

La Perdrix d'Or itself seemed to be celebrating both golden partridge and the guns who killed them. Paintings of partridge or sporting prints of shooting parties in autumn, with birds and yellow leaves cascading out of the sky, adorned the dark-red walls. There were silver partridges and vases of red Michaelmas daisies on the white tablecloths and, like Sally B-T's governors' dinners, the most delicious smells of wine, herbs and garlic were drifting up from the kitchen.

The menu was in French, always Janna's Achilles heel, but Freddie the waiter charmingly translated for her.

'The goat's cheese fritters are out of this world,' said Hengist, 'although they might give you even worse nightmares if you fall asleep during your finance meeting.'

'And the Dover sole's fresh in today,' said Freddie.

'I'll have that,' said Janna with a sigh of relief.

Janna always liked people who looked straight at you, but Hengist unnerved her; those amused appraising eyes never left her face. He was just so attractive. Determined not to be a partridge to his twelve bore, she went on the offensive.

'You can't order venison. Poor deer.'

'A poor deer got into the garden last night and

demolished the remainder of Sally's roses. He'd have gobbled up your lovely suit in seconds.'

Getting hotter by the minute, Janna was too embarrassed about the make-up on her camisole top to undo her jacket.

'How did you turn Bagley round?'

'Fired a lot of masters. Found several old codgers already dead in the staffroom, which saved me the trouble. We were horribly under-subscribed. Every time the telephone rang, it was someone resigning or removing a pupil. The children were running wild.'

'Sounds familiar.'

'They're still pretty wild,' admitted Hengist. 'You think you've got delinquents at Larks. I've got the offspring of celebrities and high achievers, who are often just as neglected and screwed up. The divorce rate among the parents is frighteningly high.

'My first move was to set off the fire alarm at midnight on my first Saturday of term,' he went on. 'Ten Upper Sixth boys were so drunk, they couldn't get out of bed. In chapel on Monday, I named them all, then fired the lot. The parents, whom I'd alerted, were waiting outside. Then I told the rest of the school, "Your last five days of bad behaviour are up." I think it shocked them. None of the boys kicked out were very bright,' he added. 'One should never fire clever pupils.'

Janna didn't know how to take this patter. Hengist, like jesting Pilate, flitted from subject to subject, never waiting for an answer.

Then he switched tack, unnerving her further by asking her all about herself, her cottage and about Larks. She was too proud to tell him about the antagonism of the staff, but he was so sympathetic, interested and constructively helpful and the cheese fritters were so delicious, particularly washed down by more champagne, Janna was having such a nice time she was ashamed.

'How d'you cope with the workload?' she asked.

'I have a brilliant PA, Miss Painswick, who's a dragon to everyone but me and drives my wife Sally crackers. I appointed a deputy head, Alex Bruce, from the maintained system, who understands red tape and I've no doubt one day will strangle me with it like Laocoön. He *likes* filling in forms. He's a friend of your nemesis, Rod Hyde, same awful class. And I've got a brilliant bursar, Ian Cartwright; he's just back from Africa having extracted two years' unpaid school fees from a Nigerian prince.'

'With so many people looking after you,' asked Janna waspishly, 'what on earth do you find to do?'

'Given the quality of my staff,' murmured Hengist, 'my job consists largely of keeping out of the way,' and again smiled so sweetly and unrepentantly Janna melted.

'Do you have many women teachers?' she asked as she attacked her sole.

'Alex Bruce's wife, an Olympic-level pest, teaches religious studies, which includes everything except the Bible. Miss Wormly teaches English and we've got a head of science with absolutely no sense of humour, known as "No-Joke Joan". She also runs our only girls' house: Boudicca, a "thankless task". Miss Sweet, the undermatron of Boudicca, takes sex education, poor thing. The girls, who are sexually light years ahead, help her along.'

He's got a divinely deep husky voice, even if I do disapprove of everything he says, thought Janna, unbuttoning her jacket.

'You ought to employ more women,' she said fretfully.

'I'm sure. You don't want a job, do you?'

'I'd rather die than work for an independent school.' Then, feeling she'd been rude: 'This sole is wonderful. How can I stop truancy? It's shocking among the boys.'

'What do they like best?'

'After Hallé Berry, probably football.'

'Start a football club.'

'We haven't got any pitches. Lots of land, nearly ten acres, but we can't afford to have it levelled.'

'I'll introduce you to Randal Stancombe. You're so pretty and he's so rich, he'll give you some money.'

'Do you have a football club at Bagley?'

'No, we're a rugger school.'

'Of course,' said Janna sarcastically. 'I suppose you played rugby for *your* school.'

'Mr Brett-Taylor played rugby for England,' said Freddie. 'Everything all right, sir?'

When he'd gone, Janna asked if there were lots of drugs at Bagley.

'Probably. We only expel on a third offence. Why squander twenty thousand a year? A boy was sacked from Fleetley last week because they found cannabis in his study. He's expected to get straight As and is an Oxbridge cert, so we took him straightaway. His parents are so grateful, they'll probably pay for a new sports pavilion.'

'I can't afford to exclude,' said Janna crossly. 'I get fined five grand every time.'

'Whatever happened to the word "expel"?' sighed Hengist. He quoted softly:

> 'Shall I come, sweet Love, to thee,
> When the evening beams are set?
> Shall I not excluded be?'

Stretching out a big suntanned hand, on the little finger of which glinted a big gold signet ring, he gently stroked Janna's cheek.

'Pretty, you are. Don't work yourself into a frazzle over Larks.'

'Don't patronize me.' Blushing furiously, Janna jerked her head away. 'We're just hopelessly

127

underfunded. Bloody rural Larkshire. Can you really introduce me to Randal Stancombe?'

'Of course. Randal wants to build us a vocational wing. When I was young, vocation meant pretty girls becoming nuns and plain ones going off to be missionaries in Africa. Now it means thick boys training to be plumbers and thick girls learning to run travel agencies.'

'I know what "vocation" means,' spat Janna. 'I didn't know you took any thick children.'

'Rupert Campbell-Black's son Xav is destined to get straight Us,' confessed Hengist. 'In compensation, it wildly impresses parents to catch a glimpse of Rupert on Speech Day.'

Janna was getting so flushed with drink, she took off her jacket – sod the spilt make-up. People kept stopping at their table to say hello to Hengist, and praise something he'd written in the *Telegraph* or said on television.

Each time, he introduced Janna, then gave the other person twenty dazzling seconds of charm, before saying they must forgive him, but he and Janna had things to discuss.

'My children aren't thick,' protested Janna when they were alone again. 'They know the players and fixtures of Larkminster Rovers inside out. All I want to do is make a difference to children in a community who don't have the advantages I had. Education is about empowering children to access parts of themselves they haven't accessed,' she concluded sententiously.

Hengist raised an eyebrow. 'Can it really be English language you teach?'

'Oh, shut up,' said Janna so loudly lunchers looked round. 'No, I don't want any dessert. My teachers stop talking when I come into the room: would I had the same effect on the children. Show them any kindness and they spit and swear at you. But now, the wildest of them all, Feral Jackson, comes to tea with me on Saturdays,' she added proudly, 'with Graffi and Paris. Paris is a looked-after kid, I must show you some of his poems, they're brilliant.'

Poor little duck, she's adorable when she gets passionate, thought Hengist, only half listening, examining Janna's glowing freckles, the fox-brown eyes, the full trembling mouth, the piled-up Titian hair, which seemed to want to escape as much as she did. Lovely boobs too, quivering in that pink satin thing.

'My children have such terrible lives,' she was saying. 'My old school, Redfords in the West Riding, was an oasis of warmth and friendliness. I want that at Larks.' Tears were now pouring down her cheeks. 'I'm so sorry.' She blew her nose on her napkin.

'I know your old head, Stew Wilby,' said Hengist. 'Met him at conferences. Brilliant man, a visionary but a pragmatist like me.'

He took Janna's hands, stroking, comforting, as if she were a spaniel frightened by gunfire in one of the sporting prints.

'I'll help all I can. S and C Services worry me. I'm not sure they're kosher.'

'Ashton Douglas's vile, and Rod Hyde's a bully,' sniffed Janna.

'Sally likes most people, but she can't bear him,' agreed Hengist. 'Says he's so pompous and stands too close, with terrible coffee breath.'

'How did you find someone as lovely as Sally?' asked Janna wistfully.

'Have you time for another drink?' Hengist waved to Freddie.

'Oh, please. Could I have a gin and orange instead, please?'

Anything, she was appalled to find herself thinking, to extend lunch. Hengist was like the kingfisher or the rainbow, you longed for him to stay longer. Without realizing, she pulled the toggle off her hair.

'Sally, at twenty-one,' began Hengist, bringing her back to earth, 'had so many admirers. She was so pretty – still is – but her father, another head, didn't approve of me. Thought I was a bit of a rugger-bugger and hell-raiser, appalled when I didn't get a first. Anyway, Sally turned me down. I was devastated. My own father, however, told me not to be a drip. Said Sally was the best girl I was likely to meet, I must try again.

'So I invited her to the dogs the following night. She wore a pale blue flowing hippy dress. We backed a brindle greyhound called Cheerful Reply. After a drink or two in the bar, we joked that if Cheerful Reply won, Sally would marry me.

'Darling, it was a photo finish between Cheerful Reply and a dog called Bombay Biscuit. So we had several more drinks and a nail-biting quarter of an hour waiting for the result, which was Cheerful Reply ahead by a shiny black nose.

'Euphoric, probably at winning all that money, Sally agreed to marry me. I've never known such happiness: even better than being selected for England.'

'Lucky Sally,' sighed Janna.

'Lucky me. My parents were living in Cambridge at the time,' went on Hengist. 'I took the Green Line bus home, sitting up with the driver, so excited and tanked up, I told him everything and he said:

'"Isn't it amizing how racing dogs influence events?" Wasn't that perfect?' Hengist burst out laughing. 'Sally and I have had greyhounds ever since.'

'What a wonderful story.' Janna shook her head. 'I'd love a dog, but I'm out all day.'

'Take it into school, you're the head, the children would love it. Homesick children at Bagley are always asking if they can take Elaine, our greyhound, for a walk.'

He waved for the bill. As Janna gulped her gin and orange, he paid with American Express, then got a tenner out of his notecase for Freddie.

'Thank you so much,' Janna told the boy. 'Is this a full-time job?'

'No, I'm starting at New College next week.'

'Well done. Where did you go to school?'

'Bagley Hall,' said Freddie.

'One of our nicest boys,' murmured Hengist as he and Janna went out into the sunshine. 'His father walked out, so his mother worked all hours to pay the fees.'

'Why the hell didn't she send him to a comprehensive?'

'Because Freddie was happy with us. A lot of our parents are poor,' said Hengist sharply. 'They just believe in spending money on their children's education rather than cars, holidays and second houses.'

Wow, he can bite, thought Janna.

'Don't forget your spoon.' Handing her the box, Hengist smiled down at her. It was as though the sun had shot out from the blackest cloud. 'Come and see my school,' he said. 'Please.'

'Well, very quickly,' said Janna ungraciously. 'I'll follow you in my car.'

14

I am way over the limit both physically and mentally, thought Janna as, determined to keep up with Hengist, she careered down twisting, narrow, high-walled and high-hedged lanes made slippery by a recent shower of rain.

Bagley Hall, surrounded by exuberant wooded hills, sprawled over a green plain like one of those villages glimpsed from a train where you imagine you might start a thrilling new life.

The school itself was dominated by a big, golden Georgian house, known as the Mansion, which formed one side of a quadrangle. Behind were scattered numerous old and carefully matched modern Cotswold stone buildings, to accommodate 800 pupils and at least 150 staff.

Girls and particularly boys craned to look as Hengist whisked Janna round endless, many of them surprisingly pokey, classrooms. These were compensated for by a library to rival the Bodleian, entire buildings devoted to music or art, a magnificent theatre and a soaring chapel with Burne-Jones windows glowing like captured rainbows.

'Science etc. is over there.' Hengist waved dismissively at an ugly pile through the trees. 'A subject about which I can never get excited; besides, it's the domain of my deputy head, Alex Bruce.'

Outside, he showed her a swimming pool nearly as big as Windermere, running tracks and a golf course. Smooth green pitches stretched eastwards to infinity. To the north, a large bronze of a fierce-looking general on a splendid charger looked out onto an avenue of limes.

'That's General Bagley, our founder, famous for putting down troublemakers after the Black Hole of Calcutta and being effective at the Battle of Plassey.

'Our house is two hundred yards to the west, hidden by the trees,' he added, 'and very pretty. We're very lucky. You'll see it when you come to dinner.' Then, when she raised an eyebrow at his presumption: 'To meet Randal Stancombe. That's Rupert Campbell-Black's adopted son, Xavier, originally from Bogotá.' Hengist lowered his voice as a sullen, overweight black boy surrounded by a lot of chattering white thirteen-year-olds splashed past through the puddles on a cross-country run.

'Xavier's acting up at the moment,' explained Hengist. 'Hard to fade into the background if you belong to such a high-profile white family. Adolescents so detest being conspicuous and Xav's not helped by having a ravishing younger sister, Bianca, of a much lighter colour.'

'Poor lad being saddled with such an uncaring father.' Janna was getting crosser by the minute. 'Having plucked him out of Bogotá, how could Rupert have shunted him off to the vile prison of a boarding school?'

'He wanted to come here,' said Hengist mildly. 'People do, you know, and his step-brother and -sister both did time.'

When he showed Janna the new sports hall, she really flipped.

'It's a disgrace, kids getting such privileges because they've got wealthy parents. No wonder society's divided. Think how Graffi would thrive in the art

133

department and Paris in the library. Think how Feral would scorch round those running tracks.'

'There's no reason why they shouldn't.'

But Janna was in full flood: 'Why should rich kids have such an easy route in life?' Furious, she snarled up at him, an incensed Jack Russell taking on a lofty Great Dane.

'Janna, Jann-ah,' drawled Hengist, 'by "easy route", I presume you mean being put into "upper-class care". Surely you don't want your precious Larks children subjected to such a "vile prison"? That ain't logic.'

'Stop taking the piss. You know exactly what I mean. I want kids of all classes to go to day schools together, have access to these kinds of facilities and fulfil their potential. All this system does is make your odious stuck-up little toffs despise my kids and make them feel inferior.'

'Dear, dear,' sighed Hengist, stopping to pick up a Mars bar wrapper. 'So it's wicked of me to improve my school because it demoralizes children who don't come here.'

Then he noticed the tears of rage in her eyes and the violet circles beneath them. They had reached a lake fringed with brown-tipped reeds. Falling leaves were joining golden carp in the water. Next moment, a chocolate Labrador surfaced, shaking himself all over Hengist's yellow cords.

On the opposite bank, a blonde head appeared between the fringed branches of a weeping willow and shot back again.

'Dora,' shouted Hengist.

Very reluctantly, a pretty little girl with blonde plaits and binoculars round her neck emerged, followed by an even prettier one, with dark gold skin, laughing brown eyes and glossy black curls.

They were poised to bolt back to school, but Hengist beckoned them over:

'Meet two of my odious stuck-up little toffs, Dora

Belvedon and Bianca Campbell-Black, two new girls this term. How are you both getting on?'

'Really well,' said Dora, eyes swivelling towards the chocolate Labrador, who was now chasing a mallard.

Both girls were wearing sea-blue jerseys, white shirts, blue and beige striped ties and beige pleated skirts, which Bianca had hitched to succulent mid-thigh.

'This is Miss Curtis, the new head of Larks,' Hengist introduced Janna. 'Shouldn't you be playing some sort of game?'

'PE, but we both had headaches and needed fresh air.' Frantic to change the subject, Dora turned to Janna, 'How are you getting on at Larks?' she asked politely.

'Very well,' lied Janna. 'Are you Sophy Belvedon's sister-in-law?'

Dora brightened. 'I am.'

'Sophy and I taught at a school in Yorkshire,' explained Janna.

'She and my brother Alizarin have got a sweet little baby called Dulcie. All my brothers are breeding,' sighed Dora. 'I'm an aunt four times over; such an expense at Christmas!'

'How's Feral Jackson?' asked Bianca. 'I think he's cool.'

'So does Feral,' said Janna.

'That was an excellent essay you wrote on Prince Rupert, Dora, you obviously liked his dog,' said Hengist. 'And I've been hearing about your dancing, Bianca, I hope you're going to teach me the Argentine tango.'

'It's dead sexy. Women dance really close and rub their legs against men's. Daddy wants to learn it.'

'Is he going to win the St Leger?'

'I hope so.'

'I don't recognize this dog,' Hengist patted Cadbury, who'd bounced up again. 'Whose is it?'

'One of the masters, we don't know all their names

yet,' said Dora quickly. 'But we offered to walk him. We'd better get back, he might be worried. Bye, sir. Bye, Miss Curtis. Best of luck at Larks.'

Dog and children scampered off.

'That was a near one,' muttered Bianca. 'We'd better dye Cadbury black. Do you think Mr B-T and Miss Curtis fancy each other? She's very pretty, and he's not bad for a wrinkly.'

Janna, however, was off again. 'How can Rupert Campbell-Black send that adorable scrap to a boarding school?'

'Bianca's a day girl,' said Hengist.

'I thought they all boarded.'

'Not at all. We've got several day pupils, and lots of them go home at weekends, so they can drink and smoke unobserved.' Then he added: 'Come and see my pride and joy.'

The gold hands of the chapel clock already pointed to twenty to four.

I ought to go back. Why am I allowing myself to be swept away by this man? thought Janna as she ran to keep up with his long, effortless stride.

Hengist, who loved trees passionately and was always sloping off in the spring and autumn to rejoice in the changing colours, led her down the pitches to a little wood called Badger's Retreat, which was filled with both newly planted saplings and venerable trees. On the far side, as a complete surprise, the ground dropped sharply down into a broad green ride with beech woods towering on either side and a glorious view of villages, fields and soft blue woods on the horizon.

Janna gasped.

'Lovely, isn't it? Some criminal idiot back in the fifties gave planning permission to build here.' Hengist's voice shook with anger. 'Desirable residences with a view. Every time Bagley runs into trouble, there's talk of selling it off. The moment I got here, I planted

136

more trees to discourage this. Those enormous holes are badger sets. If anyone built houses, the badgers would burrow up through the floors.

'This is what we call the Family Tree,' he added, pointing to a huge sycamore with a single base, out of which three separate trees hoisted a great umbrella of yellowing leaves into the sky. Like three bodies locked in muscular embrace, their trunks gleamed from the recent rain.

'This is the father.' Hengist tapped the biggest trunk, which, from behind, was pressing its chest and pelvis against the mother trunk, with its branches around her and around the child trunk, which was leaning back against its mother. The branches of all three were stretching southwards towards the sun, many of them resting on the ground, as though they were teaching each other to play the piano. The bark, acid green with lichen, was cracked in many places to reveal a rhubarb-pink trunk.

'How beautiful,' breathed Janna, 'like a marvellous sculpture.'

'Like a family, struggling for freedom,' said Hengist, 'yet inextricably entwined and protecting each other. When we first came here, we noticed it, the way families cling together and hide their problems. It was May, and the new leaves were thick and overlapping, like parrots' plumage, concealing trunks and branches.

'We have a daughter, Oriana, who works for the BBC as a foreign correspondent. We did have a son, Mungo, but he died of meningitis.'

Betraying his desolation for only a second, Hengist pulled off a sepia sycamore key.

'I used to tell Oriana she could open any door with one of these and you can too, my darling.' He put the key in Janna's hand, closing her fingers over it.

I must not fancy this man, she told herself.

'Oh look,' said Hengist, 'the Lower Sixth has been here.'

In the long pale grass lay an empty vodka bottle and several fag ends. 'The retakes must have been harder than expected,' he added, picking up a couple of red cartridge cases.

As Janna glanced at her watch and said, 'Help, it's nearly a quarter past four,' Hengist could feel a black cloud of depression engulfing her.

'Thank you for lunch and the spoon,' she stammered as he opened her car door.

'I'd like to help, and I hope it's not just facilities you and I are going to share,' said Hengist, kissing her on the cheek.

'Hum,' said Dora Belvedon, nearly falling out of the biology lab window, 'Mr B-T definitely fancies her.'

15

Hengist Brett-Taylor had been born fifty-one years ago in Herefordshire. His parents were upper-middle-class Liberals and academics: his mother specializing in plants, his father a revered early English history don at Cambridge, hence the choice of Hengist's Christian name. Hengist had been educated at Fleetley and, between 1969 and 1972, read history at Cambridge. Here he got a double Blue for cricket and rugger and later played rugger for England, clinching the Five Nations Cup with a legendary drop goal from just inside his own half. As a result of too much sport and an overactive social life, Hengist, to his parents' horror, only scraped a 2.1.

At a May Ball at Cambridge, Hengist met Sally, a headmaster's daughter, as beautiful as she was straight. Their wedding took place in the chapel at Radley, where Hengist had started teaching history in autumn 1972. A daughter, Oriana, was born in 1973. Hengist had hoped for a son who would play rugger for England and whom he intended to call Orion.

Hengist prospered at Radley and was overjoyed in 1976 when Sally produced a son, Mungo. The birth was so difficult that Sally and Hengist decided two children were enough.

In 1979, Hengist returned to teach history and rugger at his old school, Fleetley, which now rivalled

Winchester and Westminster in academic achievement. Fleetley's head, David 'Hatchet' Hawkley, was determined to keep the school single sex, believing that girls distract boys from work.

In 1984, tragedy struck when little Mungo died of meningitis. This nearly derailed Sally and Hengist's marriage, particularly as Sally had just discovered that her husband had been dallying with David Hawkley's ravishing and promiscuous wife, Pippa.

Although Fleetley took only boys, as a huge concession, because Hengist and Sally couldn't bear to be separated from their now only child, David Hawkley had allowed the eleven-year-old Oriana into the Junior School. A contributory factor was that Oriana was far brighter than any of the boys in her class.

Gradually, Sally unfroze and she and Hengist mended their marriage. In 1989, however, Pippa Hawkley had been killed in a riding accident and, going through her desk, a hitherto unsuspecting David Hawkley discovered passionate letters from Hengist, which also contained the odd dismissive crack about David himself. Hengist, therefore, departed from Fleetley under an unpublicized cloud, which not even Oriana gaining straight As in twelve GCSEs could lift.

In 1995, later than if he hadn't screwed up at Fleetley, Hengist had been appointed headmaster of the notorious and wildly out-of-control Bagley Hall. Applying the same foxiness and energy that he displayed on the rugby field, Hengist miraculously turned Bagley round in six years.

Bagley was now snapping at Fleetley and Westminster's heels in the league tables, and lynching every other school at rugger and cricket. Hengist had signed on for another five years until summer 2005 but, easily bored, was looking for new challenges. His ambition was to thrash David Hawkley in the league tables and take over Fleetley when David retired. But he was also toying with the idea of politics. His chairman of governors, steely Jupiter Belvedon, the great white Tory hope, was only too aware that Hengist, as a media star, would add a desperately needed dollop of charisma to the party.

Oriana, meanwhile, had got a first at Oxford and joined the BBC. Although attached to her parents, she couldn't handle the claustrophobia of their love and expectation, and had pushed off abroad as a foreign correspondent. Despite a somewhat contentious relationship, Hengist missed Oriana dreadfully.

One of the reasons Hengist had turned Bagley round was because he was a genius at recruitment. He had so many celebrities among his parents that, in summer, the school helicopter pad wore out more quickly than the wickets.

Interviews with prospective parents took place in Hengist's study, usually in front of a big fire with papers spread all over his desk and everyone relaxing on squashy sofas. Hengist also insisted on the prospective pupil being present and addressing him or her as much as the parents.

To the fathers, who remembered catches flying into his big hands like robins and his dark mane streaming out as he thundered like the Lloyd's Bank horse down the pitch at Twickenham, Hengist was an icon. The mothers just fantasized about sleeping with him. The children said, 'I like that man, I'd like to go to that school.'

As a result Bagley was overbooked until 2010.

Hengist was a great teacher because he was a great communicator. But, because it involved too much hard work, he preferred to leave the GCSE and A level pupils to his heads of department and teach the new boys and girls so he could get to know them. Hengist believed in praising, and always fired off half a dozen postcards a day telling staff or pupils they had done well.

He was a genius at inspiring staff and delegating, but

hopelessly bored by admin and red tape, which was why, to relieve himself of this burden, he had appointed Alex Bruce from the maintained sector as his deputy head.

Hengist was aware that the charitable status awarded to the independent schools, which saved them millions of pounds a year, was under threat from the Government unless they could prove they were sharing their facilities with the community and in particular with the local state schools.

Bagley already had a distinguished history of pupils helping in neighbouring hospitals. From the Lower Fifth onwards, each child was allotted a couple of OAPs whose gardens they weeded and errands they ran. But this wasn't quite enough.

What more charming and advantageous diversion, reflected Hengist, to mix philanthropy with pleasure and help out Larks and that adorable crosspatch. And it would so irritate the heads of the other local schools.

16

Larks was revving up for its prospective-parents' evening. All the displays were in place. There was terrific work on the walls, including Pearl's A star essay on dressing the three witches in Macbeth. Year Ten had turned a room into a spaceship. Year Eight were doing agriculture in geography, and although Robbie Rushton had been far too lazy and bolshie to provide any input, his deputy Adele, whom he'd employed to disguise his imperfections, had weighed in and, with the help of the children, created a farm with coloured cut-outs of animals, machinery and a farmhouse kitchen with bread, milk, butter, cheese and a ham on the table.

Graffi, who fancied Adele and had drawn most of the animals and a farmer and his wife, had also created a glorious country scene in reception. This included wild flowers and trees, and larks in their nest, in the young emerald-green wheat or soaring into a red-streaked sky. In the east, he had painted a yawning sun crawling out of bed, and in the west, weary stars wriggling thankfully under the duvet.

Janna had craftily made it seem a great privilege for forty of the better-behaved children to be allowed back into school to welcome and provide tours for visiting parents. Those who'd helped put up displays had been rewarded with Mars bars and letters home requesting their presence.

This had caused sneering from the troublemakers, who'd not been chosen, but who, when a smell of roasting chicken crept out of Debbie's kitchen and Bob Marley began booming over the tannoy at going-home time, felt that they might be missing something – if only the chance to trash.

Feral had been truanting again, but Graffi, Pearl and Kylie had been among the chosen. Alas, Mr Blenchley, angry with Paris for cheeking Rod Hyde, had refused to let him out. Without Paris and Feral, Graffi needed to defend his work more fiercely than ever and, like a little tiger, prowled up and down reception.

The staff had divided into helpers and hinderers. Among the former were Miss Cambola and Mags Gablecross, who had taken children into the fields to try and record trilling larks.

'He's too high, miss,' was the considered opinion, but everyone got muddy and had a laugh.

Wally had painted till he dropped. Countries of the World in lime green now decorated the turquoise corridor walls. Even languid Jason had come to Janna's aid.

'I gather you had lunch with Hengist. How did you find him?'

'With difficulty. I got terribly lost.'

'Charming bloke.'

'If you like arrogant Adonises.'

'Did he mention me?'

'He feels you'll fit in very well.'

Missing the sarcasm, Jason looked delighted.

'Any help needed this evening, I'll be around.'

'If you could provide some evidence of work in progress in the drama department?'

Once Jason decided to lend a hand, Gloria and all the other pretty women on the staff did too.

Lance, although unable to galvanize his class, had himself created a project of life in Tudor England and spent days blackening beams and colouring in doublet and hose.

The hinderers were in a state of mutiny because Janna had ordered them to be on parade. Mike Pitts had left everything to Jessamy, his little Asian teaching assistant. Robbie was sulking because Adele had done so well. Skunk Illingworth carried on reading the *New Scientist*.

Around teatime, Janna caught Cara bitching into her mobile. 'Nobody'll turn up. I'll be away by eight.'

'That is such a defeatist attitude. You've made no effort,' Janna had told her furiously. Shaking with rage, she returned to her office. 'I'm going to kill Cara Sharpe.'

'Kill her tomorrow,' said Debbie, putting a plate of chicken sandwiches, a blackberry yoghurt and a cup of tea on Janna's desk. 'You must keep up your strength.'

'You are champion, the most champion thing that's happened to Larks, your food's utterly transformed the place, and you've added tarragon.' Janna bit gratefully into a sandwich. Then, picking up the *Gazette*: 'Let's look at our ad.'

But, to her horror, there was nothing there: no advertisement nor any part of her glowing report on Larks's future plans.

'I cannot believe it!' The *Gazette* flapped like a captured seagull as she flipped through it a second and third time – nothing. Even more galling, there were big ads and reports on the splendour and overflowing rolls at Searston Abbey, St Jimmy's and the choir school, who were all having parents' evenings this same night.

Colin 'Col' Peters, the *Gazette* editor, was all injured innocence when Janna called him.

'We never received any copy, Miss Curtis.'

'I put it through the letterbox.'

'I'm sorry. We have no record. If we had, we'd have billed you. We're not in the habit of turning away business.'

145

'I don't believe you. At least send a reporter down here this evening.'

'I'm afraid they're all on other jobs. *Such* a busy night.'

Janna smashed the telephone back on its cradle. What was going on in this town? Keep calm, count to ten, she told herself as she changed into a new dress, the blue of grape hyacinths, which had long, tight sleeves and clung to the bust and waist before flowing into a full skirt. It was demure, but very sexy. Sadly, she felt as sexy as a corpse. Her face, in the mirror, was drained of all colour and confidence.

Smile, Janna, even when you're playing to empty houses.

She hadn't even the heart to chide Gloria who, to wow any fathers, had rolled up in a pink vest and a white groin-length skirt showing off a shocking pink thong.

'Gloria certainly believes in transparency,' observed Mags Gablecross.

As she waited in reception, Janna's mood was not improved by the arrival of Monster Norman and Satan Simmons.

'Who told you to come along?'

'Mrs Sharpe,' sneered Satan.

'I've come to meet my mother,' said Monster.

'If you put a foot out of line . . .' hissed Janna.

'Everything looks splendid,' boomed Miss Uglow, taking up residence in her RE classroom with the latest P. D. James and a bag of bulls' eyes.

'Just remember to be polite to the new parents,' Janna urged the children. 'Show them you're proud of your school, so they'll want to send their kids here.'

The coffee was brewing. Debbie's chicken sandwiches and homemade shortbread were laid out on plates. Fresh rolls awaited the sausages warming in the oven for people who'd come straight from work. The church clock struck seven-thirty.

'Shall we dance?' asked Jason Fenton to Gloria the gymnast, as over the tannoy Bob Marley reassured them that every little thing was going to be all right.

But it wasn't, because no one came. You couldn't even blame the weather. It was a lovely evening, dove grey in the east, rose doré in the west and the first stars competing with Wally's lights up the drive.

'People'll turn up soon. They'll have seen our "Welcome to Larks" sign outside,' Janna reassured the children.

After ten minutes, Graffi abandoned his display in reception and ran down the drive to check. Immediately, Satan and Monster moved in.

'"Due to pesticide and fertilizer, there are few larks about these days,"' read Satan in a silly voice.

'And even fewer prospective parents,' wrote Monster underneath with a marker pen, just as Graffi returned, gloomily shaking his shaggy head.

'No one's coming, miss. Street's empty.'

'They'll probably come on to us from other schools.'

'Here's someone,' cried Kylie Rose in excitement.

But it was only Cara, Mike, Robbie, Sam and Skunk, trooping in from the Ghost and Castle.

'I hope you're not going to insist we hang around if no one turns up,' said Mike.

'Those are for the parents,' protested Pearl as Robbie and Skunk started wolfing chicken sandwiches. 'Tell them off, miss.'

Janna couldn't bear seeing the excitement draining out of the children's faces. Even worse, Rod Hyde kept ringing up.

'We've had two hundred already and they're still flowing in. How are you doing?'

'Oh, go away,' said Janna, fighting back the tears.

'What a waste of money heating the school on such a warm night,' chided Cara.

The boys, also believing in transparency, had started flicking water at the white shirts of the girls, revealing

147

their bras underneath. There was a crash as a window was smashed. Any moment there would be a mass exodus down the wisteria.

Unwilling to take on Graffi, Monster led Satan off to trash Year Eight's farm and, spitting at a cringing Adele, ignoring the screams of the girls, they swept everything off the farmhouse table and hurled a bread board and a papier mâché loaf out of the window. Chucking the farmer and his wife on the floor, they stamped on pigs, sheep and hens, kicked over milk pails and ripped the beautifully constructed tractor to pieces.

'Don't,' yelled Janna, racing up and seizing Monster's arm. Next moment, Graffi erupted into the room, hurling Satan to the ground.

'Fight, fight, fight,' yelled Year Eight, tears drying on their faces as they gathered round.

'Someone's coming,' squealed Kylie Rose.

'It's your mother, Monster,' yelled Graffi, catching him off guard and smashing a fist into Monster's round, pasty face.

Not wanting to have his ears boxed (Stormin' Norman could be as tough on her son as on other people's children), Monster scrambled to his feet, wiping his bloody nose.

Downstairs, Russell Lambert, Ashton Douglas and Crispin Thomas walked into comparative calm. Ashton had gone casual, wearing a beige cashmere V-necked jersey next to his pink-and-white skin, which made his features more formless than ever. Crispin ducked as a cardboard pig flew over the stairwell.

'This is very disappointing,' said Russell as Janna ran downstairs to meet them. 'Sam Spink tells me you've had no one in.'

Crash went another window.

'Turn up the volume,' hissed Janna to Mags Gablecross.

'"Hark, Hark! the Lark",' sang Bryn Terfel,

148

fortissimo, making everyone jump out of their skins.

'Is it a good idea' – Ashton looked disapprovingly at Paris's copied-out poems and Graffi's countryside mural – 'to gwaffiti newly painted walls?'

Explosions from the science lab indicated Year Ten were having fun. As Debbie and her helpers put plates of hot dogs and more chicken sandwiches on the table, Skunk, Robbie and Sam fell on them.

'How caring of Debbie to realize we'd missed supper.'

'Those are for the parents,' repeated Pearl indignantly.

'What happened to the advertisement in the Gazette?' asked Ashton.

'They didn't print it, claimed they never got it.'

'It's always wise to check these things,' said Russell heavily, 'shame to squander so much money and time on displays which no one sees.'

I must not cry, Janna told herself.

Five minutes crawled past. Mike Pitts was nose to nose with Ashton Douglas.

'Shall we call it a night?' he was saying. 'Frankly, I've got better things to do.'

'So glad I didn't waste time glamming up my department,' sneered Cara; then, shooting a venomous glance at Janna: 'Some people accused me of letting Larks down.'

'Ay had to pay someone to mind Cameron,' grumbled Chantal Peck. 'Ay'm going to put in expenses. Told you it would flop on an *EastEnders* night.'

'Please give it another five minutes,' begged Janna.

Noticing the ill-suppressed satisfaction on the faces of Ashton, Crispin and Russell, she told herself numbly: I don't understand why, but they are willing me to fail.

17

Then, suddenly, like the Angel Gabriel emerging from a day in the City, resplendent in a pinstriped suit, dark blue shirt and pretty pink and yellow checked tie, eyes sparking with malice, in sauntered Hengist Brett-Taylor.

'Janna, darling, how are you?'

Striding down reception, he took her hands and, bending down, kissed her on both cheeks.

'It all looks fantastic. My God, you've cheered this place up, and this mural is simply breathtaking. Of course, it's "Larks Ascending" – and the music too,' as, on cue, the tape launched into Vaughan Williams. 'Who's responsible?'

'Well, everyone, but the mastermind's been Graffi Williams here.'

'Brilliant, brilliant.' Hengist grasped Graffi's hands. 'I love the sun and the stars and that beautiful Shelley quote: "The world should listen then, as I am listening now", the prayer of all writers, me included. This is inspiring stuff.' Then he gave a shout of laughter. 'I love the old man with the beard, got that pompous ass Rod Hyde to a T.'

Hengist had been buoyed up by a very successful meeting with two of his high Tory conspirators, who were standing in the doorway and whom he now beckoned over.

'First, this is Jupiter Belvedon, your MP and chairman of my governors at Bagley.'

'Oh, goodness.' Janna found herself shaking hands with a dark, thin-faced, haughty-looking man in his early forties, familiar from posters all round the town, and forgot to bristle because she was so grateful to see anyone. 'Hi,' she gasped, 'welcome to Larks.'

'And Rupert Campbell-Black,' added Hengist.

'Blimey,' whispered Pearl.

'Wicked,' sighed Kylie. 'Oh, wicked!'

'Wicked indeed,' breathed Janna, because Rupert was so beautiful: like moonlight on the Taj Mahal or Monet's Irises, or a beech wood in autumn sunshine, which you'd dismissed as clichés because you'd seen them so often in photographs, in the flesh, they – and he – took your breath away.

The antithesis of Ashton Douglas, there was nothing soft in Rupert's face, from the smooth, wide forehead, the long watchful Oxford blue eyes, the hard, high cheekbones, Greek nose, short upper lip and curling but determined mouth. Around Hengist's height, somewhere up in the clouds to Janna, he was broad-shouldered, lean and long-legged.

Only his voice was soft, light and very clipped as he said:

'You don't look like a headmistress. I wouldn't have run away from school at fourteen if they'd looked like you.' Then, glancing down at the battered cardboard collie under his arm: 'Have you lost a dog? This one just flew out of the window.'

Prejudice evaporating, Janna burst out laughing.

'Would you like some shortbread?' asked Gloria.

'Or a chicken sandwich?' said Debbie the cook.

'Or a coffee?' said Rowan.

'Or an 'ot dog?' Chantal Peck rushed forward with a plate.

'I've got one already.' Rupert patted the collie's head.

151

'I'd adore one, I'm starving,' said Hengist.

'So am I,' said Jupiter.

Rupert shook his sleek blond head. 'I'm OK.'

'You bet you are,' murmured Gloria.

Even Cara Sharpe was looking quite moony.

Jason was feeling very upstaged, particularly as Hengist hadn't recognized him.

'Rupert, as you know, is one of my parents, and a director of Venturer Television,' Hengist told a stunned Janna.

'Has Venturer been in yet?' asked Rupert, who'd noticed Janna was trembling. 'No? I'll give them a ring.'

'Nor have any prospective parents,' said Monster Norman smugly. 'You're the only people who've shown up.'

'D'you have any kiddies, your honourable?' Chantal asked Jupiter.

'One boy.'

'Thinking of sending him to Larks?'

'He doesn't really talk yet.'

'We've got an excellent special-needs department.'

'Even so, he might have difficulty keeping up,' said Jupiter gravely, 'he's only fourteen months.'

'Same as my grandson, Cameron. Frankly, Jupiter, I wouldn't send Cameron anywhere else than Larks.'

Crash went another window. Overhead, it sounded like elephants playing rugby.

'How are you, little one?' Hengist murmured to Janna.

'Hellish. They've trashed the farm we built upstairs; no one's come. I've let the kids down.'

'Leave it to me. You're right about Paris Alvaston. I've just read his poem about a lark; it's miraculous.'

'Hi,' murmured Rupert into his mobile, 'I'm at Larks, get your asses down here.' Then, after a pause: 'Can you rally some parents?' Switching off, he turned to Janna. 'They were on their way to St Jimmy's; they won't be long.'

'I want to see round the school,' said Hengist, who was now talking to the children, praising and discovering who'd done what. 'Are you all going to take me? What's that, England?' He pointed to one of Wally's newly painted acid-green countries.

'No, Africa, dumb-dumb,' giggled Pearl.

'God, these are good.' Grabbing another hot dog, Hengist set off like the Pied Piper, trailing children, all wanting to hold his hand. Reluctantly, Ashton, Russell and Crispin followed him.

Going into classroom B20, he found a scene of total devastation, and Adele trying to comfort the sobbing twelve-year-olds.

There was a pause, then Hengist said, 'This is absolutely brilliant. Look, Ashton, look, Russell, they've re-created a farm in the Balkans.' Putting huge arms round the sobbing little girls, he went on, 'Of course you're sad your farm's been bombed, but you've really captured the pathos of war.

'Look at the poor farm animals and birds.' Hengist pointed with half a hot dog. 'Animals are always the first casualties of war. Look at that poor lamb with its legs blown off and the cow who's been disembowelled, and everything's been swept off the table.'

Hengist righted the farmer and his wife who'd lost an arm. 'They were just enjoying their tea, poor darlings, when the bomb fell. So sad.'

'Are you responsible?' He turned to a shell-shocked Adele. 'I can only congratulate you; such vision and courage, to destroy something so precious. That tractor's wonderful too. What's your name? Miss Stevens, just the kind of primitive machinery they'd have in Bosnia.'

'Graffi made that,' piped up Janna proudly.

'We did it too.' Monster and Satan edged forward. 'We trashed it.'

Janna was poised to annihilate them, but wily old Hengist pumped their hands. 'Well done, a real team effort.'

Robbie was simply furious, longing to push forward to take credit, but Hengist had moved on to Life in Tudor England and, as a fellow historian, was praising a blushing Lance:

'Just the right scarlet for that doublet, a very Elizabethan scarlet.'

Jupiter, meanwhile, was hell-bent on discomfiting Russell, Ashton and Crispin, who were all allied to the hung Labour/Lib Dem county council, who so frustrated his Tory ambition.

'And we'll hang them out to dry at the next election,' he murmured to Rupert as they paused to admire Mrs Gablecross's French café and enquire after her husband, the Chief Inspector, an old friend of them both.

Word had, by this time, got around that Rupert was at Larks and there was a further chance to get on telly, so there was a mass exodus from the other schools with parents and children storming up the drive. A reporter who'd only been at the *Gazette* for a week, tipped off by a Venturer cameraman, also belted over to Larks with his photographer. Hengist immediately introduced them to Janna, then took them by the arm, showing them the Larks Ascending display and the bombed farm.

Satan Simmons and Monster Norman were soon being interviewed.

'We built it up, then trashed it to create a wartime situation,' Monster was saying.

'Like the Chapman brothers or Rachel Whiteread,' said the reporter.

'Yeah, yeah, whatever.'

Photographs were also taken of Rupert, Jupiter and Hengist with Janna. Parents were everywhere, demanding autographs: 'You sending your kids here,

Rupert? How's Taggie? Any tips for Cheltenham?'

'We didn't get food at St Jimmy's or Searston Abbey,' said the other parents as they fell on Debbie's hot dogs. 'Lovely atmosphere here. I like these old buildings. More ambience. Hello, Jupiter. He's our MP.'

Jupiter, who reminded Janna of the lean and hungry Cassius, told the *Gazette* that as Shadow Education Minister and Larkminster's MP, he took a great interest in local schools.

'I am delighted Janna Curtis appears to be turning round this one, after only a few weeks. Good to have a young, energetic and charismatic head. You're to be congratulated, Ashton.' He smiled coolly at a seething Ashton Douglas. 'I hope you're providing adequate financial support. Janna tells me she needs textbooks, computers, playing fields and a new roof.'

'We can't have raindrops falling on our head or anyone else's,' said Rupert, looking up from the *Evening Standard*.

Janna got the giggles.

'Ashton, well done,' said Hengist, coming out of a side door, trailing children. 'You must be delighted you chose Janna. I've never seen such a change.'

Ashton looked as though he'd swallowed a wasp.

Venturer Television arrived, filmed the sea of parents and then interviewed Hengist about his interest in Larks.

'Janna and I have been discussing plans to share our facilities,' Hengist told them. 'The council sold off Larks's playing fields, so we'd like to offer them access to ours, and to our libraries, art departments, science labs and running tracks. We're very early in discussions, but it's an exciting project. We'll both learn from each other.'

'We'll teach them fist-foiting, shooting and Formula One driving,' yelled Graffi and was shushed.

'When will this happen?' asked the Venturer presenter.

'I'm off to America and we've got half-term, but very soon after that, I hope. To merit our charitable status, we independent schools must increasingly demonstrate we're of benefit to the community,' Hengist concluded smoothly. 'We've always offered bursaries to bright children; we're merely carrying on a tradition.'

'First I've heard of it.' Russell Lambert was puffing out his cheeks.

'Janna and I' – Hengist smiled in her direction – 'had a working lunch yesterday. She's made a great start, but as one who had problems at the beginning with Bagley, I'd like to offer my support.'

'Rod Hyde's already doing a grand job,' snapped Ashton, 'and I'm not sure how Larks staff will feel about bonding with an independent.'

'We'll have to find out,' said Hengist coolly, 'but three heads are always better than one.'

'Come on, I need a drink.' Rupert was getting bored. 'Can I keep this dog?'

Briefly, Hengist drew Janna aside: 'Pretty dress. At last she rose, and twitched her mantle blue: tomorrow to fresh woods, and pastures new.'

'I don't know what you're playing at,' muttered an utterly confused Janna, 'but thank you for rescuing us.'

'I'll ring you tomorrow.'

'Goodbye, goodbye.' Reluctantly, the children waved Hengist off.

'I'll be in touch,' Jupiter told Janna, then, handing his card to Graffi: 'I'd like to see more of your stuff.

'That was rather injudicious,' he added a minute later as the black polished shoes of the three men rustled through red and gold leaves towards the car park. 'Do you honestly want Bagley overrun by a lot of yobbos?'

'I want the world to know how good and philanthropic my school is. Caring conservatism must show it has balls,' said Hengist mockingly.

'Are you sure Bagley won't corrupt those innocent

Larks hooligans?' asked Rupert. 'Do you really want bricks heaved through your Burne-Jones windows?'

' "We must love one another or die",' replied Hengist sanctimoniously.

'I hope you don't want to get into Janna Curtis's knickers,' warned Jupiter, pressing the remote control to open the doors of his Bentley. 'The Tory party can't afford any more sleaze.'

'I like this dog.' Rupert patted his cardboard collie. 'It can round up the Tory unfaithful.'

Paris lay on top of his bed at Oaktree Court. A girl in the room opposite had been screaming for nearly an hour. Fucking Blenchley, not to let him out, when Janna had been kind enough to pin up his poem beside those of Shakespeare, Milton and Shelley. He murmured longingly:

'Teach me half the gladness
That thy brain must know;
Such harmonious madness
From my lips would flow,
The world should listen then, as I am listening now.'

He would have liked to shag Benita who slept next door, but if ever he left his room, a red light went on in the warden's office.

Shutting his eyes, he dreamt of making love to Janna: 'such harmonious madness'. He must get out of this place.

Waving the *Gazette* next morning, Gillian Grimston, head of Searston Abbey, telephoned Rod Hyde. 'That swine Hengist Brett-Taylor's never offered us a blade of grass. It's just because Janna Curtis wears tight jumpers and bats her eyelashes.'

'Hengist has always been a ladies' man.'

'I'd hardly call Janna Curtis a lady.'

'It'll all end in tears,' said Rod Hyde grimly, thinking of his stolen hat.

Nor was Randal Stancombe pleased. He didn't fork out £20,000 a year for Jade's school fees only for her to mix with riff-raff.

18

The following evening, Janna recounted the latest events to her new friend Lily Hamilton as they sat at Lily's kitchen table making sloe gin, selecting blue sloes from a pile Lily had picked earlier in the day, pricking each one with a needle before dropping it into a waiting bottle. Lily was progressing much faster because Janna kept pricking her fingers or missing the bottle whenever she got onto the subject of Ashton or Cara or Russell.

'They were foul. If Hengist and his friends hadn't rolled up . . .'

Lily smiled. 'I told you Hengist was nice.'

'I reckon he was more interested in bugging Ashton,' said Janna firmly, but the glow of gratitude still warmed her.

'You're returning your sloes to the pile,' chided Lily.

'Oh help, sorry.'

Just as she was topping up their glasses, Janna's mobile rang.

'Is that Janna?' asked an incredibly plummy voice. 'It's Sally Brett-Taylor. We were wondering if you'd come and dine on October the twenty-sixth. Hengist so enjoyed his lunch with you, and we'll try and rustle up some fun locals for you to meet. As it's a Friday, we won't bother to dress.'

And be running around nude, reflected Janna, then said she'd love to.

'Lovely, eight for eight-thirty, bye-ee.'

'Bye-ee, bye-ee,' muttered Janna as she hung up. 'That was Mrs Brett-Taylor,' she told Lily. 'She sounds very jolly hockey sticks.'

'She's a sweet thing,' said Lily. 'Terribly kind, keeps Hengist on the rails, remembering names, edging him out of parties if he's getting drunk or indiscreet.'

Janna was further touched on Monday to receive a cheque for three thousand pounds from Venturer Television.

'Hope this might buy a few textbooks,' Rupert had written, 'and your children might enjoy this film.'

It was *Gladiator*, which Janna allowed all the excited children to watch that afternoon as a reward for their good behaviour.

As a result of the prospective-parents' evening, thirty parents put their names down for Larks in autumn 2002 and the editor of the *Gazette* nearly sacked his news editor when a most flattering piece about Larks Comp appeared on the front page. This was accompanied by a smiling picture of Rupert, Hengist, Jupiter and Janna.

Inside were pictures of Graffi, Pearl, Monster and Satan surveying the trashed farm and a large headline: 'Larks Ascending'.

An overjoyed Janna bought twelve copies of the paper and sent photocopies to all the parents. Even more excitingly, the *Gazette* published Paris's poem 'To a Skylark', no longer a blithe spirit, whose trill was a burglar alarm, warning of the pillaging of the countryside.

'Paris Alvaston', wrote Hengist in his diary.

Poor Paris was unmercifully ragged at the children's home.

Sam Spink, meanwhile, called a union meeting to protest against Larks accepting any favours from the private sector. Alex Bruce, deputy head of Bagley, who'd come from the maintained sector, was equally unamused. His friend Rod Hyde had briefed him on the 'challenging behaviour' of Larks's pupils.

'Do we really want these hooligans to invade Bagley? You're always complaining of overwork, Senior Team Leader,' he reproved Hengist. 'Why not let me mentor Janna Curtis? I could slot in a visit to Larks on Fridays.'

'I'm only overworked by things I don't enjoy and Janna Curtis is very pretty,' said Hengist and laughed in Alex's shocked face.

After the parents' evening, Hengist had telephoned Janna as promised.

'I'm deadly serious about Larks and Bagley getting together. But I've got a hellish October. Lectures in Sydney and Rome, a headmasters' conference in Boston, not to mention half-term, so let's aim at early November.'

With that, he had drifted off and, like everyone else, been distracted by the American bombing of Al-Qaeda in Afghanistan, particularly as his daughter Oriana was reporting for the BBC from there.

Larks's pupils, whose spirits had been lifted by Hengist's visit and watching *Gladiator*, fell back into their old ways. Janna seemed to spend her time wrestling with red tape, refereeing fights, putting buckets under leaks and sparring with Rod Hyde, who said:

'Typical Hengist B-T behaviour, swanning in to cash in on the publicity. That's the last you'll see of him.'

It was so humiliating to have nothing to report when the *Gazette* and other papers rang for news of the bonding, and heartrending when the children kept asking when they'd get a chance to play football on a decent pitch. Janna was too proud to call Hengist, but as the leaves changed colour and tumbled from the trees, she felt enraged he hadn't rung and was determined to look as glamorous as possible at his wife's dinner party.

This was preceded by a day from hell.

In the morning, guilty that she hadn't tapped any

local fat cats for sponsorship, Janna had visited Grant Tyler, a Larkminster electronics giant who, with his long, yellow face ending in a pointed chin, looked just like a parsnip.

'And what do I get out of sponsoring Larks?' he had demanded rudely.

'Some of our clever children could do work experience here,' said Janna brightly, 'and might want to work for you as a career.'

Mr Tyler's face had turned from parsnip yellow to the purple of aubergine. 'If you think I'd let your ragamuffins over my threshold—' he had roared, and Janna had walked out leaving him in mid-sentence.

Later in the day she gave Cara Sharpe a final warning for bullying a little Bangladeshi pupil who'd been unable to produce a note explaining her absence because her mother didn't speak or write English.

Janna was also worried about Feral, who'd been truanting persistently. She'd sort him out next week. But tonight she was leaving on time to shower and wash her hair at home and remove the red veins in her eyes with an iced eye pad, before putting on a lovely new off-the-shoulder black dress: all the things she had had time to do before a date with Stew in the old days.

As she came out of Larks, fireworks, anticipating a forthcoming Bonfire Night tomorrow week, were popping all over town. Walking towards the car park, she heard a terrified whine, followed by shouts of laughter. Tiptoeing further into the garden, stumbling down Smokers' Bank, she froze in horror to discover Monster Norman and Satan Simmons in the long, pale grasses above the pond. No doubt carried away by their success in trashing the cardboard animals, they were now trying the real thing and torturing a little dog. They had tied its front legs together; Monster was winding a rope round its muzzle. Satan was swearing as he tied a large rocket to its tail. Monster was also smoking. Having stubbed his cigarette out on the shoulder of the

162

desperately writhing animal, he groped for a lighter and set fire to the rocket's blue paper.

'Stop that,' screamed Janna as both boys leapt out of the flight path.

Seeing her storming down the bank, they bolted, howling with laughter, down the hill over the wall. Next moment, the rocket exploded. Unable to soar into the air, it thrashed around on the ground, shooting out green and bright pink stars, dragging the dog with it.

Whipping off her coat, Janna flung it over the wretched animal, gathering it up, dunking it in the pond. As the sparks finally fizzled out, the dog wriggled. At least it was alive. In the gloom she could see its red and white fur singed on its face, sides and paws. It was a small mongrel with brown ears and a brown patch over one eye. Freeing its muzzle, untying the rocket with frantically trembling hands, Janna carried it up the bank to her car. It was hardly breathing now. Finding Wally and help would waste time. Laying the dog on the back seat, trying not to upset the poor little thing by sobbing, soothing it with: 'Good boy, brave boy, hang on a bit longer, darling,' she hurtled round to the Animal Hospital, off the High Street.

Here a sympathetic vet said it was their first Guy Fawkes casualty, but they were expecting a lot more; that the dog had been very badly burned and would probably lose his tail and an eye.

'It's only just breathing, hasn't got a collar, probably a stray, terribly thin, kinder to put it down.'

The dog, who suddenly seemed to symbolize Larks, gave a whimper.

'Try and save him,' pleaded Janna.

'I'll see what I can do.' The vet looked regretfully at her watch. 'I'm supposed to be at a dinner party.'

'Oh Christ, so am I,' said Janna. 'Can I drop by later?'

'Ring if you'd prefer. You'd better get something on those burns.'

Weeping with rage and horror, Janna plunged into the night. At least she had a proper reason to exclude Monster and Satan, except they'd both deny it. There was plenty of the dog's blood on her, but probably not on them.

Heavens, it was a quarter past eight. She had no time to change or wash her hair. In a lay-by, she ripped off her bloodstained T-shirt, leaving on her old olive-green cardigan and black skirt. Her stockings were laddered to bits. She'd look as poor and scruffy as the toffs would expect a state-school teacher to be, she thought savagely.

She was so distraught, she didn't reach Bagley until nine, where her animosity escalated as various incredibly polite children gave her directions.

'If you like, I'll hop in and guide you,' a little Hooray Henry said finally. 'Should get a good dinner. Mrs B-T's a terrific cook.' Then, noticing the bloodstained T-shirt in the back, he reached nervously for the door handle, until Janna told him about the dog.

'They ought to be shot, or rockets tied to their dicks. That's diabolical. We always give our greyhounds tranquillizers at home when there are fireworks around – at least we did,' he said sadly.

'Here we are,' he announced as the headlamps lit up brilliant red and crimson dogwood and maple and drifts of white cyclamen on either side of the drive.

As they passed arches trailing last year's roses and yew hedges cut into fantastic shapes, including a greyhound, Janna knew she'd come to the right house, which reared up, greyish yellow, shrouded in creeper, with some sash and some narrow casement windows, topped by roofs and turrets on different levels.

'It's a bit of a mishmash,' said her companion. 'Part Elizabethan, part Queen Anne, but very nice.'

A mongrel of a house, thought Janna, but strangely appealing, like the little dog fighting for his life.

'I hope your dog recovers,' said the boy, running

164

round and opening the door for her, 'and you have a good evening.'

'Thank you so much. What's your name?'

'Dicky Belvedon.' As he rang the bell for her, she realized he was Dora's twin.

'How are you getting back?'

'I'll walk. It's not far, and I can have a smoke in peace.'

A plump, middle-aged woman answered the door. Relieved that Hengist's wife wasn't glamorous, Janna was about to apologize for being late, when a truly pretty blonde ran out.

'Hello, Janna, I recognize you from your picture, I'm Sally B-T.'

After her, slipping all over the floorboards, wagging her tail, dark eyes shining, long nose snaking into Janna's hand, came Elaine, the white greyhound. Seeing such a happy, healthy dog, Janna burst into tears.

'You poor darling.' Sally turned, waved to the crowd in the room behind her to have another drink and whisked Janna upstairs. 'What's happened?'

Collapsing on the four-poster in the prettiest blue, lilac and pink bedroom, Janna explained about the dog.

'They're operating now. He was so defenceless and it was Larks children that did it. What can have happened to kids to turn them into such brutes?'

'They don't know any better. But poor little dog, and you've burnt your poor hands. They must be agony. We'll ring the sick bay and something for them.'

'I'm fine, honestly. I'm so sorry I didn't have time to change.'

There was a knock on the door, and a large glass of gin and orange, followed by Hengist, came round the door.

'Everything OK?'

'No! Poor Janna's had the most awful time.'

Sally, decided Janna – all her antagonism evaporating – was simply sweet. She was terribly Sloaney in her pie-frill collar and tartan blanket skirt, with wonderful rings on her rather wrinkled hands. But she was so friendly and kind.

'Now, please, borrow anything,' she told Janna. 'I'm afraid my make-up's not very exciting. A dash of lipstick and mascara is about my limit, but help yourself. And here's a nice cream shirt, if you're too hot in that cardigan. The bathroom's next door. Don't hurry.'

Having downed half the gin and orange, Janna felt perkier and the urge to spy. The curtains of the huge four-poster were patterned with sky-blue and pink delphiniums. On Sally's bedside table were Joanna Trollope and Penny Vincenzi, on Hengist's, French poetry and a biography of Louis XIV. A big dressing gown in forest-green towelling (to match his eyes) hung on the bathroom door. Janna imagined it wrapped round his hot, wet body. *The Joy of Sex* and *Fanny Hill* were well-thumbed in the shelves. Old maps of Greece and Italy covered the bathroom walls. Water gushed out of a lion's mouth into a big marble basin.

Janna took her hair down, but it looked so lank and straggly she put it up again. Sally's base was too pink, so she merely applied a little cherry-red lipstick to her mouth and blanched cheeks, and took off the shine with a pale blue swansdown powder puff dipped in a cut-glass bowl.

She now needed some perfume. Beautiful was pushing it. She'd smelt it on Sally. Instead, she slapped on a cologne called English Fern and was immediately transported back to La Perdrix d'Or and the wonder of her lunch with Hengist.

Comus, with damp, crinkled pages, was open beside a glass vase of yellow roses. 'What hath night to do with sleep,' read Janna.

You could say that again. She glared at her hollow cheeks and even hollower eyes. Sally's cream shirt falling to her knees like a nightdress made her look even more drained, but anything was better than the dreary cardigan.

Pale but interesting, Janna, she told herself. If that dog pulls through, I'm going to keep him.

19

Hearing the neighing and yelping of the upper middle classes three drinks up, Janna nearly turned and ran. Entering the double doors she found everyone up the other end examining some picture and paused in reluctant admiration because the huge lounge was so warm and welcoming.

Flames leapt merrily in the big stone fireplace. A crimson Persian carpet covered most of the polished floorboards. Battered sofas, armchairs and window seats in fading vermilion, old rose and magenta begged her to curl up on them. Poppies, vines and pomegranates rioting over the scarlet wallpaper battled for space with marvellous pictures. Was that really a Samuel Palmer of moonlit apple blossom? In bookshelves up to the ceiling fat biographies, history, classics, lots of poetry, gardening and art books, all higgledy piggledy and falling out, pleaded to be read. More books jostled with photographs of former pupils on every table, music scores rose from the floor in piles around the grand piano.

Any space left was crammed with family memorabilia: an old-fashioned gramophone with a convolvulus shaped speaking trumpet, a papier mâché HMV dog, busts of Wagner and Louis XIV, a staring female figurehead taken from a nineteenth-century fishing ship, a ravishing marble of Demeter with a sweat band restraining her curls – every object with a story.

This blaze of colour was reflected in a wooden mirror over the fireplace and softened by lamplight falling on great bunches of cream roses.

Never if I pored over *House & Garden* for a million years could I produce a room as beautiful, thought Janna wistfully, then angrily that independent heads must be grossly overpaid to afford places like this.

Hengist seemed to have read her mind, because he swung round and bore down on her with another vat of gin and orange.

'You poor darling, poor little dog, bloody bastards, I'd like to ram great lighted rockets up their arses.'

He was wearing a shirt in ultramarine denim, which turned his dark-green eyes a deep Prussian blue. From the breast pocket he produced a tube and a silver sheet of pills.

'The sick bay sent this over for your poor hands. Let me put some on at once.'

'It's only one hand, and it's fine.' Janna snatched the tube, knowing she'd tremble far more if he touched her.

Hengist's suntan had faded; his face was sallow and rumpled rather than golden and godlike. The trips to the States and Sydney must have been punishing, but his spirits were high and his eyes filled with amusement and expectation.

'It's so nice to see you again. I can't wait to open my facilities – such a dreadful word – to your children and particularly you.'

Bloody patronizing Little Lord Bountiful, thought Janna, wincing as she applied the gel, then wiped her hands on her skirt.

'Now swallow these,' ordered Hengist, pushing out two Anadin Ultra. When Janna looked mutinous he added, 'Or I'll hold your nose and stroke your throat.'

Feeding the pills into her mouth, letting his fingers

rest on her lips a second too long, he held out the gin and orange for her to wash them down.

'Good girl. Now what are we going to argue about this evening: dyspraxia, ethnic diversity, gifted children?'

'Are my kids ever going to be allowed to play on your pitches?' asked Janna furiously.

'Oh, sweetheart, of course they are.'

'No one believes you.' The hurt and humiliation poured out of her. 'Ashton Douglas, Rod Hyde, Mike Pitts, Crispin Thomas are all sneering at me.'

'Bugger Ashton,' said Hengist, 'although he'd rather enjoy it. I swear the first – no, second week in November. The red carpet awaits. Feral, Graffi, Paris, whoever you like.'

Janna, who'd been staring fixedly at his strong, smooth neck and emerging six o'clock shadow, raised her eyes and found such affection and tenderness on his face, she was quite unable to speak. Thank God, Sally rescued her.

'Janna, come and meet everybody. Be careful, this carpet is a high-heel hazard. You've met Elaine?'

'I have.' Janna ran her hand over the pink silken belly; Elaine, showing herself off to advantage on a russet chaise longue, opened a liquid dark eye and waved a tail in greeting.

The buckets of gin and orange were kicking in and Janna was cheering up, there was so much to look at. The watchful, saturnine Jupiter Belvedon actually pressed both planed cheeks against hers before telling her how much he'd enjoyed visiting her school. He then introduced Hanna, his lovely blonde Norwegian wife, who was as warm and curvy as he was cold and thin, and who must be a colossal asset to him in his constituency.

'Hanna's responsible for those exquisite flower paintings in our bedroom,' explained a hovering Sally.

'They're beautiful,' said Janna. 'My next-door neighbour, Lily Hamilton, has lots of them too.' Then she blushed as she remembered how cruelly Jupiter had turfed Lily out of a lovely house. Fortunately Jupiter, having parked her, had moved off so Janna was able to reassure Hanna that Lily was fine and a wonderful neighbour.

'What's she up to?' asked Hanna.

'Making sloe gin. Keeping us all entertained.'

'I miss her so much,' sighed Hanna.

I am behaving really well at a smart Tory dinner, Janna told herself in amazement. Then, goodness, jungle drums! Sally was introducing her to Randal Stancombe.

Just as black panthers and leopards, sighted in woods and along river banks and terrorizing whole communities, often turn out to be domestic cats with fluffed-out winter fur, Stancombe, despite his fearsome reputation, was in the flesh much less alarming than she'd imagined. He was certainly sexy, with a handsome predator's face, scorching dark eyes that seemed to burn off Janna's clothes, blow-dried glossy black curls and a mahogany suntan, set off to advantage by a linen shirt even whiter than Elaine. Asphyxiated by his musky aftershave and blinded by his jewels, Janna snatched away her burnt hand before it was crushed by his rings.

'Delighted to meet you, Jan, Henge says you're doing a great job at Larks, catch up with you later,' and he turned back to his companion, quite understandably, because she was the most glorious, pampered, expensive-looking beauty with shining chestnut hair, creamy skin, wide hazel eyes and luscious smooth coral lips.

This ravishing adventuress, Hengist whispered in Janna's ear, was *the* Mrs Walton he'd enticed onto the Bagley board as a parent governor, to ensure not only full houses at governors' meetings, but also that the other governors were so distracted by lust that they OKed all the decisions already made by Hengist and Jupiter.

'Very different from *my* parent governors,' giggled

Janna, thinking of Chantal Peck and Stormin' Norman. 'When did they meet?'

'About ten minutes ago.'

Feeling his laughing lips against her ear, Janna experienced a surge of happiness. Sally then whisked her off to meet Gillian Grimston, head of Searston Abbey, who had a lot of teeth like a crocodile whose mother had failed to make it wear a brace, and who was asked out a lot because of her ability to offer the Larkshire middle classes an excellent free education, rather than for her charm or good looks. She was patronizing but amiable, and commiserated with Janna on having Rod Hyde on her back.

'He's so conceited and bossy.'

She then banged on about her workload, which had cost her her marriage, and Searston Abbey, which had already raised thousands for Afghanistan war victims, thus giving Janna plenty of opportunity to watch Stancombe freefalling down Mrs Walton's cleavage and only just disguising his irritation when Jupiter joined them.

Determined to crack every aspect of society, Stancombe was not only pressing Hengist to make him a Bagley governor, but having watched Jupiter's rocket-like ascent was anxious to buy into that camp and be a formative influence in Jupiter's breakaway Tory party. Jupiter, who liked Stancombe's money better than Stancombe, was playing hard to get.

'The Afghan Fund is part of our caring ethos,' droned on Gillian Grimston, wishing Mrs Walton were one of her mothers.

'I'd rather have an Afghan hound,' giggled Janna. Oh dear, she was getting drunk again.

'Dinner,' announced Sally.

The dining room was equally seductive, with bottle-green jungle-patterned wallpaper, and chairs upholstered in ivy-green velvet round an oak table as dark and polished as treacle toffee.

Light came from red candles flickering amid more white roses and a chandelier overhead like a forest of icicles, which set the regiments of silver and glass glittering.

Ancestors under picture lights looked down from the walls, except for a portrait by Emma Sergeant over the wooden fireplace, which showed the young Hengist, solemn-faced, dark eyes raised to heaven, poised to kick his legendary drop goal at Twickenham. Pausing to admire it, Janna felt Sally's arm through hers.

'I insisted on hanging it there. It was painted some time after the event. Hengist thinks it's awfully showing off, but I so love it. Hope you didn't get too stuck with Gillian. She's a good old thing and probably a useful ally. Are you OK? Hands not too sore?'

'You are kind,' sighed Janna.

Even kinder, Sally had invited two single men to sit either side of Janna. One was Emlyn Davies, a blond giant with a battered face who taught history and rugger. The other, Piers Fleming, was head of English. Dark and romantic-looking, like Shelley's younger brother, wearing a steel-blue smoking jacket, he confessed he had great difficulty keeping the Bagley girls at bay.

'I'd screw the lot, if I weren't going to be banged up for under-age sex. Some of them are so gorgeous and so precocious, and worst of all' – he nodded across at Stancombe, who was being reluctantly prised away from Mrs Walton – 'is Randal's daughter Jade, and no one can expel her because Daddy's poised to give the school a multi-million pound science block – bloody waste of money.'

They then got onto the more edifying subject of English literature.

Noticing Hengist at the head of the table flanked by lovely Hanna Belvedon and even lovelier Mrs Walton, whose taffeta dress, the stinging emerald of a mallard's head, seemed to caress her body with such love, Janna's spirits drooped. Then Hengist smiled at her and mouthed, 'Everything OK?' And suddenly it was.

Two big glass bowls of glistening black beluga caviar resting on crushed ice were placed on the table, eliciting moans of greed all round. Accompanying them were little brown pancakes, bowls of sour cream, chopped shallot, hard-boiled egg and wedges of lemon.

'Oh, thank you,' said Mrs Walton, as her glass steamed up with the addition of iced vodka. 'Thank goodness I'm staying here and can get legless.'

'Shame with such lovely legs,' Stancombe leered across the table.

How the hell do I eat this lot? wondered Janna.

As if reading her panic, Sally called down the table, 'Do make up Janna's blinis for her, Piers, her hands must be so sore.'

'My favourite food,' confessed Jupiter.

'Where did it come from?' asked Gillian Grimston.

'Moscow,' said Hengist. 'Anatole, one of our pupils and the son of the Russian Minister of Affaires, chucked an empty vodka bottle out of an attic window and nearly concussed the chaplain—'

'And was, I presume, excluded?' Gillian looked shocked.

'Good God, no,' said Hengist, 'Anatole's a lovely boy. Always pays his own school fees in cash – probably laundered – out of a money belt. If only other parents were as prompt.'

'My cheque's in the post,' murmured Mrs Walton.

'Anyway, Anatole's mother was so grateful, she immediately sent us a ton of caviar.'

'Jupiter would kill for caviar,' said Hanna as her husband put two huge spoonfuls on his plate.

And much else, thought Janna. Not Cassius, she decided, he's more Octavius Caesar to Hengist's Mark Antony.

Janna wasn't sure about the caviar. She drowned it in

174

lemon juice and took huge slugs of vodka. Perhaps she should give hers to the emaciated man across the table, who had a tired, bony face and flopping very light red hair, and was already piling a second helping onto his blue glass plate.

'Rufus Anderson, head of geography.' Piers lowered his voice. 'Head in the clouds, more likely, always leaving coursework on trains. Eats hugely at dinner parties because his wife, Sheena, doesn't cook and whizzes up to London to a high-powered Fleet Street job, leaving Rufus to look after the kids. Note his sloping shoulders weighed down by baby slings.'

'Then they should get an au pair,' said Janna sharply. 'Her career is just as important as his.'

'Not at Bagley, it isn't. Wives are expected to be helpmates. Sheena's hopping that Emlyn on your left was offered a job as a housemaster last year and Rufus wasn't. Rufus is miles cleverer than Emlyn or me. Sheena doesn't appreciate she's the only thing in the way of her husband's advancement. That's her down the table hanging like a vampire on Stancombe's every word.'

As Mrs Walton was soft, passive and voluptuous, Sheena Anderson was rapacious and hard. She had sleek black jaw-length hair, a hawklike face only adorned by eyeliner and a lean, restless body. No jewellery softened her short sleeveless black dress.

'I'd love to interview you for the *Guardian*,' she was telling Randal Stancombe.

'They always give me a rough time.'

'Not if I wrote the piece. You could approve copy.'

Like Jack-the-lad-in-a-box, Stancombe kept texting, emailing, doing sums on his palm top, leaping out of his seat to telephone or receive calls, leaving his mountain of caviar untouched.

'We could do it one evening over dinner,' urged Sheena.

But Stancombe was checking his messages. 'Bear

175

with me a minute, Sheen,' and he shot into the hall again. Through the doorway, he could be heard saying, 'Sure, sure, great, great, call you later.' Switching off his mobile, he punched the air. 'Yeah!'

'Good news?' enquired Sally as he slid back into his seat.

'Just secured a plot of land in Colorado, Sal, a ski resort to be exact.'

Janna caught Jupiter's eye and just managed not to laugh.

Gillian Grimston, who'd been subjected to Stancombe's back, was not used to being ignored. 'Where is this resort?' she asked.

'I'm not at liberty to reveal as yet, Gilly.' Stancombe flashed his teeth. 'In fact, bear with me again, Sal and Henge, if I make another call,' and he retreated again.

'That's how he keeps his figure,' said Piers.

Sheena, much to Sally's disapproval, had whipped out and was muttering into a tape recorder.

'How did you get started?' she asked when Stancombe returned.

'As a barrow boy. One of my customer's husbands gave me a job as an office boy in a property company. Kept my ear to the ground. Gave the CEO hot tips until he promoted me to head of the agency division. Two years later I took away all my contacts and started Randal Stancombe Properties. Rest is history. According to the Rich List, in Central London alone we own eight hundred buildings let to blue-chip companies.'

Everyone was listening.

'Despite heavy borrowings at the last count the port-folio must be worth more than two billion.'

Mrs Walton was gazing across the table in wonder. That would sort out the school fees.

'How many million times a million is that?' hissed Janna. 'He should be on the stage.'

'Better on television,' hissed back Piers. 'You could turn him off.'

'To what do you attribute your success?' asked Sheena, who'd left the tape recorder running.

'Hard work, seven days and seven nights a week.'

Stancombe checked his messages again. It was his thin line of moustache, Janna decided, like an upside-down child's drawing of a bird in flight, which gave him a gigolo look.

'Don't you ever play?' purred Mrs Walton.

'According to Freud,' said Janna idly, 'work and love are the only things that matter.'

'And children.' Hanna smiled at Jupiter, thinking how she'd like to paint those white roses.

Stancombe glanced down at his abandoned coal heap of caviar, realizing everyone had finished.

'I've had sufficient. I OD'd on beluga in St Petersburg last week.'

'Christ, what a waste,' exploded Jupiter.

'Did you buy a resortski?' enquired Janna.

Sheena was well named, she decided; she had a sheen of desirability about her but was very opinion-ated. As conversation became general and moved on to the war, she kept regurgitating whole paragraphs from a piece she had written on American imperialism earlier in the week.

'Hell, isn't she?' muttered Piers.

As he moved on to William Morris on October: 'How can I ever have enough of life and love?' Janna had noticed a sweet little girl gathering up the blue glass plates. Then she realized it was Dora Belvedon, Jupiter's stepsister, who'd emerged from the weeping willow by the lake with Bianca Campbell-Black, the day Hengist had shown her over Bagley.

Now she was bringing sliced roast beef in a rich red wine sauce round on a silver salver.

'Hello, Dora, you'd better tell me what fork to use.'

Dora's mouth lifted at the corner.

'It's very good, I tried some in the kitchen. I hear you met my brother Dicky earlier. I do hope that poor dog recovers.'

Dora loved waiting for Hengist and Sally. If she lurked and kept quiet, guests often forgot she was there, and revealed lots of saleable gossip.

Stancombe for a start was utterly gross, but good copy, and there'd been a lot about Janna Curtis in the press recently. She didn't look pretty tonight with that schoolmarmish hair and shapeless white smock. Mrs Walton, on the other hand, was gorgeous. Stancombe clearly thought so, which might make a story: Dora bustled back to the kitchen, and taking a pad out of her coat pocket wrote 'Randy Randal' and vowed to ring the papers tomorrow.

20

The beef and the creamy swede purée were so utterly delicious, Janna, Sheena and Mrs Walton all simultaneously vowed to take more trouble.

'Thomas Hood's also brilliant on autumn,' Piers was saying.

'You mustn't monopolize Janna,' Sally called down the table.

'He wasn't, we've had a smashing time comparing notes,' protested Janna, who had deliberately concentrated on Piers because the man on her other side was shy-makingly attractive. Outwardly unruffled as a great lion dozing in the afternoon sun, he had a spellbinding voice: deep, lilting and very Welsh, a square, ruddy face, thick blond curly hair, and lazy navy-blue eyes which turned down at the corners.

'Welcome to Larkshire,' said Emlyn Davies as she turned towards him. 'How are you enjoying being a head?'

'Not as much as I'd hoped,' confessed Janna. 'I keep looking back wistfully to the times when my biggest worry was getting a class through GCSE.'

Encouraged by his genuine interest, she was soon telling him all about Larks.

'I made Paris and Feral mentors,' she said finally. 'I thought giving them some responsibility might make them more responsible. You know Feral?'

179

'Everyone knows Feral.'

'He and Paris are so gorgeous. All the girls are dying to be mentored by them, but Feral's never in school and Paris has his nose in a book and tells them to eff off.'

'Can you buttle, Emlyn?' asked Sally a shade imperiously, 'No one's got a drink at your end.'

'Feral's a dazzling footballer,' continued Janna when Emlyn returned. 'If this bonding between us and Bagley takes off, would you keep an eye on him?'

'I teach rugby.'

'Feral could adjust, he's so fast and can do anything with a ball. If he felt he was achieving, he might come in more often. If Feral stays away, half the school does too and we'll never rise in the league tables.'

Emlyn put a huge hand over hers. 'League tables are shit, so many heads fiddle them. Schools like St Jimmy's and Searston Abbey don't improve: they just reject low achievers. Why should anyone want difficult children if they push you to the bottom?

'When you think of the disadvantages with which your kids from the Shakespeare Estate start, it's as much a miracle to get five per cent of them through as it is for us and St Jimmy's and Gillian to clock up ninety per cent. League tables are about humiliation, delving into laundry baskets and washing dirty linen in public.'

Janna was delighted by the rage in his voice.

'How does an independent teacher understand these things?'

'I taught in comprehensives for nearly nine years.'

'How could you have switched over?' cried Janna in outrage.

'A number of reasons. I like teaching history and the national curriculum's so prohibitive. Nor do I like being bossed around by the Council of Europe. I also like teaching rugby. Bagley was unbeaten last season. Gives you a buzz. I like the salary I get. I adore Hengist and I'm very idle. Here, I get plenty of time to play golf and fool around – "displacement activity" our deputy head Alex Bruce calls it.' He smiled lazily down at her.

'Most Welshmen are small, dark and handsome,' he added, patting his beer gut. 'I'm fair, fat and funny.'

Not handsome, decided Janna, but decidedly attractive.

She hoped he'd ask her out. As if reading her thoughts, he said, 'You must come out with us one evening. We drink at the Rat and Groom. If you're going to be coming to Bagley a lot, someone ought to give you a minibus.'

'I'm not very good at getting sponsorship,' sighed Janna, remembering Mr Tyler who'd looked like a parsnip. 'I get bogged down by administration.' She took a slug of red. 'I'm even wearing my admini skirt.'

Then she noticed the red and white hairs on the black wool, gave a sob, and told Emlyn all about the poor little dog.

'I'm going to call in on the way home. Oh dear.' As she wiped her eyes, smudging Sally's mascara, her elbow slid off the table.

'I'll drive you, I haven't drunk much,' said Emlyn, adding, with a slight edge to his voice, 'Don't want to screw up in front of the boss and his wife.'

'How *kind* of you,' cried Janna, hoping Emlyn might stop her thinking so much of Hengist.

'Can I come too and see this dog?' asked Dora, who was hovering with second helpings. 'Have some more potatoes, Mr Davies, keep up your strength. We had a Labrador called Visitor,' she told Janna, 'who adored fireworks, saw them as coloured shooting. He used to sit barking at them, encouraging them on.'

'Get on, Dora,' ordered Hengist, 'and you move on too, Emlyn, I want to sit next to Janna.'

All the men moved on two places, which meant

Randal ended up on Janna's right and, to his delight, on Mrs Walton's left.

Hengist was shocked how wan Janna looked. He didn't tell her about the uproar there had been from Bagley parents reluctant to have Larks tearaways let loose among their darlings.

'How are your hands?'

'Numbed by booze and painkillers. I'm having a lovely time tonight, sorry I snapped at you earlier.'

'It was fear biting.'

'Everything's been getting on top of me.'

Except a good man, thought Hengist. Then he said, 'There's a dinner at the Winter Gardens – tomorrow week – to plan Larkminster's Jubilee celebrations. All the local bigwigs'll be there. Sally can't make it. Come with me; I've got to speak so I can officially announce the twinning of Larks and Bagley.'

'How lovely. Sure I won't lower the tone?'

'Don't be silly. That's a date then. How did you like Emlyn?'

'Wonderful.'

'He is. We didn't lose a match on the South African tour; the boys had a ball but never overstepped the mark. They call him Attila the Hunk. A lot of people raised eyebrows when I tried to make him a house-master, but the boys adore him and so do the parents. Sadly he refused – said the rugger teams give him enough hassle. You know he played rugger for Wales?'

'Goodness,' said Janna.

'He used to be very chippy, but with success the chips go.'

'Am I chippy?'

'Very, that's why I want to ensure you're wildly successful.' And he smiled with such affection, Janna had to smile back.

'Oh dear, dear,' Piers muttered to Sheena. 'Little Miss Curtis is going to get hurt.'

182

'What d'you think of Stancombe?' Hengist had lowered his voice.

'Challenging,' said Janna.

'And deeply silly. Parents have to kill to get into one's school; once in, men like Stancombe compete to build science blocks, sports pavilions.'

'And an indoor riding school,' said Dora, putting out pudding plates.

Hengist laughed and patted her arm. 'Dora keeps me young.'

Stancombe had moved on to art. 'I'm a big art person, Ruth. I frequently make large donations to the Tate; they're talking of naming a staircase after me.'

'I'll slide down your banister any time,' murmured Mrs Walton.

'How about making a generous donation to Larkminster Comp?' asked Emlyn idly. 'And give them a minibus.'

'Oh, hush,' said Janna, blushes surging up her freckles.

'What a good idea.' Mrs Walton smiled. 'Then they could name the bus after you.'

'Even a second-hand one,' suggested Hengist. 'If Larks is bonding with Bagley, they'll need transport.'

'I'll think about it.'

'Oh, go on, Randal,' cooed Mrs Walton.

Stancombe was trapped. A muscle was rippling his bronzed cheek, but he was so anxious to impress her.

'Right, you're on, Jan.'

'Oh, thank you,' gasped Janna. 'Thank you so much.'

'Make a note of it, so you don't forget,' insisted Mrs Walton.

'Larks minibus,' wrote Stancombe on his palmtop, then looked across at Mrs Walton, the hunter setting the deer in his sights. 'You owe me,' he mouthed.

'I hope he won't pull out of this science block,' whispered Hengist. 'Alex Bruce insists it'll look good

183

on the prospectus, but oh dear me, builders in hard hats here for over a year and a sea of mud. I'll probably have to take Stancombe's dunderhead son as a quid pro quo, but I'm not having him on my board. And if he wants to get into Boodle's, he'll have to buy the building.'

'Why are you so ungrateful?' asked a shocked Janna.

'At heart, I don't trust him.'

A vibration in Stancombe's trouser pocket signalled an incoming call. Fascinated by Stancombe's mobile, the very latest model, which could actually take pictures and even flashed up on the screen a little photograph of who was calling, Dora shimmied forward to offer Stancombe more wine. Then she nearly dropped the bottle as a disgusting photo of a naked blonde with her legs apart indicated one of Stancombe's girlfriends was on the line. Stancombe hastily killed the call, and started taking photographs of everyone at the table, which gave him the excuse to immortalize Mrs Walton.

All the same, thought Dora, it was a wonderful invention and would hugely help her journalistic investigations to have a little camera inside her mobile. What a good thing too that revolting Stancombe was off his grub. His untouched beef would make a terrific doggie bag for Cadbury, who didn't like caviar.

'My daughter Jade is in a relationship with Cosmo Rannaldini, Dame Hermione Harefield's son,' Stancombe was proudly telling Mrs Walton. 'Dame Hermione was very gracious when Jade went to visit. As Milly and Jade are good friends,' he continued, 'I hope you'll be able to make a long weekend skiing before Christmas.'

'I'm sure we could fit it in.' Mrs Walton's exquisite complexion flushed up so gently, Stancombe could just imagine her generous, sensual mouth round his cock.

'Come home with me tonight,' he whispered.

'I can't really, Sally's offered me a bed.'

'It's awfully kind of you to offer us a minibus,' Janna told him when he finally tore himself away to talk to her. 'I hope you haven't been compromised.'

'No way, I come from a poor family myself, Jan, seven of us in a tiny flat. Your kids deserve a leg-up.'

'I'm particularly grateful for Feral Jackson's sake . . .' began Janna.

Stancombe choked on his drink. He'd been so knocked sideways by Mrs Walton, he'd been manoeuvred, without realizing it, into benefiting his bête noire Feral Jackson, who rampaged through the Shakespeare Estate and nearby Cavendish Plaza terrifying tenants and, only this evening, chucking around lighted fireworks.

Twigging he wasn't exactly flavour of the month, Janna suggested Feral would behave much better if he had a focus in his life.

'It'd better not be my Jade,' snarled Stancombe.

'Rugger channels boys' aggression in an awfully positive way,' said Sally, scenting trouble.

Fortunately Stancombe was distracted by Dora. He liked her shrill little voice, her gaucheness, untouched by masculine hand, her antagonism, her tiny breasts pushing through her blue dress, her figure which hadn't yet decided what it was going to do with itself. He wondered if she had any pubic hairs yet. He'd met Anthea, her mother, at Speech Day, a tiny, very pretty lady. Dora was larger than her mother already. That sort of thing made a young girl feel lumpy and elephantine. Dora would benefit from a little attention.

Dora was serving white chocolate mousse with raspberry sauce when she noticed Stancombe's hand burrowing under Mrs Walton's green silk skirt and was so shocked she piled an Everest of mousse onto Mrs Walton's plate.

'Heavens, Dora,' cried Mrs Walton, tipping half of it onto Stancombe's plate, 'are you trying to fatten me up?'

Dora watched appalled as Stancombe removed his hand to spoon up his mousse, then shoved it back up Mrs Walton's skirt.

Marching furiously back to the kitchen, Dora made another note on the pad in her coat pocket, before returning with a brimming finger bowl, which she plonked in front of Stancombe. 'Like one of these?' she hissed.

Emlyn glanced over and roared with laughter. Everyone else was distracted by a querulous knock on the door.

One of Hengist's tricks for keeping people on the jump was to exclude from dinner parties those who felt they should have been invited. A case in point was his deputy head: Alex Bruce, a fussy-looking man with spectacles and a thin, dark beard which ran round his chin into his brushed back hair, edging his peevish face like an oval picture frame. He now came bustling in:

'A word please, Senior Team Leader.'

'It can't be that important.' Hengist patted a chair. 'Have a drink and sit down. You know everyone except Janna Curtis, the marvellous new head at Larks. Janna, this is Alex Bruce, the superpower behind the throne.'

Alex nodded coldly at her, and even more coldly at Mrs Walton, whose presence on the board, making things easy for Hengist and Jupiter, he bitterly resented.

This must be Hengist's cross, thought Janna, the man he feared was going to strangle him in red tape. He certainly looked cross now.

'Joan Johnson's just been on the phone,' Alex told Hengist. 'She caught Amber Lloyd-Foxe and Cosmo Rannaldini snorting cocaine. Dame Hermione was incommunicado when I tried to call, but I took the liberty of suspending Amber Lloyd-Foxe. When I phoned her mother, Jane, she complained it was the middle of the night – it's actually only eleven-thirty – and when I appraised her of the situation, she said:

"How lovely, Amber can come to the Seychelles with us." I don't believe Jane Lloyd-Foxe was entirely sober; anyway she refused to drive over and collect Amber.'

Typical, uncaring, public-school parent, thought Janna disapprovingly.

'I'm afraid I hit the roof, Senior Team Leader,' went on Alex.

Cosmo Rannaldini up to no good with Amber Lloyd-Foxe? Randal was also looking furious: was his precious Jade being cheated on?

'Shall we go upstairs?' said Sally, glancing round at the women.

Do they still keep up that ritual? thought Janna, outraged to be dragged away, particularly when she heard Alex recommending exclusion, and Hengist replying in horror that Cosmo was an Oxbridge cert.

21

Upstairs, Sally drew Janna aside onto the blue rose-patterned window seat. 'My dear, it's so nice you're here. Jolly tough assignment, Larks, but I'm sure you'll crack it. You will come to me if I can be of any help?'

Advise me how not to fancy your husband, thought Janna.

'I'm so glad you got on with Emlyn,' went on Sally. 'You must go to the cinema with him and some of the other young masters. I'm awfully fond of naughty little Piers. And you must meet our daughter.' Sally pointed to a photograph in a silver frame on the dressing table.

'Oriana Taylor,' gasped Janna. 'My God! But she's an icon. So brave and so brilliant during September the eleventh and the war in Afghanistan. Hengist never said she was her. I didn't realize. I'd die to meet her, and so would our kids.'

'We must arrange something next time she's home. Oriana is rather left-wing,' confessed Sally. 'Bit of a trial for her father. Having profited from a first-rate education, she now thinks we're horribly elitist.' Sally smiled. 'I expect you do too. She gets into dreadful arguments with Hengist.'

'Does she live in New York full time?' asked Janna.

Sally nodded: 'We had a son; he died.' Oh, the sadness of those flat monosyllables. Sally pointed to a

188

photograph of a beautiful blond boy with Hengist's dark eyes. 'So Hengist misses her dreadfully.'

'I'm so terribly sorry,' mumbled Janna.

'I know you are,' said Sally. 'I'm just nipping downstairs to organize drinks and coffee and pay Dora.'

After that, Janna sat on Sally's four-poster and talked to Mrs Walton, who was really a joy to look at and to smell – great wafts of scent rising like incense from her body.

'Emlyn's very attractive, isn't he?'

'Extremely, but sadly spoken for.'

'He is?' asked Janna in disappointment.

'He's going to marry Hengist's daughter Oriana.'

'A shrewd career move – lucky Oriana.'

'Lucky indeed. Emlyn's so bats about her he agreed to wait until she'd tried being a foreign correspondent. Alas, she's been so good at it, she seems to have lost any desire to settle down.'

'Oh, poor Emlyn.'

'Sally isn't that displeased by the turn of events; she doesn't think Emlyn's quite good enough,' confided Mrs Walton as she repainted her lips a luscious coral. 'Despite his amiability, he's very left-wing. Hates the Tories, hates the royal family, and hates rich spoilt children. He didn't get a first either, although he's a wonderful teacher. Hengist dotes on him. They have rugger in common, but Sally feels that macho Welsh rugger bugger tradition isn't for Oriana – she needs someone more subtle and better bred. Sally tries not to show it because she's such a gent,' went on Mrs Walton, 'but she also feels Oriana isn't bats enough about Emlyn. I mean, if you had a hunk like that, would you base yourself in New York pursuing all those terrifying assignments?'

Sally wants me to go to the cinema with Emlyn because she knows I fancy Hengist rotten, decided Janna, and if I get off with Emlyn it will free Oriana and get me out of Hengist's hair.

189

Suddenly, she felt very tired. 'I must go.'

'Let's have lunch,' said Mrs Walton.

'I can't really get away.'

'Well, come to supper then.'

'I'd like that.'

'I'll ring you at Larks.'

At that moment Mrs Walton's mobile rang. It was Stancombe from downstairs.

'I'll call you,' she mouthed at Janna.

How can I ever have enough of love and life, thought Janna as she put on her dreary green cardigan.

Downstairs, she found Jupiter talking to Hengist, who had lucky Elaine stretched out on the sofa beside him with her head in his lap.

Sheena, having dispatched Rufus home to relieve the babysitter, was arguing with Piers and waiting to get a lift from Stancombe who was still on his mobile.

Then Janna started to laugh.

'All part of our caring ethos,' Gillian Grimston was droning on to Emlyn, who had fallen asleep in an armchair.

'Caring Ethos,' mused Hengist. 'Sounds like a fifth Musketeer, the priggish older brother of Athos or Porthos. Caring Ethos.' He smiled at Janna, gently setting aside Elaine's head so he could get up. 'Have a drink.'

'I'm off,' she said, 'I'll drive very slowly.'

'You will not, you've had a horrid shock. Emlyn is going to take you,' said Sally firmly.

As they left, Hengist imitated the Family Tree, standing big, strong and dark behind Sally's fairness, his arms wrapped around her: we are an item.

'Will you be home tomorrow afternoon?' he asked Janna. 'I'll drive your car back, and we can discuss where we go from here – put Saturday night in your diary.'

Everything out in the open, so unlike Stew, thought an utterly confused Janna.

'I'd like a word, Sheena,' said Sally as she closed the front door.

* * *

Trees brandished their remaining leaves in the wind like tattered orange and yellow banners. Janna tried to quiz Emlyn about Hengist and Sally but, guilty he'd spent half-term and so much money in New York with Oriana rather than with his mother and sick father in Wales, he was uncommunicative.

He didn't say much but he was sweet to make a long detour into Larkminster via the Animal Hospital. The little dog hadn't come round from the anaesthetic, said the nurse, but should pull through. They had saved the eye but probably not the tail. He'd need to spend a few days in hospital.

'And then I'll come and collect him,' said Janna.

I'm going to call him Partner, she decided, then if anyone asks me if I've got a partner, I can say yes.

Most of the Sundays carried lurid accounts of Amber Lloyd-Foxe and Cosmo Rannaldini being suspended for drugs, and everyone blamed the leak on Sheena Anderson.

22

Janna knew that if confronted Monster and Satan would deny torturing Partner. Instead she decided to unnerve them by relating the incident in detail at assembly the following Monday.

'Animals feel pain just as we do. They're more frightened because they have no idea why such evil things are happening.' Her voice broke: 'Partner was such a trusting little dog.'

'Bastards,' spat Pearl.

'Murderers,' sobbed Kylie Rose.

'The bad news is that it was so dark I'm not sure which Larks pupils were involved but the good news is I rang the hospital this morning and despite his horrific burns Partner's getting better all the time. He may still lose his tail but when he comes out of hospital he's moving in with me.'

Cheers from the children.

'I'm going to bring him into school because I know you'll love him and I'm sure he'll recognize the evil bullies who tortured him and we can report them to the police and RSPCA.'

Five minutes after assembly, Rowan gleefully reported that Satan and Monster had been seen belting down Smokers' and over the wall.

'One pair I don't mind truanting,' said Janna.

Feral, on the other hand, was another matter. Each

day he missed he slipped further behind. There was no point setting up minibuses, pitches and running tracks if he wasn't there to profit from them.

Paris and Graffi went vague when questioned so Janna dropped a line to Feral's mother asking if she might pop in to discuss her son on the way to Hengist's civic dinner. At least it would give her a chance to check out the dreaded Shakespeare Estate.

Outside she could see shrivelled pale brown leaves tumbling out of the playground sycamores and imagined them falling from Hengist's Family Tree revealing the interlocked incestuous grapplings to the white sky.

She tried not to get excited about Saturday's dinner, for hope would be hope of the wrong thing. At least it would be a change from paperwork and she could finally give her slinky new off-the-shoulder dress an airing. The night before she rubbed lots of scented body lotion into the shoulder that was going to be exposed before falling into a rare and blissful eight-hour sleep.

Waking with optimism, she popped into the hospital to take Partner a bowl of chopped chicken. Still heavily sedated, he greeted her with barks of joy and shrieks of pain as he wagged his poor burnt tail. He really was a sweet little dog, with one ear pointing skywards, a freckled fox's face, a pink nose, sad chestnut-brown eyes, short legs and a rough red and white coat.

'We'll be two short-arsed, mouthy redheads living together,' she told him, 'and exploring the country instead of working all weekend.'

Having measured his neck size and promised she'd fetch him home tomorrow, she spent a fortune in Larkminster's pet shop on a sky-blue collar and lead, a name disk, dog food, pig's ears, a blue ball and a blue quilted basket decorated with moons and suns.

Out in the street, rustling through shoals of red and gold cherry leaves, her happiness evaporated as she caught sight of a *Gazette* poster: 'Is Janna Curtis turning her back on failing Larks?'

Buying a paper, she found a smiling photograph of herself, Hengist and Jupiter at the prospective-parents' day on page three. Accompanying it was a snide story saying she was being wooed by the independent sector and had recently dined with the Brett-Taylors, Jupiter Belvedon, his wife and property tycoon Randal Stancombe. How much longer would she bother with a bog-standard school she had failed to improve?

With a scream of rage, Janna scrunched up the paper, sending three pigeons fluttering up into the rooftops. Why in hell hadn't the piece mentioned Gillian Grimston had been at dinner too?

Larks was always left open on Saturdays for the rare members of staff who might want to catch up or prepare lessons. Fortunately no one seemed to be around when Janna arrived so she would have time to prepare a denial. But as she walked down the corridors, rejoicing in the colour and vitality of the children's work on the walls – Larks was not failing – she heard crashes and screams coming from her office and broke into a run.

She was greeted by devastation as a hysterical Pearl, who'd already pulled the books out of the shelves and thrown every file on the carpet with Janna's in-tray scattered on top, was now upending desk drawers.

Her spiky rhubarb-red hair was coaxed upwards like an angry rooster, her coloured make-up was streaked by tears and studs quivered like the Pleiades on her frantically working face.

'Bitch, cunt, slag!' she howled, catching sight of Janna. 'I know you've got the 'ots for Feral, you 'orrible slag, wiv your cosy little tea parties.'

She ripped Janna's date calendar off the wall, pointing a frantically trembling finger at 3 November: '"Feral's mother seven p.m." You never bothered visiting my mum.' She started tearing the calendar to pieces.

'Stop it.' Janna tried to stay calm. 'Steady down. Whatever's brought this on?'

But a screaming Pearl had started on the pictures. Crash went *Hold the Dream* and *Desiderata* over the back of a chair, followed by the big photographs of Fountains Abbey and the Brontës' house at Haworth.

'For God's sake, you'll get glass in your eyes,' pleaded Janna, wondering the best way to grab her.

Crash, sending out another fountain of splintered glass, went Stew's photograph of all the children at Redfords.

Pearl then hurled Janna's Diorissimo against the window smashing both with a sickening crunch, followed by a bottle of ink against the white wall which spilt down over the flower-patterned sofa. Then she picked up Stew's little Staffordshire cow.

'Oh please, no,' gasped Janna.

'You sad bitch!'

Crash went the cow, hitting the fridge and fragmenting into a hundred pieces. Pearl, like a cornered cat now, rather than a furious rooster, was clawing, screaming, spitting. Slowly, slowly Janna talked her down.

'Please tell me what's the matter. I'm not cross, I'm here for you,' until Pearl collapsed sobbing on the ink-stained sofa.

'Thought you liked us, miss, but the paper says you're leaving us for those stuck-up snobs.'

A tidal wave of relief swept over Janna.

'Then they'll have to carry me out in a coffin. I love you at Larks. You're my children and I'm going to take a big photograph of you all and put that on the wall.'

Sally and Hengist, she explained, had kindly invited her to dinner to meet other teachers and people who might help Larks.

'So we can buy more textbooks and go on more jaunts and invest in some fun, young, new teachers. I'd rather live in a cage full of cobras than teach in an independent school.'

'What about the cow?' sniffed Pearl, picking up a fragment of horn from the carpet. 'Was that precious?'

'Not any more,' said Janna, realizing it was part of a past that had gone away. 'And the only reason I haven't asked you over to the cottage is because of your Saturday job, and I'm not sure how you'd cope with the walk in those heels. The boys are coming tomorrow afternoon instead to meet my new dog. Please come too, and be very gentle with him, boys can be a bit rough. Look at what I bought him at the pet shop.' She opened the carrier bags she'd left in the corridor. 'And let's have a coffee and a chocolate biscuit.'

Later, as, chattering, they made an effort to straighten the room, Pearl noticed the invitation to the civic dinner which Hengist had posted to Janna.

'That's tonight. "Jubilee Dinner". Looks a posh do. I hope we can have a street party. My mum's always going on about how great they was in seventy-seven. Look, to make up for this' – Pearl waved a blue-nailed hand round the devastation – 'I'll make you up for tonight, do your hair, give you a make-over, like. It'd be really cool. Then I could photograph you, put it on the wall like Graffi's pictures and Paris's stories and fucking goody-two-shoes Aysha's chemistry project.' Pearl was suddenly wildly excited. 'I'll find you a dress too.'

'That would be champion,' said Janna. Anything not to shatter this rapprochement. 'Let's meet at five-thirty.'

'Make it earlier,' said Pearl, suddenly authoritive. 'I did the morning stint at the salon. That's where I read the *Gazette*. I need time to do it proper. You go home and have a nice bath. I'll meet you back here at four.'

When Janna dutifully returned, Pearl refused to work her magic in front of a mirror.

'It stresses me to be watched.'

So Janna tugged her desk chair into the middle of

the office and got stuck into planning the next human resources meeting, which would cover staffing.

She was sure Ashton Douglas and Crispin would demand redundancies or her budget would never balance. But with any luck the dinosaurs like Mike Pitts, Basket, Skunk, even Cara Sharpe might consider early retirement.

'She's an evil bitch, that Cara.' Pearl peered over Janna's shoulder as she cut her hair.

'If I'm not allowed to look, neither are you,' reproved Janna, 'and not too much off.'

'My mum always says that. I'm going to lift the colour with a few highlights.'

'Not too tarty,' pleaded Janna, 'I'm trying to be an authority figure,' then cautiously enquired about the Shakespeare Estate.

Pearl shrugged. 'Council uses the place as a bin bag to dump all the bad families. Most of the dads are in the nick like mine or on nights and never see their kids.'

Finally, having washed Janna's hair in the Ladies, blow-dried it and made her up from a range of colour that would have been the envy of Titian, Pearl sprayed gold dust on her shoulders. Then, dismissing the black off-the-shoulder number Janna had brought in as too mumsy, she helped Janna into an incredibly short fern-green handkerchief dress which gave her a cleavage worthy of Mrs Walton.

'You look wicked, miss.' Pearl held up Janna's hand mirror, about the only thing unsmashed. 'Now you can look.'

Janna didn't recognize herself. Even under the office strip lighting she looked absolutely gorgeous.

'That can't be me. I look like a film star.'

'Good material to work on,' conceded Pearl.

She had covered Janna's face in light-reflecting moisturizer, then put shimmering highlights on her cheekbones, and narrowed and rounded Janna's

197

squarish chin with blusher, before blending in sparkling powder.

To make the eyes huge and vulnerable she had drawn black along the upper lash line, mingled all the golds, oranges and russets on the lids, then thickened the lashes with three layers of brown mascara.

Most seductive of all, on Janna's big mouth, instead of pale pinky coral, she had used a deep plum red gloss.

'Weee-ee.' Janna shook her head, swinging rippling cascades of rose red, emerald green and chestnut hair. 'Which flag of the world am I? You're a genius.'

'You look amazing, miss,' said Pearl happily. 'Go out and pull.'

'Where did you find all this incredible make-up?' asked Janna, suspecting it had been knocked off.

'They often pay me in make-up at the salon,' said Pearl airily.

Janna was far too kind to put Pearl down by saying the whole thing was completely OTT and was vastly relieved when Pearl wrapped a long, tasselled flamingo-pink shawl round her shoulders.

'This is lovely and the dress too.'

'My mum's,' said Pearl hastily.

'Won't she mind?'

'Doesn't know – it's my babysitting fee.'

It was only when she was driving to the Winter Gardens, praying none of the big shop owners would recognize their stolen wares on her that Janna remembered she'd promised to pop in on Feral's mother at 12 Macbeth Street. She'd been crazy to pick this weekend. It was like entering a war zone, as coloured stars exploded in dandelion clocks and rockets hissed into the russet Larkminster sky, crashing and banging to a counterpoint of jangling fire engines and screaming police sirens.

How could the people of Afghanistan cope with

incessant American bombing – or was she twice as scared because she'd had a baptism of fireworks with Partner a week ago?

The Shakespeare Estate was a concrete hell, hemmed in by a high circular wall, which separated it from the beautiful, prosperous golden town, the serenely winding river and the lush countryside beyond. Cul-de-sacs named after Shakespearean characters ran like spokes in a wheel from this circular wall into a bald piece of land, known as the Romeo Triangle, which had a much graffitied pub, broken seats and a boarded-up newsagent's. Gangs of youths in hoods with sliding walks prowled the streets chucking stones or bangers at Janna's green Polo as she drove past. Rasta and R and B music fortissimo, blaring televisions, couples having violent domestics were interrupted by the screams of prostitutes. Fireworks lit up the crazed emaciated faces of Ixions chained to the wheels of their addictions.

'Never get out of your car and walk,' Pearl had warned.

But there was no space outside number 12, so Janna was forced to park fifty yards away and totter up Macbeth Street on her high heels. All the windows of number 12 were broken or boarded-up. The front garden contained stinking, unemptied dustbins, an old fridge and a burnt-out BMW. No one answered the door, the paint of which was blistered and dented with kicks. Youths, gathering on the pavement, were hurling fireworks into next door's garden. A curtain flickered and Janna caught a glimpse of a terrified old man.

Although number 12 was in darkness, she could hear a ghetto blaster. Perhaps Feral was hiding upstairs. Ducking in terror as a rocket hissed past her head, she ran back down the garden path slap into a very large black man. He had a shaved head and was wearing black leather, a large diamond necklace, ear studs and lots of aftershave, which mercifully blotted out the stench of dustbins.

199

'What yer doing?' a bass voice with a soft Jamaican accent rumbled menacingly up from his chest.

'Looking for Feral Jackson.'

The big guy gave Janna, as made over by Pearl, the once-over and made an understandable mistake. 'Bit long in the tooth for him.'

'I actually have an appointment with his mother.'

'Pull the other leg – and get off my territory if you don't want your pretty face rearranged.'

Janna winced as he yanked her head upwards and flicked on his lighter. 'On second thoughts I'll forget it if you show me a good time.'

'I beg your pardon?'

'I won't cut you up' – he threatened her eyelashes with his lighter – 'if you give me a fuck.'

Whereupon Janna rose in outrage to her five feet one inch plus four-inch heels. 'How *dare* you. I am Feral's head teacher.'

The big guy looked initially flabbergasted then became very, very cosy and introduced himself as Feral's Uncle Harley.

'And you don't look like an 'ead teacher, little darling.'

'Feral hasn't been in school for three weeks.' Janna tried to steady her trembling legs. 'I'd like to see Mrs Jackson.'

'She's not in; family's gone to the pitchers to see *Shrek*.'

'I just want someone to get him up in the morning and see he does his homework.'

'Look no further,' murmured Uncle Harley.

As he walked her back to her car, approaching gangs of youths retreated like smoke. A prostitute stopped screaming at Janna and slid away like a snake.

'Feral's such a wonderful athlete,' urged Janna. 'A group of Larks children have been invited over to Bagley Hall so he'll get an opportunity to play football on decent pitches and try out their running tracks.'

'He's a lucky young man.' Uncle Harley grew even cosier. 'You got time for a drink?'

'I should be at the Winter Gardens already.'

'Sorry I mistook you.' Uncle Harley took her keys to open the car door, then, adding with massive irony, 'Not safe round here for a nice young lady,' he kissed her hand.

'I hope to see you at one of our parents' evenings.'

'Try and keep me away.'

23

Still shaking with hysterical laughter, Janna reached the Winter Gardens. The dinner was held in a side hall, whose high ceiling was covered with nudging, pinching cherubs reminiscent of the playground at Larks. In one half of the room, tables were laid for dinner and speeches. In the other, because a Lib Dem/Lab hung council had no intention of squandering ratepayers' money, indifferent red or white was being offered to a crowd of bigwigs.

Hengist had not yet arrived, but Pearl's make-over was soon having a dramatic effect. The Mayor, wearing a chain Uncle Harley would have killed for, blamed the Winter Gardens' poor acoustics for the fact he had to bend right over Janna's boobs to hear what she said.

Next minute, parsnip-faced Mr Tyler rushed up with two friends and was just apologizing for his rudeness the week before last when Stancombe appeared by her side, looking sleek and glamorous in a dinner jacket and far more relaxed than he'd been at Sally and Hengist's. 'I can't handle teachers, Jan; so patronizing, do my head in. Don't count you as one; not tonight, particularly. You look very tasty.'

He got out his mobile, took a picture of her and texted it to one of his friends, showing her the message: 'How lucky am I to be invited to functions with ladies like this?' Then, to show off further to Tyler and the Mayor: 'The minibus will be with you by a.m. Wednesday, what colour d'you fancy?'

'The coolest colour, please.' Janna accepted a top-up of white. 'You are kind, it will give our children such street cred.'

'I'm donating a minibus to Larks,' boasted Stancombe to the others, 'so Jan can transport her kids to matches and things.'

'I'll send in the boys to sort out your computers,' countered Tyler.

'I'll pick up the bill for any sports kit,' said one of his friends.

'That would be fantastic,' beamed Janna.

Thank you, Pearl, she thought, sidling away as the Mayor pinched her bottom. She'd never had such an effect on men. Tyler and his mates were clearly irked by the way Stancombe muscled in, but they all deferred to him.

Then Hengist swanned in, instantly stealing Stancombe's thunder: 'Darling, sorry I'm late. Christ, you look amazing.' He kissed her on both shimmering cheeks. 'What have you done?'

'Pearl gave me a make-over.'

'We'll make her head of make-up when we do our joint Larks–Bagley play.' He took a gulp of red and nearly spat it out.

'Christ, that's disgusting.' He waved to a waiter who scuttled over. 'Can you get me a bottle of Sancerre and a large whisky and soda, no ice, and take this arsenic away.' He handed the boy his and Janna's glasses.

'It can't be that bad, Hengist,' grumbled the Mayor.

'It's much worse,' said Hengist, putting an arm round Janna's shoulders. 'Jesus,' he added as the flamingo-pink shawl fell away.

'I'm having a Mrs Walton moment,' giggled Janna.

Hengist couldn't stop laughing.

'I can't work out if you look ten years older or younger than the little teenager you normally resemble. Come and meet everyone important. Oh dear, here come Super Bugger and Sancho Pansy from S and C,' as Ashton and Crispin paused to have their picture taken by the *Gazette*.

Crispin had put on more weight and with his petulant baby face he looked like the bullying older brother of the cherubs rampaging over the ceiling. Ashton's bland pink and white face had been given more definition by a dinner jacket and a black tie but his thinly lashed eyes were as cold green as a frozen fjord. Waiting until Hengist had been distracted by some Tory councillor, he and Crispin cornered Janna.

'You look very Chwistmassy.' Ashton examined her hair. 'Does it wash out?'

'Yes, but I don't.'

'The *Gazette* says you're joining Bagley,' snuffled Crispin.

'When did that rag ever tell the truth? Gillian Grimston was at the same dinner party. Sally invited me to meet some locals, which is more than Mike Pitts, Rod or either of you have ever done.'

'And how's the Bagley bonding going?' asked Ashton.

'Starts next week.'

'Doesn't it threaten your left-wing pwinciples to accept largesse from an independent?'

'Beggars can't be choosers. My children have been let down too often.' Janna's voice rose: 'And it's not as if you're giving us any money.'

Ashton put his head on one side. 'You should weally take a course in anger management.'

'Doesn't she look gorgeous?' It was Hengist back, waving a bottle of Sancerre, topping up Janna's glass. 'Pearl Smith did her hair and make-up. I think we've got another Barbara Daly on our hands. You should let her have a go at you, Ashton, next time you've got an important date,' he added insolently.

'I'm from the *Western Daily Press*, Miss Curtis,'

announced a hovering photographer. 'Can I get a picture of your new look? I'll take care of your shawl,' he added whisking it away and arranging her next to a marble vestal virgin with downcast eyes.

'Sacred and profane love,' murmured Hengist. 'I know which I prefer.'

'Can we have you in the photograph too, Mr B-T?' said a second photographer. 'I'm from *Cotswold Life*.'

Ashton and Crispin were hopping. So was Rod Hyde. How dare Janna look so desirable! She deserved a good spanking. Rod had rolled up with Alex Bruce and, like Alex, had rejected the right-wing regalia of a dinner jacket. Gillian Grimston immediately sat down beside them.

'As the leading professional at the Brett-Taylors' dinner party,' she said indignantly, 'why didn't the *Gazette* mention I was there?'

Why wasn't I asked in the first place? thought Alex and Rod darkly and simultaneously.

'Who's that toad-like man with bulging eyes who's just waddled in?' Janna whispered to Hengist.

'Colin "Col" Peters. Editor of the *Gazette*, failed Fleet Street, now enjoying being a big toad in a small pool.'

Janna downed her third glass of wine. 'I'm going to kill him.'

'Not tonight you're not,' said Hengist firmly.

'And the smiley-faced woman in the red trouser suit talking to him looks familiar.'

'That's Cindy Payne, the Labour county councillor in charge of education, hand in glove with Ashton Douglas. Looks like a cosy agony aunt, but she's a snake in sheep's clothing.'

'Snakes eat toads. Col Peters better watch out.'

At dinner Janna found herself sitting next to a CID Chief Inspector with a square, reddish face softened by beautiful long-lashed green eyes, and was enchanted when he turned out to be the husband of her languages teacher, Mags Gablecross.

'Such a lovely woman. If only she worked full time.'

'She says you're working wonders and the kids adore you.'

'I wish the teachers felt the same. They're so terrified of Cara Sharpe.'

'Get her out,' advised Chief Inspector Gablecross. 'She's bad news.'

After a good bitch about Cara, Janna told the Chief Inspector about her encounter with Uncle Harley, which really shocked him.

'Don't ever go near the Shakespeare Estate alone again. Harley's really dangerous and hell-bent on taking the drug trade to new markets all over the West Country.'

Janna drew in her breath. 'Oh dear.'

Across the room she saw Stancombe getting up, making apologies to his table and waving to Janna on the way out.

'See you Wednesday morning, Jan. Give the garage a spring clean.'

'Stancombe's got his eyes on the Shakespeare Estate,' observed the Chief Inspector. 'Always the same procedure. He vows he's going to build cheap houses for first-time buyers – teachers and nurses – then he razes the place to the ground and, like mushrooms, desirable residences spring up.'

He looked down in disgust at his first course of roast vegetables. 'You used to be able to turn down these things with your main course. Now they're everywhere.' He patted his gut.

Janna, who hadn't eaten all day, was tucking in.

'I was worried Stancombe might be after Larks – all those acres of lovely land,' she admitted; 'but I misjudged him, he's just given us a minibus.'

'*Timeo Danaos*,' warned the Chief Inspector.

'Will you come and talk to my kids?' asked Janna.

On Janna's left was a trendy estate agent called Desmond Reynolds, nicknamed 'Des Res', because he found so many middle-class parents desirable residences in the catchment areas of St Jimmy's and Searston Abbey.

He had little chin, talked through clenched teeth and, having discovered she came from West Yorkshire and didn't know the Lane-Foxes or the Horton-Fawkeses, lost interest.

'Five per cent of the properties I sell each year are driven by parents' desire for a better school. Stands to reason,' he went on languidly. 'Pay three hundred thousand for a house in the catchment area of St Jimmy's. In seven years you've not only saved at least a hundred and forty K per child you would have spent on Bagley school fees, but also your house will have trebled in value because you're in the catchment area of such a cracking good school.'

'Why's St Jimmy's so good?' Sulkily, Janna speared a roast potato.

'Because Rod Hyde's a cracking good head.'

'Do your children go there?'

'No, Eton.'

'I suppose people never want to buy houses in the catchment area of Larks?' asked Janna wistfully.

'Never,' said Des Res with a shudder. 'Beats me why Hengist's pairing up with them.'

Glancing round, Hengist caught the desolation on Janna's face and immediately swapped places with Des Res.

Janna took a huge gulp of wine and then a deep breath.

'Stancombe's promised the minibus for Wednesday morning.'

'Come over on Wednesday afternoon then.'

'How do I know your little toffs won't take the piss out of my kids?'

'Send the best-looking. The Wolf Pack are such celebs they'll get badgered for autographs.'

Hengist's flippancy enraged Janna but when she told him about her visit to the Shakespeare Estate he went white.

'Promise, promise never to go there again. Planes may not disappear from the Romeo Triangle but people do.'

'Uncle Harley promised to get Feral back into school.'

'Probably wants him to flog drugs to our "little toffs" when he visits Bagley.'

'Oh God, I hope not.' Then, stammering and angry: 'Desmond Reynolds said he couldn't think why you were wasting your time on Larks.'

'Ah.' Hengist forked up one of her potatoes, 'Because I believe in improving the state system. When I'm old, I want well-educated, positive, happy young adults running this country.' He smiled. 'Or it could be that I fancy you rotten.'

Janna's blush came through Pearl's war paint.

'Stop taking the piss.'

'And because you remind me of Oriana.'

'She's wonderful.'

'And terribly tricky. If only she'd take a nice job with the BBC in Bristol instead of being addicted to trouble spots.'

'I'm amazed she can tear herself away from the Shakespeare Estate.'

Hengist laughed. Then, as waitresses stormed on with strawberry pavlova: 'I'd better get back to my seat.'

Against the colourful banners of the Boys' Brigade, the Rotary Club, the Parish Council and the Honorary Corps of Elephants and Buffaloes, the chairman of the county council made a colourless speech laboriously outlining Larkminster's plans for the Jubilee.

He wasn't anticipating a visit from Her Majesty but there were plans for a Jubilee mug and the shops would be decorating their windows. No street parties were planned.

'My children would love a street party,' shouted a now drunk Janna and was shushed.

Noticing Ashton shaking his head and exchanging a pained, what-did-you-expect glance with Crispin and Rod, Hengist thought angrily: They're willing the poor child to screw up. More resolute than ever he rose to his feet.

Miss Painswick had typed out his speech in big print, so he didn't have to wear spectacles; a lock of black hair had fallen over his forehead. As he thanked the waitresses and waiters for all their hard work, they crept back into the dining room to hear him.

'The Queen has been on the throne for nigh on fifty years,' he said warmly, 'never put a foot wrong, and deserves to be celebrated. And, like myself,' he went on slightly mockingly, 'she believes there is no privilege without responsibility.

'We in the independent sector have always recognized there is no justification for our work if pupils grow up to use the benefits of their education only for their own advancement and profit. We at Bagley Hall have a tradition for community work: we go into hospitals, we give concerts in the cathedral, members of the public and other schools use our golf course and our park for cross-country running. We are also clearing ponds around Larkminster and carrying out conservation in the Malvern Hills.'

Then he launched into an attack.

'I appreciate many county councils and education authorities are actively opposed to private education. Larkshire's LEA, in the past, was too busy to answer our letters and ignored our offers of help. S and C Services have shown themselves equally pigheaded. So we approached Janna Curtis direct and to our relief found she puts her children at Larks before her prejudice.

'Larks has been described as a "head's graveyard",'

went on Hengist idly. 'One might almost believe S and C and Councillor Cindy Payne are frightened of Janna breaking the mould.'

'Prepostewous. Nothing could be further from the truth,' spluttered Ashton.

'Good,' said Hengist smoothly. 'Just to let you know that Larks will be paying their first visit to Bagley on Wednesday.'

'Oh, goodness.' Janna clapped her hands in delight.

Col Peters was writing furiously.

'This has nothing to do with Janna Curtis or helping her students,' hissed Councillor Cindy Payne to Ashton, 'it's Hengist establishing himself as a dove. If Jupiter takes over the Tories, he'll find Hengist a quick seat and give him Education and God help us all.'

Glancing over to the enemy table, Janna noticed Alex Bruce quite unable to hide his jealousy. Hunched like an old monkey throughout Hengist's speech, he had mindlessly wolfed his way through an entire plateful of petits fours. A denied Crispin was almost in tears.

No sooner had Hengist finished, to mixed applause, than the press gathered round him, except for Col Peters, editor of the *Gazette*, who pulled up a chair beside Janna, plonking a bottle of red on the table. Close up he really did look like a toad, his eyes glaucous, fixed and bulging.

'What did you think of that, Miss Curtis?'

'Fantastic.' Janna raised her glass. 'Hengist has been marvellous to us, which is more than you have. Why are you always slagging off Larks? Don't you realize my kids read your rotten paper and are utterly demoralized by your lies?'

A good row was boiling up when Janna was distracted by the peroxide-blonde wife of the chairman of the Rotary Club, who'd drunk even more than she had, and who, passing Councillor Cindy Payne in the gap between the tables, called out: 'Thank God we got Lottie, our grandchild, into Searston Abbey, Cindy, or we'd have had to go private or out of county rather than end up at that dreadful Larks.'

'They'll probably bid for specialist status now they've got Hengist B-T on board,' joked Cindy, who must have been aware of Janna's proximity.

'Crime's Larks's only speciality,' sneered the Rotary chairman's wife. 'They hold their old school reunions in the nick.'

'How dare you slag off my school!' Janna jumped to her feet. 'And you, Councillor Payne, haven't even had the courtesy to visit Larks.'

Seizing Col Peters's bottle, she was tempted to give Councillor Payne's mousy hair a red rinse, when Hengist grabbed her wrist, increasing pressure so violently she gasped and dropped the bottle, spilling red wine all over Pearl's mother's lovely dress.

'Now look what you've made me do.' She turned, spitting, on him. 'Get off me, you great brute.'

Loosening his grip only a fraction, Hengist dragged her out into the corridor and let her have it:

'When are you going to learn to behave?' he yelled. 'Have you got some sort of death wish? Do you want to wreck everything we're doing to save your school?'

Bursting into tears, Janna fled into the night.

211

24

Janna woke to find herself on the settee, her breath rising whitely as a reproving sun peered in through the window to dissect her hangover without the aid of anaesthetic. Pearl's mother's green handkerchief dress was her only protection against the bitter cold.

Whimpering and wailing, she pieced together last night's broken dreams. How could she have nearly tipped wine over Cindy Payne, sworn at Col Peters and Hengist, who'd made such a lovely speech about her, then driven home plastered?

As a contrast to such anarchic behaviour, she caught sight of the green and gold serenity of Graffi's mural of Larkshire. He had worked so hard. But now she had stormed out on Hengist, Graffi and his pals would no longer get the chance to run joyously on Bagley's green and pleasant pitches or blossom in art studio, library or concert hall. She had blown it for them and she'd never see Hengist again.

Staggering to her feet, she noticed Pearl's make-up all over the recently upholstered coral settee. Why did she ruin everything? Tottering into the kitchen, wondering if she could keep down a cup of tea, she fell over a padded blue basket and gave a moan of horror as she took in the tins of Pedigree Chum on the window ledge and the blue collar and lead with the newly engraved disk: 'Partner Curtis'. In the fridge was a Tesco's cooked chicken to tempt his appetite.

Glancing at the clock she realized she was due to collect him in three-quarters of an hour. Rescued dogs, particularly ones as traumatized as Partner, needed calm, relaxed owners and she hadn't had the decency to stay sober the night before his arrival. Bloody Larkshire Ladette. And what the hell had she done with Pearl's mother's shawl?

Partner's delighted wagging when he saw Janna was still punctuated by whimpers. His tail, which they'd managed to save and had wrapped in a net gauze dressing, was still very raw and sore.

'Bathe it constantly with cold water,' said the nurse, 'and he'll need antibiotics and painkillers for another fortnight. We ought to keep him in longer, but he's pining in here. He'll do better in a home environment.'

As Janna sank to the floor holding out her arms, Partner crept into them, licking away her tears as they poured from her reddened eyes. 'He needs me as much as I need him,' she whispered.

'Be happy for him,' said the nurse, handing her a box of medicine. 'He's such a brave little dog; we'll all miss him.'

Reluctant to leave at first, Partner perked up in the car, resting his roan nose on Janna's shoulder all the way home. He peed in excitement over the stone kitchen floor before wolfing a huge chicken lunch.

Janna's hangover was hovering like an albatross. She must plan tomorrow's staff meeting. Still cold, she lit a fire. Determined to start as she meant to go on with Partner, she brought his basket into the lounge. Ignoring it, he jumped onto the sofa beside her.

'Not on my new settee,' she said firmly, then caught sight of the streaked make-up and relented.

'Agenda for staff meeting', she read. On top was a note that Mrs Chalford, head of history, who'd been off all term with stress, would be back in school on Monday. Evidently she was a dragon and a bossy boots. The file dropped from Janna's hand.

She was woken by furious barking. Partner, although he was taking refuge under the sofa, was defending his new home against an enchanted Lily.

'What a charming dog. Part corgi, part Norwich terrier, I would say.' Then as Partner, cheered to be attributed with such smart origins, crawled out to lick her hand: 'Oh, your poor little tail. How are you feeling?' she asked Janna.

'Terrible.'

'I've brought you a hair of the dog.' Lily brandished a bottle of last year's sloe gin.

Janna shuddered. 'I'd never keep it down.'

'It's to celebrate Partner's arrival. What are you going to do with him during the day?'

'Take him and his basket to Larks.'

'It's too soon. I'll look after him here until his tail mends.'

'Oh Lily, you're an angel. Are you sure?'

'I expect he'll tree the General to start with, but the old boy needs a bit of exercise.'

'OK, I will have a glass,' said Janna.

As they toasted Partner, Lily said, 'You look terribly tired. What happened last night?'

Janna was about to tell all, when to her horror Partner went into another frenzy of barking and up rolled Graffi, Feral, Paris and this time Pearl. Janna had completely forgotten they were coming.

From Paris's point of view, the afternoons spent at Jubilee Cottage had been the happiest of his life. Afterwards, the memories of gentle football, picking apples and sweeping leaves and twigs for bonfires would be suffused by a golden glow. Best of all had been his hours by the fire with Janna toasting marshmallows and crumpets, the long, leisurely conversations about books, the quiet after the needy, anguished clamour of the children's home. Often, when younger, he had pretended to be his mother and read out loud to himself. Sitting on the floor, not quite letting his head fall onto Janna's little jeaned knees, he had listened to her reading from the *Aeneid*, Aesop's *Fables*, *Paradise Lost* – 'With thee conversing I forget all time' – with no other sound except the swish of Graffi's brushes and the crackle of Lily's apple logs.

Paris had never loved anyone as he loved Janna, but never by the flicker of a pale eyelash would he betray his feelings or embarrass her. He never had any difficulty attracting girls – they lit up like road signs in his headlights as he approached – but it was only an illusion that faded once he'd passed. For, however much they ran after him, inside him was desolation. He must be worthless and unlovable if his mother hadn't wanted to keep him.

Paris didn't have to be back at Oaktree Court until eight o'clock – nine, when he reached fourteen in January – so as the evenings closed in, he would wander the streets of Larkminster: wistful, lonely, pale as the moon, gazing into rooms lit up orange like Halloween pumpkins, bright with books, pictures, leaping fires and mothers, arms round their children's shoulders, as they helped them with their homework.

Bleakly aware that he was incapable of expressing the love that would make him lovable, that he had nothing to offer emotionally, longing for a family would overwhelm him and he would howl at the night sky, reaching for the stars beyond the branches.

What terrified Paris was once Graffi's mural was finished, there would be no excuse for them to roll up at Janna's every weekend, so he kept dreaming up extras for Graffi to include: 'Put Rod Hyde in the stocks.'

As the Wolf Pack rolled up that Sunday, blown in like

dry, curling leaves, Paris tried not to feel resentful at having to share Janna with Graffi, Feral and a chattering, first-among-equals Pearl as well as Lily, who was puffing away on the sofa, already stuck into the booze with a fox on her knee, who promptly shot terrified under the sofa.

'Meet Janna's new dog,' said Lily.

'Is it all right if we come today?' asked Graffi.

'Sure,' said Janna weakly.

In agony, Paris noticed her swollen, reddened eyes, ringed by vestiges of Pearl's eyeliner, and loved her more than ever. Had she had bad news? He'd kill anyone who hurt her. Instead he knelt down by the sofa and began to coax out the little dog.

'Come on, good boy.' At least Graffi could string out a few more afternoons adding Partner to the mural.

Janna took a reviving slug of sloe gin. 'You must all speak very quietly,' she begged, 'and avoid any sudden movements. Partner's scared of humans.'

'And I'm scared of dogs,' said Feral, keeping his distance and defiantly bouncing his football.

'It's lovely to see you again,' Janna told him, but noticed in dismay a purple bruise on his cheekbone and that one of his eyes had closed up. She prayed that Uncle Harley hadn't done him over. He was wary of her today, with no sign of that wide, charming, dodgy, insouciant smile.

Later, when conversation moved on to the subject of films, Janna asked if anyone had seen *Shrek*. They all shook their heads, which meant Uncle Harley had lied about Feral's mother taking Feral and the other children to the cinema last night.

While Graffi got down to work, Pearl, her shiny black eyes darting, wanted to hear all about last night. Janna told her, omitting the indecent proposal from Uncle Harley, the row with Col Peters, the attempted wine-drenching of Cindy Payne and the screaming match with Hengist.

'Everyone thought I looked fantastic. Lots of people didn't recognize me. Others who'd previously ignored me were all over me. I felt like a princess.'

'Meet any nice guys?' said Pearl.

Shut up, Paris wanted to scream.

'Think there'll be anything in the paper?'

'Well, they took my picture with Hengist B-T and he told a reporter about your brilliant make-up.'

'Nice guy, Hengist,' observed Graffi, mixing rose madder with burnt sienna to paint in a copper beech. 'Like to see him again.'

'Knowing the *Gazette*,' said Janna quickly, 'they're bound to print the most hideous pictures, but I'll try and get some prints. I'm afraid I spilt wine over your mother's lovely dress and left the shawl behind. I'll get it dry-cleaned.'

'Don't matter,' said Pearl.

'Probably nicked,' murmured a grinning Graffi.

'Shurrup,' snarled Pearl.

Feral was examining the mural. It had come on since his last visit, with a wedding spilling out of the cathedral, dog walkers in the water meadows and otters and fish in the turquoise river.

'It's cool,' he said, then, aggressively bouncing his football, sent Partner under the sofa again.

'Stop it, you're scaring the dog.' There was such ice in Paris's voice and eyes that Feral stopped.

'Why don't you play in the garden?' suggested Janna.

Lily struggled to her feet. 'I'm off to watch Arsenal. You coming, Feral?'

Janna was feeling really ill – perhaps Ashton had spiked her drink. She wasn't up to cooking for this lot and there was nothing in the fridge except Partner's cold chicken.

'How'd you like a Chinese?'

'Wicked,' said Pearl. 'I'll come and help you.'

Paris could have knifed her.

Looking at Pearl's heels, Janna decided to drive.

'Why don't you come with us?' Pearl asked Paris.

'I'll stay with the dog,' said Paris sulkily.

'Oh, would you?' Janna's face lit up. 'He's really taken to you. You're an angel.'

Paris thought he would live after all.

The increasingly bare woods seemed to have been invaded by swarms of yellow and orange butterflies as leaves drifted down. The sun was already sinking.

'Everywhere you look, the colours make you want to be a fashion designer,' observed Pearl as they drove towards Larkminster.

'I met Feral's Uncle Harley last night,' said Janna.

There was a long pause, then Pearl said, 'He's not a real uncle. He's kind of scary, laughing one moment, crazy wiv rage the next. People say he's got Feral's mother hooked on crack' – her voice faltered – 'so he can do what he likes wiv her.'

Listen, listen, listen, Janna urged herself, let Pearl stumble into more indiscretion.

'Don't tell anyone I told you, miss, but Harley's the Shakespeare Estate supplier. Also collects rents for Randal Stancombe. You don't want to be late paying or Uncle Harley cuts you up.' White-knuckled, Pearl's little hands were clenched on her thin thighs.

'He seemed keen for Feral to stop truanting.'

'Only so Feral can push drugs. 'Spect he heard about us bonding wiv Bagley. Means Feral'll have access to rich kids.'

Oh dear. Hengist had said the same thing.

'Uncle Harley gave Feral's brother Joey a gun for his sixteenth birfday, same as a deaf warrant. You didn't hear this from me, miss.'

As they waited outside the Chinese takeaway for their order, which included a double portion of sweet and sour prawns for Feral, Pearl grew more expansive.

'My boxer dad got a prison sentence for burglary, feeding a drug habit. He's convinced Harley shopped him. Last year' – Pearl lowered her voice, shiny robin's eyes darting round for eavesdroppers – 'Feral ran away because Uncle Harley beat him to a pulp. No one went looking for him. Frozen, bleeding to death and half starving, he was forced to crawl home. He's so proud, Feral. Never asks for help, feels he's got nuffink to offer in return. Don't say anyfing, miss. I'm not supposed to know these fings, picked them up, listening.'

'You've been so helpful, Pearl, this'll be our secret.'

'Did they really like my make-up?' asked Pearl.

When they got back to the cottage, Partner only barked once, wagging his tail as Janna went into the sitting room but staying put on the sofa beside Paris.

'Oh look,' shrieked Pearl. 'Sorry, sorry, Partner,' she whispered. 'Graffi's drawn him into the fields wiv you, miss. You've both got the same colour hair.' Then she started to giggle because Graffi had painted in Mike Pitts, Cara, Skunk and Robbie: instantly recognizable as gargoyles.

Janna tried to look reproving. 'I'll never be able to ask any of them for a drink now. Did anyone ring?'

Paris shook his head, noticing how she kept checking her mobile for messages and how she now pounced on the telephone when it rang.

Janna felt herself winded by disappointment when, instead of Hengist, it was the shrill voice of Dora Belvedon.

'You probably don't remember me, Miss Curtis. I was waiting at table when you came to dinner with Mr and Mrs Brett-Taylor and we met by the lake. I'm having tea with my Aunt Lily, she says your new dog has arrived. Could I come and see him and bring your shawl back? And I've got a letter for you from Mr Brett-Taylor . . . Miss Curtis?'

But Janna was out of the house in a flash.

Dora had been dying to steam the letter open but wily old Hengist had sealed the blue envelope with green wax, imprinted with his crest of a griffin and a lion.

Dora felt only mildly guilty she had sold the story about 'Bagley beckoning Janna Curtis' to the *Gazette*. Janna would be far happier teaching at Bagley than that horrible Larks.

'I've heard of a new CD that stops dogs being frightened of fireworks, Miss Curtis. You play it every day when they're having their dinner and they get used to the bangs.'

But Janna wasn't listening, she had torn open the envelope and it wasn't just the setting sun reddening her face.

'Darling Janna,' Hengist had written. 'Sorry I bawled you out. I just want to open every door of your advent calendar for you. Very much looking forward to seeing you on Wednesday afternoon. Bring about sixteen to twenty children; they can play football and case the joint and have tea together. I'll ring you this evening. Love, Hengist.'

She was brought back to earth by Dora's gasp of delight. 'Oh, what a sweet dog, he looks like Basil Brush.'

Suddenly Janna's hangover had vanished.

'We're coming over to Bagley next week,' she told Dora. 'Paris and Feral are indoors, and Pearl and Graffi. Do come and meet them.'

Dora sidled away. 'I've come to see Aunt Lily. She misses the family since my horrible brother Jupiter chucked her out of her house. Another time. That is a very cool dog.'

Dora had not forgiven Paris for telling her to fuck off or Feral for kicking his football between her pony Loofah's legs.

Birds were singing agitatedly as the day faded. It was getting cold, so they had tea in the kitchen. It amazed Janna that so much food should vanish so quickly. Feral had cheered up; he'd been at Lily's sloe gin, Arsenal had won convincingly and he was delighted to have an extra helping of prawns. Partner, exhausted by his social afternoon, snored in his blue basket among the moon and stars.

Radiant, able to eat and even keep down a glass of wine, Janna broke the news of the trip on Wednesday.

'Randal Stancombe's been really kind and given us our own minibus to enable us to go to plays and rugby and football matches against other schools, so please stop writing rude things on the walls of Cavendish Plaza.

'And on Wednesday,' she went on, 'a bus load of Larks pupils has been invited over to Bagley on a recce.'

'Wreck will be the operative word,' snapped Paris.

'Send Johnnie Fowler,' taunted Pearl. 'He'll break the place up. I wouldn't want to meet those stuck-up snobs,' she added sulkily.

'How would you all like to go?' said Janna.

'You'd send us?' asked Graffi slowly.

'Yep.' Janna smiled round at their incredulous faces. 'And some pupils from Year Ten, just to look round and have some tea and see what we'd like to do in the future: playing golf, using the running track. The art and the music rooms are to die for; they've even got a rock band.'

'I don't want to go,' said Paris flatly.

'You wait until you see the theatre and the library.'

'Can Kylie come?' asked Pearl.

'I don't see why not.'

'Why us?' muttered Feral. 'We're the school dregs.'

'No you're not,' said Janna crossly. 'I want to show Bagley what attractive, talented pupils Larks has and that, once and for all, our manners are just as good as theirs.'

'Yeah, right,' said Feral, licking sweet and sour sauce off his knife and rolling his huge eyes at Janna, so everyone burst out laughing. From his basket, Partner wagged his gauze-wrapped tail.

'I'd like to go,' said Graffi. 'I'd like to see Hengist again.'

'He really liked your work, Graffi, and your poems,' she added to Paris. 'Please come.'

'OK,' said Paris, 'but what's in it for them?'

'They want to break down conventional social barriers,' said Janna hopefully.

After they'd gone, Lily popped in with some lavender oil. 'Put a few drops on your pillow and you'll fall into a deep sleep. You look much better already.'

Janna was floating on air. She had a bath and sprinkled lavender oil all round her room and on her pillow, then she took Partner out for a last pee and put him in his basket in the kitchen. 'Stay there, love,' she said firmly, then forgot everything because Hengist rang.

'I'm so sorry,' she babbled, 'I just lose it when people attack Larks. I should never have said those awful things to Col Peters.'

'You were suffering from toad rage,' said Hengist.

When she floated upstairs five minutes later, she found Partner out like a light, his ginger head on her lavender-scented pillow. Even his snores didn't keep her awake.

25

Forgetting her own violent antipathy towards private education, Janna was taken aback by the fury produced by the proposed visit to Bagley. The matter was thrashed out at Monday's after-school staff meeting by which time most of the participants had digested as deadly poison the *Gazette* piece with a headline: 'Brett-Taylor confirms Bagley–Larks bonding'.

The copy, which included flip remarks from Hengist about the need to get chewing gum and hooligans off the streets, was accompanied by a glamorous photograph of himself and Janna in front of a vestal virgin. Janna was smiling coyly. Hengist's lazy look of lust was so angled as to be aimed straight down her cleavage.

'Just as though they were playing Valmont and Madame de Merteuil in some amateur dramatics,' spat Cara.

The piece ended with a paragraph about Janna's make-up being created by a Year Nine student, fourteen-year-old Pearl Smith.

'"We like to encourage enterprise in Larks's pupils," joked Miss Curtis.'

Pearl had borrowed a fiver off Wally and rushed out and bought ten copies and a cuttings book.

As staff gathered in explosive mood, down below they could see Janna drifting round the playground chatting, laughing, bidding farewell to the children, adding a last handful of crumbs to the bird table, and praising the new litter prefects who were shoving junk into bin bags.

As she came in Wally, who'd been making garage space for the new minibus, warned her the mood was ugly:

'Don't take any nonsense.'

Already two minutes late, Janna was further delayed by a telephone call.

'It's Harriet from Harriet's Boutique. We were so delighted to see you in today's *Gazette* in one of our gowns.'

'It was a present,' stammered Janna, convinced now that Pearl had nicked the dress. Harriet's was very pricey.

'You looked so lovely,' went on Harriet, 'we wondered if as a great favour, we could blow up the photograph and put it in our window – it would be such a boost to our Christmas display.'

Janna was still laughing as she went into the staffroom. The wind had whipped up her colour and ruffled her hair. She looked absurdly young.

The subject for discussion had been going to be the creation of a Senior Management Team (SMT), or lack of it, because Janna was dragging her heels about appointing a second deputy head to succeed Phil Pierce. If she'd had a flicker of support from any of the heads of department besides Mags Gablecross and Maria Cambola, she might have made more effort.

Now the staff had additional cause for outrage. Rain lashed the windows and relentlessly dripped into three buckets. The only cheery note was a blue vase of scarlet anemones which a grateful parent had given Janna, and which she had plonked in the middle of the staffroom table.

On Janna's right, Skunk Illingworth nearly gassed her with his goaty armpits. On her left, Mike Pitts crunched Polos to hide any drink fumes. Why in hell didn't he kill two birds and drink crème de menthe?

Beyond Mike was Cara Sharpe, who had ripped up the *Gazette* piece. Now, shivering with fury, she was marking essays on the sources of comedy in *A Midsummer Night's Dream* with a red Pentel. Beyond her, Robbie Rushton was spitting blood and applying for a new driving licence. Opposite him presided a returning Mrs Chalford, whom Janna already disliked intensely.

A self-important know-all, she had a smug oblong face and wore a brown trouser suit with a red Paisley scarf coiled round her neck like a python. Insisting on being called 'Chally', she looked as likely to have been suffering from stress as a Sherman tank.

Next to her sat Miss Basket, the menopausal misfit, who had not forgiven Janna for refusing two invitations to supper. She was so red in the face Janna wanted to shove her outside to provide autumn colour.

'Restore work/life balance', 'No one forgets a good teacher', shouted posters on the wall. The younger staff were waiting expectantly for fireworks. Mags Gablecross looked up from the blue and purple striped scarf she was knitting for her future son-in-law and winked at Janna; Jason was reading *The Stage*, Gloria *Hello!*, Cambola the score of *Beatrice and Benedict*. Trevor Harry, head of PE, shook with righteous rage. How dare that shit Brett-Taylor suggest the only exercise Larks pupils got was running away from the police? Old Mr Mates, who taught science, was asleep.

As a heavyweight and official spokesman, Mrs Chalford kicked off. 'I wish to object in the strongest possible terms to learning future plans for our school from the pages of the local rag: future plans which are anathema to the majority of my colleagues who are opposed to any partnership with the private sector. To take only sixteen students is also totally against our caring ethos of equal opportunity for all.'

'The idea has been around since the prospective-parents' meeting,' said Janna reasonably, 'when Mr Brett-Taylor visited Larks.'

'Such bonding is a flagrantly right-wing initiative,' accused Mrs Chalford.

'Not at all, it's a New Labour initiative.'

'I agree with Chally,' butted in Robbie Rushton, who used every steering group or meeting to puncture the atmosphere. 'It is a disgrace that schools charging parents twenty thousand pounds a year should be subsidized for bonding with their impoverished state-school neighbours. Any Labour Government worth its name should be working night and day to abolish the educational apartheid of the independents.'

'Sin-dependents,' murmured Janna.

'As a socialist, I am amazed you're committed to the project,' added Sam Spink.

'Think of the children,' said Janna. 'There is no play-ing field here where they can let off steam and build up team spirit. Every suggestion box is filled with pleas for more football, more games with other schools. Nor do I want our children to turn into grossly overweight couch potatoes.'

'I object,' said Trevor Harris.

'Later, Trev.' Janna raised her hand. 'As S and C won't help, we have to go elsewhere. If Bagley are prepared to share their facilities with us, we should be gracious enough to accept them for the sake of the children.'

'How are we going to get there?' snapped Mike Pitts.

'Randal Stancombe has given us a minibus,' said Janna. 'It's arriving on Wednesday.'

'That capitalist snake,' hissed Robbie.

'As someone from a desperately deprived back-ground who has clambered out of the poverty trap, I think Randal should be applauded for giving others a chance in life,' snapped Janna.

'Why doesn't he set a good example by sending his children to maintained schools?' said Chally.

'You'll get a chance to ask him on Wednesday; we're

having a photo call at Bagley.' Janna took a gulp of water. 'The minibus arrives at midday. We're going over to Bagley in the afternoon. I'd like volunteers to pioneer this first trip.'

The dead silence that followed was only broken by the furious scratch of Cara's pen.

'Hopeless. 1/10', she scrawled across an essay that looked suspiciously like Paris's.

'You amaze me,' she said shrilly. 'After the way you've constantly complained about the cost of supply staff, you're now prepared to impose a further drain on the budget?'

'It'll only be Wednesday afternoons to begin with,' said Janna. 'Later we're going to aim for Saturdays.'

'You cannot expect dedicated, overworked professionals to squander valuable time on something of which they utterly disapprove,' intoned Chally.

'Hear, hear,' agreed most of the room.

'Quite frankly, if I left my post for half a day to commit to this project, which I don't believe in anyway,' said Mike Pitts, 'I'd return to worse problems.'

'I'm sure we'd all like an afternoon off and a chance to see the Burne-Jones windows, but I, for one, thought we were trying to restore work-life balance, not jeopardize it,' pronounced Chally.

'What's in it for Lord Bountiful?' sneered Robbie.

'If you mean Mr Brett-Taylor,' said Janna icily, 'he genuinely wants to help.'

'Rubbish,' hissed Cara. 'He's only interested in his charitable status. Caring conservatism is a classic oxymoron.'

Janna's fingers drummed in counterpoint to the rain dripping into the buckets.

'She's about to lose it,' murmured Jason to Gloria.

'You cannot expect instant decisions without adequate consultation,' reproved Chally.

Mags Gablecross got another ball of mauve wool out of her bag:

'I'd like to go,' she said. 'I'm off on Wednesdays so it won't disrupt the timetable.'

'I'd like to go too,' said Miss Cambola, who was now orchestrating 'Ding, Dong, Merrily' for the Christmas concert. 'I gather the acoustics for the new music hall are stupendous. I'd like some of our young musicians to join the Bagley orchestra. Cosmo, son of my late countryman, Roberto Rannaldini, is their conductor. His mother, Dame Hermione Harefield, has the most beautiful voice of her generation.'

'Oh, thank you both.' Janna tried to control her shaking. 'We need one more.'

'I'd like to go too,' drawled Jason. He'd score brownie points if he were seen to be giving support to Hengist's pet scheme.

'You've already gone over to Rome,' hissed Cara.

'Thank you, Master Fenton,' sighed Janna.

'I'd like to go as well,' piped up Gloria to Robbie's rage. 'Chance of a lifetime to see their facilities, pick up good practice, must be open-minded, I had an aunt who went to public school.' She smiled adoringly at Jason. 'I'd like to see Bagley.'

'So would I,' sighed Lydia, and was bleached pale by a laser beam of venom from Cara, who then turned on Jason, hissing, 'Who's going to cover for you, Jason?'

'I will,' said Lydia.

She turned even paler when Cara added viciously, 'You know it's Year Nine E.'

'Not quite as challenging as it sounds.' Janna smiled at Lydia. 'The Wolf Pack are coming to Bagley.'

'The Wolf Pack?' Cara's mad escalating laugh made everyone jump. The grey-green roots of her lank black hair gave an impression of poison welling out of her skull. Her red mouth was slack and twitching; her mad malevolent eyes rolled in every direction. Selecting an anemone from the blue vase and ripping off its petals with scarlet talons, she hissed, 'The Wolf Pack? D'you want Larks to be even more of a joke?'

'I've chosen kids who don't normally get recognition and whom I trust,' said Janna simply.

'Just because they've been enjoying cosy weekend tea parties at your cottage. They'll trash the place.'

'Other kids are going: several from Year Ten, plus Aysha, Rocky and Johnnie Fowler.'

'Johnnie Fowler!' said Skunk incredulously.

'Johnnie hasn't been in trouble since he chucked a chair at me on my second day. He's a marvellous cricketer.'

'Who's going to control them?' mocked Cara, selecting another anemone.

'They're very fond of Hengist and have huge respect for Wally who's going to drive the bus.'

'Wally as well?' snapped Mike. 'Without a by-your-leave you hijack our site manager. What happens if there's a fire or a fight?'

'Fend for yourself for a change,' snapped back Janna. 'Use the fire extinguisher on both.'

'I wish to register a protest against our students being exposed to snobbish and reactionary peer pressure,' said Robbie pompously.

'Have you got parental permission?' accused Chally.

'I was on the phone first thing this morning,' said Janna triumphantly, 'and didn't get a single refusal. Even Aysha's mother agreed. Parental consent forms have gone home with the kids this evening.'

'How long will you be at Bagley?' demanded Sam Spink, who'd been making copious notes.

'We'll arrive after lunch, at about one-fifteen, and be home about half-five.'

'That could be two and a half extra hours. I'll have to consult the branch secretary. Unfortunately I'm away on Wednesday.'

'What takes you away this time?' said Janna irritably.

'A course on self-assertiveness.'

'Whatever for?' Jason grinned. 'You're far too bossy as it is.'

'How dare you?' spluttered Sam.

Janna decided she was rather going to miss Jason when he moved to Bagley.

Chally looked at her watch. 'It's nearly five o'clock, which leaves no time to discuss the lack of a Senior Management Team. We must have more democratic rule and the opportunity to make informed decisions.'

Her scarf looks set as fast as Hengist's sealing wax, thought Janna. I'm going to see him the day after tomorrow. She fell into a daydream.

'Sorry to railroad you,' she piped up two minutes later as Chally paused for breath, 'but I'm convinced it will boost the children's morale. We're planning a joint play next term.'

Cara gave such a howl of rage, teachers on either side shrank away. 'As head of drama and English I should be consulted on every development.'

'Loosen up, Cara,' drawled Jason, 'it's a great idea.' Then, smiling round the room: 'Means I won't lose touch with you when I move to Bagley.'

'Shall we call it a day?' asked Mike Pitts, who needed a drink.

'Have the rest of Nine E been given the option of going or just your Hell's Angels?' asked Robbie.

Janna gathered up her files. 'That's uncalled for.'

'I'm sure Simon Simmons and Martin Norman would love to go,' said Cara ominously.

'They wouldn't,' replied Janna sweetly. 'Both Mrs Norman and Mrs Simmons told me categorically Monster and Satan don't do detentions on Wednesdays, so I hardly think they'd be available to go to Bagley.'

Then she regretted it, instinctively crossing herself as Cara shot her a look of pure loathing. Ripped anemone petals lay like drops of blood on the table. She wants to kill me, thought Janna.

26

Hengist, who, unlike Chally, regarded debate as the enemy of progress and had no desire to discuss anything with his (dreadful word) colleagues, often used chapel to issue orders to subordinates who couldn't answer back.

It was thus on Tuesday morning that he broke the news of the Larks invasion. He softened the blow by asking Primrose Duddon, form prefect of the Lower Fifth, to read a specially selected lesson from St Luke's Gospel.

Primrose Duddon was clever, earnest, noble-browed and already ample-breasted, which ensured normally inattentive schoolboys listened as she read about the Lord throwing a party and, when all his smart friends refused, dispatching his servants into the lanes to invite 'hither the poor, and the maimed, and the halt and the blind'.

'Like some ghastly soup kitchen,' observed Dora Belvedon.

Primrose, reflected Dora, who was sitting in the choir stalls, didn't need the exquisite silver lectern decorated with oak leaves framing the Bagley emblem of a lion sheltering a fawn; she could have rested the Bible on her boobs.

Dora loved chapel. She loved the carved angels in the niches, the flickering lights attached to the dark polished choir stalls, the soaring voices echoing off the wooden vaulted ceiling and the luminous glowing windows, particularly the one opposite, full of birds and animals inhabiting the Tree of Life.

'"For all the saints who from their labours rest,"' sang Dora.

Because she could sight-read and sing in tune, she had been picked for the choir and could thus observe the feuds and blossoming romances of both staff and pupils. Opposite sat her favourite master, Emlyn Davies, far too big and broad-shouldered for his choir stall. Black under the eyes from worry about his darling Oriana who was reporting from Afghanistan, he was surreptitiously selecting the rugby teams for a needle match against Fleetley on Saturday.

Next door were his friends, the elegant, charming head of modern languages, Artie Deverell, who was reading the Spectator, and Theo Graham, head of classics, who was bald, wrinkled and sarcastic but revered by his pupils because his lessons were so entertaining.

Next to Theo, looking pained, sat deputy head Alex Bruce, known as Mr Fussy because he was always whingeing about something and who was now pinching the bridge of his nose between finger and thumb. Next to Alex was his friend, Biffo Rudge, head of maths, who got so carried away coaching the school eight, he was always riding his bike into the River Fleet. Biffo, a cherry-red-faced bully, with bristling hair like an upside-down nail brush, had a crush on Dora's poor twin brother, Dicky, and (if Dicky were to be believed) dressed up in a black leather dress very late in the evening. Next to Mr Fussy and Biffo was their ally, Joan Johnson, No-Joke Joan, Dora's housemistress, who was hell-bent on making Boudicca, the only girls' house, outstrip the boys' houses academically.

There was no way Joan was going to let Dora rest from her labours like the saints.

In the row in front, romantic-looking Piers Fleming, head of English, was asleep. Not surprising. When Dora had crept out at six o'clock to walk her chocolate Labrador, Cadbury (who was currently living a clandestine existence with the school beagles), she had seen Piers scuttling in, probably from shagging Sheena Anderson in London. Sheena's husband Rufus, head of geography, having dressed and fed himself and his children, and got them to school, was now frantically preparing his first lesson. Piers smelt of Paco Rabanne, reflected Dora, Rufus of baby sick. One could see why Sheena preferred the former.

If she leant back, Dora had an excellent view round the silver lectern of the Lower Fifth – Bagley's equivalent of Year Nine – and the naughtiest form in the school.

Although it contained boffins like Primrose Duddon, and 'Boffin' Brooks, who was both geek and boffin, the Lower Fifth boasted the luscious, long-limbed Bagley Babes. Otherwise known as the Three Disgraces, they included Dora's heroine, Amber Lloyd-Foxe, who had a mane of flaxen hair, exeats on Saturday morning to hunt with the Beaufort and who was now reading love letters from boys at Eton, Harrow and Radley. The second Bagley Babe was Milly Walton: emollient, charming and auburn-haired but over-shadowed by her ravishing mother Ruth.

Making up the trio was Jade Stancombe, Randal's 'little princess', who had long, shiny dark hair and was as bitchy as she was beautiful. Jade's street cred had rocketed because of her on-off relationship with Cosmo Rannaldini and because she'd been recently rushed from a party to hospital with alcoholic poison-ing to blot out the 'pain of my parents' separation'. Jade had in fact been spoilt rotten all her life, and was miffed because her parents were, for a second, think-ing of their impending divorce rather than her.

Everyone was scared of Jade. Milly and Amber loved

her for her cast-offs – she seldom wore even cashmere twice – and for trips in the Stancombe jet, though you had to be prepared to endure Randal's groping.

The Bagley Babes indulged in lots of hugging and kissing and, from the humming of vibrators after dark, you'd think bees were swarming. As a new girl, Dora got fed up with making toast and running errands for Jade, and applying fake tan to the small of her very sleek back. She drew the line at shaving Jade's Brazilian.

As well as the Bagley Babes, the Lower Fifths were enlivened by Lando France-Lynch, the Hon. Jack Waterlane and Amber's twin brother, Junior Lloyd-Foxe, who all had Coutts cheque cards and accounts at Ladbrokes and whose sparse intellect was compensated for by their dazzling athletic ability, which had led them to forming their own cricket team: the Chinless Wanderers. With life also revolving round the school stables where they kept their horses and the beagle pack, little time was left for academic pursuit.

And if Babes and Wanderers weren't enough in one form, there was Cosmo Rannaldini, machiavellian master of the universe, and his pop group the Cosmonaughties. Jade Stancombe thought Cosmo was 'sex on cloven hoofs'. Dora thought he was the most horrible boy in the school.

Known as the Bagley Byron, Cosmo had the same lustrous black curls as the poet, but his pale, cruel face was leaner and his dark, soulful eyes less protruding.

'Oh God, our help in ages pissed,' sang Cosmo. Only five foot seven, our little Prince of Darkness had two bodyguards. The first was Anatole, son of the Russian Minister of Affaires, whose vodka bottle chucked out of an attic window was responsible for the glazed expression on the chaplain's face. The second was Lubemir, from Albania, who claimed his family were asylum-seekers, but whose safe-breaking skills and habit of paying school fees with rare works of art suggested rather an affiliation with the Mafia. Pupils tended to seek asylum as Lubemir approached. No one was going to beat up Cosmo with those two around.

Next to the Cosmonaughties sat Xavier Campbell-Black, hunched and miserable. Dora tried to like him because he was the brother of her best friend Bianca, but she'd been horrified recently to see him beating up his horse. Although if you were fat and ugly, and had a heart-rendingly pretty sister after whom every boy in the school lusted, you probably had to take it out on something.

Last hymn over, Dora fell to her knees and really prayed for the safety of Cadbury and Loofah and her dear Bianca, who kept waving and giggling at her from the body of the chapel, and for her brother Dicky, who was always being bullied or jumped on because he was so small and pretty.

Dicky had a much better voice than Dora, but had deliberately sung flat at the compulsory audition, because he'd get even more jumped on if he had to wear chorister's robes.

'Grant me lots of good stories to sell,' prayed Dora.

The twenty pounds from the *Gazette* for the story of Janna dining with the Brett-Taylors wouldn't keep Cadbury in Butcher's Tripe or pay the massive mobile bill from chattering to Bianca. How could she talk to her press contacts without a phone? Life was very hard.

The glazed chaplain was just blessing everyone, when a hitherto absent Hengist swept in, bounding up the steps of the pulpit, as always raising blood pressures and fluttering pulses as he smiled round.

'If I may keep you a moment,' he began in his deep, infinitely thrilling voice. 'You all heard the lesson: "Go out quickly into the streets and lanes of the city, and bring in hither the poor, and the maimed, and the halt, the blind."

'Well, just as the Lord invited the poor to his party, we will be inviting those less fortunate than you to our school tomorrow, when sixteen pupils from

Larkminster Comprehensive will spend the afternoon with us.'

A rumble of mirth, interest, disapproval and incredulity swept round the chapel.

'These are children often from tragically impoverished backgrounds, who have only played football on concrete between tower blocks, who often care for handicapped, senile, abusing or drug-addictive parents, who after long days at school have to clean the family home, look after brothers and sisters, iron, cook, shop and hold down evening or weekend jobs to make ends meet.'

Glancing round, moved by his own eloquence, Hengist noticed Cosmo Rannaldini, long lashes sweeping his high cheekbones, playing an imaginary violin, and snapped:

'Save that for the orchestra, Cosmo. Sixteen children from Years Ten and Nine will visit us,' he went on. 'You will recognize them from their crimson sweatshirts and black tracksuits.'

'And yobbo accents,' said Jade Stancombe.

'Takes one to know one,' murmured Amber Lloyd-Foxe.

'A list of both staff and pupils selected to look after our visitors will be found on the noticeboard,' added Hengist. 'I know you and Larks have been sneering at each other for generations, but tomorrow you will have a chance to break down traditional class barriers, and to treat your visitors with the kindness and consideration of which I know you are capable.

'As those selected are too old to kick off with Pass the Parcel, and too young – officially that is' – Hengist raised a thick black eyebrow – 'to break the ice with a large vodka and tonic, we will begin with a team-building exercise in Middle Field, supervised by Mr Anderson and Mr Fleming, which I think you'll enjoy, followed by a tour of the school in general and early supper in the General Bagley Room.

'Tomorrow is only a recce. In future Larks will be spending more time with us and sharing our magnificent facilities. So please look out for anyone looking lost in a crimson sweatshirt and remember our Bagley emblem of the lion protecting the fawn and our motto: "May the strong defend the weak".'

Dora was absolutely livid when she consulted the noticeboard and discovered the Bagley Babes, the Cosmonaughties and the Chinless Wanderers had been chosen to entertain Larks rather than her form. Think of the stories she'd miss.

She was not, however, as furious as Alex Bruce when he saw the list of staff and pupils and realized Hengist had ridden roughshod across his timetable.

Fortunately Miss Painswick, the dragon who guarded Hengist, was off with flu, and Alex was able to storm into Hengist's darkly panelled book-lined office, which was on the first floor of the Mansion and, like the bridge of a ship, enabled Hengist to overlook the playing fields and escape if he saw anyone he didn't like coming up the drive.

Alex's mood was not improved to find Hengist reading *The Times* and listening to some noisy symphony on Radio 3.

'I must protest, S.T.L., on the peremptory way you have imposed your will, hijacking members of staff without any consultation. Who is going to take Piers and Rufus's classes now?'

'Oh, go away, Alex,' said Hengist irritably. 'We must try and learn how the other ninety-five per cent live in this country.'

Alex cracked his knuckles. 'Before you rush into this scheme, S.T.L., we should apply to join the Government Building Bridges programme which for a start would entitle us to some funding.'

'Any initiative from this Government involves far too much red tape.'

'Our parents will be understandably displeased,' continued Alex. 'How can we justify putting up our fees – I got a most offensive letter from Rupert Campbell-Black this very morning – if we reject potential funding?'

Then, as Hengist turned to the crossword:

'I don't expect you realize, grant money could be particularly advantageous to the maintained school involved, funding transport costs and cover for teachers. If you're anticipating any expensive joint productions, you could be depriving your' – Alex was about to say 'precious' but changed it to – '"friend" Janna Curtis of fifty thousand pounds.'

'Good God.' Hengist put down his pen. 'That's not bad.'

'And there's no reason we ourselves shouldn't apply for a grant retrospectively.'

'Then look into it, you're so good at that sort of thing. Now, if you please.'

But Biffo Rudge, also unchecked by Miss Painswick, had barged in, redder in the face than ever, bellowing, 'Our parents will be up in arms that fees they're struggling to raise are being squandered on the very students from whom they wish their children to be distanced.'

Bringing up the rear, like Boudicca leading her troops into battle, came No-Joke Joan, who had just learnt from the noticeboard that the Bagley Babes, none of whom were working hard enough, had been enlisted. Nor did she trust them with Feral Jackson or Paris Alvaston. Couldn't Hengist select three other young women?

'My decision is final,' said Hengist, turning up Brahms's First.

'But S.T.L. . . . .' Joan longed to defy Hengist, but her ally Alex Bruce, who'd got her in post at Bagley, was shaking his head.

'Make a note of it – our time will come,' he murmured

as a delighted Hengist swooped on an incoming call, then to his horror realized it was Dora's mother, the awful Lady Belvedon whom Painswick would never have let through.

'Quite frankly, Hengist,' she was squawking, 'I don't bankrupt myself as a poor widow in order that Dicky and Dora pick up common accents. The late Sir Raymond would turn in his grave. I also insist the party doesn't include Feral Jackson, who's been up before me and spent several weeks of the summer holidays in a Young Offenders' Institute; a most vindictive fellow.'

Hengist filled in five across and let her run. If he kept saying, 'Yes, yes, yes,' a glowering Biffo, Alex and Joan might go away.

Having ascertained from the noticeboard that the Cosmonaughties, the Chinless Wanderers and the Bagley Babes were all rather surprisingly included in the party to entertain Larks, Cosmo Rannaldini decided to give physics a miss.

Humming Prokofiev's Piano Concerto No. 1, which he was playing and conducting in a concert at the weekend, he sauntered across the quad to the school office to discover Painswick, Hengist's secretary, was off sick. She must be ill to desert Hengist. Instead, Painswick's junior, the ravishing but daffy Jessica, whom Hengist only employed to keep visiting fathers sweet and because her typos made him laugh, was in charge. Jessica was an old friend of Cosmo, having worked as a production secretary on his late father's last film. Jessica wanted to pop down to Bagley village to buy a birthday card for her nan. So Cosmo offered to man the office.

Having checked the weekly bulletins and Hengist's diary, he tapped into Painswick's computer to find out who was coming from Larks, and whistled. Talk about the dregs: not just Johnnie Fowler and his hell-cat girlfriend Kitten Meadows, and Rocky who went berserk if he didn't take his Ritalin – that had possibilities – but all the Wolf Pack.

Feral was four inches taller than Cosmo and had once hit him across Waitrose's drink department. Cosmo did not want his crown as the Byron of Bagley taken away.

He therefore proceeded to email the entire school and most of the parents in histrionic terms, listing the dramatis personae, warning that barbarians were at the gate and that Bagley could anticipate the worst mass rape since the Sabine Women.

'A marauding army of Sharons and Kevs will plunder your cattle and your mobiles. Lock up your Rolexes, iPods and your credit cards; pull up the drawbridge; get the oil boiling on the Aga: we will fight to the death.'

He was just enlarging Janna and Hengist's photo in the Gazette to stick on the noticeboard when Dora Belvedon sidled in.

'What do *you* want?'

'To be part of the welcome party when Larks comes over,' said Dora piously. 'It's so important to break down social barriers.'

'Bollocks,' said Cosmo, 'you want to flog the story to the press.'

Unlike his current squeeze Jade Stancombe who considered Dora to be 'a mouthy disrespectful brat', Cosmo rather liked little Miss Belvedon. Her blond plaits were coming untied, her blue-green eyes were suspicious and disapproving and her little nose stuck in the air, but her pursed mouth was sweet. He liked her fearlessness, resourcefulness and jaundiced view of life. She could be trained up as a useful accomplice. And if he won over Dora he could gain outwardly unthreatening access to the desirable Bianca.

'You were waiting at dinner when Janna dined with the B-Ts,' said Cosmo, offering Dora one of Painswick's humbugs.

'So?'

'Must be something going on between Hengist and Janna for him to allow scum like this in here.'

'If you'll stop bullying my brother Dicky . . .'

'Yeah, yeah, whatever. So what gives with Janna and Hengist?'

'She's got a ginormous crush on him. I delivered a sealed love note to her house on Sunday; it was like chucking petrol on a bonfire: whoosh!'

'Is Randal Stancombe after her too?' Cosmo got a fiver out of the inside pocket of his tweed jacket. 'Giving her that minibus?'

'No.' Dora accepted the fiver. 'He was showing off to Mrs Walton. He had his hand up her skirt all dinner – disgusting letch.'

'Lucky Stancombe.'

Dora accepted another fiver, and another after the revelation that Piers Fleming had come in at six that morning.

'Piers likes Sheena Anderson. He put his hands between her bosoms when no one was looking. Thank you.' She shoved yet another fiver into her bra.

'What a decadent world we live in,' sighed Cosmo. 'If we can instigate a punch-up or, better still, a broken jaw tomorrow, it'll make every national. You pick up what you can behind the scenes. Here's my mobile number. I'd better have yours. If you're good, I'll buy you a mobile that takes photographs, then you can photograph the Duddon valley in the shower.'

Sally Brett-Taylor picked up a telephone and rang Larks.

'Janna, my dear, we're so looking forward to seeing you tomorrow. Tell me, what do your chaps really like best to eat?'

Sally was such a brick, reflected Janna, you could chuck her through a window.

241

27

The morning of Larks's visit began for Hengist with a glorious fuck. His favourite breakfast aperitif was going down on his beautiful wife, licking her clitoris, seeing it and the surrounding labia swelling pink, hearing her squeaks and gasps of pleasure, then her breath coming faster until she flooded into his mouth, so slippery with excitement that he could instantly slide his cock inside her.

Sally was like a clearing in the jungle no one but he had ever discovered. No one else knew the joy of making love to her. No one had warmer, softer, sweeter-smelling flesh, or higher, more rounded breasts and bottom, or prettier legs.

Sally's clothes were so straight. No one seeing the silk shirts tucked into the wool skirts which fell just below her knees suspected the luscious underwear: the suspender belts, French knickers and pretty bras in pastel satins; the Reger beneath the Jaeger. Strait is the gate; once through it was all pleasure, which left Hengist purring and utterly relaxed.

Downstairs he switched on the percolator, threw a croissant into the Aga, later smothering it with Oxford marmalade, chatted to Elaine the greyhound and turned on BBC 1 to hear Oriana's latest brief bulletin from Kabul, protesting on the plight of Afghan women. Thank God, she was alive.

Sally knew her husband was excited about Larks's visit. In turn, recognizing the slight widening and worry in Sally's eyes, Hengist murmured that Janna was only an Oriana substitute. 'I like someone to spar with – chippy, chippy, bang, bang – and she's so desperate to make Larks succeed.'

Sally understood Hengist's craving for novelty. She watched his confident lope, head thrown back, wind lifting his dark hair, shoulders squared. Last leaves were tumbling out of the trees, tossed in every direction, gathering round the bole of a big chestnut, whirling like the tigers circling until they turned into melted butter in *Little Black Sambo*. Sally's heart swelled as she saw Hengist suddenly dance and skip as he rustled through the dry leaves.

She must get on. There was lots to do: organizing smoked salmon and scrambled egg and puds for the Larks pupils; arranging a wrapped bottle of champagne and a light lunch for Randal Stancombe; and masterminding an Old Bagleian reunion dinner this evening.

Swinging out of sight, Hengist ruffled the hair and asked after the parents of two Upper Fourth boys, before grappling briefly with the second fifteen's scrum half and then discussing with him Bagley's chances against Fleetley on Saturday.

'We'll bury them, sir.'

Mist was curling ghostly round the last fires of the beeches as he stopped to joke with gardeners, busy putting the flower beds to rest; ferns hanging limp and dark and a few pinched 'Iceberg' roses being the last inhabitants.

Robins and blackbirds stood round indignantly glaring at a squirrel who, having taken over their bird table, was wolfing all their food. Hengist shooed it off. It was after all the duty of the strong to protect the weak.

It was going to be a beautiful day. The sun was

breaking through as he settled into his big office chair, upholstered in burgundy leather, which had once belonged to the Archbishop of Singapore. Radio 3 was playing Brahms's Third Symphony, written when the composer was hopelessly in love, as Hengist leafed through his post. He so adored not being pestered to do things by Miss Painswick.

Then his telephone rang. Jessica wasn't good at fielding calls. This one was from a father, furious that his tone-deaf daughter hadn't been awarded a music scholarship.

No sooner had Hengist put down the telephone than Jessica rushed in to say the *Daily Telegraph* was on the line.

'We wondered what had happened to your copy,' asked John Clare, the hugely respected and influential education editor.

'What copy?'

'On the contribution of competitive sport to the public-school ethos.'

'Christ, when was it due?'

'Yesterday.'

'Jesus, I'm sorry.'

'I can give you till four o'clock.'

'Fuck, fuck, fuck,' yelled Hengist. Painswick would have reminded him. He dialled Emlyn Davies. 'You'll have to kick-start this Larks operation.'

'I've got rugby all afternoon.'

'Not any more you haven't. I'll get shot of this piece as fast as I can.'

'Absolutely fucking typical,' roared Emlyn as he slammed down the telephone.

Next Hengist dialled Alex Bruce.

'I've got to borrow Radcliffe. Someone's got to type this piece.'

'Why can't Jessica?'

'Jessica's not safe. Remember "There's no such word as cunt"?'

Alex Bruce winced. 'High time you learnt to use a computer.'

'You know technology makes me cry.'

'Absolutely typical,' screamed Alex slamming down the telephone and, turning to Mrs Radcliffe, his PA: 'Hengist wants you to type out his article.'

Mrs Radcliffe tried not to look pleased. Hengist was so attractive and so appreciative.

Rufus then rang in and said he wouldn't be able to organize the team-building exercise as one of his children had chicken pox and needed looking after.

'Why can't your wife do it?' snapped Hengist.

'She's in London.'

28

'What is the dress code?' Gloria had asked for the hundredth time.

'Trousers, jumper, warm jacket and flat shoes to run around in,' Janna had replied firmly.

Then, early on Wednesday morning, watched by a bleary-eyed Partner, she had proceeded to wash her hair and scatter rejected clothes all over the bedroom before settling for shiny brown cowboy boots, cowgirl dress in woven pink and blue wool and a dark red jacket with a rich red, fake-fur collar. It looked wacky but sexy and elicited wolf whistles from all the children when she arrived at Larks.

'You said we had to wear trousers,' reproached Gloria, who'd shoehorned herself into her tightest jeans, but added a Sloaney twinset, Alice band and Puffa.

Jason, rolling up in a tweed jacket, grey flannels, a striped shirt and round-necked dark blue jersey, looked as though he'd already crossed over. Mags Gablecross, in a lilac coat and skirt that reminded everyone what a pretty woman she was, was having great difficulty not laughing at Cambola, who looked equipped for a Ruritanian shooting party in a moss-green belted jacket, plus fours and a Tyrolean trilby trimmed with a bright blue jay's feather.

Knowing the other staff were waiting for things to go

wrong, Janna had organized everything to the nth degree. Then Chally came bustling smugly into the office. 'Cara's just rung.'

'Yes?' said Janna through gritted teeth.

'The poor dear's sick.'

'Is she ever anything else,' said Janna, instantly regretting it as Chally bridled.

'Let's pretend you never said that. Cara's been signed off with stress for at least a week.'

'She could have rung in earlier,' snapped Janna, thinking of a hundred children with their minds and mouths open and only young Lydia and martyred Basket to cope.

'It was perhaps a mistake for both you and Jason to desert the English department.'

'Cara was perfectly OK last night.'

'Outwardly, perhaps,' reproved Chally. 'Inwardly she was humiliated by your announcing a joint play with Bagley. She feels her authority slipping away – we all do.'

Janna was tempted to throttle Chally with today's bright orange scarf. It was too late to get in a supply teacher.

Instead Wally rigged up a new film of *A Midsummer Night's Dream* in the main hall for the children to watch and then write an essay about.

Janna hugged him. 'Thank God for you.'

Stancombe's minibus was already twenty minutes late. The selected children were getting edgy. No matter that they'd knocked off Bagley's caps for generations. That had been on the streets of Larkminster. Now they faced an away fixture in toff country. Those not chosen to go were jealous and taunting. Fights were breaking out all over the playground.

Matters weren't helped by Kylie Rose turning up in a pretty mauve pansy-patterned wool dress and a little blue velvet jacket, saying she hadn't realized they had to wear uniform.

'And you look wicked, miss,' she added to get the attention off herself.

'She just wants to hook a toff boyfriend,' said Pearl furiously, 'and we're stuck in bloody uniform.'

'That's enough, Pearl,' said Janna. 'And take off those hoop earrings. A dog could jump through them. All right, Aysha?'

Aysha, the cleverest girl in the school, nodded. Despite dark hair hidden by a headscarf, her features were serene and lovely. Inside she fought panic. Her father, in Pakistan on business, was due back any day. Her much more liberal mother had bravely signed today's consent form. If her father found out he would beat both of them.

The boys, wearing massive trainers and tracksuits with the hoods up, were swigging tap water from Evian bottles, unwilling to reveal they couldn't afford spring water.

'Have you taken your Ritalin, Rocky?' asked Janna.

Other boys had discovered that crushed Ritalin snorted gave you a high as good as cocaine and had been offering Rocky ten quid for his daily intake. Rocky liked money to buy chocolate and fizzy drinks, which made him even crazier.

Rocky also had a huge crush on Kylie who led him round like a great curly-polled red bull.

'I want to go on the bus,' he was now grumbling.

'We all do.' Trying to keep her temper, Janna got out her mobile to learn that Stancombe had an important lunch in London, but would arrive at Bagley around three-thirty, officially to hand over the bus, which would be arriving any second.

'It's not coming, it's all a hype,' taunted Monster Norman.

Graffi, Feral and Paris retreated behind a holly bush for a cigarette, which became a second and a third as they all waited.

Then, just when they'd given up, Kylie shouted:

'Here it comes, here it comes, and it's ginormous!'

The bus, the same crimson as Larks's sweatshirts, had black leather upholstery, an upright lavatory like an upended coffin, a television and seated at least twenty-four. On the sides, so no one could mistake its benefactor, was printed in gold letters: 'Larkminster Comprehensive School Bus donated by Randal Stancombe Properties'. On the front the destination said: 'Bagley Hall'.

'Wicked!' yelled the children.

But as they surged forward, struggling to be first up the steps, Satan shouted: 'Yer mother,' to Feral. Next moment Feral had jumped on Satan and Monster on Johnnie Fowler, at the same time aiming a kick at Paris. Graffi leapt to Paris's defence. Everyone was yelling and pitching in, when suddenly the driver climbed down out of the bus. Instantly every child retreated in terror. Then, as he swept off his baseball cap, revealing a dark, shaven head and lighting up the grey day with his diamonds and his white teeth, Janna recognized Feral's Uncle Harley.

'Miss Curtis.' He took her hand. 'As beautiful as ever.'

'What are you doing here?'

'I do a bit of work for Mr Stancombe. Sorry I'm late, the garage was changing the number plates.'

'It's wonderful, thank you so much,' cried Janna as the selected children climbed on in a most orderly fashion.

Janna was about to leap on too, when Rowan came running across the playground: 'Toilets are blocked again, and Mrs Norman's on the warpath.'

A second later, Stormin' Norman came charging across the playground.

'Why isn't my Martin on that bus? Why's he bein' discriminated against, you cheeky cow?' The fist poised to smash into Janna's face stopped in mid-air. 'Mornin', Harley, just discussin' logistics wiv Janna.'

'Fuck off,' ordered Harley, who'd been showing Wally how the bus worked.

Amazingly, Stormin' Norman did.

'You wouldn't like a job here?' asked Janna.

Harley flashed his teeth and advised her to get going. He'd sort everything this end.

'He's dead sexy, your uncle,' said Gloria as Feral tried to get lost against the black leather.

'Quick, miss. Baldie Hyde's just driven up,' shouted Graffi.

Janna needed no further encouragement. Cheered off by other pupils who ran down the drive, banging its sides, the bus pulled away, quite jerkily at first, as Wally became accustomed to the gears.

'I'm going to be sick,' announced Kylie. 'Can we open a window?' '

'Nah,' said Pearl. 'It'd fuck my hair.'

As the bus crossed over the River Fleet into the country, pupils charged up and down, trying out the coffin lavatory, fiddling with the windows, standing on the seats to test the luggage rack.

Mags Gablecross, knitting a shawl for a prospective grandchild, handed round a tub of Heroes. Miss Cambola got everyone singing: first 'Swing Low Sweet Chariot', then 'It really ain't surprising That we're rising, rising, rising.'

'Up the fucking social scale,' sang Graffi to howls of laughter.

Outside, the red ploughed fields were covered in flocks of birds having staff meetings.

'Miss, miss, Johnnie Fowler and Kitten Meadows have been in the toilet for five minutes,' cried Kylie.

Janna smiled and walked up and down encouraging everyone.

Paris, ecstatic to be in her company for a whole day, thought she'd never looked more beautiful. The red fur softened her little freckled face. Her perfume made him sneeze and his senses reel, particularly when she sat down and took his hand.

'You'll flip when you see the library. Have you written any more poems?'

'Not a lot.' Actually he was wrestling with one about Janna herself called 'Perihelion'. Such a beautiful word, it meant the point in its orbit when a planet was nearest the sun. He was the planet that craved its moment of perihelion close to his sun: Janna, her flaming hair spread out like the sun's rays.

Love had sabotaged his cool, but he tried to be more inscrutable than ever, gazing out at old man's beard glittering like cast-aside angels' wings in the hedgerows.

'Here's Bagley, playground of the rich,' said Graffi, catching sight of the big gold house through the thinning trees.

Getting out her powder compact Janna took the shine off her freckled nose and, in the driving mirror, met Wally's wise, kindly eyes, which missed nothing. 'Be careful,' they said.

The bus swung left, through pillars topped with stone lions, up a drive past red and white cows, muddy horses, black-faced sheep, ancient trees in khaki fields; past heroic sculptures; past a signpost pointing the way to the bursar's office, the science laboratory, the music hall, the sick bay, the headmaster's rooms – Janna gave a shiver. Would there be room for her?

All around, Bagley pupils were walking to classes, girls in sea-blue jerseys, soft beige pleated skirts and slip-on shoes, the boys in tweed jackets and grey flannels. Passing eternal playing fields on the right and the big square Mansion on the left, Wally turned left, then left again up a little drive through a big oak front door into a quadrangle in the centre of which a bronze lion tenderly sheltered a fawn between its paws.

'Bleedin' 'ell,' said Feral, 'it's a fuckin' castle.'

'Bigger than Mr Darcy's house,' conceded Pearl.

'It's Goffic,' breathed Johnnie Fowler, gazing up at the pointed turrets and narrow windows.

'Ah, isn't that lion sweet,' cried Kylie.

As the bus doors buckled, aware of hundreds of eyes looking down at them from offices and classrooms, the Larks children swarmed out into the sunshine, steeling themselves for mockery.

Then, as though one of the heroic sculptures, perhaps Thor, God of Thunder, had come to life, curly-haired, square-jawed, massive-shouldered and battling to curb his fury, Emlyn Davies strode out to meet them.

On Saturday, the five Bagley rugby teams had away matches against Fleetley, the school from which Hengist had departed under a cloud and the one he most wanted to bury.

Emlyn had intended spending the afternoon fine-tuning each team, trying out different moves and combinations of players, before making a final selection. Hengist would be the first to raise hell if Bagley didn't wipe the floor with Fleetley, but had now dragged Emlyn away to oversee his latest self-indulgent distribution of largesse, leaving that pompous woofter Denzil Harper, head of PE, in charge. Sometimes Emlyn loathed Hengist. Everyone had to pick up the fucking pieces.

He had just broken the news that Hengist was irrevocably tied up all afternoon to a stricken Janna and her bitterly disappointed children, when Hengist made him look a complete prat by erupting into the quad, dark hair on end, ink all over his hands.

'*Mea culpa, mea culpa.* I'm so sorry, children. I failed to hand in an essay yesterday and have to stay in all afternoon to write it.' Then, seizing Janna's quivering hands, he kissed her on both flaming cheeks. 'Darling, I'm mortified, how delicious you look. Diorissimo, isn't it?'

Then he turned his spotlight charm on the other

teachers – kissing Mags and telling her on what good form her husband Tim had been the other night; praising a piece on Boccherini Miss Cambola had written for last week's *Classical Music*: 'I'd no idea he was such a fascinating character!'; urging Gloria to try out the newest equipment in the gym: 'I'd so value your opinion. What pretty women teach at Larks! And young Jason, hello. I can't remember whether you're in Year Nine or Year Ten,' followed by a shout of laughter, which cracked up the children.

Jason, who'd quickly put his striped shirt collar inside the crew neck of his dark blue jersey because Hengist had, tried to be a good sport.

Then, turning to the children, Hengist explained that with Miss Painswick away and his excitement about their visit, he'd completely forgotten to write his piece for the *Telegraph* about 'the importance of competitive games'. 'You lot, being obsessed with football, know all about that,' he went on, shaking hands with each of them.

'I know Miss Curtis has only chosen special people: Johnnie Fowler, the great cricketer, you must try out the indoor school later. And Aysha, the budding Stephen Hawking, what part of Pakistan d'you come from? I know it well,' followed by a couple of sentences in Urdu.

'And Feral, the ace footballer, whom I am determined to convert to rugger, you're the right build. Lily Hamilton, an old friend, and a fan of yours, Feral, tells me you support Arsenal. And here's Graffi, another old friend, how's the mural of Larkminster going? Janna says it's fantastic. I've just bought a Keith Vaughan for the common room. I'll show it to you later.

'And here's Pearl, who transformed Janna last Saturday, an amazing effort, although you had a lovely subject' – quick smile at Janna – 'will you help us with make-up for our play next term? We're planning to join forces. You must look at our theatre.'

'Yes, please, sir.' Pearl, the cross robin, had suddenly turned into a lovebird.

Yesterday Janna had emailed Hengist photographs of every child with little biogs, but never expected him to memorize them. She felt overwhelmed with gratitude.

Noting how she was blushing, Paris thought: the smarmy bastard, he's miles too old for her. Then Hengist swung round, his smile so warm and sympathetic.

'And you must be Paris. I love your poems. Janna showed me "The Spire and the Lime Tree". I gather you can also mimic anyone, so you must have a big part in our joint play. You'll find a terrific drama section in the library. Have a look at Wilde, Coward and Tennessee Williams, great writers, great dialogue, great parts for you.'

The boy's looks set him apart, thought Hengist. He has the same sad eyes, pallor, long nose and greyhound grace of Elaine, and I bet he can run away from life just as fast.

And Paris was bowled over like the rest.

Hengist was so good at putting people at their ease: he fired questions and used names to punctuate a sentence, to illustrate how clever he was to remember you out of the thousands of people he met. He had reached Kylie and rocked everyone by asking after little Cameron.

Kylie blossomed like the mauve pansies on her pretty dress. 'He's very well, fank you, sir.'

'Must be hard looking after him and getting your homework done, Kylie, but I gather you're coping brilliantly.'

Janna couldn't fault him. He had screwed up, but as she watched the antagonism and fear melt out of her children, she could only forgive him.

'I'm going to leave you in the large, capable hands of Mr Davies who, until he wrecked his knee, used to play rugger for Wales, which won't impress you, Feral, but will our Welsh Graffi, look you. Everyone wants to be taught history by Mr Davies. His classes are hopelessly over-subscribed. He's easily our most popular master, and has taken the afternoon off to organize your fun and games.'

Emlyn, who'd just been told that Rufus, who'd set up the entire team-building activity, had ratted, refused to be mollified. He was also brick red with hangover and not nearly as attractive in daylight, thought Janna.

Emlyn, in fact, had got wasted last night because he was worried sick about Oriana. God knows what the Taliban might do to one so fearless and beautiful. Then Sally had had the gall to email him first thing. Oriana was safe and sent love. Why the fuck couldn't Oriana call him herself instead of ducking out, like her father, leaving someone else to break the news to the kids.

'Mr Davies will take you over to Middle Field to meet our Bagley lot,' Hengist was now saying. 'He's got some rather vigorous game to help you get acquainted. Randal Stancombe is jetting in during the afternoon, so you'll get a chance to thank him for that splendid bus. Then you're free to explore the school; someone will show you round. Don't forget the library, Paris. I'll see you all later. I better get back to my prep.'

'Isn't he awesome?' sighed Kylie Rose.

29

'I'm afraid I won't remember any of your names,' said
Emlyn sarcastically as he led them out of the quad, past
the lake and the River Fleet in the distance, down to a
little white cricket pavilion. Behind this lay Middle
Field, which divided Pitch One from the first holes of
the golf course and consisted of four acres of rough
grass dotted with little copses. Middle Field was also
used by the CCF for training exercises. Bagley pupils
enjoying peaceful smokes or snoggings were often disturbed by flying balls or invading armies.

On Pitch One, the armies of Larks and Bagley now
lined up glaring at one another.

Feral, to appear more menacing, had, like Paris and
Graffi, left up the hood of his black tracksuit. Then he
clocked the three Bagley Babes, who looked as though
they'd been fed on peaches and fillet steak all their
lives, who had glossy hair cascading from side partings
to below their boobs and gym-honed bodies in cobalt-
blue tracksuits and pale ochre T-shirts, which evoked
the sea and sand of endless holidays.

Nodding haughtily at Amber, then Milly, then Jade,
Feral murmured, 'I am going to have that one, that
one and that one.'

'No doubt yelling Sharpeville at the moment of
orgasm,' murmured back Paris.

Then Feral reached for the knife in his tracksuit

trousers as he recognized sneering, supercilious Cosmo Rannaldini flanked by his two heavies.

'I am Anatole from Russia,' announced the first heavy in a voice as deep as the Caspian Sea, as his narrowed, dark eyes slid over Kylie, Kitten and Pearl.

'And I am Lubemir from Albania,' said the second, whose black hairline rested on his thick eyebrows like a front on the horizon and whose Slav face was rendered more sinister by dark glasses and even darker stubble.

'And we're Lando France-Lynch, Jack Waterlane and Junior Lloyd-Foxe, from the broom cupboard,' quipped Amber's mousy-haired, merry-faced twin brother.

'Those three are nice,' whispered Kylie, who was also vastly relieved that some of the Bagley contingent were quite plain. There was a boy called Spotty Wilkins who had more spots than face and a geek in granny specs with buck teeth and a huge air of self-importance, who, humming and swaying back and forth, introduced himself as: 'Bernard Brooks from East Horsley, but most people call me "Boffin".'

'Boffin from leafy East Horsley,' murmured Paris, catching Boffin's singsong curate's voice so perfectly, the Bagley Babes started giggling.

'Look at the knockers on that one.' Graffi gazed at Primrose Duddon in wonder. 'Stick out more 'n Boffin's teef.'

'And this is Xavier Campbell-Black,' announced Emlyn because Xav was too shy to introduce himself.

Remembering Rupert from the prospective-parents' evening, all the Larks girls swung round in excitement, which faded as they realized the heavy, hunched, sullen Xavier bore no resemblance to his gilded father.

Next moment the mighty unbeaten first and second fifteens pounded past.

'Sir, Sir,' they shouted to Emlyn, 'we've been dragged out on a fucking cross-country run. We're supposed to be practising ball skills.'

'Buck up, keep moving,' shouted Denzil Harper, head of PE, running effortlessly beside them. A recent Alex Bruce appointment, sporting a snow-white T-shirt and earrings, Denzil had a shaved head and a chunky, muscular body.

I'll kill Hengist and Rufus, vowed Emlyn, if that woofter Denzil injures any of them.

'I want you to split into groups of six,' he told the waiting children, 'mixing both schools as much as possible.'

This meant everyone chose their best friends. Instantly the Wolf Pack drew together, determined to show those fucking Hoorays (Lando France-Lynch indeed) how thick they were.

'Come on, Rocky.' Kind Kylie pulled him into their group.

'We don't want him,' hissed Pearl, 'Rocky couldn't build a team if it sat on his face. Grab Aysha.'

As Jade was Cosmo's girlfriend, the Bagley Babes automatically teamed up with the Cosmonaughties. Johnnie Fowler, who wouldn't let sexy Kitten Meadows out of his sight, formed up with four members of Larks Year Ten; the Chinless Wanderers – Lando, Junior and the Hon. Jack – with Bagley mates from the form above. Rejects like Spotty Wilkins and Xavier edged miserably together for comfort.

'A fat lot of mingling that is,' roared Emlyn and proceeded to number members in each group from one to six, and to their outrage ordered the 'ones' to form one group, the 'twos' another, and so on until crimson sweatshirts and sea-blue tracksuits were totally mingled.

Outside the cricket pavilion on a trestle table lay a building pack for each group.

'These packs contain simple – depending on your intelligence – instructions on how to build your own hot air balloon,' shouted Emlyn, 'and as you can't fly a balloon without a control tower, here are newspapers for you to create one.'

'This is going to be fun.' Janna smiled anxiously at the mutinous, contemptuous, incredulous faces as Mags Gablecross and Jason rushed round handing out copies of the broadsheets.

'I can't understand papers like this,' grumbled Kitten, unenthusiastically opening the *Observer*, 'too many long words.'

'To build your balloon,' continued Emlyn, 'you'll also need coloured sheets of tissue paper, cardboard and scissors, which are assembled here on the table. But you win these by passing a number of tests.'

Then, as Janna and Gloria handed out pads of crosswords, puzzles and teasers, Emlyn explained: 'Every time you solve a page of these, you race up to us in the cricket pavilion and if it's correct you'll win yourself either cardboard, scissors or glue, or a sheet of coloured tissue paper. You'll need at least six of those to build your balloon.'

Like the labours of Hercules, thought Paris.

'The other way you can win the stuff you need,' called out Mags, who'd been reading the instructions, 'is by taking part in an orienteering treasure hunt.'

'We're not in the bloody Lower Fourth,' grumbled Cosmo.

'One would not know from your behaviour,' snapped Emlyn. 'You may not have noticed, but amid the autumn colour of Middle Field are hung fifteen orange flags with staplers and directions to the next map reference attached. Here are the maps.' He lobbed them at each team. 'In the frames round them you will find fifteen boxes which each need to be punched with the appropriate map reference. These will entitle you to more tissue paper, glue, etc.'

'Are we going to find treasure?' Amber eyed up Feral.

'Once you've built your balloons,' added Emlyn, 'and you've got an hour and a half, members of the staff will provide hot air.'

'Again,' shouted Junior Lloyd-Foxe to shouts of laughter.

'OK, joke over. Provide hot air to enable them to fly. And there'll be a competition to see whose balloon flies farthest, and for the prettiest and the first finished.'

'And to think I could be curled up in a nice warm classroom learning calculus and being molested by Biffo Rudge.'

'Shut up, Cosmo. Anyone undertaking the treasure hunt must go round in twos in case you get lost.'

'Sounds fun,' Amber smouldered at Feral. 'Shit, I forgot to ring Peregrine.' She groped for her mobile.

'Put that away,' roared Emlyn, 'we're about to start.'

'What is the matter with Attila?' sighed Amber.

Graffi, meanwhile, was immersed in the *Telegraph* racing pages.

Peering over his shoulder, Junior said, 'Singer Songwriter's a good horse.'

'Shining Sixpence's a better one,' said Graffi. 'My dad does work for his trainer. We orta have a bet.'

'I'll ring Ladbrokes,' murmured Junior. 'Hear that, Lando and Jack?' he called out. 'Shining Sixpence in the three o'clock.'

Next moment Lubemir and Anatole were also on their mobiles.

'Shall I put a tenner on each way for you?' Junior asked Graffi.

Aware it would feed the family for a week, Graffi said yes. He'd have to become a rent boy. That Milly Walton was hot.

'Blimey. "He left pubic hair on my mouse",' read Kitten, now engrossed in the *Observer*. 'I didn't know posh papers wrote about this sort of fing. What's "coprophilia"?'

'A kind of cheese, I fink,' said Kylie.

Janna turned on her angrily. 'Concentrate.' Emlyn's increasingly short fuse was getting to her. How on earth had she found him so attractive? With his gut spilling over too-tight chinos, blond hair like an electrocuted haystack, heavy stubbly jaw and angry bloodshot eyes, he looked more like Desperate Dan.

Seeing his beloved Kitten in the same group as evil Cosmo, Johnnie Fowler grabbed Cosmo's collar.

'Don't you lay a finger on my woman.'

'Don't insult my libido,' said Cosmo icily.

'Yer wot?' Johnnie clenched tattooed, ringed fingers.

Nonchalantly, Cosmo sidled off whistling Prokofiev One. Separated from Anatole and Lubemir, however, he felt vulnerable. He was, in addition, outraged to be teamed with not just Kitten but also Amber, who was making eyes at his arch enemy, Feral, and Lando, who was so thick he made pig shit look like consommé.

Deeply competitive, accustomed to automatic victory, Boffin Brooks was even more outraged to be lumbered with Lubemir, the Hon. Jack, Kylie and the unspeakable neanderthal Rocky, who refused to leave Kylie's side.

'For Christ's sake keep Rocky away from any glue or he'll sniff it,' warned Kylie. 'And the scissors too. If his Ritalin wears off, he'll cut your head off.'

Like a vicar doorstepped by the *News of the World*, Boffin shuddered.

Paris, icier and more remote by the minute to hide his shyness, was in a group which included the even more shy Aysha, monosyllabic Xavier Campbell-Black, Anatole who was reading Pushkin and swigging vodka out of an Evian bottle, and Jade Stancombe.

As Cosmo's friend and his girlfriend respectively, there was no love lost between Anatole and Jade, who made no secret of the fact she had joined the worst group.

'"Woman! when I behold thee flippant, vain, Inconstant, childish, proud, and full of fancies..."'

murmured Paris, who'd been reading Keats. Jade was beautiful, but what a bitch.

How he envied Graffi who, oblivious of class difference, was creating his usual party atmosphere, laughing with the ravishing Milly Walton and Junior Lloyd-Foxe, whose father Billy worked for the BBC and brought home riveting gossip about celebs ('Richard and Judy are *so* nice').

Also in their group were Pearl and Spotty Wilkins.

'You could use a concealer on those spots,' Pearl was telling him kindly as they waited for the off.

'You start on those puzzles, Junior,' suggested Graffi, 'and win us some sheets of paper. Pearl's clever, she'll help you.'

'Five, four, three, two, one,' yelled Emlyn, brandishing the starting pistol, then as the chapel clock struck two he pulled the trigger, making members of both schools leap out of their skins, thinking the other had opened fire.

'You have a go at these brainteasers, Feral,' suggested Lando France-Lynch.

'Ain't got a brain to tease, man,' said Feral.

'Nor have I,' agreed Lando.

Amber smiled at Feral. 'Why don't you and I do some orienteering? Hand over the map,' she added to a furious Cosmo, 'you and Lando can work out the puzzles with Kitten and wind up her jealous boyfriend.'

'Ven two people stand on the same piece of paper in the same house and can't see each other, vere vould they stand?' A perplexed Anatole looked up from another page of puzzles.

'Haven't a clue,' said Jade in a bored voice.

'If they put the sheet of paper under a door, shut it and stood on the paper on either side, they couldn't see each other,' suggested Aysha timidly.

'Brilliant,' chorused Paris, Xav and Anatole.

Admiring her sweet blushing face framed by its black

262

headscarf, Xav wondered what Aysha would look like with her hair unleashed. Not liking attention off her for a second, Jade announced she was going to build the control tower.

'Daddy's got several around the world,' she boasted, picking up the *Sunday Telegraph* business section. 'Oh look, there's a picture of Daddy.'

Ignoring her, Paris was whipping through the crossword even faster than Boffin Brooks.

'Despicable person, five letters beginning with "C"?'

'"Cosmo",' volunteered Lando.

Paris smiled faintly. 'Nice one, but I guess it's "creep". Pleasant facility, seven letters beginning with "A".'

'"Asshole",' drawled Lando.

Aysha blushed. 'Could it be "amenity"?'

'Could indeed, well done, Aysha.' Paris tore off the page, sending her and Xav scurrying off to claim more tissue paper.

The Threes were being held up by Graffi's desire to build a round balloon, rather than one in the recommended cylinder shape.

'It's the wrong way,' protested Junior.

'No it ain't.'

'Bloody is,' said Pearl. 'Graffi's so wilful.'

'Trust me, give me the fucking scissors, and go off and win some more tissue paper in case I screw up,' ordered Graffi.

Tempers and papers were beginning to fray. Under Boffin Brooks's fussy guidance, his team had concocted a scarlet and black cylinder from five sheets of paper, and were now trying to attach round ends to top and bottom.

'You stupid idiot,' screamed Boffin as Rocky's big fist went straight through the tissue paper.

'Don't pick on him, you great bully,' screamed Kylie.

Jade, bored of building her control tower, was putting the boot in.

'You stupid cow,' she cried as Aysha, trying to join their balloon's two emerald and royal blue sides together with trembling hands, also tore the paper.

'Don't talk to her like that,' yelled Xav.

Jade turned on him. 'I can talk to anyone however I like. You know who my boyfriend is.'

'I don't care,' lied Xav defiantly.

'You'll regret this,' hissed Jade.

'Kill each other later,' said Anatole, who was now immersed in the Sunday Times business section. 'Ve have balloon to build.'

'You're not being much help.'

A full dress row was quelled by the descent of Mags Gablecross, who chided them for wasting their human resources.

'You've completed the puzzles. Anatole and Jade, go off orienteering; Paris, get on with the balloon and Xav and Aysha, help him after you've finished the control tower.'

Janna and Jason stood at the trestle table handing out tissue paper and cardboard, checking maps to see if each box had been punched correctly.

'You're cheating again, Lubemir, go back and get two to eight punched properly and you too, Rocky, these have all been punched with the same staple. You need fifteen different ones.'

Feral and Amber raced hand in hand through Middle Field, their footsteps muffled by the thick yellow and orange leaf patchwork. They had punched nearly all their map references and collapsed on the roots of a big sycamore to catch their breath.

Amber's tousled mane was falling over eyes, the rich

ochre of winter willows. Her breasts heaved beneath her sand-coloured T-shirt.

'Lovely tan,' said Feral.

Amber stroked his cheek. 'Not as lovely as yours.'

Feral laughed, clapping her hand to his face.

'You been away,' teased Amber.

'Inside,' said Feral.

'Poor you, was it hell?'

'Hell, being banged up.'

'What did you do?'

'Mugged a stuck-up bitch; only took her bag and her mobile.'

'My father was always in gaol for hellraising on the showjumping circuit in the old days. You should compare notes. You're so sexy, Master Feral.'

Feral stretched out a hand and touched a nipple sticking through her bra and T-shirt and very gently ran his finger round and round it, until Amber was trembling with longing to be kissed. He had such white even teeth, such a wonderful smile, such curly black eyelashes.

'It's so important to overcome traditional barriers,' murmured Amber.

Feral found her colouring so exquisite against the yellow hazel, and faded tawny oak, he said, 'You suit autumn.' Putting a hand on her tracksuit trousers, he repeatedly tapped a finger against her clitoris. 'Like that?'

'Amazing.'

Unable to bear the tension, Amber leapt to her feet and stumbled deliberately in a rabbit hole, allowing Feral to catch her. For a second they gazed at each other, burst out laughing, then he kissed her. He smelled so lovely and tasted faintly of peppermint, his tongue flickering as delicately as his fingers had, then growing more and more insistent until her legs would have given way if his arms hadn't held her like steel bands.

'Oh Feral,' gasped Amber, 'talk about lift-off,' then, as his snake hips writhed against hers and his cock seemed about to burst through his trousers: 'I don't think you're entirely in control of your tower.'

'Stop taking the piss, man.'

'Oh, wow,' moaned Amber. As Feral's hand crept inside her T-shirt, her hand in turn slid down his flat belly and thighs and encountered hard steel.

'Ah,' she whispered. 'I see you also dress on the left.'

'I don't take chances.'

Letting her go, Feral whipped out his knife, running his finger down the blade, smiling at her. Amber stood her ground, determined to show no fear. Neither jumped much as they heard Boffin Brooks's strangulated whine.

'Number eight ought to be around here somewhere.'

Reaching up Feral cut through the string which tied stapler and flag to an overhead branch and chucked them into a wild rose bush. Then, putting away his knife, he pulled Amber behind a big oak tree, hand over her mouth to stop her laughing.

'We don't want Boffin catching up wiv us.'

'I've never snogged anyone black before,' murmured Amber, prising off his hand and pulling his head down. 'What have I been missing?'

30

Earlier, in London, Randal Stancombe and Rufus Anderson's wayward wife Sheena lunched on smoked salmon and champagne in one of his many apartments.

'It'll be an excellent photo opportunity,' Sheena reassured him, 'and brilliant for your profile both locally and nationally to help a school that serves an estate with such a high level of deprivation. People will recognize your sincerity about cleaning up the area. If the rest of the press are expected at Bagley at three-thirty I suppose we ought to go,' she added regretfully.

'We could have another drink,' said Stancombe, unbuttoning her dress. Sheena was very tasty and it was one way of finding out if she'd hidden a tape recorder anywhere.

Back at Bagley, the Lower Fourth were studying Tennyson. Poor Miss Wormley, whom the class referred to as Worm Woman, had made the mistake of asking Dora Belvedon for her views on the Lady of Shalott.

'Well, Sir Lancelot with his flowing black curls and his broad brow was pretty cool,' began Dora, 'like a young Mr Brett-Taylor. But next minute he's described as flashing into the crystal mirror. We had a flasher in Limesbridge when we lived there. Our gardener, actually. He was always waving his willy at people, so it must have been a shock for the Lady of Shalott, she'd led such a sheltered life. No wonder she suddenly got her period.'

'Don't be silly, Dora.' Miss Wormley had gone very pink.

'She did too. "The mirror cracked from side to side; 'The curse has come upon me,' cried The Lady of Shalott." They called a period "the curse" in medieval times when my mother was young, so she wasn't going to be much good to Sir Lancelot that day. No wonder he kicked on.'

Apart from Dora's brother Dicky, who had his burning face in his hands, the rest of the Lower Fourth were in ecstasy. They loved it when Dora got into her stride. Dora, however, was frantic to escape.

'I simply must go to the loo, Miss Wormley, I've got a frightful tummy upset. I'll burst all over the floor if I don't.'

And Wormley let her go. Anything to be spared more literary interpretation.

By the time the Lower Fourths had moved on to the next poem, about a snob called Lady Clara Vere de Vere, Dora was falling out of the lavatory window, binoculars trained on Middle Field as the teams shrieked, yelled and raced about.

There was Xavier Campbell-Black actually laughing – that must be a first – with a girl in Eastern clothes. Kylie Rose and the Hon. Jack were having a very heavy snog behind a holly bush. Jack was so dopey, Dora hoped he'd remember to use a condom. Lord Waterlane would go ballistic if he got Kylie pregnant. If only she had a camera, the *Mail* would love that story – talk about Posh and Complications. That dickhead Boffin was grumbling to Mr Davies about something. Dora could just make out Graffi and Milly Walton building a tower together. Janna was looking bleak, probably missing Hengist. And Amber, Dora's heroine, was sauntering out of Middle Field, doing up her bra, straightening her clothes, followed by – yuk! – Feral Jackson. How could Amber fancy him? She wouldn't if she knew he'd kicked a football through Loofah's legs. Dora got out her mobile to ring the press.

Great cheers rent the air as Junior Lloyd-Foxe got a text to say Shining Sixpence had won by five lengths.

'I'm terribly sorry I only got him at ten to one. That's a hundred and thirty quid I owe you,' he told Graffi. 'Thanks for the tip. Bloody good.'

Graffi's balloon would clearly be the most beautiful but not the first completed.

'Come on, Graffi, we must beat that twat Boffin,' pleaded Pearl.

'Rocky and Kylie'll hold him back,' muttered Graffi, gluing on extra strips of violet.

'We must beat that horrible Cosmo.'

'Feral and Lando will hold him back even more.'

'Feral makes up for it by running quick.'

Cosmo, in fact, was white with rage. He'd always fancied Amber, and she'd pushed off with that snake Feral, leaving him with Lando (who was immersed in week-old racing pages) and only Kitten Meadows to bully, who kept rolling her eyes, clapping her hands over her mouth and giggling.

'Why do you laugh when it's not funny?' he asked evilly.

'Dunno.'

'That's not an answer.'

Kitten flushed, looking round for Johnnie to protect her, but Johnnie, part of Primrose Duddon's team, was gazing longingly at Pitch One. To hit a six on it would be really something.

Having cut out a doughnut-shaped piece of cardboard to reinforce the bottom disk of violet tissue paper, Graffi shoved his fist through the paper.

'This is where the hot air goes in, Milly.' He lowered his voice. 'You ever come into town?'

'It could be arranged. Here's my mobile number.' Milly wrote it on a fragment of daffodil-yellow tissue paper, shoving it into Graffi's jeans pocket, fingers splaying over his thigh.

'Stop wasting time,' said an envious Spotty Wilkins.

'Your balloon's the prettiest,' said Milly.

Graffi's smile was unwavering. 'No, you're the prettiest.'

To reinforce his team's balloon, Rocky had also been instructed to cut a piece of cardboard shaped like a doughnut and now pretended to eat it. Everyone laughed so Rocky started really to eat it.

'Stop that, you stupid idiot,' screamed Boffin.

'Leave Rocky alone, you great bully,' shouted Kylie. Then, as Rocky went on chewing the cardboard: 'Stop that, you stupid asshole.'

'Now who's being both bullying and offensive,' said a shocked Boffin.

'Rocky's my friend, I'm allowed,' snapped Kylie, adding as an afterthought: 'You're the asshole.'

'Very well said, Kylie,' brayed the Hon. Jack.

Jade Stancombe wasn't happy. Cosmo had ignored her all afternoon. Amber had pulled the divinely wayward Feral. Graffi was so busy gazing at Milly he'd put a fist through his balloon and was frantically patching. The enigmatic Paris, whose beauty was undeniable, was ignoring her. Paris was in fact watching Janna and Emlyn, wondering how that great ape could train his binoculars on a distant rugby game when the loveliest woman in the world stood beside him.

My poor father has spent a fortune on a bus to enable Larks and Bagley to indulge in an orgy, thought Jade furiously, and no one's asked me to join in.

'Why are you staring at me?' she rudely asked Paris,

who shrugged and turned back to the balloon to which Lando and Anatole, delighted at their winnings, were proving surprisingly good at adding finishing touches.

Aysha and Xavier were also working well, Aysha deftly gluing the paper Xavier had cut out as they built a beautiful control tower, nearly three feet high with crenellated turrets.

The hour and a half was nearly up. Shrieks of rage, frustration and triumph rent the air.

'I feel like the end of a jumble sale,' said Mags, looking at the empty trestle table from which every scrap of tissue paper had been whipped.

'Finished,' yelled Primrose Duddon, whose team, even with Johnnie on board, had indulged in no dalliance or illicit boozing and had completed their orange and Prussian-blue balloon to loud cheers. As there was no sign of Stancombe, Emlyn presented Primrose with a red rosette.

'Well done,' he told her, then, turning to Janna: 'Should we release the balloons as they come in?'

'More impact if they all go off together,' said Janna, and was nearly sent flying by a furious Boffin.

'Sir, sir, someone's been cheating, cutting free the staplers in the wood so I've been unable to complete our map. Objection! Objection!'

'It's only a game,' said Emlyn, mindful of the gathering press. 'No one's getting any prizes.'

Graffi's round balloon, in diamonds of primrose yellow, shocking pink and violet, was judged to be the most beautiful; Xav and Aysha's control tower the finest; Cosmo's tower the biggest and tallest, which, everyone agreed, figured. Nearly all the participants were chatting and laughing now.

As the balloons were lined up on the edge of the cricket pitch, the chapel weathercock, which had been watching proceedings, swung away as the warm south wind, which would have swept the balloons over the

271

golf course, changed to north-east. Now, with luck, it would carry them over the Mansion.

'Stick 'em up.'

Feral reached instinctively for his knife as Gloria ran out brandishing two hot-air paint-strippers, followed by Cambola, Jason and Janna bearing hairdriers. Emlyn then handed out cardboard tubes to plug into the cardboard hole in the bottom of each balloon.

'Too phallic for words,' muttered Cosmo as the nozzles of hairdriers and paint-strippers were applied to the lower end of the cardboard tubes.

Emlyn was studying the building pack.

'Are all staff wearing protective gloves and all balloons held firmly by a team member?' he shouted.

'Yes,' went up the cry.

'Well, turn on the heat.'

Scarlet and black, navy and emerald, Prussian blue and orange, shocking pink, violet and yellow, mauve and dark green: the balloons bobbed like tropical fish.

Mauve and dark green, held by Paris as Janna's hairdrier poured hot air inside it, quivered most. Jade put her hand round the cardboard tube, pretending to toss it off, then, encountering an icy look from Paris, blushed and let go.

'Do you like the bus my father gave you?' she demanded.

'It's absolutely wonderful,' cried Janna, 'it'll change our lives. We can't thank him enough.'

'The balloons should take four minutes to fill up,' advised Emlyn.

Kitten stood well back. 'I'm sure the glue's going to catch fire.'

'Out of nuffink, just bits of paper and glue, we've made somefing beautiful,' said Kylie in a choked voice. Like we could be, she thought.

The press had now arrived in force and, with no sign of Stancombe, photographed balloons and happy, excited children.

'Everyone ready?' yelled Emlyn.

'No,' protested Lando France-Lynch.

'He's never been able to get it up,' shouted Junior.

'They'll never fly either,' mocked Cosmo and, as everyone was concentrating on the balloons, whipped Amber's mobile from her pocket.

'Ten, nine, eight, seven, six,' shouted Emlyn. 'Five, four, three, two, one, lift-off.'

Away went the balloons, the tropical fish metamorphosing into a swarm of coloured butterflies, flying over the gold trees into the bright blue autumn sky.

Lubemir and Boffin's black and red balloon caught on the spikes of a sycamore, triggering off a stream of Albanian expletives until a gust of wind freed it to bob after the others. Sailing south-west over the Mansion, Primrose's orange and Prussian-blue prizewinner stalled on the gold weathercock.

'First time she's bounced on top of a cock,' giggled Amber.

'Let's see how far they go,' said Feral, taking her hand and together they raced through trees and school buildings, followed by a whooping Milly and Graffi, Lubemir and Pearl and, after exchanging shy smiles, by Aysha and Xavier.

'Black shit sticks together,' observed Cosmo. Jade laughed and slid her hand into his.

'Xav has just been very rude to me, I think he needs taking down a peg or two.'

'Or three, or four, or five,' agreed Cosmo. 'It will be arranged.'

'The Montgolfiers always maintained—' began Boffin.

'Oh, shut up, Boffin,' said Primrose.

Janna and Paris stood side by side watching until the last balloon floated out of sight.

'They're a symbol of Larks,' whispered Janna. 'We're going to take off and really fly and so will the partnership with us and Bagley—' Her voice broke.

Turning, Paris saw tears spilling over her lower lashes. Taking the hairdrier from her, he put it on a trestle table, then somehow his hand slid into hers and they smiled at each other.

'God speed,' cried out Janna, as the last emerald and navy balloon bobbed briefly between the tall chimneys, 'such a wonderful omen.'

Paris didn't know when to let go of her hand, so he left it to her.

Interesting, reflected Cosmo, who was standing behind them. Miss Curtis clearly likes toyboys as well as wrinklies.

The rugby fifteens, probably wrecked from all that pounding on hard ground, had gone in, so Emlyn also observed Janna and Paris. She's very near the edge, he decided, and so besotted with Hengist, she's unaware of the havoc she's wreaking on that poor boy.

'That was a great success,' he said loudly.

Janna let go of Paris's hand, and was soon telling the hovering press that 'Larks and Bagley's partnership couldn't have been illustrated taking off in a more romantic and beautiful way.'

31

Stancombe still hadn't turned up, but the Larks and Bagley balloonists, over orange juice and slices of Mrs Axford's cherry cake in the pavilion, were getting on much too well to care. Nor did they notice Cosmo slipping Amber's mobile into the pocket of Feral's tracksuit top, which he'd left hanging on the back of his chair.

Amber and Milly were wildly impressed when they discovered Pearl had done Janna's Winter Garden make-up.

'I mean she's pretty for a wrinkly today, but in that picture with Hengist, she looks like Meg Ryan, and you can see Hengist really, really fancies her,' said Amber.

'Will you make me up one day?' begged Milly.

'Pearl's going to do the make-up for a joint production,' said Amber.

'Then I can quite confidently play Helen of Troy,' giggled Milly.

Pearl was in heaven.

'What d'you want to see this afternoon?' asked Amber.

'The theatre, and Graffi's desperate to see the art department. He's dead talented.'

'Dead lush as well,' sighed Milly.

'Not as lush as Feral,' said Amber.

'Feral's my boyfriend,' said Pearl sharply.

'Ah,' said Amber.

If Feral were taken, which was indeed a body blow, she'd better call Peregrine. She patted her pockets. Where the hell was her mobile?

Johnnie Fowler, who'd been too uptight to have any lunch, had a fourth piece of cherry cake as he discussed safe-breaking and drugs with Lubemir.

'I tried to kill Miss when I were high on crack, so I went cold turkey.'

'Ve vould have allowed you to kill Alex Bruce,' said Lubemir. He turned to Feral: 'Vat vould you like to do this afternoon?'

'Amber Lloyd-Foxe.' Feral shook his head in wonder. 'She's the hottest girl I've seen in years.'

Amber, however, had slid out of the dining room, raided the art department and was racing towards the car park.

Dora, spitting with rage, was leaning out of the science lab window as Stancombe's crimson and gold helicopter finally landed on the grass, to be greeted by a diminished press corps fed up with waiting. As Larks's splendid minibus glided onto the field for the official presentation, no one realized that Amber Lloyd-Foxe had graffitied the back with silver spray paint.

Larks pupils lined up in two rows like ball boys at Wimbledon as Stancombe leapt lithely down onto the grass. Even today, when he'd cultivated an au naturel Richard Branson look – carefully ruffled hair, open-necked check shirt, designer jeans and a shadow of stubble, he didn't get it quite right. The tan was too mahogany and the Dolce & Gabbana label deliberately worn outside his belt.

Striding out to meet him, Alex Bruce explained why Hengist was tied up. Stancombe was incensed.

'You'd have thought . . .'

'I know, I know, I'm afraid our Senior Team Leader is a lawlessness unto himself.'

Next moment, Sheena Anderson had jumped down, and a gust from the helicopter took her black dress over her head to reveal black hold-ups, a neat Brazilian and a wodge of white loo paper shoved between her legs. This was greeted by whoops and wolf whistles. Cosmo whipped out his camera. Dora nearly fell out of the window as a furious Sheena tugged down her skirt.

'Funny place to keep your hanky,' observed Pearl.

'Stan came,' murmured Paris.

Feral laughed. 'You OK, mate?'

'We had a load of press here at three-thirty. They've rather drifted away,' Alex told Stancombe. 'Let's get on with the presentation.'

Rocky, who'd already torn the gold paper off the magnum of champagne, very reluctantly relinquished it so Kylie could present it to Stancombe who, accustomed to the tropical heat of his apartments, was now shivering uncontrollably in the north-east wind.

Janna then came forward to shake his hand.

'It's the most beautiful bus in the world, it's wonderful of you. We are all so grateful.'

A second later Jade, putting on a little girl's voice and crying, 'Daddy, Daddy,' ran across the grass to get in on the act.

'Hi Jadey, how's my little princess?' Stancombe kissed her lingeringly on the mouth.

'Gross,' muttered Milly.

'Can we have a photograph of you and Jade?' asked the Gazette.

Meanwhile the helicopter pilot, who'd been kept waiting hours the other end, had charged off to the Gents, whereupon Larks and Bagley pupils swarmed onto the helicopter, examining, pressing buttons, bouncing on the pale beige upholstery, helping themselves to coloured cigarettes.

'Put it back,' said Paris furiously as Feral pocketed a gold ashtray. Sulkily Feral did. A second later, the same ashtray slid into Lubemir's pocket alongside a silver cigarette case. Everyone would blame the yobbos from Larks.

Outside Jade said, 'You know Amber and Milly, don't you, Daddy?'

'Of course.' Stancombe shook their hands. 'And I'd like you to meet Sheena Anderson.' Then, anxious to explain Sheena's presence to Milly: 'Sheen's doing an in-depth profile on me for the *Guardian*.'

'We know Mrs Anderson,' said Milly pointedly.

'How's Flavia?' asked Amber even more pointedly.

'Fine,' snapped Sheena.

'We heard she's got chicken pox even worse than Rebecca. She's got a temperature of a hundred and four,' Milly renewed the attack. 'Mr Anderson was so worried he had to duck out of supervising our balloon-building today.'

'Rufus is such a caring father,' said Jade, who always gave her father's girlfriends a hard time.

Sheena was simply livid.

'How's your mother, Milly?' Stancombe's voice thickened.

'She's really well.'

'Give her my best.'

Why the hell didn't the bitch answer his phone calls?

Bagley and Larks were getting bored. The press were getting restless.

'Why have you given Larkminster Comprehensive such a magnificent bus when you haven't been a huge supporter of the school in the past?' asked the Venturer presenter.

Stancombe, ruffling his hair for the camera, said:

'I feel it's important for disadvantaged youngsters to escape from the poverty trap and, as a consequence, a life of crime.'

As Larks faces fell or set into sullen lines, Janna's eyes met Emlyn's and was comforted to see rage. Stancombe then put an arm round Jade.

'My daughter is a very privileged young lady to be at

a school like Bagley. But I've always taught her to treat those less fortunate with kindness.'

'You have, Daddy,' agreed Jade fondly.

'Jade sounds much posher than her dad,' Graffi whispered to Milly. 'Can you learn Posh as well as Spanish, French and German at Bagley?'

'That's what lots of the parents pay for,' said Milly.

Stancombe was kicking himself. By arriving late he had lost crucial coverage. He never should have shagged Sheena – and Larks kids had invaded his chopper. Feral Jackson had just leapt out, pulling at the elastic of a pair of black and red panties as though shooting a catapult at Paris, who was laughing his head off.

Then Stancombe gave a bellow. On the back of the minibus someone had sprayed the words 'Rough Trade Counter' in huge silver letters. The press was going mad photographing it. Alex Bruce was having a coronary.

Lurking in the bushes Amber chucked the can of silver spray paint into the nettles. That would teach young Feral to make a play when he was already in a relationship – and yet, and yet, those kisses had been so magical . . . And what the hell had she done with her mobile?

Fed up with Sheena sticking her tape recorder in every-where, the press were packing up.

'We'd like the two heads with the pupils,' said a *Daily Telegraph* photographer. 'Any chance we can drag Hengist out?'

'He insisted on not being interrupted.'

'Then we'd better have you in the picture, Mr Bruce.'

Alex was just combing his beard in the minibus wing mirror when Hengist rolled up.

'Randal, you're a brick coming all this way.'

'Randal, you're a brick,' murmured Paris, cracking up Bagley as well as Larks pupils.

As Hengist, Janna, Stancombe and the Larks children, still humiliated and angered by his comments, posed together, a peal of bells floated across the soft autumnal air.

'How lovely,' sighed Janna. 'It must be Wally in the chapel.'

'Thought you only rang bells like that to warn people war had broken out,' quipped Stancombe.

'It already has,' said Paris bleakly.

'OK, chaps.' Hengist waved at the press. 'Got to get back to work. Help yourselves to a cup of tea and a piece of cake inside. Alex'll look after you. Randal, thanks for coming, and I'd like a word with you, Sheena.'

All amiability was wiped off Hengist's face as he drew her aside.

'Glad you're back. Rufus, as you're no doubt aware, is looking after your children, probably contracting chicken pox – or more likely shingles, after the pressure to which you subject him – which means he'll be off for more weeks. Now you're back, you can bloody well take over.'

Sheena flared up immediately. 'The *Guardian* have commissioned this piece. I'm flying straight back to London with Randal to file copy.'

'You can write it from home. Rufus was supposed to supervise operations today. He's paid to look after Bagley's children, not his own.'

Sheena glanced up at Hengist, so handsome, so hard, so contemptuous, and ached with reluctant longing.

'I earn four times as much as my husband,' she said furiously. 'Only way we can make ends meet on his piddling salary since you passed him over as housemaster.'

'Since we passed you over as a housemaster's wife. There's nothing wrong with Rufus. If you're capable of earning that kind of money, why the hell don't you get a nanny?'

Quivering with rage, Sheena caught up with Stancombe.

'That bastard B-T's ordered me home to look after the kids.'

'Got a point. Mother's place is with her kids when they're sick.'

'I can't write against that din.'

'You promised I could see copy.'

'I will if there's time; they want it this evening. I'm going to bury the Brett-Taylors if it kills me.'

32

Pearl and Graffi were in ecstasy. The drama department were doing *Bugsy Malone* and researching all that thirties kit and make-up. Graffi, having discovered the art department, was going berserk with a spray gun. Miss Cambola had already had a lovely time exploring the music library. Now, wandering round with Kylie, she suddenly heard a pianist pouring forth his soul in a ravishing fountain of sound. Miss Cambola stiffened like a pointer.

'This I must see.' Pushing her way into the music hall, followed by an enraptured Kylie, she found Cosmo at the piano, black curls flying, pale face maniacal as he thundered up and down the keys, producing notes of such crystal beauty, yet somehow managing with his head and occasional free hand to conduct the orchestra as well.

'Stop, stop.' The orchestra slithered to a nervous halt. Cosmo was hurling abuse at them when he heard a footstep and swung round. 'Get out,' he screamed. 'Get fucking out, out, out.'

But Miss Cambola strode on undeterred.

'Maestro,' she cried, sweeping off her Tyrolean hat like a principal boy and seizing Cosmo's pale hand. She kissed it lovingly. 'You can only be the son of Roberto Rannaldini, the greatest conductor of the twentieth century, if not all time.'

Cosmo was mollified. Whatever his contempt for humans, he loved music and was soon gabbling away in Italian. Miss Cambola then introduced Kylie Rose.

'She has an extraordinarily beautiful voice.'

'I must hear it. What instrument do you play, signora?'

'The trumpet,' replied Cambola.

'There's a spare here.'

'The Battle of Waterloo was won on the playing fields of Eton and various other good public schools,' wrote Hengist.

Normally he rattled off journalism. Today he was struggling, especially as Painswick wasn't here to do his research and find out how many acres of playing fields had been sold off in the last twenty years – or hectares. Stupid word. 'Hectors' ought to be sorting out Greeks on the ringing plains of windy Troy.

'Crash, bang, wallop, de dum, de, dah – de, dum, de dah,' anyone would think the Rolling Stones were warming up in the corridor. Hengist glanced irritably up at the timetable. 'Orchestra rehearsal: Cosmo Rannaldini.'

Sixty seconds later, Hengist roared into the music hall—

'For Christ's sake, Cosmo, take that bloody din down.'

Only to find Cambola, Tyrolean hat on the back of her head, jamming away on a trumpet.

Feral, who had a great capacity for kissing the joy as it flies, had just jolted Ex-Regimental Sergeant Major Bilson, who ran the small arms range, by hitting everything in sight. Feral in turn had been fascinated to learn that the sixth-form pupils listed on the walls had sharpened up their shooting here before immediately setting off for two world wars to kill real people and be killed themselves.

Now he was playing golf in the fading light with his new friends Anatole, Lubemir and the Hon. Jack, who seemed a good bloke for a toff and who also supported Arsenal.

'You played before?' Jack asked Feral after a few holes.

'No, man.'

'Christ, well, keep practising, Tiger.'

'My father will sponsor you,' said Anatole. 'We will bury Americans.'

'Golf is excellent game,' said Lubemir. 'You can combine other pleasures, enjoy country air . . .' and, reaching into the bole of an oak tree, he produced what looked like a large stock cube wrapped in cellophane.

'Don't do drugs, man,' said Feral.

'Have a slug of this, then.'

'Nice guy, Emlyn,' observed Feral as neat vodka bit into his throat.

'Tough as sheet,' grumbled Lubemir. 'As punishment he make you run round the pitch in the middle of the night. But you can have a laugh with him. And he takes the teams to the pub when they win matches.'

'Good teacher,' Jack said, who was looking for his ball in the long pale grass. 'Annoying sometimes; always got a reason why the English didn't really win a battle.'

They were passing Badger's Retreat and the Family Tree, its three bodies writhing together in love and resentment. Down below in the valley, lights of farms and cottages were twinkling.

'Very left wing, Emlyn,' Jack went on disapprovingly.

'What's his woman like?' asked Feral.

'Good-looking but even more of a leftie than Emlyn. Wants to abolish public schools, hunting and the House of Lords – what the fuck would my father do all day?'

Feral was teeing up a ball, white as his eyeballs,

284

squinting towards the distant green as he'd watched Tiger do so often on television.

'This is a five,' said Lubemir, passing the spliff to Anatole.

'Oriana is in Afghanistan,' said Anatole approvingly. 'Talking about war, always attacking American imperialism, very good girl.'

'Emlyn must be worried,' said Feral.

'That's why he's so bad-tempered.'

Johnnie Fowler, Kitten and Gloria were having a lovely time working out in the gym with Denzil. Alex Bruce, by contrast, was having a dreadful day. He'd failed to get on television. Hengist had stolen Mrs Radcliffe for another draft. He was furious with Emlyn for sloping off to fine tune the rugby team, leaving that coven of thieves playing golf with Feral Jackson. God knows what they were plotting. Alex had ordered Boffin Brooks, the one dependable boy in the school, not to let Paris Alvaston out of his sight.

Paris was now in the library. He had never seen such rows of temptation, magic carpets waiting to fly him to distant worlds. He had found the plays of Noël Coward and Oscar Wilde. How could anyone be so funny? But Paris couldn't really concentrate; he wanted to write sonnets to Janna. She had held his hand and let him see her cry. If only Boffin would fuck off and stop rabbiting on about IT.

Paris took down a copy of Donne's poems.

> I am two fools, I know,
> For loving, and for saying so
> In whining poetry.

Summed it up really.

Boffin, bored with books, insisted on showing Paris the science lab. Here Dora, forcibly removed from the window by No-Joke Joan, was furiously writing an essay on 'The Journey of the Sperm'.

'The sperms venture inside the womb' – her Biro was nearly ripping the paper – 'trying to swim towards the eggs – yuk – eventually they find them and fertilize them.'

'Do they do the breast stroke or do they crawl?' asked Bianca.

'Dog paddle, I would think. Just imagine all those tiny tadpoles swimming around to produce one. Yuk. Imagine our parents doing that.'

'Being adopted, I don't know who my parents were,' sighed Bianca.

'Must have been beautiful to produce you. My brother Dicky says you're the prettiest girl in the school. Oh, look, here comes that tosser Boffin and Paris Alvaston.'

Dora and Bianca watched Boffin sidle off to chat up No-Joke Joan.

'The old buzzard's looking quite starry-eyed. Boffin's her favourite pupil.'

'He's gorgeous-looking, Paris,' observed Bianca.

Paris's face was as still as a statue, the white streak down the side of his tracksuit trousers emphasizing the lean length of his leg.

'Hengist said we've got to be nice to them,' said Dora, then, edging up to Paris: 'Would you like to take part in an experiment?'

'Depends.'

Dora handed him a piece of stiff white paper and a bottle of blue-black ink. 'Now, drop some ink on the paper.'

So Paris shook out a dark-blue blob, which trembled, then settled.

'Now dip the bit of paper in this flask of water.'

'What for?'

'Trust me. Good. Now watch.'

When the paper was removed from the water the dark blob had metamorphosed into a royal-blue, turquoise and olive-green oval.

286

'Look,' cried Dora in excitement, 'it's a peacock feather.'

'That's cool,' said Paris, examining it.

'You can all turn from blobs into peacock feathers if you work hard enough,' said a marching-up Joan. 'Now get on with your work, Dora. What are you writing?'

'The Journey of the Sperm.'

'Finding the eggs,' piped up Bianca. 'Dora wanted to know if the eggs were free range.'

'No, the sperm is,' said Paris.

Dora and Bianca got the giggles.

'Don't be sillier than you need be,' snapped Joan.

'I'm going to blow her up soon,' muttered Dora as she handed the peacock feather to Paris.

Paris put it in his pocket, thinking how nice it would be to have a little sister like Dora.

High tea was held in the General Bagley Room, which was used by the debating and literary societies, and for visiting non-crowd-pulling speakers. It was a charming room with flame-red walls, grey silk curtains, framed prize-winning pictures from the art department and a lovely view from the window of the General astride his charger gazing down the Long Walk.

As Hengist still hadn't finished his piece, Sally stood in for him and made the Larks children feel even more special by offering them a great mountain of delectable scrambled egg, dripping with butter and cream and served with smoked salmon and wholemeal toast. Larks, who had never tasted anything so delicious, went back for second and third helpings. A big cheese and onion pie had been set aside for the vegetarians, but everyone tucked into that too and into salads, slices of melon with glacé cherries, fruit salad and chocolate brownies.

'Yum, yum, yum,' said Milly. 'You must come over more often. We don't usually get food like this.'

'Such a happy day,' Mags Gablecross was telling Sally.

'I feel as though I've had a week's holiday. The kids are overwhelmed by such kindness.'

Mags was like a hot-water bottle on a cold night, thought Janna, who was ashamed of feeling so depressed when they were all enjoying themselves. Even Emlyn had shrugged off his ill humour. The teams looked sharper than he'd expected and he was electrified by Feral. If ever there was a natural talent . . . That golf swing was utterly instinctive; he couldn't wait to get him onto the rugby field. Where was he? he wondered.

All around, the children were chattering nineteen to the dozen, arguing about GCSE subjects, football and clothes.

Boffin Brooks, who strongly disapproved of smoked salmon being wasted on such ruffians, noting Aysha and Xav sitting together, contented but not speaking, decided to join them. He was so caring about ethnic minorities.

'Mustn't neglect you two,' he said loudly.

Patronizing bastard, thought Xav, who'd never met anyone as adorable as Aysha. She had the same timidity and sweetness as his mother and he was sure she had the same rippling dark hair beneath her headscarf. He longed to tell her what he couldn't tell his parents: how lonely it was being black in a white family, particularly when, unlike Rupert, he wasn't good at anything.

'There is a myth that independent students don't work hard,' Boffin was saying sententiously. 'In fact I rise at six-thirty and am often still at my computer at eleven at night.'

And I clean the house, cook, wash, iron, shop, go to the mosque, learn from the Koran and do my homework, thought Aysha; and my father still beats me. But Xavier had protected her from Jade. She didn't know how to thank him. He had such a nice face when he wasn't scowling.

'Qualifications are indeed the only things that matter,' went on Boffin.

'No they ain't.' Graffi squeezed Milly's hand. 'Straight As don't teach you how to hang doors or unblock a bog.'

'I agree,' said the Hon. Jack. 'We're learning about agriculture in geography. Bloody waste of time. My father's got a farm. Rufus can't teach me anything new.'

Kylie felt Jack's big hand edging up her thigh. The hand of a lord's son. Her mother would be in raptures.

'I don't like maffs because I don't like our maffs teacher,' said Rocky in his hoarse voice.

'You wouldn't like ours any better,' said Amber. 'He shifts his cock from one leg of his trousers to another, and buries great silent sulphuric farts in his thick tweed trousers. He's called Biffo; ought to be "Whiffo".'

Rocky broke into his hoarse laugh and, unable to stop, lumbered to his feet.

'I'd like to fank everyone at Bagley for having us. Free cheers to Bagley. Hip, hip, hooray; hip, hip, hooray; hip, hip, hooray.'

'You must play Bottom next time we do a production of *A Midsummer Night's Dream*,' suggested Cosmo.

'Where's Feral?' said Pearl fretfully.

'You will come out wiv me, won't you?' Graffi murmured to Milly. After his winnings today he could take her to La Perdrix d'Or.

'Course I will. You've got the same lovely accent as Mr Davies. Everyone's got crushes on him, but you've got me over mine.'

33

Hengist felt drained but Christ-like. He had faxed his piece and the *Telegraph* loved it. One shouldn't be so dependent on approval. In the drinks cupboard he found a box of Maltesers given him by some pupil and, realizing he hadn't had any lunch, broke the cellophane and started eating them. His thoughts turned to Janna arriving with her children.

'Round about her "there is a rabble Of the filthy, sturdy, unkillable infants of the very poor",' he quoted idly. '"They shall inherit the earth."'

Poor child, he'd neglected her shamelessly. He decided to text her: 'Settle your children, then escape and have a drink.'

Shiny-faced, shadowed beneath the eyes, lipstick bitten off, Janna longed to repair her face, but, scared Hengist would have pushed off somewhere else, loathing herself for such abject acquiescence, she was knocking on his big oak door five minutes later.

'How's it gone? I'm so sorry, darling.' Hengist thrust a large glass of gin and orange into her hand.

He'd remembered, but then he'd remembered Kylie had a baby called Cameron. It was so unprofessional to sulk, she must just be cool.

'Your kids have been so nice,' she began. 'The balloons were brilliant, and they've had a really good

290

time since then trying things out. I'm so proud of them,' she added defiantly.

'So you should be.'

His was such a beautiful room: rich dark panelling soaring into the ornate ceiling, William Morris animal tiles round the leaping log fire, red lamps casting a warm glow, lovely photographs on the desk of Sally, Oriana and Elaine, a stuffed bear in a mortar board, overcrowded bookshelves. Noting dilapidated, leather-bound copies of Horace, Aristotle, Saint-Simon and Gibbon, all containing bookmarks, Janna wondered if he'd really read and referred to them all.

Apart from the Keith Vaughan of a thundery twilight, yet to be dispatched to the Common Room, all other available wall space was covered by sepia photographs of past teams, past scholars, past heads, past glories. Such a stultifying emphasis on tradition.

'We've got an old boys' reunion tonight,' said Hengist. 'It's to encourage them to send their sons and daughters here.'

'"This is the Chapel: here, my son, Your father thought the thoughts of youth,"' quoted Janna scornfully.

She ran her hands over a bronze replica of the lion in the quad, dropping his head to lick the little fawn:

'More likely to gobble it up.'

'Debatable,' agreed Hengist.

He looked tired, with great bags under his eyes, but he seemed very happy as he abstractedly went on eating Maltesers.

On a side table Janna suddenly caught sight of a perfectly dreadful figurine of a headless naked woman, with a noose around her long neck and forests of armpit and pubic hair.

'Goodness.'

'Goodness, as Mae West said, has nothing to do with it. Alex Bruce's wife made it for my birthday to remind me not to oppress women.'

291

'What's she like?'

'Gha-a-a-astly.' Hengist shuddered. 'She carries political correctness ad absurdum and has the relentless cheeriness and verbal diarrhoea of a weather girl. One longs to throw a green baize cloth over her.'

There was a pause. The room was so cosy after the chill winter evening, the flames dancing merrily.

'Dreadful forgetting the *Telegraph* piece, I'm so sorry.' Hengist upended the box of Maltesers.

'Did they like it?'

'John Clare said he did. It probably thumped the right tubs. I ought to write more.'

'I ought to read more,' Janna said fretfully. 'I haven't read a single novel since I came to Larks. I truly hate being a head.'

The guilt she felt about being away from school all afternoon was kicking in. She could no longer bury it beneath her longing to see Hengist again. He's not remotely interested in me, she thought bleakly.

'I don't deserve to be one,' she went on. 'I can't make peace with my staff. They'll never forgive me for having a lovely time today.'

'Don't be silly,' said Hengist gently. 'I like your children very much and I look forward to knowing them and their headmistress a great deal better.'

'You do?' Janna glanced up, and Hengist was mortified to see her trembling bottom lip and the despair in her big brown eyes.

They were interrupted by an almighty crash, scattering glass everywhere, followed by a second and a further shower of fragments.

Janna screamed; Hengist leapt forward, pulling her against him and out of the way. For a few blissful seconds, his arms closed around her and she felt the softness of dark green cashmere and his heart pounding, and breathed in a faint smell of lemon aftershave and Maltesers.

Then he looked down and she looked up. Both for a

second were distracted from the disaster as his beautiful mouth hovered above hers, then reality kicked in.

'Was that some kind of terrorist attack?' she gasped.

Something had smashed the vast bay window overlooking the pitches and to the splintered glass all over the floor were added the shattered remnants of Poppet Bruce's figurine.

'I've found a bit of bush.' Hengist brandished a fragment. 'At least Mrs Bruce's masterpiece is no more. It's an ill window, I suppose.' He grinned in such delight, Janna burst out laughing.

'This is the culprit,' Hengist fished a golf ball out of the fireplace. Striding to the now gaping window, he peered into the dusk, roaring: 'What the hell are you playing at? Christ!' he added as he slowly took in how far the ball must have travelled. Picking up his binoculars, usually used for birdwatching, he caught sight of a distant crimson sweatshirt and a huge, wide grin.

'Your Feral Jackson is the culprit behind the culprit.'

'Oh God.' Janna was appalled. 'We'll pay for it.'

'Feral can pay for it himself when he wins the Masters, if we haven't converted him to rugger by then. God, that was a long way.'

'I'm so sorry, I must take my children home.'

'Feral won't have had supper yet.'

'You've got your old boys' reunion.'

Hengist shrugged. 'We've always got something. Have another drink, it's only five o'clock.' He ran a hand over her hair. 'Sorry you were frightened, but it was a lovely hug.'

34

Over in the General Bagley Room, Graffi and Feral were chatting so much they hadn't noticed Paris's self-absorption.

Feral had come to Bagley determined to trash everything in sight, but he'd had fun; he'd outshot and outdriven everyone else; and he had a new friend called Amber who'd given him her mobile number. Would he have the guts to ring her?

Suddenly the jangling jolly theme tune of show-jumping on the BBC rang out.

'That's my mobile,' cried Amber in delight. 'Where is it?'

'Here,' said Cosmo, picking up Feral's black tracksuit top and, before Feral could stop him, whipping a mobile out of the inside pocket. The room went quiet. Cosmo switched it on.

'Hi, is that Peregrine? Hang on a minute. What's your mobile doing in Feral's fleece?' he asked Amber.

'I never touched it.' Feral jumped to his feet, amiability turning to menace, fists clenched, Graffi and Paris beside him.

'I gave it to Feral to look after when we were racing round the wood,' said Amber quickly. 'It was safer with him.'

For a second she and Cosmo glared at each other.

'You said you'd lost it.'

'And now I've found it. Hi, Perry, how are you?'

Graffi pulled a protesting Feral back into his chair.

'I didn't take no mobile.'

'Cool it, man, she gave it to you to look after, she said so.'

'She didn't,' said Feral stonily. 'That was a plant to frame me.'

'What did you go inside for last summer, Feral?' asked Cosmo chattily. 'For nicking a mobile wasn't it?'

Paris stood up and, strolling down the row, pulled Cosmo to his feet. 'Don't even go down that road, you sick bastard,' he said softly. In a trice, Emlyn was beside him.

'It's Janna's day. Don't spoil it for her.'

Paris glowered round, slowly his fist uncurled and dropped to his side. 'You sick bastard,' he repeated.

Boffin, who'd missed this scrap, was still pontificating. 'We do a lot for charity,' he was telling Aysha in his nasal whine. 'We raised twenty thousand pounds for netball courts in Soweto with sponsored runs and cycle rides. Senior students act as mentors to the local primary school. Primrose is very active in this field. We run errands for senior citizens and tend their gardens. We raise a lot for the NSPCC, for cancer patients and other disadvantaged groups.'

Pausing for breath, he smiled smugly round at the Larks contingent. 'And of course today, we've set aside an entire afternoon to entertain you folks.'

'An entire afternoon to entertain you folks,' whined Paris in perfect imitation.

Milly's giggle immediately died. There was a terrible silence.

'Boffin,' said a horrified Amber.

Pearl rose to her feet, hoop earrings flying.

'You lot 'ad us over today,' she yelled. 'If you just did it for bleedin' charity, you can stick it up your ass'ole. In fact you're just a lot of fuckin' ass'oles. Upper class'oles in fact.'

'Upper class-holes,' sighed Cosmo in ecstasy. 'Isn't that perfect. Oh, Pearl of great price.'

Paris, however, had jumped onto the table, padded his way catlike through the debris of supper and leapt off at Boffin's side, lifting him up by his lapels.

'Take that back,' he hissed.

'Paris,' thundered Emlyn.

'How dare you patronize us.'

Next moment there was a crunch as Paris's knuckles connected with Boffin's buck teeth and hoisted him across the room.

'Stop it.' Emlyn grabbed Paris, clamping his arms behind his back; then, turning on Boffin, who was moaning on the floor, mouth filling up with blood: 'Get up, you deserve everything you got.'

Emlyn proceeded to whistle up Lando and Jack. 'Get him out of here quickly, take him to the sick bay.'

'Wait 'til my father hears about this,' mumbled Boffin, spitting out teeth.

'Save him the cash for a brace,' shouted Lando. 'You should send him a bill, Paris.'

Boffin's remarks had been so cringe-making that everyone cheered as Lando, aided by Jack, Mags and Jason, smuggled him out of a side door.

'Be quiet, everyone,' rapped out Emlyn as Hengist walked in with Janna, who looked as though a smoothing iron had been run over her glowing face.

'I just love being a head,' she was saying. 'It's like being a gardener with slightly too many plants to look after.'

Paris had felt no pain from Boffin's teeth, but he'd rather have roasted in hell than witness the adoring way Janna was smiling up at Hengist.

Out they swarmed into the twilight, rain like the spray from some giant waterfall cooling their hot faces.

Wally, who'd had a wonderful time trying out the bells, hobnobbing with Mrs Axford and talking to

RSM Bilson about his son in Iraq, was revving up the bus.

The two schools were bidding each other fond farewells and the Larks pupils were surging onto the minibus when a BMW came hurtling up the drive, screamed to a halt and one of the prettiest women Paris had ever seen leapt out. She was very tall and slim with big anxious eyes and a mass of dark wavy hair. Jeans might have been invented for her.

'"Her eyes as stars of twilight fair; Like twilight's, too, her dusky hair",' he muttered in wonder.

'Christ, look at her,' gasped Feral.

'It's Rupert Campbell-Black's wife, Taggie,' cried an excited Kylie, a great reader of *Hello!*

For a moment, Taggie looked around in anguish, then Bianca came dancing down the steps into her mother's arms.

'I'm sorry, darling,' gasped Taggie. 'The traffic was terrible and I forgot my mobile. I'm so sorry, how are you, how did the dance class go?'

Chucking her stuff in the back, running round to the other side, Bianca waved goodbye to Dora. 'See you tomorrow, I'll text you the moment I get home.'

For a second a shadow flitted across Taggie's face. 'Is Xav around?'

'No,' said Bianca, then irritably: 'He'll be doing prep or watching television. Come on.'

'OK,' sighed Taggie, slotting a seatbelt over the most delectable bosom.

'Oh, that I vas that seatbelt,' sighed Anatole.

'You did give Xav Daddy's and my love?'

'Yes, yes.' For a second, Bianca's sweet face hardened. 'Let's go, we're holding up the bus.'

Neither she nor Taggie saw Xavier lurking under a nearby oriental plane, desperate to catch a glimpse of his mother. He mustn't be a wimp and run to her. Cosmo, alas, had seen him.

'I hear you insulted Jade,' he said softly. 'Getting a

297

bit above yourself, aren't you, black shit? You'll pay for it later.'

A furious Alex caught up with Hengist just as he was leaving his office. 'That window will cost a fortune to replace.'

'I know, but did you see how far the ball travelled? Boy's a natural, and surely we're insured.'

'Not for my wife's gift,' spluttered Alex. 'It's irreplaceable. I know how much care she put into it.' Then an almost coy expression flickered across his face. 'Although if you asked her very nicely, she might model you another one.'

'Sweet of her but I'm sure there are worthier recipients than I.'

You bastard, thought Alex.

'A very successful visit, I feel,' said Hengist, whisking off down the stairs.

On the journey back Wally stopped to pick up Graffi's balloon, which was roosting in a hedge like a bird of paradise. The children sang the whole time except when Janna went up to the front and clapped her hands.

'Thank you for behaving so beautifully. I'm right proud of all of you. The Bagley teachers were really complimentary, and thank you for mixing so well with the Bagley kids. Would you like to go back again soon?'

'Yes please,' rose the cry.

Paris didn't sing. He gazed out of the window at the skeletal trees against the russet glow of Larkminster and the cathedral spire, so like one of Rowan Merton's sharpened pencils that he wanted to pick it up and write volumes about his despair.

Imagine running out of school into the arms and soft bosom of a mother as loving as Taggie, who would ask him about his day and sweep him home to tea. Or think of turning right to Wilmington, feeding Partner, cooking supper with Janna and falling asleep in her arms: 'Pillowed upon my fair love's ripening breast'.

Oh God, he wanted a family and a home.

Rocky, after his exertions, had fallen asleep on Kylie's shoulder.

'I really like Jack Waterlane,' she was telling Pearl. 'He was so sweet to Rocky.'

'Same intellectual level,' muttered Graffi.

'Never seen such lovely men as that Emlyn, so macho,' gushed Gloria, 'and that Hengist and that Denzil, who I can assure you is not G.A.Y.'

Feeling there was safety in numbers Wally dropped the children off on the edge of the Shakespeare Estate. Janna shivered at the sight of Oaktree Court, a great Victorian pile with fluorescent lighting and bars on the windows. Paris jumped out, shuffling towards the front door without looking behind or uttering a word of thanks. He couldn't trust himself not to cry.

Humming Prokofiev One, Miss Cambola was joyfully ringing possible dates for a joint concert with Bagley.

'Time for a drink?' Mags asked Janna as they reached Larks.

'Just let me check my messages.'

'Mess' was the operative word. All the displays in reception had been trashed. Rowan had left a note on her desk:

'Did you mean to switch off your mobile? Ring Ashton the moment you get in. Ditto Russell. Ditto Crispin. Ditto Rod Hyde; he left at 6.30. Girls' toilets blocked as well now. Martin Norman rushed to hospital after fight in playground. Three windows broken. Satan on roof chucking down tiles.'

'I'll come and have that drink,' said Janna, just finding time to open a note from Lydia: 'Lovely day; kids very good. We all missed you but heaven without Cara, please burn this.'

Mercifully the Ghost and Castle was empty, except

for the skeleton propping up the bar. No disaffected Larks staff in sight. Funny how I lived in the pub when I was at Redfords, thought Janna. Her hair still felt on fire where Hengist had stroked it. Mags insisted on buying the drinks and, between gulps, carrying on knitting the scarf for her future son-in-law.

Mags had the beautiful complexion and sweet unruffled serenity, thought Janna, that a Raphael Madonna might have achieved in middle age if her life had not been torn apart by the tragedy of a son's death.

'Thank you ever so much for coming.'

Mags smiled. 'It was a huge success. You're right to be proud of your children. You've given them so much confidence. Both sides were amazed how much they liked each other.'

Mags prayed the saga of Boffin's teeth wouldn't reach the press. She wondered if she should tell Janna about it, then Janna put everything out of her mind by asking her if she'd like to be deputy head.

'You'd be so good, Mags. The kids love and trust you, and so do the staff. Your lessons are so popular and you don't grind axes all day.'

Looking at Janna's little face, at the pallor beneath the dark freckles and the eyes that never seemed far from tears these days, Mags was deeply touched.

'That's the sweetest compliment I've ever been paid. If you're part-time, people regard you as a dilettante. But truly two and a half days a week are enough for me, so I can be there for Tim when he's on a big case and comes home wiped out, and for the children and soon, fingers crossed, the grandchildren who will all want a part of me and expect me to drop everything. And we've got Diane's wedding coming up. I'm better all round if I don't spread myself too thin.

'I'll support you all the way,' she went on, 'and the others aren't that antagonistic. Sam Spink is a trouble-making cow, but you get that in any school. Forget the Dinosaurs. The rest of the staff like you very much, they're just terrified and poisoned by Cara. You must get rid of her.'

'Hengist and your nice husband said the same thing.'

'Cara made a play for Hengist once, asked him to dance. He rejected her with a finesse only he's capable of.'

'Really?' Janna longed to know more, but didn't want to appear too keen. 'I think Cara's mad. Did you see her ripping apart those anemones? Do you think there's a conspiracy against me?'

Mags looked up, startled.

'The *Gazette* won't leave me alone. There was a piece yesterday about the staff leaving in droves. Russell and S and C deliberately thwart my every move. They seem to be willing me to fail.'

'I'll have a word with Tim,' said Mags thoughtfully. 'You know I disagree passionately with private education, but I have to say both teachers and pupils were terrific today.'

Over at Bagley, Cosmo, Lubemir and Anatole were enjoying their game: shoving Xavier's dark head down the lavatory, holding him under as they pulled the chain.

'Might wash you white, black shit. Black shit should go down the bog,' taunted Cosmo, giving Xav a vicious kick in the ribs.

'Don't bruise him,' reproved Anatole.

'Bruises don't show up on black shit.'

'He is not getting whiter.' Lubemir yanked Xav out by the hair to examine his face. 'Try some bleach.' He emptied half a bottle of Domestos into the water before ramming Xav's head back again.

Xav squeezed shut his eyes so the bleach couldn't burn them but, forced to open his mouth to breathe, gulped and choked as bleach went down his throat.

Cosmo meanwhile, having wolfed down some muesli

and a crushed bloc of lavatory freshener, retched and, yanking aside Xav's head, threw up into the lavatory bowl before shoving Xav back again.

'In you go, black bastard.'

Xav thought he'd choke with revulsion and his lungs would explode with pain. Death would be better than this.

Please God, let me die.

Mags had left her Renault outside the Ghost and Castle. As Janna wandered back to Larks's car park, she found the words: 'Go back to Yorkshire you dirty bitch', scrawled in scarlet lipstick across her windscreen.

I mustn't panic, she told herself. It couldn't be Cara, she was off sick. Heart thumping, terrified her brakes had been tampered with, or a mad murderer might rise up in the back to strangle her, she drove very slowly back to Wilmington.

As she leapt out of her car, Partner hurtled out of Lily's house, then stopped at her feet, whimpering and crying.

'I'm so sorry to leave you so long, love,' she said, gathering him up, bitterly ashamed that he was trembling as violently as she was.

Lily admitted that the little dog had missed her dreadfully.

'He's fine with me for a bit, then he seems to panic you're not coming back.'

'I'll take him into Larks tomorrow,' said Janna. 'I guess I need a guard dog.'

35

Janna was so tired, neither terror of Cara nor dreams of Hengist kept her awake. It seemed only a second later that her alarm clock was battering her brain. Six o'clock already. Tugging a pillow over her head for five more minutes, she was roused at a quarter to seven by Partner tugging off her duvet with his teeth.

Thanking him profusely, showering, dressing, wolfing a piece of toast and marmalade, she took her cup of coffee, torch and dog out for a quick run across the fields, soaking her trousers with dew, tripping over molehills, splashing through streams.

'In winter I get up at night And dress by yellow candle-light.'

Partner charged ahead, barking joyfully, chasing rabbits, but as they returned to the cottage, his tummy dragged along the ground, his pointed ear and the remaining plumes on his tail drooped lower and lower at the prospect of Janna abandoning him.

'It's all right, darling, you're coming too.'

Hope springing eternal, Partner gazed up, ginger head on one side, onyx eyes shining, then went berserk, squeaking and jumping four feet off the ground. As she put his basket and a bag of biscuits in the car, he rushed off to collect his lead, then leapt into his basket in the back.

There was an apricot glow in the east. As they passed

303

the signpost for Bagley, she wondered if Hengist ever thought of her. She kept remembering his powerful body thrust against hers. She must find herself a boyfriend.

'I've got you,' she called back to Partner, who swished his tail, then as she crossed the bridge into Larkminster, her mobile beeped. Glancing at the screen, she read: 'Yr toff Bagley friends won't save you, you rancid old tart' and nearly ran into one of the Victorian lamp-posts. She must go to the police.

Shaking uncontrollably, moaning with terror, she sought refuge in the boarded-up newsagent's next to the Ghost and Castle. As she picked up the papers, she was fractionally cheered when the owner, Mrs Kamani, who was always grumbling about the children shop-lifting, suddenly announced how delightful they'd been on television last night.

Having installed Partner with a Bonio in his basket under her desk, Janna distracted herself from the foul text message by checking on yesterday's press coverage. It was pretty good except for the *Gazette*, which angled its report on caring Stancombe giving Larks a £25,000 minibus and taking time out from his impossibly busy schedule to fly down to Bagley.

As the purpose of his generosity had been to rescue Larks pupils from the poverty of their ambitions and a life of crime, Stancombe had felt it sadly ironic that after these same pupils had stormed the helicopter during the opening ceremony, several gold ashtrays, a silver cigarette case and a bottle of champagne had gone missing.

'Rubbish,' howled Janna. 'The helicopter was also swarming with Bagley pupils.'

The piece was illustrated by a glamorous picture of Stancombe and Jade, of Larks and Bagley children looking bored, and of Janna, as usual, smiling coyly up at Hengist.

When was Col Peters going to ease up?

Thank God the television coverage would be seen by millions more people than read the *Gazette*.

Most of our parents can't read anyway, Janna was shocked to find herself thinking. The rest of the press had followed Venturer's lead, photographing Kylie in her flowered dress: 'We thought Bagley would be stuck-up snobs, but they were really nice people.'

The *Guardian* had clearly dropped Sheena's piece on Stancombe, who'd be livid. They had however included a charming photo of the black children: Xav, Aysha and Feral, sending Aysha's proud but panic-stricken mother out to buy every copy in case her husband saw it on his return from Pakistan.

Only that most scurrilous of tabloids the *Scorpion* excelled itself by showing Cosmo's somewhat fuzzy pictures of the geography master's wife flashing her Brazilian as she descended from Stancombe's chopper and of 'Rough Trade Counter' on the back of the bus, which had a caption: 'This is what snooty Bagley really thought of Larks'. However, this hadn't stopped 'Toff Love', the caption on a picture of Kylie Rose, 'a 13-year-old single parent', breaking down social barriers with the Hon. Jack Waterlane behind a holly bush.

'Jack's lush,' enthused Kylie Rose . . .

Janna couldn't stop laughing. What would Hengist say? She was brought back to earth by a call from Crispin Thomas furiously cataloguing her iniquities. How could Janna have deserted her post? One would have thought Nelson had gone ashore to frolic with Lady Hamilton during the Battle of Trafalgar.

'If you grant a handful of kids absurd privileges, the rest will act up.'

Janna left the telephone on her desk, made a cup of coffee, and when she picked it up again, Crispin was still snuffling.

'If Rod Hyde hadn't held the fort yesterday . . .'

Oh God, another text message was coming through. Janna steeled herself, but it was from Hengist.

'Hurrah for Toff Love. Ignore *Gazette*, coverage great and should take Sheena down a few square pegs. A bientot. H B-T.'

Trying to keep the silly grin off her face, Janna found Crispin still yakking: 'I'm surprised you have nothing to say to justify such a lapse. It will be top of the agenda at the governors' meeting next week.'

As Wally came in whistling Prokofiev One, Janna handed him a bottle of whisky.

'What's this for? I had a great time. The wife loved seeing us on TV and taped the programme. That Emlyn Davies is a smashing bloke. And that's a nice little dog. Is this Partner? Looks like a cross between a fox and a woodlouse. Come on, boy.'

Partner cowered in his basket.

Then Rowan raced in weighed down by Tesco carrier bags.

'How did it go? Lovely piece on Venturer; the kids looked so happy and you looked so pretty, and you were great, Wally. Oh! This must be Partner, isn't he adorable? Look at his sweet face. He must be part Cairn, part Norfolk. Look at his poor bare tail, but I'm sure it'll grow back. Goodness he's sweet.'

Thus encouraged, Partner edged forward.

'We had a lovely day at Bagley Hall,' announced Janna at assembly. 'Later, we'll tell you about it and the wonderful things planned for the future. But first, I want to introduce a new member of Larks. I hope you'll be very kind to him; it's so hard starting late in the term.

'Many of you have been asking what happened to the little dog who nearly died when some cruel boys tied a rocket to his tail. The answer is he recovered, he's living with me in Wilmington and he's so clever, when I overslept this morning, he pulled the duvet off my bed to wake me up. But he gets frightened on his own during the day and howls, thinking he's been abandoned again. So he's going to come to school every day to be our mascot, bringing us luck. His name is Partner,' she added as Rowan carried him proudly up onto the stage and handed him over.

'I want you all to say "Howdy, Partner", like the cowboys.'

'Howdy, Partner,' roared the delighted children.

Partner quivered at such a big crowd, particularly when Janna carried him down the steps so Year Seven in the front row could stroke him. Then suddenly he caught sight of Paris, who had hugged him and so gently bathed his sore tail and, leaping down, he jumped into Paris's arms.

'Now we really know how much time Paris Alvaston spends at our Senior Team Leader's cottage,' muttered Red Robbie, who was furious that Gloria had had such a lovely time in a capitalist playground yesterday.

'That remark should be withdrawn,' cried an outraged Cambola. She strode up to the piano. 'Now we will sing "All Things Bright and Beautiful", with special emphasis on the Lord God loving all creatures great and small.'

Cambola started playing. The children started singing, but had great difficulty carrying on when Partner put back his ginger head, like the fox in Aesop's fable, and howled until Miss Cambola rose from the piano and conducted him with her pencil, so he howled even louder and the singing broke up because everyone was laughing so much.

As a dog who could end assembly five minutes early, Partner's fame was assured.

36

Cara had only been off sick five minutes before a flood of Larks teachers, realizing how wonderful school was without her venomous demoralizing presence and unable to face the prospect of her return, handed in their notice. These included Adele, Robbie Rushton's deputy, who would now have no means of supporting two little children; Jessamy, Mike Pitts's teaching assistant; Gloria, the gymnast; Lydia and Lance, the newly qualified teachers; and, most surprisingly, Miss Basket, who, because no one else would employ her, everyone thought would ensure her pension by clinging on by her bitten fingernails to the end of time.

Lydia summed up the exodus:

'I love Larks and you, Janna, but I can't handle Cara any more. I feel sick with terror every morning. She's supposed to watch my teaching and encourage me, but I haven't had a page of notes since I've been here. And she punishes me by inciting her favourites to act up. Kitten Meadows stood with her hands on her hips and said, "You're just jealous because I'm hotter than you," then spat in my face. When I complained, Cara just laughed and said, "If you can't handle sassy girls!"

'We're supposed to go to the deputy head if we've got a problem with her, but as he's shagging her anyway, he'd just grass me up, then she'd murder me.

'I'm scared of her, Janna. Please let me leave at Christmas.'

'I'll see what I can do, but please reconsider.' Janna felt bitterly ashamed that she hadn't protected poor Lydia, who'd been so plump and pretty when she'd joined the school, and was now a thin, pale, trembling wraith.

She must tackle Cara, but how?

It was the same at governors' meetings. Although Cara, as a teacher governor, left the room when staff, salary or financial matters were discussed, Stormin' Norman, like Mike Pitts, would report back any snide remarks and Cara would put in the stiletto.

Janna herself grew increasingly fearful as the obscene telephone calls continued. One night her tyres were let down; on another a circle of barbed wire rested against her windscreen.

Some people are terrified of snakes, others of spiders. Janna was terrified of madness. As an imaginative child often left alone at night when her mother went out cleaning, she'd lived in fear that the inhabitants of a nearby lunatic asylum would escape across the fields and come screaming and scrabbling at her bedroom window. Later, dotty Miss Havisham and Mr Rochester's first wife, imprisoned upstairs with her crazy mirthless laugh, had haunted Janna's nightmares. For years, she wouldn't touch apples in case they'd been poisoned by the evil queen in Snow White. Most frightening of all was the wicked witch in The Wizard of Oz, who, in her sudden appearances and wanton capacity for disruption, reminded her most of Cara.

Thank God for brave little Partner, curled up on her bed or at her feet. Janna longed to put on Dorothy's shiny red shoes, gather him up like Toto and escape down the Yellow Brick Road – but first she must stand up to the governors . . .

Cara in fact limped in a week later, flanked by Satan, Monster and sassy Kitten Meadows, and in time for the after-school governors' meeting. This was held in Cara's classroom, whose walls were covered with masks of everyone from Tony Blair to Maria Callas, gazing sightlessly down from the black walls. Blood-stained rubber knives, instead of scarlet anemones, stood in a blue vase on the table.

Cara looked so deathly pale and red-eyed, and her rasping voice was so pathetically muted, Janna wondered why she had ever been scared of her.

'That's green base and red eyeshadow,' muttered a passing Pearl scornfully.

Fear is the parent of cruelty, but also of sycophancy. Thus staff and pupils were so terrified that Cara, through her KGB system, would learn they had been slagging her off that she returned to a heroine's welcome of cards, flowers and bottles of wine.

There was also a full house at the governors' meeting.

Sir Hugo Betts had had a good lunch and was fighting sleep. Sol the undertaker had just had the satisfaction of burying a very rich local businessman. Cara was flanked by a solicitous Stormin' Norman and by Crispin, who was wearing dark glasses to hide a stye and flustering Miss Basket who, in the absence of Rowan at the dentist, was taking the minutes on her laptop and kept begging people to 'slow down please'. Basket was also terrified that Cara might have bugged Janna's office and found out why she was leaving.

Ashton Douglas was flipping distastefully through a pile of cuttings on the Bagley jaunt. Sir Hugo Betts put on a second pair of spectacles to admire Sheena's Brazilian. Russell Lambert, his mouth sinking at the corners like the mask of tragedy on the wall, exuded disapproval, particularly at Partner curled up on Janna's knee.

Ashton kicked off, deploring Janna's involvement in the trip to Bagley, 'against the advice and pwinciples of your colleagues and your Labour/Lib Dem county council, who you know are violently opposed to integwation. The result was an unprecedented outbweak of destruction and a lamentable pwess.'

'It was not lamentable, except for the *Gazette*,' protested Janna. 'I've had so many nice emails. It's been so good for the kids' morale.'

Support then came from an unexpected source.

'My Kylie had the most wonderful day of her life,' enthused Chantal Peck.

'We noticed,' said Stormin' Norman sourly.

'Sally Brett-Taylor was most gracious to Kylie Rose, encouraging her to persevere with her singing, because it's a flexible career for a single mother. Cosmo, Dame Hermione Harefield's son, also said Kylie's voice is remarkable. The day was a 'uge success.'

'Because your slag of a daughter got orf with an 'Ooray.' Stormin' Norman was brandishing her short umbrella like a baseball bat.

Chantal, however, decided to rise above this insult.

'Jack is a charmer,' she said icily. 'He's already texted Kylie Rose seventeen times.'

'I'm sure he'd love you as a muvver-in-law,' snarled Stormin'.

'Ladies, ladies,' said Russell smoothly. 'Cara wishes to make a point.'

'I don't feel,' quavered Cara, 'that whoever planned this ill-judged trip appreciated the fragile egos of our students. Anarchy broke out because those left behind felt undervalued.'

''Ear, 'ear,' growled Stormin'.

'We have great plans for the future,' said Janna quickly, 'for a joint concert and a joint play next term. The theatre at Bagley is big enough for all our parents and children, so no one will feel excluded.'

'Except the Larks head of drama and English,' said Cara pathetically.

'Please slow down,' wailed Miss Basket.

'We can't spend an entire meeting discussing Bagley Hall and Larks,' said Ashton.

'I would like to register,' boomed Russell Lambert, 'that I found all the publicity so distasteful, I'm contemplating stepping down.'

Janna murmured:

> 'He, stepping down
> By zigzag paths, and juts of pointed rock,
> Came on the shining levels of the lake . . .'

Her thoughts were wandering. Odd that King Arthur and St Joseph, two of the most famous cuckolds in the world, were also regarded as the most noble of men.

'Janna,' said Ashton sharply.

'Sorry, I was miles away,' mumbled Janna, which didn't help.

'We have decided to form a sub-committee to discuss the Larks–Bagley partnership,' went on Ashton.

'Why not a Government enquiry?' quipped Sol the undertaker, winking at Janna.

'Let us move on to the high level of truancy,' went on Russell . . .

'It's down ten per cent,' protested Janna.

'That's not enough.'

'Anyone like one of my choccy biccies?' said Cara, getting a packet out of her bag. 'So many presents and I got forty-two get-well cards.'

'No one's used to you ever taking time off,' gushed Miss Basket, blushing even redder as she met Janna's eye.

'Could we instead move on to wedundancy?' said Ashton.

As teacher governors were excluded from discussions about staff or financial matters, Russell asked Basket and Cara to leave.

'I can speak for all of us in saying how pleased we are you're back, Cara.'

'Hear, hear,' cried Miss Basket.

'Thank you,' whispered Cara.

Crispin leapt up to open the door for them, adding: 'Cara's a lovely woman, such a dedicated teacher.'

'I hope she hasn't come back too soon,' said Russell. 'She looks very pulled down.'

'Wedundancies,' said Ashton. 'I'll make notes now Miss Basket's gone. We've examined your budget situation, Janna. Your only hope is to instigate at least eight wedundancies.'

Janna, who was drawing a picture of Crispin as a pig in a trilby, replied that it was sorted.

Ashton looked up, startled.

'Nine people handed in their notice this week.'

'Whatever for?' said Russell.

Janna took a deep breath. She might as well be hung for a Sharpe as a lamb.

'They're all terrified of Cara.'

'Nonsense,' said Ashton.

'This is disgraceful,' exploded Russell. 'Look at all the cards and flowers greeting her return.'

'Those people were sucking up to her, as his minions fawn over Saddam Hussein. Cara shamelessly favours certain children over others.' Janna looked straight at Stormin' Norman. 'That's why they sent her cards.'

'These are very serious accusations,' said Ashton.

'And very serious transgressions. I have already given Cara three formal warnings for intimidating children, and made a note of numerous others. I also assumed that teacher governors left the room during human resources discussions, so that the rest of the board could talk off the record in the strictest confidence.'

'Of course,' said Russell heartily. 'Within these four walls.'

'I'd therefore like to reiterate that Cara Sharpe is poisoning our school.'

There was a squawk of a tape running out.

'Ha,' said Janna. 'So this meeting is being recorded.'

313

Pouncing on Stormin's bag, she whipped out a recorder and played it back.

'"Cara Sharpe is poisoning our school",' said the tape.

'I must have left it on by mistake,' puffed Stormin', for once discomforted.

'I'm sure,' said Janna. 'Just for the record, I'm keeping this.' Removing the tape, she dropped it into her bag. Then she turned furiously on Ashton and Russell. 'I don't understand you. Because of my ailing budget you demand redundancies. But when nine teachers hand in their notices, which will cost you nothing compared with the vast amount you'll have to fork out if you have to make people redundant, you don't seem remotely pleased. This saves money, which I thought was your top priority.'

'I agree,' said Sol. 'Janna's achieved what you wanted, cheaply and painlessly, so stop whingeing.'

'Hear, hear,' said Sir Hugo, waking up.

The meeting broke up in uproar.

Only after she had escaped did Janna start shivering. How long would it take Cara to get her revenge?

When she finally got home several hours later, the outside light came on to illuminate a front door daubed with red paint: 'Get out of Larkshire, cradle-snatching bitch'.

Far more dreadful, Partner was frantically sniffing at something on the step. It was a little black cat with its throat cut, its poor body still warm. The nutters were out to get her.

Running into the house, she rang Mags Gablecross and left a terrified, pleading message.

37

After a night with her four-poster shoved against the bedroom door, Janna was passionately relieved first thing to get a call from Chief Inspector Gablecross. He and Mags had been away meeting fellow in-laws and only just checked their messages. Could he pop in around eleven-thirty after break, when hopefully most staff and children would be in lessons?

Janna liked the Chief Inspector as much as when she first met him. The world immediately seemed a better and safer place. Face to face across her desk, rather than side by side at the Winter Gardens dinner, she noticed the shrewdness of his curly lashed green eyes. His rugby player's body, running not unpleasantly to fat, and his slow, soft, gentle voice, evoking the drinking of cider in pubs on the edge of fields of buttercups, reminded her a lot of Emlyn Davies.

And after Janna had reiterated how much she liked and admired Mags, and Gablecross had said how much he liked Partner, who was now chewing on a dried pig's ear, and didn't Janna think he was part dachshund, part corgi, Janna shut the door and told him everything from the daubed windscreen to the murdered cat.

'Cara should be having a rest period,' Janna said finally, 'but she's taking Nine E, which includes the Wolf Pack, because Lydia stayed at home. She's really conscientious but she couldn't hack it now Cara's back.'

Janna was badly frightened, observed Gablecross, but fighting like a little terrier. He admired her guts.

'Could you show me round the school?'

The Chief Inspector had an even more dramatic effect on the children than Uncle Harley. The din in the corridors subsided as though a radio had been turned off. Pupils slid into classrooms. Guilty parties shot into the toilets. Satan Simmons leapt out of a window he'd just broken and set off bleeding like a pig down the drive.

Year Nine E were reading *The Mayor of Casterbridge*, which Paris thought was a fabulous book. Was it possible that his own father had sold him and his mother at a fair, and his mother, unable to support him, had left him on the children's home steps? He was touched Henshaw the Mayor loved Elizabeth-Jane just as much when he discovered she wasn't his natural daughter. Perhaps some father could one day love him. He also liked Hardy's pessimism. He'd have made a good *EastEnders* scriptwriter.

Paris, on the other hand, was churning inside. Lydia, who normally took this class, had thoughtlessly asked the pupils to write an essay about their family tree and bring in photos of their parents and themselves as babies.

Most of the children on the Shakespeare Estate hadn't seen their fathers for years, if ever. Cara was joyfully poised to skin Lydia alive for such gross insensitivity, but meanwhile she intended to have fun and with a cackle picked up Rocky's photograph.

'What a hideous baby you were.'

As Rocky's face fell like a chastised Rottweiler, the class tittered out of fear, rather than agreement.

'You were an even uglier baby, Feral,' went on Cara, 'and goodness me, where did your mother meet your father, Pearl?'

'In the dole queue,' said Pearl sulkily.

''Spect it's the only time they did meet,' taunted Satan. In the front row with Kitten Meadows, who'd had a row with Johnnie Fowler, he was egging Cara on. 'Pearl's father's inside.'

'And when my dad comes out, he'll get you if you don't stop fucking bugging me,' spat Pearl.

'Don't swear.' Cara turned with such venom, Pearl shrank away.

Cara had reached Paris. Beside him Graffi, stressed that he had a zit bigger than the Millennium Dome, was texting Milly, whom he was meeting for a first date after school. Paris had had a lousy week. He'd borrowed a copy of *Private Lives* from Bagley library without asking and last night, kids in the home had ripped it to pieces. Inside it had been signed 'To Hengist, love Noël'. He'd meant to give it back, but now no one would believe him. He wasn't sleeping because of Janna; he'd been watching her all week and knew she was unhappy. He'd hardly spoken to her since the Bagley trip, but he'd been taking Partner for walks round the school grounds.

Cara was poised for the kill. Kitten and Satan were grinning in anticipation.

'I see you've forgotten to bring in any photographs or produce an essay, Paris.' Then, when Paris didn't answer: 'Have you lost your tongue?'

'I don't have parents to write about,' he muttered.

'He don't know who they are and he hasn't got no photographs of himself as a baby nor a family tree,' protested Graffi furiously.

'How unfortunate,' drawled Cara, then cruelly intoned:

'"Rattle his bones over the stones; He's only a pauper, whom nobody owns!"'

Only a few grasped the significance of the lines. Fear of Cara inhibited even the Wolf Pack.

Cara detested Paris for his beauty, his brains and,

317

most of all, for his adoration of Janna. She had seen his lovelorn looks and had pieced together torn-up notes in the bin. Stalking Janna herself, she'd had to be very careful not to be apprehended by him.

Gablecross and Janna had just slid into the classroom and witnessed Cara's narrow scarlet back quivering like a cobra poised to strike. At the sight of Gablecross, Feral edged towards the window.

'Where are you off to, Feral Jackson? Sit down,' screeched Cara. Then, turning back to Paris, with her mad laugh: 'I'm not surprised your mother didn't want to keep you. If you only had a fraction more charm . . . Still, I'm sure Janna is like a mother to you, or would you rather be her toyboy?'

Cara had lost it, evil seemed to gush out of her. The class edged away. Only Paris stood his ground. Janna was poised to move in, but Gablecross put his hand on her arm.

'Can't you give me an answer?' screamed Cara. 'You insolent lout.'

'Shut up,' yelled Paris. 'Janna's the loveliest woman in the world. You're just a jealous old bitch.'

Next moment, a mobile rang and Graffi snatched it up. His shoulders hunched in ecstasy: 'Milly, lovely!' As Cara swung round to silence him, he thrust out his palm in a lordly fashion: 'Talk to the hand, dearie.'

Paris made the mistake of laughing. Next moment Cara had whacked him so hard that she left a red handprint darkening on his face; then, as he ducked, balling his fists to strike her, she lashed at him again with the back of her hand. Unable to stay neutral a moment longer, Partner wriggled out of Janna's clutches and, yapping furiously, rushed forward to defend his friend.

'You fucking animal,' screamed Cara, snatching up a pair of scissors lying on the table and jabbing first at Partner, then at Paris.

'Put that down,' thundered Gablecross.

A heavy man but as quick on his feet as Feral's idol,

Thierry Henry, he was across the room grabbing Cara's arms from behind and slapping on handcuffs.

'Let me go,' she screeched.

'Cara Sharpe, I am arresting you. You do not have to say anything, but . . .'

'Just like *The Bill*,' cried Kylie in ecstasy.

Janna called Russell Lambert.

'You'd better call an emergency governors' meeting. I've got rid of ten teachers now. I've just fired Cara Sharpe.'

'Hey ho, the witch is dead,' sang the children, racing along the corridors and round the playground and for once no one hushed them. By the afternoon, a raving mad Cara down at the police station had, between bouts of wild laughter, confessed to everything from graffitiing Janna's windscreen to leaving the murdered black cat outside Jubilee Cottage. By late afternoon the teachers, realizing Cara had really gone, started sidling into Janna's office, saying that, after a lot of heart-searching, they'd decided not to resign. Even arch red Robbie Rushton announced that he couldn't live with himself deserting a sinking ship.

Refraining from expressing doubt that anyone else could live with him, Janna took him and everyone else back, and then went out and got drunk with them all in the Ghost and Castle. Mike Pitts bought her a huge gin and orange, and confided that he actually approved of the Larks–Bagley partnership and it would be grand if they could get a football team up and running, then admitted he'd played once for Brentford.

Partner had a wonderful evening, picking up the general euphoria, being fed crisps and pork scratchings, sitting on the bar stool being fussed over as everyone discussed his possible parentage.

'He can take over from Cara as a teacher governor,' said Mags. 'Essential not to have a spy or a sneak.'

Partner dusted the bar stool with his increasingly plumey tail.

The only real resistance to Cara's sacking came from Satan and Monster, who, revved up on crack and armed with crowbars the following morning, threatened Janna on her way to assembly. Partner, however, had barked so furiously before flying at Satan's ankles that both Satan and Monster had fled down the drive. Enough people witnessed this display of canine courage to secure Satan's exclusion and Monster's long-term suspension.

With Monster, Satan and Cara out of the way, children terrorized in the past came flooding back into school over the next few weeks, and attendance went up by twenty per cent.

Partner, who had acquired cult status by seeing off the forces of darkness, also proved a huge help in the battle against truancy. Each week, the class with the best attendance was rewarded with the task of looking after Partner for the next week. Partner adored children and, as long as Janna left her door open and he could pop back and check she was there, was quite happy. He was soon heading and pushing footballs around with his nose and delivering praise postcards, an idea Janna had picked up from Hengist, and certificates of merit. With one child holding one end of the skipping rope, and Charlie Topolski, who was in a wheelchair, holding the other, Partner learnt to skip. When he got tired, he would leap onto Charlie's knee, lick his cheek and curl up.

Because he had suffered himself, the little dog seemed to know instinctively how to comfort a lonely child. Bad readers grew in confidence when allowed to read to Partner. When a school photograph was taken, he took pride of place on Janna's knee.

38

Janna decided to postpone crossing the bridge of redundancies which, if it were anything like the bridge over the River Fleet in the rush hour, would take for ever. Right now she needed a head of English and drama.

In the past Janna had not felt confident enough to bring in her own people. Now Larks was so much happier, she felt justified in approaching Vicky Fairchild, an aptly named beauty of twenty-nine, who looked nearer sixteen. Vicky had long, dark hair, which fell in a thick fringe over melting, dark brown eyes and a pearly complexion, which grew more luminous with tiredness. She was incredibly slender, making the much shorter Janna feel like a bull terrier, and as a member of Janna's department at Redfords, had been an admirer and a huge support.

When Janna rang her to offer her head of drama, adding that as Vicky would have to give in her notice, she presumably couldn't start until the summer, Vicky instantly revealed she was leaving Redfords at Christmas.

'It was so horrible there without you, Jannie.' Then, in her sweet, breathy little girl's voice: 'And I haven't been well. Nothing serious.'

Vicky had also decided to leave because she'd planned to join her boyfriend, Matt, in Bermuda, but that hadn't worked out, so she'd simply adore to come to Larks.

'I love the Cotswolds and I've read all about you forming a partnership with Bagley – that's so cool, I bet they've got a glorious theatre, and Hengist B-T is so inspirational. You've done so well, Jannie, you always know how to motivate people.'

'Larks is a very tough school,' confessed Janna.

'So was Redfords to start with. Oh Janna, thank you so, so much, it's such a compliment.'

The governors had been rather stuffy about the sacking of Cara – wasn't it rather a coincidence that Chief Inspector Gablecross had been in the building when one of Janna's favourites, Paris Alvaston, started acting up? Shouldn't Janna be advertising Cara's job? But the special interview panel of susceptible males – Sir Hugo, Sol the undertaker, Russell and Mike Pitts as deputy head – soon forgot their doubts when they clapped eyes on Vicky, glowing in a scarlet suit and long black boots as shiny as her hair.

'This is my dream job,' she told them. 'I really feel I can make a difference. A good drama production can unite an entire school, and raise their profile sky high in the area.'

'She was so interested in Larks,' said Russell Lambert, smoothing his pewter-grey hair, which, translated, meant that Vicky, briefed by Janna, knew Russell's name and occupation as head of the local planning committee and that the *Guardian* had once described him as 'Larks's personable chair'.

As part of the interview, Vicky had to be watched teaching a class. Janna craftily threw her to the Wolf Pack and troublemakers of Year Nine E. Thus Paris, Graffi, Feral and Johnnie sat in the front row, their dropped jaws resting on their trainers. Pearl, Kylie and even sassy Kitten Meadows were equally captivated as Vicky talked about the havoc caused by gang warfare and how Juliet had been let down by her parents and Friar Lawrence.

Then she showed them clips from the fights in the Leonardo di Caprio film, and suggested how brilliant it would be if Bagley and Larks did a joint *Romeo and Juliet* with Bagley as the Montagues and Larks as the Capulets.

'Wiv the Hon. Jack and Kylie Rose as Romeo and Juliet and both sets of parents going ballistic,' shouted Graffi to much laughter.

It was a happy, productive class. If Vicky could handle the Wolf Pack, reasoned the interview panel, she would take on anything, and promptly appointed her.

Effusive in her gratitude, Vicky floated off with Russell to meet Des Res, the smooth local estate agent who'd been so dismissive about Larks at the Winter Gardens dinner. Janna prayed Des wouldn't disillusion Vicky, but she rang ecstatically from the train.

'Des has found me a heavenly flat in the Close and we bumped into Ashton Douglas: such a darling. So is Des. What did you do to upset him, Jannie? I said I wouldn't hear a word against you.'

Lucky to have the kind of beauty that opened doors. Janna glanced at her increasingly lined face in her office mirror. She in turn was lucky to have a friend like Vicky to stick up for her.

'I'm so sad we didn't have more time to gossip,' went on Vicky. 'Everyone at Redfords is desperate to know how you're getting on.'

'How's Stew?' asked Janna, testing the emotional water.

'Sent his love. He's such a letch, pulled me onto his knee at a party the other day, and he had this huge erection. I don't know how Beth puts up with him.'

Janna was surprised at the pain, as though a lovely Chippendale chair of her past had turned out to be a fake.

'I'm so excited about my new flat – and it's dirt cheap,' added Vicky.

Next day, Janna received a note through her letterbox at home from Des Res. He had several clients who'd be very interested in Jubilee Cottage, would she like a free valuation?

'Is this a hint?' wrote back Janna furiously. 'I'll give you a free assessment – you're an absolute shit.'

Having posted the letter, she got her hand stuck trying to retrieve it, and had to hang about until the postman came to open the pillar box.

As a result of Vicky's interview, it was decided that Bagley and Larks would stage a production of *Romeo and Juliet* during the spring term.

Christmas is the cruellest time for children in care. Bombarded constantly by images on television or in the high street of loving families and piles of gold-wrapped presents round glittering Christmas trees, aware that they have no parents or parents that can't look after them, the children rampage, rage, roar and weep at their loss. There is no refuge from their unhappiness.

Janna had tentatively suggested Paris should spend Christmas with her and Partner, with Aunt Lily and the Wolf Pack coming in on Christmas Day, but Paris had flatly refused, still mortified by Cara's cruel jibes about his ambition to become Janna's toyboy and terrified that, alone in the house, he might not be able to control his passion.

So Janna went to Yorkshire to stay with Auntie Glad and Paris remained at Oaktree Court, the sound and fury only redeemed by a navy blue sweater sent him by Janna, which he hid under his bed in case the other inmates nicked it, and by steeping himself in the beauty and sadness of *Romeo and Juliet*.

'Heaven is here,' he kept murmuring:

'Where Juliet/Janna lives, and every cat and dog
And little mouse, every unworthy thing,
Live here in heaven and may look on her;
But Romeo/Paris may not.'

If he couldn't have Janna, at least let her be proud of
him as Romeo.

39

Vicky arrived in January 2002, and cured truancy among boys almost overnight. Fathers suddenly seemed wildly keen to come in and paint classrooms. Rod Hyde, Ashton and Russell continually described Vicky as a breath of fresh air.

Janna was ashamed of feeling a little disconsolate. She knew her children at Larks were what mattered, but it would have been nice to have a man in her life, particularly as Hengist had been away and inattentive and even more particularly when Vicky came rushing into her office on a late, grey January afternoon, crying:

'Hengist Brett-Taylor has just dropped in and mistook me for one of the kids. He said girls at Larks were getting prettier and prettier, and isn't he drop-dead gorgeous?'

'So was Satan in *Paradise Lost*,' snapped Janna. Was she becoming a disagreeable old crone like Cara? 'Where is he?'

'Oh, he's gone. I said you were closeted with Ashton Douglas, so he said, "Rather Janna than me," and he'd ring you. So exciting we're starting casting Romeo and Juliet tomorrow.'

'"We?"' Janna tried to keep the indignation out of her voice.

'The drama departments: Jason Fenton and me. Emlyn Davies. And Hengist wants to have input.'

'So do I,' said Janna grimly.

The auditions took place in the General Bagley Room on a bitterly cold morning. Even with the play cut by nearly a half by Bagley's head of English, Piers Fleming, there were excellent parts not just for the two lovers but for Romeo's friends, Mercutio and Benvolio; Juliet's parents, Lord and Lady Capulet; Friar Lawrence; not to mention Juliet's volatile cousin, Tybalt, Prince of Cats; and Juliet's nurse.

Two hundred children had applied to take part but, as Year Ten and upwards would be occupied with GCSE and A level work through the spring term, it was decided to cast mostly from Year Nine, and name the production 'Cloud Nine'.

Determined Larks shouldn't let the side down, Janna, and Vicky to a lesser extent, had been giving Larks's pupils a crash course in the play and equipping them with speeches to learn or read out. Lit up by her subject, Janna inspired not just Paris, but many others to have a go.

Some had other motives. Kylie was anxious to snog the Hon. Jack again. Rocky went everywhere Kylie did. Pearl was desperate to do the make-up.

Feral wanted to see if Amber Lloyd-Foxe was as disturbing as he remembered. Graffi grasped any opportunity to see Milly. Aysha, forbidden by her heavy father, now back in England, to take part in such immoral frivolity, still longed to see Xavier again. Monster Norman, back in school but missing Satan Simmons and with a massive crush on Vicky, came along for the ride.

The judging panel, sitting at an oblong table armed with pens, notebooks and copies of the text, consisted of Emlyn, who'd been asked by Hengist to keep a lid on everything in case 'naughty little Piers', head of English, went off at half cock. Or whole cock, reflected Emlyn, noticing the way Piers was snuggling up to

Vicky, who was reeking of Trésor and ravishing in a raspberry-pink polo neck and short, tight black skirt. On Vicky's other side, whispering into her ear in an increasingly posh voice and looking very public school in a tweed jacket and dung-coloured cords, was Jason.

Piers and Jason had obviously bonded and would need some reining in, particularly where the budget was concerned, or they'd have David Linley designing Juliet's balcony and Stella McCartney her dresses. Beyond Piers was Janna; achingly aware she hadn't seen Hengist since the day of the balloon launch. He'd rung occasionally pleading overwork but now, grabbing the seat on her right, seemed unsettlingly enchanted to see her. Hengist was in fact eaten up with jealousy because his great rival and old boss David Hawkley, head of Fleetley, had been given a peerage in the New Year's Honours list, and been described in *The Times* that morning as the greatest headmaster of the twentieth/twenty-first century.

Hengist wanted to howl. Instead he stroked Partner, who was half asleep on Janna's knee, and said how he'd missed her and they must have lunch and catch up.

Pupils, meanwhile, hung around gossiping, waiting for the off. The Bagley Babes, Amber, Milly and Jade, all with ski tans paid for by Randal Stancombe, were sitting with Graffi, Feral, Paris, Kylie and Rocky. Jack Waterlane, Junior and Lando had parked themselves in the row behind, also inhabited by a sneering Cosmo, and Anatole the Russian, who was drinking neat vodka out of a teacup.

As Dora Belvedon sidled in, Jade demanded:

'What are you doing here?'

'We were having sex education with Miss Sweet,' replied Dora. 'She was showing us how to roll condoms onto courgettes with the help of K-Y Jelly and got so embarrassed when Bianca asked her what fellatio was that she ran away and we got a free period. So Hengist said I could stay if I was extremely quiet.'

She plonked herself down between Cosmo and Anatole.

'You're incapable of being quiet,' spat Jade.

'Fellatio, fellatio, wherefore art thou fellatio,' sighed Cosmo, who wanted to conduct his beloved orchestra throughout the production but also to play the short, spectacular part of Tybalt.

Feral glanced up at a painting of rugby players leaping in the line-out to distract himself from Amber's thighs. Covered by barely six inches of fawn pleated skirt, they were utterly gorgeous.

'Silly using courgettes as willies,' went on Dora. 'We'll all get a shock when we discover the real thing's red, or pinkish, or purple. They're called zucchini in Italy, I believe.'

'Zucc orf,' said Paris, who'd been miles away in Verona.

To capture his Hooray Henry voice he'd been listening to a tape of Prince Charles; now he was trying to capture the nuances of Jack Waterlane and Lando France-Lynch's voices as they idly discussed snow polo.

'Christ, it's cold, throw another new boy on the fire,' grumbled Cosmo.

Outside, in sympathy, flakes of snow were beginning to settle on General Bagley and his charger.

'All right' – Hengist helped himself to Vicky's tin of Quality Street – 'let's get started, try and keep in alphabetical order. Kirsty, you're first.'

Kirsty Abbot, covered in spots and puppy fat, waddled on and delivered Juliet's speech: '"Gallop apace, you fiery-footed steeds,"' as though she were taking the register at a primary school. Her audience tried not to laugh. Hengist let her run for sixty seconds.

'Thank you, Kirsty.'

'Useless,' scoffed Jade.

'I'd quite like to play Juliet. I learnt the part while I was skiing,' sighed Amber, 'hissing down the white mountains shouting: "Romeo, Romeo! wherefore art thou Romeo?" nearly setting off an avalanche.' She glanced at Feral under her lashes and yanked her skirt an inch higher.

'Paris Alvaston,' shouted Hengist.

I am Giovanni the lad, Paris was psyching himself up. I've gatecrashed the Capulets' ball, which is dripping with upmarket totty, including Rosaline, the beautiful cold bitch who's rejected me and is now wrapped round a rival. Suddenly I catch sight of little Juliet and realize everything I've felt before has been a mockery. When she leaves the party, I follow her, hanging around her garden, trampling on her father's plants.

As he walked to the centre of the room and turned, he could hear the thud of Partner's tail. For a few seconds he stood absolutely still, eyes shut as if in a trance, then, glancing up at the window, said as softly as the falling snow: '"He jests at scars, that never felt a wound."'

And the room went still.

'But, soft! what light through yonder window
    breaks?
It is the east, and Juliet is the sun . . .
See how she leans her cheek upon her hand!
O! that I were a glove upon that hand,
That I might touch that cheek.'

His voice was so filled with tenderness and longing, even Partner wagged his tail again. The only accompaniment was the tick of the clock. Paris then switched to the end of the play, when he discovered Juliet apparently dead in the Capulet tomb.

'"Eyes, look your last! Arms, take your last embrace!"'

Glancing at Janna, Hengist saw her face soaked in tears, and took her hand.

'We've got our Romeo,' he whispered.

As a burst of astonished clapping and foot-stamping

greeted Paris's return to his seat, Feral turned to him in amazement.

'You was wicked, man.'

Graffi, Jack Waterlane and Lando thumped him on the back.

Cosmo, his sallow face alight with malice, was less impressed.

'Talk about Kev and Juliet,' he drawled. 'No wonder the Capulets were devastated their daughter had fallen for such a yob.'

'Shut up, Cosmo,' snapped Hengist.

Paris was unmoved.

'I can do it Hooray Henry, if you like.' Shoving one clenched fist into the palm of the other, talking through gritted teeth, he strolled back to the centre of the room. '"But, sawft! what light through yonder window breaks?"' and sounded so like Prince Charles, everyone howled with laughter.

Wriggling free, Partner scampered towards Paris, who gathered him up, burying his grin in Partner's fur.

'Well done, Paris,' called out Vicky. 'Those one-to-one rehearsals we've been doing have really paid off.'

A hit so early in the proceedings cheered everyone.

'Now we've got to find him a decent Juliet,' said Jason.

Next moment Alex Bruce rolled up, on whom Stancombe had been putting pressure.

'There's a certain young lady, Alex, who'd be devastated if she doesn't land the lead role in this production.'

Stancombe was threatening not to put up the umpteen million pounds to finance the science block. Alex didn't think he could swing his favourite Boffin Brooks to play Romeo, but he was determined Jade should get Juliet.

Walking into the General Bagley Room, he was furious to find Hengist, who'd claimed he was far too busy to show the Archbishop of some African state round the school, stuffing toffees and giggling with Janna Curtis.

Draining his teacup of vodka, Anatole's turn was next.

'He's got to have a decent part too,' murmured Hengist to Janna, 'so we get another jetload of caviar.'

Anatole was in fact very clever and loved Pushkin, Lermontov and Shakespeare as much as vodka and Marlboro Lights.

'I must give it some velly,' he announced and proceeded to make a wonderfully exuberant Mercutio, teasing Tybalt to fight a duel with him: '"Tybalt, you rat-catcher, vill you valk?"'

Then, after Tybalt's sword had run him through, his audience, willing him to live, could feel his vitality ebbing away as he swore a plague on both Capulet and Montague houses.

Again, Janna fighting back tears, was hugged by an equally overjoyed Hengist.

'Darling, we've got our Mercutio, and vats of caviar. Anatole's father might even bring Mr Putin to the first night.'

Dora, who'd been given a mobile cum camera by Cosmo for Christmas, was taking pictures. Alex Bruce, not a fan of Anatole, had just bustled off when a heavily pregnant woman in a flowered smock, socks and Jesus sandals waddled in.

'Who's that?' hissed Graffi. 'She's about to pop.'

'Very appropriately she's called Poppet Bruce,' giggled Dora. 'That's Mr Fussy's wife. She is *so* pants. She teaches RE and never mentions poor Jesus. She's also nicknamed "Maternity Won't Leave" because she keeps having babies. Can you imagine sleeping with Mr Fussy that many times? Then everyone prays she'll never come back, but she always does. She's the worst person I know.'

'Worse than No-Joke Joan?' asked Amber, applying lip gloss.

'There'd be a photo finish,' said Dora darkly.

From his expression as Poppet approached the panel, looking eager, Hengist clearly felt the same about her.

'Hope you don't mind my joining you,' she said. 'R and J has such strong RE overtones with Friar Lawrence and an under-age marriage, I hope I may make suggestions.'

'You're welcome today,' said Hengist coolly, 'but too many cooks . . . I'd leave it to the production team.'

Poppet's lips tightened as she pressed her bulge against the table, waiting for someone to give her their seat. Terrified she might explode, Jason leapt to his feet.

'Come and sit down, Mrs Bruce.' Vicky patted Jason's chair. 'I'm Vicky Fairchild, Larks's head of drama. Of course we welcome input. We're planning to have Arab/Israeli overtones in the street fighting and put the play in modern dress with perhaps Friar Lawrence as a mullah.'

'Are we?' muttered Janna to Hengist, who muttered back: 'Friar Lawrence of Arabia.'

To Poppet's noisy approval and much clashing of bracelets, Boffin Brooks read two of Friar Lawrence's speeches in the high fluting voice of a curate at choral evensong.

'Excellent, excellent, Boffin, although I wish you'd read for Romeo.'

'Only with a recycled carrier bag over his head,' muttered Cosmo.

'Essential, in the bedroom scene and with the rise of STDs,' Poppet was now saying, 'that Romeo is shown to wear a condom.'

'And has a green courgette as a willy,' said Milly, 'which Friar Lawrence has grown in his garden.'

'Ah, here's Jade,' cried Boffin.

'Oh good,' said Poppet.

Jade Stancombe's legs were longer and her pleated skirt shorter even than Amber's; her cream silk shirt and blue cashmere jersey clung to her lovely rapacious body.

'"What's in a name? that which we call a rose By any other name would smell as sweet,"' began Jade, over-acting appallingly.

Everyone tried not to giggle.

'She's dreadful,' whispered Dora.

'"Thou knowest the mask of night is on my face,"' went on Jade.

'And a whole lot of Clarins,' hissed Dora.

'"The more I give to thee, The more I have, for both are infinite,"' concluded Jade, rolling her eyes and clutching her cashmere bosom.

'Bravo, bravo! That was very convincing, Jade,' called out Poppet.

By contrast, Amber, with her hair piled up, her charming lascivious smile and air of insouciance, decided to go for Lady Capulet – 'just for a laugh' – and was brilliant.

'You're booked,' called out Piers. 'Lady C was only twenty-seven.'

Emlyn wondered how long this was going to last. He had a two-hour period on Hitler and the Nazis and rugby practice for the first and second fifteen after that.

Ah, here was Feral. God, the boy was beautiful. There was a chorus of wolf whistles as he prowled in to audition for Tybalt, 'Prince of Cats', the furious play-ground bully who picks fights with everyone, who has comparatively few lines but huge impact on the play.

Coached by Paris until he was word perfect, not caring if he got the part, Feral kept exploding into violence:

'What, drawn, and talk of peace! I hate the word,
As I hate hell, all Montagues and thee:
Have at thee, coward!'

He was booed, hissed, then cheered to the stuccoed ceiling as he sauntered back, grinning, to sit beside Amber.

Cosmo, whose heart was set on playing Tybalt, was not amused.

'Why not give Cosmo Capulet?' Piers was muttering across Janna to Hengist. 'He's the biggest shit in the play, which figures, then Jack Waterlane might just manage the Prince, if I cut his lines to nothing.'

'Good idea,' said Hengist. 'Yes, Vicky?' as she perched on the end of the table beside him.

'At the Capulet ball, why don't we get a wonderful little dancer to play Romeo's ex-girlfriend, Rosaline, and do a fantastically sexy dance with Tybalt, if Feral gets the part – he's an incredible dancer. Then, after being wildly jealous, Paris takes one look at Juliet, and Rosaline is forgotten. It makes the coup de foudre so much more dramatic.'

That was my idea, thought Janna indignantly, particularly when Hengist congratulated Vicky and put forward little Bianca Campbell-Black, who was being tipped as the next Darcey Bussell.

'Let's audition her. At least it would ensure Rupert rolled up on the opening night.'

'Kylie could sing with the band at the ball,' went on Vicky, 'she's got a lovely voice, and Cosmo's Cosmonaughties must be the band.' She smiled winningly at Cosmo, who smouldered back. He must pull Vicky before the opening night.

Pearl, everyone agreed, would be in charge of make-up.

The auditions were nearly over.

Primrose Duddon of the huge boobs, who'd been taking a Grade 7 piano examination, was now making a pitch for the coveted comedy role of Juliet's nurse. Squawking, slapping her thighs, overacting worse than Jade, she reminded Janna of Sam Spink.

'Thank you, Primrose,' said Hengist after a minute.

They were down to the Ws and no one had been out-standing enough to play Juliet. They couldn't have Jade. Then Milly Walton wandered in. Like Amber, she'd only come along for a laugh and a chance to see Graffi. Her auburn curls were scraped back, her ski tan shiny and Graffi had kissed off all her lipstick in a nearby classroom.

'"My bounty is as boundless as the sea,"' she said thoughtfully. '"My love as deep; the more I give to thee, The more I have, for both are infinite."'

Then she turned to Graffi and smiled and Graffi's shaggy black locks rose up on the back of his neck, and his toes turned over. Even Paris took his nose out of *The Iliad*.

Hengist turned to Janna, running the back of his hand down her cheek. 'That's our Juliet. Ruth, her mother, will be so pleased. She's always worried about overshadowing Milly.'

I can't help it, thought Janna, when he strokes me I have to purr.

Graffi, being Williams, was the last to go. He was still clapping Milly when a terrible thought struck him. If Paris got Romeo and Milly got Juliet, Paris would spend the whole play kissing and shagging her. Paris was much too good-looking. Graffi hated the thought of his woman making out with someone else.

He had been going to pitch for Benvolio but, nipping off into the nearby dining room, he grabbed a white damask napkin from the table laid for the African Archbishop, folded it into a triangle and wrapped it round his forehead, tying two ends behind his head. Then he grabbed a drying-up cloth from the kitchens, tying it round his waist. Leafing through the text, he found the place and bustled in as Juliet's nurse, the most irritating woman in literature, and brought the house down.

'The nurse in drag, why didn't we think of it?' said Hengist.

336

'We can cut a lot, but he's hilarious,' agreed Piers.

Then, after all the teasing and horseplay, Graffi's grief when he found his beloved Juliet apparently dead – the scene Primrose Duddon had dreadfully over-played – was truly touching.

Hengist hugged Janna once more.

'Your boy's come good, darling.' Then, rising to his feet: 'Thank you very much, you all did very well. Think we've found some real stars. Go off and have lunch and we'll let you know.'

40

When the cast list was pinned on the noticeboards of both schools two days later, whoops of excitement and not a little jeering at Larks greeted the news that Paris would be playing Romeo; Feral, Tybalt; Graffi, the Nurse; and Kylie Rose both the Chorus and a blues singer at the Capulets' masked ball.

Janna was particularly gratified that Rocky had been cast as the Capulet heavy who bit his thumb (the Shakespearean equivalent of giving a middle finger) to the Montagues and Monster had landed the small, crucial part of the apothecary who sells deadly poison to Romeo, 'and probably will,' quipped Graffi. Monster was chuffed to bits at the prospect of his own chemist's, open on Sundays, with druggies hanging around. Other members of Year Nine would be filling in as members of the Watch, guards, street fighters, paparazzi and guests at the ball.

The casting over at Bagley caused more ructions. Primrose Duddon, much championed by Poppet and No-Joke Joan, was hopping that Graffi, not she, would be playing the Nurse.

'There are only four parts for young women in the play and the most characterful one's gone to a male student.'

Stancombe was outraged that Juliet had been given to Milly rather than Jade – and so was Jade, particularly when bloody Cosmo applauded the decision, claiming that by no stretch of the imagination or shrinking of the vagina could Jade ever pass as a thirteen-year-old virgin.

Jade was, in fact, over Cosmo. Now it was Paris who robbed her of sleep. She detested indifference and loathed her fellow Bagley Babe Milly for landing the part and the chance to snog and more with Paris for the next two months, particularly as she herself had been cast as Lady Montague, Romeo's mother.

'And this play ain't *Oedipus Rex*,' mocked Cosmo.

Nor had Jade realized Lady Montague only had two lines.

After prolonged hysterics through splayed fingers, it was agreed she could swap with Amber and play the much longer and meatier part of Lady Capulet.

'Lady C was a sassy, glamorous woman in her late twenties,' Vicky explained to Jade. 'And as you're married to a rich peer, with a wedding and a funeral in the offing, there's scope for a fantastic wardrobe.'

Amber, who'd been bribed with a Joseph dress she could keep after the play, was only too happy to play Lady Montague instead, particularly since Pearl, now in charge of make-up, was threatening to add arsenic to the face powder of anyone who flirted with Feral.

Cosmo had been outraged only to be offered Capulet, rather than Tybalt, until he discovered subtleties and ironies in the part as Capulet changed from a kind, tolerant father and genial host to an evil bully. He was delighted that the Cosmonaughties would be playing at the Capulets' ball with Kylie as their lead singer. He intended to bill the school £1500 a night and as the group would be providing the music for a sizzling dance routine performed by Feral and Bianca, Cosmo would be able to clock to the second the comings and goings of the divine Bianca.

Xavier, still terrified of Cosmo, and having learnt that Aysha's father had forbidden her to take part, had refused to get involved with the production. Everyone therefore was relieved Bianca was participating, which would at least ensure the presence of her crowd-pulling parents on the opening night.

'I can't wait to meet Rupert Campbell-Black,' gushed Vicky.

As soon as the play was cast Vicky, a genius at delegating – often a euphemism for extreme laziness – called a staff meeting to discuss what help she needed with the play.

The Larks art department was soon coaxed into designing scenery; Gloria into coaching Bianca and Feral in their dance routine; design and technology into producing costumes and props. Cambola was in cahoots with Cosmo over the music. Johnnie Fowler's father Gary, when sober, was an ace electrician and agreed to help with the lighting.

Once Gary Fowler was involved, other fathers felt impelled to follow suit. Most of them DIY experts, they were soon building and painting scenery, and their wives and girlfriends, having clocked Vicky and determined to keep an eye on their other halves, were giving a hand with costumes – over which there was fierce debate.

Anatole, who had sensational legs, wanted doublet and hose. This meant long skirts for the women, deduced Jade, which meant her even more sensational legs would be hidden, so she pushed for modern dress and won.

'Alex Bruce has a finger in every tart,' grumbled Anatole, who in the end was delighted to wear a Red Army mess jacket and tight black trousers with a red stripe down the side. Other boys in the cast wore paramilitary uniform: berets, peaked caps or red and white keffiyehs borrowed from fathers and masters. Chief Inspector Gablecross provided policemen's uniforms for the Watch. This meant more could be spent on female members of the cast.

Janna contented herself with giving lessons to Year Nine on the background of the play, pointing out its topicality; how innocent people were always caught up in the crossfire of war – particularly domestic violence.

'"Poor sacrifices of our enmity," Old Capulet called them, who'd caused a few in his time.'

Determined Larks would be word perfect, she also helped cast members learn their parts.

Rehearsals took place at Bagley every Tuesday and Wednesday after school from 4.00 to 5.30 p.m., and often in the lunch hour but only using the actors that were needed, which involved endless round trips for Wally.

Caught up in Vicky's enthusiasm, none of the teachers seemed to mind covering for her. Basket had a massive crush. Even Sam Spink was looking quite moony and presented Vicky with a pair of Piglet character socks, causing squeals of delight.

'Piglet is my most favourite character.'

Even though the school was a happier place, Janna herself was still ridiculously overstretched. There was always some desperately crying child needing comfort over cigarette burns or cracked ribs. There was always some furious parent: 'My daughter was top in English last term, why isn't she playing Juliet?'

February brought incessant rain, pouring in through the roof on classes and on coursework, and the heating broke down. The classes not involved in the play were also very jealous. Janna tried to compensate by organizing trips to the ballet or ice skating or football, but she understood how they felt and found it hard to not feel jealous herself. Hengist, so adorable on casting day, had not been in touch since.

Vicky, on the other hand, flaunting those vogue words 'Transparency and Accountability', insisted on keeping her boss up to date with events, particularly late one evening, when she dropped in on a very cold, still-working Janna and announced:

341

'"My boys", as I call Emlyn, Piers and Jason, are working so hard. Hengist is constantly popping in to see if I'm OK and Sally Brett-Taylor is being so supportive. She's insisting on making Juliet's dress. We discussed it over a drink last night. Jade Stancombe's ordered a dress for the Capulet ball from Amanda Wakeley, which costs well into four figures, which made Ian Cartwright, the darling old bursar, frightfully uptight till I calmed him down.

'His wife Patience is a pet; she teaches riding at Bagley. His 'mistress of the horse', Hengist calls her, claiming Patience couldn't be anyone else's mistress because she's so plain, naughty man! But Patience has agreed to teach Paris to ride, so he can clatter up the gangway when he storms back from exile, believing Juliet's dead.'

'Paris is terrified of horses,' interrupted Janna icily. 'There's no way he should be forced to ride.'

Ignoring her, Vicky glanced over her shoulder:

'What are you wrestling with? Oh, figures. You ought to talk to Ian. Ian Cartwright. He'd be able to sort them out for you. He's been ringing round other independent bursars, checking their fees all week. I thought I might ask him and Patience to supper, and Hengist and Sally and Emlyn, of course. Emlyn is such a tower of strength. I hope you'll come too, Jannie. You ought to get out more, you look so tired.'

Stop patronizing me, Janna wanted to scream.

'I've no time for jaunts,' she snapped, turning back to her computer. 'Sorry, I must get on.'

The following week, however, Vicky forgot to book the bus for Year Ten's ice-skating trip. As a result, dreadful fights broke out. Not only were Year Nine having all the fun and the kudos, no one could organize anything for Year Ten.

When Janna summoned Vicky back from Bagley and bawled her out, Vicky sobbed and sobbed, rivalling the overflowing River Fleet, and fled into the dusk.

Arriving home from work around midnight, Janna was splashing up the path, lamenting yet again that rain had stopped stars, when Partner went into a frenzy of barking. Lily's cottage was in darkness. Catching sight of a huddled figure in the porch, Janna gasped with terror – had Cara escaped from prison?

'Who's there?'

She was overwhelmed with a divine smell of spring. It was a still-sobbing Vicky, thrusting out a huge bunch of narcissi.

'I'm so sorry to let you down, Jannie. I wanted you to be proud of me and put Larks on the map. I've been so thoughtless.'

So Janna opened a bottle and they ended up crying on each other's shoulders, and Vicky staying the night. But once again, as Janna made up a bed on the sofa, the goalposts changed.

'I never meant to make you jealous, Jannie. Has Hengist upset you? He can be so dismissive. Piers and Jason were saying only the other day, it's a shame you've had no input.'

Vicky looked so enchanting curled up under Janna's duvet, cuddling Janna's only hot-water bottle.

And I meant to slap you down for neglecting Year Ten and your tutor group, thought an exasperated Janna, and vowed once again to spend more time at Bagley.

But the following day, Ashton Douglas and Crispin Thomas summoned her to their plush S and C Services headquarters, overlooking an angry, grey and still rising River Fleet.

Even though the appointment was for midday, not a cup of coffee nor a drink was on offer. Janna's spirits were lowered by a huge wall chart, showing Larks at the bottom of the league tables of Larkshire schools.

Both men had big desks side by side. Crispin, who had gained another chin over Christmas and whose pink pullover had shrunk in the wash, was fussily arranging papers. Ashton, wafting his cloyingly sweet chloroform scent, his apple blossom complexion flushed up by tropical central heating, had removed his jacket to flaunt his trim waistline.

S and C must be making a fortune, decided Janna, judging by the fuck-off lighting, the leather sofas in beiges and browns and the suede cushions to match suede cubes on which to rest your feet.

The pictures on the walls were even more impressive. The bunch of red tulips was certainly by Matthew Smith and the lookalike photograph of Beckham by Alison Jackson. Also blown up over the fireplace was the artwork for S and C's latest logo of a grown-up's hand on a child's back both propelling forward and comforting: a symbol of support and challenge, except the hand was placed a little too low. Janna shuddered.

Ashton was examining his very clean fingernails, the diamond set in the gold band on his third finger catching the light.

'This is wather embarrassing, but we feel you ought to spend less time at Bagley in future.'

Janna's bag tipped over, spilling out biros, lipstick, hairbrush, perfume, Bonios for Partner and diary onto the thick pale beige carpet.

'I've hardly been near the place,' she squeaked, dropping to the floor to claw back her belongings. 'I've been too busy.'

'Maybe.' Ashton sighed with pleasure. 'But I'm afwaid people are talking about you and Hengist.'

Retrieving a tampon from under Crispin's desk, Janna banged her head.

'I know you feel demonized by the Gazette,' went on Ashton, 'but you have a good fwiend in Col Peters. These are the pictures he refused to publish, and instead handed over to us.'

Playing the ace, Ashton produced out of his

crocodile notecase a photograph of Janna in Hengist's arms, her cheek rammed against his, her eyes closed in ecstasy. She was wearing a dark blue shirt; a painting of leaping rugby players could be seen in the background.

'This is ridiculous,' she protested. 'This was at an audition surrounded by hundreds of teachers and children. Who took it, for heaven's sake?'

'We're not at liberty.'

'Well, I want to know. Hengist and I were knocked out – Paris Alvaston had just auditioned. We'd found our Romeo. You'll see how brilliant he is on the opening night.'

'Rather unbridled enthusiasm,' observed Crispin. God, he was loving this. 'Particularly when you put it beside this,' and pointed to another shot of Hengist's hand stroking Janna's cheek and then two cuttings of her smiling adoringly up at Hengist at the Winter Gardens civic dinner and on the air-balloon day.

'The cumulative effect is unfortunate,' said Ashton sympathetically. 'We understand. It's so easy for lonely unmarried women of a certain age to develop these cwushes. Hengist is very charismatic, but Sally Bwett-Taylor is such a good egg.'

'There is absolutely nothing between Hengist and me,' said Janna furiously, her face feeling as though it had just come out of the microwave. 'Head teachers have common problems and practice to discuss. Hengist has been genuinely kind and constructive.'

'In future I'd go to Wod Hyde,' urged Ashton. 'He is after all your official mentor. You don't want tittle-tattle to sabotage the excellent work Larks's teachers are doing at Bagley. Vicky Fairchild is first class. Give her her head.'

'I am her Head,' spat Janna.

'No need to be facetious. Just leave Hengist alone.'

Blinded by tears, Janna fumbled her way out to the

car park. Ironically, Hengist seemed to feel the same as S and C; he hadn't been in touch for weeks.

Partner, leaping on his hind legs, grinning and scrabbling in ecstasy, body shaken by frenziedly wagging tail, stopped her chucking herself into the swift-flowing river.

You're the only male in my life from now on, she vowed grimly. Vicky can get on with it.

41

Paris was missing Janna desperately. He had to be back in the children's home by nine and was thus denied any of the jolly after-rehearsal get-togethers. He'd invested so much in the play because he thought Janna would be there all the time. He longed to talk to her about his part. Vicky never listened and wanted to impose her own views. Graffi was so busy painting scenery, designing posters, camping it up as the Nurse and snogging Milly, he had abandoned Janna's mural which was nearly finished anyway, so the tea parties at Jubilee Cottage had been scrapped.

The Bagley Babes all fancied Paris like mad, but miffed he was always reading and wouldn't respond, they took the piss out of him instead. Milly was convinced he'd been put off by her costume, which was white muslin, high-waisted, sleeveless, with a buttercup-yellow sash like a little girl's party dress.

'It's so drippy. It's only because Sally Brett-Taylor's made it and Vicky's so far up her,' stormed Milly.

Sally in turn was charmed by Vicky, disloyally thinking how nice it would be to have a daughter with whom you could discuss girly things and who didn't always disagree. She had invited Vicky to supper with Emlyn the night Ireland thrashed Wales, and Emlyn, unable ever to envisage his country's rugby revival, arrived utterly legless. Hengist had had to drive him home before the crème brûlée and let him into his flat. Sally only just stopped herself unbuttoning to Vicky that Emlyn wasn't really the ideal son-in-law. Emlyn also seemed the only male in Bagley not besotted with Vicky. The bursar was making a complete idiot of himself hanging round the rehearsal rooms.

But, as February gave way to March, most of the cast were shaping up splendidly. Feral as Tybalt was an unexpected, if reluctant, star.

'"Why, uncle, 'tis a shame", such a crap line,' he grumbled to Paris.

'Think of Uncle Harley.'

'Everything he does is a shame,' shuddered Feral, then, launching back into his part: '"To strike him dead, I hold it not a sin."'

He was gratified one of the highlights of the evening was going to be his dance with Bianca Campbell-Black at the Capulets' ball.

Normally football was Feral's passion. At every opportunity, down on the grass went the fleece, down twelve feet away went the school bag. Instantly a ball would be kicked between them. But, having agreed *Dirty Dancing* was their favourite film, Bianca and Feral practised their sexy Argentine tango routine, with Bianca rubbing her legs up Feral's, with increasing excitement.

After one particularly successful rehearsal, during which the room seemed to fill up with lustful school-boys who should have been in lessons and an accompanying Cosmo broke two strings of his guitar, Feral sloped off for a quick game of football while Bianca returned to the changing rooms.

No one was about for her to chatter to – a great deprivation for Bianca. She was just wriggling out of her sweaty leotard when she felt herself grabbed from behind.

'You shouldn't dance so sexily,' said a smoky, bitchy voice as hands crept over her little breasts.

It was Cosmo, who was very strong. Next moment, he'd yanked her against him, clamping her between his legs and bending over her shoulder, forced his lips down on hers.

'Lemme go.' A revolted Bianca, despite writhing like an eel, was unable from this angle to knee him in the groin, even when he plunged his tongue deep down her throat. Retching, gagging, she struggled harder.

Then she heard a crash as a bench was knocked over and Cosmo was dragged off and punched in the face, sending him toppling backwards into a rail of dresses. Feral then opened the window and, gathering Cosmo up, hurled him out onto Sally Brett-Taylor's precious bed of spotted hellebores.

'Keep your filthy hands off her,' he howled. Tugging the window shut, he turned to Bianca, who was struggling to replace her leotard. Seizing Jade Stancombe's big soft dark blue towel, Feral wrapped it round her frantically shuddering body.

'You OK, little darlin'?'

'Yes. No.' Fighting back the tears, Bianca rubbed the back of her hand across her bruised mouth again and again. Cosmo's tongue had been so disgustingly hard, wet and bobbly underneath, her mouth felt raped.

Feral put an arm round her, then, flourishing an imaginary sword with the other: '"To strike him dead, I hold it not a sin."'

'"Why, uncle, 'tis a shame",' mumbled Bianca.

'It is too.' Feral felt so sorry for her. 'Let's go and find your teddy bear.'

He tried to joke and Bianca had giggled through her tears, but he wanted to kill Cosmo. Bianca was only twelve, but holding her had released some highly unavuncular feelings in Feral.

He so wished Janna was here to advise him and steady the ship.

Vicky seemed to read his mind. As they were waiting in the drizzle for the minibus back to Larks, she could

349

be heard grumbling to Cambola: 'I can't understand why Janna opted out of this production. When she was at Redfords, she never missed a rehearsal. I suppose she was there longer and felt closer to the pupils.'

Seeing the hurt in the children's faces, Cambola snapped that Janna was frantically busy.

'She was never too busy at Redfords,' said Vicky smugly.

Pearl, meanwhile, was taking her responsibility for make-up very seriously and had managed to persuade Paris to let her dye his pale eyelashes and apply dark brown eyeliner before he and Milly were photographed by Cosmo for Graffi's posters.

Cosmo would never forgive Feral, but he was enough of a perfectionist to want to get the best out of Paris and Milly. The results had an unearthly beauty, and posters of the star-crossed lovers were soon plastered all over Larkminster. Tickets designed by Graffi, with a dagger plunged into a bleeding heart, were also selling well.

Paris, as a result, was being teased rotten both at Larks and Oaktree Court, particularly when the inmates got hold of a poster, gave it golden ringlets and a scarlet rosebud mouth and scrawled 'Homo and Juliet, good on you, Woofter' underneath.

'You haven't arrived until you've been graffitied,' Graffi told him airily.

At the beginning of March, three weeks before the opening night, Year Nine and Bagley Lower Fifth had to decide what GCSE subjects they wanted to take in 2004. Ninety per cent opted to take drama with Vicky, almost as many as those who wanted to take history with Emlyn Davies. After such a vote of confidence, Vicky felt entitled to put pressure on Paris to gallop up the gangway to the stage and when he baulked, to suggest they use a stand-in.

'Cosmo, Lando, Junior, Jack Waterlane, all great riders, could put on your jacket and breeches, thunder up the gangway in the half-light, chuck their reins to Dora, jump across the orchestra onto the stage and exit right into Capulet's tomb. Next scene, which is the interior of Capulet's tomb, you barge in having re-appropriated your clothes.'

'That would work,' mused Jason.

If Emlyn were here, Vicky wouldn't have dared, thought Paris, who was at breaking point.

'I'm not having a stand-in and I'm not doing this fucking play,' he snarled and walked out.

Dora caught up with him halfway down the drive and took his hand. 'Just come and meet Mrs Cartwright – the bursar's wife – she's lovely. They live in the Old Coach House, through the woods.'

The faded leaves on the path matched the brown ploughed fields; other fields were the same pale fawn as the sheep that had been grazing them. The woodland floor was turned emerald by wild garlic leaves.

Dora led a grey-faced, frantically trembling Paris into the yard, where hunters and polo ponies with clipped manes stared out over the bottle-green half-doors. A smell of leather and dung made him want to throw up.

'This is Mrs Cartwright,' said Dora. 'She's a brilliant horsewoman.'

Paris looked unenthusiastically at the big-boned, large-nosed maroon-complexioned woman in the clashing scarlet Puffa.

'Hello Paris,' brayed Patience Cartwright, holding out a rough mottled hand that had never seen a manicure. 'I hear you're a wonderful Romeo.'

Not only did she look like a horse, she sounded like one.

'I don't ride,' he said icily.

'This is Beluga,' said Dora. 'He's extremely kind and loves people, unlike Loofah, my pony' – she stroked the brown and white nose of a small skewbald leaning meanly out of the next box – 'who doesn't.'

'The thing to do is to get on Beluga's back in the middle of the field for a few moments,' advised Patience, 'so if you fall orf it's nice and sawft.'

Paris quarter-smiled. At least he could bone up on his Hooray accent.

'Here's a carrot to sawften him up,' giggled Dora.

The saddle was very slippery and the ground below seemed miles down in Australia, but Beluga had a thick black mane to cling on to. Beluga was also lazy and devoted to Plover, Patience's mare, and therefore quite happy plodding round the fields on a lead rein.

After days of downpour it was a wonderfully gentle, sunny day. Woodpeckers laughed inanely in trees already glowing russet, amethyst and warm brown with swelling buds; the singing birds exhorted him not to be frightened. Very gradually Paris unfroze; sweat dried on his pinched face.

'You're doing really well,' encouraged Patience. 'If ever you want him to stop, just pull very gently on the reins.'

A cock pheasant waddled across their path, showing off ginger, scarlet and bright green plumage and a neat white collar.

'The shooting season's over. Such a relief for him,' said Patience.

'Just like Boffin Brooks as Friar Lawrence,' observed Paris. 'Same silly beaky face and fussy walk.'

Patience brayed with laughter.

'Boffin's a little beast.' She lowered her voice furtively as though a passing rabbit might grass her up. 'He drives my husband Ian mad suggesting to Alex Bruce ways the school could economize. He'd have the stables turned into an IT suite, whatever that might be.'

'Can we go a bit faster?' asked Paris.

'Of course, if you're sure.'

Paris nodded, taking a firmer grip on Beluga's mane. Patience bypassed the trot, which was bumpy, going straight into a much smoother canter up a green ride flanked with hazels. Paris gave a gasp of terror, but by the time they'd reached the gate on the crest of the hill, he'd settled into the rhythm.

'Can we canter back to the stables?' he asked twenty minutes later.

And they did.

Paris slid off, trembling violently, hanging on to Beluga as his legs collapsed like plasticene. 'Thanks, horse.'

'Awfully well done,' said Patience. 'You're really good with animals. Dora was saying how Elaine Brett-Taylor loves you.'

'Well done,' said Dora, who'd been up in the hayloft watching through binoculars. 'Looks as though you've ridden for ever.'

'Different ball game clattering up the gangway surrounded by a yelling audience,' grumbled Paris.

'We've got three weeks,' said Patience soothingly. 'Come and have a cup of tea.'

She led him into a messy kitchen, with bridles hanging from a clothes horse, plates and mugs still in the sink and ironing, reminding him of Janna's in-tray, rising to the ceiling.

'Christ!' Paris had caught sight of a photograph of a stunningly beautiful girl on the dresser.

'That's my sister, Emerald,' announced Dora, 'and to muddle you completely, she's Mrs Cartwright's daughter.'

How on earth could a dog like Patience give birth to something so exquisite, wondered Paris, then blushed when Patience read his mind and laughed.

'They always say the fairest flowers grow on the foulest dung heaps, but actually we adopted Emerald and when she sought out her natural mother, she turned out to be Dora's mother, Anthea.'

'The old tart,' chuntered Dora, 'having sex before marriage.'

353

'Dora,' reproved Patience, seeing Paris grinning.

'We adopted both Emerald and Sophy, who's a schoolmistress,' explained Patience, 'and longs to move to the country. She's a great friend of your head-mistress, Janna Curtis. I keep hoping to see her at rehearsals so I can introduce myself and ask Janna to supper.'

Glancing out of the window towards Bagley, appreciating the extent and complexity of its spread of buildings, Paris felt himself flushing as he always did when Janna's name was mentioned.

'I must go,' said Dora wistfully. 'Joan's taking prep. Where's Northcliffe?'

'Our golden retriever,' Patience explained to Paris. 'Gone to work with Ian.'

'Cadbury's still living with the beagles,' sighed Dora. 'I wish he could live here.'

'Not sure if Northcliffe would like that, he's awfully territorial. I'll ask Ian.' Patience had taken off her red Puffa to reveal a purple knitted jersey on inside out.

After Dora had gone, she made very strong tea and toast and then surreptitiously scraped mould off some pear jelly entitled 'Poppet Bruce 2000', before discovering to her relief some chocolate spread and a coconut cake stuffed with glacé cherries.

'Were they very young when you adopted them?' asked Paris.

'Very, we were so lucky, and they've both got heavenly babas of their own now. It's so crucial for adopted people to have their first blood relation.'

Euphoric that he'd conquered his phobia of horses, Paris, over a second cup of tea and third slice of cake, found himself most uncharacteristically unbuttoning to Patience about his fruitlessly advertising for a family.

'There was no takers. Guess I looked too likely to knife them in their beds.'

'That's horrible.' Patience looked as though she was going to cry. 'Anyone would feel privileged and overjoyed to have you for a son. Everyone thinks so highly of you at Bagley. Your Romeo is the talk of the staffroom.'

Paris shrugged.

'I do hope' – Patience blushed an even darker maroon – 'you'll drop in and see us, like Dora does, even if you don't want to go on riding.'

Seeing Paris's eyes straying to a bookshelf crammed with poetry, much more thumbed than the cookery books, she explained: 'My husband loves poetry. Matthew Arnold's his favourite. I'm awfully badly read, but Arnold wrote a lovely poem called 'Sohrab and Rustum', which has a sweet horse in it called Ruksh who sheds real tears' – Patience's voice trembled – 'when his master unknowingly slays his own son in battle. You must read it.'

'Horses cry when their masters die in the *Iliad*,' said Paris, reaching out his hand for more coconut cake, then pausing.

'Please have it,' begged Patience. 'We used to say whoever had the last piece got a handsome husband and a thousand a year, which wouldn't go very far these days.'

'I could use it,' said Paris.

'I do hope you'll have another go on Beluga. I think you're a natural.'

42

Gradually as March splashed into its third week and Bagley was lit up by daffodils, the excitement began to bite. Wally borrowed a lorry to transport props and scenery made by Larks parents, which included a four-poster painted with flowers for Juliet and a wrought-iron balcony: 'More suited to a Weybridge hacienda,' said Hengist, 'but perfect for sixteenth-century Verona.'

The dress rehearsal in front of pupils from both schools was scheduled for Wednesday evening; the big night for governors, parents and friends would take place on Thursday.

Larks participants spent Wednesday afternoon over at Bagley taking part in a dry run to fine-tune performances, scene shifts and lighting. Glimpses of Paris's naked back view would add excitement to the bedroom scenes. Johnnie Fowler, in charge of his dad's lighting, was determined to catch Paris full frontal.

Amber, meanwhile, was shouting at Alex Bruce:

'I'll pay for my own fucking dress, it was only five hundred pounds,' which is the difference between them and us, thought Graffi, who'd never been paid by Junior for Shining Sixpence's winnings.

All the cast were jittery and Vicky didn't help by ringing in with a migraine. 'So sorry, I've overdone things. I'll try and stagger in later.'

Emlyn took a deep breath and counted to ten.

'Right, let's get started. We all know this is a play about conflict rather than love.'

'Why can't Miss come in instead of Vicky?' sighed Kylie.

The day continued full of spats.

Jade Stancombe, insisting on wearing four-inch heels, fell down the stairs. A waiter carrying full glasses of coloured water bumped into a bodyguard, soaking the stage, which resulted in Feral and Bianca nearly doing the splits in their tango. Juliet's bed collapsed during her night of passion with Romeo. Everyone burst out laughing when Feral's moustache fell off during a fight.

The instant Juliet's bed had been repaired and her wedding night resumed, Poppet Bruce marched in brandishing a packet of rainbow-coloured Durex.

'R and J are having underage sex; Paris must be publicly seen to be wearing a condom.'

'Surely that's wardrobe's department?' grinned Jason.

'The audience won't see him in the dark,' snarled Emlyn. 'Get out, Poppet.'

'That is not how you should address your deputy team leader's wife,' spluttered Poppet, then, as Emlyn rose to his mighty height, flounced out slamming the door.

'Romeo, Romeo,' sighed Milly, 'wherefore fart thou, Romeo,' producing more giggles.

'Shut up, Milly,' howled Emlyn.

Paris gritted his teeth. His ride up the aisle and his last impassioned speech were still to come.

'"The day is hot, the Capulets abroad . . ."' Junior Lloyd-Foxe, who had the part of Benvolio, delivered his best and most ominous line.

Next moment, Feral and Cosmo were on the floor, howling, punching, clawing like tomcats.

'Take your hands off her, you sick bastard.'

357

'Don't give yourself airs, you fucking golliwog.'

'Don't black Cosmo's eyes,' begged Jason as Feral lunged and missed.

'Pack it in,' yelled Emlyn and, when they didn't, he emptied a dusty fire bucket over them. This, as they retreated, spluttering and swearing, did nothing to aid Paris's concentration.

Somehow he managed to gallop Beluga up to the orchestra pit and keep control when Cosmo, to spook the horse, deliberately launched the brass into a deafening tantivy. Chucking his reins to Dora, Paris managed to leap off without touching the floor, run up the plank laid across the pit and dive into Juliet's tomb to a round of applause.

'I don't need no fucking stand-in,' he hissed at Cosmo.

Now Juliet lay before him in her coffin and the half-light. He had just launched into his impassioned soliloquy about the colour still in her lovely face, when he realized Milly, bet by Amber, had slipped on a red Comic Relief nose, and raised a hand to hit her.

'Don't,' thundered Emlyn, so Paris swore at him, spat on the floor and stalked off the set.

'You stupid bitch,' yelled Emlyn. 'How dare you wind him up like that?'

'It was only a joke to loosen him up,' wailed Milly. 'It's not me he's kissing, it's Juliet. I'm fed up with pandering to him. "Paris, Paris, don't upset Paris." What about my needs?'

Graffi, in his Nurse's costume, rushed onto the stage and flung his arms round Milly. 'There, there, lovely, it's OK. Don't bully her,' he shouted at Emlyn.

Milly was touched but rather wished her knight in shining armour wasn't wearing drag and a grey granny wig.

'But soft what brick through yonder window breaks,' intoned Amber.

Although he was consistently bottom in maths, Jack

Waterlane had worked out that between appearances on stage, he and Kylie had at least an hour unaccounted for. He had therefore whipped her into the biology lab and hung his red jacket on a skeleton, then they both froze as Poppet Bruce, exuding bossy bustle in her eco-monitor role, rushed by flicking off the lab lights and seemingly giving them her blessing.

'Gosh, we've just had underage sex,' sighed Jack as he lay in Kylie's arms. 'My father had to have sex before polo matches – relaxed him – 'spect I'll win an Oscar now. I love you, Kylie Rose.'

'I love you, Jack,' said Kylie.

It was an hour to the dress rehearsal. No one could find Paris. He hadn't even been to make-up. Everyone was panicking.

'Sometimes he disappears on trains for days,' said Feral, then, turning on Amber and Milly: 'Why'd you wind him up, you stupid cows?'

Patience Cartwright found Paris in Beluga's box, throwing up into an empty water bucket, wiping his face with hay from the rack. At first he wouldn't speak and carried on retching, but when Patience brought him a glass of water, he told her about the red nose, mumbling that he found it so hard without Janna.

'She got me into Shakespeare. Explained things. But she hasn't been to rehearsals for weeks, 'spect she's too busy.'

He slumped against Beluga, his face grey and defeated.

'She probably doesn't want to cramp Vicky's style.'

'Vicky's a stupid bitch.'

Patience felt ashamed at her elation; Ian was besotted with Vicky.

'You've got to be terrified to be any good,' she reassured Paris. 'I once competed at the Horse of the

Year Show, and I was so worried about letting Bentley, my horse, down, I spent three hours in the lav. They had to drag me out and then we won our class. I crept into the rehearsal room the other day: you're miles the best in the cast. I'm sure Milly was trying to relax you.'

'I can't kiss her tasting of puke.'

'I always keep spare toothbrushes and toothpaste in case a pupil needs it, and Ian confiscated some peppermint chewing gum yesterday, you can have that.'

'You weren't just saying I was OK?'

He looked so forlorn and despairing, Patience longed to hug him. 'You'll be sensational.'

As soon as he'd gone, Patience called Emlyn. 'Paris is on his way back. I don't mean to interfere, but he needs Janna, he's so alone.'

The dress rehearsal was a great success. When the cheers and clapping finally died down, the cast yelled for Mr Davies: 'Attila! Attila! Attila!' They stamped their feet until, loose-limbed and bleary-eyed, Emlyn shambled onto the stage, where Graffi presented him with a big bottle of red, 'from Larks as a mark of our gratitude'.

'Mr Davies builds us up,' shouted Rocky. 'He puts the boot in, but he's always looking for fings to praise.'

'Why, thank you, Rocky.' Emlyn was touched. 'What about Miss Fairchild and Mr Fenton?'

'We've got fings for them tomorrow, but you do all the work,' said Pearl.

Emlyn was so tired, he would have loved to unwind over a few beers with his friend Artie Deverell, the head of modern languages. Instead he threw the bottle of red into his dirty Renault Estate and drove over to Larks where, although it was after eleven, lights were still blazing.

Inside he thought what a good job Janna was doing. The building might be falling down, but newly painted walls and noticeboards were covered in praise post-cards, brightly coloured work and crammed with pictures of the children and their activities: a new baby brother yesterday, a birthday today. Along the corridor, *Romeo and Juliet* posters proudly flaunted yellow 'sold-out' stickers.

Janna was in her office, squealing with frustration as she tried to put back a cupboard, which, as a result of the damp, had fallen off the wall. Her fathers weren't as diligent about do-it-yourself when Vicky wasn't around.

Nor was putting back screws without a screwdriver very easy. 'Bugger, bugger, bugger,' yelled Janna, as a 50p piece slipped out of the groove. The handle of her tweezers had been no more successful.

Then she shrieked as a dark figure filled the door-way. Partner woke up, went berserk, then, recognizing Emlyn's soft Welsh accent, dragged his blue rug across the floor in welcome.

'Fucking cupboard.' Janna gave it a kick. 'How did it go?'

'Wonderfully. They all did so well. Your kids presented this to me.' He dumped the bottle of red on Janna's desk. 'Why don't you open it?'

Rootling round in Wally's toolbox, Emlyn then located four big screws and a box of matches. Putting matches in the holes to make them smaller, he banged in the screws with a hammer.

'That is so cool,' cried an amazed Janna as the cupboard stayed put.

'Can't beat a good screw.' Emlyn took the corkscrew from her.

Noticing the bags under his bloodshot eyes, she said apologetically, 'You must be shattered.'

'No more than you,' said Emlyn, noticing the bags under her bloodshot eyes.

'Why the hell do we teach?' asked Janna, getting two glasses out of a second cupboard.

Emlyn was reading the letter on her laptop.

'Dear Mrs Todd, I thought you'd be pleased that Charlie wrote a wonderful essay on Oliver Cromwell this morning.'

The wine was unbelievably disgusting. If they hadn't needed a drink so badly, Emlyn would have chucked it down the bog.

'I don't think Larks children have much pocket money,' said Janna defensively.

'It was a sweet thought.' Emlyn collapsed on the sofa which still bore Pearl's ink stain. Partner jumped onto his knee.

'Now tell me how it really went.'

When he'd finished, Emlyn said, 'You should have been there.'

'I'm coming tomorrow.'

'Not good enough. I'm told you were always in the thick of things at Redfords. Why have you backed off?'

'I'm frantic,' said Janna defensively.

'Everyone's frantic.'

'Everyone adores Vicky.' Janna tried not to sound bitter. 'I put people's backs up.'

'Vicky lacks your vision,' said Emlyn flatly, 'and she doesn't understand the play. Jason's been terrific, but it's you the kids love. They're dying to show you how far they've come, that they're carrying out your ideas – which Vicky claims are hers.'

'How was Paris?' A defiant, shame-faced Janna wanted to change the subject.

'All to pieces; nearly lost it. Amber, Milly and Jade are fed up they're getting no reaction from him. Why did you stop coming?'

Getting up, he looked at the school photograph. Hands shoved into his pockets, he showed off a surprisingly taut, high, beautiful bottom. He had terrific shoulders too and the bulldog face had charm if you liked bulldogs. Janna longed to throw herself into his arms and tell him how Ashton and Crispin had

362

warned her off. Instead she said, 'I've got a school to save.'

Emlyn could see how reduced in bounce she was and longed to comfort her. In the old days he'd have taken her home for a joyful romp in bed. But there was the cool, white body of Oriana to consider. 'I have been faithful to thee, Cynara! in my fashion.'

Janna anyway was too vulnerable and too nice for half measures.

'Let's go and have supper,' he said instead. 'I know somewhere still open.'

'I've got far too much to do,' snapped Janna, 'but thanks all the same.'

'We all miss you,' said Emlyn as he went out. 'Particularly Paris.'

Returning to Jubilee Cottage, Janna and Partner wandered into the garden. The rain, at last, had stopped and the stars for the first time in days were scattered across the sky like a sweep of white daffodils.

'Give me my Romeo,' she cried out:

'And, when he shall die,
Take him and cut him out in little stars,
And he will make the face of heaven so fine
That all the world will be in love with night.'

Oh Hengist! Oh Emlyn! She was so lonely for love and a pair of arms round her.

Even though it was nearly midnight, she rang first Mr Blenchley and then Nadine, Paris's social worker.

'I've got a few spare tickets. It'd mean so much to Paris if you came along.'

43

Paris was gratified next day to get lots of cards, including one from Aunt Lily and another from Nadine, delivered to school by hand: 'So looking forward to seeing you tonight.' Normally she wasn't remotely interested in his academic progress, only his social welfare. There was even a card from the children in the home: 'Sorry we took the piss.'

Patience sent him a silver horseshoe and some chewing gum. Dora had bought him a fluffy black cat, which, entitled 'Dora's pussy', became the subject of much ribaldry. Cadbury sent him a good-lick card.

After last night's success, the cast were cheerful and over-excited.

'You've got to calm down,' Emlyn kept telling them.

It was a glorious evening, with the setting sun flaming the flooded playing fields below a vermilion and Cambridge-blue sky, which was considered a good omen, as the Montagues' uniform was flame red and the Capulets' pale blue.

All afternoon Pearl worked her magic on the cast, particularly Jade, who couldn't stop admiring herself in the mirror. Amber was less sanguine.

'Pearl's still convinced Feral's got the hots for me,' she whispered to Milly, 'but frankly he can't take his big eyes off Bianca C-B. So humiliating to be cuckolded by someone from the Lower Fourth.'

'"There's no trust, No faith, no honesty in men,"' sighed Milly.

Amber was not cast down. Both Eton and Radley boyfriends had sent her huge bunches of flowers and their undying love.

'I'd still like a night with Feral,' she confessed. 'Do you think Paris is gay?'

'That could explain it,' said Milly in delight. 'All the time he's fantasizing I'm Feral, not me. I still fancy him rotten.'

'One can't not,' agreed Amber.

'He stares and stares but it's to observe, not to lust. If Sally Bloody-Taylor hadn't forced me into such a prissy dress with that gross sash, I might have scored.'

Paris was shivering uncontrollably. Thank God he wore a flimsy white shirt in the first act, so the circles of sweat wouldn't show. Already he could hear strains of Tchaikovsky as the orchestra warmed up.

Emlyn was everywhere, calmly encouraging, dealing with last minute crises. 'No, the Prince can't wear gel, Jack, go and wash it out.'

As Mr Khan had shot off to Pakistan on business, Aysha had bravely applied to be a stage hand. Hearing the news from Bianca, Xavier Campbell-Black had applied as well. They had only been working with the cast for a week. Occasionally Xav's hand touched Aysha's as they shifted balconies, beds and coffins around. There were twenty scenes to be set up. They were both very nervous. Aysha looked more beautiful than ever in a shalwar kameez of midnight-blue silk.

Xav had avoided Cosmo and his minions since they tried to drown him in the bog. Now as he and Aysha made sure that Paris's plank was in place, stacked in a corner of the pit ready to form a bridge across the orchestra, Cosmo shouted nastily:

'Good thing you and Miss Khan are black, so the

audience needn't see you when you're shifting scenes.'

Next moment, Feral had grabbed Cosmo's dark curls, holding a knife to his throat. 'Take that back,' he hissed.

'I'll have that.' Emlyn grabbed the knife. He also confiscated Anatole's vodka. 'You can get drunk after you're killed off.'

' "Why, uncle, 'tis a shame",' grumbled Anatole.

Jade had got forty-eight red roses from her father, and a huge bunch of pink lilies that she'd sent herself and made a lot of fuss wondering who they came from. Stancombe also sent yellow orchids to Milly. Milly's mother was not as biddable as Stancombe would have liked. He had wanted to arrive with her in the helicopter this evening, but perversely she insisted that, as a governor, she should make her own way.

'When's Hengist going to make me a governor?' grumbled Stancombe.

'When a vacancy occurs. No one resigns because meetings are such fun,' said Mrs Walton.

Mags Gablecross and Sally B-T were working flat out on final alterations to costumes.

'Where's Vicky?' demanded Monster fretfully.

'Gone to the hairdresser's,' said Mags dryly. 'She felt the need to pamper herself before her big night.'

'I bought her these flowers,' protested Monster.

'How very thoughtful of you,' said Sally, recognizing five of her rare irises and the only spotted hellebores not squashed earlier by Cosmo. 'I'll put them in water for Vicky.'

Mrs Kamani, thrilled to be sent a ticket, had closed her newsagent's especially early and was now sitting in the second row next to Vicky's proud parents.

Janna crept into the dressing room, where everything seemed chaos. So many ravishing girls and boys. Whatever happened to spots and puppy fat? Such

366

smooth flesh to make up, she thought wistfully, no crevasses for it to sink into.

Milly's streaked ponytail was being brushed out by Sally, before being put up with a white rose. Bianca Campbell-Black, watched surreptitiously by every boy in the room, was being zipped into her scarlet spangled dress.

Feral paced up and down, muttering, '"Have at thee, coward!"' He must remember to speak up.

'Who's coming tonight, apart from my mum?' asked Kylie as Pearl toned down her flushed post-orgasmic face.

'Press, parents, friends of the school.'

'Din't know we had any friends,' said Graffi.

'"Why Uncle, 'tis a shame",' muttered Feral.

'I'm going to throw up again,' said Paris.

'No you're not.' Hengist swept in resplendent in a beautifully cut pinstripe suit, sky-blue shirt and dark blue spotted tie. 'The audience are arriving. I want you all down in the General Bagley Room. Take the back stairs so no one sees you.'

On the way they passed props tables groaning with policemen's helmets, Sally's old scent bottles filled with coloured water for Monster's chemist shop, pots of rosemary, camomile and foxglove for Friar Lawrence's garden, phials of fake blood, retractable knives and pistols, which Emlyn constantly checked for the real thing.

Self-conscious yet astounded how newly beautiful Pearl had made so many of them, the cast took up their positions in rising tiers on three sides of a square. Amber and Jade had become glamorous society hostesses, Milly an innocent vast-eyed angel, towards whom even Paris felt a flicker of lust.

'I look almost as good as Mummy,' sighed Milly.

Graffi, aged up with wrinkles, parsnip-yellow bags under the eyes, a shaggy grey wig and a Norland

Nurse's uniform, with a fob watch on his starched bosom, looked nearly fifty and decidedly unattractive. Milly loved him but she wished once again he looked as sexy as Feral who, with his lithe beautiful body encased in black, his amazing tawny eyes elongated to his temples and with a suggestion of ebony whisker, looked indeed the Prince of Cats. Paris had refused blusher or lipstick, but Pearl, with bronzing gel, had warmed his deathly pallor to the olive glow of an Old Master and defined his pale unblinking eyes with eyeliner and mascara. He looked drop dead gorgeous with his officer's peaked cap shoved onto the back of his head.

'I must not fancy Paris,' pleaded Milly.

Standing facing his young audience, Hengist smiled.

'You all look fantastic.' Then, sternly: 'But remember your job tonight is to entertain. Invite the audience on stage with you, invite them to become part of this amazing story. It's all about eye contact, even if you're a bad guy or one of the crowd – look out at the audience.

'Up until now, no one's given more than seventy-five per cent. Tonight I want one hundred and fifty per cent. It's already a great show. I want it to be a brilliant show. I want you to change what the audience feels about you. Your parents are out there, longing to be proud of you.'

Not for Paris, thought Janna in anguish.

'Stand up,' ordered Hengist.

As the children struggled to their feet, the girls swaying on their high heels, his voice became almost messianic:

'Shut your eyes. You are young, you are beautiful, you're energetic, you have ability and gifts. You have time to entertain.'

'Yeah, man.' Rocky punched the air with his fist.

Kylie suppressed a nervous giggle. Aysha was horrified to feel her hand creeping into Xav's, and nearly fainted when he squeezed it back.

'Make the audience want to be what you are,'

Hengist's voice dropped seductively: 'Make them adore you. Your job is to break their hearts.'

Against the force of Hengist's personality, Feral wrenched open his eyes and caught Bianca gazing at him; then she smiled shyly. Feral was jolted, he must get a grip on himself. Quickly he looked away. Cosmo, intercepting this exchange, was determined to negate it.

'Good luck, God bless you all,' ended Hengist to a round of applause. Hovering at the back, glancing at the rapt, inspired faces of the children, Janna was reminded once again why he was head of one of the best schools in the country. He could have sent entire armies over the top.

And he looked so divine. The strong features, the ebony eyebrows, the high colour, the slicked-down hair already leaping upwards, the vitality tamed by the dark-grey establishment suit. An arrogant public-school shit, and yet, and yet . . .

'My only love sprung from my only hate', she thought helplessly, stepping out from behind a tier of seats, then leaping back as Pearl shouted, 'Miss, Miss,' and all the children took up the cry.

But Janna had fled, racing down the corridor, losing herself in the crowd gathering in the foyer outside the theatre. All round the walls were Cosmo's blown-up photographs of the cast. Janna swelled with pride. Paris, Feral and Kylie looked so beautiful.

Even more beautiful to the Larks parents was a splendid array of free drink. Two coachloads had been ferried over from the Shakespeare Estate by the heroic Wally and were fast losing their shyness. There was Pearl's mother and her very young lover, who didn't look capable of beating Pearl or anyone else up, and Chantal Peck in gold lurex and a high state of excitement, telling everyone she was a parent governor. Stormin' Norman, in a black trouser suit, had been spoiling for a fight, but her aggression evaporated when she saw the blow-up of Monster as the apothecary. The small stocky man with black curls and naughty laughing eyes, drinking red wine out of a pint mug, must be Dafydd Williams, Graffi's dad.

Out of loyalty to Vicky, but not bothering to change out of very casual clothes, Skunk Illingworth, Sam Spink, Robbie Rushton and Chally had overcome their loathing of private education enough to get stuck into Hengist's drink.

Bagley parents, however, were in the ascendancy.

'Darling darling, kiss kiss, yock yock, ha, ha ha, ski-ing, the Seychelles, the Caribbean, Egypt, Aspen, Florida, Klosters. Are you going to the Argentine Open? Must come over to kitchen sups,' to show they'd got a dining room. Listening to the confident yelling and exchange of proper names, Janna had forgotten how much she detested the upper middle classes.

It was still light outside; through the open windows, birds were competing with the orchestra. Chantal and Stormin' Norman were pointing out celebs.

'Look, there's Rupert Campbell-Black, ain't he beautiful?'

'Best owner-trainer in the country,' agreed Dafydd, 'and there's Billy Lloyd-Foxe,' as Amber's father, clutching two large whiskies, pushed his way through the throng.

'Never miss him on *Question of Sport*,' said Stormin'. ''Ello Billy, don't drink it all at once.'

Billy grinned back at them: 'I hate running out.'

Dafydd was over the moon and in turn helped himself to two mugs of red.

'And there's Jupiter Belvedon, our Member,' squeaked Chantal. 'Evening, Jupe.'

Jupiter nodded coolly as he joined the group round Rupert Campbell-Black.

'Pity I didn't bring my autograph book,' sighed Chantal.

Such was Janna's paranoia, having been warned off

by Ashton and Crispin and imagining everyone would be dubbing her a whore, that she was amazed so many parents hailed her.

'She's so nice, she's our head.'

Maybe all those home visits were paying off.

Randal Stancombe, hovering hopefully round the Campbell-Black clique, kissed Janna on both cheeks. Mrs Walton, ravishing as ever in a Lindka Cierach cream velvet suit, to which she had pinned a big pink rose, Calèche rising like morning mist from her ravine of a cleavage, rushed up and insisted she and Janna have lunch soon.

'I am so thrilled Milly's playing Juliet,' she whispered. 'Randal's livid that poisonous Jade didn't get it. Have you met Taggie Campbell-Black? She can't sleep for worrying Xav's going to move the wrong chair, or Bianca forget her dance steps.'

Janna smiled up at Taggie, who, slender as a young birch, with a dark cloud of hair, kind, silver-grey eyes and soft pink lips, seemed infinitely sweeter and more beautiful than Mrs Walton.

'I gather Bianca's champion,' she said. 'She's doing her dance with one of my most adorable pupils.'

'Is that Feral? Bianca chatters about him all day. Rupert's getting very jealous. But we're so pleased Xav's got involved. Darling, you've met Janna,' Taggie called out to Rupert who, detesting school events, was cringing behind a pillar talking into two mobiles.

Peering out nervously, he waved at Janna.

'I've still got that sheepdog that fell on my head when I visited your school – much better behaved than my dogs.'

Absurdly flattered to be remembered, Janna was thanking him once again for sending *Gladiator* and the huge cheque, when she lost her audience as Rupert muttered, 'Oh God,' and shot behind his pillar again, as a large woman, outcleavaging Ruth Walton and with the wide innocent eyes of a doll, appeared in the doorway awaiting adulation.

'There's Dime Kiri,' shouted Stormin' Norman, who was well away. ''Ello Dime Kiri.'

'That ain't Dime Kiri,' chided Chantal as the large woman expanded like a bullfrog, 'that's Dime Hermy-own, stupid. 'Ello, Dime Hermy-own.'

'It's Dame Hermione, Cosmo's mother, silly old bat. Hengist can't stand her,' said Ruth Walton with rare venom as Randal shot forward to kiss Dame Hermione's hand, determined to harpoon this great whale to open his hypermarket.

'Can I take your photograph, Miss Curtis?' said a shrill voice. It was Dora, ostensibly covering the play for the Bagley school mag. 'Oh bugger, here comes my mother, she's crazy about Rupert.'

'Christ!' Rupert had now disappeared round the other side of the pillar to avoid Lady Belvedon, a very slim pretty blonde, crying: 'Rupert, Rupert.'

'Did I hear Rupert's name?' cried Dame Hermione roguishly and, leaving Stancombe in mid-supermarket pitch, rushed off in pursuit.

Advanced on from right and left, Rupert bolted for the bar.

'Poor Rupert, he's so naughty,' laughed Taggie, then, lowering her voice: 'He can't stand Dame Hermione or Anthea Belvedon, but they're like cats and always crawl over people who are allergic to them.'

'Oh look, he's now been clobbered by Poppet Bruce,' giggled Dora. 'I expect she'll invite him to her workshop on behaviour management.'

Strains of Prokoviev's *Romeo and Juliet* were rising above the din of chat as the five-minute bell went.

'God, I loathe school plays,' grumbled Amber and Junior's mother, Janey, a blonde Fleet Street journalist who'd seen better days. 'This one's going to be even direr, since Bagley bonded with that grotty comprehensive . . .'

Ruth Walton laughed.

'This is the grotty comp's headmistress, Janna Curtis.'

'Oh dear,' said Janey, filling up Janna's glass from her brimming half-pint mug, 'I'm so sorry. You're much too pretty and young for a head. I'm covering this for the *Mail*. I'll say you're charismatic and deeply capable.' Then, as Uncle Harley sauntered in looking sleek and dangerous: 'Who's that utterly ravishing man covered in diamonds?'

'Some African prince,' said Janna slyly.

At least someone's come for Feral, she thought as she waved at Harley. She was also delighted Nadine and Mr Blenchley from Oaktree Court had showed up.

'Christ.' Rupert had joined them again. 'Hermione, Lady Belvedon and that ghastly Poppet: I thought the three witches came in *Macbeth*.'

There was an explosion of flashes as Hengist swept in with Anatole's father the Russian Minister and his glamorous wife, who was wearing a floor-length fur.

'It must have accounted for a hundred bears,' said Dora furiously, 'I'm going to blow her up.'

'I feel one has a duty to support these functions,' Lady Belvedon was telling Stancombe, then squawked as the long pink tongue of Elaine, the greyhound, relieved her of the vol-au-vent she was clutching.

The sixty-second bell was ringing imperiously. As everyone surged into the theatre, Taggie turned shyly to Janna.

'Good luck. I'm so sick with nerves for Bianca, I can't imagine what it would be like to worry about a whole school. You've done so well, Xav and Bianca have really taken to your Larks children.'

If only all posh people were like you, thought Janna, noticing Graffi's dad tucking a bottle of red wine inside his jacket.

'Thank you for helping our Graffi with his muriel,' said his wife.

'You must come and see it,' said Janna happily, then any joy was drained out of her as she saw the Tusk Force: Russell, Crispin, Rod Hyde and Ashton Douglas, in a dark purple smoking jacket, with an uncharacteristically adoring expression on his bland, pink face.

'Dame Hermione.' He seized both her hands. 'You were the most wonderful Elisabetta I ever saw. Pawis nineteen eighty-five.'

'You're very kind.' Hermione bowed gracefully. 'Perhaps you could rustle me up another glass of bubbly?'

'Indeed.' Ashton belted off.

'You're looking very iconic this evening, Dame Hermione,' snuffled fat Crispin.

'Where's Vicky?' asked Russell.

'Backstage.' Rod Hyde's voice thickened. 'The good general is always with his troops.'

Catapulted forward by the crowd, Janna couldn't avoid them.

'Good evening, gentlemen,' she said coolly.

They nodded back equally coolly.

'Good of you to turn up.'

'We felt we must support Vicky,' said Ashton.

Janna glanced at her ticket. 'I must find my seat.'

Next moment, a big warm hand grabbed hers. 'Gotcha,' said a familiar deep husky voice. 'Come and watch with me.'

'I'm sitting with Tim and Mags Gablecross,' shrieked Janna, aware of Ashton and Co's delighted disapproval and wriggling like a stray cat to escape.

'The Gablecrosses won't mind,' said Hengist. 'We started this together, I want to share it with you,' and he dragged her off to sit in the middle of the tenth row, making everyone move up.

'Sally's backstage, doing last-minute repairs,' he told Janna. 'Half our girls are so besotted with your Feral, the other half with your Paris. They've all had to have their costumes taken in.'

Oh God, thought Janna in panic as a flurry of 'Excuse me, sorry, excuse me' indicated that the Tusk Force had taken the seats directly behind her.

I haven't seen Hengist since I last saw you, Janna wanted to scream at them, but then she thought defiantly: I don't care, I don't care. Maybe it's three glasses of wine on an empty stomach, but I still really adore him.

Giving her a slug of Courvoisier from a silver hipflask, Hengist introduced her to two masters on her right.

These were Artie Deverell, the handsome, languid, gentle head of modern languages, whom Mags Gablecross, who taught the same subject, had fallen in love with on balloon day, and Theo Graham, the bald and very wrinkled head of classics, revered for his translation of Euripides.

'I've got Jack Waterlane, Junior, Lando and Lubemir in my house,' whispered Artie. 'Theo's got Cosmo and Anatole, so we both have our crosses.'

The Russian Minister and his wife were seated on Hengist's left. Next moment, everyone jumped out of their skins as Dame Hermione started singing along to Prokofiev.

'Lurex tremendous,' murmured Hengist as Chantal Peck swept up to the front.

44

It was a wonderful theatre, stark and forbidding, with black brick walls forty feet high and black leather seats. Saxophones and clarinets glittered like jewels in the pit; pearly drum skins gleamed in the half-light.

The only prop in front of the crimson curtains was a big cardboard television with the screen cut out. As Prokofiev's menacing 'March of the Capulets' faded away, Kylie Rose appeared inside the now lit-up screen as a presenter.

'"Two households, both alaike in dignity . . ."' She held up cards saying Bagley and Larks:

'In fair Verona, where we lay our scene.
From forth the fatal loins of these two foes
A pair of star-crossed lovers take their laife.'

'Christ,' muttered Rupert, 'she's been here half a term and she talks like Anthea Belvedon.'

Chantal was in ecstasy: Kylie looked so dignified.

Back creaked the crimson curtains to a howl of police sirens and a burst of clapping. Against Graffi's fantastic backdrop of mosques, tumbling twin towers, tower blocks and army barracks strangled by barbed wire was a street in Verona with an ice-cream van, AC Milan posters, a large bullet-pocked Shakespeare Estate sign, and a signpost saying 'Bagley 5 miles, City

376

Centre ½ mile'. There was the Ghost and Castle and Mrs Kamani's newsagent's with a broken window.

Oh God, thought Janna, but, rising out of her seat, she could see Mrs Kamani laughing. Revelling in the roars of applause, Janna forgot her nerves. This was no school production; it was slick, yet bursting with exuberance and passion. Larks's confidence had grown so much, they were as assured as their Bagley counterparts.

Here was Rocky lumbering out of the Ghost and Castle and turning on the Montagues.

'"No, sir, I do not bite my fumb at you, sir, but I bite my fumb, sir. When I have fought the men, I will be civil with the maids, and cut off their heads."'

'"The heads of the maids?"' demanded Junior.

'"Ay, the heads of the maids or their maidenheads."' Rocky leered round; the audience laughed.

Then Feral erupted onto the stage to huge cheers and boos.

'"What, drawn, and talk of peace! I hate the word,"' he spat, his fury scattering the Montagues, then paused.

Although the cast knew he'd dried, the audience thought it was terrific timing.

'"I hate the word,"' repeated Feral, recovering, '"As I hate hell, all Montagues, and thee. Have at thee, coward!"' And guns were flashing and blanks ringing out.

'That's Bianca's boyfriend,' whispered Taggie. 'Isn't he gorgeous?'

'Very black,' muttered back Rupert.

Paris stood apart in the wings, psyching himself up, mindlessly chewing gum. I am Romeo; I am in Verona; I am empowered; I am lovesick for a woman who hardly knows I exist. *Plus ça change*, he thought bitterly, I am about to crash a ball and fall in love for the first and last time in my life.

'Good luck, Paris.' Vicky's clap on the back nearly

377

shot him onto the stage. 'Remember to speak up.'

Roars of applause greeted each new set, particularly the Capulets' ballroom with long-legged beauties in masks and paparazzi hiding, like Rupert, behind every pillar.

'That's my Jade in cerise,' said Stancombe loudly to Dame Hermione.

'That's my Cosmo playing Lord Capulet in a navy military jacket,' said Hermione even more loudly.

'Shut up,' said Janna.

'Don't wepwove Dame Hermione,' hissed a horrified Ashton.

Cosmo, having played the genial host, whipped off his jacket and joined the Cosmonaughties and Kylie Rose in a number he'd composed called 'Cocks and Rubbers', the words of which were fortunately obscured by the din of the band. Looking at Cosmo's pale dangerous face, ebony curls flopping maniacally as he lashed his guitar, Janna thought: That is one whole lot of gorgeous trouble.

Then the stage cleared for Feral and Bianca's tango. Never taking their eyes off each other, talking through their bodies as they danced, their red-hot passion branded the floorboards. Rupert, woken by his wife just in time to watch them, led the bravoes and thunderous applause. This resulted in two encores, which broke the mood for Paris's big entrance.

'Oh poor boy,' muttered Janna in anguish as the applause petered out.

'He'll be OK,' whispered Hengist.

And Janna moved her body against his so the comforting hand he'd laid on top of hers couldn't be seen from behind by Ashton and Crispin. Any minute, she imagined Crispin's fourth chin resting on her shoulder so he could peep over.

Despite a balloon bursting and Rocky now dressed as a waiter nudging him in the back, saying hoarsely:

'Nibbles anyone?' Paris remained motionless, waiting until he'd got everyone's attention, gazing in wonder at the young girl in white muslin standing with the shy dignity of the daughter of the house at the foot of the stairs.

Pausing for five seconds on that first '"Oh!"' then, glancing up at the flambeaux flickering round the room, he murmured: '"She doth teach the torches to burn bright!"'

'Christ,' murmured Theo and Artie.

I must have that boy at Bagley, thought Hengist.

Offered another swig of Courvoisier from his flask, Janna shook her head, refusing to be distracted for a second. As Paris ended his speech, vowing he'd never seen true beauty till this night, you could have heard a pin and also the jaw of Dora Belvedon drop.

At the moment Paris fell in love with his Juliet, Dora felt herself blasted by similar lightning, as if she was seeing Paris for the first time, and he had become as beautiful, remote and beyond her reach as a stained-glass saint in the chapel.

He was even more heartbreaking in the balcony scene. Cosmo had given her five rolls of film to capture misbehaviour to flog to the nationals. Dora used them all on Paris. Even when Anatole and Feral were being killed off, she could only think of him. The wound made by Cupid's arrow was like the one in Mercutio's side.

'"Not so deep as a well, nor so wide as a church door, but 'tis enough, 'twill serve."'

Dora moaned in terror. She had lost control of her life.

In the dark beside Hengist, Janna had never been prouder or happier, breathing in lemon aftershave, rejoicing as his shout of laughter and the thunderclap of his big hands set off the rest of the audience.

In the interval, reality reasserted itself. Janna resisted

going backstage, terrified of intruding. She'd lost so much confidence. She'd just found Tim and Mags and a large glass of wine, when Vicky emerged to hearty cheering from the Tusk Force.

She looked enchanting in jeans and an old petrol-blue jersey, her hair in a ponytail, make-up lightly but carefully applied. Janna was ashamed to find herself wondering if Vicky had got Pearl to add the smudge on her cheek and the violet shadows beneath her eyes.

'So sorry I'm not dressed, everyone,' she cried, 'it's hard to rush round backstage in high heels and glad rags. Is it all right? I'm so close to it!'

The Tusk Force, except for Crispin who had a mouth full of cocktail sausages, assured her it was simply wonderful.

Janna steeled herself to invade the ring of admirers. 'Brilliant, Vicky, congratulations.'

'Your productions were so wonderful at Redfords' – Vicky hugged Janna – 'I so wanted not to let you down.'

'No danger of that,' said Ashton, 'Pawis Alvaston is headed for stardom, I would say.'

'I must rush and have a word with Mummy and Daddy in the auditorium.'

'I hope you'll bring them to the party later,' said a passing Hengist, 'they must be very proud.'

Even with Feral and Anatole killed off, the second half was full of incident. Boffin Brooks had surreptitiously put back the lines cut out of his long speeches as the Friar, and the audience started slow handclapping.

Johnnie Fowler-Upper, as he was now known, had a heavenly time in the bedroom scene, lighting up Juliet's Barbie dolls and Justin Timberlake posters, the Hon. Jack and Kylie snogging illicitly in another corner of the stage, Milly's boobs twice, Paris nude three times, the beauty of his slender wide-shouldered body causing several masters and Ashton to drop their binoculars.

'Very tasteful and dignified,' cried Chantal, seizing Hermione's opera glasses. 'May word, what a botty.'

Hoots of laughter greeted Monster's chemist shop offering Durex at £10 and Viagra at 50p. The mood was brought back on course by Cosmo, no longer the brutal father, but deranged with grief over his daughter. '"Death lies on her, like an untimely frost Upon the sweetest flower of all the field."'

Then, not on stage until the next act, Cosmo belted off to conduct the orchestra as they broke into galloping music. Suddenly the audience was startled by a clatter of hooves, the doors flew open and Paris thundered up the gangway. Unfazed by the screams and cheers, Beluga reached the pit and slithered to a halt, but as Paris chucked his reins to a starry-eyed, blushing Dora, he realized someone – no doubt Cosmo – had removed his plank.

Should he jump off and race round backstage, which would wreck the momentum, or risk falling into the pit? He chose the latter and scrambled onto Beluga's slippery saddle.

'Careful,' cried Dora in anguish as he took a massive leap, crashing onto the ill-lit stage, struggling to his feet before disappearing into the Capulets' mausoleum.

'Oh, my brave lad,' gasped Janna.

Even when Paris launched into the 'Eyes, look your last! Arms, take your last embrace!' speech and someone yelled: 'She's not dead yet, you berk,' he held the mood.

Tears were pouring down Janna's face and even Rupert was blowing his nose on Taggie's paper handkerchief as Paris drank purple flavoured water out of Sally's scent bottle, which had once contained Beautiful, and collapsed on Milly, gasping:

'"Thus with a kiss, I die",' and did.

'Well done,' whispered Milly, 'you've made it.'

45

The cast were called back again and again – all beaming – except Paris, who looked drained and utterly shell-shocked, but who got the biggest cheer of the night every time he took a bow.

My boy, thought Janna in ecstasy, and her heart nearly burst as Feral and Bianca bounded on hand in hand and slid into a ten-second tango routine, with Feral arching Bianca back until her black ringlets touched the floor, to stampings and cries of, 'More, more.'

Emlyn ensured that there was thunderous applause for every participant from Pearl for her make-up, Graffi for his sets, and Johnnie Fowler for his lighting:

'You should work in a strip club, Johnnie.'

The stagehands filed on until everyone had clapped their hands raw. But at the first pause, Ashton and Rod Hyde called out: 'Director!'

Whereupon the cast all put on their red noses and Primrose Duddon made a glowing breathy speech, handing out bottles to Emlyn, Jason, Sally Brett-Taylor, Mags and Cambola to thank them for all their hard work. Wally was also praised for being a tower of strength and ferrying everyone about in the wonderful Randal Stancombe bus. Wally was then presented with the definitive book on bell-ringing.

'But most importantly' – even Primrose had a crush on Vicky – 'I'd like to thank our wonderful director, Vicky Fairchild.'

Everyone stamped and yelled as Vicky ran on, accepted a vast bunch of pink roses and launched into an orgy of gratitude, for the wonderful chance she'd been given, for the children and teachers at Bagley and Larks, 'and particularly' – dimple, dimple – 'Hengist and Sally for making us so welcome and for all my dear friends at Larks for covering for me. I know I've played hookey a lot but I was so anxious to make a difference.

'And I'd like to thank dear Ashton and Crispin, at Support and Challenge, and dear Russell and all the governors, for being so supportive, and my parents who've come all the way from Harrogate.'

Audience and cast were getting restless. Cosmo, if he hadn't been trapped on stage, would have started up the orchestra.

'Oh come on, Vicky,' muttered Janna.

'Hush.' Hengist patted her arm. 'Let the little poppet enjoy her moment of glory.'

'If you'll just bear with me,' twinkled Vicky.

'Anytime you like, darlin',' yelled Graffi's father, who after the interval had smuggled in an entire bottle of champagne.

Vicky giggled enchantingly.

But Rocky had had enough. Shambling in front of Vicky, he raised a huge red hand. 'And I'd like to fank Miss Curtis, Janna, for believing in us, and making us feel we could do fings and for turning our school round,' he shouted.

This was greeted with cheers, Tarzan howls and fists punched in the air by both Larks and Bagley.

'Get that nutter off the stage,' howled Ashton.

'I was just coming to Janna,' said Vicky tartly.

With all the cuts, the play had lasted only ninety minutes, but it felt like midnight as Janna fought her way backstage to embrace and congratulate a euphoric cast in various states of undress.

'I am right proud. I never believed in a million years you could do so brilliantly.'

In his purple-stained shirt, a burning-hot Paris trembled as she hugged him, but couldn't speak or smile. His head was still in Juliet's tomb, but he was gratified that Nadine and Mr Blenchley, both of whom he loathed, rolled up to congratulate him at the same time as Patience, who in her raucous voice told them how bravely he'd overcome his terror of horses and even more brilliantly circumnavigated the missing plank.

'Plank's been relocated on his shoulder,' murmured Cosmo who, nevertheless, was feeling vulnerable. Judging by the way Feral and Graffi, still in his nurse's uniform, kept scowling in his direction, they were planning revenge.

Cosmo had lost his guards. However much he snapped his fingers, Anatole and Lubemir were ignoring him. Back in the General Bagley Room, where a splendid party was under way, they were happily getting drunk with the opposition.

'"Tybalt, you rat-catcher, vill you valk,"' said Anatole for the hundredth time.

Feral grinned, making a feint with a bread knife.

'We can't stop them drinking after such a magnificent performance,' Sally Brett-Taylor was telling Janna as big bowls of lasagne and sticks of bread were placed on a side table. 'But let's at least give them plenty of blotting paper.'

'An Italian dish – appropriate for *Romeo and Juliet,*' Boffin was saying pompously. 'Although at the Capulets' ball they would probably have eaten boar.'

'Unlike us who have to listen to one,' said Anatole, sprinkling Parmesan over Boffin's hair.

Paris, having survived his ride up the aisle, would have liked to retreat to Beluga's stable, thank the kind horse and relive with him every moment of the play. As it was, when he slunk into the party, everyone wanted a piece of him. With such a bone structure, what did it matter if he was monosyllabic?

'Cosmo will invite you back to River House for the weekend,' gushed Dame Hermione.

Cosmo, flipping through the film in Dora's camera, was enraged to find only pictures of Paris.

'They'll be worth a fortune when he gets an Oscar,' protested Dora.

'We need cash now,' snarled Cosmo.

Cosmo was right, thought Dora in panic. How could she support Cadbury or Loofah if she didn't sell stories? What had become of her? She normally had three helpings of lasagne; now she couldn't eat a thing. She couldn't take her eyes off Paris. He was as beautiful as the wild cherry blossom floodlit outside the window. She longed to tell him how wonderful he'd been, but the words stuck in her throat. The hurt was dreadful.

A record player was pounding out music from *Grease*. Amber and Pearl, sharing a surreptitious spliff and a bottle of white, were drowning their sorrows.

'We've lucked out there,' observed Amber as Feral and Bianca, unspeaking, making love with their eyes, danced on and on.

'She's only twelve,' snapped Pearl.

'"Younger than she are happy mothers made",' quipped Amber.

Aysha had gone home. A dazed, deliriously happy Xav gazed out of the window, breathing in the scent of Sally's narcissi, as sweet and delicate as Aysha, who had held his hand.

Janna moved from actor to parent to teacher to technician, praising and thanking. Not realizing Cosmo had been instrumental in Paris not walking the plank, she thanked him too.

She had a lovely chat with Theo Graham and Artie

Deverell. Theo seemed keen on teaching Paris Latin and Greek, and quoted Keats about feeling 'like some watcher of the skies When a new planet swims into his ken'.

Artie seemed equally keen to teach Paris modern languages.

'That boy is separate,' he said. 'You can't watch anyone else when he's on stage.'

'Or off it,' sighed Theo.

Kylie unplugged herself for a second from Jack Waterlane's embrace to ask Janna, 'People aren't just saying Larks did good, miss, because we didn't fight or trash anyfing?'

'You weren't good,' said Janna, then, as Kylie's face fell: 'You were utterly sensational.'

'Better'n Redfords?'

'A million times,' said Janna truthfully.

She was pleased when Emlyn, who'd been clearing up the stage, hove into sight clutching a large whisky and asking if she'd had anything to eat.

'Yes,' lied Janna. 'You were the real star. That play was only brilliant because you held everything together.'

'Not for much longer. The Wolf Pack are spoiling for a punch-up.'

'We'd better get them home,' said Janna. 'I'll alert Wally.'

On the way, she was accosted by Stormin' Norman, very drunk and singing Vicky's praises. 'Vicks realized Martin was visually and aurally impaired, put him in the front row and his school work's gone from strengf to strengf.'

Next Janna passed Vicky, surrounded by more admirers than Paris.

'If I had had my way,' she was telling Randal Stancombe, 'your Jade would have been Juliet.' Meeting Janna's eyes, she blushed. 'Well, Jannie, are you proud of us?'

To conceal her galloping disillusionment, Janna was shocked by her own effusiveness. 'It was all great. You did so well.'

'Send us Victoria, Sweetie and Gloria, Long to reign over us,' sang a drunken Lando and Junior.

'It was priceless,' said Vicky, dimpling again. 'Anatole insisted on introducing me to his father, who asked me what I taught. Quick as a flash, dear Anatole said: "She teaches the torches to burn bright, Dad." Wasn't that darling? I must tell Hengist.'

'Hengist has gone,' said Alex Bruce sourly. 'Pushed off to dinner at Head House with the Russian Minister, Rupert and Jupiter. He wouldn't waste time bothering with riff-raff like us.'

Vicky's lips tightened. Janna felt wiped out with tiredness and wondered if it would be letting the side down to go home, but first she must find Wally.

In her search, she bumped into Jason, congratulated him warmly and asked how he was getting on.

'Bloody tiring. I like the work, but you're on call twenty-four hours a day. You can't bunk off at three-thirty like we did at Larks. Thank God it's the end of term.'

'Thank you for working so hard on the play.'

Jason glanced back at Vicky still holding court.

'Come back, Cara,' he said acidly, 'all is forgiven.'

Janna gave a gasp. 'Then I'm not imagining things?'

'You are not. Nothing sucks like success. You turned Larks round. You made the kids understand the play. I know how much Emlyn, Piers and I put in, and how lazy little Vicky has claimed credit for everything. She thanks too much; such women are dangerous . . . And she's after Emlyn.'

'Oh dear.' Janna loathed that. 'He's much too nice.'

'But lonely without Oriana. You two should have dinner.'

Outside, Janna met Patience and thanked her for befriending Paris.

'We love him.' Patience lowered her donkey bray as Nadine and Mr Blenchley went down the steps: 'I just wish we could get him out of that horrible children's home.'

'Oh, so do I.'

'He's such a gentle soul.'

As they spoke, the fist of the gentle soul powered into Little Cosmo's jaw, sending him flying across an empty dining room. Scrambling to his feet in terror, Cosmo managed to leap out of a nearby window, landing this time on Sally's beloved white narcissi and budding crown imperials, followed by a yelling Paris, Feral and Graffi, only slightly impeded by his nurse's costume.

They were all beating the hell out of Cosmo and the crown imperials when Emlyn and the guards of the Russian Minister rolled up, yanking them off by their shirts.

'Lemme go, you fuckers,' howled Paris, escaping back into the fray. 'Lemme get at you, you fucker. How dare you move that plank?'

'How dare you grope my woman?' yelled Feral, also wriggling free.

'Lemme get at him,' bawled Graffi, fob watch and white cap flying.

'Let's all get at him,' shouted the Chinless Wanderers, leaping out of the window and pitching in.

'Stop it,' bellowed Emlyn, hauling Graffi off by the starched white collar of his costume, then, launching into Welsh: 'Back off. Your da's drunk, I need your help to carry him onto the coach before he throws up.'

Swearing and spitting, Graffi backed off.

It was a very warm night. No one could explain why Cosmo was discovered in the flower bed next morning with bruising and mild concussion, but otherwise unhurt, which was more than could be said for Sally's beloved narcissi, trillium grandiflora and crown imperials. Thanks to Emlyn and the Minister's guards, none of this reached the press, which, as a result, was excellent.

Venturer had filmed the whole production, five minutes of which was aired, including Paris's gallop up the gangway and the tango of Feral and Bianca, whose father was, after all, a Venturer director.

46

Mrs Kamani was so pleased to be invited and featured in *Romeo and Juliet*, she gave every Larks child an Easter egg. Janna organized a treasure hunt around the grounds, but she continually had to replace eggs, because they kept being tracked down and gobbled up by Partner.

Everyone had a wonderful time, as did Hengist and Sally, who spent Easter with Anatole's family in Russia.

'We had a treasure hunt for Fabergé eggs,' laughed Sally. 'Hengist and I found one each. Simply heavenly.'

All of which was too much for poor Alex Bruce, still festering over Hengist's lack of concern over Poppet's smashed figurine and being excluded from Hengist's private party after *Romeo and Juliet*, particularly when he discovered that feline smoothie Artie Deverell had been invited.

Then Emlyn Davies, who never showed any respect, announced that as he'd been working all hours on the play, he intended to take two days off to play golf and go racing.

It was high time, decided Alex, to impose some discipline. Staff therefore returned for the summer to find glass panels fitted into their classroom doors so Alex could monitor their lessons.

Theo Graham, head of classics, led the mutiny, promptly hanging his old tweed coat over the panel.

Alex then emailed all staff saying he would be monitoring random classes. Again, Theo led the resistance.

'I've been teaching for nearly forty years; no one's sitting in on my lessons.'

'Well, at least submit a plan for each lesson,' persisted Alex. 'This is required practice in the maintained sector.'

'I don't care, my lesson plans are in here.' Theo tapped his bald head. 'I don't need to write them down.'

Alex was furious and later in April, when Hengist went to America (ostensibly to attend a conference of heads; actually to join Jupiter in talking up their New Reform Party, as it was now officially known, to American senators), Alex decided to introduce daily staff meetings before chapel to discuss targets. This caused uproar.

On the first day only Alex's supporters – Joan Johnson and Biffo Rudge, head of maths – arrived on time: Biffo, because he wanted to seize the most comfortable big brown velvet armchair; Joan, big, meaty, dominating, because she believed in targets. Both she and Biffo rolled up armed with clipboards.

Miss Sweet, sex educator and undermatron of Boudicca, also arrived on time because she was terrified of Joan, as did little Miss Wormley, who was feeling sick at the mid-morning prospect of initiating Amber, Cosmo *et alii* into the erotic subtleties of 'The Love Song of J. Alfred Prufrock'.

The view from the staffroom was already causing controversy. It looked north-west over the shoulder of General Bagley and his charger down the long lime walk, which was just opening into palest acid-green leaf, to the golf course and woods beyond. It was a view which had restored the sanity of many a staff member since the mid nineteenth century, but which was now under threat because Alex Bruce was applying for planning permission to build on this site a new Science Emporium, financed by Randal Stancombe.

Hengist, who would have gone berserk if Alex had threatened a twig on his beloved Badger's Retreat, was comparatively indifferent to the positioning of the new Science Emporium – it had to go somewhere, preferably as far as possible from his office, which faced east, or from Head House, which was tucked away on the other bosky side of the campus, facing south.

And if push came to shove, General Bagley could always be relocated to the lawn below Hengist's office, where more people could admire him. He'd enjoy watching rugger and cricket far more than rats being dissected, and he'd be facing the East and India, where his great career had been carved out.

Alex and Poppet thought General Bagley, who'd won glory at the Battle of Plassey and wreaking vengeance after the Black Hole of Calcutta, was a dreadful old Empire-builder and wanted to get rid of his sculpture altogether.

From eight thirty-five, on the morning of Alex's first meeting, other staff drifted in, grumbling about having no time to walk their dogs, ostentatiously carrying on marking work and preparing lessons. Theo Graham, having scowled at Biffo for pinching the only chair which eased his bad back, perched on the window seat, reading a handful of Paris's poems sent him by Janna. They were very good, particularly one about a dandelion clock, glittering silver then puffed away to decide men's fates. Will she accept my proposal, will I get this job, will I get into Cambridge, is this cancer malignant, it is, it isn't, it is, it isn't. Thank God. My life will go on, but not the dandelion stalk, all its silken feathers flown, given no life in water after such a momentous forecast, chucked down to die on the dusty road.

'Have a look at this.' Theo handed the poem to Artie Deverell who'd just wandered in in a dark blue silk dressing gown, carrying a cup of black coffee, and who, putting the poem in his pocket, stretched out on the staffroom sofa and went back to sleep.

The room was almost full up, so Alex proceeded to involve the staff in a brainstorming session.

'Where d'you think you'll be in five years' time, Theo?'

'In a coffin, with any luck,' growled Theo.

'Don't be fatuous,' snapped Alex.

A disturbance was then created by Emlyn strolling in, still in pyjamas, eating a bowl of cornflakes and reading the Sun.

'We're trying to discuss targets and aims, Emlyn,' Alex told him icily. 'Tell us, if you please, the most important ingredient in your teaching plan.'

'A bullet-proof vest,' said Emlyn. 'Crucial for anyone who teaches Cosmo and Anatole.'

'And what is your goal when teaching the Lower Fifths?'

'To get out alive,' grunted Emlyn, not looking up from page three.

'Try to be serious.' Alex was fast losing patience. 'What is the most satisfying part of your lesson?'

'A large gin and tonic afterwards,' snapped back Emlyn.

'And the worst thing about Bagley Hall?' asked Alex through gritted teeth.

'Answering bloody stupid questions like this.'

'And the best?'

'Playing golf and getting wasted with Artie.' Emlyn blew a kiss to the sleeping Mr Deverell.

Alex was beside himself, particularly as Mrs Axford, the school cook, chose that moment to march in:

'Here's your sausage sandwich, Emlyn.'

Emlyn smiled sweetly up at her. 'Thanks so much, lovely.'

'Now we all know why you are so fat, Emlyn,' exploded Alex.

'No we don't,' said Emlyn amiably. 'It's because every time your wife takes me to bed she gives me a biscuit.'

The meeting broke up in disarray and howls of laughter.

The next day, Hengist flew back from America and enraged Alex Bruce by cancelling the meetings, adding they were the stupidest idea he'd ever heard and that good housemasters should be looking after their houses at that hour.

Hengist then embarked on the poaching of Paris Alvaston and the possibility of offering him a free place at Bagley in the Michaelmas term. In this he was much encouraged by the governors, who'd been entranced by *Romeo and Juliet*, and by the number of masters pixillated by Paris's white beauty, in particular Theo Graham and Artie Deverell, who were also impressed by Paris's poems.

Hengist, whose motives were invariably mixed, also wanted to take on a boy who would outshine Alex's favourite, Boffin Brooks, and scupper No-Joke Joan's smug prediction that her girls would soon be out-stripping his boys. David Hawkley had also been the subject of a flattering *Sunday Times* profile, and since the death of Mungo from meningitis and with Oriana constantly abroad, Hengist's longing for a son had increased.

Towards the end of the month, therefore, a secret afternoon meeting was held in the tranquillity of Head House to discuss the logistics of Paris's transfer.

Sitting round the highly polished dining-room table, admiring the bottle-green jungle wallpaper and Emma Sergeant's painting of Hengist's legendary drop goal, were Ian Cartwright, the bursar, Crispin Thomas, representing S and C, Nadine, Paris's social worker, Mr Blenchley, who managed Oaktree Court, Janna, who was spitting with Hengist for trying to poach her star pupil, and Hengist himself, who'd been playing tennis

394

and was wearing a dark blue fleece, white shorts and trainers and showing off irritatingly good, already brown, legs.

It was a warm, muggy afternoon; a robin sang in a bronze poplar tree; the cuckoo called from a nearby ash grove; young cow parsley leaves and the emerald-green plumage of the wild garlic spilt in jubilation over shaven green lawns. Beyond, in the park, acid-green domes of young trees rose against a navy-blue cloud, from which fell fringes of rain.

Sally had provided a sumptuous tea of cucumber and tomato sandwiches, a chocolate cake, warm from the oven and thickly spread with butter icing, and Earl Grey in a glittering Georgian silver teapot.

'Who's going to be mother?' snuffled Crispin.

'Who better than you?' mocked Hengist.

Nadine hastily grabbed the teapot. 'I will.'

The next question was who was going to be mother and father to Paris. Having poured out and piled up her plate, Nadine, who was wearing a black trouser suit which couldn't disguise thighs fatter than duffel bags and who, with her short curly fringe, glassy, expression-less eyes and long face, looked like a badly stuffed sheep, proceeded to consult her notes.

She reported that since *Romeo and Juliet*, Paris had had a rough time at Oaktree Court.

'He's too strong to be beaten up, but the inmates have ganged up and trashed his room, torn up his homework, shoved his books, many of them from Bagley library, down the toilet, stolen his school bag and thrown his denim jacket, which you gave him for his birthday, Janna' – Janna blushed as Crispin raised an eyebrow – 'into the boiler.

'As a result, Paris's behaviour has been very challenging. Last week he nearly strangled a boy who ran off with a snow fountain of the Eiffel Tower, the only gift left him by his birth mother.

'If he moved to Bagley,' continued Nadine in her

sing-song voice, helping herself to another tomato sandwich, 'conflict at Oaktree Court would escalate and he would be subject to peer pressure on two fronts. We therefore feel that if he were to go to Bagley, he should leave the care home and be fostered. Over to you, Gordon.'

In his shiny grey suit, with his brutal pasty face, nicotine-stained hands and dirty nails, Mr Blenchley looked both seedy and sinister. He had reached an age when his black and silver stubble merely gave the impression he had forgotten to shave. Hengist, Janna and Ian Cartwright shuddered collectively.

Mr Blenchley then said in his thick, clogged voice that he'd be extremely sorry to lose Paris.

'The lad's been with us for nearly four years; reckon we can congratulate ourselves. Before that he had over twenty placements. In some ways a difficult boy, inscrutable, but very able, needs challenging.'

Mr Blenchley was in fact desperate to get shot of Paris. In the past, the lad had been too terrified of being parted from his friends at Larks, the only family he knew, to blow any whistles. But at five foot nine, whippy and well muscled, Paris could no longer be intimidated into accepting that doors stealthily sliding over nylon carpets and creaking floorboards in the dead of night were the work of ghosts – or that predatory fingers creeping inside pyjama trousers and under little nightdresses were figments of the imagination.

'It costs fourteen hundred pounds a week to keep you at Oaktree Court, you ungrateful little shit,' he had shouted at Paris that very morning.

To which Paris had shouted back, 'Give me the fucking money then.'

'What we feel Paris needs,' chipped in Nadine, 'is a sympathetic foster family, a middle-aged couple whose kids perhaps have grown up. It will be challenging, coming from an institution, however admirable, and a maintained school like Larks, then mixing with the protected, privileged students at Bagley. Paris gets ten pounds a month clothes allowance.'

'Jade Stancombe gets about a thousand,' sighed Hengist.

Janna gazed out into the park at the young green trees in their little wooden playpens. Even trees that soared twenty-five feet still retained their wooden cages. Paris would have no such protection.

'Children of Paris's age seldom find a home,' said Crispin, who'd been too busy filling his face to contribute to the debate, 'because potential adopters think they're too damaged.'

'Paris isn't damaged,' cried Janna in outrage. 'He's a sweet boy, so kind to the little ones and intensely loyal to his friends.' Then, as hateful Crispin smirked again, she went on: 'It would be like trapping a skylark to send him to Bagley, away from Feral and Graffi. What he needs is love and some kind of permanence.'

'I agree,' said Nadine. 'Ideally Paris Alvaston needs a forever family to facilitate the adjustment.'

Hengist had put his chocolate butter icing on the side of his plate. Was he watching his figure or keeping the best bit till last? He kept glancing across the table trying to make Janna laugh each time Nadine murdered the English language, but she refused to meet his eye. She was unable to forgive him for not consulting her before offering Paris a place or for looking so revoltingly sexy in those shorts that she wanted him to drag her upstairs and shag her insensible.

And yet, and yet, however much she loathed the idea of private education, she had to recognize Bagley would give Paris a step up the ladder that Larks never could. But if Oaktree Court had given him such hell for getting posh, surely Bagley would roast him for being a yob?

If only she could foster him herself and provide him with a haven at weekends, half-term and during the holidays. Then she'd have someone to love and to cherish; they'd have such fun together.

But I'm too busy, she thought despairingly.

The spring holidays might never have been. The dark circles were back under her bloodshot eyes. She had 400 kids, 399 if Paris went to Bagley, and a school to save.

'You haven't had any cake.' Ian Cartwright, silly old blimp, was about to slide the last piece onto her plate. 'It's awfully good.'

Janna shook her head. She didn't want anything from Bagley. As the meeting roved on over pros and cons, she fought sleep, finally nodding off only to wake with a start, crying, 'Bagley won't hurt Paris, will they?' making the others stare at her in amazement.

Fortunately, at that moment, Sally Brett-Taylor wandered in, rivalling the spring's freshness in a pale-green cashmere jumper, asking if the teapot needed more hot water and discreetly giving Hengist an escape route by reminding him his next appointment was waiting. Everyone gathered up their papers.

'To sum up,' snuffled Crispin, licking chocolate icing off his fingers, 'unless we can find a foster family for Paris, you wouldn't recommend a move to Bagley.'

'That's right,' said Nadine. 'I think the contrast would be too extreme.'

'Beautiful garden, Mrs Brett-Taylor,' said Mr Blenchley, gazing out on Sally's riot of tulips, irises and fritillaries. 'Do you have a sprinkler system?'

'I prefer to water plants myself.' Sally smiled. 'That way you get to know them individually.'

Like my children, thought Janna. Why did everything at the moment make her cry?

47

Hengist returned from Rutminster Cathedral, where the school choir had been singing at Evensong, around nine. On the bus home he had sat next to Dora Belvedon, who, having somehow discovered the meeting had taken place, was desperate for Paris to come to Bagley.

'Just think, he'll mention you and Bagley one day in his acceptance speech at the Oscars.'

Hengist was greeted by a squirming, pirouetting Elaine, who left white hairs all over the trousers of his dark suit, the jacket of which Hengist hung on the banisters before removing his tie and pouring himself a large whisky.

He found Sally at the drawing-room piano playing the beautiful second movement of Schubert's D Major Sonata, which was slower and easier than the first. Only holding up her cheek to be kissed, she didn't stop. Hengist slumped on the sofa with Elaine to listen, watching the lamplight falling on his wife's pale hair, on Mungo's photograph and on a big bunch of white tulips, which shed petals each time she played more vigorously.

Swearing under her breath at the occasional wrong note in the difficult cross rhythms and vowing to set aside time to practise in the future, Sally reached the end.

'How would you feel about adopting Paris Alvaston?' asked Hengist.

Sally looked down at her hands, closed the music and shut the piano with a snap.

'Or, for a start, fostering him?'

'Not fair to him,' said Sally, with unexpected harshness. 'He'll be conspicuous enough coming from Larks; imagine being the head's son.'

'Easier than if he was our actual child. No one could blame him for my cringe-making idiosyncrasies. Nor would he be upset by other children slagging us off.'

Rising and crossing the room, he massaged Sally's rigid shoulders for a moment, then slid his hands down inside her pale-green jersey, which had been washed in Lux so many times.

'We don't have the time,' said Sally angrily. 'You want Fleetley, the Ministry of Education; you want to write. You have eight hundred children and an army of staff. You're always away and poor Elaine doesn't get enough walks.'

Elaine thumped her bony tail in agreement.

'Paris deserves better,' she went on. 'He needs time, individual attention and a live-in father.' And I don't see enough of you, she nearly added.

As his hands crept downwards, she willed her nipples not to respond. He had such a hold over her.

'It'd only be the holidays, half-terms and weekends,' protested Hengist. 'Give Oriana a bit of competition – a sibling to rival. She might come home more often.'

'Why did she stay away so much in the first place?' At heart, Sally felt she had failed as a mother to the absentee Oriana. Why should she fare any better with Paris?

'The voice of reason,' said Hengist irritably. 'He's such a lovely boy and such a potential star. I could bask in his reflected glory in my dotage.'

As his hands slid over her breasts, he felt the nipples hardening, and Sally felt liquid ripples between her legs.

'I was thinking of you,' whispered Hengist. 'You can always make time. Those geeks today had never eaten anything like your chocolate cake.'

'Janna and Ian Cartwright aren't geeks,' protested Sally, 'although she was looking awfully peaky, poor child.'

'Paris would be company. Mungo—' he began.

'Don't,' gasped Sally. The pain was still unbearable.

'Sorry. I just can't bear the thought of the poor boy being abandoned to that grotesque Blenchley, who I'm sure's a paedophile. His nails looked as though they were steeped in dried blood. Did you know that twenty-five per cent of the homeless are care leavers who've been cast out on the world?'

'Stop it.' Sally clapped her hands to her ears. 'I'll think about it.'

'Elaine loves Paris.' Hengist's hand slipped under the waistband of her skirt, over her flat stomach, to lose itself in warm flesh. 'I'm going to ring Mrs Axford and tell her to wait dinner half an hour.'

Despite his brusque, bossy exterior, Ian Cartwright liked children and, as a fine cricketer and rugby player, had always wanted a son. Since his adopted daughters Emerald and Sophy had married and had their own children, the house had seemed very empty.

Arriving home from the meeting, he could smell shepherd's pie, made from the remains of the cold meat from Sunday's shoulder of lamb. If one carved narrow slices, there was always plenty over. He found Patience crimson in the face, reading *Horse & Hound* as she spread mashed potato over the lamb.

'Good day?' she asked.

'Interesting.' Ian poured them both a glass from the bottle of red with which she was jazzing up the mince. 'Hengist wants to offer a free place to Paris Alvaston.'

'That's wonderful.' Patience tested the broccoli with a fork. 'How brilliant of Hengist.'

'Paris is having a bloody time at the children's home. They're looking for a family to foster him.'

'Oh, poor boy. If only we weren't so old.'

'We may not be. They want an older couple, who, if it worked, might consider adopting him to bridge the gap when he'd normally leave care and be chucked out on the streets.'

Out of the window, Ian could see Northcliffe, the golden retriever who had a tendency to go walkabout round the campus, cantering back across the fields, pausing to pick up a twig as a peace offering.

'Social services won't let him come to Bagley unless they can find someone. "Family find" is the awful expression.'

'Oh, Ian.' Patience sat down. 'Are you sure? We've only just got ourselves sorted.'

'You mean clawed our way back from financial ruin,' said Ian with a mirthless laugh. 'I won't be so stupid again.'

'I'd love to give it a try,' mused Patience. 'Dora simply adores him, so does Northcliffe. But I'm sure he'd find us too square. I don't know anything about Liverpool or pop music or Larkminster Rovers or computers.'

'Why don't we ask him?' said Ian.

They were brought back to earth by the smell of burnt broccoli.

First thing, Ian rang Nadine, who dropped in later in the day and was most enthusiastic.

'Paris loves coming to you. Your daughters and their kids visit often, so he'd have an extended family. You've been cleared by the Criminal Records Bureau; you've experienced the ups and downs of adoption. It could take several months, however, because you'd have to go on a course and undergo some counselling and some extensive interviews, I'm afraid.'

'We've been there. Last time they kept asking about

our sex lives,' brayed Patience. 'We're a bit past that now.'

Ian frowned. 'I'm sure Nadine doesn't want to hear about that.'

'Paris's behaviour will probably be very challenging,' said Nadine. 'Looked-after kids invariably test their carers to the limit, just to prove they really care.'

'Just like rescued dogs,' said Patience happily. 'I must start reading the football reports.'

'I can't bear to think of poor Paris trapped in that children's home with that repellent man,' announced Sally the following evening. 'I'm sure we could make time.'

'Too late,' said Hengist, almost accusingly. 'Fools have rushed in. Ian and Patience have offered. They've got to undergo loads of ghastly trials, like the labours of Hercules. But Nadine is taking Paris to "meet with" them shortly. "None but the brave deserves the fair",' he added bitterly and Sally felt reproached.

News of the poaching of Paris flashed round the staffroom.

'Just like a feminist version of the Trojan Wars,' sighed Artie Deverell. 'Lucky, lucky Cartwrights, but bags I be Helen of Troy.'

Dora was in ecstasy:

'I'll come and help you dirty up your house,' she told Patience. 'Social workers don't like prospective foster homes to be too pristine.'

403

48

The first meeting with the Cartwrights was excruciatingly embarrassing. Paris had only had mugs of tea in the kitchen before, but this time Patience had put on a skirt and make-up and heels she had great difficulty walking in, and had plunged into a drawing-room rat race of best china, silver, bread and butter and strawberry jam and 'Would you like milk, sugar, lemon or another slice of walnut cake?' all to be balanced on one's knees or the cat-shredded arm of a chair.

The drawing room, like Lily Hamilton's, seemed overcrowded with dark furniture, suggesting departure from a much larger house. Every shelf and table was crowded with ornaments or yellowing silver or blossom from the pink cherry outside rammed into vases.

Paris wished Ian and Nadine would bugger off and he could sort things out with Patience. Hitherto he'd only seen Ian flitting round Bagley being bossy about overspending and drooling over Vicky Fairchild. He seemed very old and straight, smelt like Mike Pitts of peppermint and stiff whiskies and kept barking, 'Mind out,' as Northcliffe's plumy tail endangered a precious teacup. He was like Captain Mainwaring in *Dad's Army*; Paris couldn't imagine him wearing jeans or taking him to McDonald's.

'I'm afraid it's bought,' confessed Patience when

Nadine congratulated her on her walnut cake. 'I'm not much of a cook.'

Anything would be better than Oaktree Court, thought Paris, where, as if Nigella and Jamie Oliver had never existed, Auntie Sylvia boiled mince, diced carrots and onion in water until they were cooked and turned cod the grey of the ancient pair of knickers, almost divorced from its elastic, which a wagging, singing Northcliffe had just laid at Nadine's big feet.

'Oh Northie,' giggled Patience, grabbing the pants and shoving them under a cushion.

'The most important thing is to hold back and listen,' Nadine had urged Patience, who, however, came from a generation and class who regarded it as a crime not to keep conversation going, however inane, and proceeded to do so.

How the hell was he going to put up with a lifetime of this, wondered Paris. If only he could turn on the television and watch Chelsea play Liverpool.

'This is our granddaughter, Dulcie,' said Patience, picking up a photograph of an adorable child with blond curls. 'She's a darling.'

Paris loved children. The best part of the home had always been making up games and stories for the littlest ones and comforting them when they cried. A few years ago, abuse had been rife; now the pendulum had swung. No careworker was ever on for more than forty-eight hours and the majority were so terrified of being accused of abuse, they wouldn't even take on to their lap a child who'd grazed a knee or been torn away from its parents. Desolation ruled. And if you dared complain of past abuse, you'd be bombarded by social workers, counsellors and therapists, prising you open, gouging out your secrets. Easier to trust no one and keep your trap shut.

There was another long pause.

'Our daughters Emerald and Sophy both married painters,' announced Patience, to explain the large, strange pictures rubbing shoulders with the hunting prints and landscapes on the walls.

'You were in the army, Colonel Cartwright,' accused Nadine, pointing to an oil of a lot of screaming women being mown down by a firing squad and their blood watering the young barley. 'Is this your taste?'

'Certainly not. It was painted by my son-in-law. He's actually a war artist, with work in the Tate.'

'You mustn't be so defensive,' chided Nadine.

Ian turned purple.

'Emerald's a sculptor,' said Patience quickly. 'She made me this adorable little maquette of Northcliffe for my birthday. You can almost see his tail wagging.'

'How old were they when you adopted Emerald and Sophy?'

'Just babies.' Patience reached for more photographs.

Those children had clearly inspired love, reflected Paris. Could he do the same? He was terrified they'd discover, beneath his cool, that he was as needy and desperate to escape as those mongrels pathetically scrabbling at the bars in a dog's home.

'We've got to go through some gruelling interviews,' Patience told him. 'We won't know if we're suitable as parents until August, which is a bore, but more importantly you might hate the thought of living with us.' She tried to stop her voice shaking.

Out in the yard a horse neighed, calling out to its stable mate who'd been taken out for a ride.

'Dunno,' muttered Paris, pulling at a piece of cotton on his chair and releasing an avalanche of horsehair. 'Oh shit.'

'Paris, that's not very nice,' reproved Nadine.

Shut up, Paris wanted to scream, because he didn't know what to say, and was even more terrified that if they found out about his red-haze temper, his light fingers, his capacity for demolition, that he occasionally wet the bed, and was racked by fearful, screaming nightmares, they'd chuck him out after a week, a care leaver destined for homelessness.

'We'd so love you to come and live with us,' stammered Patience, missing the cup as she topped up Nadine's tea. 'But first you must get to know us.'

'That's enough,' snapped Ian. 'Let Paris make up his own mind; there's no hurry.'

'You will come and see us next week?' persisted Patience.

'For Christ's sake,' exploded Ian.

Oh God, they'll reject Ian and me because we don't get on, thought Patience in panic.

'Careful not to invade Paris's personal space,' reproved Nadine.

Paris scowled round at her. 'I can go if I like,' he said curtly.

The following Saturday, they asked Paris if he'd like to go to the cinema, but he said he'd prefer to muck about at home, and spent a couple of hours looking at Ian's military collection, which contained pieces of shrapnel, shells and bullets, and even a bit of marble from Hitler's desk.

'Rupert Brooke and I were at the same school,' volunteered Ian and, secretly thrilled by Paris's interest, presented him with a paperback of First World War poems.

Later, as the evenings were drawing out, Patience took him out to watch the Bagley herd being milked and took a picture of him with Ian and Northcliffe.

Paris's next visit was a disaster. Examining the photographs of beautiful Emerald in the drawing room, he knocked off and smashed the maquette she had modelled of Northcliffe. In terror, he shoved the pieces under the sofa, but missed the tail, which had fallen on a rug.

'I'd better go,' he told Patience, edging towards the door.

'You haven't had any tea – I've got Cornish pasties and chips.'

'Don't want anything.'

'I'll drive you back.'

'I want to walk.'

'Oh look, Northcliffe's tail's fallen off again. I must stick it back.' When she found the other pieces under the sofa, her face fell, then she smiled. 'Doesn't matter, I'm sure Emo can make me another one. I'm always breaking things. I smashed a vase this morning.'

Paris flared up:

'Why aren't you mad at me? You must be, you loved that dog.'

'It's only an ornament that's broken – not a promise or a heart.'

'Oh, for Christ's sake.' Paris stormed out and, crying helplessly, ran all the six miles back to Oaktree Court.

Two days later, he received a letter from Patience.

'Please come to tea next Saturday. Longing to see you.'

It wasn't natural to be so forgiving.

Nadine dropped him off, jollying him along, interrogating him all the way, as though she were forcibly opening an oyster with a chisel. He didn't tell her he was only intending to stay five minutes. Working himself into a rage, heart crashing, his breath coming in great gasps, he marched into an empty kitchen, rehearsing his speech: 'Look, it's not going to work. I want to chuck the whole thing: I can't handle Bagley and sod Hengist and Theo Graham and fucking Homer and Virgil.

'Get out the way,' he yelled, aiming a kick as Northcliffe, carrying a feather duster, bounded towards him in delight.

He was about to sweep all Patience's recipe books

onto the floor, and then start smashing plates and mugs so they'd definitely never want to see him again, when he caught sight of his own photographs in a silver frame on the dresser: one of him with Northcliffe, another of him as Romeo. Yet another of him, with Dora and Beluga, Romeo's fiery steed, had been put in a big frame beside pictures of Emerald and Sophy.

Paris blushed and blushed, a huge smile spreading over his face, as Patience bustled in:

'Oh, hello, Paris.' Then, catching sight of the photographs, she added humbly: 'We hope you don't think we're jumping the gun.'

Paris kicked the kitchen table and shook his head.

'It's fine.'

'Thank goodness. Plover's sister's about to foal, the vet's on his way, I thought you might like to help.'

'OK.' Paris then screwed up courage to ask how the interviews were going.

'Pretty well,' said Patience, putting on her red Puffa. 'They do ask extraordinary questions. If normal couples went through such hassle, they'd never have children. But it's all worth it,' she added hastily.

After the foal had been born, all covered in blood and gore, the vet and Patience had shared a bottle of white wine with Paris and congratulated him on having such a calming effect on the frightened mare. When Nadine rolled up, Patience hastily dropped the bottle in the bin.

As he was leaving, she shouted he'd left his jacket, and as she picked it up from the kitchen chair, a photograph of her and Ian fluttered out.

'Must have picked it up by mistake,' muttered Paris. 'No, that's a lie, I wanted one until I moved in, like.'

'Keep it,' said an enraptured Patience.

Watching him go off into the hazy blue evening, Patience hugged herself. Until he moved in, like. She ran to the gate to wave him off.

Back at the home, Paris hid the photo between his

under-blanket and the mattress, because he didn't seem to be wetting the bed any more and because Patience and Ian were pretty old and ugly, and he couldn't bear the other kids taking the piss or, even worse, tearing up the photo.

As bursars work extremely hard, Paris saw more of Patience than Ian, who was nervous but determined things should work.

'What'm I supposed to call you?' Paris asked him on the next visit.

'You could call me "Colonel Cartwright", but that's a bit formal, and "Uncle" is silly because I'm not. Would it be OK, if we pass the tests, to describe you as "Paris, our foster son", which would be true, then if things go very well, we can drop the foster.'

'That's good,' agreed Paris. 'I'll call you Mr Ian, if that's OK.'

'Good start,' said Ian.

'As we know each other better, you can call me Patience.'

Paris really smiled for the first time.

'Going to need a lot, if you're taking me on.'

'Next week, why don't we go to IKEA and choose some stuff for your room?' Treading on eggshells, trying not to presume, she added hastily: 'If we don't pass the test, you can always use the room when you come and stay.'

49

In the middle of May, when Bagley was looking at its most seductive, with the setting sun warming the golden stone, cow parsley lacing the endless pitches and the trees still in their radiant young, green beauty, Hengist formally offered Paris a place.

On the wall of Hengist's study, Paris was intensely flattered to see, alongside other triumphs, a framed photograph of himself as Romeo. Then Hengist had added he was also offering a boarding place to Feral, so he and Paris needn't be parted, and when Paris accepted, trying to keep the excitement out of his voice and face, Hengist offered him a glass of champagne to celebrate.

'Patience and Ian are a super couple.' Hengist sat down on the dark red Paisley window seat beside a reclining Elaine, and beckoned Paris to join them. 'A super couple, salt of the earth, although one's not, according to Poppet Bruce, supposed to have salt in anything these days. You'll have fun when their daughters come down – Emerald is stunning – and with young Dora hanging around and lots of horses and a charming dog. But if you find it hard to discuss things with them, speak instead to Theo Graham, who's going to be your new housemaster. Beneath the rather crusty exterior Theo's a sweet man.

'But if you ever think of running away from Bagley'

– Hengist was lovingly smoothing Elaine's white, velvet ears – 'I want you to promise to pop in on Sally and me first, and we'll give you some sandwiches and a can of Coke for the journey. Give me your hand and your promise,' and his big suntanned hand enveloped Paris's, which was almost as white and slender as Elaine's.

Paris promised. He'd never met anyone as charismatic as Hengist. The thick, dark hair, olive skin, heavy-lidded eyes, beautiful clothes, the element of danger, the desire not exactly to corrupt but to stir up and subvert reminded him so much of Lord Henry Wotton in *The Portrait of Dorian Gray*. The same sweet, seductive scent of lilac, so memorable in the book, was now drifting in through the window, overpowering the clean, healthy, soapy smell of hawthorn.

Paris had been jealous of Hengist in the past, because Janna smelt so lovely and always seemed to be laughing when Hengist was around. Paris still thought and dreamt of her constantly. At the end of term, they would be split up, but at least before that, at the end of June, she would be coming on the geography field trip, when Larks and Bagley would be taking off together for Wales, and he might slay a dragon for her. He was very proud Hengist had chosen him, and with Feral by his side, he could face anything.

Hengist, predictably, was not just enlisting Feral entirely for Paris's benefit. As a dazzling athlete, who'd really profit from decent coaching and pitches, Feral would bring glory to Bagley. Nor could Hengist resist unsettling that pompous ass Biffo Rudge by installing a gloriously priapic black boy in his house.

Alas, the next day, Feral was summoned off the cricket field, having just been bowled after knocking up a useful fifty in twenty minutes, and flabbergasted Hengist by turning down his offer of a place.

'Kind of you, man, but I don't like the thought of being locked up in the evening.'

He didn't add that he was worried his family would fall apart if he wasn't there to hold it together.

'"Why, uncle, 'tis a shame",' said Paris when he heard the news. Although devastated by Feral's refusal, he wasn't prepared to betray regret or try and talk him round.

'As I'm locked up already, I might as well accept a more upmarket gaol.'

Nor was everyone pleased about Paris going to Bagley. Joan Johnson thought free places should have been offered to clever Aysha, or Kylie for her pretty voice, or Pearl for her artistic skills.

And if the masters at Bagley were excited, the staff at Larks were outraged that Paris would be thrown to the wolves of private education.

Emerald and Sophy Belvedon, who liked to dump their own children on Granny Patience whenever they needed a break, also expressed doubts.

'He'll be bringing his rough friends home and breaking the place up. He's already smashed my maquette of Northcliffe,' raged Emerald. 'And I hope Daddy's not going to get any silly ideas like Jupiter about sons inheriting everything.'

Sophy was more worried that teenagers were wildly expensive and that her parents had just got straight financially after Ian going bankrupt in the nineties.

Janna, meanwhile, had not made it up with Hengist. Ringing up to ask her to lunch, he received an earful, but refused to admit he'd pulled a fast one by poaching Paris.

'Darling, from the moment we met at La Perdrix d'Or, you kept telling me how wonderfully clever Paris was, thrusting his poems and essays at me, saying he needed to escape from the poverty trap. I honestly thought that was what you wanted.'

'Oh, go to hell.' Janna slammed down the telephone.

She was having a very tough summer. The GCSEs loomed and unless their results improved, they would again be branded one of the worst schools in the West. Exams also meant the gym would be out of action, so the children couldn't work off any energy. The Wolf Pack were demoralized and acting up because Paris was leaving. Half the staff were moonlighting and exhausted and tetchy, after four or five hours marking GCSE papers every night.

After the good publicity generated by *Romeo and Juliet,* many parents had put Larks as their first choice. Then the wretched council had changed the bus route, which meant buses no longer stopped outside the school gates and parents, worried about kidnapping and sexual abuse, changed their minds.

One step forward, one step back.

But despite not a week passing without a slagging off in the *Gazette,* Janna felt the school was steadily improving. Thanks to frequent visits from Gablecross's constabulary, there was much less fighting in the playground or in the corridors. Teachers were mostly able to teach. Mrs Kamani no longer complained of shoplifting and rowdy behaviour. Even Miss Miserden, the old biddy who lived at the bottom of the drive, stopped grumbling about Feral's football after Graffi rescued her cat Scamp from the top branch of a pear tree. The children had also been on some terrific jaunts to the seaside, to the Blackpool illuminations, to Longleat and the London Eye. A production of *Oliver!* was planned for next term.

Vicky, who would direct it, was not enjoying the summer term as much as her spring one. She couldn't slope off to Bagley all the time and had to face up to the rough and tumble of Larks.

In the last week in May, in the middle of the GCSEs, having gained Mike Pitts's permission and claiming it was 'vital for her professional development', Vicky sloped off for two days at a National Theatre workshop.

In her absence, Janna discovered a shambles of homework unmarked and work unset. Worse still, Vicky was hardly engaging with her tutor group, with the result that one girl was being so badly bullied, she tried to hang herself with a pair of tights during break.

Janna, who had already received a warning from the girl's mother, had ordered Vicky to sort it out. Vicky had clearly done nothing.

Bitter shame that she herself hadn't prevented it fuelled Janna's anger. Vicky was due back on the Wednesday morning before half-term, then rang in to tell Rowan her train had broken down and she wouldn't be back till after lunch.

She had eventually floated in around two-forty-five, Little Miss Demure in a navy blue suit, with her shining clean hair drawn into a neat bun, pale cheeks flushed, wafting Trésor. Immediately, she started wittering on about 'cutting-edge productions' and 'unique opportunities to discover my own creativity'.

Janna let her run, then let rip, epitomizing every cliché about redheads and fiery tempers. Partner shot under the sofa.

'I trusted you, Vicky. How dare you bunk off like this? Year Eight is totally under-rehearsed for their play on Parents' Day. Year Eleven can't quote a single line from A View from the Bridge and they've got Eng. lit. tomorrow. You left no lesson plans for this morning.'

'I rang in,' bridled Vicky.

'You should have come back. Lottie Hargreaves, one of your tutor group, tried to hang herself. We've had the police here all morning. I told you to keep an eye on her. You've let me down!'

'And you've let me down,' shouted back Vicky. 'You never warned me this school was completely out of control. A parent slapped my face the other day.'

'Why didn't you report it?'

'I didn't want to sneak.' Vicky burst into tears and fled.

Overnight, Janna cooled down. The fact remained she needed Vicky. Whatever her limitations, she had reduced truancy among the boys, and with so many children taking drama and English GCSEs next year because of her, Janna couldn't really sack her. She'd better call her in first thing, before she caused too much havoc.

She was greeted on the morrow by a furious Rowan.

'You're not going to like this.'

It was a letter from Bagley's personnel department asking for a reference for Vicky who had applied for a job teaching English and drama. Janna flipped and rang Hengist who, as Painswick had gone to the dentist, picked up the telephone. Bruckner's Eight was on fortissimo. Hengist only turned it down fractionally and when Janna started screaming at him, became quite sharp. Education was a free-for-all. Vicky was entitled to work where she wanted. As long as her notice was in by 31 May, which was tomorrow, she could start in the autumn.

'Anyway, I can't see why you're making such a fuss. You seemed pretty anxious to be shot of the poor child yesterday. I also wanted to make things easy for Paris,' he went on, even more infuriatingly, 'who will feel happier if he's acquainted with a member of staff.'

Out of the window, Janna could see a Year Eleven pupil so deep in last-minute revision, she bumped into an oak tree.

'"All my pretty chickens and their dam, At one fell swoop?"' she said tonelessly. 'How dare you poach my staff and pupils without asking?'

'Because I knew you'd try and stop me,' said Hengist unrepentantly.

'Vicky has ensured three-quarters of Year Ten will be taking drama GCSE next year.'

'That's great. We can hold joint Larks–Bagley classes. Means I'll see more of you.'

After that, Janna's shouting could be heard all

416

over Larks, and Partner took refuge in Rowan's office.

'I'm not going to talk to you until you cool down,' said Hengist and hung up.

'We're well shot of her, she's an applause junkie and a dozy bitch,' said Rowan, rushing in with a box of tissues and a cup of black coffee laced with brandy. 'Give her a good reference to show you're magnanimous. Lord Brett-Taylor can pick up the pieces when she fucks up.'

'Rowan,' said Janna in awe, 'I've never heard you swear before.'

Janna's magnanimity was sorely tested when she and Vicky met.

'I'm tired of sticking up for you, Jannie.'

'Who first approached you?' asked Janna numbly.

'I don't remember, but Hengist, Emlyn and nice Alex Bruce, such a sweetie, all suggested I'd be an asset to Bagley, and frankly' – Vicky smiled helplessly – 'Hengist is so charismatic, I can't resist the chance of working with him. And if I can ease Paris's transition and Hengist believes I can . . .' Then, misinterpreting the anguish on Janna's face: 'But don't worry, I won't let you down over the geography field trip. Emlyn's going and Hengist even said he might drop in. He's arranged for us to stay in some Welsh stately castle. I can't wait.'

Vicky didn't add that she herself had applied for the job, and at her first interview over lunch with Hengist on Wednesday, had presented him with a rare work on rugby football or that yesterday, after Janna had carpeted her, she had driven over to Bagley and sobbed on Alex's narrow shoulder, telling him:

'Larks is out of control: a Year Nine boy tried to rape me' (mild lunge from Monster) 'and I was punched by a parent' (mild lunge from a mother whose husband Vicky had inveigled into Larks to paint cupboards).

'I loved Jannie so much in Yorkshire,' Vicky had continued to sob. 'She was such fun. Now she seems to have lost her creativity. She's so hard now.'

Dora Belvedon, busy weeding up wallflowers under the window, heard everything, which the following day appeared in the *Gazette* as 'Star teacher and pupil to leave Larks'.

Red Robbie, who'd been hoping to get his leg over Vicky on the geography field trip, was so shocked by her defection to an independent, he flatly refused to go.

Janna also received lots of flak.

'Just learnt of your tragic loss,' emailed Rod Hyde, 'you must try and hang on to your good staff.'

'I don't know what we'll do without our little Vicky to bring sunshine into our life,' moaned Basket.

Monster proceeded to trash the drama department.

I'm just jealous of Vicky having constant access to Hengist and Paris, thought Janna in despair. She wished she could pour her heart out to Emlyn, but he'd taken the opportunity of half-term to fly to Afghanistan to see Oriana.

Janna spent most of the break sobbing for her mother. She had to face up to the fact that hard work cannot blot out loneliness for ever.

The only positive thing she did was to telephone her friend Sophy Belvedon. Sophy was Ian and Patience's daughter, married to Alizarin, the brother of Jupiter, Dora and Dicky. Sophy was also an English and drama teacher, with whom Janna had worked in Yorkshire, who now lived in London.

Sophy was her usual cheerful, adorable self.

'It's so lovely to hear from you. Mum says you're making a brilliant job of Larks. It must be so beautiful down there now.'

'How's Dulcie?' asked Janna. 'She must be nearly eighteen months now.'

'She's heaven, but I'm not sure being a full-time mother's quite me. I'm so turning into a cabbage, leaves are sprouting out of my head. I'm sure some

German's going to make me into sauerkraut.'

'You don't want a job, do you?'

'God, I'd love one.'

'Head of English and drama in the autumn.'

'Oh yes, yes please.'

'It's a pretty rough school.'

'Couldn't be rougher than London. Someone chucked a brick through our drawing-room window yesterday. We could get an au pair or perhaps Mum could look after Dulcie during the day. Might put her and Dad off their latest mad project of fostering a looked-after kid of fourteen.'

Alex Bruce, while delighted by the annexing of Vicky, bitterly regretted that Hengist's ability to poach clever children and staff was only equalled by his irrational refusal to boot out the stupid children of his friends.

The Chinless Wanderers: Lando, Jack and Junior, although dazzling at games, were predicted to get straight Us in their GCSE exams in two years' time. Xavier Campbell-Black bumped sulkily along the bottom of the class and his sister Bianca, even more intellectually challenged, had recently revealed that she didn't know on which side Hitler fought in the last war.

Alex was anxious to single out any pupils on the Grade C/D borderline and give them early coaching. Anyone below that level would endanger Bagley's place in the league tables and should be asked to leave.

'Bianca will stay,' said Hengist firmly. 'She's destined to be the next Darcey Bussell. Screw the league tables. We must cultivate individual excellence.'

'You said you wanted to beat Fleetley and ward off any challenge from St Jimmy's.'

'Maybe I did. The secret of greatness is to admit one is in the wrong.'

Hengist's inconsistency drove Alex crackers.

'Thank God this school is in a safe pair of hands,' he told Miss Painswick.

'Thank God for a handy pair of safes,' smirked Little Cosmo, as he and Lubemir cracked the combination of the safe in the school office, photostatted the 2002 GCSE and A level papers stored inside and flogged them for five hundred pounds a go to needy candidates.

'We need never work again,' crowed Cosmo, 'and we're doing our bit for Bagley by ensuring it does really well in the league tables.'

Having insinuated himself as a regular in the school office by plying Miss Painswick with chocolates and Dame Hermione's latest CDs, Cosmo also overheard Alex chuntering over Bianca's lack of intellect.

After his success at photographing the stars of *Romeo and Juliet*, Cosmo had been asked to do the pictures for the school prospectus and achieved an excellent multi-cultural mix by putting Anatole, Lubemir, Nordic blonde Amber and Bianca on the cover. No one could sack Bianca if she was in the prospectus.

Cosmo also found the proofs of the prospectus on Painswick's computer and added 'binge-drinking, buggery and Bruce-baiting' to the list of pupils' favourite activities. Fortunately this was picked up and deleted by an amused Hengist.

Alex also had to accept the fact that during Wimbledon, which coincided with the last fortnight of term, Hengist would be virtually incommunicado, claiming to be writing a crucial piece for *The Times*, when all you could hear was the thwack of tennis balls and the rattle of applause.

This year, Anatole's father dropped in for 'an important meeting' and to thwack and rattle were added the chink of bottles and roars of laughter as he and Hengist enjoyed the dazzling Miss Kournikova in the first round.

Hengist fiddled, while Alex burnt with resentment.

50

Field trips are very hard work and enmeshed in red tape, so once Red Robbie refused to go as a matter of principle, the rest of Larks's staff were only too glad to use their disapproval of the private sector as an excuse to opt out. Anyway, they were far too busy marking exams and writing reports.

So Janna buried her pride and pleaded with Robbie to change his mind: 'Next term Year Nine will begin their two-year GCSE course. This trip will whet their appetite not just for geography but for history and English. There are wonderful activities planned. They'll learn self-esteem and the ability to relate to people of a different background.'

Robbie had folded his arms and gazed mutinously up at the damp patch in the ceiling, until Janna lost it.

'You're just terrified of being shown up because Rufus Anderson's such a brilliant head of geography.'

This caused a rumpus, with the senior staff blanking Janna and Sam Spink marching in accusing Janna of humiliating Robbie.

'Good,' snapped Janna.

So in the end, Janna only had Vicky who, having sworn she wouldn't let Janna down, couldn't back out, and Gloria who had a crush on Emlyn, and Skunk Illingworth who would do anything for a freebie and who also had a crush on Vicky, and Cambola who was always game for a jaunt. Mags would have come but her new grandchild was about to be born and the ever dependable Wally had his son, Ben, home on leave.

Batting for Bagley were Rufus and a couple of his young geography teachers, No-Joke Joan who also had a crush on Vicky and didn't want to let any of her young women loose unchaperoned with Cosmo and all those dreadful Larks youths around, and, of course, Emlyn.

As Paris was moving to Bagley, it was felt the field trip would be a good way for him to bond with future form-mates. He was already enduring endless flak at Oaktree Court and at Larks for becoming a stuck-up snob, and as social services hadn't yet confirmed Patience and Ian as his foster parents, it was a time of deep uncertainty.

Paris refused again to betray how gutted he was that Feral – and Graffi as well – had refused to join him on the field trip. Graffi's father was off sick and heavily on the booze again; Feral's domestic life was always shadowy; but both boys were needed at home. Both vowed, as a band of brothers, they would always be friends of Paris, but he knew it would never be the same.

Without the other two he also felt less sanguine about protecting himself against Cosmo and his body-guards. The female remnants of the Wolf Pack were unlikely to provide support. Pearl would probably go off like a firecracker. Kylie had not only persuaded Chantal to look after Cameron while they were away, but, at the prospect of Kylie becoming the future Lady Waterlane, to also bankroll a snazzy new wardrobe. This included a glamorous dress because everyone had been told to bring something 'eveningy' for a mystery destination on the last night of the trip.

Paris, fretting about his lack of wardrobe, was extremely touched when Ian took him aside and gave him sixty pounds, gruffly bidding him not to spend it all at once. Carrying this out to the letter, Paris nicked some T-shirts and trainers and sauntered out of Gap in unpaid-for dark-grey jeans, which he promptly slashed across the knees and thighs to age them up.

On the morning of departure, Janna was drying her hair when Emlyn rang and said he was dreadfully sorry, he couldn't make the trip. Whereupon Janna, mostly from disappointment and because Emlyn was the only person who could control this mob, lost her temper and bawled him out.

As she paused for breath, Emlyn repeated how sorry he was but that his father had died in the night, from lungs wrecked by a life down the mines, and he was on his way home to Wales to look after his mother and organize the funeral.

A mortified Janna was frantically apologizing when Emlyn displayed a flicker of his old self:

'Now the even worse news. Biffo Rudge has been press-ganged into going in my place. He'll be as anxious to chaperone his boys as Joan is. I'm sorry, lovely, I'll buy you dinner when I get back.'

'I'm the one who's sorry,' wailed Janna, 'I know how you loved him.'

The weather was hot and jungly. The journey in three coaches seemed to take forever. Paris read *Le Rouge et Le Noir*; Rocky the *Mirror* with one finger; Cosmo read the score of *Harold in Italy*; Jade and Milly read each other's palms; Boffin read *A Brief History of Time* and, as litter monitor, bawled out everyone for dropping sweet papers. Amber read text messages from admiring boyfriends; Kylie, who felt sick on buses, tried to look at the pictures in *Hello!* and had to stop near St Jimmy's on the outskirts of Larkminster to throw up.

'You don't think she's up the duff again?' Pearl murmured to Paris.

Whereupon Rocky, realizing he'd left behind his

Ritalin, leapt into the driver's seat and drove the bus back to Larks to collect it. Everyone was too petrified of a Ritalinless Rocky to stop him. When the outraged bus driver took over on the second journey, it was noticed how many desirable residences Randal Stancombe was building within the catchment area of Rod Hyde's school.

'These are the sorts of houses you can afford if you don't have to fork out for school fees,' observed Cosmo nastily.

Before leaving, both schools had received individual pep talks on the importance of good behaviour and overcoming the traditional animosities which divide private and state schools.

Cosmo, cash rich from flogging exam papers, had listened in amusement. He liked Emlyn, but they would be much freer without him. Biffo couldn't control an ant. Cosmo had packed a first-aid kit of vodka, brandy, cocaine, grass, Alka-Seltzer, a hundred condoms, the morning-after pill and amyl nitrate, and had had a bet with Anatole that he'd pull both Gloria and Vicky by the end of the trip.

He also fancied a threesome with Milly and Amber, was going to bully Xavier to a jelly and unsettle Paris, to whom he intended to give a rough ride next term, particularly as the Bagley Babes had just announced that, in the absence of Feral and Graffi, their target on the trip was to pull Paris.

As the coaches moved into open country, Cosmo proceeded to ring up Dora, ordering her at pain of death not to forget to water his marijuana plants – not that they would need it, as rain was now chucking itself like lover's gravel against the bus window.

Poor little Dora, being ordered around by a pig like Cosmo, thought an indignant Pearl, who was sitting across the gangway. Pearl was utterly miserable; her little stepbrother was teething and her mother had discovered fifteen pounds missing from her bag, which Pearl had nicked to pay for a long-sleeved olive-green T-shirt from New Look. This had meant her mother's toyboy couldn't go to the pub, whereupon her mother had hit Pearl and screamed that 'she could bleedin' leave home if there was any more trouble'.

The long sleeves had been needed to cover Pearl's arms, which she'd attacked with a razor and which now throbbed unbearably. Cosmo smiled evilly across at her. He was vile but dead sexy, with his night-dark eyes and his satanic pirate's smile.

Down the bus, Biffo Rudge, noisily crunching an apple as sulphuric farts ruffled his long khaki shorts, was sharing a seat with a pile of Lower Fifth reports.

Cosmo proceeded to convulse pupils from both schools by holding up behind Biffo's seat the air freshener from the lavatory. As the bus crossed over into Herefordshire, plunging into thick forest with glimpses of silver rivers gleaming in the valleys below, Biffo fell asleep. Whereupon Cosmo seized the pile of reports, found his own and wrote 'towering genius' and 'undeniably brilliant' all over it. Buoyed up by the mounting mirth of his audience, Cosmo dug out Boffin's report and scribbled 'deeply irritating', 'unimaginative' and 'stupid twat' all over it, before crying, 'You dropped this, sir,' as Biffo woke up.

At the back of the coach, Vicky had palled up very pointedly with Gloria: 'Such a relief to have someone fun and my age on the trip.'

Now they whispered and played silly games: 'In ten seconds – who would you rather go to bed with, Biffo or Skunk?' followed by squeals of laughter.

Occasionally they cast covetous eyes at Rufus, head of geography, but he was too busy calling his wife and mother, who was looking after the children, even to notice them.

As Cambola was in another coach, Janna was forced to sit with Joan who, despite taking up most of the seat, insisted on clamping a beefy thigh against Janna's.

'All my Lower Fifth students have opted for triple science,' she announced, adding that she was off to a conference in Atlanta at the end of term. 'I'm giving a paper on the Place of the Runner Bean in Teaching Genetics,' she boomed. 'The runner bean is the perfect plant to illustrate multiple pregnancies.'

'Why not Kylie Rose?' murmured Amber to Milly. 'Did you know, Joan rejected seventeen possible gardeners provided by the bursar this week because none of them was ugly enough for us not to jump on him?'

Despite a desire to get off with the opposite sex, Janna noticed a look of relief on the Larks girls' faces when, after an interminable drive, they discovered they would be sleeping in one youth hostel near a river on the edge of a wood, while the boys would be housed four miles away in another.

'Thank goodness,' said Primrose Duddon, 'boys always gobble up all the food.'

In fact the food was awful, spag bol full of gristle, vegetables boiled into abdication and great blocks of jam roly-poly.

'Talk about Calorie Towers,' grumbled Amber.

After supper, if you could call it that, the rain stopped so they dried off the benches outside and Joan brought out her guitar and, led by Cambola, they sang round a dispirited camp fire.

'To think I got myself sacked from the Brownies to end up here,' muttered Amber. 'I need a drink.'

'You'll get cocoa at ten o'clock,' said Joan tartly.

At ten-fifteen, she went round with a basket confiscating mobiles. 'You've all got a long day tomorrow.'

So the Bagley Babes unearthed their second mobiles and rang their boyfriends.

'If anyone tries to escape,' boomed Joan as she

marched up and down the rows of beds, 'there'll be trouble.'

'I don't know why we came on this jaunt,' moaned Milly. 'Tomorrow we'll start digging a tunnel.'

As the lights were turned off and everyone stretched out on their hard beds, Kylie, who'd thought by now she'd be curled up with the Hon. Jack, started to cry that she was missing Cameron and Chantal.

'I miss my dog and my horse more than my parents or even my boyfriend,' said Amber, which made Kylie cry even louder, so Jade pelted her with pillows.

For the staff, Janna noted nervously that there were a double and three single rooms.

Joan looked warmly at Vicky. 'I'm happy to share.'

'No, no. You deserve the privilege of a room of your own,' Vicky simpered. 'Gloria and I don't at all mind bunking up.'

Janna, who had watched the girls' faces during that dismal dinner, prayed things would improve tomorrow. Hearing sobs, she went into the dormitory and sitting down on Kylie's bed, patted her heaving shoulder.

'Shall I tell you a story?'

'Please, miss.'

'"O, young Lochinvar is come out of the west, Through all the wide Border his steed was the best",' began Janna in her sweet, soft voice, which in the dark sounded like that of a young girl.

She can't be more than early thirties, thought Amber. It was such a good story, she managed to stay awake to the very end.

51

Things did get better.

'The students have bonded so well that the teachers are redundant,' Skunk Illingworth announced the following evening, froth gathering on his moustache like snow on a blackthorn hedge as he downed a pint of real ale.

He, Biffo and Rufus had sloped off to the local pub, leaving the pupils happy to write up their field notes because, thanks to Bagley's head of geography, they had discovered geography could be really interesting. Rufus, red-blond hair flopping, bony freckled face alight, had charged round Herefordshire, a piece of rock in one hand, a hammer in the other, book open in the grass, explaining the mysteries of the natural world to his enraptured listeners.

Earlier in the day, one group, including Paris, Boffin and Kylie, had carried out a tourist survey in a neighbouring forest. Unfortunately, on a dripping Wednesday morning, there was only a handful of tourists, who got fed up being repeatedly asked the same question. Kylie had even disturbed a couple in flagrante in the maturing bracken.

'When I asked Mr and Mrs Brown from Scunthorpe whether they had travelled here by train, coach or bicycle,' she was now writing in her round, careful hand, 'they told me to f— off.'

Everyone had then piled into the coaches and moved on to the next location, the source of the Fleet, which here was an eight-foot-wide brook, but which swelled into a great river as it passed Bagley, curled round Larkminster and Larks, then flowed on into Rutshire, past Cosmo's mother's house, through Lando France-Lynch's father's land, then skirting Xav's father's land in Gloucestershire.

If I could only climb into a boat and row home, thought Xav, who, that morning, had been punched very hard by Lubemir.

'Each group was allocated a section of the river,' wrote Primrose Duddon in a red and mauve striped notebook. 'We had to test our hypothesis on a "meander", which means the river bending several times, and on a "riffle", which is a fast-flowing, straight section. We rolled up a piece of tin foil, then checked how fast it floated down river.'

Pearl had kicked off her shoes and watched the ball of foil. It was snagged by tawny rushes, then floated on through the brown peaty water. Then she had collapsed on the warm wet grass, waiting for a teacher to tell her to get up. She was about to turn on her stopwatch and see how fast another ball of foil was floating down the far bank, when she felt a hand, as warm as the sun, on her bare legs.

'This is a "riffle",' murmured Cosmo as he ran his hand slowly up her bare legs, roving over her bottom, gently exploring in and out of her shorts. 'And this is definitely a "meander".'

He then lay down beside her on the bank, wickedly squinting sideways at her, stroking her rainbow hair, kissing her forehead, burying his tongue in her ear, murmuring endearments in Italian, his night-dark eyes blotting out the sun. As she turned her head towards him, he kissed her, slowly sucking each lip, then dividing them with his tongue.

A roar of rage interrupted Pearl's moment of bliss.

'Cosmo Rannaldini. Stop that at once.' Then the roar diminished as Joan realized Cosmo was only molesting a Larks student. 'But stop it all the same. You're supposed to be testing the velocity of the river, not the speed of your seduction technique.'

Pearl couldn't wait to tell Kylie.

'Cosmo snogged me. He is so brilliant, my knees gave way and I was lying down.'

The Chinless Wanderers, who weren't remotely interested in riffles and who regarded rivers as places in which you caught salmon or retrieved polo balls, were smoking and listening to the test match. Further down the bank Paris read *Le Rouge et Le Noir*, totally engrossed in Julien Sorel's seduction of the beautiful, much older Madame de Renal leading to passionate mutual love – maybe Janna wasn't such an impossibility.

He had bonded least of the Larks contingent. He was sick of Bagley chat about gap years in Argentina and their parents' splitting up. There was also something sickening about the country, he thought, or the evils man imposed on it. Last year, he'd been haunted by the funeral pyres burning innocent sheep and cattle.

This year it was the rabbits lying in the footpath dying from myxomatosis, desperately trying to crawl away as their bulging eyes were pecked out by huge killer gulls. The girls screamed in horror; Paris turned away retching; Jack Waterlane picked up a log and put one rabbit out of its misery, then another, then another, shouting at the gulls before returning to put a comforting arm round a sobbing Kylie.

Jack wasn't quite such a prat as he seemed, decided Paris.

The gulls were a symbol of the way Cosmo pecked away at Xavier and himself, if given a chance.

Before supper that evening, Paris wandered off from the hostel into the wood to read in peace. Hearing raised voices, he was about to sidle to the right, when he clocked Lubemir's very distinctive accent: 'Fetch eet, black sheet.'

Edging forward through the green curtain of a willow, Paris found a clearing in which Cosmo and Lubemir were playing football. To the left, like an enemy ambush, lurked a huge bed of nettles, giving off a rank, bitter smell as the still hot evening sun burnt off the rain. Beside them stood Xav, fat, hunched, terrified, as Cosmo powered the ball into the nettles.

'Pick it up, black shit.'

Desperate to avoid a beating, wincing from the stings, Xav plunged in and picked up the ball, only for Lubemir to boot it back again. 'Fetch eet, you fat creep.'

For a moment defiance flared: 'Why should I?'

'Because your black skin's too rhinoceros-like to feel stings. Pick it up,' demanded Cosmo.

Paris strolled into the clearing. 'Get it your fucking self.'

'Don't speak to me like that, yob,' said Lubemir insolently.

Paris dropped *Le Rouge et Le Noir*. A second later, his right hook had sent Lubemir flying into the nettles.

Bellowing at the pain, Lubemir yelled, 'Get heem,' to Cosmo.

Cosmo, however, who believed guards should guard themselves, was examining his nails.

Turning on Cosmo, Paris grabbed him by his bright blue Ralph Lauren shirt.

'Want to make the same journey?' he hissed, yanking Cosmo towards the nettles. 'I thought not. Well, fucking lay off Xav.'

Picking up *Le Rouge et Le Noir*, he stalked back to the hostel, with Xav panting to keep up.

'Thanks very, very much.'

''S OK. Cosmo's a wimp if you face up to him.'

Xav didn't believe him, but he felt a little better.

* * *

431

'Dear Mum,' wrote Kylie, another twenty-four hours later:

> We're having a brilliant time. We've been clay-pigeon shooting, rock climbing and we cycled to a museum. We've also been to an art gallery, which Graffi would have loved. Everyone friendly – Bagley really nice, Jack gorgeous. We write up our notes in the evening when the teachers go to the pub, so we can get out the booze and the weed. Today some kids went riding. Cosmo raced his horse up behind Paris's and made it bolt. Paris fell off.

Paris hadn't any parents to write to. He'd started a card of a red dragon's tongue, symbol of the Welsh language, to Patience and Ian, then, not knowing how to address them on the envelope and deciding it was counting chickens, had torn it up. His head ached after his fall; if only he was with Janna in the pub.

Janna enjoyed these pub sessions, discussing the children, comparing state and private school practice.

'We work much harder in the independent sector,' moaned one of Rufus's young geography teachers. 'At least you lot can work at home. We're on call twenty-four hours a day and most weekends.'

'You have loads longer holidays and we've got so many teachers off with stress,' said Gloria, returning with another bottle. 'The ones who aren't work ten times as hard.'

'Hengist doesn't believe in stress or "generalized anxiety" as it's now known.' Rufus shook his head. 'He expects people to come in every day.'

'Except for himself,' grumbled Biffo.

'You won't be able to run to your union when you join us next term,' Joan teased an increasingly alarmed Vicky.

'Hengist is a despot,' complained Biffo. 'When

Emlyn had to pull out, he virtually ordered me to take his place.'

'Poor Emlyn, his father's being buried tomorrow.' Janna found that he was seldom far from her thoughts. She kept wanting to call and comfort him, but felt it would be intrusive. She had arranged a wreath and a card of sympathy signed by everyone on the trip.

'Hengist is driving down to Wales for the funeral – to show support,' said Joan dismissively.

'And distribute largesse. The great international in a Welsh rugger town,' said Biffo even more dismissively.

'I think it's lovely of Hengist to go,' protested Janna. 'Emlyn adores him. He is Emlyn's future father-in-law and it'll mean a huge amount to the family.'

'Hengist's probably rather relieved Sally won't have to walk down the aisle on the arm of Emlyn's dad,' observed Joan. 'He's a crashing snob.'

'He is not,' said Janna furiously. 'Hengist gets on with people from all backgrounds.'

'Hark at you defending him,' simpered Vicky. 'I thought the two of you had fallen out.'

Paris had spent Ian's sixty pounds on a pair of shorts, a Prussian-blue shirt and a Liverpool baseball cap, which someone had nicked. As a result, on the third day he got too much sun canoeing. On the way back to the hostel, he started feeling horribly sick and sweaty; his head, after yesterday's fall, ached abominably. Stepping down from the bus, his legs buckled and he fainted.

He came round to find himself on the grass under a spreading chestnut tree, with a rolled towel under his head and Janna fussing over him, and thought he'd gone to heaven. As the bus had drawn up nearer Calorie Towers than the boys' hostel, he was moved to Janna's bed and a doctor summoned, who diagnosed sunstroke.

'With a fair skin like yours, you should never go out without a hat. Realistically you should go home.'

But with Janna holding his hand, mopping his forehead with her own pale blue flannel and looking down with such concern, Paris definitely wanted to stay.

'Perhaps it's better if you're not moved.' The doctor turned to Janna. 'As long as you can keep him cool and quiet?'

'He can sleep in my bed,' said Janna. 'I'm so sorry, love.' She squeezed Paris's hand. 'I should have noticed you weren't wearing a hat.'

She had been swimming and was still in a sopping-wet primrose-yellow bikini, through which goose pimples were protruding like bubble wrap.

'Get something warm on,' advised the doctor, looking admiringly at her speckled body, 'you've had a shock. Don't want you getting a chill.'

Peel off that bikini in here, thought Paris longingly and said:

'I can't take your room.'

'You certainly can and I'm not leaving you either.'

Paris, for the first time in his life, knew the bliss of being cosseted. The Bagley Babes nipped down to the greengrocer's and brought him strawberries and raspberries. Vicky rolled up with lemon sorbet, Gloria with a melon. Paris was embarrassed, yet touched they were so worried. Even Lubemir and Anatole sent apologies and the Chinless Wanderers promised to get him a better horse next time. Finally, Xav shuffled in and offered Paris his mobile.

'You might want to ring someone. No one except my mother rings me.'

'I'll ring you.'

Xav grinned. 'You can't if I haven't got a mobile.' Then, staring at the floor and kicking a table: 'Thanks for sticking up for me. I'm really glad you're coming to Bagley next term.'

Shyly, they exchanged a high five.

* * *

434

Having shooed everyone out, Janna gazed out of the window across the river. She could see thirty or so red and white cows standing together, whisking flies off each other's faces. That's what a good school should be, she thought wistfully, everyone protecting each other.

Despite another deluge, it was still terribly hot. Paris was getting drowsy. As she leant over to straighten his pillow, he could feel the smooth firmness, like almost ripe plums, of her breasts. Soaking the blue flannel in iced water, she trickled it over his forehead, shoulders and chest, like a caress.

'Please don't go away, read to me.'

Janna picked up Matthew Arnold, which had fallen out of his shorts pocket. 'To Paris with love from Patience and Ian', she read on the flyleaf and felt happier that they were kind, educated people who would look after him. She read:

'But the majestic river floated on,
Out of the mist and hum of that low land,
Into the frosty starlight, and there moved,
Rejoicing, through the hushed Chorasmian waste,
Under the solitary moon; he flowed
Right for the polar star . . .'

'I wonder if he was a riffle or a meander,' mumbled Paris.

He could smell Janna's scent on her sheets. On the table were bottles: magic potions to make her even more beautiful. Gradually Janna's soft, young voice merged with the rain-swollen stream pouring into the river outside. He was asleep.

Oh, the length of those blond lashes. Not wanting him to catch cold, Janna pulled the blanket over him and couldn't resist bending over and dropping a kiss on his damp forehead.

'Good night, sweet Arctic Prince.' If only she'd been able to adopt him.

Paris opened his eyes a millimetre, next moment a tentacle hand had closed round her neck.

'Get away with you,' she protested.

Lifting his head, dizzy this time with longing, Paris kissed her. For a second her lips went rigid, then they relaxed and opened and kissed him back. Then she seemed to shake herself, prised away his hand and laid it on his chest.

'You're delirious,' she told him firmly. 'I must check on everyone else and find myself somewhere to sleep.'

'I love you, miss,' called out Paris, as he drifted into sleep.

52

'You've got to be better by tonight,' Jade Stancombe told Paris next morning as she dropped a box of white chocolates onto his bed. 'We're off to our mystery destination.'

She was followed by Cosmo, who'd clocked the burgeoning friendship between Xav and Paris and, wanting to punish Xav further, decided to take Paris away from him. Cosmo therefore rolled up with mangoes, peaches and Paris's baseball cap, which he claimed he'd found down the seat of a bus.

'But that won't keep the sun off back and front though, like this will,' and he plonked a panama on Paris's head.

'I don't want your fucking hat.'

'You will when you see how much it suits you.'

Paris was about to chuck it in the bin when Janna walked in: 'Oh Paris, you look gorgeous.'

'Just like Jude Law,' agreed Cosmo.

So Paris kept it.

Pearl was terribly excited.

'If you make me up for the mystery party this evening,' Jade had told her, 'you can borrow and keep one of my dresses.'

Then, when Pearl said she hadn't brought much make-up, Jade suggested they buy some in Hereford

437

and proceeded to spend £300, also splashing out £550 on an aquamarine and diamond ring.

'I've brought a nice blue wraparound cardigan with me. You can have that too, Pearl, if you do my hair as well.'

It didn't look as though anyone would need cardigans: the weather was getting steadily hotter and muggier; huge white clouds rose like whipped cream on the horizon.

Terrified of being sent home, Paris kept telling everyone how much better he felt.

'You can come,' said Janna, 'if you take it really easy and keep that hat on.'

The panama was almost unbearably becoming. With the brim over his nose, he could have drifted out of *Brideshead* or *The Great Gatsby*.

But I'm Julien Sorel, he told himself. When I'm sixty, Janna'll be eighty, not a huge gap. Anyway, with her hair in a ponytail and freckles joining up on her face, she looked about fourteen.

As the coaches splashed through huge puddles, they seemed to be galloping back in time. Meadowsweet overran the emerald-green meadows, brown rivers struggled through great tangles of water lilies and dense primeval forests swarmed down the hills.

'That's a riffle, that's a meander,' yelled the children.

'God it's hot, are you OK, Paris?' asked the girls repeatedly.

Joan, the eternal chaperone, marched up and down the coach in search of bad behaviour. Boffin, still engrossed in *A Brief History of Time*, hummed a Bach prelude in a reedy tenor.

'Prince Harry's been done for drink driving,' said Amber, drinking Bourbon out of a Coke bottle, 'he's my hero.'

'Pity he's got a girlfriend,' sighed Milly. 'Boffin Brooks tried to snog me this morning. He must have month-old pilchards lodged in his brace. Where d'you think we're going tonight? It's so exciting.'

Jade stretched out long, newly bronzed and waxed legs.

'Good book?' she asked Paris.

'Very,' said Paris, not looking up.

Rufus was telling Kylie about whales.

'They'll be extinct quite soon.'

'That's really sad.' Kylie's big eyes filled with tears. 'Just like the dildo.'

Pearl had been sad too on the trip to Hereford because Cosmo had gone off in another coach with Vicky. Now he was back sitting beside her, reading *Classical Music* magazine, smiling wickedly, caressing the outside curve of her breast with his little finger.

And so, after four nights of rigorously enforced celibacy, the coaches rolled over the border into Wales. Biffo Rudge sat at the front, directing the driver.

'Here we are,' he shouted as they rounded the corner. On the other side of a wide river, hazily reflected in its water like a forgotten child's fortress, stood Castle Gafellyn against the darkening green trees.

As they crossed the river and drove through huge wrought-iron gates, flanked by rampant lions, they saw that the stern grey walls ahead were softened by rambling pink roses and pale blue hydrangeas.

'Castle Gafellyn was a most important military outpost,' read Biffo from Emlyn's notes. 'An early owner burnt it down to stop it falling into the predatory hands of the English.' He pointed to a square green field framed by crumbling stone walls. 'This was the enclosure into which livestock was herded at night to protect it from the wolves.'

'Sounds just like us,' said Pearl, sticking her tongue out at Cosmo.

I'll teach you, he thought.

'This is the sort of property in which the Macbeths

439

might have resided,' announced Boffin, 'repelling other warlords and of course the English.'

The moat circling the castle was as green, still and smooth as mint jelly; all around dark forest encroached like stealthily invading armies. Like Burnham Wood advancing on Dunsinane, thought Paris, glancing at Janna, whose eyes were wide, her hands clasped in excitement like a child at her first pantomime. She deserved some fun; if only he could provide it.

Once inside, the children swarmed about, peering out through narrow, vertical windows, racing up winding stone staircases leading to turrets. Tapestries, swords and armour covered the walls. Meissen and Ming softened every alcove.

The owner, smooth, pewter-grey-haired, butterscotch-tanned, roving-eyed, was a childhood friend of Hengist called Bertie Wallace, who seemed deeply amused by the whole invasion.

'When one's ancestors have been accustomed to invading English hordes, Larks and Bagley seem very small beer,' he observed dryly as the children fell on tomato sandwiches and rainbow cake.

'It would have been fun to dine in the great hall, but it's so hot, I thought you'd prefer the garden room which opens onto the terrace. Hengist used to stay here as a child,' he told the somewhat awestruck teachers. 'His parents were friends of my parents who sold the place to pay death duties. My wife and I bought it back and are planning to turn it into an hotel, but first it's got to be extensively rebuilt and redecorated. Then I read about Larks joining forces with Bagley and thought you might like to stay here as a climax' – he smiled knowingly at Janna – 'to your trip.'

'You are so kind,' stammered Janna. 'What a treat. The kids have behaved very well so far. I hope they don't get carried away.'

'In olden days, castles like this would have had

rushes and meadowsweet all over the floor instead of carpets,' pronounced Boffin.

A flurry of notes and a burst of *Rigoletto* indicated that Cambola had found the piano. Shrieks of joy echoed round the garden as the children discovered a croquet lawn and the swimming pool, a rippling turquoise expanse of water, framed by limes in sweet scented flower, heavy with the murmuring of bees.

'We can go skinny-dipping later,' purred Amber.

'Or fatty-dipping, in Xavier's case,' said Cosmo evilly.

Bertie, soft-voiced and rakish, was decidedly attractive. Janna could imagine him and Hengist getting up to all sorts of tricks and because he was Hengist's friend, she wanted to make a good impression.

'I cannot think of a more wonderful end to our trip. And it will really help them to relate to history and Macbeth. "This castle hath a pleasant seat; the air Nimbly and sweetly recommends itself Unto our gentle senses",' she quoted happily.

' "This guest of summer, The temple-haunting martlet, does approve By his lov'd mansionry that the heaven's breath Smells wooingly here",' quoted back Bertie. 'I used to be an actor. Hengist told me I'd like you.'

Janna squirmed with pleasure.

A smell of mint was drifting from the kitchen.

'We've got smoked salmon, duck and puds. Do you think they'll like that?'

'Adore it, that's absolutely perfect. Thank you, particularly' – she thought of Calorie Towers – 'after the food they've been having.'

'I'm sorry I won't be with you,' said Bertie. 'A friend's having a dinner party five miles away, so after the servants have served up your dinner and it's mostly cold, I hope you'll forgive me if I hijack them to help my friend. They can clear up first thing. You'll probably feel freer on your own.'

'You're awfully trusting.'

Vicky and Gloria, who, seeing Bertie, had raced to their rooms to tart up, now drifted in.

'What a lovely property,' gushed Vicky.

'I could say the same for you two,' quipped Bertie. 'What amazing taste Hengist has in women.'

'We're expecting him later,' said Vicky. 'Oh, tomato sarnies, how yummy. I've just checked on Paris, Janna, he seems OK.'

Calm down, Janna told herself fiercely. What if Hengist was rolling up just to pull Vicky, who would wear something amazing tonight? 'You are old, Father William.'

Janna's room, at the end of a long corridor, was tauntingly romantic. The big four-poster with deep blue curtains embroidered with silver stars needed only a handsome prince. Other delights included a pale yellow Chinese screen, painted with narrow-eyed warriors, a bottle of champagne in ice and a dapple-grey rocking horse with a rose-red saddle. On the wall was a tapestry of Diana the huntress, her chariot drawn by a purposeful stag who looked very like Joan. Joan, putting an arm round Janna's waist this morning, had definitely slid a hand upwards to grab a breast.

Janna and Joan: perhaps that was her destiny. Collapsing on the bed, she noticed even the blanket had a coat of arms, a golden ram with a motto, 'Fidelis et Constans'. 'An Atkinson Blanket, made in England', said the label. Janna Curtis, made in Wales. Hengist was on the way. Would he be faithful and constant to Sally? She liked Sally so much; how hideous it would be if Hengist were to cheat on her with Vicky.

In another part of the castle, Cosmo, who intended to enjoy his evening, was lacing the fruit cup with vodka and brandy. By studying the guidebook, he had located, ten miles away, a renowned observatory with some adjoining historic troglodyte caves. His suggestion that Skunk and Biffo should give them a ring had resulted in both of them, plus Boffin and Rufus's two minions, being invited to supper to view some rare eclipse and visit the troglodyte caves.

Cosmo had also arranged for his mother to invite Joan and Cambola to *Ariadne auf Naxos* in which she was singing in Cardiff, which would occupy them for several hours.

Rufus should have stayed at the castle too, but getting no answer from his wife Sheena on her mobile or at home, where she should have been with the children, he had panicked and decided to miss dinner and slope home for the evening.

Situation excellent, which meant only Janna, Vicky and Gloria left in charge. If Hengist did show up, reflected Cosmo, Janna would be oblivious to everything else, so his plan to seduce Vicky and Gloria looked feasible.

Cosmo emptied another bottle of vodka into the fruit cup.

53

Before dinner everyone met on the terrace. The pupils in particular were amazed how unfamiliar and glamorous they looked in their party dresses. Jade, made up by Pearl, in a clinging white dress slashed to the waist from top and bottom, showing off St Tropez tan applied by Pearl, her hair plaited and threaded with flowers by Pearl, looked over the top but sensational.

Pearl glowed like a pearl, her normally pinched, sharp, pale little face softened and flushed by sun, love and Jade's flowered dress and pale blue wraparound cardigan.

'Designer clothes are certainly worf the price,' she admitted.

'Because I've got designs on you,' said Cosmo, patting her bottom.

Janna had washed and curled her hair, oiled her body and hidden sleepless nights with a lot of eye make-up. In her bronze speckled dress, which moulded her body and merged with her freckles, she looked like the Little Mermaid.

The children thought she looked stunning, but not as stunning as Vicky, who wore flamingo pink and who, perhaps trying to appear sophisticated for Hengist, had piled up and knotted a pink rose into her dark hair.

Everyone was agreeing they were having a fantastic

time, when Bertie Wallace wandered in with a call for Joan Johnson.

'She's gone to the opera,' said Janna.

'It's Hengist.'

'I'll take it.' Vicky grabbed the cordless. 'Hengist, this place is a-mazing. Thank you so much. The kids are ecstatic. You stayed here as a child, Bertie told us. Are you coming over? Oh, what a shame. Of course, I understand. Research is all. Tintern Abbey. My favourite poem: "That time is past, And all its aching joys are now no more, And dizzy raptures."

'OK, I'll give your love to everyone,' and after a pause: 'Mmm, me too.' Catching sight of Janna's anguished face she added, 'Do you want a word with Janna?' who shook her head frantically. 'OK, thanks for ringing, enjoy your evening.' She handed the cordless back to Bertie. 'Hengist isn't coming, what a pity. He's staying near Tintern Abbey doing some research.'

'"Why, uncle, 'tis a shame",' murmured Anatole.

'Bloody isn't,' murmured back Cosmo. 'When the cat goes arty, the mice begin to party.'

'Where's Tintin Abbey?' asked the Hon. Jack. 'I always liked Tintin.'

'Have a drink,' said Cosmo, handing Janna a huge glass of fruit cup.

How even more amusing to seduce Miss Curtis, who didn't dwarf him and who was looking unusually tempting. Now that really would crucify Master Alvaston.

Fucking Hengist! Paris, also watching Janna, was aware of a dimmer switch turning off the glow in her face. If only he could comfort her.

The sun at thirty degrees was reddening the castle walls; a short shower of rain had scattered pink rose petals over the grass. Delphinium and campanula rose in blue and violet spires. A most heavenly smell of roasting duck mingled with the sweet, heady scent of lime blossom and philadelphus. Vicky and Gloria, succumbing to laced fruit cup and Anatole's deep-voiced blandishments, were getting noisy and sillier.

'I'm dreadfully sorry,' whispered Janna, 'I've got an absolutely blinding headache – a migraine actually. They come on suddenly, I can't see out of one eye.'

'I had one on the opening night of *Romeo and Juliet*,' cried Vicky, 'it was all I could do to stagger in. Poor you. Gloria and I'll hold the fort – or rather the castle.'

Everyone was very solicitous.

'Go and lie down, miss, come back when you feel better.'

'Shall I bring you some iced water?'

Janna could see secret relief in many faces. Without her, joy would be truly unconfined. Paris insisted on accompanying her back to her room.

Let me stay, he wanted to beg. I'll lie down beside you and stroke your forehead as you did mine yesterday.

'Too much sun,' mumbled Janna.

'Do you need a doctor?'

'I'm fine. You go and have fun. I'll probably join you again in half an hour.'

'Sure you're OK?'

The intensity in his face alarmed her. She shouldn't have led him on yesterday. She'd only just managed to shut the door on him and bolt it when the tears poured forth. She was overwhelmed with despair at not seeing Hengist and shock that she could no longer conceal the fact she was hopelessly in love with him.

But what the hell was she playing at? Hengist was a married man, no doubt as faithful and constant to sweet Sally as the Atkinson blanket into which she was sobbing. He was also out of her league. She'd tried to cross the class barriers and found, as the Little Mermaid had when she tried to walk on shore, that she was treading on knives.

Then an imperious knock on the door sent her through the roof. It must be Paris back again. She should never have kissed him, but he'd looked so adorable. The knock became a tantivy. Nervously she opened the door a centimetre, but found the shadowy landing was deserted – perhaps it was the Gafellyn ghost.

The banging had become more insistent, coming from the far side of the room. Padding over the flagstones, she found a bottle-green wool curtain and behind it a rounded Norman door, buckling on its hinges. Oh God, was it Joan or raffish Bertie?

Someone was declaiming the Porter's speech in a strong Welsh accent. '"Knock, knock, knock . . ."'

Janna opened this second door an inch, breathed in lemon aftershave and almost fainted as the door was thrust open, nearly concussing her. In the dim light she slowly made out a faded Prussian-blue shirt, a sunburnt throat, and eyes, slittier with laughter than the Chinese Warriors. It was Hengist. Ducking his head, he powered his way into the room and pulled her into his arms.

'I thought you were staying near Tintern Abbey.'

'I was, but I couldn't bear the thought of all those aching joys being past. I suddenly wanted a dizzy rapture.'

'I thought you fancied Vicky,' sobbed Janna.

She was so small in her bare feet, Hengist had to pull her chin upwards in order to smile down into her reproachful, bewildered, tearful, mascara-stained face.

'Dear God,' he said, 'from the beginning you've been the one I wanted, the object of my desire.' And when he drew her against him, he was like a great, warm, solid wall; where his shirt was unbuttoned, she felt the burning heat of his body and was shaken by the relentless pounding of his heart.

Then his beautiful, wilful mouth swooped down on hers and she no longer doubted his passion as he kissed her on and on, his big hands closing round her small waist, then moving upwards to caress her high bouncy breasts, then moving down to cup her equally bouncy bottom. Finally, gasping for breath, he buried his face in her clean, silky curls.

'You utterly gorgeous child. Christ, I've fought this.' Then, laughing half ruefully: 'This is an awfully big adventure weekend.'

Janna escaped and paced round the room, heart battling with her head.

'How did you get in here?'

'By a secret passage. It comes out on the edge of the woods. Bertie and I were at school together; I used to stay in the holidays. I can get into every room in this castle.'

'And probably did,' snapped Janna, raging with insecurity, frightened her legs wouldn't hold her any more. 'I cannot believe this.'

'You soon will.' Hengist swiftly unzipped her speckled dress, unhooked her bra, then, gathering her up, dropped her on the blue and silver patchwork quilt.

'We can't,' stammered Janna. 'Sally? The party? How did you know I was here?'

'I tried to ring you but your mobile was switched off. Bertie said you'd sloped off with a headache. You have the sweetest body, look at those adorable boobs.'

Lying down beside her, he swept back her hair, kissed her forehead and little snub nose, then her lips again, then her nipples, slowly, luxuriously, sensuously. The hand creeping lazily between her legs was so sure.

'Down comes the drawbridge,' he murmured, pulling off her knickers.

In turn he smelt so clean and healthy, and his face was so smooth and newly shaven – Janna was so used to beards and grating stubble – his glorious broad-shouldered body so powerful, his hair so springy yet silky. As he stroked and fingered her, leaving her quivering with longing, he made no attempt to undress himself.

448

'I really like Sally,' muttered Janna.

'Hush. Sally's my problem.'

As he drew her into a fairy-tale world inside the star-spangled blue curtains, any principle fled. Through the narrow window, she could see Venus, a glittering silver medal pinned on the deepening blue breast of the night.

'You do want this, darling?' Hengist's hand was roving further afield.

'Oh please, yes,' Janna gasped. 'I'm stunned, that's all. I didn't realize it was an option. I haven't slept with anyone since Stew.'

'I should hope not – you were saving yourself for me.'

'I'm out of practice.'

'We must exchange best practice,' murmured Hengist, spitting on his fingers, finding her clitoris, caressing so gently and expertly.

'I'll give you best practice,' cried a fired-up Janna.

Wriggling out of his embrace, she took over, shoving Hengist back on the bed. Removing his loafers, kissing his bare feet, swiftly unbuttoning his shirt, kissing the dark brown tuft of chest hair, she licked his nipples and his belly button as she undid his belt and unzipped and removed his trousers. For a moment his red check boxer shorts were pegged by a splendidly excited cock, then he eased free and was divinely naked beneath her.

Clambering over his body like a squirrel, she kissed, caressed, sucked and licked until he was moaning in delight.

'For a head, Miss Curtis, you give exquisite head. Aaah . . .' Reaching down, he grabbed her waist and, pulling her up the bed, plunged his splendid rock-hard penis up inside her, which she had no problem accepting in full because she was so bubbling over with excitement.

'Aaah,' groaned Hengist again as her muscles gripped and released him, squeezing and coaxing, 'like the Bourbons, you've forgotten nothing. I'm going to be so selfish, darling, I cannot hold out a second longer, you'll have to catch the next bus. Oh, my Christ,' he shouted, 'here comes the drop goal,' and exploded inside her.

For an age it seemed, they lay giggling and in shared ecstasy.

'Hang out our banners on the outward walls; The cry is still, "he comes",' sighed Hengist. 'Oh my darling. That was even better than scoring at Twickenham.'

As he turned to kiss her, she was made happier by the intense happiness on his face.

'Now, I'm going to make you come lots,' he whispered. And he did.

Time stopped – fantastic, mind-blowing sex blotting out everything.

Under a weeping willow, whose leaves caressed her far more tenderly, Pearl was seduced by Cosmo, a coupling as brutal and perfunctory as Janna's had been ecstatic.

Retreating into the castle to wash, Pearl reflected it was a shame Cosmo had used a condom or she might have fallen pregnant and qualified for a free flat. At least Cosmo had said he loved her. She hoped Jade wouldn't be angry her wraparound cardigan had been torn.

54

After a glorious dinner, the plates had been stacked and everyone had drifted into the garden to dance under the stars, to snog in the bushes and, because it was such a hot, muggy night, to strip off and leap into the pool. Vicky and Gloria were far too drunk and giggly to worry that it was too soon after dinner to swim.

The scent of philadelphus and lime flower grew headier; more moths dived like kamikaze pilots into the lights round the pool; Jack and Kylie had retreated to the shrubbery; Lando and Junior were playing croquet, trying to hit each other's ankles.

Bertie, who'd gone off to see his mistress, had no intention of returning before dawn.

Paris, wearing just shorts, lay on the grass, admiring the stars; Venus was setting. Above him, the constellation Hercules, arms outstretched, mighty thighs apart, wrestled with his labours. Paris was worried about Janna; she'd been gone three hours. He decided to check her room.

He would have liked to clean his teeth, but someone had nicked his toothbrush. Returning to the dining room, he grabbed and bit into a Granny Smith, poured Janna a glass of orange juice loaded with ice, and set out. Normally at this hour, he'd be confined to his room at Oaktree Court, and he luxuriated in the cold

451

dew beneath his feet and the night air warm on his bare shoulders.

Gradually the screams and shouts round the pool receded. In the moat below, the water-lily leaves gleamed like armour; to the right loomed the castle. Janna's lights were turned off; she must be asleep. O, that he were the pillow beneath her head.

Then he froze as a man appeared at her window, naked to the waist with a magnificent chest and heroic head thrown back, smiling triumphantly and stretching his arms in ecstasy. Not Hercules down from the skies – but Hengist. Then he turned and was engulfed once more in the darkness of the room.

Paris slumped against the castle, body drenched in sweat, heart crashing, ice frantically clattering against the glass in his hand. The whore, the slag! How could she? Women complained of headaches when they didn't want sex – and she'd kissed him first yesterday and not gone into a flurry of outrage, but had parted her lips when he'd kissed her back.

Paris gave a howl and hurled the glass against the wall. Bagley and Larks – 'a plague on both your houses'. In a daze, he staggered back into the castle, heading for the bar. Grabbing a bottle of vodka, he filled a half-pint glass, splashed bitter lemon on the top and downed it in one, then downed a second, spluttering:

'The bitch, the slag.'

Picking up a patterned orange Chinese vase cringing in an alcove, he hurled it against a big gilt mirror, splintering them both. A Tang dog flew out of the window. Gathering up a mahogany side table, Paris hurled it at the bar, smashing glasses, bottles, then swept more glasses onto the floor.

'Fucking slag.'

A bamboo plant had taken off, crashing down onto the keys of the piano, as Rocky wandered in, his mad bull's face crimson, his red curls askew, a bottle of Grand Marnier in his hand.

'What yer doing, man?'

'Wrecking this pervy nob's castle.'

'Right,' yelled Rocky, picking up a large flower arrangement and hurling it against a tallboy. Then he ran into the dining room and started on the debris of duck carcasses and bowls of potatoes and raspberries stacked on the sideboard. There was a sickening crunch as a pile of Rockingham plates fell to the floor. Like Duncan's blood, summer pudding was soon dripping down the pale blue Chinese wallpaper.

Outside, the music was too loud and the dancers and swimmers having too much fun to notice. Someone had found a big yellow ball and Lando and Junior were playing water polo.

Telling herself that first sex with a guy was never very good, still sore from Cosmo's cavalier seeing-to, Pearl wandered back to the party, pausing in horror to see her new boyfriend ferociously snogging Vicky Fairchild, his hand unzipping her flamingo-pink dress.

Going over, Pearl tapped him on the shoulder:

'D'you mind?'

'Piss off,' said Cosmo, with such venom that Pearl shrank away, looking desperately round for someone to tell, but everyone was snogging or swimming.

Running down a grassy path, she bumped into a reeling, half-dressed Jade, who asked:

'Where in hell's Paris?'

'Dunno. Cosmo's a fucking bastard.'

Jade stopped, swaying in her tracks, smiling cruelly.

'What have you and Cosmo been a-doing of? He just texted me.' Jade unearthed her mobile from her bra and held it out.

'Mission acc-come-plished pearls a slag', read Pearl and gave a shriek of rage. 'The bastard. He said he loved me, that I was the biggest fing in his life.'

'You might have been five seconds before he shagged you. Cosmo doesn't let grass grow under his feet, only in window boxes.'

453

Next moment, Pearl heard the distinctive double beat of a message on her own mobile and read: 'Sorry its over cosmo'.

'Wot dyou mean', texted back Pearl.

'Thanks for terrific sex shame youve just become my X', came back the reply.

'Bstrd how am I supposed to handle this', Pearl replied.

'Ask joan for alka seltzer. now fuck off', texted Cosmo.

Leaving the castle ransacked, Paris found everyone skinny-dipping in the pool. He felt like Actaeon spying on Diana and her nymphs.

A naked Vicky, whose hair had come down, was giggling hysterically and pretending to swim away from Cosmo, who'd just returned from texting. Yanking her back by her hair, Cosmo's hands closed over her breasts.

Very drunk, Paris laboriously undid his belt and stepped out of his shorts. The Bagley Babes, frolicking like Rhine Maidens, gasped as he paused, sleek, white and beautiful. Actaeon had become a moon-blanched Endymion. The only flaw was the tattoo of the Eiffel Tower on his shoulder.

'Jesus,' said Amber.

Letting go of Vicky, leaving her dog-paddling frantically in the deep end, Cosmo scrambled out of the pool, grabbed his camera from his jeans and took a roll of film.

Paris, a glass of neat vodka in his hand, stood gazing into the pool in despair and loathing, then wandered off. After two attempts, a naked Jade managed to struggle out of the pool and ran after him.

'Paris, make love to me,' she called out.

'Fuck off.'

'How come you're so mean to me?'

'Because you're a bitch.'

When Jade slapped his face, Paris slapped her back, then, grabbing her arm, pulled her behind the changing rooms into the shrubbery. He shoved her on the grass and fell on top of her, yelling in pain as her hand clamped around his sunburnt neck, pulling him down to kiss her. Her lovely sleek body writhed beneath his. Her eyes were glazed with lust and booze, Pearl's so carefully applied make-up streaked by water. The coupling, like Cosmo and Pearl's, was violent, fierce, messy and meaningless. The moment it was over, Paris pulled out and walked off.

Bumping into his friend, Pearl, who sobbed hysterically that Cosmo had dumped her by text and told the entire party, he could only say: 'You shouldn't go with trash: sorry, I wish I cared.'

Five minutes later, Pearl stumbled over Jade, passed out on the grass, puked-up raspberries and cream gleaming like blood in the moonlight. Jade was so far gone, she didn't even stir when Pearl produced a kitchen knife and sawed off her twelve-inch plait, threaded with flowers. Then Pearl attacked her own wrist, gasping at the pain and joy of release.

Amber, wet from the pool, caught up with Paris.

'What goings on, Mr Alvaston.'

So Paris pulled her into his arms and shut up her patrician babble by kissing her. He didn't care any more.

'I like you,' he told Amber.

'And I like you.'

It was like being serviced by a unicorn, Amber reflected hazily, or a statue half come to life. Paris's face was dead, devoid of any tenderness. At one moment he called her 'Janna', at another his features seemed about to disintegrate in tears, then set like stone again.

'Oh Christ, oh Christ.'

It was not, as you might say, satisfactory. At least he said 'thank you' as he got to his feet and wandered off.

If he found Milly, thought Paris, he could chalk up a

Bagley Babe hat-trick, as Feral had always wanted to do. God, he missed Feral; only Feral would have understood his agony. Then he heard the sound of sobbing. It was Xavier, slumped on a bench, head in his hands, an empty bottle of rum beside him.

'Dad'll never be proud of me. I failed to pull Jade and why haven't I got the guts to kill Cosmo?'

'I'm sorry. I can't help you,' said Paris.

55

Joan and Cambola sang tunes from *Ariadne* all the way home, putting down the hood of the convertible Joan had hired so they could admire the stars. Dame Hermione had been wonderfully gracious and invited them back to her hotel for a cold supper of chicken gelé, wild berries, white chocolate sauce and Pouilly-Fumé. When Miss Cambola had pointed out Cosmo's musical genius, Hermione had replied that Cosmo was 'such a kind boy and very, very sensitive'.

'He gets that from you,' suggested Cambola.

'Indeed.' Hermione bowed her head, then, turning her big, brown eyes on an excited Joan: 'High-spirited maybe, but genius must be untamed.'

It had been after midnight when they'd left Cardiff and her presence.

Overhead, Draco the Dragon, not Welsh this time, had been joined by the Swan and the Lyre, on which Joan would have loved to serenade Dame Hermione. Wild honeysuckle and elderflower bashed in the narrow lanes by her car released a sweet yet disturbingly acrid, sexy smell. The night air was a pashmina round their shoulders. The roads were quiet. Joan took Cambola's hand. They agreed that Skunk and Biffo would have been home hours ago and that Janna was a sensible young woman to leave in charge.

'Janna is like Toscanini,' mused Cambola, 'many

wrong things, but redeemed by so much passion and vitality.'

As they drove towards the castle, they heard sounds of revelry by night. Striding down to the pool, Joan's first reaction was delight to see such charming young women frolicking naked in the pool. But her delight turned to horror when she realized they were not only her girls, but Vicky and Gloria also stripped off and extremely the worse for wear. Vicky was wrapped round Anatole, and Gloria snogging unashamedly in the shallow end with Hermione's 'very, very sensitive' little son, who, when Joan bellowed with rage for everyone to stop, gave her a V-sign.

Not making a great deal of potential deputy headway, Joan marched inside to be greeted by devastation. Summer pudding had incarnadined the exquisite blue wallpaper, a glazed brown duck carcass had nested in the chandelier. Empty alcoves reproached her. A raspberry pavlova had been rammed, like a custard pie, into the face of a replica of Michelangelo's David.

Bellowing with rage, blowing her whistle, crunching on smashed Meissen, Ming and Venetian glass, Joan stormed upstairs to find doors ajar and the beds of Jade, Milly and Amber empty. Primrose Duddon wasn't in her room either, nor were Kylie, Pearl or Kitten Meadows.

Red and more fiery than any Welsh dragon, Joan hammered on Janna's door.

'Kerist' – Hengist leapt out of bed – 'it's that porter from Macbeth again. How time flies when you're really enjoying yourself.'

'The moon's gone, get on the balcony,' hissed Janna, kicking his Prussian-blue shirt and white trousers under the bed.

Wrapping herself in a towel for a second time that evening, she opened her door an inch and again was nearly concussed as it was thrust open to reveal Joan bellowing like a Herefordshire bull. Hastily, Janna leapt backwards, aware she must reek of Hengist, his fingerprints luminous on her quivering, sated body.

'How could you let this happen? Downstairs has been totally wrecked. Students and teachers are frolicking naked in the pool. None of my students are in their rooms. As duty officer you're totally to blame.'

Retreating further from a fountain of spit, Janna mumbled she'd been struck down by migraine.

'The worst ever. I lay down for half an hour before dinner; I must have dropped off.'

'Well, get dressed at once,' thundered Joan, 'your students aren't in their beds either.'

Turning, Janna caught a glimpse of the rocking horse, hooded like a prisoner by Hengist's underpants and, fighting laughter, slammed the door and locked it. Equally weak with laughter, Hengist slid in from the balcony.

'Oh dear,' he sighed, 'but quite inevitable after segregating them in separate youth hostels all week. I don't expect they've come to much harm. And quite frankly, that was so miraculous, darling, nothing else matters. I suppose I'd better beat it.'

He was buttoning up his shirt and pausing to kiss Janna, when his mobile rang. It was Joan covering her tracks.

'Sorry to wake you, headmaster, just to alert you that anarchy has broken out at Castle Gafellyn. Janna Curtis was left in charge but deserted her post, claiming a headache. Both Vicky and Gloria are drunk and incapable. Half our students are missing.'

'And where were you and Biffo and Rufus whilst all this was happening?' asked Hengist icily. 'You went to the opera in Cardiff?' After a pause: 'Biffo and Skunk and Boffin went to some troglodyte caves? Surely that was taking coals to Newcastle? Well, you should all have bloody well been there.'

Then, after another long pause: 'Bertie's an old

friend and very reasonable. I'm sure the bracelet will turn up.' Reaching out for Janna's pubes, he pulled her towards him, sliding his hand between her legs. 'Try to limit the damage. You've got yourself into this mess; don't call the police. I'm at Tintern Abbey and over the limit, or I'd drive straight over.'

Switching off his mobile, he kissed Janna lingeringly.

'I'd better scarper or we'll both be in trouble. Stick to the migraine story. Joan hasn't got a hairy leg to stand on.'

His feet groped around for his loafers.

'Where are you going?'

'Back down the secret passage. It comes out at the edge of Hanging Wood quarter of a mile away; my car's hidden in the trees. I utterly adore you, that was the best fuck I've ever had.'

'I feel drunk,' sighed Janna, 'and I haven't had a drop.'

'I'll call you,' said Hengist and was gone.

Groggily, Janna dressed. She couldn't stop giggling. She was no doubt about to be sacked, but she didn't care.

I love Hengist, Hengist loves me and two heads are definitely better in bed than one.

Joan meanwhile had stepped over a supine Rocky on the landing, located Lando France-Lynch watching polo on Sky and finally tracked down an orgy in Jack Waterlane's bedroom. Here she found Johnnie Fowler, Monster Norman, Jack, Kylie, Kitten, Junior, Amber, Milly, Cosmo and Anatole, who she'd last seen behaving abominably in the pool, and oh horrors, Primrose Duddon, among the writhing bodies.

Inspired by an internationally prize-winning installation entitled 'Shagpile', which showed models of naked men piled on top of and plugged into each other like Lego, the geography trip participants were trying to create a replica of fornicating bodies.

'Vaitress,' shouted Anatole, falling off the pile and waving an empty vodka bottle at Joan, 'can you get us another drink?'

'How dare you?' thundered Joan.

'Come and join our team-building exercise, miss.' Johnnie Fowler took a hand off Amber's left breast and patted the bed.

'Stop it, all of you, what the hell d'you think you're doing?'

'Don't swear, miss,' giggled Kitten from the middle of the pile.

'You told us to overcome traditional animosities and bond with Larks,' panted Junior, 'and what better way of doing it?' He kissed Kitten's shoulder. 'You beautiful thing.'

'Help,' shrieked Kylie, bucking frantically then collapsing on top of Jack, 'I'm overcoming.'

'Have you seen the state of downstairs?' yelled Joan. 'Thousands of pounds' worth of damage has been done.'

'Not by us,' chorused Shagpile II.

Drawing a dick the length of a conger eel out of a glassy-eyed Milly, Cosmo said chattily, 'Could have been Rocky. He was trashing the place as I passed, probably forgot to take his Ritalin.'

Downstairs, amid the debris, Cambola had swept earth from the hurled bamboo plant off the piano keys and, armed with a large brandy, was singing along as she picked out tunes from *Ariadne*.

Paris, having shed his shorts earlier, couldn't find them. Suspecting Cosmo, he nicked a pair marked Anatole Rostov from the Cosmonaughties' bedroom. Anatole wouldn't miss them; he'd brought six other pairs. Wandering into the garden, overwhelmed by vodka, despair and loveless sex, Paris passed Joan having a squawking match with Vicky.

'You will certainly lose your job, young lady.'

'Doesn't matter, I've got another one to go to.'

'Don't be too sure of that.'

Driven out of Jack's bedroom, Shagpile II were indulging in another shrieking stint of skinny-dipping. Reaching the pool, Paris stopped in his tracks to find Janna counting heads. As though nothing had happened, she turned and smiled at him.

'Oh, there you are. Are you OK?'

Paris was about to shout that she was a fucking slag, when he caught sight of a body in the shallow end, deathly pale even in the moonlight, hair streaming, stick legs askew, and realized it was Pearl surrounded by a flickering halo of blood. At first he thought she must have started her period and to save her humiliation looked round for a towel. Then he realized the blood was gushing from her wrists and, leaping into the water, he dragged her to the side. Hoisting her onto the flagstones, he yelled: 'Quick, she's cut herself.'

Janna rushed forward.

'Oh, poor child. Ring for an ambulance.' Crouching down, she put an ear to Pearl's chest. 'She's breathing, but unconscious, and terribly cold.'

Miss Cambola came running into the garden. 'We must make a tourniquet.' Tearing off her orange and black scarf, she wound it round and round Pearl's arm. 'Put your finger on the knot,' she ordered Paris. Then, turning to Janna: 'We must get her straight to hospital for a blood transfusion. If we meet the ambulance coming the other way, at least we save time.'

'I'll drive, I haven't been drinking,' said Janna. 'What the hell happened?' she asked as a suddenly sobered-up Amber, Junior and Paris helped her and Cambola carry Pearl to Joan's convertible.

'Fucking Cosmo. Shagged her, texted everyone to say she was a slag, then dumped her by text,' said Amber.

Jade, back in her bedroom, was calling her father. 'Daddy, Daddy, I'm having a horrible time. Paris

462

Alvaston tried to rape me, he came on so strong and I didn't want to reject him because he's a yob and Xavier Campbell-Black tried to rape me too. I didn't want to be unkind, but he was drunk and went at me like an animal. I had to knee him in the balls. And, oh Daddy, someone's cut off all my hair, I look hideous. Everyone's drunk; all the teachers are shagging and skinny-dipping.'

'Calm down, princess. Who's in charge?'

'Joan but she bunked off with Cambola to hear Cosmo's mum in some opera and Skunk and Biffo went to look at some lousy eclipse and Rufus's gone home, he thinks his wife's bunked off.'

'Who's in charge?'

'Janna, but she bunked off to bed and now she's taken some girl who's slashed her wrists to hospital. We're staying in such a lovely old castle and Rocky's gone berserk and broken the place up. Everything's out of control. My diamond bracelet's been nicked and oh, my hair, Daddy.'

'Did anyone actually rape you, princess?'

'No, but they tried.'

'Go to bed and I'll fly down and collect you first thing.'

Stancombe came off the telephone and turned to Rufus's wife, Sheena, stretched out beside him on black satin sheets.

'Mission accomplished,' he said triumphantly. 'There's no way the blessed Janna and Larks will survive this disaster.'

'The pupils have bonded so well,' mocked Cosmo as, back in their bedroom, he and Lubemir heated up an electric kettle to light their spliffs on the element, 'that the teachers felt redundant and soon will be declared so.'

'I wonder how the Lower Sixth are getting on with their tour of the battlefields,' pondered Lubemir.

'Ought to start by studying the one downstairs,' said Cosmo.

Alex and Poppet Bruce had spent the day walking in Wales. They had booked into a nearby hotel but, seeing lights still on in the castle, decided to drop in to see Biffo, Skunk, Joan and dear little Vicky and enjoy some free drink.

They found Joan in a state of shock. Desperately guarding her position, fulminating to hide her guilt she had been skiving, she whisked them as quickly as possible out into the garden.

'Where are the students?' asked Alex.

'In their beds.'

'What on earth happened?' asked Poppet, who loved trouble.

'A young woman, Pearl Smith, slashed her wrists. Janna Curtis has rushed her to Casualty. I've been trying to ring Pearl's emergency contact number in Larkminster, but the telephone appears to be cut off.'

'Why did she try to end her life?' pressed Poppet.

'Oh, some love affair,' replied Joan. Dame Hermione would never forgive her if she shopped Cosmo. Anxious to get off the subject: 'And Jade Stancombe has behaved in a most reprehensible way. She was observed in flagrante with both Paris Alvaston and Xavier Campbell-Black. She must be excluded.'

Alex Bruce turned pale.

'We can't exclude Jade. We'd jeopardize our Science Emporium. Stancombe's been supportive when we've fired anyone else's kids, but he wouldn't like it if we excluded Jade. We must limit the damage. Don't call the police or the parents or the ambulance.'

'Janna Curtis insisted on taking Pearl to hospital,' said Joan.

'Well, I suppose Pearl is her responsibility.'

At that moment Biffo and Skunk strode in, laughing heartily.

'Alex, Poppet, how good to see you. We've seen the most dramatic eclipse,' said Biffo. Then, lest Alex should think they'd been skiving, he added that they'd taken Boffin, Alex's favourite pupil with them. 'He couldn't believe his eyes. We've packed him off to bed. No doubt he'll debrief you tomorrow, Alex. I could do with a Scotch, couldn't you, Skunk?'

Joan was just debriefing them about the last six hours, heaping blame on Janna, when Bertie Wallace, hot from his mistress, walked in, whereupon Joan heaped blame on Rocky.

'Quite an achievement,' said Bertie, surveying the devastation. 'Rocky should get a job with the council demolishing old buildings. Fortunately for me, this house is in my wife's name. I doubt if she'll be quite so sanguine, but I expect it's insured.'

Janna rang Joan from the hospital. Pearl, thank God, was out of danger. They had given her stitches and a blood transfusion. She was conscious and Janna had spoken to her. Then she asked if she could have a quick word with Paris.

'I know he's worried.'

Even though it was nearly three a.m., Paris was awake, lying on top of his duvet, gazing at the ceiling. He took the telephone into a deserted bedroom.

'I thought you'd like to know Pearl's going to be OK and you probably saved her life.' Then, when Paris didn't answer: 'She's all right, Paris.'

'You're fucking not.'

'I beg your pardon?'

'If you hadn't sloped off to bed with a made-up headache and Hengist Fucking Brett-Taylor, none of this would have happened, you dirty bitch.'

'What are you talking about?'

'I saw Hengist at your window, stripped off and flaunting his six-pack, you fucking slag.'

'Oh Paris,' pleaded Janna in horror, but he had hung up.

56

Bagley pupils who'd been on the field trip were gated until the end of term, which was only a few days away. As Dora Belvedon had not been among the participants, it fell to Sheena Anderson to sell the story of 'Toff School in Mass Orgy', complete with gory details of skinny-dipping, group sex, trashing of our precious heritage and, finally, of a young woman nearly dying from a suicide attempt.

The person who carried the can was Janna. She was the only head on the trip, and the catastrophe had occurred when she was in charge. She had let the maintained sector down. Hengist was very sympathetic to her plight and had bollocked his staff for leaving her exposed, but he was not prepared, 'for both our sakes, darling', to reveal his part in distracting Janna during the evening.

Parents were fortunately mollified by magnificent exam results released in August, in which Bagley, helped no doubt by Cosmo's leaked papers, had drawn away from St Jimmy's and edged towards Fleetley.

Larks did infinitely better than the previous year: up from four per cent to ten per cent of the pupils getting the requisite five A–C grades known as the Magic Five, but they were still near the bottom of the Larkshire league. Any satisfaction was doused by Ashton Douglas's call.

'Vewy disappointing wesults, Janna. We'll need a post-mortem on these and the geography field trip.'

On the credit side, Pearl bounced back quickly – cheered by all the sympathy and by a large bunch of pink roses on Dame Hermione's account, plus a card from her 'very sensitive' little son saying: 'Sorry, I was a rat. Love, Cosmo.'

Remembering how she had smashed Janna's Staffordshire cow, Pearl organized a whip-round from both Bagley and Larks children who'd been on the field trip and raised enough money to buy an even prettier Herefordshire cow from Larkminster Antiques.

'Miss loves cows.'

'She don't love Chally or Basket or Spink or Joan,' grumbled Graffi, but he designed a beautiful card, saying 'You're a star' in gold and purple sequins and everyone signed it and wrote fond messages inside apologizing that the trip had gone pear-shaped, but insisting they had had the best time ever, and thanking her for all her kindness.

Janna, overwhelmed, stroked the spotted red and white cow, and blushed and wept with joy over the card. Only after she'd read it half a dozen times did she notice Paris's name was missing.

When asked, Pearl had also blushed. 'Paris gets funny.'

I doubt it, thought Janna.

Paris had blanked her for the rest of the term and when she'd given him a lovely edition of Housman's poems as a leaving present, had just put it back on her desk. How would he treat Hengist, she wondered, when he got to Bagley?

Paris had also fallen out with Feral who, resentful the field trip had been a riot, grew crosser when Paris refused to debrief him and Graffi.

'Did you shag Amber and Jade?'

'Fuck off.'

'Did you shag Vicky or Gloria? Did you shag Miss?'

'I don't want to talk about it.'

Feral then queried the wisdom of moving in with Ian and Patience. 'Be careful, man. People only foster in order to abuse. That Ian looks a fascist perv and she's an ugly cow. I suppose you can always phone Childline.'

Paris, fuelled by rage, misery and apprehension, hit Feral across the playground. The fight went to ten rounds and was not made up. Once again, longing for his lost mother overcame Paris. Two days before the end of term, he vanished, taking to the trains to find her. After two days of panic, social services in Larkminster received a call from a stationmaster in Land's End saying Paris was stopping the night with him and his wife, but would be put on the train back to Birmingham tomorrow. Seeing Nadine's stuffed-sheep face on the platform at New Street, however, beside grim bully Blenchley and Crispin snuffling in disapproval, Paris jumped trains and went off to Edinburgh.

'Children dumped by their mothers never stop looking for them,' said Nadine, which hardly helped a desperately nervous Patience.

So Paris never said goodbye to Larks, even when he was safely returned to Oaktree Court and started packing up his few belongings in the expectation of moving to the Cartwrights. Janna felt wiped out by guilt. She should have levelled with both Patience and Nadine that Paris had only been thrown off course and was likely to act up appallingly because he'd been let down by yet another mother figure.

'I needn't say I was in bed with you,' she begged Hengist, when he visited Jubilee Cottage after the field trip. 'I can just say some lover rolled up.'

'You're in enough trouble as it is,' said Hengist firmly. 'Some bloody counsellor will worm it out of Paris and then we'll be really in the shit. We deserve a

468

little happiness. It's going to be difficult enough to see each other as it is.'

So, just as Paris felt horribly guilty but let Rocky take the rap for trashing Gafellyn Castle, Janna also kept quiet. Hengist had bewitched her, as blindingly dazzling as low winter sun reflected in icy puddles. She found it impossible not to revel in such unfamiliar happiness.

Throughout the long, hot summer, she was amazed and gratified how often he managed to see her. Luckily, hers was the last cottage in the village, with no house opposite, and Lily's wise sapphire-blue eyes were too short-sighted to recognize Hengist when he crept in during darkening evenings, wearing a confiscated baseball cap, shades and shoes wet from the increasingly heavy dews.

He frequently rolled up with one of Elaine's Bonios for Partner, who, instead of barking, whimpered and wriggled his little body with joy.

When Hengist was unable to see her, he rang, having learnt from his pupils to acquire a second pay-as-you-go mobile so Painswick couldn't trace his calls. He wouldn't, however, write to Janna when he was away. 'Too risky. I trust you, darling, but not the press.' Instead he gave her poetry books with pages marked:

Ah, love, let us be true
To one another! For the world, which seems
To lie before us like a land of dreams,
So various, so beautiful, so new . . .

'I feel dreadfully guilty about Sally,' Janna told him repeatedly, but Hengist always claimed that was his department.

'I'm not going to lie and say Sally doesn't understand me or sleep with me or love me as I love her. But this is so utterly divine . . .' He buried his lips in Janna's freckled shoulder. 'That's why we must be so careful not to get caught.'

Lovers, like Stew in the past, had refused to say they loved her. Hengist said it all the time. The downside – like jesting Pilate – was that he could never stay for more than an hour or two.

They were in bed one early August afternoon when a naked Janna glanced out of the window and shot back as Alex Bruce jogged by, head held high, spectacles misting up, showing off a spare figure and skinny legs.

'D'you think he's spying?'

'No, determined to win the school steeplechase.'

'When's that?'

'Last Sunday in September. It's Biffo's baby, both staff and pupils take part in a six-mile run round Bagley village and the surrounding countryside. Excellent way of giving unfit masters coronaries. Biffo takes it incredibly seriously. Alex is a lousy games player – can't see a ball – so he's desperate to triumph at cross country. Robot the Bruce. I must keep Paris away from his deplorable wife, Poppet, who'd love to counsel our guilty secret out of him. Anyway, I can think of better ways of keeping fit.' He pulled Janna on top of him.

Hengist was as generous with presents as with his affections: Ralph Lauren shirts; a dusty pink cashmere twinset; a topaz brooch and matching earrings; a little Staffordshire dog; a CD of *Beatrice and Benedict*, Berlioz's lovely opera based on *Much Ado*, because Janna reminded him of the mettlesome lippy Beatrice; a watercolour by Emily Patrick; endless books he'd loved that he hoped she'd enjoy.

Janna was also in heaven because the long summer holiday was the first time she'd had a chance to play house, tend her garden, listen to the Proms and explore the countryside with Partner, who grew in confidence every day. Often she picked blackberries so ripe and luscious in the hedgerows you could fill a bowl in ten minutes. But deep in the wood, the same berries were small, hard and green and would never reach fruition – like so many of her children, trapped by poverty. She vowed once again to start homework and breakfast clubs next term and campaign for a football pitch for Feral.

One muggy afternoon in August, she stood and gazed out of her bedroom window at the yellow shaven fields, the darkening olive-green woods and the gaudy butter-flies, glutting themselves on the amethyst spears of 'my buddleia', she thought happily.

She had just been to court with Feral, who, refusing to admit how heartbroken he was at Paris's defection, had got hammered and totalled a stolen car. Bitterly ashamed of his dyslexia and that he could hardly read or write, he was panicking how he could avoid utter humiliation next term without Paris to translate, explain and do his homework.

Even with Dora's frightfully disapproving mother Lady Belvedon on the bench, Janna's impassioned plea that it would be disastrous for Feral to miss the start of his GCSE course, and that she could vouch for his character, won over the other magistrates. When Feral got away with a suspended sentence, his relief was palpable. He clammed up, however, whenever Janna asked him about Paris or his family.

Taking off her rose-patterned suit, worn to charm the magistrates, Janna paused to glance in the mirror. Love seemed to have made her body curvier and softer. Last autumn's headmistress's bob had grown out, thank goodness; her red curls now nearly reached her nipples. If Hengist thought she was beautiful, maybe she was. He was not due till tomorrow, so she could veg out tonight and watch the four hours of *The Bill* that she'd taped.

'Bugger, bugger,' said a voice.

Returning to the window, Janna found her

neighbour Lily, who'd been staying with friends in the Dordogne for a fortnight, forcing a mower through a hayfield of lawn.

'Get on, you utterly bloody thing,' Lily yelled as the mower stalled on a particularly shaggy corner, then hit a bone – probably Partner's, thought Janna guiltily – went into a furious clatter and stopped completely.

'Bugger you.' Lily kicked it several times to no effect. 'My bloody corns!' Then, frantically tugging a wire: 'Don't do this to me, I can't afford to get you mended.'

Next moment, Lily had collapsed onto a rickety garden bench and burst into terrible rasping sobs. Janna was appalled. Ramrod-straight, endlessly kind and merry, outwardly invincible, only occasionally grumbling about her arthritis, Lily seemed indomitable. It was like seeing Big Ben crumbling. Lily was such a good listener and had been such a comfort that Janna wanted to race downstairs, fling her arms round her and return some of the comfort, but felt Lily might feel embarrassed.

Partner, with no such reserve, shot downstairs and out into the garden through the gap in the fence. Dummying past an outraged General, he leapt onto his friend Lily's knee to lick away her tears.

Grabbing a bottle of white from the fridge, Janna followed more reflectively. Feral was flat broke and had nothing to keep him out of mischief. He'd always got on with Lily when the Wolf Pack came over on Saturday afternoons. Janna would get Lily's mower mended, and Feral could mow her lawn.

She found Lily drying her eyes with Partner's ears, her face ravaged by tears. It was sweet of Janna to suggest Feral, but she could honestly manage.

'Oh please, he's so sad about Paris, and he's desperately broke, you'd be doing him a favour.'

'I always liked Feral,' admitted Lily. 'He had such amazing ball control when he played football on my lawn. He never broke a flower.'

'Well, that's settled then. Let's open this bottle.'

'We mustn't forget to watch Christian Woodford's programme at six-thirty,' said Lily.

The Brigadier, who lived a few doors away, had evidently been asked by Rupert Campbell-Black to do a programme on Dunkirk.

'How exciting,' cried Janna. 'I'll just go and ring Feral.'

Lily's heart sank. She couldn't afford to have her mower mended, let alone pay Feral. Ever since she had been kicked out of her lovely riverside house Lily had existed in this damp, rented cottage on a hopelessly dwindling fixed income – with shares yielding one per cent.

Despite her outward insouciance, Lily was in despair. Although she adored her nephews and nieces, particularly Dora, their constant visits exhausted her physically and financially. She was reduced to selling silver and pictures every month to keep herself in drink and the faddy black and white General in chicken. Some days Lily herself existed on 'pussy's pieces', bought for General from the fishmonger and blackberries picked on walks.

There was another space on the drawing-room wall where she'd last week sold a little Sutherland drawing to pay some bills. Now she'd have to find extra cash to pay Feral and give him a good tea.

57

Feral looked as though he needed a good tea when he rolled up two days later. He wore a black baseball cap back to front, black loose jeans, a black T-shirt. Was he in mourning for Paris or did he think black suited him? Rangier than ever, he'd shot up three inches. His tawny brown eyes roved round the kitchen, checking in every corner for ways to escape.

It had been raining heavily. A few muddy gashes, a few roses clouted on the ankles, a clematis taken out altogether and a lot of bad language later, the lawn was mowed and the terrace swept. Lily gave Feral a pie made of potatoes, onions and cheese sauce, blackberry crumble and a glass of sloe gin. He had seconds of everything, as they discussed Arsenal and Larkminster Rovers' prospects for the coming season.

'Football makes me look forward to autumn,' said Lily, 'as foxhunting used to in the old days.'

The Premiership was due to start on Saturday and the joy of Arsenal winning, or despair at them losing, lasted Feral all week, until excitement about the next game kicked in. But it wouldn't be the same without Paris and the endless arguments they'd had about the relative merits of Emile Heskey or Thierry Henry.

'Paris loved Liverpool,' said Lily idly. 'How's he getting on with his new family?'

'Dunno.'

'You must miss him.'

Feral shrugged.

'How's Graffi?'

'His dad's out of work.'

There was a pause.

'You must meet my friend Brigadier Woodford, who lives four houses away. He might need someone to do odd jobs for him. Rupert Campbell-Black had him on television two nights ago; he was excellent, talking about Dunkirk. Did you come across Rupert's children Xav and Bianca when you went to Bagley?'

'Xav's a no-good nigger,' observed Feral. 'She and I did a dance routine in *Romeo and Juliet*.'

He was desperate to ask after Bianca who, since March, had tangoed through his dreams, but couldn't bring himself to. Instead, he volunteered the information that Randal Stancombe was looking for squatters. 'Pays four pounds an hour, puts them in to bring down the price of a house he wants to buy.'

Lily observed the swallows gathering on the telegraph wires. 'Perhaps I should apply.'

'Bit rough for a lady,' grinned Feral, helping himself to another spoonful of crumble.

Stiffly Lily got to her feet. Taking off her huge sapphire engagement ring and putting it on the draining board, she turned on the hot tap and added washing-up liquid.

'Haven't you got a dishwasher?'

'There's only me. Wouldn't want to risk my best china.'

General the cat appeared at the window. He landed with a thud then ferociously attacked a wooden leg of the kitchen table as the telephone rang. It was Dora. Bianca's friend, thought Feral longingly – as if Rupert Campbell-Anti-Black would let me anywhere near his darling daughter. Fucking upper classes.

'Of course,' Lily was saying, 'no, bring Cadbury, that's fine, perhaps not Loofah as Feral's just mown my

475

lawn most excellently. Yes, stay the night, we can watch *Midsomer Murders*.'

Putting the telephone down, Lily turned back to Feral, lines deepening on her no longer smiling face, utterly exhausted. Feral's tea had taken a lot out of her, and there wasn't any cheese pie or crumble left for Dora's supper. Then she glanced at the draining board. Her ring had gone. She was sure she'd left it there. She should never have put temptation in Feral's way. The great sapphire had been bought to match the blue of her eyes, by a husband she'd loved so much. She glanced at his faded photograph, smiling out at her, and wondered what to do. The sapphire had been like a safety net to keep from the door the wolf, but not the Wolf Pack.

Slowly, painfully, she opened the silver clasp of her red leather purse and with trembling, arthritic fingers gave Feral a tenner for mowing. Then, taking a basket, she went into the garden. It had been a wonderful year for plums; glowing ruby-red, they weighed down the trees like weeping willows. How often recently had she dined on bread and plum jam? Slowly she filled up the basket, swearing and sobbing as a sleepy wasp landed on her third finger where the sapphire had been. Back in the house, she found Feral puffing on a spliff and watching the sports news.

She held out the basket. 'Do you like plums?'

'Never had one.'

'Well, don't break those beautiful white teeth on the stones.' Then, as Feral rolled his eyes: 'You might be able to sell them. I'll decant them into a cardboard box.'

'Fanks, man,' said Feral. With his first glimmer of a smile: 'I could sell them to Paris to put in his mouf, now he's gone all posh at Bagley.'

Lily laughed. Rootling around for an old Whiskas x 12 box, shaking out a spider, she filled it with plums. Handing them to Feral, she noticed the sapphire ring back on the draining board. Dizzy with relief, she had to fight back the tears. For a moment, their eyes met. Again Feral half smiled and shrugged. Then he handed Lily the spliff. Taking a giant puff, she practically burst her lungs.

'You need help wiv Dora's bed?' said Feral.

'You are kind. Actually it's already made up, a teenage friend stayed for a dance last week, only in bed an hour, so I'm afraid I made it up again.'

There was a pause.

'Would you like to come back next week? The grass still grows quickly at this time of year.'

'I'll fink about it,' said Feral.

He longed to feel welcome in an adult world. He needed people to talk to, to feel respect.

'Oh, OK,' he said.

As Brigadier Woodford, who was reading the lesson, drove Lily to Evensong in the next village, they spotted Feral. He was slumped by the side of the road with his Whiskas box, holding up a torn-off piece of cardboard, on which he had written 'Plumes for Sal'.

'"Bring me my white plume",' quipped the Brigadier, slowing down. 'First-rate job you made of Lily's lawn. Well done,' he told Feral and although his garden was awash with plums, he bought a pound's worth. 'Can't resist Lily's plums.'

The collection could have a pound, instead of two, he decided as he drove on. He had skipped lunch at the Dog and Duck, so he could afford to ask Lily to have dinner with him on the way home.

'Your Dunkirk programme was such a triumph,' Lily told him.

'They did seem pleased.'

'With all those Second World War anniversaries coming up, I'm sure Rupert'll ask you to do some more.'

The Brigadier, who had been brought up to be

self-deprecating, loved having someone to tell things to. Gratifying how many people at Evensong, even the parson, who was a notorious pacifist, made a point of saying how good he'd been.

'Rupert's going to pay me two hundred pounds,' he confided to Lily. 'Quite extraordinary for a ten-minute waffle. That's twelve hundred an hour.'

'Randal Stancombe will evidently pay us four pounds an hour for squatting.'

'Have to get a new hip before I tried any of that,' grinned the Brigadier.

By the time he'd levered himself out of the car on arrival at the Dog and Duck, to open Lily's door, she'd already clambered out. Good thing there was no shortage of single women in later life. If a husband came home these days, he would be far too crocked to leap into the wardrobe or pull on his clothes in a hurry. He'd had such wonderful escapades when he was young: wives of commanding officers or even of a visiting general. He didn't think his wife Betsy had ever found out, but she'd looked sad sometimes. He'd made it up by nursing her to the end, although he'd often been rather irritable. Now he harboured a secret passion for Lily: so beautiful, so plucky. He suspected she was even broker than he was and wished he could help.

Although over eighty, the Brigadier was tall and upright, with a high colour which tanned quickly and thick hair, brushed back in two wings, in the same steel grey as his moustache.

Lily had refused his invitation to dinner at first because Dora was staying, so the Brigadier had invited them both to the Dog and Duck, where Dora admired the 'gorgeous springer spaniel' on the inn sign, and where it was sheltered enough to eat outside and admire an orange moon floating free of the darkening woods.

Dora, as usual, was brimming over with chat as she

fed crisps to Cadbury and tucked into roast chicken, chips and peas.

'Only time to grab a sandwich at lunchtime,' she announced in her piercing voice. 'Patience and I have been getting Paris's room ready. He loves Liverpool, so we put posters of Owen, Gerrard and Emile Heskey on the walls and she's bought him a Liverpool shirt and a red Liverpool mug which says 'You're not drinkin' any more' on the bottom, and a lovely bookshelf and a tuck box with a key, so he can keep private things.

'He's so lucky,' went on Dora, dipping a chip in tomato ketchup. 'That room's got a terrific view of the stables and Patience has painted it a lovely warm corn colour. Ian's been so preoccupied letting the school to a bishops' conference, and getting fees out of parents like my mother who won't pay up, that Patience has been able to splurge. Fortunately, her aunt kicked the bucket and left her some money.'

The Brigadier, famished after no lunch, had nearly finished his shepherd's pie; Dora, getting behind, began feeding strips of chicken to Cadbury.

'Anyway,' she continued, 'Patience has also bought him a television, a radio, a laptop, a tape deck, a mobile and loads of uniform. Ian wanted her to buy it second-hand. Patience wasn't having any of it, so it's all new.'

'Eat up, Dora, darling,' chided Lily, 'it'll get cold.'

'I'll eat your chips if you like,' said the Brigadier, filling his and Lily's glasses with an excellent red.

'And he's got a double bed,' added Dora, aware the entire pub was now listening, 'so he can have women in, with a patchwork quilt. Patience put lots of Emerald and Sophy's old children's books in the bookshelf: *Babar* and *The Happy Prince*, which is what Patience wants Paris to be. I think he's more like Little Kay in *The Snow Queen*. We mustn't let his heart turn into a block of ice. Can I turn my fork over to eat my peas? It's quicker.'

The rising moon had grown paler.

'Not too cold?' asked the Brigadier.

'I'm fine. That was gorgeous. Thank you so much.' Dora shoved her knife and fork together. 'I'm truly full up.' She beamed at him. 'Well, I wouldn't mind some chocolate ice cream, if you insist.'

A second later, she was back to the subject of Paris.

'I only hope he's very grateful because Ian and Patience have gone through so much to become foster parents – oodles of medical tests, and they've got to practise safe sex – sounds like a duet' – Dora pretended to play the piano on the table – 'so that Patience doesn't get pregnant. She's a bit ancient for that, I would say.'

A woman at the next table choked on her quiche. Lily's eyes met the Brigadier's and, as they tried not to laugh, she attempted to steer Dora onto safer subjects.

'How many bishops has Ian let the school to?'

'Millions,' giggled Dora. 'The Bishop of Cotchester's sleeping in Cosmo's study. I hope he'll remember to water Cosmo's marijuana plants.'

58

Head boy at Rugby, a rugger blue with a second at Cambridge, commanding officer of a tank regiment, managing director of a highly successful Yorkshire engineering company, Ian Cartwright had had few setbacks in life until ousted by a boardroom coup staged by directors fed up with his brusque, despotic manner.

He then fell on desperately hard times, lost everything through foolish investment, descended into heavy drinking and nervous breakdown, only surviving on the money his staunch wife Patience earned working in a bar. The nightmare had ended two years ago, when Ian had landed the job as bursar of Bagley Hall, a Hengist appointment, which had been an unqualified success: the previous incumbent having cooked the books. Ian, who was utterly straight, industrious and excellent with figures, soon got the reputation of a man who could 'get things done', which was also a euphemism for being at everyone's beck and call.

Having been delivered from the hell of poverty, Ian was passionately grateful to his deliverer and in truth it was partly to impress Hengist that he had been keen to foster Paris.

Ian had also longed for a son with whom to discuss internationals, test matches and nineteenth-century poetry, who would look up to him, replenish his whisky, bring in logs and share manly tasks.

Although apprehensive, he was determined to do right by Paris and kept quoting *Timon of Athens*: ''Tis not enough to help the feeble up, But to support him after.'

Alas, Paris, already in explosive mood, arrived at the Cartwrights' at Ian's busiest time. Bills for school fees had been dispatched on the first day of the holidays and should have been paid – in theory – before the children set foot in school for the autumn term.

This had resulted in a flood of furious letters from parents outraged not only by the increased fees but at having to foot the bill for the demolition of Gafellyn Castle – letters which Hengist, having buggered off to Umbria, had left Ian to answer.

The majority of staff had swanned off on long holidays, leaving Ian to oversee the installation of new kitchens and damp courses and replace faulty windows in their houses and classrooms. No-Joke Joan rang every day from Lesbos to find out if Ian's maintenance men had unjammed the Tampax machine in Boudicca and whether he had looked at her suggestions for a second young women's boarding house.

Little Vicky Fairchild, on whom Ian had a crush, had already wheedled herself a charming flat overlooking the playing fields with a new en suite bathroom; where-upon all the young staff followed suit and wanted one too. In addition, it was Ian's duty in the holidays to let the school to bring in revenue. For the fifth year running, the Church of England had held their conference at Bagley, charming chaps who all wanted to play golf and ride Patience's horses, which ran away with them, which added to the pressure.

In the second half, the school had been taken over by a group of Orthodox Jews, charming chaps too, a source of excellent jokes, but who as part of their religion insisted that their quarters should be plunged into darkness at ten o'clock. They had therefore wrenched out and mislaid most of the infrared lights that automatically came on in the passages as night fell.

Any conference involved a lot of tidying up for Ian's ground staff and maintenance men to prepare the school for the new term. Ian didn't mind, he relished hard work and found Hengist, who only raised hell if his expenses were curbed and the pitches were not mown, a dream boss. The job would have been perfect except for the endless bullying interference of Alex Bruce. Hell-bent on modernizing the school, Alex had insisted Ian learn to use a computer so he could do his own letters and figures and dispense with Jenny Winters, his kind, pretty and brilliantly efficient PA.

Ian was subsequently having a nightmare mastering the beastly machine, which seemed to have tripled his workload.

Normally, as bursar, after he had chased up the parents for payments and settled in the school, he and Patience would have taken their annual three-week holiday in the second half of September. This year, with all the expense of kitting out Paris, they couldn't afford to go.

In late August, when the Cartwrights finally got permission to foster, an exhausted, uptight Ian was hardly in the right mood to welcome and make allowances for Paris. Patience as a reaction became over-conciliatory and dithery, filling every silence with chat, until Ian put her down out of nerves.

Paris was equally uptight, at moving to both a new home and a new school. He loved his new room. He loved his bathroom and, after the fight for often cold showers at Oaktree Court, luxuriated for hours reading in scented baths. He loved his laptop, tape deck and mobile, but since he'd fallen out with the Wolf Pack and Janna, he had no one to ring. The bliss of reading and writing in peace and being able to watch *Richard and Judy* or *Top of the Pops* to the end, without someone throwing a punch or snatching the remote, rather palled when you had all day in which to do it.

After the permanent din of the home where inmates shouted and screamed and were shoved in the quiet room, he found the repressed formality of the Cartwrights unnerving. Nadine had urged them to provide a stable environment with clear boundaries. Ian, tetchy and at full stretch, would return in the evening and order Paris around like an errand boy.

There was the disastrous occasion when Ian asked him to dig some potatoes, and Paris by mistake dug up all the precious half-grown artichokes. Or when Paris was ordered to collect the *Sunday Telegraph* from Bagley village and, settling down to read the football reports on a gravestone in Bagley churchyard on the way home, had crumpled and muddled up all the pages.

Ian, in addition, felt it was his duty to improve others. He started off on Paris's appearance. Sleeveless T-shirts were to be discouraged when they showed off a tattoo of the Eiffel Tower. Soon he was nagging Paris to remove his jewellery. As Paris's ear studs, plaited leather bracelet and necklace of wooden beads, threaded onto a bootlace, had all been presents from Feral, Paris had no intention of complying.

Mealtimes together were also a torment as Ian corrected Paris's pronunciation and table manners.

'It's beetroot, not bee-roo, Paris, and bu-er has a double "t" in the middle. Spoons go on the right and forks on the left and try not to hold your knife like a pencil.'

Patience's erratic time-keeping often meant Paris was summoned to lay the table in the middle of *EastEnders* or *Holby City*. Asparagus lost any initial charm when you were reproached for taking a knife and fork to it.

Even worse horrors occurred at breakfast: plunging your silver spoon into a cavern of phlegm because Patience had under-boiled your egg. It was also impossible to make conversation if your table manners and pronunciation were constantly criticized.

'Leave him alone,' pleaded Patience. 'You're making the poor boy self-conscious.'

'I'm only doing it so he doesn't get teased when he goes to Bagley.'

So Paris left his food and fell into silence. Plates brought to his room when Ian was away were found untouched and gathering flies.

For the first few days he sat with them in the evening, listening to the Proms, watching programmes on archaeological digs and wrecks being brought up from the bottom of the sea. One evening they borrowed and watched a tape of Brigadier Woodford's excellent programme on Dunkirk.

'Woodford lives near Lily Hamilton and Janna Curtis. Evidently he's an awfully nice chap,' observed Ian.

Paris felt the inevitable stab of anguish on hearing Janna's name. Patience felt reproachful. Both Hengist and Janna had promised to be around and help ease Paris's first weeks at Bagley but neither had been near the place, not even a telephone call.

Paris missed the Wolf Pack and Janna dreadfully. Patience couldn't stem his loneliness. She felt she was looking after someone's dog who pines constantly for his master. Trying to make Paris feel at home, she showed him family albums of her daughters Sophy and Emerald from when they were first adopted, through schooldays and eventually marriage and grandchildren.

'My life is recorded in social service files, not family albums,' said Paris bleakly.

'Not any more,' said Patience brightly. 'You'll be in our albums.'

Not if your poxy husband has his way, thought Paris.

The stingy bugger, furious that his wife had spent so much money on mobiles, laptops and new clothes for

Paris, insisted Patience sew the name tapes on herself, rather than avail herself of a school service that only charged 50p a tape. Paris watched her pricking her big red fingers, straining her eyes as she threaded needles.

'At least you're not called something long like Orlando France-Lynch, or Xavier Campbell-Black. Bianca and Xavier are adopted,' bumbled on Patience.

'I know.'

'Bianca's such a happy little soul,' sighed Patience. 'Mind you' – she lowered her voice – 'Sophy was always much happier and easier than Emerald. Maybe it's younger children.'

To make Paris feel at home, Patience had asked Emerald down for the weekend – sadly Emerald's charming, larky husband Jonathan was in Berlin and unable to accompany her. And the baby Raymond, who might have broken the ice, was left in London with the nanny. Paris found Emerald as beadily bitchy as she was beautiful. She clearly hated seeing him ensconced in the spare room with Liverpool posters rather than her own paintings on the walls.

The evening was chilly, and Ian, showing off, had ordered Paris to fetch logs and coal for a fire. Paris, engrossed in Great Expectations, had told Ian to 'piss off' and been sent to his room.

A furious Emerald had followed him.

'How dare you cheek Daddy after all he's done for you, you horrible brat.'

'You could be horrid as a teenager,' protested Patience when Emerald returned downstairs.

'He's a yob,' said Emerald. 'He comes from the gutter and he'll go back there.'

Paris much preferred Emerald's plump, jolly sister, Sophy, Janna's friend, who was going to replace Vicky at Larks in the autumn term. But feeling Sophy might be spying or trying to heal the breach between himself and Janna, whose letters he had continued to tear up, he shut himself in his room whenever she dropped in.

Lying in the bath Paris watched a snail, which had climbed all the way up the wall of the house to escape the incessant rain, its trail glittering in the morning sun, its horns hitting the buffers of the gutter.

Like me, he thought, from the gutter to the gutter.

Term approached. Paris grew more edgy and withdrawn as Bagley staff, back from their holidays, also popped in to check if their windows and sinks had been repaired and to register if he had two heads.

'You're a saint, Patience, adopting at your and Ian's age, and looking after the horses as well. You look exhausted. I hope you're getting paid. Of course he does have a free place.'

And Paris, who'd perfected the art of eavesdropping in care, lurking on stairs and doorways (which was the only way he could learn if he or his friends were being moved on), heard everything.

Watching Patience struggling across the yard with buckets and haynets, he longed to help, but didn't know how to offer.

He would never have survived without Dora, back from a turbulent week in Spain with her brother Dicky, her mother and one of her mother's admirers, a High Court judge.

'Although he was paying for all of us, Mummy didn't want to sleep with him so she insisted on sharing with me, which was so pants. He barged in one night plastered, forgetting I was there, so I whacked him with a black plastic bull.'

Dora's round face and her plump little legs and arms had caught the sun and, rather than plaiting it, she had pulled back her long, blond hair into a ponytail. She was still a tomboy, but as she rolled up with Cadbury and took up residence on his bed, Paris reflected that she might one day have possibilities.

When he tried on his school suit for the first time, both Patience and Dora gasped as its dark severity set off to perfection his pale marble features and lean elegant body. Paris liked the slate grey overcoat. With shades on, he'd look like Feral's Uncle Harley.

'You look cool,' admitted Dora. She consulted the list. 'Two pairs of slip-on shoes. Try a pair on.'

'What am I going to slip on – a banana skin?'

'Are they comfortable?' asked Patience anxiously.

'Very. Change to have a pair that doesn't pinch or let in water.'

A din in the yard outside suggested a pupil had arrived early to drop off a horse. Patience disappeared to welcome them. Dora, who was cleaning tack, remained on Paris's bed, rather randomly applying saddle soap to Plover's bridle.

That tweed jacket must be a cast-off of Ian's, thought Paris. Christ, it was from Harrods, still with the label on, and those pale blue shirts were really cool. It was as though he was being kitted out by Wardrobe for a new play, but who knew if it would be a tragedy or a comedy?

'Let's see your duvets,' asked Dora.

'Thomas the Tank Engine and Beatrix Potter with Peter Rabbit cock-sucking a carrot,' grumbled Paris. 'I am going to get so much piss taken out of me.'

He was now skimming through the Bagley Code of Conduct with increasing alarm. There were pages of rules about not downloading porn.

'I wanted to download some stuff for Patience about Northcliffe' – Dora went very pink – 'but when I logged into golden retriever, it was so disgusting: women actually weeing on men. I don't understand the human race.'

Paris grinned and read on.

'"No one can leave the school without permission." How do they stop me?'

'Give you a detention, make you do hearty things like digging the garden and not watching television. The second time they cancel your leave-outs.'

'That'd be a relief, if Ian doesn't loosen up. "Once a week", he read, "all scholars must participate in an activity that involves serving others in the community."'

'Cosmo helps out at Larkminster Hospital,' said Dora. 'He's shagging one of the nurses.'

'Servicing others,' murmured Paris.

'Best way is to find a nice old biddy, weed her garden, then you get crumpets and cake for tea and to watch Neighbours. Feral's working for my aunt, Lily Hamilton, mowing her lawn. They get on really well. Janna fixed it up.'

'The happy highways where I went And cannot come again', thought Paris, wincing at the pain.

'"No hats to be worn inside",' he went on. 'That's crazy.'

'They're talking about woolly hats and baseball caps and you're not allowed jewellery.'

'I'm not taking mine off. "In cases of bullying, both victim and bully get counselling."' Paris shivered. He'd heard a chilling rumour about the Pitbull Club in which older boys arranged fights between new boys and bet large sums of money on which one would first beat the other to a pulp.

'What the hell am I supposed to do in my free time?' he added in outrage. 'It says here, "Any scholar caught supplying drugs or having sex gets sacked."'

'Not always.' Dora went to Paris's basin to wash silver polish off Plover's bit. 'You're sacked if you're caught having sex with a girl. If it's a boy, you'd only get three hours' gardening.'

'How d'they work that out?'

'Boys don't get pregnant; it's meant to act as a detergent,' Dora went on helpfully.

'God, listen to this: "Swearing, spitting, chewing gum all incur five-pound penalties." This is a police state. What about smoking and drinking?'

'Fiver first time you're caught, then they double up.'

'What do they do with the money?'

'Goes to charity. Alex Bruce was hopping last term when brilliant Hengist sent the entire six and a half thousand to Greyhound Rescue. But as that tosser Boffin Brooks keeps saying' – Dora put her hands together sanctimoniously – 'one only has to behave oneself.'

59

Determined to familiarize Paris with everything, Dora gave him a map and a tour of the school.

'Here's the gym, here's the music school, here's the sick bay. Most important, here's the tuck shop.'

Hengist had put him in Theo Graham's house, a two-storey neo-Gothic building covered in Virginia creeper, which was north-east of the Mansion with a view over the golf course.

'Here's your bedroom-cum-study,' went on Dora, leading him down a corridor. 'They're known as cells.'

The room was tiny – Paris could touch the walls with both hands – and contained a single bed, a desk for his books and laptop and a small cupboard and shelves for his clothes. The joint window was to be shared with the boy in the next cell.

'Who is it? Oh, Smart, he's a rugger bugger; hope he doesn't want the window open all the time. Next year you'll go upstairs to a bigger room of your own. I'll bring your Liverpool posters over later.

'This is Cosmo's cell.' She opened a door on the way out.

'Why's he got a room twice as big as anyone else?'

'Because he's Cosmo. Once he moves in his stuff it'll look like something out of the Arabian nights.

'This is Anatole's.' Giggling, Dora showed Paris the next cell. 'He's got a map of the world as his duvet cover and always sits on the United States because he loathes the Americans so much.'

And I've got Thomas the Tank Engine and Peter Rabbit, thought Paris. How could Patience?

'Oh look, there's Mummy's car outside,' said Dora as they wandered back to the stables.

Although Anthea Belvedon was wildly jealous of Dora's addiction to Paris and the Cartwrights, it freed her for assignations of her own. Today she had had lunch with Randal Stancombe, who was so attractive, and who hadn't a high opinion of Paris, who'd evidently tried to rape Jade on the field trip.

Having rolled up to collect Dora, Anthea was looking distastefully at the mess in Patience's kitchen (riding boots on the table, washing up still in the sink) while enquiring how Paris was getting on.

'Really well,' said Patience, terrified Paris might walk in.

'Emerald found him gauche and awfully tricky,' went on Anthea. 'Dora said you were awfully upset Paris never said a word of thanks about his lovely room. The working classes never know how to express gratitude, of course.'

'I wasn't upset,' squeaked Patience furiously. 'It's his right to have a nice room.'

'But such an expense: Sky, tape decks and computers – Dora says you emptied Dixons.'

'Mummy, I did not,' screamed Dora, who was standing appalled in the doorway.

Paris had bolted upstairs. Giving a sob, he hurled his precious Liverpool mug against the wall. Then he smashed a china dog, ripped the poster of Heskey off the wall and tipped over the bookshelf.

Hearing crashes, Patience lumbered upstairs, hammering on the door against which Paris had shoved a big armchair.

'Paris, listen.'

'Fuck off,' hissed Paris, grabbing his laptop.

'Anthea's a complete bitch; honestly, she's jealous because Dora loves being here and adores you. We don't expect you to say thank you for anything. We give you things because we love having you here.'

Oh God, it was coming out all wrong. But Paris put down his laptop.

'It'll be shepherd's pie and just you and me tonight; we can eat it in front of the telly.'

'So my crap table manners won't show. I don't want any supper.'

The window was open. Paris slid down the Virginia creeper and off across the yard.

It was only after ten-thirty, when Ian returned home, that Patience realized Paris had taken the car and just managed to stop Ian ringing the police.

'We'll lose him.'

'Bloody good riddance.'

When they went out looking for him they found the car undamaged behind a haystack.

Paris staggered in, plastered, at midnight.

'Go to bed at once, we'll discuss this in the morning,' shouted Ian.

Alex Bruce often rose at six to train for the school steeplechase and to spy on other masters, particularly Hengist's cronies, Artie Deverell and Theo Graham, who were both gay; Emlyn, who was engaged to Hengist's daughter Oriana (sort of); and, more recently, the brusque, dismissive Ian Cartwright: all the King's men.

Hearing shouts from the Old Coach House, Alex broke his journey, jogging up the path, letting himself into the kitchen.

'Can I help?'

He found Dora Belvedon taking everything in, Patience by the Aga, looking miserable, and Ian, as boiling over with rage as Paris was icy with fury.

They all turned to Alex: not an attractive sight. A

493

fringe like a false eyelash hung damply on his fore-head, his drenched yellow T-shirt clung to his hollow chest, sweat parted the black hairs on his skinny thighs.

'Can I help?' he repeated.

'No,' snapped Ian.

'You OK, Paris Alvaston?'

'Fine, just fuck off.'

'Paris,' thundered Ian.

'If you'd started at Bagley, young man,' began Alex, 'you'd be fined five pounds for that. I will not allow foul language. I shall leave your foster parents to deal with you.'

'Lando France-Lynch owed the swear fund eight hundred and fifty pounds last term,' piped up Dora, taking croissants out of the Aga and throwing them on the kitchen table. 'Would you like one, Mr Bruce? You look as though you need feeding up.'

Paris went up to his room and slammed the door so hard all the china and glass crowded on the shelves below rattled and clinked. Ian shut himself away in the drawing room with his confounded computer.

Later, tipped off no doubt by Alex, Nadine the social worker popped in. 'Gather you're having a problem with Paris, Patience.'

'I'm afraid my husband's working and Paris has just gone out. Would you like a cup of tea?'

'Thank you. You must open up.'

'We're fine, we love Paris.'

'Don't expect him to love you. When you foster a teenager at best you can expect to be a mentor or an authority figure.'

Did Nadine ever wear anything else but that funereal black, wondered Patience as she switched on the kettle. Getting a packet of chocolate biscuits out of the cup-board, she noticed mice had eaten a hole in one end, and hastily decanted the biscuits onto a plate.

'I know you want to rescue a young life and Paris longs for a family,' bleated Nadine. 'But your expectations are unrealistic. At an age when most adolescents are trying to escape from their parents and forge their own identity, you're going against the grain and trying to form ties. It's not easy.'

Then, seeing the tears spilling down Patience's tired red face: 'He's going to need a lot of counselling.'

It was nearly midnight. Paris still hadn't come home.

'Thank God he's boarding and'll be out of our hair by tomorrow,' exploded Ian. 'How dare he tell Alex Bruce to fuck off.'

Patience felt ashamed that momentarily she agreed with her husband. She felt bitterly let down that neither Hengist nor Janna had yet made contact. She turned out the horses and collapsed into bed.

It was a very warm, muggy night. Moths flying in through the window kept torching themselves on Ian's halogen lamp. Ian winced but there was no time to rescue them. It was after eleven and he was still wrestling with his infernal computer to provide Alex tomorrow with a list of parents who still hadn't paid up. As the whisky bottle emptied, he grew more clumsy. Scrumpled-up paper shared the threadbare Persian carpet with a snoring Northcliffe.

Ian glanced up at the photograph of himself in the Combined Services rugger team, strong muscular arms folded, hair and moustache still black and glossy, eyes clear and confident. He hadn't met Patience then. She was a good old girl, but she no longer stirred his loins, and tomorrow there would be no sweet Jenny Winters to sort out every problem and flash delightful pink flesh and thong as she bent over to pull out a file. On Radio 3, Rupert's older son, Marcus Campbell-Black, was playing a Mozart piano concerto so exquisitely it brought tears to Ian's eyes – a piece Mozart had evidently knocked off to pay bills. Would he had such talent.

Ian hadn't slept properly for weeks. How could he

hold down the job of bursar if he wasn't on the ball? He was sixty-one, not twenty-six. He hadn't touched the pile of messages. Boudicca's Tampax machine was still jammed. But at least he'd reached the end of the list of the defaulting parents and tapped in Commander Wilkins, Spotty's father, who'd paid last year with a hogshead of brandy.

Lord Waterlane, Jack's father, had in the past filled up the school deep freezes with venison and grouse, which made marvellous shepherd's pie. Anatole paid his own fees with roubles, Lubemir's father with a Pissarro which turned out to be a fake.

Having been destitute himself recently, Ian felt so sorry for the parents who worked all hours, forgoing cars and holidays and luxuries, to scrape the fees together, and for the grandparents who often paid them and who'd been equally strapped by pension scandals and the collapse of the stock market.

But he didn't feel sorry for Cosmo's mother, the great diva Dame Hermione, who, in lieu of a year's fees, had offered to give a recital to the school with Cosmo accompanying her.

'Normally, Ian, I never charge less than a hundred thousand pounds for a gig, so Bagley's getting a real bargain.'

Lando's parents seemed to be always broke too. Daisy, his mother, had offered to paint Sally Brett-Taylor for free last year. Nor did Amber and Junior's parents, both on high salaries, ever seem to have any money.

Anthea Belvedon, the prettiest little thing, played every trick in the book to avoid forking out since she was widowed two years ago. He'd have to summon her next week. He had a special Paisley emerald-green silk handkerchief, faintly flavoured with lavender, to mop up pretty mothers' tears. What a shame Mrs Walton had shacked up with Randal Stancombe, who'd paid Milly's fees this term. Comforting Mrs Walton had been an even more exquisite pleasure than glimpsing Jenny Winters's thong.

Bagley, overall, was in great financial shape. Since the geography field trip, the waiting list had doubled, as eager offspring pestered their parents to send them to such a fun palace. Hengist, routing the Education Secretary on *Question Time* last week, had brought another flood of applications. The school was booked solid till 2012. If only Hengist were as good at picking staff. How dare Alex Bruce steal Jenny Winters?

Thank God for that. Ian switched off the computer. But as he emptied the last drop of whisky into a mug entitled Master of the House, he noticed an envelope on the floor. Inside was a cheque signed by Boffin Brooks's frightful father Gordon for five thousand pounds. (Two thousand less than normal because of Boffin's scholarship.) Gordon always paid at the last moment to avoid both a two per cent penalty and losing interest.

Like most first-generation public-school parents, Sir Gordon Brooks clamoured for his kilo of flesh and would have gone berserk and straight to his good friend Alex Bruce if he'd been chased for non-payment, or if Ian had forgotten to put CBE (for services to export) on the receipt. Why didn't someone export Gordon?

Ian mopped his brow with his shirtsleeve in relief. But when he switched on the computer to delete Gordon's name, he couldn't find the file.

Drenched in sweat, heart pounding, blood swept into his brain in a tidal wave, trying to force its way out. Lightning jagged before his eyes. He was going to have a stroke. Nothing. He'd deleted the fucking thing – two whole days' work with his slow typing. He was far too drunk to type it out again.

'I can't go on.' Ian's head crashed into his sweating hands. He'd get fired; they'd be destitute again. Snoring Northcliffe and Patience's horses would have to go.

He jumped, hearing a crash and rattle downstairs, and shoved the empty whisky bottle under the half-completed Times crossword. Hearing a step and a thump of a tail, he swung round. Paris trying to creep in had sent a walking stick flying.

'Where the hell have you been?'

The boy looked whiter than ever – a ghost postillion struck by lightning, haunting the Old Coach House.

'For a walk.'

'Too bloody late.'

Seeing despair rather than rage in Ian's bloodshot eyes, however, Paris asked if he were OK.

'No, I'm not, just wiped a bloody file,' mumbled Ian. 'Need it for Alex Bruce first thing.'

He banged his fist on the table. Everything jumped: the mug tipping over, spilling the last of the whisky on his written notes; *Times* crossword page fluttering down to reveal the empty bottle.

'I can't go on.' Picking up the keyboard, Ian was about to smash it.

Paris, rather encouraged by such loss of control, leapt forward. 'Cool it, for fuck's sake. Get up.' He tugged the keyboard from Ian. 'Lemme have a go.'

Sliding into Ian's seat, he went into MS-DOS and typed in the command to bring up the list of files.

'What's the name of the one you lost?'

'"Unpaid fees 2002 autumn".' Ian slumped against the wall. He didn't dare to hope. Oh, please God.

A blond moth fluttered on a suicide mission towards the lamp. Cupping his hands, Paris caught it. He got up and shoved it into the honeysuckle outside, before shutting the window. Returning to Ian's chair, he scrolled down.

'Reports, expulsions, health, recreations, staff performance, that looks in-eresting – or, as you would say, "intr'sting".' His eyes slid towards Ian. '"Unpaid fees 2002 autumn." Got it.'

Ian gave a gasp of relief:

'Are you sure?'

'Quite,' said Paris, reinstating the file back on the computer in its original format. 'Do you need to change anything?' Then, scrolling down the list: 'There's that bitch Anthea Belvedon, Campbell-Black, Harefield, Lloyd-Foxe, Waterlane, always the rich buggers that don't pay up.'

'You shouldn't be reading that, it's confidential.'

'I have the shortest memory.'

'Can you delete Gordon Brooks, Boffin's father? He's paid.'

As Paris found the name, highlighted it and hit the delete button, his fingers made an even more exquisite sound than Marcus Campbell-Black.

'Let's print it out,' suggested Ian. 'I can add latecomers in biro. Thank God, Paris, you've saved my life, probably my job.'

Slumped on a moth-eaten sofa covered in a tartan rug, Ian looked utterly exhausted, his eyes red hollows, his cheeks and nose a maze of purple veins, the lines round his mouth like cracks in dry paths.

'Would you like a nightcap?' he asked, desperate for one himself.

Paris grinned. How could a face so shuttered and cold one moment be so enchantingly warm, almost loving, the next?

'Thought caps weren't allowed to be worn indoors at Bagley.'

Getting the joke, Ian laughed.

'All those rules must seem a bit alarming. Have to have that jewellery off, I'm afraid. Wear it when you come back here for leave-outs.'

Ian rose unsteadily and wandered to the much depleted drinks cupboard, pouring a brandy and ginger for Paris and the rest of the brandy for himself, taking a great gulp.

'Thank you, Paris, so much.' Then, seeing the boy's eyes straying towards the crossword: 'Finish it if you like. Got stuck on a Tennyson quote. "Heavily hangs the broad . . .", nine letters, "over its grave in' the earth so chilly.'"

'Sunflower,' murmured Paris.

'Of course, well done. "Heavily hangs the hollyhock, Heavily hangs the tiger-lily." Beautiful poem.'

Paris smirked. 'Any time, Ian. And if you have trouble with that computer, ring me or text me on my mobile and I'll whiz out of chemistry and sort it.'

'I suppose those wretched mobiles have their uses,' conceded Ian. 'Sorry, the last few weeks have been rough. All a bit nervous. Promise to telephone or pop into my office if there're any problems.'

'Thank you,' said Paris, feeling much happier.

When Ian looked at his computer next morning, Paris had written, with some scarlet nail polish which Emerald had left in the bathroom, on the frame of the computer screen: 'To remind you to save it.'

60

Paris's first weeks at Bagley were hell. At Larks he'd bunked off any lesson he disliked and been free after three-thirty. Now he was flat out from the moment the bell fractured his skull at six-forty-five until lights out at ten, kept endlessly busy racing from chapel to lessons to games to prep and losing his way despite Dora's map. Used to being easily the cleverest pupil at Larks, he found himself woefully behind in most subjects and, with smaller classes, there was nowhere to hide. Nor had he dreamt rugby would be so brutal, but with Anatole and Lubemir in the scrum, he couldn't expect much else.

His rarity appeal had also gone. An arctic fox occasionally peeping out of the frozen tundra loses his mystery when he's caged in the zoo. Stripped of his lucky jewellery, disfigured by a savaging from the school barber and by his first spots ever (from existing on chocolate, rather than Patience's cooking), he had never felt less attractive. Ian's assault on his pronunciation and table manners had made him miserably self-conscious both in class and at mealtimes.

His first evening was a nightmare, with so many pupils rolling up in flash cars or helicopters with their glamorous parents yelling about mooring the yacht off Sardinia, or stalking in Scotland, or villas in Dubai where the jet-skiing had been out of this world.

Paris nearly died of embarrassment when Patience insisted on humping his stuff across the school into Theo's house, putting Thomas the Tank Engine on his duvet and braying 'hello' to all the other pupils.

'Theo's terrified of parents,' she whispered. 'Probably won't appear for hours. Now let's put up your posters.'

'I'm fine,' hissed Paris.

'Just want to settle you in. Where shall I put this fruit cake?'

'I'll sort it,' Paris almost shrieked. 'I'm OK, just go.'

The moment she left, he was frantically stripping off the duvet cover when his next-door neighbour, Smart, who already had a ginger moustache above his broad grin, wandered in, shouting, 'I'm Smart. Thomas the Tank Engine, fantastic, wish I'd thought of that. Where's the Fat Controller?'

So Paris left it on, and put up a poster of Tennyson between Michael Owen and Emile Heskey.

'Coming to supper?' asked Smart.

Paris wasn't hungry, but he needed an ally. In the dining room, the din was hideous, as they all yakked in their Sloaney way about polo in Sotogrande and the sailing lessons Daddy'd organized in Rock, or chatted to new conquests on their mobiles, or flagged up photographs of them. Paris noticed Xav, sitting alone, sullen and miserable, and felt a louse for avoiding his eye. He also realized he'd made enemies on the field trip. He'd never texted Jade or Amber after shagging them – not having a mobile at the time was no excuse. Boffin, twitchy at the prospect of being usurped by a cleverer boy, was reading the *New Scientist*. Cosmo was smiling his evil smile.

'Hengist really must install a runway, it takes such ages by chopper,' said a familiar bitchy voice.

It was Jade Stancombe, flaunting a butterscotch tan and a ravishing new short tortoiseshell-streaked haircut. Nicky Clarke had repaired the ravages of the

502

sawn-off plait with something far more becoming to Jade's thin, predatory face. Mobile glued to her ear, chatting to some new admirer, she swung round, clocked Cosmo, exchanged a long eye-meet and, walking over, bent down and French kissed him for thirty seconds, sending a shiver through the room. Jade and Cosmo were an item again.

'Love your hair, Jade,' chorused everyone sycophantically.

'Brings out the latent homosexual in all of us,' murmured Cosmo. 'You obviously haven't been abused by the school barber, like our friend Paris.'

Everyone turned round and looked at Paris, who, not giving them time to hail or reject him, chucked down his napkin and, food untouched, stalked out.

'Don't go,' called Amber.

Resisting a temptation to bolt back to the Old Coach House, Paris returned to Theo's house where he found some post on his bed.

Seeing Janna's writing on a dove-grey envelope, Paris dropped it in the bin. Beneath was a parcel from Cosmo, containing a copy of *Tom Brown's Schooldays*. Inside Cosmo had written 'À bientôt, Flashman'.

Finally there was a letter from Sally Brett-Taylor. 'Good luck. Come and have tea with us very soon. Hope your years at Bagley are happy and rewarding.'

Like fuck, thought Paris.

'"The years like great black oxen tread the world,"' he declaimed. '"And I am broken by their passing feet."'

'At this moment, you can't envisage a day let alone a week at Bagley being tolerable,' said a flat, rasping, mocking voice. 'I'm sorry I wasn't here to welcome you. I'm allergic to parents.'

'Lucky I don't have any.'

'Come and have a drink. Who are you next to? Oh, Smart. A misnomer actually. But he's good-hearted and an excellent rugger player.'

Months spent every summer in Greece and Italy poring over relics and ruins with never a drop of suntan oil had browned and creased Theo Graham's bald head and face like a conker soaked in vinegar. He had jug ears, jagged teeth and, like many schoolmasters, looked older than his sixty years, but his eyes were kind, shrewd and lively.

'This is my lair,' he said, leading Paris into his study, which reeked worse than a public bar of fags and booze, but which was almost entirely lined with literature, history and philosophy in the original Greek and Latin: ancient books with leather binding or faded dilapidated jackets. As well as a huge desk and an upright piano, the room was densely populated with busts of emperors and great thinkers and sculptures of gods, goddesses, heroes, nymphs, centaurs and caryatids, all poised to embark on some splendid orgy after dark. Paris's eyes were on stalks.

'I hear you're interested in learning Latin and Greek,' said Theo, rootling around under the papers on the desk to find a corkscrew. 'Well, you've come from the Old Coach House to an old coach's house,' and he smiled with great affection.

Adding to the chaos, a huge fluffy marmalade cat padded across the room and landed on the desk, sending half the contents flying.

'At least he's unearthed the corkscrew.' Theo pounced on it. 'His name is Hindsight, so we can all benefit from him.'

Having poured a large glass of red for Paris and an even larger whisky for himself, Theo settled a thunderously purring Hindsight on his knee and asked Paris what other subjects he was intending to take for GCSE. When Paris reeled off English, English lit., French, Spanish, history, geography, drama, business studies, science and maths, Theo heaved a sigh of relief.

'Thank God, none of those new subjects like leisure and tourism. How could one prefer a hotel to Homer?'

Paris took a slug of red and thought for a minute, then said, 'If I could have a night in the bridal suite with Bianca Campbell-Black, sir, I might prefer a hotel, but the *Iliad*'s one of the best books I've ever read.'

'Good,' said Theo happily, 'we should get along.'

Hengist had given a lot of thought to the right house for Paris. Biffo would have got drunk and probably pounced on him. The Bruces would have killed him with petty regulations and counselling. Artie Deverell, gentle, handsome, clever, tolerant, charming, adored by pupils and parents (particularly the latter, who invited him to stay in their villas in Tuscany and Provence for weeks on end), would have been ideal. But Deverell's was always hopelessly over-subscribed, which Graham's never was.

Theo, crotchety, very shy, dreadful with parents and liable to take his hearing aid out on Speech Day, had a house with only a dozen boys. One to whom he was utterly devoted was Cosmo, who returned this devotion. Cosmo was clever and made Theo laugh. As one of the few people who could control Cosmo, Theo also believed that with parents like Dame Hermione and the evil, late Roberto Rannaldini, the boy was entitled to be a monster. Theo also took out his hearing aid when Cosmo and the Cosmonaughties were giving tongue.

If Cosmo started bullying Paris, deduced Hengist, Theo would pick up on it.

Theo drove Alex Bruce crackers calling his Chinese pupils 'Chinks', his Russians 'Little Commies' and banging any child if they were being particularly stupid on the head with an atlas of the ancient world.

Unlike Ian Cartwright he had refused to succumb to Alex's bullying and chucked his first laptop in the lake, continuing to tap away with two fingers on an ancient manual typewriter until Cosmo, terrified the only master who understood him would be eased out, taught him to use a computer.

Theo incurred disapproval because he smoked and drank too much.

'Why am I late?' he would ask his classes.

'Because you drank too much last night, sir,' they would chorus.

A typical holiday in the past would have been riding round Umbria on a donkey reading Plato's *Republic*. Now he took gentler vacations, occasionally grumbling about a bad back. In fact only he knew he had an inoperable tumour in his spine, which was why he drank so much: to ease the pain.

Apart from translating the plays of Euripides and now embarking on those of Sophocles, Theo looked after the classical library and school museum and was in charge of the archives, which chronicled the achievements of illustrious former pupils. Alex Bruce was desperate to scrap the museum and the library and replace them with an IT suite.

'Tradition is the enemy of progress,' he was fond of saying.

Alex was driven demented by Theo, but he was powerless to fire him because Theo got even the dimmest child through GCSE and, because of this and his wonderfully entertaining teaching, his lessons were always crowded out.

One of Bagley's favourite pastimes was watching Artie Deverell and Theo argue. For the duration of an entire cricket match they had been observed marching up and down the boundary waving their arms and shouting over whether Catullus had really been wiped out by love when he wrote his poems or merely portraying someone thus afflicted.

David Hawkley, headmaster of Fleetley, another great classical scholar, had dedicated his translation of Catullus to Theo and every Christmas sent him a litre of malt whisky. This irritated Hengist who longed to be admired by David Hawkley.

'Extraordinary, these new GCSEs,' Theo was now

complaining to Paris. 'I gather they're thinking of linking RE and PE as one subject. The mind boggles until one remembers all those old jokes about when the high jump was first invented.'

'When was it?'

'When Jesus cleared the temple.'

Paris laughed.

'Or the first cricket match,' went on Theo, 'when Jesus stood up before the eleven and was bold – or bowled. Interesting that they're always described as schoolboy jokes, never schoolgirl.'

'If you'd been on a geography field trip with Joan Johnson, you'd understand,' said Paris.

At the same time that first evening as Paris was, to his amazement, really enjoying having a drink with Theo, Anthea Belvedon was delivering her son Dicky back to Alex Bruce's house. Here she sought out Poppet Bruce: 'Have you a mo?'

'Of course, Anthea. One of the reasons I'm nicknamed "Poppet" is because people are always "popping in" on me.' Poppet gave a soppy smile.

'My late husband nicknamed me "Hopey",' countered Anthea, 'because I always give people hope.'

After a minute on the importance of reminding Dicky to use his foot-rot cream because he'd infected Anthea's High Court judge on holiday, Anthea moved briskly on to Paris and the riches the Cartwrights had heaped on him:

'Would that I could do the same for my Dora and Dicky.'

'But I thought the Cartwrights were broke,' mused Poppet. 'I hope they're not spending Bagley money.'

'So do I.' Anthea sighed gustily. 'Surely a free place does not mean a free-for-all?'

'I'll have a discreet word with Alex.'

'You won't mention my name.'

'We haven't spoken,' said Poppet.

507

The upshot twenty-four hours later was a fired-up Patience barging into Alex's office brandishing bills and cheque stubs.

'How dare you accuse Ian of cooking the books? It's actionable. He's the most honest man in the world. He's been flat out through the summer holidays and we've given up our three-week holiday in France this year so we can be home to give Paris a proper start. You and your wife can bloody well apologize to him.'

'We do feel you're in danger of spoiling Paris Alvaston,' spluttered a discomfited Alex. 'His behaviour so far has been very challenging . . .'

Ian, in turn, was later apoplectic with Patience.

'How could you have shouted at Alex? I could have given him a perfectly reasonable explanation. Of course it looks odd you squandering so much on Paris. He could easily have worn a second-hand suit. How can I ask for a rise now?'

Dora, who suspected her mother of sneaking, had also spent too much money on Paris. She must sell some more stories.

Flipping through the papers in the library to assess her market on the first Saturday of term, she came across a piece about parents of truants being given gaol sentences.

If she bunked off for a week, would her utterly bloody mother go to prison? Although her awful old High Court judge boyfriend would probably get her off.

Dispirited, and unable to keep away, Dora wandered off to see Paris. A warm west wind was chasing chestnut leaves round the quad; green spiky husks were opening to drop gleaming brown conkers; the shaggy pelt of Virginia creeper flung round the Gothic turrets of Theo Graham's house was turning crimson.

She found Paris pretending to tackle a distressing amount of homework while listening to Liverpool against Everton on Radio Five, and expressing fury that he'd officially been given Xavier as a 'buddy' to show him the ropes. Talk about linking two social misfits.

Lucky Xav, thought Dora wistfully, but out loud said:

'It won't be so bad, you needn't see much of him after the first week and he might invite you to Penscombe. It's gorgeous. Fabulous horses and Rupert and Taggie are really lovely.'

'And Bianca's even lovelier,' said Paris bitchily. 'Only reason to brown-nose her lousy brother is to get a crack at her.'

Dora couldn't speak for the hurt, as though a huge wasp had plunged its sting deep into her heart, flooding poison through her veins. She knew Paris didn't adore her as she adored him, but he'd never mentioned Bianca, so she'd assumed he wasn't interested.

Seeing her stricken face, her blue eyes widening in bewilderment, Paris felt as though he'd kicked a puppy.

'Oh fuck off,' he snapped. 'You're getting on my tits.'

But as Dora stumbled out, tripping over a pile of books, Paris was livid with himself. He liked Xav as well. Why did he have this urge to hurt and destroy people who were kind to him? He longed to explain to Patience, Dora, even Xav how sad and lonely he was and how sadness came out as anger, but the less you gave people the less they had to hurt you with.

Even Liverpool winning in the dying moments couldn't lift his spirits. On the hall table he found a parcel and a card saying: 'Dear Paris, good luck. Sorry this is late. Love Dora'.

Inside was a really cool Black Watch tartan duvet cover and two pillowcases.

Switching on his mobile, he dialled Dora's number.

'The person you are dialling knows you are calling,' said the message, 'and doesn't give a fuck.'

Meanwhile, on her way out, Dora passed Cosmo's king-sized cell. Glancing in, she saw it now accommodated a baby grand and, on the walls, a Picasso Blue Clown, oriental rugs, an antique gilt mirror and portraits of Cosmo's heroes: the Marquis de Sade, Wagner, Byron and his father, the late Roberto Rannaldini. On the king-sized bed covered with fur rugs lay a dark blue cushion embroidered with the words: 'It's hard to be humble and go to Bagley.'

Seated at the piano, Cosmo was playing and singing Mahler Lieder in a deep, hypnotic baritone of exceptional beauty. He was sporting a black overcoat with an astrakhan collar made famous by his late father, and which much became his night-dark eyes and sallow features.

Hearing a sob, he glanced round to find Dora's sweet plump face dissolving in misery.

'Dora, darling.' Pulling her inside, he shut the door and patted the bed.

'It's very cruel to have fur rugs.'

'I am very cruel. Now, whatever's the matter?' Cosmo stroked her blond hair and retied the blue ribbon on one of her plaits.

'I loathe my mother, I'm sure she shopped the Cartwrights to Poppet, implying they'd been using Bagley money kitting out Paris, whereas Patience has paid for everything out of some money her aunt left her.'

'Patience Carthorse,' drawled Cosmo. 'She ought to be pulling beer barrels round London.'

'She's lovely.'

'Not the word I had in mind. You must be blind and deaf.' Cosmo handed Dora a Bacardi and Coke from his fridge and relit his spliff. 'What else is the matter?'

'Paris is in love with Bianca.'

'And the rest.'

'He told me to fuck off. I gave him a new duvet cover today and earlier a video of *Macbeth*.'

'Young Alvaston needs sorting out,' said Cosmo thoughtfully. He had been reading in the *Observer* that Cherie Blair was offering to defend school bullies in court. What an admirable woman. His mission this term was to make Paris Alvaston's life hell and with Xav as his buddy . . . what an opportunity to kick the shit out of both of them.

It was also high time he bedded Vicky Fairchild.

61

Vicky was not enjoying her first term at Bagley. The workload was appalling and there was no Sam Spink to fight her corner. After cajoling the lovely flat and bathroom out of Ian Cartwright, her charm objective wasn't working as well as she'd hoped. So many of the masters were gay or married and tied up with families. Piers, the head of her department, was rumoured to be having an affair with Rufus's wife, Sheena. Vicky and Jason had seen through each other long ago. Emlyn, easily the most attractive, and with a strange relationship with Oriana from which Vicky was sure he could be detached, was polite but cool, which exhausted the best heterosexual bachelors.

Hengist and Sally were kind, but Olympian and remote, like Jupiter and Juno, and hadn't invited her to a single dinner party.

There were enough boys in the school in love with her and girls, madly admiring, to feed her ego, but she wanted a husband or a steady partner to love and cherish.

Vicky found her thoughts straying rather too often to Cosmo Rannaldini, sexy little beast, with whom she had gone much too far on the field trip. Now he sat, staring at her, a wicked smile snaking round his full lips, unnerving her as she tried to initiate him and the rest of Middle Five B into *The Pardoner's Tale*. Anatole and

Lubemir, meanwhile, were playing poker. Milly was painting her nails; Amber was writing to one of her numerous boyfriends; the Chinless Wanderers were studying the *Sun*, deciding which horses to back, except for Lando, lazy great beast, who was asleep.

'Can you tell me, Lando, what Chaucer is trying to say here?' she asked sharply.

Lando opened an eye. 'Can you tell me who the fuck Chaucer is?'

The class fell about.

'Don't use horrible language, Lando, that's another fiver for the swear box. And don't be so obtuse.'

Lando stretched out a large polo-stick-calloused hand for the Collins dictionary. 'What does "obtuse" mean?'

Vicky's lips tightened. She found the Middle Fifths very difficult and not nearly admiring enough – particularly Paris, who, as they had both come from Larks, should have supported her. His stroppy behaviour was becoming the talk of the staffroom with Hengist showing a curious reluctance to put the boot in.

Vicky showed no such reluctance when in the Middle Fifths' next English lesson, three days later, she asked them to describe a happy family experience in the holidays, using simile, metaphor, oxymoron and personification.

'Please, Miss Fairchild,' whispered Milly, 'Paris doesn't have a family.'

'Of course he does. He has the bursar and his wife, his new foster family,' said Vicky, so that everyone looked at Paris. 'You could write a most interesting essay on adjusting to your new placement, Paris, and how Bagley compares with Larks.'

'"Why, this is hell, nor am I out of it",' spat Paris.

'My mother,' piped up Amber, 'says placement is the most difficult part of a dinner party. She always forgets to do a seating plan, and is pissed by the time we get into the dining room. Why doesn't one learn important things like that in maths?'

'I hardly think Biffo'd be an expert,' said Milly. 'It's even worse if you're a single woman. If my mother asks Randal to dinner, is it coming on too strong to put him at the head of the table, or will he be miffed he's not on her right?'

'Don't be silly, Milly,' exploded Vicky.

'Silly Milly,' echoed Jade, sticking her tongue out at Milly.

'Write it as a play, Paris,' suggested Vicky, 'then we could all take parts.'

'Or as a poem,' quipped Cosmo. 'Living with the bursar could not be worser.'

'Shut it,' hissed Paris.

'Paris in fact is quite a poet,' went on Cosmo, dramatically whipping out a rainbow-coloured notebook. 'Listen to this epic about a snail,' which he proceeded to declaim in a camp Cockney accent:

'"O Snile, your gli-ering trile, leads from the gu-er up to anuvver gu-er on which to bang your 'orns."'

As Paris gave a howl of rage, uneasy laughter broke out round the room.

Milly put a hand on Paris's arm. 'Ignore him.'

'Here's another little gem,' continued Cosmo, turning the page, knowing instinctively that Vicky didn't like Paris. 'Here's what our new boy thinks of Bagley:

'Death is like a boarding school
From which you never come home
Where your name is carved on a gravestone
Rather than sewn inside your clothes.'

'Doesn't scan,' complained Boffin.

'You bastard,' whispered Paris, turning on Cosmo.

'I think it's rather good,' said Primrose Duddon with a shiver.

'I think it's very good,' came a voice from the back of the class.

It was Piers Fleming, head of English, who'd

dropped in to listen to Vicky's class. 'May I?' He grabbed the rainbow-covered notebook and read both the snail poem and the death poem again, but in a normal and beautiful voice.

'The second one,' he went on, 'reminds me of Robert Frost describing a disused graveyard:

> 'The verses in it say and say:
> "The ones who living come today
> To read the stones and go away
> Tomorrow dead will come to stay."

'It has the same icy hand on the heart. I'm going to put forward your poems for the school anthology,' he told Paris. 'We publish it every three years. You're probably too modest to submit your own stuff, so thank you, Cosmo, so much, for drawing it to my attention.'

Cosmo was hopping.

As the bell went and the Middle Fifths packed up, Piers very kindly suggested to Vicky she might fare better with one of the less demanding sets. If Piers and Vicky had seen the Middle Fifths at their next lesson, however, they might have changed their opinion, as the entire set listened enraptured to Theo Graham introducing some of their GCSE Latin texts.

'Poets were like rock stars around the first century ad,' he was now telling them as, hip hitched onto the side of a desk, he puffed away on a forbidden cigarette. 'Just as you lot might enliven an evening with a video or a takeaway or by hiring a stripagram for a party, the Romans sent out for a slave to read poetry.

'Some poets like Martial, who was charming and very witty, recited their own poems at dinner parties, but most of them were read by slaves. You didn't make money as a poet in those days, but people could sponsor you. Horace was earlier, of course, but he was such a good poet – we'll be looking at his stuff in a minute – that a rich Etruscan gave him a farm and a huge estate.'

'Just think if he'd liked your poems, Paris,' giggled Amber. Paris grinned and gave her a middle finger.

Lighting one cigarette from another, Theo shuffled down the row and lifted a lock of Amber's blond hair.

'You'd have been in trouble as a slave, miss, because Italians liked blondes, so lots of society ladies dyed their hair blond, and when it fell out, they shaved the heads of the blonde slaves and used the hair as a wig.

'That's probably why Pyrrha in our first poem was considered such a beauty, Horace describes her as braiding her flaxen locks.'

'Paris would have cleaned up as a poet *and* a blond,' said Milly.

Feeling much happier, Paris came out of Theo's class slap into Poppet Bruce, who was always nagging him to drop in on her and Alex and pour out his soul. Now she wanted him to go public.

'Could you address our Talks Society next week? If a talk is too daunting, I could always interview you.' Paris raised a pale eyebrow. 'It would be such a broadening experience for our group to hear your views on your foster placement and being in care.'

The lad was certainly good-looking, decided Poppet, and the same age as their daughter, Charisma. She was very touched when Paris put a hand in his pocket and handed her a tenner.

'How kind, but you don't have to pay to join our little society.'

'No, it's for the two fines I'm about to get,' said Paris icily. 'You just want me to slag off Patience and Ian, to give you and Mr Fussy ammunition against them. So fuck off.' Then he spat at her feet, just falling short of her grubby sandalled toenails.

Poppet didn't miss a beat.

'I know you're hurting, Paris, and don't really mean it.'

'Hurt is a transitive verb,' snapped Paris, 'and I do.'

Despite half the staff competing to make him tell them if anything was wrong, Paris felt it was as weak to admit terror as to display love and dependency. And so he waited for Cosmo. Whether it was a bomb in the tube or on Big Ben, the terrorists would strike sooner or later. He had already found a rubber snake in his bed and still kept hearing rumours about the notorious Pitbull Club.

It was after midnight on the second Saturday of term. Theo, after downing a bottle of whisky in his room, had passed out, his snores ripping open the night. Smart, in the next-door cell, had long since wanked himself to sleep over a photograph of Jade Stancombe. Paris could hear the Virginia creeper flapping limp hands against the window, floorboards creaking, Tarquin's ravishing strides, doors softly opening and closing. Just like Oaktree Court. Starting to shake, already drenched in sweat, he pulled Thomas the Tank Engine over his head. The chattering of his teeth would wake the dead.

Suddenly the duvet was wrenched off him and a torch brighter than the full moon shoved in his face.

'Get up, pretty boy.'

'Fuck off.'

'Get up,' repeated the voice.

In the dim light, he could make out a hooded figure, then groaned as the torch was rammed into his ribs.

'You're invited to the Pitbull Club. Move it.'

Paris froze, nearly shitting himself, heart crashing.

'Leave me alone,' he croaked, kicking out at another hooded figure that appeared on the right.

'Come on, Gay Paree.' He knew that voice. Next moment its owner had grabbed his hair, tugging him viciously to his feet.

'New boy's initiation. Let's see how brave you are,' mocked another slighter figure hovering behind.

The figure on the left jabbed him with the torch again. Paris moaned, then, reaching behind him, grabbed the knife from under his pillow. Leaping at the first figure, catching him off balance, pulling him against his own body, clamping him with his left hand, he put the knife against his throat.

The torch crashed to the floor.

The muscular, almost square body, left him in no doubt about the identity of the tormentor.

'Get out, unless you want your throat cut, Albanian pig.'

'Put him down,' ordered the larger of the figures on the right, who had a deep voice, and was moving in. Paris caught a waft of brandy.

'Don't come anywhere near me,' he spat, then, running the blade down Lubemir's cheek, split it open, drawing blood. 'I'm not just shaving him. Next time I'll cut deeper.' Kneeing Lubemir in the kidneys, he sent him crashing to the floor.

'Get him,' said the smaller figure on the right – with less conviction as, in the light from the fallen torch, Paris approached with knife poised.

'You don't scare me,' snarled Paris. 'I'll cut up the lot of you, and you'll lose more than your plait this time, Miss Stancombe.'

Jade gave a gasp, and fled, followed by Lubemir and Anatole.

Down in the cellar, the leader of the pack in his astrakhan coat was admiring his reflection as he snorted coke from a framed mirror lying on an ancient desk. His eyes were glittering but no less cruel.

Other figures stood round self-consciously, rather apprehensively, drinking from bottles or smoking.

Millbank, a new boy in blue-striped pyjamas, almost fainting in terror, was loosely tied to a chair. He had bitten his lip through trying not to cry. Despite the heat from the boilers, he shivered uncontrollably.

'Where's Paris?' snapped Cosmo.

'Won't come,' said Anatole.

'How pathetic is that. Three against one.'

'I'm not risking it,' said Lubemir, removing a blood-saturated handkerchief from his slashed cheek. 'He knows who we all are.'

'How?' Cosmo was hoovering up every last speck of cocaine.

'He listen,' said Anatole. 'How you think he's such a good mimic?'

'I'm going back to Boudicca,' bleated Jade. 'It was bloody scary.'

Cosmo grabbed her arm. 'You're not going anywhere.' Then: 'You can bugger off,' he told Millbank. 'You got off lightly, but don't breathe a word' – he jerked his head at Lubemir, who held the cigarette he'd just lit to Millbank's jumping cheek – 'or we'll really sort you out. Understand?'

'Yes,' sobbed Millbank and fled.

Cosmo turned to the others.

'Are you honestly telling me three of you couldn't sort out that etiolated wimp?'

'He pulled a knife on us,' protested Lubemir.

'Oh dear,' sighed Cosmo, 'I do hope he didn't hold it like a pencil.'

62

Alex Bruce was incensed when Hengist gave any pupil who applied permission to go on the Countryside March. Far too many of the applicants had retakes the next day and would be exhausted and probably hungover.

'And is championing blood sports really part of our Bagley ethos?' asked Alex querulously.

'Damn right it is,' snapped Hengist. 'Bagley Beagles have been going for nearly a hundred years and' – he waved a hand in the direction of Badger's Retreat – 'isn't that country worth saving?'

Patience asked Paris if he'd like to join her on the march.

'Rupert Campbell-Black, Ricky France-Lynch and Billy Lloyd-Foxe are all going. Rupert's taking his dogs. It should be a fun day out.'

Paris replied coldly that he didn't approve of blood sports.

'Alex and Poppet don't either,' said Patience with rare edge. 'It's not just blood sports, it's the whole tapestry and livelihood of the countryside, which this Government is hell-bent on destroying, totally undermining the poor farmers. If hunting goes, thousands of people will lose their jobs, and thousands and thousands more horses and hounds will be put down.

People who make such a fuss about killing foxes don't give a stuff about the horrors of factory farming or the dreadful transport of live animals.' Realizing she was shouting, Patience stopped in embarrassment.

'Still bloody cruel.' Paris stalked towards the door. 'Is Ian going?'

'No, he's dining with a supplier.'

'I'll dogsit,' said Paris as a peace offering.

Later he kicked himself when Dora told him that Xav and Bianca were also going, adding:

'Bianca's such an applause junkie, she can't resist crowds and photographers.'

Deliverance seemed at hand when Xav asked Paris to join them. Alas, social services stepped in. Paris couldn't join their party because Rupert hadn't been cleared by the Criminal Records Bureau.

'I can't imagine he ever would be,' said Alex nastily.

Boffin Brooks rose at six most mornings ostensibly to conjugate Latin verbs but in reality to spy on his housemates. Early on the Saturday before the Countryside March, he caught Xav in bed smoking a spliff and reading a porn mag. Noting the ecstasy with which Xav was inhaling, like a chief drawing on a peace pipe, Boffin launched into a sermon in his nasal whine:

'People smoke to look cool, Xavier, or because they're forced to by bullies or peer pressure.'

Boffin's spectacles enlarged his bulging eyes. Shaving his meagre ginger stubble, he had deheaded several spots, reducing his face to an erupting volcanic landscape. His full red lips were salivating at the prospect of reading that disgusting porn mag before he handed it over to Alex.

'I might be fractionally more lenient, Xavier, if you told me who sold you the stuff.'

'I'm not grassing up anyone, so piss off.' Inhaling deeply, Xav blew smoke rings at Boffin.

Boffin looked pained.

'It must be in your blood, Xavier. Colombia not only trains and supports the IRA and many other forms of terrorism, but also destroys billions of lives as the drug centre of the world.'

'Nice place for a weekend break.'

'Only place you won't be this weekend is the Countryside March. My only recourse is to report you to Mr Bruce,' at which point Xav launched himself at Boffin.

'You little idiot,' Hengist yelled at Xavier later in the morning. 'I know how you wanted to go on that march. Why on earth did you screw up? Drugs are not allowed and that's the second time Boffin's teeth have been knocked out in a year. How can I do anything but gate you? Your father will be devastated.'

My father couldn't give a stuff, thought Xav despairingly. He'll just regard it as another cock-up on my part.

My first leave-out and no one to look after me – thank God, thought Paris as Patience and Ian left the house.

He brushed Northcliffe, partly from self-interest to keep the dog's pale gold hair off his clothes; then he lit a fag and, pouring himself a glass of red, collapsed on the sofa in front of the television, where he was shortly joined by Northcliffe, who was not allowed up when Ian was around. Liverpool had won yesterday, so Paris flicked over to mock the Countryside March for a second and stayed to pray.

'There's Dora,' he shouted in excitement, shoving Northcliffe's face towards the screen as, dressed in jodhpurs and a hacking jacket, Dora marched proudly past chattering to Junior and the Hon. Jack, who were blatantly smoking and shouting to pretty girls among the mass of spectators lining the route.

They were followed by Isa Lovell, former champion jockey, now Rupert Campbell-Black's trainer, with his swarthy gypsy face, and by Rupert Campbell-Black himself, still the handsomest man in England, his eyes the colour of blue Smarties, his face expressionless as he ignored the cheers of the crowd. He was accompanied by half a dozen dogs: lurchers, terriers and Labradors, who kept stopping to fight each other and attack dogs in the crowd, until Rupert called them back.

Inside, Rupert was raging and desolate that Xav as part of the clan wasn't beside him. Instead, running to keep up, was Junior and Amber's father, Billy Lloyd-Foxe, laughing helplessly, grey curls astray, wearing a tweed coat with no buttons and an equally buttonless shirt, held together by his tie.

Reporting the march for the BBC, shouting over the tooting of hunting horns, Billy was giving an unashamedly biased commentary. 'This is the country-side fighting back, making its protest seen and heard, with the largest march London has ever seen.'

Even Paris couldn't restrain a cheer for the three couple of the Bagley Beagles, sterns waving like wheat in a high wind, and in their midst, a large grinning chocolate Labrador pausing to gobble up a discarded Cornish pasty.

'Cadbury,' shouted Paris. Even Northcliffe opened an eye.

In charge of the beagles, blowing their hunting horns, flicking their token whips, were Amber and Lando, glamorous in their teal-blue coats, breeches and black boots.

'I shagged that girl last summer,' said Paris, topping up his glass. He wished he could remember more about it.

And *look* at her: an utterly stunning blonde with the same cool face, blue eyes and ferociously determined mouth as Rupert. It must be his daughter Tabitha, the silver medallist, and that must be her husband Wolfgang who produced films, to whom Xav had promised to introduce Paris: 'So he can discover you.'

Close on their heels came a group who'd clearly had an excellent lunch. According to the commentator, they were former members of the England polo team. Except for Lando's father Ricky, who had a closed, carved, ascetic face and very high cheekbones, they all had handsome, flushed, expensive faces. Two of them, identical twins in their thirties, were holding lead reins attached to the wrists of a beautiful girl. Paris gasped. It was Bianca, inspiring as many cheers and wolf whistles as her father.

She had tied a scarlet bandanna round her dark ringlets and wore a flame-red wool shirt and dark blue breeches which clung to her impossibly supple and slender figure. Her lovely even complexion, the colour of strong tea, was faintly touched with colour. But neither twin could restrain her wonderful wildness. You could more easily have trapped a sunbeam as she skipped and danced, her laughing dark eyes making love to every man in the crowd.

Bloody hell. Paris refilled his glass. For, just behind Bianca and the twins, advancing fast, waving a 'Bring back Blair-Baiting' poster, his black curls flowing out from under his flat cap like Sir Lancelot, strode Cosmo.

'Fuck him,' said Paris, then his heart lifted as Patience came into view. 'There's your mistress,' he chided Northcliffe who was burying a Bonio in the camellia by the window.

Patience might resemble a scarecrow, but she looked so sweet and carefree as she laughed and gossiped to the Hon. Jack's father, David Waterlane and – my God – to Sally Brett-Taylor. It was brave of her to stick her neck out. All three of them were walking backwards now to watch and clap a piper who was leading a large contingent from Scotland, marching behind.

He could just imagine them: knights and ladies of the court, straight out of Tennyson, riding through medieval England on their great horses, a bobbing flotilla of white placards lit by the turning plane trees and Patience part of it. How dare Ian put her down so much? And what a tragedy for Xav not to be there.

I loathe what they stand for, he thought despairingly, but I long to be accepted by them. And Bianca was the only person who might get him over Janna, whom he still missed unbearably. He tried not to think of her. He hadn't glanced at the *Gazette* for weeks, nor been in touch with anyone from Larks. His mobile was dying from lack of use.

If only Janna were here with him now, discussing some poem, casually ruffling his hair. But if Sally was on the march, that satyr Hengist was probably now at Jubilee Cottage shagging her. Jesus, it crucified him. Paris was about to open another bottle when he realized Rupert was addressing the crowds in Whitehall. The clipped, arrogant, carrying voice hardly needed a microphone.

'We will not let a politically correct but morally corrupt Government dictate to us. We will fight to the death for what we believe in: England, freedom and the countryside.'

'What about Wales, Scotland and Northern Ireland?' reproached Sally Brett-Taylor, over the roar of approval.

'And of course the colonies,' grinned Rupert, chucking an empty hipflask to an adoring fan who rushed off to the nearest pub to refill it.

God, he's a cool bastard, thought Paris, and Xav was his only route to Bianca. Picking up the Cartwrights' telephone he rang Xav. 'Patience and Ian are out. Why don't you come over? Got any weed?'

'Some really strong skunk; it'll blow your mind.'

Happily Alex and Poppet had gone out and the deputy housemaster, Joe Meakin, who was new to the job and engrossed in the Sunday papers, was in charge.

'Can I nip over to the Old Coach House? Paris

Alvaston's on his own and a bit down, adjusting to a new school and all.'

'OK, don't be late,' said Mr Meakin, glad that Xavier had found a friend. The poor boy seemed so isolated.

'I'll sign myself out,' said Xav, and didn't.

Collecting the skunk, he put a pillow in his bed.

63

'Are you sure it's safe?' he asked Paris ten minutes later. 'If I'm busted again I'll get sacked.'

'Quite safe. Ian's out to dinner; Patience is on the march.'

Having finished the red, Paris handed Xav a glass of Ian's whisky and had one himself.

'Your dad made a good speech; I taped it. I understand now why you wanted to go.'

Xav's face sank into sullenness.

'They wouldn't want a black bastard like me around.'

'Don't talk crap, they all cheered Bianca. Have a look,' said Paris winding back the tape. He wanted to watch her again. 'And hurry up with that smoke. Ian's obviously been watering the whisky; it tastes like gnat's piss. Who are those dirty old men holding Bianca's lead reins?'

Xav looked up from the tobacco and the skunk which he was shredding into a king-sized Rizla.

'The Carlisle twins. Good blokes. The two in front are Bas Baddington and Drew Benedict, friends of my dad's who played polo for England. All terrific studs, who like to wind up Dad, who was the biggest stud of all, by chatting up Bianca. He goes ballistic,' Xav added wistfully. 'He hates people chatting up Mum too. Give me a slug of that Courvoisier; you're right about the whisky.' He emptied it into a nearby plant pot.

* * *

'You may not be the brain of Britain,' giggled Paris half an hour later, 'but you're a genius at rolling spliffs.'

Xav had obviously had plenty of practice, and he'd been right about the skunk: it blew their minds, putting them in a really mellow and expansive mood.

There wasn't anything on television and Patience and Ian had crap videos, so they put on a Marilyn Manson CD and, ignoring shouts of 'Turn it down' from all over the campus, they danced. Xav, rocking with the abandon that he drained glasses, was soon rolling another spliff.

After that they got the munchies. Paris remembered a shepherd's pie Patience had left in the fridge, which he put in the oven, and the remains of a boeuf bourguignon, which he fed to Northcliffe. He also found a nice bottle of white and a plate of smoked salmon sandwiches under clingfilm, which they wolfed down, dropping the crusts on the carpet.

Oh help! Paris noticed a cigarette burn on one of Emerald's poncy embroidered cushions and two more on the sofa. He'd sort it later. Drugs made him feel he could conquer anything, be the best guy Cameron Diaz had ever slept with, win the poetry prize, score five goals for Liverpool, have Little Cosmo pleading to be his best friend. Then you came down and descended into the abyss when you wanted to hurt and destroy anyone who loved you.

'Why were you in care?' asked Xav.

'My mum dumped me on the doorstep of a children's home in Alvaston and fucked off. They named me after the town. They reckoned I was about two, so they gave me a birthday on January the thirtieth. Makes me the water carrier – or wine carrier.' He filled Xav's glass with Pouilly-Fumé. 'Aquarians are supposed to be aloof and charismatic. I've worked on it ever since. What happened to you?'

528

Xav drew deeply on his spliff, eyes like black threads, face impassive, a Hiawatha with puppy fat.

'I was born with a squint and a birthmark, which, probably correctly, is the sign of the devil to the Colombian Indians. So they chucked me into the gutter to die. They shoot stray children along with dogs in Bogotá, so the place looks tidy when foreign leaders roll up. I was rescued by a nun who worked in an orphanage.' Xav's voice grew more bitter. 'Bianca was brought in as a baby when I was about twenty months. She came from a good family, strict Catholics, who forced Bianca's mother to give her up. Dad and Mum had placed an order for her and flown over from England; the nuns threw me in as a job lot. I know nothing about my parents. Bianca's posh but I'm a yob: I can tell that when I look in the mirror.'

Emptying the entire glass of wine, Xav choked. Paris bashed him on the back and said:

'You've got the poshest voice I've ever heard. Birthmark's gone, so's the squint.'

Xav glared glassily at Paris. 'Gets worse when I'm pissed.'

'D'you feel Indian or English?'

'Indian mostly. I love booze, drugs and fast horses. But I've got no stop button. Once I start I can't stop.'

'Your father can't mind that with horses.'

'My father is the most embarrassing person I've ever met. He doesn't give a shit. Wherever he goes everyone gazes at him and Mum and Bianca, and sees how like film stars they are. Then they look at me, and think: Why's that ugly black bastard hanging round them?

'They used to spit at Mum when I was young,' continued Xav bitterly. 'They thought she'd been with a black man. They used to finger my hair and ask her if she ever washed it. I wash the fucking stuff every day. Boy, Mum got angry.' For a second, Xav's heavy face lifted. 'She used to yell at people. But no one ever asked Dad questions about me, because they're too scared

529

of him. So he's never realized there was a problem.'

Xav was rolling a third joint, breaking cardboard off a cigarette packet for them to smoke through.

'Least you've got parents,' said Paris.

The bottle of white was empty. The only thing left seemed to be a bottle of medium-dry sherry. He filled up their glasses.

'Let's drink to yobbos.'

'Yobbos,' shouted Xav, draining his glass. 'Put on some more music.'

Putting on Limp Bizkit, turning up the volume, Paris opened the curtains on a sky full of stars and lit-up windows all over the campus.

'Hear that, you fuckers,' he yelled over the din. 'God stands up for bastards.' Then, as the chapel clock chimed eleven o'clock: 'I've got an idea how we can screw up Biffo's steeplechase.'

On balance, Ian felt the evening had been a success. He had lied to Patience. He hadn't been dining with a supplier, but with Poppet and Alex Bruce, whom he'd taken to *Fidelio* in Bristol – on tickets admittedly given him by a supplier.

This had been to melt the distinct *froideur* which had grown between him and Alex since Patience's shouting match. As Alex wielded more power, Ian was increasingly edgy about losing his job. He knew Patience would disapprove of this move almost as much as Alex disapproved of her going on the march, so he had kept her in the dark.

Fidelio had been ravishing, with a Bagley old girl, Flora Seymour, singing Leonora quite magically. But although the opera was about liberation from tyranny, he didn't feel Poppet and Alex were fans of Beethoven – too militaristic perhaps.

'I prefer Eastern music,' admitted Poppet. 'Or early music on period instruments.'

Both Bruces had worn open-toed sandals and Alex,

tieless, had displayed fearful short sleeves when he removed his jacket. They had certainly tucked into the smoked chicken, roast beef, avocado and spinach salad and apricot tart Ian had ordered for the interval, and between them downed the bottle of Beaune.

Ian, who couldn't drink because he'd agreed to drive them, couldn't stop thinking of that bottle of Pouilly-Fumé in the fridge at the Old Coach House.

On the way home, Poppet and Alex talked insufferably smugly about their daughter Charisma, who went to Searston Abbey.

'Of course she's G and T,' boasted Poppet, which turned out to be 'gifted and talented', rather than 'gin and tonic', and which made Ian long for a drink even more.

As they crossed the border into Larkshire, it was still mild enough to have the windows open. Conversation moved on to the challenging behaviour of Paris.

'He's very troubled,' said Poppet firmly, 'and I'm afraid Janna Curtis gave him an inflated sense of his own ability.'

Ian didn't rise, saying they were finding Paris much easier and he seemed to be getting on well with Xavier.

'I'm not liking that,' mused Poppet. 'Xav is very troubled too. I blame Rupert. Xav gets a detention for challenging behaviour and instead of dropping everything to sort out his son, Rupert swans off on the Countryside March.'

'I asked Rupert to discuss Xav's special educational needs recently,' added Alex petulantly, 'and he said: "All Xav needs is a kick up the arse. He's a lazy little sod, like I was at school."'

In the dark, Ian suppressed a smile.

'Rupert of course is troubled,' sighed Poppet, 'and a very private person.'

Only because he runs like hell the moment you appear on the horizon, thought Ian.

Swinging the car in between the stone lions at the

bottom of the school drive, Ian was surprised at the number of lights still on. Must be pupils revising for tomorrow's retakes. Someone was playing loud music. Through the trees he could see lights in the Old Coach House; perhaps Patience was home.

'I've got a nice bottle of Pouilly-Fumé and some sandwiches in the fridge,' he told the Bruces. 'It's a long time since supper.'

Paris, if up, could open the bottle for them and hand things round.

'Well, if you insist,' said Poppet.

'Christ,' whispered Paris, who'd been looking out of the window, 'Ian's home and he's brought Mr and Mrs Fussy.' Turning off Limp Bizkit, he chucked the remains of the spliff into the waste-paper basket.

Then he noticed more burns: in the 'Mother's Place is in the Wrong' cushion and on Ian's bridge table and on another of Emerald's cushions, shit, shit, shit. Paris turned the cushions over and shoved a pile of *Horse & Hounds* on the bridge table.

'Gather up the empties at once, man,' he begged, but, cross-eyed and giggling on the sofa, Xav was too far gone.

'Oh, for God's sake.' Paris scooped up at least four bottles and shoved them in Patience's little sewing cupboard, producing a chink and crash of glass, which indicated Ian was already secreting bottles there.

Paris was just trying to identify a smell of burning and shoving a swaying Xav out by the back door when they went slap into Ian, Alex and Poppet coming in through the garage.

'Mr and Mrs Fussy,' said a beaming Xav. 'Have you had a good evening?'

Seeing him momentarily handsome, showing excellent teeth and softened features, Alex thought for a moment Xav had turned into the egregious Feral Jackson. Then he caught sight of the shadow of a birthmark in the overhead light.

'Xavier Campbell-Black,' he thundered, 'why aren't you in bed?'

'Chill, man, I've been counselling Paris. I didn't realize it was so late.'

'You were ordered not to leave your house.'

'I got permission.'

'Something's burning,' said Poppet, fascinated to witness such chaos.

Wrenching open the oven, Ian found a blackened shepherd's pie. Opening the fridge, he discovered the bottle of Pouilly-Fumé and the sandwiches missing and, striding into the drawing room, found an utterly depleted drinks cupboard and took in the mess.

'Paris, come in here at once,' he bellowed.

Everyone unfortunately followed him, whereupon the waste-paper basket containing Paris's discarded spliff, not wanting to be left out, burst into flames.

'Fire, fire,' giggled Xav, emptying the last of the sherry over it, which turned the flame blue. 'Just like the Christmas pudding at home,' he added wistfully.

'We'll be forgetting that drink and sandwiches,' said Alex grimly, 'and take you straight home.' He seized Xav by the arm and turned to Paris. 'And I want you in my office before chapel tomorrow to explain yourself.'

Thank God, the burnt shepherd's pie had blotted out the smell of dope.

Giggling hysterically, Xav tripped over a side table, sending flying a 'World's Best Dad' mug and a Staffordshire dog, and fell flat on his face.

'For God's sake,' exploded Ian.

Xav was as unyielding as a bag of concrete as Paris lugged him to his feet. 'Getta grip,' he hissed. 'I'll help him out, sir.' Anything to escape from Ian's fury.

Outside, the peace of the soft September starlight was disturbed by a tantivy of horns and joyful off-key singing.

'The dusky night rides down the sky,
And ushers in the morn;
The hounds all join in glorious cry,
The huntsman winds his horn.'

' "And a-hunting we will go, a-hunting we will go, a-hunting we will go," ' joined in Xav. Lunging forward he yelled, 'Taxi, taxi, take me to paradise,' as a lorry, driven by Patience, with Dora, Jack, Lando and Junior, and several beagles falling out of the windows, came roaring up the drive.

' "The dusky night rides down the sky, the huntsman . . ." ' began Patience. Screeching to a halt outside the Old Coach House and seeing Xav and Paris, she cried, 'Hello, boys, we've all had such a wonderful day.'

The Bruces, however, lurking in the shadows, felt otherwise, particularly when the beagles poured out of the back of the lorry after Joan's Burmese cat before relieving themselves all over the lawns and the flower beds. The calm of the night was disturbed again as Poppet Bruce's open-toed sandals encountered Northcliffe's regurgitated boeuf bourguignon.

Paris fled to bed, trying to blot out the sounds of Patience and Ian arguing furiously downstairs.

Oh hell, there was the main section of the *Sunday Times* on his bed all crumpled up by Northcliffe, which Ian hadn't read yet and would be crosser about than the booze. The paper lay open at a piece listing the advantages of boarding school which included 'the widening of horizons, the development of autonomy, and the relief from tensions commonly built up in a nuclear family around adolescence'.

Paris buried his face in his pillow. 'I've been catapulted into a nuclear family,' he groaned, 'but I'm the bomb.'

64

As a result of the Countryside March, Bagley received excellent coverage. Many papers carried pictures of Amber, Lando and the beagle pack. The front page of the *Western Daily Press* showed Sally and Patience waving placards. Dora was ecstatic over Nigel Dempster's picture of herself and Cadbury. It would be so good for all her press contacts to be able to put a face to her name. There was however a bitchy piece in the *Scorpion* on the shortness of Rupert Campbell-Black's fuse. Was it due to lack of support from his two sons, Marcus, who was gay and allergic to horses, and his adopted son Xavier, who'd been gated by Bagley Hall (fees £22,000 a year) for undisclosed bad behaviour?

The star of the day was definitely Bianca, who, combining her mother's beauty and her father's ability to dazzle, was considered to be carrying the Campbell-Black torch. This did nothing for Xav's self-esteem, but his street cred rocketed when news leaked out via Dora and the Evening Standard that instead of marching, he and Paris had been busted for drunken trashing of the bursar's house.

This, according to the Bruces and a reproachful Nadine, would never have happened if Patience hadn't abandoned Paris so early in his foster placement to defend evil blood sports. Poppet promptly emailed the

Cartwrights the telephone number of P.U.K.E., 'which stands for Prevention, Understanding, Knowledge, Education, a support group which takes a non-judgemental view of binge drinking'. 'Call them,' urged Poppet.

Patience put the email in the bin.

Paris and Xav were heavily fined and as punishment had to knock in endless posts and blue and brown flags for Sunday's steeplechase. This enabled them to ear-mark an outwardly impenetrable clump of rhododendrons and laurels about seventy-five yards from the start.

Xav had planned to invite Paris back to Penscombe that Sunday but the whole school was ordered to stay at Bagley to take part in the steeplechase or at least witness Alex Bruce achieve his personal best.

On a grey dank Sunday afternoon, with fog forecast, the Biffo Rudge Trophy for the first member of staff past the post and the Gordon Brooks Cup for the first pupil, donated by Boffin's father, glittered on a trestle table, reflecting the turning gold limes surrounding Mansion Lawn. Silver shields for the next five in both categories were stacked in a cardboard box.

The six-mile course itself was shaped like the frame of a tennis racquet. Contestants left Mansion Lawn, ran under General Bagley Arch, down the east side of the drive, past thick rhododendron clumps, turned left at the lion gates and continued in a big circle round the villages of Bagley, Wilmington and Sedgeley, turning left again at the lion gates, pounding up the west side of the drive under the arch to the tapes in front of the Mansion.

In chapel that morning, Biffo, nailbrush hair bristling even more fiercely, had sternly set out the rules:

'Students in the past have let down the school and themselves, straying into public houses, cafés and shops along the route. But your target is to be the first back here, where Gordon Brooks and I will be holding the tape. Occasionally pupils have taken short cuts, pretending they have completed the course. Wardens everywhere will be monitoring such transgressions. Any cheating or flouting of rules will be severely punished. Above all act on your own initiative. Don't let anything or anyone distract you from your goal.'

Despite this, all the pubs and shops along the route were staying open expecting excellent business. Janna, Lily and Brigadier Woodford had heaved deckchairs and several bottles and Melton Mowbray pork pies onto the Brigadier's flat roof to enjoy the spectacle.

As kick-off time approached, competitors gathered on Mansion lawn, chatting, shivering, running on the spot and jogging round in little circles.

The smart money for pupils was on Kippy Musgrave, a Lower Fifth beauty, already fleeter than a whippet from running away from lustful masters. Denzil Harper, the ultra-fit head of PE who ran marathons for the county, was favourite for the Rudge Cup, a rather stocky hare who had reckoned without Alex Bruce's tortoise, according to Boffin Brooks.

'I don't approve of gambling, sir, but I've put a whole week's pocket money on your being first past the tape.'

Boffin, his spectacles misting up in an orgy of toadyism, sporting long grey shorts which failed to disguise a bottom wider than his shoulders, breath reeking of breakfast kipper, was also determined to be in the first six.

Members of the first fifteen, including the glamorous captain, Tarquin Courtney, had perfected that rugby star walk, sticking out their chests, straightening their legs backward with each stride to make their thighs judder. Big bruisers, they outwardly treated the whole steeplechase as a joke but underneath, like Alex, they were hell-bent on winning.

Alex himself was in a trance. One must go inside

oneself. Following Bianca's example, he had tied a red bandanna round his head; he was flexing his thigh muscles backwards as he swayed and hummed. Poppet, jogging on the spot in shorts and a purple vest, displaying Black Forests of armpit hair, was chopping up bananas for Alex and other runners from his house.

'We want Bruce students in the first six.'

Their G and T daughter Charisma was waiting along the route to ply Alex and Boffin with glucose tablets. Anxious to beat as many masters as possible, No-Joke Joan had, like Alex, been jogging round the campus for weeks.

'Have you seen her thighs?' asked Artie Deverell faintly. 'Like barons of beef.'

'Our Joan would be more interested in the baroness,' murmured back Theo, who was increasingly grateful for swigs from Ian Cartwright's hipflask. Patience, beside them, had gone purple with cold; Ian, looking bleak, had still not forgiven Paris, who hadn't been near the Old Coach House since Sunday and whom he couldn't see anywhere. Probably too ashamed to show his face.

'I want ten pounds on Paris Alvaston for a win,' Dora, currently on three mobiles to various newspapers, told Lando who was keeping a book.

'Don't waste your money, he's two hundred to one.'

'I don't care.'

A chorus of wolf whistles greeted Vicky running out in a clinging pale pink fleece and pink pleated skirt, her hair in bunches.

'I am *so* nervous,' she told Poppet.

Alex detranced enough to say: 'Why not run behind me, little Vicky, until you get into your stride?'

She couldn't fail to be inspired by his tall good figure ahead of her.

'"Mark my footsteps, good my page!"' mocked Cosmo, still in his astrakhan coat.

'Line up everyone,' shouted Biffo as the big hand of the chapel clock edged towards five to three.

In a long race with over three hundred runners, it didn't matter if everyone started at once, but Mansion Lawn was now entirely covered with competitors. The Mansion itself dozed in a shaft of sunlight which had broken through the clouds.

'Where the hell's Hengist?' muttered Biffo to Joan as he fingered the starting pistol. 'Why is he always deliberately insultingly late?'

'He looked over his shoulder For athletes at their games,' murmured Theo, noticing that Cosmo had at last tossed his astrakhan coat to Dora, and, oh dear, was sliding a thieving hand between Vicky's thighs. There was Smart, stubbing out a fag, but where was Paris? Theo hoped he hadn't done a bunk. Hengist, who was keeping a paternal eye on the boy, had suggested Paris would benefit from a few hours' Latin and Greek coaching a week. Theo sighed. The temptation would be irresistible.

Ah, here at last was Hengist, flushed from a good lunch, laughing, joking, but in no hurry and making no apologies.

Biffo longed to turn the pistol on him.

'Get ready, everyone,' he bellowed. 'Two minutes to the off.'

Alex Bruce had been doing a quick interview with Radio Larkshire.

'Forgive me, the race awaits.'

'Of course, deputy headmaster.'

As Alex strode towards the start line, he passed Emlyn, who'd just enjoyed a long lunch at Hengist's.

'Why aren't you taking part?' he demanded.

'With stars like you, Alex?' Then, when Alex looked simply furious: 'Best of luck.'

Fifty yards down the drive, Paris and Xavier waited in their rhododendron hideout. Paris was watching the start through binoculars. 'One minute to three. Mr

Fussy's crouching down with one knee bent, and the other stretched out like the Olympics. Now he's bowing his head. God, he's a twat. OK,' he whispered to Xav.

Crash went the starting pistol, which Paris and Xav had bought on the internet from Bristol last week.

Off set the runners, pounding down the drive, past the rhododendron clump, spilling out onto the roughly mown grass on the left, stepping up their speed to be first through the lion gates.

'Stop,' thundered Biffo, brandishing his unfired pistol, 'that was a false start. Stop the race,' he shouted into his walkie-talkie to Mr Meakin who, desperate to redeem himself after letting Xav out last weekend, rushed forward waving his arms: 'Stop, stop.'

But the leading runners and Tarquin Courtney, who thought Meakin was a wimp and had been ordered not to be distracted by anything, waved two fingers at him and pounded on.

A second later, another avalanche of runners including Vicky and Cosmo sent Meakin flying into a hawthorn bush.

'Blessed are the Meakin for they shall inherit the earth,' shouted Cosmo.

Not until a hundred and fifty or so pupils and masters, including Alex Bruce, had flowed out of the gates did Biffo manage to convince the wardens of the false start.

'Just like the National in nineteen ninety-three,' whinnied Jack Waterlane, who'd been planning to run off and see Kylie, 'except the front runners are halfway to Wilmington.'

Alex Bruce walked back to the Mansion, gibbering with rage, froth flying from his lips.

'Get everyone back. The race must be rerun.'

'Too late,' sighed Hengist. 'Unfair disadvantage to those who've run a mile already; they'll be exhausted.'

'I and many others have been training for months to achieve a pitch of fitness.'

'I know, Alex,' said Hengist sympathetically, 'it's too bad. I felt the same when I did my Achilles tendon just before the England–France game. Run it tomorrow.'

'The sixth form are off to CCF camp.'

'Then we'll have another steeplechase next term.'

'The weather is too unreliable.'

'Who fired that pistol?' spluttered an approaching Biffo.

'Better call a stewards' enquiry,' said Emlyn gravely.

Theo and Artie were having great difficulty keeping straight faces.

'Poor Mr Fussy,' said Patience, 'he was so keen to win.'

'What's going on,' whispered Xav from the dark of the bushes.

'Obviously a terrific row,' said Paris, who'd climbed a rhododendron bush to peer out. 'Biffo's gone purple and is waving his hands. Hengist is trying not to laugh. Poppet Bruce is jumping up and down, saying this is what she hates about competitive games. Her husband's more competitive than anyone.' Paris dropped back on the ground.

'It couldn't have gone better,' said Xav in ecstasy.

'Hush, here comes Boffin Brooks on a bike, we'd better stay put.'

Pedalling furiously, Boffin reached the back runners on the outskirts of Wilmington village.

'Stop, stop,' he yelled, riding straight through them. 'The race is being rerun, stop.'

'Fuck off, Boff,' said Junior, 'it's not the Tour de France.'

'Get off that bike, we were told not to cheat,' called out Lando, coming out of the Dog and Duck clutching four gin and tonics.

'Everyone's got to go back and start again,' panted Boffin.

'Oh, shut up,' grumbled Junior, 'you just want

541

Mr Fussy to win. Throw him in the ditch, Anatole.'

'You're not allowed to drink spirits,' squealed Boffin.

'It's vater, you prat,' said Anatole, chucking Boffin and his bike into the stream that ran along the street.

Five minutes later, help was at hand. Joan had jumped into her British racing green MGB, which the girls in her house had nicknamed Van Dyke, and, hooting imperiously, had overtaken the front runners in Wilmington High Street. Just below a cheering Janna, Lily and Brigadier Woodford, she turned Van Dyke sideways to block the road where it narrowed, before going into the country. The red light of her great roaring face turned everyone back.

'The school buses are on their way to transport you back to the start,' she told them.

'If I have a heart attack,' said Cosmo in outrage, 'I shall get Cherie Booth to represent me.'

Back at Mansion Lawn Alex Bruce was still arguing with Hengist.

'This is a Bagley tradition we must not lose, headmaster.'

'You never stop saying tradition is the enemy of progress,' snapped Hengist, who for once felt outmanoeuvred.

'Someone fired that pistol,' said Biffo furiously. 'I am absolutely determined to get to the bottom of—'

'Kippy Musgrave,' shouted a voice in the crowd to howls of mirth.

'Who said that?' roared Biffo.

Hengist bit his lip. Emlyn, Theo and Artie, standing on the Mansion steps, were openly laughing.

Xav and Paris were in heaven.

'We did it, we fucked the steeplechase.'

They were just about to slope off into the woods and chuck the starting pistol, wiped clean of fingerprints, into a bramble bush when, to their horror, runners came sulkily shuffling back.

'It's bloody unfair, I was in the lead.'

'Dotheboys Hall! I'm going to sue the school.'

'If any masters or boys have coronaries, Alex, I'll hold you personally responsible,' said an outraged Hengist, who'd planned to slope off to Jubilee Cottage. Now he'd be presenting cups at midnight.

Pretending he needed to collect a file, he retreated to his office to ring Janna.

'Sorry, darling, I was so longing to see you, but I can't make it.'

'Probably just as well, Lily and Brigadier Woodford are downstairs getting plastered. I do miss you. But it was terribly funny.'

'Wasn't it? Robot the Bruce is not amused. They'll be pounding past your door again in a few minutes.'

The sun had set, peeping out under a line of dark clouds like a light left on in the next room, as the weary winners, six of them bunched together, finally hobbled through the lion gates into the home straight. A hundred yards behind them, out of eyeshot, concealed by a bend in the road, came the second batch.

Just before the latter turned into the gates, a new willowy, white-blond competitor shot out of the rhododendrons, followed by a smaller, plumper, dark companion. Not having exerted themselves all afternoon, they were fresh enough to catch up with the front runners, and the white-blond boy in a glorious burst of speed began to overtake them.

Perched on the window seat in Hengist's study, peering through the gloom, Theo caught sight of Paris and yelled for the others.

'He's leading. God, he's going to do it, come on, Paris.'

The window seat nearly collapsed as Artie, Emlyn, Hengist, Patience, Ian and Elaine joined Theo, yelling their heads off as Paris passed a panting heaving Denzil and flung his breast against the tape. Xav coming in eleventh was just in the medals.

'Exactly like *Chariots of Fire*,' sighed Dora. She got out her calculator. 'I've made two thousand pounds.'

The joy in Ian's face was enough. Patience was crying openly as Paris accepted the Brooks Cup from an outraged and twitching Gordon Brooks.

'What a triumph, well done, Paris,' said Hengist, shaking him by the hand.

Paris was so overwhelmed by the reception he forgot to scowl at his headmaster. Boffin Brooks and Alex, who were in the second batch and just missed medals, were absolutely livid.

'Never saw Paris Alvaston during the race,' panted Alex.

'Neither did I,' said Boffin.

'It was such a muddle, I'm surprised anyone saw anyone, particularly in the dusk,' said Hengist smoothly.

'I paced myself,' Paris, playing up for the cameras, told Venturer Television. 'Long before I came to Bagley, I perfected my technique running away from the police.'

'I'm convinced it was my counselling,' Vicky was telling everyone.

Back at the Old Coach House, Ian was so delighted he opened a bottle of champagne and shared it with Patience, Dora and Paris.

Perhaps they do like me after all, thought Paris.

Later Hengist rang Janna.

'Paris won; I hope you're pleased. He was so elated he forgot he loathed me. I think we're winning, darling.'

65

As Middle Five B shuffled towards history the following morning, Milly Walton rushed up and kissed Paris.

'Well done, terrific news, you deserve it.'

'Well done,' said Primrose Duddon, blushing scarlet.

'Well done,' said Jade, smiling at him for the first time that term.

'What you talking about?'

'Go and check the noticeboard.'

'Well done, Paris,' said Tarquin Courtney, captain of rugby and of athletics, who had passed his driving test and kept a Porsche in the car park. He knows my name, thought Paris in wonder. Then he went cold. Looking up at the noticeboard, he discovered that after his triumph in the steeplechase, he'd been selected for the athletics team against Fleetley on Saturday.

'This is the one Hengist always wants to win,' confided Tarquin. 'There's training this afternoon. We can sort out whether you're best at sprint or middle distance.'

Oh shit, thought Paris, particularly as next moment Ian charged out of the bursar's office and thumped him on the back.

'Well done, old boy. Patience and I thought we'd drive over to Fleetley to cheer you on. We'll take a picnic. If the weather's foul we can always eat it in the car.'

'What the hell am I going to do?' Paris asked Xav five minutes later.

'Aren't they always pushing steroids outside Larks? You could take some and test positive.'

'Don't be fucking stupid.'

Wandering off down the cloisters Paris went slap into Emlyn, to whom he'd spoken very little since the beginning of term. He wasn't in Emlyn's set for history, and Theo, unable to bear the thought of Paris's beautiful straight nose being broken, had so far managed to get him out of rugby. But Paris trusted Emlyn.

'Can I have a word, sir?'

Thirty seconds later he was in the safety of Emlyn's classroom. Stalin's poster smirked down from underneath his thatch of black moustache. I'll be shunted off to the Gulag any minute, thought Paris.

'I screwed up,' he told Emlyn flatly. 'I didn't win the steeplechase. I lurked in the bushes and slid into the back of the leaders.'

'I thought as much.' Emlyn dropped four Alka-Seltzers into a glass of water. Yesterday's lunch with Hengist had run into dinner.

Emlyn then got a pile of essays on Hitler out of his briefcase and started to mark the one on the top with a yellow pen entitled Afghanistan Airlines.

Bastard, thought Paris, as Emlyn put a thick red tick halfway down the margin.

'Sit down,' snapped Emlyn. 'Theo showed me that essay you wrote on the *Aeneid*. It was very good. Shame he encouraged you to wimp out of rugby. I suppose he sees you hurling discuses or driving chariots. If you come and play for my under-fifteen side, I'll get you out of athletics.'

'How?' asked Paris sulkily.

'As Hengist still runs this school, rugby takes precedence. It'd also please Ian. He'd go berserk if he knew you'd been cheating in the steeplechase and anything's better than the total humiliation of running next Saturday.'

Emlyn had reached the end of Cosmo's essay, and wrote: 'A+. You obviously identify with the Führer.'

'OK,' said Paris.

'If you play on my team' – Emlyn grimaced as he downed half the glass of Alka-Seltzer – 'you must give one hundred per cent.'

Emlyn might not have been so co-operative if he hadn't yesterday morning received a telephone call from Janna, saying she was worried about Paris and could Emlyn keep an eye on him.

'Keep an eye on him yourself,' Emlyn had told her disapprovingly. 'How many times have you seen him this term?'

'I've been frantic,' replied a flustered Janna. 'We've got Ofsted any minute, and S and C are still refusing to give me any more money.'

So Emlyn said he'd see what he could do, adding, 'Let's have dinner and catch up and I'll tell you how to bamboozle Ofsted. I'll call you.'

As a fine former rugger player, Ian was thrilled, particularly when Emlyn gave Paris private coaching in the basics required of an all-rounder before his first game.

Tackling Emlyn, Paris felt like a flea trying to topple a charging rhino. Emlyn also gave him some videos of internationals to watch with Ian, but Paris still thought it was a strange, brutal, muddy game compared with football. And he already had pierced ears, without having them bitten through.

For the first game, Paris rolled up with hair tangled and unkempt, wearing shirt and shorts still muddy from his brief run in the steeplechase. Nor did he give a hundred per cent because he was terrified of getting hurt.

'If you play hard enough, you won't realize you're

hurt till afterwards,' Emlyn assured him at half-time, and once the game was finished took him aside.

'Have you got a girlfriend, Paris?'

Paris went scarlet, kicked the grass and shook his head.

'I should think not, if you go round looking that scruffy. Don't think your hair's seen a brush since the beginning of term.'

'Such a fucking awful haircut' – Paris spat on the grass – 'doesn't deserve one.'

The next game, Paris rolled up with his hair brushed, boots polished, clean shorts. The snow-white collar of his sea-blue and brown striped rugby shirt emphasized his deathly pallor. He was in a foul temper and soon into fights, quite prepared to thump and knee in the groin anyone of either side who bumped into him.

Emlyn kept up a stream of reproof: 'Don't hang on to the ball, don't tackle so high, those boots are to kick balls, not heads in. Rugby's not a free-for-all, it's a team game.'

He was about to send Paris off when the boy scooped up the ball, sauntered towards the posts, kicked a perfect drop goal and raised a middle finger at the other players.

That evening Emlyn called Lando and Junior over to his flat for a beer. The two boys loved the big living room, which had a huge comfortable sofa, a massive television with Sky for all the sport, shelves crammed with books on rugby and history, and a view, once the leaves fell, of General Bagley and the Lime Walk.

Pictures included a few watercolours of Wales, photographs of rugby fifteens, portraits of Emlyn's heroes: J. P. R. Williams, Gareth Edwards and Cliff Morgan; and in a corner a group photo of himself, a giant towering over giants in the Welsh rugby team. The record shelves were dominated by opera and male voice choirs. On his desk were photographs of his late father, mother and sisters, and the exquisite Oriana, who seemed more distant than his father. If he didn't see her soon, his dick would fall off.

'Which one of you would like to take on Paris Alvaston?' he asked the boys.

'How?' asked Lando.

'In a fight.'

Both boys looked startled.

'We've got to break the ice around him somehow.'

'I will,' said Lando. 'I'm pissed off with the stroppy, arrogant little git.'

The following afternoon was cold, grey and dank with a vicious wind. The Colts were playing to the right of Badger's Retreat, separated from other games by a thick row of conifers.

Passing the Family Tree, seeing Oriana's initials on the trunk, Emlyn was overwhelmed with longing. She hadn't written for three weeks. Was she still in Afghanistan? If he flew out at Christmas, would she be too caught up with work to find time for him? His face hardened. It was a day to take no prisoners.

Within minutes of kick-off, Paris was landing punches, spitting and swearing. Groped too vigorously in a tackle, he turned on Spotty Wilkins, throwing him to the ground, fingers round his throat: 'Keep your fucking hands off me.'

Lando and Junior pulled him off.

Emlyn blew his whistle and formed the boys into a circle.

'I see you're spoiling for a fight, Paris.'

'I've had it with those fuckers.'

'Good,' said Emlyn coolly, 'Lando is only too happy to beat the shit out of you now.'

Lando stepped into the ring, long dark eyes for once alert, massive shoulders, scrum cap and gumshield giving him an inhuman look of Frankenstein's

549

monster, body hard as teak, four inches taller and two stone heavier than Paris.

'Come on, wimp, I'm waiting.'

'This is worse than the Pitbull Club,' hissed Paris, turning on Emlyn. 'You'll get the sack for this.'

'I doubt it,' said Junior, trying to balance the ball on his curly head. 'It's your word against ours and there are lots of trees in the way. Go on, bury him, Lando.'

Lando took a step towards an expressionless but inwardly quaking Paris. Emlyn was also quaking inside that he'd taken such a risk.

'You can either fight Lando,' he said quietly as Paris raised two trembling fists, 'or become one of the squad, and fight for them rather than against them. You're potentially a bloody good player, you've got the build, the eye and the short-term speed. We'd all be on your side.'

Paris glanced round the group; Junior, Jack, Anatole, Lubemir, Lando, Smartie, Spotty and the rest: all impassive, watchful, much stronger and bigger than him. Then he looked at Emlyn, an implacable giant, with the big smile for once wiped off his face. The pause seemed to go on for ever. He heard a whistle from a nearby pitch and the rumble and hoot of a distant train on which he could be off searching for his mother. But she had left him. Ian and Patience were his only hope. He held a shaking hand out towards Lando.

'OK,' he muttered. 'I've behaved like a twat, I'm sorry.'

'Well done.' Emlyn clapped a huge hand on his shoulder. 'That's the hardest thing you'll ever have to do in rugby.'

'The lads gave him a round of applause,' Emlyn told Janna over a bottle of red in the Dog and Duck that evening. 'They also gave him a lot of ball in the second half, and he played a blinder.'

'You took a hell of a gamble,' reproved Janna. 'Poor

550

Paris could have been beaten to a pulp. You should have been fired.'

'I know.'

'How can you justify such bully-boy tactics?'

'I pray a lot.'

Miffed she wasn't more grateful, he asked her what was the matter.

'Bloody *Gazette* ran a libellous piece today saying: "In a county of too many schools, Larks would be a suitable case for closure."'

'They're only flying kites.'

'Not with Ofsted about to finish us off.'

Janna was also shocked by the change in Emlyn. The fat jester had gone; so had the double chin. His cheeks were hollowed and new lines of suffering formed trenches round his normally laughing mouth. No longer ruddy and bloated, he looked like Ulysses the wanderer returning from an endless and scarring war.

He was wearing too-loose chinos held up by a Welsh international rugby tie, a dark blue shirt and a much darned grey sleeveless pullover which Janna guessed had belonged to his father, about whom over more glasses of red he talked with great pain.

'Like John Mortimer in *A Voyage Around my Father* – that should be a set book – I just feel lonely now he's gone, and racked by lost opportunity. Why didn't I tell him I loved him more often? I betrayed him by going to Bagley – he could never understand it; and although Dad and Oriana were in the same camp, they never really got on. He couldn't comprehend anyone who'd been brought up with every advantage being so ungrateful.'

'How's your mum?' asked Janna.

'Crucified, bewildered, stoical. They'd been together forty years.'

Janna let him talk. It was a pleasure to watch him and to listen. Now the spare flesh had gone, he had such a strong fine face and, after a summer back in the valleys, his lovely lilting voice seemed deeper, with the Welsh open vowels more pronounced.

Oriana, it seemed, had provided little comfort when he'd flown out to see her in the summer holidays.

'She doesn't have the same relationship with her father.'

'But Hengist adores her,' said Janna unguardedly.

Fortunately Emlyn was too preoccupied to notice.

'Maybe, but she doesn't admire what he stands for. She can't understand how sad and guilty I feel. She's too taken up with the present, devastated at the plight of the Afghans. She's got a lead to Bin Laden, and plans to infiltrate herself into some Taliban spy ring. She could easily pass for a boy.'

'Oh poor Emlyn.' Janna topped up his glass. 'Sally and Hengist' – she felt her voice thickening – 'must be out of their minds with worry.'

'I'm sure. But they keep themselves busy. Hengist has been at some conference in Geneva all week. He's expected back this evening.'

Janna was just smirking inwardly because she was going to see him tomorrow, when Emlyn added,

'Why have you fallen out with Paris?'

Janna's glass stopped on the way to her mouth. Careful, she told herself, Emlyn doesn't miss things.

'He was dangerously crazy about you. I always suspected he accepted that place at Bagley as the only possible escape route. He's giving Patience and Ian a really hard time. Trashed their place a few Sundays back, and although he seems to get on with Theo, he's been arguing and swearing and spitting at other teachers.'

'He was used to arguing and swearing and spitting at Larks. I bet you played up at school.'

'I was utterly angelic,' said Emlyn piously. 'I spent my entire school career as still as still' – briefly his face broke into a smile – 'outside the headmaster's office.'

Janna laughed, but her mind was racing.

'Everything Paris loved has been taken away from him,' said Emlyn, his huge hands taking Janna's. 'He lost his mother; endless schools and care homes where he made friends; teachers; foster parents: all taken away. Oaktree Court, however much he loathed it, was familiar. His life's been like living in an airport. All the love and understanding you gave him, I guess he misconstrued it. It's hard for teachers. We have to be so careful not to inspire passion in kids who have had no love, and lead them on to yet another rejection.'

Not just in kids, thought Janna, removing her hands, which felt so comfortable in his.

'Let's get legless,' said Emlyn, about to get another bottle.

Janna shook her head: 'I've got Ofsted in a fortnight. Hengist calls it "Orfsted".'

God, what a slip.

Emlyn looked at her speculatively.

'What happened on the geography field trip?'

Suddenly he was much too big for their corner table, his eyes boring into her.

'I went to bed with a migraine.' At his look of scepticism, she insisted, 'I did truly. I was so tired; I nodded off and missed everything. You're always nodding off,' she added defensively.

'We're not talking about me. Paris was evidently good as gold until the last night. But he's so angry now. Did you turn him down?'

'I don't have to answer these questions,' said Janna furiously.

'Course you don't, lovely, but you're so instinctively warm and tactile. Perhaps he misinterpreted the maternal nature of your affections.'

'Now Paris has got a new school, I'm sure he'll settle down and find himself a nice lass.'

* * *

A few days later, Dora was lurking in the main hall, hoping to bump into Paris. She knew his timetable backwards. He was so preoccupied with learning rugby with Emlyn, he hardly noticed her. Late for English, because he'd been practising drop goals, he came hurtling through the yellow lime leaves carpeting Mansion Lawn.

'Shut your eyes,' she called out.

'If it's not seeing the new moon through glass, I'm not interested. Last time I wished for an A star for my Simon Armitage essay, effing Vicky only gave me a C plus.'

'Much better than that.' Seizing Paris by the arm, joltingly aware how he'd thickened out and muscled up since term began, Dora dragged him down the cloisters. 'Now you can look.'

The board was painted in dark blue gloss, like the board outside Larks. Here the gold lettering said 'Notices'. At Larks it said: 'Head Teacher: Janna Curtis'. Oh Christ, when would it stop hurting?

'You don't seem very pleased.'

'What for? I'm late for English.'

'Here, stupid.' Dora pointed to a list of names.

In Emlyn's square, clear writing, Paris read, 'France-Lynch (Capt), Waterlane, Lloyd-Foxe, Smart, Rostov . . . Alvaston.' *ALVASTON!*

He couldn't speak; he shut his eyes as warmth flowed through him. He hadn't let Ian, Theo or Hengist down. He'd been picked to play for the Colts on Saturday. Even better, it was a needle match against St Jimmy's, who'd always sneered at Larks and hated Bagley even more. As the first, second and third fifteens would also be playing, the residual resentment between maintained and independent would come bubbling to the surface.

'How d'you feel about St Jimmy's being your first fixture?' asked Dora.

'Great!' Paris punched the air. 'Set a yob to catch a

yob. I've always wanted to wipe the smirk off Baldie Hyde's face.'

'Ian and Patience will be *au dessus de la lune*,' said Dora, rushing off to ring the papers.

66

Saturday dawned meanly with the sun skulking like a conspirator behind charcoal-grey clouds, which provided the perfect backdrop for the gold leaves tumbling steadily out of the trees. Distant Pitch Four, where the Colts were playing, was hidden by a net curtain of mist. Despite this, a glamorous photograph of Paris as Romeo, sold to the *Express* by Dora, captioned 'Scrumpet' and announcing his rugby debut and desire to bury St Jimmy's, had attracted a sprinkling of press and a largish crowd.

'Only been playing a few weeks,' crowed Ian, who was watching with Patience, Artie Deverell and Theo, who in an old Prince of Wales check coat and a trilby on the back of his bald head looked like a bookie. Artie noticed with a stab of anguish how grey, now his Tuscany tan had faded, his friend looked in the open air. But Theo was in high spirits and getting stuck into Patience's bullshots. Five other boys from his little house, other than Paris, Anatole and Smart, were playing on various sides and only two from Alex Bruce's. Boffin Brooks, officious little shit, was one of the touch judges in the Colts game.

Then Theo growled: 'Here comes Rod Hyde, hubristic as ever,' as Rod, having travelled in the first coach singing revivalist hymns with his teams, strode about self-importantly, clapping leather-gloved hands on the shoulders of his 'men' – literally. They looked twice as old and hulking as their Bagley counterparts. Rod was wearing a new black leather coat, tightly belted, to show off his manly figure, and a new big black hat under the brim of which his eyes crinkled at the prettier mothers.

'Mr Hyde who never turns back into nice Dr Jekyll,' observed Theo sourly. 'Ah, here's little Vicky Fairchild with a pretty foot in both camps,' as Vicky, seductive in a long purple coat and a black fur hat, paused to kiss first Poppet and Alex and then Rod and Sheila Hyde.

'Isn't it thrilling Paris is playing?'

'I'm sure your counselling has helped,' said Poppet eagerly.

'I do feel I'm easing his passage,' smiled Vicky.

'The ambition of every Bagley master,' murmured Artie Deverell as the Colts ran onto the field.

'Come on, Bagley,' shouted Bianca and Dora.

'Go for it, Paris,' yelled Dora's brother Dicky. 'God, he looks shit scared. So would I be. Those St Jimmy Colts will never see fifteen again. Look at their moustaches and chest hair. They should have been made to produce their passports. Brute Stevens, their captain, is reputed to have a wife and three children,' he added as, locked together, the St Jimmy's scrum sent Bagley reeling backward.

'Hengist's little laboratory rat is going to be carved up,' said Cosmo approvingly as Paris fluffed three passes and holding onto the fourth was brought crashing down by Brute Stevens.

'That was high,' muttered the crowd. The referee took no notice.

Was it coincidence or had Brute Stevens been deliberately ordered to harass Paris, never Rod's favourite pupil? For the second time as Paris leapt for the ball in the line-out, Brute rammed a thumb down the pockets of Paris's shorts, nearly pulling them off. Around the ground, binoculars rose to a score of masters' eyes.

'Come on, St Jimmy's,' yelled the caring and concerned parents – hearties in Barbours or blazers with badges on their breast pockets, their wives in peaked caps or woolly hats, cheeks purpling against the cold, working up a good hate against Bagley. How dare any school have such splendid buildings, such an excess of land, such arrogant pupils and such a cavalier headmaster, who hadn't deigned to make an appearance so they could ignore him. Even the white goal posts and the helicopter pad said H for Hengist.

Sally Brett-Taylor, in a dark blue Puffa, navy-blue and gold Hermès scarf tied under the chin, her exquisite complexion unmarred by the elements, had reached Pitch Four, and was being fractionally more gracious to Sheila Hyde than she would be to the wife of the head of a major public school.

'How good of you to come. The chaps so love a crowd. No, Joan's taken the girls' hockey team to Westonbirt; she'll be so sorry to miss you. Hengist'll be out soon. He always feels personally responsible for all four matches. Oh, come on, Bagley. Come on, Colts. Emlyn's been working so hard on them. Well out, Paris. Well done, Smartie. Come on, Junior, come on. Oh, bad luck,' as the whistle went.

Hengist, who'd been in his study with Jupiter thrashing out New Reform's law-and-order policy, which could more profitably have been applied to the Bagley Colts, arrived to find Pitch Four in an uproar, St Jimmy's leading 28–7 and Emlyn in a towering rage.

'We've done all the attacking and had ninety per cent of the ball,' he told Hengist, 'but the bloody bent ref from St Jimmy's is disallowing everything. He's given six penalties against us, none against St Jimmy's. If they knew how to kick straight, the score would be double. Boffin Brooks is touch judge, and can't see a fucking thing – or chooses not to.'

Rod Hyde meanwhile was leaping up and down, bellowing on his side: 'Well played, Wayne, well done,

Kevin. Oh, good tackle, Brute. Come on, St Jimmy's,' clapping his great leather-gloved hands together like a walrus.

Bagley Colts, fast losing their tempers, were dramatically down to ten men, five – Junior, Lando, Smartie, Anatole and Spotty Wilkins – having been banished to the sin bin. The rest, like uncut stallions at Windsor Horse Show, were circling the ref.

'I was not orfside,' Jack was yelling, 'and that try was good. Can't you bloody well see?'

'Sin bin,' yelled back the ref.

As the roar of the crowd merged with the whirr of a helicopter, Rod was in ecstasy. Who were the yobbos and the bad sports now? Alex Bruce was also trying not to look smug. If that blockhead Emlyn Davies had introduced a few of Bruce's boys into the Colts, things would be very different. The Colts' moods were not improved at half-time as they sucked lemons and emptied water bottles to be told all the other Bagley sides were wiping the floor.

'High tackle,' yelled Ian Cartwright early on in the second half as Brute put a beefy arm round Paris's neck, yanking him to the ground. 'Did you see that, Hengist?'

But no one had seen anything because Mrs Walton, utterly ravishing and smothered in blond furs, had just rolled up with Randal Stancombe to watch the Colts before taking Milly and Jade to Sardinia for the weekend.

I hope she's happy, thought Hengist as, smiling, he strode down the touchline to welcome them. He was wearing a fawn coat, his hair, always curlier in damp weather, falling over the dark brown velvet collar. St Jimmy mothers, turning as he passed, had to agree reluctantly that he looked even better in the flesh.

Randal was in joshing mood. 'With all your resources and expertise, Hengist, surely the Colts should be thrashing St Jimmy's.'

'Randal!' Rod Hyde strode up, pumping Stancombe's hand.

'You're doing too damn well, Rod.'

'We've been bringing on our young players,' said Rod smugly. 'Congratulations on that takeover, must have taken a lot of time and vision.'

'What takeover?' said Hengist, wrenching his eyes away from Mrs Walton.

He ought to know, thought Randal angrily.

'Both takeovers,' he replied lightly, putting an arm round Mrs Walton. 'Ruth's about to move in with me.'

'If you walk through a head hold your storm up high,' sang Dicky, who'd been drinking vodka in the rhododendrons with Xavier.

Revved up by Emlyn at half-time, the Bagley Colts fought back, and no one fought with more guts than Paris, battered by the terrible strength of the opposition. Tries from Lando and Junior, one of them converted by Lubemir, followed by a stylish drop goal from Anatole, brought the score up to 28–22. Victory was at last within Bagley's reach.

The mist was coming down again; the light fading; the other games were over.

'Come on, Paris,' howled his fan club as he scooped up the ball. Escaping from a tangle of red, blue and brown jerseys and muddy shorts, he streaked down the pitch, pale hair flying, cheers in his ears. Seeing Brute Stevens pounding in like a mad bull from the right, he jinked to the left, bounding along the touchline, burying the ball triumphantly over the line at Boffin's feet.

'Disallow that if you dare, you sad bastard,' he panted, then, raising the ball triumphantly, waved it to the crowds to roars of applause.

In the closing seconds of the game, he had put Bagley almost level. Junior's conversion would clinch it. As photographers raced to get their pictures, Northcliffe broke free, bounding towards Paris, picking up a horse chestnut leaf as a prize. Paris could see Patience wiping her eyes, Ian joyfully brandishing his shooting stick, Theo waving his bookie's hat in the air and Dora and Bianca jumping up and down.

Jack and Anatole charged out of the sin bin to ruffle Paris's hair, and clap him on the back. 'Well done, man.'

Hengist sloped off to report the triumph to Janna.

But against all this din, the whistle kept on blowing and not for the end of the match. After a long consultation with Boffin, the ref was walking in Paris's direction.

'I'm afraid the pass was forward and your foot was in touch.'

Paris's muddy face contorted in fury.

'Do you actually know the fucking rules of the game?' he yelled. 'It was not forward and I was not in touch.'

'Don't argue with the ref, you posh bastard,' yelled Brute Stevens.

All the Colts were now shouting at the ref. From all round the ground came booing. Emlyn looked on stonily but impotently.

'I have never witnessed such appalling sportsmanship,' exploded Rod Hyde.

'Come on, we've still got two minutes,' pleaded Smartie.

Once again, Bagley stormed St Jimmy's' end. But tiredness and fury made them fumble.

'Come on, Paris,' he heard Bianca Campbell-Black screaming. Then the whistle blew long and plaintive, the train moving out of the station away from him, and it was over.

Rod Hyde had not been so happy since Margaret Thatcher was booted out of Downing Street. The maintained sector were proving themselves both intellectually and physically superior to the independents. He was already writing the piece in his head for

Education Guardian. He was so proud of his students. 'Well done, well done.

'Bad luck,' he called out jovially to Emlyn. 'Several of our best players were off from injury. If we'd had our full side, you wouldn't have stood a chance.'

'Come and have tea in the common room,' Sally said hastily to Sheila Hyde.

'We were robbed,' a sobbing Dora was telling the *Mail on Sunday.*

Paris walked back, covered from top to toe in red-brown Larkshire mud, Northcliffe beside him.

'Beautiful, isn't he,' murmured Artie to Theo. 'And, God, he's brave.'

'Paris played a very gallant game,' insisted Ian.

'He did,' agreed Biffo grudgingly. 'There's no denying a first-rate public school can straighten out the most wayward lad.'

Through the twilight, he could see Paris stealthily approaching the little group round Rod Hyde and the ref who, relishing their moment of glory, were loath to leave the pitch.

'Read the fucking rule book next time,' hissed Paris and, smashing his fist into the face of the ref, sent him crashing to the ground.

There was a horrified pause, interrupted by a burst of cheering from the Bagley Colts.

'Hit him again, he's still moving,' yelled Lando as the ambulance hurtled across the pitch.

67

Hengist loved post-mortems after games. He and Emlyn would play back videos, pinpoint achievements, discuss tactics for next week. Emlyn always saw the cause, while others watched the effect. When everyone else was cheering a try, he could tell you fifteen seconds back what moves had created it. After it was over, he could recount the whole game. He believed if you could get boys to use their brains and think, they'd be much better players and enjoy the game so much more. The boys loved Emlyn for his deep commitment, his expertise, his dedication to transmit the skills he had learnt, his extreme seriousness beneath the jokey exterior.

There was no jokiness in his face that evening as he knocked on Hengist's door.

'Oh dear,' said Hengist a minute later. Throwing a log on the fire, he took a couple of cans of beer out of the fridge.

'I hope you don't mind, I told Paris to report to me up here,' said Emlyn.

Paris climbed the stairs. His neck felt dislocated by Brute's tackles; his knees locked together; his heart battered every bruised rib. Slower and slower he climbed, mocked on all sides by framed photographs of glorious former fifteens.

Inside Hengist's study, Elaine, reclining upside down

on a dark green sofa, lifted her tail. Flames dancing and crackling in the red-tiled William Morris fireplace were a cheerful contrast to the bleak faces of the two men, huge shoulders against the big bay window, through which Feral had once driven a golf ball. In the distance could be seen the orange glow of Larkminster.

'Shut the door,' snapped Emlyn.

Hengist retreated to his archbishop's chair, picking up a copy of Matthew Arnold's poems, which fell open at 'Rugby Chapel'.

> Coldly, sadly descends
> The autumn evening [read Hengist]. The field
> Strewn with its dank yellow drifts
> Of withered leaves, and the elms,
> Fade into dimness apace,
> Silent . . .

He must get on with his biography of Thomas and Matthew Arnold. Jupiter was so demanding. Hengist wondered if he really wanted to go into politics.

Emlyn, his normally genial face like granite, paced up and down for a moment, and then let loose his thunderbolt. How dare Paris let down his side, his house and his school and behave like a hooligan on the field.

'And you've let the independent system down, behaving like a yob in front of Rod Hyde, who you know will make political capital out of the whole thing.' Emlyn mimicked Rod for a second. '"We could have told you he'd revert to type."'

After another two minutes of the same rant Hengist, who was a kind man, felt Emlyn was being too brutal. To lighten the mood, Elaine got to her feet and started running on the spot on the window seat, ripping the red Paisley upholstery with her long claws.

'I really feel—' murmured Hengist.

'With respect, headmaster, don't interfere,' snarled

Emlyn, then turned on Paris again. 'You realize knocking out a ref is a criminal offence. He could suffer brain damage.'

'No brain to damage.'

'Don't be bloody cheeky,' howled Emlyn, 'just get out of my sight.'

'It's not a laughing matter,' said Hengist sternly, flipping over a page, he read:

> Ah, love, let us be true
> To one another! for the world, which seems
> To lie before us like a land of dreams . . .

It was the same poem he had marked in Janna's copy. Poor Paris, he wondered, was he still hopelessly in love with her?

'Get out,' roared Emlyn.

Elaine shot under a sofa as Paris limped towards the door, shoulders hunched, the picture of desolation. He'd been so proud of being in the team; now he'd blown it. He'd let Bianca down too; he'd heard her screaming for him. Just as his desperately trembling hand reached for the polished brass doorknob, Emlyn drained his beer can and called after him.

'I also have to thank you.' Paris froze. 'If you hadn't knocked out that ref, I'd have been forced to do it myself.'

For a second Paris scowled round at him, then he smiled, slowly, infinitely sweetly. 'Brute Stevens accused me of being a "posh bastard", so I must be making some progress,' and he was gone.

'Christ, how can anyone resist that boy,' sighed Hengist.

From then on Paris began to enjoy Bagley. He played regularly for the Colts. More importantly, Theo Graham began giving him four hours' Latin and Greek coaching a week.

As Theo devoted to him that gift of teaching, that insight into another mind, that patience and ability to inspire and ignite, Paris had his first real glimpse of the enchanted world of the classics and became not altogether of this world. He lost things, he drifted in late, he forgot to eat. He was in love.

Theo was battling to finish his translation of the seven existing plays of Sophocles. Knowing Paris to be confused about his identity, he gave him *Oedipus Rex*, one of the plays he had completed, to read.

'Not only the greatest play ever written,' he told Paris at their first session in his crowded study, 'it's also all about adoption and of the dire consequences of not telling a child it's adopted.

'As an abandoned child' – what Paris loved about Theo was that he never pussyfooted around a subject – 'you must wonder if every man you meet is your father, or every woman you're attracted to is your mother.'

'Perhaps that's why I fancy Bianca,' said Paris dryly, 'who's so young she couldn't possibly be my mother.'

Theo himself had reached an age when he no longer expected reciprocated love, just something to look forward to and dream about at night to distract him from the often terrible pain in his back.

The shadows under Paris's eyes were the pale mauve of harebells, his eyes the grey of overcast skies. He had the straight nose and pallor of an Elgin marble, which Theo would never give back to the Greeks.

Theo now had a second goal, not just to live long enough to complete his translation of Sophocles, but also to get Paris into Cambridge.

68

The week before Larks faced Ofsted, as if deliberately to derail Janna, Ashton and Crispin had finally summoned her to S and C headquarters for the intended pep talk.

A lovely Hockney of a kingfisher-blue swimming pool brightened the beiges of the Evil Office, no doubt reminding the pair of the fortnight they'd just enjoyed in Tangier. Both were tanned, although Ashton must have plastered himself in factor 100 to stop his pink and white skin burning. Crispin was fatter than ever, his primrose-yellow shirt straining at the buttons to reveal his waxed chest. A new goatee beard failed to hide an extra chin. The sun had bleached both goatee and his hair a rather startling orange. The room reeked of Ashton's chloroform scent as he launched straight into the attack.

'S and C were bwought in to waise educational standards in Larkshire but we have just had to pay a massive three-hundred-and-ninety-thousand-pound fine out of our annual management fee purely because you and a handful of rural schools failed to reach their targets. Your GCSE figures were among the lowest in Larkshire.'

'Much higher than last year. We rose six per cent.'

'Not enough. You've let us down.'

'Are you aware' – Crispin glanced at his typed notes

567

– 'your governors called an unofficial meeting because the parents were in such despair over the results and the lack of information provided?'

'Only a few parents,' said Janna, thinking of the pile of cards at the end of the summer term. 'How dare the governors hold secret meetings? It's illegal.'

'A measure of their fwustration,' sighed Ashton.

He's getting a real buzz out of this, thought Janna, looking at his hateful soft features and unblinking serpent's eyes. Putting out a delicately manicured hand, Ashton helped himself to a white chocolate from a shiny mauve box. Crispin's piggy lips watered.

'Your projected intake is also disastwous,' went on Ashton.

'The county council sabotaged that by changing the bus routes,' said Janna quickly. 'No parent is going to allow their eleven-year-olds to walk three-quarters of a mile from the school gates – particularly in winter. We were just getting known as a rapidly improving school then crap press ruins it. A lot of parents changed their minds about coming to Larks after the hopelessly biased reports on the geography field trip.'

'Oh my dear, I was coming to that.' Ashton nibbled another chocolate and finding it lime-centred, lobbed it, to Crispin's distress, into the bin. 'That disaster was of your own making. In this vewy office we warned you not to bond with Hengist B-T. Carried away by his glamour, you flew too near the sun. You were the only head in charge that fatal night. If Alex Bwuce hadn't arrived and taken control, you'd all have lost your jobs. You're lucky Wandal Stancombe didn't have Paris and Xavier Campbell-Black up on a wape charge. Jade Stancombe was evidently so traumatized she couldn't bear to go through the experience again in court.'

'Jade's been going through the same experience since she was twelve. She's a slut.'

'Dear, dear, your language! And after all Wandal's

done for you. I hope you're making enough use of that minibus.'

Janna decided to go on the attack.

'I'll never improve my school until you give me more money. We must have more teachers. We must have the roof repaired: reception was flooded last week. We must have more books and more computers—'

'Must, must, must,' interrupted Ashton smoothly: 'I'm amazed you can ask when you've just lost us nearly four hundred thousand pounds. I'd concentwate on pulling yourself together as much as possible before Ofsted next week.'

'The new refuge for asylum-seekers hasn't helped either,' protested Janna, getting to her feet. 'They're great kids, but we're getting six and seven a week, most of them with no English. You just settle them in and find them friends, so they don't totally destabilize established classes, then they move on again. Many of them come from war zones and are used to carrying guns.'

'Then they must feel thoroughly at home at Larks,' said Crispin nastily, 'and at least they're easing your surplus-places situation, so don't knock it.'

'I bet Rod Hyde hasn't been lumbered with them.'

'That's because Wod's school is overflowing, and if you're going to use words like "lumbered"' – Ashton pretended to look shocked – 'you shouldn't be in teaching. What was Larks's mission statement about cultivating every child's special excellence?'

'Oh eff off,' screamed Janna and stormed out.

'Good luck with Ofsted,' a highly satisfied Ashton called after her.

69

Janna's determination to conquer Ofsted was not helped by the panicking of her entire staff. At breaktime the day before, even an old hand like Skunk Illingworth was grumbling that he'd stayed up until four in the morning typing out the three-term development plan of the entire science department.

'I didn't,' scoffed Red Robbie, who was ringing jobs in the *TES*. 'All inspectors are failed teachers.'

'Takes one to know one,' muttered Wally who seemed to have painted the entire school, even the bird table, a brighter canary yellow.

During the same breaktime, Enid the librarian had fallen asleep on the sofa clutching a cup of coffee, which dripped onto her fawn flares. She had worked the entire weekend rolling back the date stamp, slapping it on every book in sight to indicate extensive borrowing, even bringing in her own rampageous children to rough up unread volumes. If only Paris were still here: he'd never stopped reading.

The pupils, on the other hand, were gleeful at the prospect of seeing their teachers going through the hoop, particularly silly old Basket who was one long panic attack. Dr Boon, the appropriately named local GP, was getting writer's cramp scribbling sick notes and prescriptions for tranquillizers.

'It may seem obvious,' said Janna as she gave the

remaining staff a last-minute briefing, 'but I trust by now you've all familiarized yourselves with the files of every child in your class or tutor group. Please emphasize our positive use of the whiteboard and IT, even if most of our computers need updating. Show the inspectors the children's best work. Tell them the good things about our school. Dress attractively but conservatively – no minis or cleavages.' She looked pointedly at Gloria. 'Be friendly; they're not ogres.'

By which time most of the staff had gone into Red Robbie mode, folding their arms and gazing truculently up at the tobacco-stained staffroom ceiling.

'And when you go to the toilet' – Janna addressed their thrust-out chins – 'for God's sake check, before slagging anyone off, that an inspector isn't lurking in the next-door booth. Finally, the inspectors will be based in the interview room, so if any of the more volatile parents roll up, head them off and ask them to come back later.' Janna forced a smile. 'Frankly you're a terrific bunch so just be yourselves and good luck to you all.'

As well as pupils, teachers and parents, the inspectors would be interviewing the governors, who were sharpening their claws, particularly after Janna had ticked them off at the last meeting for caballing behind her back.

'And please don't badmouth the school,' she had added, 'when we're trying so hard to save it.'

'Could have fooled me,' muttered Stormin' Norman, who was marshalling disaffected parents to put in the boot.

'We just hope you'll keep your students under control,' had been Russell's last word. 'It's we who have to carry the can.'

At least Janna's friends hadn't let her down. Mags Gablecross and Year Nine had produced a marvellous Spanish display of sombreros, tambourines and brave bulls tossing terrified matadors.

Cambola was magicking celestial sounds out of the choir and an orchestra which she'd started. '"If the trumpet gives an uncertain sound",' she exhorted them, '"how shall he prepare himself to the battle?"'

'Every child matters. Our ethos is to cultivate each child's special excellence and bolster their self-esteem so they confront the future with confidence,' intoned Lydia, Lance and Gloria. 'Every child matters, our ethos is to . . .'

'Please let me not let Larks down,' prayed pretty, very plump Sophy Belvedon, Patience and Ian's daughter, who had taken Vicky's place as head of English and drama and who had proved a huge success.

Mike Pitts, meanwhile, was overdosing on Gold Spot, scurf drifting on his shiny blazered shoulders. Skunk Illingworth ponged so dreadfully, Janna engaged in stench warfare and placed on his desk a deodorant, which he merely returned to her desk.

'This must be yours, headmistress.'

I'm a head's mistress, thought Janna wearily, or would be if I ever got a chance to see him.

Determined not to look like a school-marm, she had invested in a lovely ivy-green suit and a pretty frilled shirt in wild rose pink, which she had laid out with new tights last thing, before falling to her knees: 'Oh dear God, look after my school tomorrow.'

After a restless night, she arrived at Larks at half past seven. Partner, sporting a crimson bow, his red winter coat thickening, bounced ahead, happy to find Debbie, whom he loved and who meant titbits, had already put on a slow cooking goat curry, and was now in reception watering a jungle of potted plants forming the background of the Save the Tiger project. In and out of them drifted gaudy parrots, howler monkeys, sly snakes and splendid amber-eyed tigers. Graffi, who had drawn and cut them out of cardboard for Year Seven to colour, was touching up the tigers' stripes with black gloss.

'That looks grand,' sighed Janna. 'Bless you, Graffi.'

To add authenticity to the tiger display, the schizoid central heating had opted for tropical. Graffi had already removed his crimson sweatshirt. Noticing a big purple bruise on his arm, Janna hoped his father wasn't drinking again.

Reception had also been brightened by flags representing the nationalities of every child in the school. Two more had been added after yet another influx of asylum-seekers on Friday.

Beside the main desk like a welcome committee was a second display entitled 'Movers and Shakers', which included life-size cut-outs of Kennedy, Martin Luther King and Margaret Thatcher.

'Here's hassle,' hissed Graffi as Chally bustled in, her dark brown suit topped with a yellow autumn-leaf-patterned scarf, which Janna found herself sycophantically admiring.

'Yes, everyone likes it,' replied Chally smugly. Having sniffed Debbie's goat curry approvingly – 'a caring gesture to our Afro-Caribbean brethren' – she predictably bristled at 'Movers and Shakers'.

'Black women are deplorably under-represented.'

'Not any more they ain't,' grinned Graffi, splashing black gloss over the faces of Margaret Thatcher, Germaine Greer and Florence Nightingale. 'Florence was a lesbian as well, which makes her even more PC. Silly old bitch getting her effnics in a twist,' he murmured as an apoplectic Chally was fortunately distracted by one of Johnnie Fowler's BNP posters and made a fearful fuss about breaking a nail when she ripped it off the wall.

The young teachers, Lance, Lydia and Sophy Belvedon, yawned as they straightened displays, checked spelling, jazzed up lesson plans and prayed the children would be in a good mood.

'It all looks lovely,' repeated Janna.

In her office the sun had shrugged off its polar-bear

coat of dirty white cloud and was shining on the new yellow paint. She was touched to receive good-luck cards from all the Bagley children who'd been on the geography field trip except Paris, and from Sally Brett-Taylor, but worried that the central heating was growing increasingly tropical. She longed to take off her jacket but before the inspector arrived at nine she had to take assembly.

'"Every little thing gonna be all right,"' sang Bob Marley over the public-address system.

'We won't bother with a hymn or a talk today,' she told the packed hall, 'but I'd just like you all to put your hands together, shut your eyes and ask God to look after our school.

'On the other hand,' she continued thirty seconds later, 'God will need your help. The inspectors will be with us for several days, so please be nice to them. Try not to shove or shout, or swear, or drop litter, or your gum.' Glancing around at their anxious faces: 'And try to look happy.'

'How can I look happy when I'm trying to remember all these fings,' grumbled Rocky.

'Above all,' urged Janna, 'be yourselves.'

On cue she received a text from Hengist: 'Above all, *don't* be yourself,' she read, 'or you'll duff up any inspector who criticizes your beloved children. Good luck. When am I going to see you? H'.

Laughing, Janna looked up at the children and said, 'As you file out, I'd like all teachers to double-check the appearance of their classes. Do up your shirt buttons, Kitten, and pull down your skirt. Tuck in your shirt, Johnnie; pull up your socks, Martin. Have you all brushed your hair and cleaned your nails? Miss Basket isn't in? OK, I'll check Nine A.'

She was just working her way down the row of black, yellow, brown, pink and freckled hands, all with commendably clean nails, when she felt Partner's tail bashing her legs, heard whoops of laughter and found herself examining a huge hand, whitened by scars from rugby studs, and with big square nails and fingers.

Looking up, she found Emlyn grinning down at her.

'Oh Emlyn, you are daft.'

''Lo, Mr Davies, 'lo Mr Davies.' The children swarmed joyfully around him. 'When are we going to Bagley again?'

'When you learn to behave.' Emlyn produced a big bunch of reddy-brown chrysanthemums from behind his back, 'For your office, lovely, and to match your hair. And these are for your inspectors.' From his pockets he produced packets of herbal, peppermint and fruit tea and a jar of decaffeinated coffee. 'If you don't have any, they're sure to want it.'

'You are so dear,' gasped Janna.

'And you look so pretty in your green suit, just smile and wow them. I must go.' As he kissed Janna on the cheek, all the children whooped again.

'Now, you be particularly good, Miss Curtis has worked her heart out for you lot.'

He was so reassuring and made everything seem so normal, Janna longed for him to stay.

'You're blushing, miss,' accused Pearl.

'It's the central heating,' said Janna hastily. 'Now hurry back to your classrooms, they'll be here in a minute.'

Dear Emlyn, thought Janna, then groaned as her head of PE approached in patent-leather thigh boots, leather shorts and a see-through black shirt.

'You told me to cover up,' protested Gloria. 'That Emlyn's right hunky, isn't he?'

Gloria, it seemed, had, out of nerves, gone out clubbing, and hadn't had time to go home and change.

'Well, for God's sake,' said an exasperated Janna, 'nip down to New Look and get a less transparent top.'

'It's nearly nine,' warned Rowan. 'You're a disgrace, Gloria.'

'You'd better take my shirt,' snarled Janna, dragging

Gloria into her office. 'I'll just have to keep my jacket on.'

'I'm ever so sorry. Such a pretty blouse, are you sure?'

'No, I'm bloody not. Put it on.'

In fact Janna's wild rose pink shirt straining over Gloria's thrusting thirty-eight-inch boobs looked even more flagrantly provocative than the see-through black.

Bugger, thought Janna buttoning her wool suit, the temperature was rising by the second.

As Wally gave her brown boots a last polish, there was an enraged banging on the door and Chally barged in.

'Oh, there you are, Wally. Everyone is so stressed, the women's toilet smells like a sewage farm. Can you please put more air freshener in there?'

'And in Skunk Illingworth's classroom,' snapped Janna.

'And I don't know' – Chally's lips tightened – 'who put all those Penhaligon's toiletries in there, the inspector will think we're rolling in money.'

'I did.' Janna was fed up with Chally. 'They were a present. Do you want me to put up a sign saying "Gifted Toiletries"?'

'They're here, they're here.'

Rowan rushed in removing her suit jacket to show off a charming cream linen shirt, straightening Janna's papers, shoving her buckling in-tray under the sofa, then, like a teenager's mum before a dance, straightening Partner's bow tie, before he rushed off sending cardboard, black-faced Margaret Thatcher flying in his haste to welcome the visitors.

As Bob Marley was replaced by Schubert's *Marche Militaire*, such a brisk jaunty tune, Janna found herself marching down the corridor. In reception, the inspector was crouched down admiring the largest of Graffi's tigers.

'This is a very fine beast,' he said. Rising to his feet,

he took Janna's trembling hand. 'Wade Hargreaves, and, from your photographs, you must be Janna Curtis.'

Janna had expected an ogre but the man smiling down at her was tall, slim, in his late thirties and with the genial friendliness of a yellow Labrador.

'Welcome to Larks,' said Janna in relief.

'Oh Christ,' muttered Mike Pitts, going green and reversing into his office, 'it's Wade Hargreaves. I sacked him when I was head of maths at Rutminster Comp.'

Wade Hargreaves was accompanied by, amongst others, a spinster called Miss Spicer, who had one of Chalford's draped scarves, short spiky hair, a lantern jaw, disapproving coffee-bean brown eyes and who, having demanded a cup of peppermint tea, seemed disappointed when it was provided. Well done, Emlyn.

From then onwards Janna felt the sharp constant pain of a steel toothcomb being plunged into the scalp and tugged through tangled hair as Wade Hargreaves's team went everywhere, talked to everyone and asked for every lesson plan, file and balance sheet to be taken into the interview room. Brandishing clipboards they moved around devouring timetables, schemes of work, attendance figures, the first tentative coursework of Year Ten, and listening to Sam Spink in her Hogwarts' character socks, her massive thighs spilling over her chair like suet as she charted the inadequacies of Larks's workload agreement.

Mike Pitts, unable to face Wade Hargreaves, disappeared home with stress. By contrast Mags Gablecross was everywhere, guiding, supporting, comforting staff who felt they had cocked up.

'I could have done it so much better,' sobbed Lydia. 'I made a tape about Simon Armitage to nudge my memory but Johnnie Fowler got hold of it and played it back to the class and Miss Spicer.'

'I got Ten C too revved up about Billy the Kid,' said Lance dolefully. 'One of the asylum-seekers pulled out

577

a gun and Miss Spicer said I must remember that the Indians not the cowboys were the heroes.'

But there were good moments.

'Until Miss came, I had no grown-ups to talk to,' Pearl told Wade Hargreaves. 'No one respected me. Now school remembers my birthday, I get a card and a Mars bar and a song in assembly. She's going to help me take a make-up course.'

'Miss is there for the mums,' said Kylie. 'She helps them fill in forms for the social and the courts. She listens when their partners leave them or they can't pay their rent. She filled in my brovver's driving licence for him, and she remembered Cameron's birfday. Lots of teachers don't know all our names. Miss even knows all our babies' names.'

'We get letters to take home in Urdu,' said Aysha, 'so Mum and Dad can understand what's going on. Mum came to parents' day for the first time; there was cake and orange juice and she talked to other mums.'

70

Assembly the following morning was a great success. Kylie Rose lifted the hair on the back of everyone's neck singing 'It's a Wonderful World'. Aysha in her headscarf read from the Koran, Graffi from the New Testament – 'Judge not that ye be not judged' – which made Wade and even Miss Spicer smile. Danijela, one of the new asylum-seekers, read a Bosnian prayer, then the choir sang 'How Lovely are Thy Dwellings' so beautifully as the morning sun streamed through the stained-glass St Michael that even Miss Spicer wiped away a tear and Wade grinned across at Janna.

He was a terrific listener, as still as a wildlife cameraman who knows the only way to score is to move quietly. He and Miss Spicer were unfazed when Graffi's father, who'd been in the pub all day, dropped into the interview room for a quiet kip before going home. Or when Pearl's boxer father, just out of gaol, rolled up to get even with one of the pushers outside the school gates and try and catch a glimpse of his wife and her toyboy friend.

Debbie had been thrilled yesterday when the inspectors lunched in the canteen and had second helpings both of goat curry and rhubarb crumble and were constantly requesting more flapjacks for the interview room.

Things were dicey when they caught up with Feral,

sulky because he was having a one-to-one lesson with Sophy Belvedon in the individual learning unit, which had once been the changing rooms before the football pitch was sold off.

Sophy, realizing Feral would only attempt to read if he were interested, had blown up both Sunday's football reports on Arsenal and pages from a biography of Sol Campbell.

'You're not thick, Feral,' Sophy was telling him. 'People are stupidly characterized these days as gifted, able or with needs.'

'I've got needs all right. I need a fag and a shag,' said Feral, grabbing Sophy and burying his sleek face in her splendid breasts.

'I don't think my husband Alizarin would like that.' Sophy edged away her legs and hips, leaving her bosom in Feral's strong grip. 'He's six foot four and built like an oak tree.' Then, as Feral reluctantly released her: 'Not that you're not utterly gorgeous.'

'Wiv needs.' Feral batted his long eyelashes. He liked Sophy but he found it humiliating to be taught on his own. It was all Paris's fault for deserting him.

Wade and Miss Spicer asked Feral a little about work and then about the other teachers.

'Miss went to court with me in August; her evidence got me off. She got me a job working for two coffindodgers, mowing, chopping logs and fings; later me and Lily got wasted on sloe gin.

'Most of the teachers are shit here,' Feral went on. 'Chalford's shit, so're Robbie and Skunk, Miss Basket's crap too, she ought to be able to control us. Mrs Gablecross is nice, we can talk to her about anyfing. I need a fag.' Feral shook an empty pack in irritation. 'That no-good mother-fucking nigger-basher Monster Norman pinched my last one.'

'You can't call him that,' said Miss Spicer faintly.

'*You* can't call him that,' corrected Feral mockingly, 'but I can, 'cos I'm black and underprivileged. As a representative of an underprivileged effnic minority, I can call him anyfing I like.'

Sophy tried not to laugh, particularly when Miss Spicer rallied and asked Feral if he felt underprivileged.

'People call you "black shit".' Feral tipped back his chair, testing their reaction through narrowed speculative eyes. 'But if you play football well enough, you earn eighty grand a week and in a few seasons go from being "black shit" to God. That's why I'm gonna become a footballer. Put a recommendation in your report' – he tapped Miss Spicer's clipboard – 'that Larks needs a football pitch.'

'Thank you, Feral and Mrs Belvedon,' said Wade.

Checking the dining room at lunchtime on the second day, Janna's heart sank to see Miss Spicer and a jolly blond member of the team called Mrs Mills tucking into toad in the hole and deep in conversation with Rocky. Did he know that Larkshire had one of the highest rates of teenage pregnancies in the country?'

'Sure,' replied Rocky. 'That's 'cos Kylie Rose lives here.'

'I don't think that's quite right,' said Mrs Mills, who was dieting and reluctantly setting aside a piece of gold, utterly delicious, batter. 'Do you find sex education enlightening, Rocky?'

'Sex education is wicked, man.' Rocky bit suggestively on a sausage. 'They never stop banging on about STDs but they tell you lotsa ways to have sex – blow jobs, going down and fings, anal sex – without getting girls up the duff.'

'That's enough, Rocky,' said Janna firmly. 'Go and get yourself some dessert, you know you like jam roly-poly.'

'Sorry about that,' said Janna, 'Rocky gets carried away. Can I get you some sweet?'

Both Miss Spicer and Mrs Mills felt they'd had enough.

'Would you like to hear my poem about a skylark?' asked Rocky, returning.

'That sounds nice,' said Mrs Mills bravely.

'I heard a skylark singing so sweetly in the sky,' began Rocky, seeing relief dawning on the faces of his listeners, 'but when I looked to find him, he dumped right in my eye.'

'I think I'd like to see the D and T department now,' said Mrs Mills.

'I'll take you there,' said Janna and was just expounding on the splendid work being done when they heard screams. Rounding the corner they nearly fell over Pearl, who was lying on top of Kitten Meadows, holding clumps of her hair in order to smash her head on the stone floor.

'Take it back.'

'No,' squealed Kitten.

'Take it fucking back.' Smash.

'No.' Clawing at Pearl's face with long silver nails, Kitten drew blood. 'You always look fucking crap.'

'Fucking don't.' Pearl smashed her fist into Kitten's face, whereupon Kitten hit Pearl on her left breast.

'Ow,' screamed Pearl.

'Please stop,' called out Basket faintly from the safety of her classroom.

As a crowd gathered – 'C'mon, Pearl, c'mon, Kitten' – Wade Hargreaves emerged from a history lesson, so Janna dived in on the right, ducking blows, trying to prise the contestants apart.

A second later, Sophy Belvedon had rushed up and dived in on the left. As Kitten tried to elbow her in the ribs, she said: 'Won't work, I'm much too fat to feel anything.'

'Stop it, both of you,' yelled Janna.

At that moment Wally arrived and with his superior strength dragged off a spitting, wriggling Pearl.

'Take her to my office,' panted Janna. 'You can go to the gym,' she told Kitten, 'and both of you will have

582

detentions tonight and tomorrow.' Then, when they furiously protested, continuing trying to kick out at each other: 'That's final, now get out of my sight.'

Having administered smelling salts to Basket, Janna, aware that a button had been ripped off her suit and her neatly piled-up hair had come down, retreated to the Ladies where she met Sophy coming out, and said, 'Thanks so much for your help.'

'That Basket's a wet hen.'

'Hush.' Janna put her finger to her lips. Seeing an engaged sign on one of the doors she crept into the next-door booth. Climbing onto the seat and peering over the partition she discovered Miss Spicer knitting and reading *Good Housekeeping* and was so startled she fell back into the lavatory bowl with a shriek.

'Checking for spies?' asked Miss Spicer dryly.

'Sort of.'

'One needs a break from inspection.'

'And from being a head,' sighed Janna.

'Hello,' added Miss Spicer as Partner's snout appeared under her door. 'That is a delightful dog, he seems to know instinctively when a child is sad. He was trailing that pretty fair-haired Bosnian girl this morning.'

Shaking her wet boot Janna climbed down.

'That's probably because we made Danijela our bird girl. Every morning she takes out a tin of scraps which contains rich pickings from the kitchen. We couldn't think why the birds were standing indignantly round with their wings on their hips until we discovered' – Janna's voice quivered – 'Danijela was emptying the tin into her school bag for her friends in the refuge.'

'Can't take on everyone's burdens,' said Miss Spicer briskly, but her coffee-bean eyes were kind as she washed her hands vigorously before applying Bluebell hand cream. Then, painting her small mouth bright orange and rearranging the folds of her scarf, she announced she was off to the Appletree annexe to monitor some science lessons.

Miss Spicer had an eventful day. She was observing one of Mr Mates's experiments when the roof of Appletree finally caved in on her and Year Ten E, who emerged unhurt but much aged by grey, dust-filled hair.

'It worked with the other division,' bleated a shaken Mr Mates, who had to be reassured that the collapsing roof had nothing to do with his experiment.

'How lousy are thy dwellings, oh S and C,' sang Cambola, whose music department next door had also been submerged.

'They'll have to give us a new roof now,' said Mags Gablecross.

Next day Pearl gave Wade Hargreaves even more pressing reasons.

'I spend half an hour straightening my hair every morning, then the rain pours through the roof and it goes all kinky; that's why Kitten Meadows said my hair was crap and that's why I hit her. If we had new roofs this wouldn't happen.

'My dad's a boxer,' she went on, 'so it's in my genes to land punches. Fights isn't Miss's fault. She's great, and so's Mrs Belvedon, the new English teacher.'

'I'm just going to watch Mrs Belvedon giving Year Eight a lesson on *The Tempest*,' said Wade.

'Oh bugger,' grumbled Sophy, retrieving some dropped folders, then, as Year Eight giggled: 'You'll have to move your table, Stefan and Josef, I'm much too fat to get through that gap.'

'You do sound posh, miss.'

'If you think I'm posh you should hear my mother.'

'Paris is living with her?' asked Kata from Kosovo longingly. 'How's he getting on?'

'Fine.' Sophy was amazed by Larks's ongoing obsession with their lost leader. 'Now to Caliban. My husband Alizarin has done a painting of him.' On the whiteboard appeared a picture of a ferocious-looking beast, half wild boar, half gorilla, but with the saddest eyes.

'See his long nails for digging up pig nuts for his master. Caliban is a really sympathetic character,' Sophy went on, 'he's a bit ugly, but he longs to help and be loved and he says beautiful poetic things. Some horrid sailors are shipwrecked on his island and get poor Caliban drunk, so he makes a fool of himself. He adores Miranda, his boss's daughter.'

A picture of a pretty blonde in a ruff and long Elizabethan dress appeared on the whiteboard. 'But she's in love with someone else, and I'm sure you all know how it hurts when you love someone who doesn't love you.'

Wade Hargreaves couldn't imagine anyone not loving Sophy.

'And I bet lots of you boys when you go to parties feel shy of chatting up girls, so you drink too much and fall over – well, that's Caliban.'

'He's gentle giant like King Kong,' piped up Kata.

'Exactly.'

'And Monster Norman, except he's horrible.'

'No, no.' Sophy looked round nervously. 'Anyway, this is Alizarin's picture, and now I want you all to produce your own idea of Caliban. You've got paints on each table and plasticene and paper. Try not to paint each other. Anyone who comes up with an interesting idea can have one or two of these.' She waved a tin of Quality Street. 'Now: ready, steady, go.'

Sitting at the back of the class Wade and Miss Spicer made notes on their clipboards and watched Sophy advising, praising, laughing, screaming with joy – 'That is so good!' – and occasionally remonstrating: 'Don't put that blue brush back in the white pot, Jasper.'

The children, particularly the ones who couldn't speak English, were having a ball. As they slapped on paint or modelled in plasticene or clay, a wonderful zoo emerged.

'I can't do his nails,' wailed Kata.

On cue in pattered Partner and obligingly held up a paw so they could see his claws.

'Good boy.' Sophy hugged him and rewarded him with the Quality Street green-wrapped triangle which was all chocolate.

'That is really cool, Anwar,' she cried, pausing beside a Pakistani boy's desk. 'You've made Caliban look happy because he's asleep. That's in the text: he was so hurt by humans, only in dreams did he find happiness, and when he woke he cried to dream again. This is so good. Brilliant colours too. Lay it out on that chair to dry.'

What a lovely young woman, thought Wade wistfully. Shortly afterwards he was so impressed by another painting of Caliban he sat down on Anwar's picture to study it and was left with red, blue, green and purple splodges all over the seat of his elegant beige suit.

The children screamed with laughter.

'Oh, goodness,' wailed Sophy, 'you look more like a mandrill than a nimble marmoset. I'm so sorry. I'll get it dry cleaned or take it home and wash it for you.'

'Don't give it a thought, I might start a fashion.'

Janna, who'd just been forced into giving Monster a detention for cheeking some other member of the inspection team, was vastly cheered when she peered into Sophy's classroom and saw even Miss Spicer laughing.

As the bell rang for break, Year Eight bore Wade off to the playground to show him the bird table.

'That's a robin.'

'No, stupid, it's a bullfinch.'

'This is the pond,' said Kata, leading him out into the garden. 'We're going to clean it to encourage wild lives. Wally's made a ladder so anything drowning can climb out. And he's going to build a duck house and a bridge to the island.'

'Perhaps Miss Curtis will get you some fish.'

How nice he is, thought Janna, watching from the window, but we mustn't be lulled into a false security.

'Would you like a cup of tea?' she asked as he returned from his tour to her office.

She'd just put on the kettle, when Stormin' Norman roared in. 'You know Martin don't do detentions on a Thursday. You're depriving him of his liberty.'

She was about to punch Janna, who was protesting that surely it was Wednesdays, when Wade stepped out from behind the door, where he'd been admiring some stills from *Romeo and Juliet.*

'I wouldn't.'

'And 'oo the fuck are you?' yelled Stormin' Norman. 'Another of 'er fucking fancy men?' But at least her fist stopped in mid-air.

They were interrupted by the arrival of Chally, bright red in the face.

'One of the Croatians has exposed himself to Year Seven. I said, "We don't do things like that here, Roman, put it away," but he laughed in my face so I called back-up.'

'Front-up, more likely,' said Janna, trying not to laugh.

'This is serious, Senior Team Leader.'

They were distracted yet again by a yell and the crash of plasterboard. Pearl's boxer father had rolled up drunk again and discovered Graffi's father, whom he suspected of once pleasuring his wife, fast asleep in the interview room.

'I told you it was in my genes,' said Pearl smugly as the police arrived to remove both her father and Stormin' Norman.

71

On Friday afternoon Wade called a meeting after school
to report on his team's findings. Russell, Ashton and
Crispin arrived early. As the interview room had been
temporarily totalled by Pearl's boxer dad, they were
ushered into Janna's office, where they drank tea,
guzzled Debbie's chocolate cake and rubbed their hands
in anticipation of a serious drubbing for little Miss Curtis.

Crispin, who was perched on the sofa beside Ashton,
murmured that Debbie was an excellent cook.

'She'll be looking for a job tomorrow,' murmured
back Ashton. 'I'll put in a good word at County Hall.
Perhaps she could come and do for me.'

As Mike Pitts was still off with stress, Mags had been
asked by Janna to stand in for him. Pacing up and
down outside, Mags had never felt so tired. She was so
worried for Janna, who never failed to wear her
generous heart on her sleeve.

'Any room for a little one?' said Cindy Payne, the
Larkshire county councillor in charge of education,
parking her red-trouser-suited bottom on the sofa
between Crispin and Ashton. Both men would have
liked to edge away but were too firmly wedged.

Russell had commandeered a big upright chair. In
his hand was another letter of complaint from Miss
Miserden about Larks hooligans swearing and kicking
balls into her garden.

'Thought you might like to see this, Inspector.'

Wade, sitting at an imported table shifting papers and flanked by Miss Spicer and Mrs Mills, hardly glanced at the letter before handing it back.

'Sorry to keep you.' Janna rushed in followed by Partner. She settled down at her desk, ramming her hands between her thighs to conceal their trembling. So many things had gone wrong; so many bricks dropped; so many children out of control. Mags, sliding into a little red armchair beside her, squeezed her arm.

Through the window they could see the children running home through the pouring rain, their coats over their heads. After the row at the last governors' meeting, Russell's eyes refused to meet Janna's.

'Hope you survived,' he said heartily to the three inspectors.

'Extremely well,' said Wade, then turning to Janna, 'thank you for your hospitality. We have been made most welcome and given every assistance in forming our opinions.'

Then he unleashed both barrels. Larks in a word was being used by S and C and the county council as a pupil referral unit, or rather a dumping ground for all the rubbish kids with behaviour problems that were expelled from other schools.

'After four days, however, my team and I were delighted to see what efforts are being made by the staff to tackle attendance, unauthorized absence and deplorable behaviour. Support for vulnerable pupils is excellent, as is mentoring. Despite standards being constantly eroded by the behaviour of certain parents and a very disruptive band of children, bad behaviour is dealt with swiftly. Special needs are catered for well within very limited resources. Overall adherence to the curriculum has also been observed.'

Slowly, slowly, Janna felt her foot leaving the bottom of the sea as she drifted upwards towards the sunlight.

Wade consulted his notes. 'The teaching of the older staff is less than satisfactory. Their lessons are often dull, their marking unhelpful.' He pinpointed Chally, Mike Pitts, who had once sacked him, Skunk, Basket, Sam Spink and Robbie. Janna bit her lip: all her *bêtes noires.*

'On the other hand, language teaching was excellent.' Wade smiled at Mags. 'So was Miss Cambola's music and Mr Mates's science.' He then praised Janna's appointments: the new deputy head of history and the head of D and T, and in particular Sophy Belvedon. 'Quite excellent, we much enjoyed her English lesson bringing in both art and drama disciplines.

'Despite the appallingly deprived lives of so many of the children, this is a happy school, a haven which makes many of their lives bearable.'

Russell was rotating his signet ring; Cindy's little dark eyes were like those of an angry swan; Crispin, swelling like a balloon about to pop, seized the last piece of chocolate cake. Janna put her burning face in her hands. She must be dreaming.

'Janna Curtis' – Wade smiled at Janna's bowed head – 'is clearly very popular with pupils and parents for whom she appears to act as a Citizens' Advice Bureau, and by all the staff except the reactionary and the work-shy. She has also had considerable success winning over the community.'

He also praised the excellent displays in reception and on the walls and particularly the hard work and cheerful contribution of Wally and Debbie.

'I shall miss her flapjacks. The beautiful grounds are in good order,' he went on, 'although the children need a playing field.'

Everyone jumped as a football smacked the window.

Much of Wade's disapproval was reserved for the state of the buildings – one of which had collapsed on a member of the inspection team – the atrocious damp, erratic central heating and leaking roofs.

'Which leads me back to the appalling poverty of resources,' he said bleakly. 'We get the impression that both S and C Services and the county council, for some reason, have been deliberately withholding money. From the minutes, the governors appear to have been totally unsupportive to Janna Curtis' – Wade glared at Russell – 'ganging up and scapegoating her. In this they have been hugely aided by a local press so unrelentingly damaging that one might imagine conspiracy.'

As Partner gnawed on an old beef bone given him by Debbie, Ashton lost it.

'Get that bloody dog out of here.' He aimed a kick at Partner, who yelped.

Wade raised an eyebrow. 'If Larks fails,' he concluded, 'it will not be Janna Curtis's fault. As I've said, like its name, Larks is a happy place.'

Janna sat stunned, then, leaping to her feet, ran round and shook hands with a smiling Miss Spicer and Mrs Mills. She turned to Wade and, unable to stop herself, flung her arms round his neck and kissed him, leaving pink lipstick marks on both cheeks.

'Oh, thank you all, thank you, thank you,' she cried tearfully.

'Janna kissed me when we met, jumping from the chair she sat in,' sighed Wade and then beamed. 'I'm sure you want to pass on the good news to your staff,' he told her. 'I'll be sending you a full report.'

'Thanks so much.' Janna bolted, unable to face the rage of the Gang of Four, who retreated to the Evil Office to lick terrible wounds.

'Curtis clearly dropped her knickers,' said Crispin pouring four large brandies.

'I've never been so insulted in my life,' spluttered Cindy Payne. 'Can we sue?'

'I can only resign,' said Russell. 'Scapegoated indeed. That trollop.'

'You stay put,' ordered Ashton. 'We've got work to do.'

Hengist brought round two bottles of Veuve Clicquot, lit Lily of the Valley scented candles and to the accompaniment of *Capriccio* on Radio 3 gave Janna a bath.

Slowly, lingeringly, he ran soap over her breasts and up between her legs, groping and fingering, then slapped her lightly on the bottom. 'Are you going to be good tonight?'

After he'd dried her, they collapsed in front of the sitting-room fire, made all the more cosy by the relentless patter of the rain outside.

'I cannot believe it,' sighed Janna. 'Wade's looks went everywhere and he seemed to like what e'er he looked on.'

'Your Ofsteady boyfriend, clearly a man of discernment,' said Hengist.

'He virtually accused S and C of malpractice. Cindy looked so pained, Crispin misery-ate most of Debbie's chocolate cake and Ashton went totally silent, but his eyes . . .' Janna shuddered. 'Then he kicked Partner. Spicer was so nice in the end and Wade – well!'

'You bewitched him,' said Hengist.

Pushing her back on the fluffy rug, he ran his tongue along the tender undersides of her breasts, but Janna couldn't get into the mood for sex.

'He loved me for the dangers I had passed,' she murmured, echoing Othello. 'And I loved him that he did pity me. This is the only witchcraft I have used. He realized I'd been scapegoated.'

'I wish you wouldn't butcher a perfectly good noun,' sighed Hengist. 'Scapegoated is worse than showcase.'

'It was the scapegoat curry wot did it,' giggled Janna, 'and probably Sally's good-luck card. I feel so guilty.'

'No you don't,' said Hengist, who was bored with Ofsted. He was due at dinner five minutes ago, was getting a reputation for lateness, and wanted sex now. As if in sympathy, the rain was drumming its fingers on the window. Throwing a log on the fire, which put up a shower of orange sparks, he took Janna's ankles and parted them like scissors, then kissed his way up her warm, scented, freckled thighs.

He loved it when she went quiet, but, surprised by her lack of response – by now she should be writhing, gasping and growing damp – he looked up. She'd fallen asleep.

72

The rage and humiliation of Ashton and Crispin knew no bounds. Ashton, despite his soft features, his lisp and his pretty hands, was a thug who bullied Crispin as relentlessly as everyone else.

'I want evidence to get wid of Janna Curtis,' he ordered his deputy the following morning. 'I don't want her or Larks bouncing back.'

Janna's and Larks's euphoria over Ofsted had been sharply terminated the following week by a couple of knifings in the Shakespeare Estate and a horrific sex murder just over the border in nearby Rutminster. Bethany Watson, the sweetest ten-year-old, had been raped, strangled, then chucked under a pile of rotting hay in a cow byre, leaving a devastated and terrified community. Police were conducting house-to-house searches. Hordes of media hung around, scathingly referring to Larks as 'the Shakespeare Estate sink school'.

Larks mothers were increasingly jittery about their children having to walk home on increasingly dark evenings, because the bus stop had been moved. There were sightings of prowlers everywhere.

Chief Inspector Gablecross had been seconded to Rutminster to lead the investigation. Earlier in the term he had instructed one of his junior officers, PC Cuthbert, to keep an eye on Larks and to break up fights in the playground or at going-home time, when tensions grew high.

PC Cuthbert, despite his blond curls and fresh face, was tough, ambitious, zero-tolerant and determined to rid the town of crime. Influenced by Tim Gablecross and his wife Mags, he was unusual among his colleagues in that he liked Larks kids and felt they had a raw deal. His presence had been a definite plus.

Another plus of the term had been Lily's lectures to the newly formed Wildlife Club. Frantic not to let S and C sell off any part of Larks's beautiful land, Janna had been determined to establish them as a wildlife sanctuary and had been much heartened by Wade Hargreaves's approval.

Lily would arrive with a bootful of plum jam dough-nuts and ancient binoculars weighed down with Ascot, Kempton and Goodwood labels and bear the Wildlife Club off on rambles round the grounds, identifying coloured leaves falling from the trees and birds that flocked to the bird table.

They had also sighted roe deer, muntjac, squirrels, rabbits, several foxes and, on a very mild afternoon, an adder asleep on a sunlit pile of leaves, which provoked screams of terror from the children and Monster into picking up a branch.

'Don't hurt him,' Lily had cried. 'Adders are a pro-tected species.'

'His parents must've had unprotected sex to pro-duce him,' observed Feral. 'Nasty killing machine.'

'They ought to practise safe sex,' said Kylie, 'then they wouldn't produce any more babies.'

'Unlike you,' said Johnnie Fowler.

The adder had retreated into the blond grasses.

The pond had also become a focus of interest. The children loved swaying across Wally's narrow bridge to the island on which stood a pale blue duck house, surrounded by willows and white poplars garlanded with brambles and wild roses.

Here, to Lily's great excitement, they sighted a greyish-brown creature covered in red warts, which turned out to be a very rare natterjack toad.

'Looks like somefing the witches'd cook wiv in *Macbeth*,' said Pearl.

'They probably did.' Lily bent down to admire the toad's bright green eyes. 'Natterjacks weren't protected in those days. You must take a photograph, Graffi. Thank you,' she added, as Feral hoisted her to her feet.

Partner, who was devoted to Lily, always accompanied them on these jaunts. The Wildlife Club adored them because Lily was easily distracted into telling them stories about her days in the Wrens, the exotic places she'd visited with her late husband the ambassador and about her wild nieces and nephews who were mostly artists.

The children had instantly taken to Lily because of her genuine kindness, sense of fun and her friendship with Feral who, now her lawn no longer needed mowing, was chopping logs, bringing in coal and sharing spliffs and a passion for Arsenal.

Feral would call her on one of his stolen mobiles: ''Lo, Lily, how yer doin', man?' and chat for hours about Sol and Thierry's latest exploits. Lily had started a scrapbook of Arsenal cuttings and encouraged Feral to practise and play as much as possible. Both were secretly very proud of this friendship.

It was Sam Spink, discovering Lily was being paid forty pounds in cash per nature ramble out of the school tin, who predictably sneaked to Ashton Douglas that Lily was entering the school when she hadn't been cleared by the Criminal Records Bureau to work with children.

Ashton promptly banned Lily from Larks on the very November day when a contingent from Bagley Hall was coming over to take part in a ramble. With the honour of Larks at stake, Lily had done a huge amount of cooking, and was understandably upset.

'Hardly likely at my age to jump on children in broad daylight.'

'Quite right,' agreed Johnnie Fowler. 'Lily's too old to be a kiddy-fiddler.'

'We want Lily,' chorused the Wildlife Club.

But S and C were adamant.

'When it's a question of children's safety . . .' Ashton told an enraged Janna. 'Can't think how it's gone on so long.'

'Can't be too careful,' said Sam Spink sanctimoniously.

'Sneak,' hissed Janna.

As a result No-Joke Joan stepped in to lead the ramble.

'Gratifying to have a committed professional,' enthused Chally. 'Joan is a formidable biologist.'

Joan, who'd been regaled with horror stories and instructed to spy by Alex Bruce, was curious to have a look at Larks.

Janna would have fought harder for Lily if she hadn't been besieged by parents frantic about the Rutshire prowler. Yesterday morning Chantal had rung in to report that Kylie Rose was too stressed to come in having caught sight of a suspicious bearded character in a flat cap and dark glasses photographing girls in the playground. Later in the day, three of Year Seven complained they'd seen a bearded prowler lurking between the pond and the car park. Two of the asylum-seekers from Year Eight claimed with graphic mime the same prowler had been flashing on Smokers' Bank.

Today, sightings were coming in thick and fast. What was Janna doing to safeguard the kids, demanded Kitten's mother. Chantal Peck rang to say that, like the little soldier she was, Kylie would be coming in because she didn't want to miss lessons. Or Jack Waterlane due from Bagley, thought Janna sourly.

Stormin' Norman made the next call. Did Janna realize kiddy-fiddlers went both ways and what provision had she made to protect Martin. Janna had just put the phone down when a sobbing Pearl barged in in a bloodstained shirt, having cut herself.

'My mum must be the only mum at Larks so unconcerned about her kid she hasn't phoned in to make a fuss.'

'Oh Pearl,' sighed Janna, getting out her first-aid kit.

It would need more than Dettol and plaster to heal Pearl.

In assembly, Janna tried to calm everyone's fears. 'When you're terrified, you sometimes see people who aren't there.'

'I saw him, miss, I saw his knife,' came cries from all over the hall.

'He's got a beard and a big red willy wiv a purple knob on.'

'That's enough, Kitten. Make sure you go round in groups of three or four, and never walk home alone.'

'No one wants to walk with me any more,' sobbed Pearl.

'Oh, shut up,' snapped Kitten, throwing a hymn book at her.

Pearl was about to leap on Kitten, but, distracted by Janna's news that good-looking PC Cuthbert would be along soon, she belted off to do her face.

It was a damp, cheerless day. Trees wrapped thick grey mist round their shoulders to protect their last leaves; crows cawed morosely; any minute Dracula's carriage would rumble up the drive.

Joan, as if warding off the powers of darkness, rolled up in a calf-length Barbour, lace-up khaki gumboots and a sombrero worn over a headscarf, so only the lower half of her disapproving brick-red face was visible.

'Like a rubber fetishist's daydream,' muttered Wally.

Joan was accompanied by a giggling Amber, Milly

and Jade, a sneering Boffin, a very nervous Primrose Duddon, quivering like a nun entering a brothel, the Chinless Wanderers, armed with hipflasks, and the Cosmonaughties, who had all brought wads of green-backs to purchase drugs from the pushers who only deserted the gates if PC Cuthbert hove in sight.

'Why hasn't Paris come?' wailed Larks.

'He had double Latin,' explained Amber.

'Oh, did he now,' mocked Monster. 'How fritefly posh.'

'Watch it.' Feral bounced his football fractionally faster, then, turning to Amber: 'You're looking good.'

'Almost as good as you,' murmured Amber.

'Why, you're hunkier than ever,' said Milly, hugging Graffi.

'Make sure the students keep away from the bushes,' Chally advised Joan.

Aysha, who had been worried Xav would think her ugly because she had circles under her eyes from not being able to sleep for excitement about seeing him, was devastated when he didn't turn up, although she'd probably have been too shy to speak to him.

'I want some of Lily's fruit cake,' grumbled Rocky.

'You've just had lunch, young man,' reproved Joan bossily, then, blowing her whistle, set off into the mist.

Noticing Cosmo was as fatally glamorous as ever in his astrakhan coat, Pearl couldn't resist trying to attract his attention.

'I saw the prowler yesterday. I was having a quick tinkle in the bushes, and looking round saw his long lens pointing up my bum.'

'Good thing it were only his lens,' leered Monster.

'He was horrible with a flat cap and a perv's beard and shades.' Pearl was famous for exaggeration, but as the mist thickened, everyone shivered and her words gave Milly the excuse to edge near Graffi, and Amber to sidle up to Feral, and Jack to put an arm round Kylie's shoulders. After a cold night, leaves were falling in their thousands, descending without a fight to mould and enrich the earth below.

Joan strode ahead, pointing out different species.

'Look at *Hedera helix*, commonly known as ivy, its little yellow flowers a last feast for the insects. Listen to them humming: hummmm,' she went.

'I want a doughnut,' grumbled Monster. 'Lily brings doughnuts 'n' fudge 'n' chocolate cake.'

Joan turned on him disapprovingly, 'If you want to avoid obesity, young man, you should stop eating between meals.'

'That's an affront to my human dignity,' spluttered Monster, reaching for his mobile. 'I'm telling my mum.'

On Wildlife Club days, feeding the birds was always saved until the rambling party reached the bird table.

Aysha opened the tin, tipping out stale cake, pastry crusts, bacon and birdseed, as the others filled up the nets with nuts.

'Christ, I'm starved,' grumbled Feral, whipping a piece of sponge cake. 'I missed lunch, 'spectin' Lily's doughnuts.' He glared at Joan.

As the rambling party retreated, sharing Lily's binoculars, the birds began to fly in.

'That's a fieldfare,' called out Joan. 'Listen to his cry.' She went into a series of jerky, nervous whistles. 'And here's the redwing, tirra lira, tirra lira, whit, whit. Redwings come south from colder climes. At this time chaffinches and lapwings go round in flocks, you can recognize the lapwing, tirra lira, whoop whoop. There's no need to laugh, Feral Jackson, must you mock everything?'

'Cockadoodle do,' murmured Graffi, sliding his hands inside Milly's fleece.

'Robin's still singing his rich little song.' Putting on a special face, Joan went into another frenzy of whistling and trilling, which had everyone holding their own or each other's sides. Jack and Kylie vanished into the bushes.

'I want a doughnut,' moaned Rocky.

'This is the mating call of the Feral Jackson.' Amber gave three wolf whistles.

'Don't be silly, Amber. Robin will fight over his little bit of garden.'

'Like I'd fight over you,' whispered Graffi. 'You are so beautiful,' he added as he drew Milly into a clump of laurels.

As Joan peered into some long grass, Lando offered Pearl a slug of brandy.

'How's Paris?' she asked.

'Better,' drawled Lando, 'although he can still be moody and aggressive.'

'Note the beech leaves shrivelling.' Joan was pointing in all directions. 'And evergreens in their dark dress like winter furniture: yews, bay trees and over there a Lawson cypress.'

'Joan's getting quite carried away,' muttered Amber from behind a blackthorn copse.

'So am I,' said Feral, sliding his long fingers inside her knickers.

'All animals are preparing for winter. Snails retreat into their shells, squirrels into the trees, even this dear little dog' – Joan patted Partner, who was hanging around for Lily's fudge – 'is developing his thick winter coat.'

As they reached the pond, Joan put a big red finger to her lips:

'We might see the reedling. You can identify him by his brown back and grey and black head, and sometimes orange and lavender feathers. Reedlings are often known as bearded tits.'

'Plenty of those at Larks,' quipped Johnnie Fowler.

In front of the island, a blasted tree had collapsed, half in, half out of the water, its reflection like the strong limbs, torso and thrown-back head of a sleeping god. Above it rose poplar saplings and the whiskery grey ghosts of willowherb.

'I can see a bearded tit,' shouted Rocky.

'That's a moorhen,' reproached Joan.

'Not a hen, I know hens.'

'Note the beautiful yellow and crimson leaves of the bramble.'

'I can see a bearded tit.'

Practically garrotting Rocky, Anatole grabbed Lily's binoculars. Through the willowherb, black disks encountered black disks. Despite the lack of wind, the poplar saplings were shivering to the right of the pale blue duck house, as Anatole caught sight of a bearded figure in a flat cap.

'There is bearded tit on island,' he confirmed in his deep voice.

'It's the prowler!' screamed Pearl. 'He was looking up my panties yesterday. No one believed me.'

'Perv, perv, filthy perv!' chorused the remaining children, who were soon joined by the rest of the party spilling out of the undergrowth in various states of undress and intoxication, yelling: 'Nonce, filthy perving nonce.'

As they searched the water's edge for pebbles to hurl at him, Partner rushed forward barking furiously.

'It's the prowler, miss,' repeated Pearl.

Reluctantly, Joan moved her binoculars from the water. 'Could have sworn I saw a natterjack.' Then, focusing on the island: 'Good God, there is a bloke there.' She blew her whistle. 'Calm down, students. If need be I shall make a citizen's arrest.'

Cheered on, she strode forward. But PC Cuthbert, hell-bent on promotion, who'd been hovering behind a vast cedar, was too quick for her. Racing round the pond, swaying precariously across Wally's bridge, he caught the prowler attempting to escape the same way.

The prowler was indeed wearing a flat cap and dark glasses and sporting a bushy grey beard. Hanging from his neck, binoculars and digital camera clashed against each other. Turning, nearly falling into the pond, he regained the island, calling out:

'Good afternoon, officer, I can explain everything. I've been photographing wildlife for a book I'm writing.' He had a snuffling voice that reminded PC Cuthbert of his aunt's pekingese. Probably an asthmatic.

'May I have a look at your camera, sir?'

The prowler then tried to make a run for it, and in other circumstances would have wondered if he'd gone to heaven when this forceful young constable flung him against the duck house to rousing cheers from the bank and slapped him into handcuffs. In the struggle his beard came off to reveal an orange goatee and several chins.

'I can explain everything, officer,' repeated the prowler. 'My name is in fact Crispin Thomas, Deputy Director of S and C Services, responsible for the education of Larkshire's children.'

'Funny way of showing it, sir.'

'I am actually doing undercover research into challenging behaviour and whether the curriculum is being adhered to in Larkshire's schools. Mike Pitts and Janna Curtis can certainly confirm my identity.' His voice rose as PC Cuthbert dragged him across the bridge.

'Janna's away this afternoon,' shouted Graffi, 'and she don't owe you no favours, and if it's past dinner-time, Pittsy wouldn't know you from his Aunty Vera.'

On disembarking, PC Cuthbert removed the camera from around Crispin's neck, dislodging his flat cap and grey wig to reveal startlingly orange hair.

'That's my property,' screamed Crispin, as PC Cuthbert began looking at the camera's screen.

Clicking through, he found many shots of a questionable nature, namely Pearl urinating and displaying a lot of naked bottom; of sweet little Year Seven photographed from a low angle, their skirts flying as they leapt for a ball; of Kitten Meadows giving Johnnie Fowler a blow job; of Jack Waterlane unhooking Kylie's bra; of Monster sniffing glue; of Graffi and Feral hurling tiles off the roof last Friday and Partner trying to shag Miss Miserden's cat.

An everyday story of Larks Comp – but enough to convince PC Cuthbert he had done the right thing. He wasted no time in summoning back-up in the form of a second officer to ride in the back seat of the car with the prowler.

'I am arresting you on suspicion of taking indecent photographs of children,' he told Crispin and proceeded to caution him.

When Crispin screamed that he was a friend of PC Cuthbert's Chief Constable and would get him sacked and, despite his handcuffs, attempted to run away, Partner rushed forward and nipped him sharply on the ankle.

'Ouch,' screamed Crispin.

'Do any of you recognize this gentleman?' demanded PC Cuthbert.

'Never seen the dirty nonce before in our lives,' lied the children. 'Lock him up.'

Puce, spluttering, swearing he'd sue for wrongful arrest, Crispin was borne off to the station. Joan thought he looked vaguely familiar but it was probably only his identikit photo in the paper. He looked a thoroughly depraved individual. How splendid if he were the Rutshire prowler.

After a very unpleasant session both in a police cell and under interrogation, Crispin was released when a furious Ashton rolled up to identify and bail him.

Chief Inspector Gablecross, who'd been working on poor little Bethany's murder all day, was also able to identify him. But Crispin still had the photographs and the false identity to explain. He was not sure the police believed his excuse about an undercover operation.

Ashton was incandescent with rage. How could Crispin screw up so monumentally?

Janna was even angrier when she and Cambola got back from a meeting with the cathedral choirmaster and learnt what had happened, particularly when Hengist rang, having heard the news, and treated the whole thing as a huge joke.

'So perfect for a self-confessed wildlife photographer to cut his teeth on Larks Year Ten and Bagley Middle Fifth. Joan is thoroughly over-excited and longing to go to court.'

'Crispin was lurking on the island to give himself ammunition against us,' stormed Janna.

'I know and he could easily have caught you and me. We must be careful. See you later, darling, and don't wear any knickers.'

73

To Larks's disappointment, the *Gazette* failed to report Crispin's arrest and subsequent release; they were too busy leading on a forthcoming review of Larkshire's secondary schools. According to inside information leaked to them, Larkminster Comp was the preferred option for closure.

Janna was on to Col Peters in a trice.

'What inside information?' she yelled.

'We cannot reveal our sources,' said Col primly.

'You bloody well should when they're libellous and vindictive. You're just putting people off sending children to Larks and utterly demoralizing my parents, teachers and children.'

'Your kids can read our newspaper? They *must* be improving.'

'Bastard!' howled Janna.

As a result Larks pupils were mocked in the street by St Jimmy's, Searston Abbey and even the choir school.

'Sink school, stink school, you're closing down, you'll soon be gone.'

After Ofsted's recommendations, Janna had hoped for more funding or at least that Appletree would be rebuilt. Instead, at the end of the month, Ashton and Crispin, in a fit of spite, ordered Appletree to be boarded up and its science, D and T and music departments to be relocated to the main building. This not only devastated the teachers – Mr Mates had had his labs in Appletree for nearly forty years – but also the pupils, who felt less valued than ever.

When Janna complained, Ashton merely replied bitchily that with so many surplus places, Larks pupils couldn't even be filling the main building.

Hostile and bewildered, the children slipped back into their old, bad ways, particularly the Wolf Pack. Pearl was disrupting every class; Kylie was miserable and doing no work because she'd just lost a baby. Feral and Graffi were truanting and acting up. The only chemistry the latter two did for the rest of the term was to make up a paste with an ammonium triodide base. This they spread thinly over the platform in the school hall the morning Rod Hyde rolled up on a fault-finding mission and insisted on taking assembly. His pacings up and down the platform triggered off such a series of explosions that, fearing a terrorist attack, there was a stampede out of the hall. Rod, punching pupils out of the way, was at the forefront. On learning the truth, he fired off a furious email to a gratified S and C: 'This school is so dreadful, it must be closed down.'

'My Rod and staff don't comfort me,' moaned Janna as she and Hengist lay in her double bed that evening, so sated with sex they could hardly lift glasses of Hengist's Veuve Clicquot to their lips.

'I had to give Graffi and Feral a detention,' she went on, 'but I had great difficulty not laughing. Pity it didn't blow Rod up. Where are you supposed to be?' she asked.

'Dining with some prep-school heads. The things I do to fill up my school.'

Tomorrow he and Sally were taking Randal and Mrs Walton to the ballet in Paris and a party at the British Embassy afterwards. Clinton and Hillary and a host of luminaries were expected.

'I have to ensure Randal meets everyone, he is such a star-fucker. He won't shut up until I nail down the poor dear Queen to open his bloody science block.'

'I'm the one who needs a science block. How's he getting on with Mrs Walton?'

'Moved her into a penthouse flat and picking up her bills, so her spirits will be lifted as well as her body.'

'Improving on previous bust,' giggled Janna.

'God, I'm going to miss you,' groaned Hengist as Janna crawled down, trickling champagne over his cock before sucking it off.

Janna was ashamed how her love affaire with Hengist insulated her at least momentarily against the horrors of Larks. Nor, she comforted herself, was any school with such a glowing Ofsted report likely to be closed down.

The morning after Hengist had left for Paris, she was horrified to see Alex Bruce, in a tracksuit, jogging up the drive on a courtesy visit.

'Thought your Year Ten bods might profit from some chemistry coaching' – Alex vigorously polished his spectacles – 'now they've started their GCSE syllabus.'

But when he insisted Year Ten remove their coats and baseball caps, spit out their chewing gum and sit at their desks rather than on top of them, they started pelting him with rulers, rubbers and pencil boxes. Then Johnnie Fowler picked up a brick and, pretending it was a grenade, lobbed it at Alex.

'Sending him belting down the drive,' Janna told Hengist when he rang that evening.

'Already training for the next steeplechase,' sighed Hengist.

'The children can't stand him.'

Nor could Alex stand them and wrote an even more damning report to S and C than Rod Hyde.

After that they were into the Christmas frenzy of reports, school plays, end-of-term parties, carol concerts and, apart from an official Christmas card, Janna didn't hear from S and C until January.

It was during mocks, whilst she was appreciating the vast amount of work needed to be put in by Year Eleven before May in order to boost Larks's place in the league tables, that a very amicable letter arrived from Ashton.

In it he wished her a very happy New Year and asked if, after school on 4 February, he could visit Larks.

'At last,' Janna told a staff meeting joyfully, 'S and C have responded to our Ofsted and are going to give us some funding.'

Exhorted by Janna, most of the children stopped trashing and vandalizing and pitched in to make the school look as attractive as possible. As a jokey reminder about the leaking roof, Year Eight had created a rainforest in reception. Janna also aimed to nudge Ashton about rebuilding Appletree and the labs.

The fourth of February dawned bitterly cold, with an east wind howling through every ill-fitting window.

'Pity we can't light a fire with all those DfES directives,' grumbled Rowan as she turned on the storage heater, which Emlyn had dropped in to keep Janna warm on long, late evenings. On a low table, she arranged the pansy-patterned tea set that the children had given Janna for Christmas.

Are pansies quite the right message for Ashton and Crispin? wondered Janna.

On her desk was a copy of the latest Review of Secondary Schools, packed with faulty statistics about Larks's results, attendance, surplus places and future intake. When confronted, smiley-faced Cindy Payne from the county council had airily dismissed them as typing errors, but had made no attempt to correct this publicly. Nor had the review made any mention of Larks's successful Ofsted.

'I must discuss it rationally with Ashton,' Janna told herself. 'I must not lose my temper.'

Thank God the children would be out of the building before he rolled up. There had been far too many fights recently. Many of the kids looked up at her window and waved as they set out for home. She mustn't let them down. Partner, knowing teacups led to biscuits, bustled in wagging ingratiatingly.

'You are *not* to bite Crispin,' said Janna sternly.

'They're here,' shouted Rowan. 'Are you sure you don't mind my sloping off? I must get Scarlet to the doctor.'

'I'll be fine.' Janna ran towards reception, proudly thinking what a contrast the riot of colour in every classroom made to the chill, grey, dying day outside. This was a good and thriving school.

Her first shock was that Ashton had brought Cindy Payne. Her second that they totally ignored all the effort that had been made, even the Indians, cowboys and big toothy horses Graffi had designed for Year Ten's American Wild West display, as they marched along the corridor to Janna's office.

'They've been working so hard,' she said lamely, then after a pause: 'Where's Crispin?'

'He's moved on,' said Ashton, discarding his former deputy as casually as he whipped off an exquisite dark blue cashmere overcoat and palest pink scarf, dropping them over a chair. A pink silk bow tie enlivened a waisted pale grey suit and silver-grey shirt. As usual, he'd drenched himself in sweet, suffocating scent as if to ward off the fetid air of Larks.

Cindy today had matched a red nose and woolly flowerpot hat to the inevitable scarlet trouser suit. But the effect was not one of cheer. Her round face had the relentless jollity of a sister in a ward of terminally ill geriatrics, but her little eyes, like Ashton's, were as cold as the day.

'Those storage heaters are very dear to run,' she said disapprovingly.

'They keep me warm at night when the central heating goes off,' snapped Janna. 'Remembering how saunaed you are at S and C, I didn't want you to catch cold.'

Stop bitching, Janna, she told herself.

Cindy's smile became more fixed, then her face really lit up as Debbie arrived with tea, which included egg sandwiches and a newly baked batch of shortbread:

'Hello, Debs! You do spoil us, what a wonderful spread.'

'What a feast,' said Ashton heartily.

'Shall I be mother?' asked Cindy, flopping onto the sofa, narrowly missing Partner who retreated sourly to Janna's knee. 'I still haven't taken off that half-stone I put on over the festive season, but I won't be able to resist Debs's legendary shortbread.'

Ashton, with an equally greedy expression on his face, was gazing at a blow-up of Paris playing Romeo.

'He got into twouble knocking out a wef last term. Old habits die hard, I suppose.'

'He's playing regularly for the Colts,' said Janna sharply.

'Don't be so defensive,' teased Cindy, hiding the pansies on hers and Ashton's plates with sandwiches. 'A sarnie for you, Janna?'

'I'm OK, thanks.'

Picking up his plate, Ashton moved on to last summer's photograph of the whole school (except for Paris, he noticed, who had probably gone off joy-riding on trains by then). But there was Paris's alter ego, Feral Jackson, another beauty, clutching his football. All the children and teachers were laughing with Janna in the middle with that blasted dog on her knee.

'Nice one of Debs,' he said idly. 'Excellent sandwiches. She's one person who won't have any difficulty getting another job.' Then, as Janna looked up, startled: 'There's weally no easy way to say this, but I'm afwaid Larks is scheduled for closure at the end of the summer term.'

Partner squeaked as Janna's stroking hand clenched on his shoulder. She felt as though she'd stepped back off a cliff with a bullet straight between her eyes.

'But you haven't even seen over it,' she whispered. 'We've spent days making it look lovely.'

'We don't need to see over a school to close it down.'

'But why?' stammered Janna.

'Do you really need us to tell you?' Ashton idly added sweetener to his tea and joined Cindy on the sofa. 'The figures speak for themselves.'

'We had a wonderful Ofsted.'

'The most wonderful Ofsted in the world can't change the fact that you have four hundred and fifty, probably four hundred by now, students wattling around in a building meant for twelve hundred. Your wesults are dreadful, truancy and vandalism are sky high.'

'The latest Review of Secondary Schools was rigged.' Janna could hardly speak through her stiff lips. 'All the figures were wrong and you averaged them over four years, so of course no improvement was discernible. You said they were typing errors, but you never publicly corrected them. We were doing fine until you changed the bus routes and leaked that rumour about Larks being targeted for closure back in November. Why didn't you hang a plague sign over the school gates?'

'You'll have a chance to appeal,' said Cindy cosily, helping herself to two pieces of shortbread. 'My word, these are good; Debbie really is a treasure. We always put our decisions for closure up for public consultation.' At Janna's blank look she added, 'We give people a chance to express their views – public meetings, letters of support, etc. – then in May, the council cabinet will meet to examine these views and put forward recommendations to the Larkshire Schools Organization Committee.'

'If any of their five members vote against closure,' said Ashton, also helping himself to shortbread, 'it'll go to adjudication in the autumn.'

'Unlikely, as you've no doubt got the committee sewn up,' accused Janna.

She looked at the trees outside, disappearing into the twilight, like her school. She was shaking so violently that Partner jumped down and, unnoticed, took refuge on Ashton's navy blue coat.

'Ever since I've been here,' she said bleakly, 'I've battled against a disaffected governing body, a totally uncooperative privatized LEA and a county council who won't give me a penny and who are in league with a vindictive local press.'

'You're making dangerous accusations,' said Ashton sharply.

'Ofsted said exactly the same thing. They knew we were capable of improving if we were given the chance. What about my children?' Janna had a sudden vision of every one of them drowning before her eyes. 'You can't close Larks down. How could anyone in S and C understand? You don't give a toss about continuity. You all move on, like Crispin, if things get rough. What about my teachers? They've made such sacrifices and worked so hard.'

'They'll be wing-fenced,' said Ashton. 'So many have left already; if any jobs are advertised in the county, they'll get first option.'

'Doesn't mean they'll get the job, now they've been tarnished with working at Larks.'

'Is it your career you're worried about?' asked Cindy as if she were dictating to a half-wit secretary. 'You're not old, you'll get plenty of job offers.'

Ashton, who'd been examining his nails, stretched out and selected a nail file from Janna's blue mug crammed with pens.

'Do drink up your tea,' urged Cindy.

Picking up the sugar bowl, Janna emptied it into her

cup, then, realizing what she'd done, let the bowl slip from her fingers, so it crashed down onto her cup, smashing them both, spilling tea everywhere.

'Years Ten and Eleven gave me this tea set for Christmas,' she said in a strange, high voice. 'Oh, fuck off, Partner,' she screamed as he leapt off Ashton's coat and tried to lick up the tea.

'There, there,' said Cindy, 'I'm sure that bowl can be mended.'

'But my school can't,' yelled Janna, bursting into tears.

'I know it's a shock when a school closes down.' Cindy struggled to her feet. 'Have you got a friend to come and be with you?'

'Don't fucking patronize me. If you think I'm giving up Larks without a fight . . .' Dropping to the floor, Janna grabbed Ashton's scarf to mop up the tea.

'Give me that.' Ashton seized it back. He was even less pleased to see his coat covered in Partner's hairs. 'Twy not to be gwatuitously unpleasant, Janna,' he continued smoothly, 'you're suffering from hurt pride. I can only advise you to go gwacefully.'

Seeing the murderous expression on Janna's face as her hand grabbed the handle of the teapot, Cindy said hastily:

'We can show ourselves out. Don't get too stressed. I can recommend an excellent counsellor.'

'Anything's better than a county councillor, you fat cow,' shrieked Janna, 'they kill schools.'

'Dear, dear, dear,' said Ashton as they hastened out into the drizzle, 'how did that malevolent hysteric ever get a job running a school? Nothing has ever convinced me more of the rightness of our decision.'

'Thank goodness Alex Bruce and Rod Hyde put in such negative reports.' Cindy tugged her red wool hat over her ears. 'I don't anticipate much opposition, do you?'

'I hope not. Hengist Brett-Taylor might act up; he always had a *tendresse* for little Miss Curtis.'

'But he's so tied up in politics. At least Cavendish Plaza and Haut Larkminster will be on our side. Closing down schools causes such a rumpus. We must rush it through as soon as possible.'

After all, one didn't want to lose one's seat on the county council or all that kudos and fat expenses.

They jumped as a window was flung open.

'You won't get away with this, you murderers!'

Two minutes later Janna ran out to a deserted car park, crying uncontrollably: 'My teachers, my children.'

A hundred yards beyond the school gate, she had to leap out of her car and throw up, mostly bile, on the pavement outside the Ghost and Castle.

'Drunk at this hour . . .' chuntered a couple disappearing into the saloon bar.

Only then did Janna realize she'd left Partner locked in her office.

'I'm so sorry,' she sobbed as she recovered him.

But as he snuggled across her thighs, attempting to be the seatbelt she had forgotten to fasten, all she could think was: My career is over. In Yorkshire, they'll say I failed, failed, failed.

She was overwhelmed by a stench of burning wax. Like Icarus, she had flown too near the sun.

74

By contrast, Brigadier Woodford had had such a wonderful piece of news, he had splashed out on two bottles of champagne (Lily's favourite drink, which she could no longer afford), two large cartons of potted shrimps, a beef and ale pie, strawberries and an even larger carton of double cream, and taken them over to Lily's to celebrate.

Lily had lit a fire and they were sitting comfortably on Lily's shabby sofa with the vast fluffy black and white General between them, accidentally brushing hands as they both simultaneously stroked him. Lily had rescued some poor crocuses trampled on the verge outside and, in a white vase in the warmth of the room, they had expanded like purple striped umbrellas with little orange handles. The Brigadier felt his heart expanding like the crocuses.

'God I miss champagne, this is such a treat,' said Lily happily. 'Now, what are we celebrating?'

'Rupert's offered me my own programme. It's going to be called *Buffers*. Each week we'll take a war or campaign in history and get four so-called experts or "old buffers", retired generals and admirals, to sit round a table having frightful rows about strategy and blame. I've got to chair it.'

The genuine delight on Lily's face nearly gave the Brigadier the courage to kiss her.

'How clever of Rupert! You're going to be a star, Christian.'

'Rupert wants to start with twelve programmes. We have to do something called a pilot first, which sounds more like the RAF. You'll have to come on it to add some glamour and talk about the Wrens.' He emptied the bottle into their glasses.

'D'you think we can manage a second?'

'Certainly, with a celebration like this.' As Lily leant across General and gave the Brigadier a peck on the cheek, he had a longing to kiss her passionately on the lips, but was worried it might dislodge his bridge. It was such a long time since he'd made a pass.

'If the pilot works, Rupert wants his father Eddie, who was in the Blues, to be one of the regulars. Said it might stop Eddie tapping him for money if he got an income from television. Frightfully amusing chap, Eddie, thought the programme was going to be called *Buggers*.'

'Probably be even more successful,' said Lily dryly.

Christian guffawed; then, because he didn't feel it was boasting with Lily, 'The Tories have asked me to open their Easter Fair. GMTV want me to go up to London to talk about the possibility of war in the Gulf and Larkminster Rovers wrote asking me to go on their board. I don't know much about soccer.'

'Feral and I will teach you,' said Lily. 'When you score a goal you have to slide to the ground and bare your breast by lifting up and shaking the front of your shirt.'

'Much more excitin' if you did,' snorted the Brigadier. As he heaved himself up to fetch another bottle, he noticed how empty the fridge was except for the strawberries and cream, and also that that dear little watercolour of the church at Limesbridge where Lily grew up was missing. He hated Lily having to sell things. What heaven if they could be together like this every night. Lily could have an 'old age serene and bright, And lovely as a Lapland night'.

General the cat opened a disapproving yellow eye but didn't shift as the cork flew across the room to the accompaniment of a hammering on the front door.

'Oh hell,' said Lily, 'let's pretend we're out.'

But there was no escape as Janna barged in, followed by Partner; nor was there any word of apology as she collapsed onto the dark blue velvet chair by the fire, shaking uncontrollably, her reddened eyes wide and staring.

'Oh Lily, oh Lily.'

'You poor child, whatever's the matter? Give her a drink, Christian.'

'They're closing my school down.'

'They can't do that.'

'They can, they can! What's going to happen to my children and my teachers and Wally?'

'That's rotten luck,' said the Brigadier, handing her a glass. 'You must fight it.'

'I know, but I don't know how to. I've been fighting since I took over.' Janna gulped down half the champagne and carried on talking.

Lily, of course, insisted she stay to supper, and divided the potted shrimps and the beef and ale pie for two into three, and buttered a lot of brown bread.

Christian tried not to feel irritated when Janna drank most of the remaining champagne but, incapable of eating, fed all her pie to Partner.

'I forgot to get him any food on the way home, and I left him shut in my office, I'm coming apart at the seams, I've got to be strong for the children. Larks is the only security they know.' She started to cry again. Partner, his front paws on her knees, tried to stem her tears with a beef-flavoured tongue.

'We'll all fight,' promised Lily. 'Hengist will kick up a hell of a rumpus, and so will Rupert. And while my nephew Jupiter isn't my favourite person, he's

618

excellent at putting the jackboot in – anything to discredit Cindy Payne and New Labour.'

'I called her a fat cow.' Janna was twisting a thread hanging out of Lily's green velvet chair cover so violently it broke off and a mass of kapok billowed out. 'Oh God, I'm sorry.'

Whatever happened to stiff upper lips, thought the Brigadier as Janna helped herself to the last of the champagne.

'I've let so many people down.' She sobbed. 'People like Sophy Belvedon and the new head of D and T who've got children and massive mortgages because they've specially bought houses in the area. I feel like a captain who's steered his great battleship onto the rocks.'

Lily patted Janna's shoulder. 'No one could have fought harder.'

The Brigadier felt ashamed. It was only because he'd so wanted to be alone with Lily.

'Oh God, I must tell Russell,' exclaimed Janna. 'So many people to tell – the children are going to be the worst. Can I use your phone?'

Her shaking hand kept misdialling Russell's number. She got the vicar and the local greengrocer before she finally reached him.

'I heard, and I'm not surprised,' he said heavily. 'I gather you were extremely offensive to Cindy when she tried to be supportive. Why must you always construe help as criticism?'

'Their help is like snake venom,' shouted Janna and hung up.

'He knew,' she said flatly. 'Ashton and Cindy must have been straight on to him.'

'I smell collusion,' said Lily. 'First, you must appoint Dora as your press officer.'

Next morning Janna had the nightmare of breaking the news to the staff, taking an extended lunch hour, gathering them into the staffroom, feeling utterly sick at the sight of their stunned faces.

'It can't be true,' muttered Lydia.

Basket burst into tears. 'I'll never get another job.'

'We're going to fight it, of course,' said Janna quickly. 'We've got two months to register protest.'

'It wasn't unexpected,' said Mike Pitts. 'When will the axe fall?'

'Ashton said the end of the summer term, but that's only a few months away.' Janna looked bewildered. 'He must mean summer two thousand and four, and that's only if the Schools Organization Committee are all in favour.'

But when she dialled Ashton to check, he assured her if the Schools Organization Committee were unanimous, Larks would close in summer 2003.

'You can't close it so soon. You particularly can't do that to Year Ten,' whispered Janna in horror, remembering how she'd walked out on her GCSE classes at Redfords. 'Year Eleven will be OK. They'll take their exams in May and we'll be able to see them through before we close down.'

Outside she could see the children in the playground. Graffi and Feral were idly kicking a ball around; Pearl and Kylie were reading the same magazine, stamping their feet to keep warm. All of them were perplexed by their extended lunch hour and, aware some storm was brewing, gathering in edgy little groups, glancing constantly up at her window. Are we in more trouble?

'We can't abandon Year Ten,' she told Ashton firmly. 'What about Aysha and Graffi and Kitten and Johnnie and Feral and Monster, they'll never get a job and out of this hell if they don't get any qualifications.'

'Your beloved Wolf Pack,' drawled Ashton.

'And at least fifty others.'

'Hardly the A team.'

'They bloody are!' yelled Janna, turning and catching Chally raising an eyebrow at Mike Pitts.

'They've been totally disrupted by all the rumour and speculation about closure,' she went on furiously, 'and the incessant bitching of other schools. They haven't completed any coursework, and they'll be chucked out at the end of the summer term into an unfamiliar school for the second year of their course. It's not bloody fair.'

'If their last SATs were anything to go by,' snapped Ashton, 'they're not likely to get any gwades anyway. Straight Us, I'd say.'

'They've got to be given a chance.'

'And you'll have a chance to air your views at the public meeting.'

'I'm afraid it's summer 2003,' she told the staff grimly, 'so we've really got a fight on our hands.'

If anything convinced her of the need to fight it was the anguish and terror of the children. Pearl, sobbing that she'd thought they'd have five terms more; an inconsolable grey-faced Danijela: 'I is only happy with you, this is my home.' 'Who will write our CVs and sign our driving licences,' wailed Year Eleven.

The boys reacted with violence, hurling more tiles off the roof, tearing off door handles, kicking over desks, trashing classrooms; soon they wouldn't have a school to close down. The *Gazette* and the television cameras were soon outside the door. The staff, panicking about lost jobs, gathered in corners, whispering and afraid, many of them blaming Janna.

But even the darkest cloud has a silver lining.

'Can I have a word?' demanded Chally later in the day, shutting Janna's door behind her and rearranging a crimson-leafed scarf before announcing she was off to take up a deputy head's post at St Jimmy's.

'Congratulations.' Janna tried not to display her delight. 'I'm really pleased for you. You'll find it inspirational working with Rod Hyde. Is one of his Senior Management Team leaving?'

'Not that I know of. They need an extra pair of capable hands. St Jimmy's is so over-subscribed.'

Probably soon with an influx of the brightest children from Larks, thought Janna in outrage, but at least I won't have to suck up to you any more, you old bat.

'Every Chally shall be exalted,' sang Cambola when Janna pulled her and Mags into her office to tell them.

'Do you think there's any hope she'll be one of those high fliers who whisks all her key people away with her?' asked Mags.

'What bliss if she took Spink, Skunk, Pittsy, Robbie and Basket,' sighed Janna.

Next moment, a red-eyed Rowan put her dark head round the door. 'Hengist Brett-Taylor on the line, Janna.'

'That should cheer up the poor little duck,' whispered Mags as she and Cambola made themselves scarce.

'Darling, darling!' Hengist was ringing from Brussels. 'I only just heard from Jupiter. Lily Hamilton rang him. She must feel really strongly; first time she's spoken to him since he threw her out of her house. God, I'm sorry, are you OK?'

'Fine.' Janna battled not to cry. 'At least Chalford's just announced she's leaving to be deputy head at St Jimmy's.'

'Two wrongs have certainly made a right there.'

'And when I called Russell last night, an hour after I knew, he'd already been told.'

'Sounds like conspiracy,' Hengist echoed Lily, 'what fun we're going to have exposing them. Don't worry, darling.'

'How can I not? What will happen to my children?'

'I'm sure Bagley can accommodate any of your Year Tens in with a shout. I'd love to have Graffi and Feral and Aysha and mouthy Pearl.' Then, when Janna didn't react: 'You could join Bagley and keep an eye on them. You're always saying how you miss teaching, and I could see more of you.' His voice had grown softer, more husky.

'How can you trivialize such a terrible thing, I'd never teach in an independent,' yelled Janna. 'You've already stolen my teachers, my brightest pupil and my heart, you're not taking anything else,' and she slammed down the receiver.

To her dismay, Hengist didn't ring back. Was she misconstruing genuine help as criticism again?

Two days later she got a letter from Sally.

'Hengist has told me. What a dreadful thing to happen. I'm so sorry. We must save Larks. Hengist has got something up his sleeve.'

75

Affection had grown so strongly between Bagley and Larks that when news of the closure hit the press, mostly via Dora, both schools joined forces to create an uproar.

Graffi's poignant design of a lark escaping from a vicious black cat, with the slogan 'Larks will survive', was soon appearing on balloons, stickers, posters, waving placards and, indeed, scrawled on walls all over Larkminster.

Hengist, to Alex Bruce's fury, blithely encouraged his pupils to join the public protests and marches against both the closure of Larks and the imminent war in Iraq, so they seemed hardly ever in school.

'We bonded with Larks in good times, sir, we're not going to desert them in bad times,' Lando told Alex sanctimoniously.

'But you've got double maths.'

'I don't care,' said Lando, and he raced off to join Graffi and Johnnie on the picket line.

Save our school, boom, boom, boom, save our school, boom, boom, boom, it was so much more fun than lessons.

Tarquin Courtney was only too happy ferrying pickets around in his Porsche. Ashton was demented, particularly when someone spray-painted ascending larks all over his pretty Regency house in the Close.

Lily and the Brigadier were also in the thick of things. In March, to the horror of her nephew Jupiter, Lily whacked a Lib Dem councillor over the head with her placard. Luckily the officer poised to arrest her was PC Cuthbert, who promptly let her off.

Together, she and the Brigadier distracted themselves from the horrors of the war and the stock market by going on marches. Save our school, boom, boom, boom. 'Why does my heart go boom, boom, boom,' sang the Brigadier. The pilot of *Buffers* had been such a resounding success, his presence at Larks demos added considerable gravitas.

Emlyn added physical weight. With Attila the Hunk on the picket line, S and C heavies melted away. With war in Iraq seemingly inevitable, Emlyn was worried sick about Oriana in Baghdad, but he hid it well. He made all his history pupils write letters of protest to County Hall praising Larks, saying how much they'd enjoyed *Romeo and Juliet*, the field trip and the nature ramble in which an S and C executive, hell-bent on closing down Larks, was found in disguise spying in the bushes.

Only Boffin Brooks got under the wire, writing and sealing his own letter, claiming Larks was the most dreadful school he'd ever encountered.

Miss Cambola led every protest, playing 'Hark, Hark! the Lark' on her trumpet. Even Cosmo surprised everyone by proposing a concert in the water meadows near the cathedral. His mother, Dame Hermione, was a friend of the Bishop.

'What could be more lovely, my lord, than classical melodies on a warm summer evening?'

When it leaked out that Cosmo was planning to feature himself and the Cosmonaughties, belting out 'Cocks and Rubbers', among their cleaner lyrics, the Bishop's secretary slipped Cosmo a thousand pounds to go away, half of which Cosmo handed over to Larks.

Poor Feral, who never thought beyond tomorrow,

which he thought would be spent at Larks, was terrified. Even incessant Arsenal victories didn't cheer him. He laboriously made his own poster: 'Saive are Skool', which the Gazette photographed him nailing up outside Larks. The photograph appeared on the front page, with 'sp' signs in the margin and a caption: 'Another reason why Larks should close'.

Stormin' Norman started a Parents' Action Group, but as most of the action consisted of thumping other parents, it soon fizzled out.

Dora was in her element with the press ringing her every day. In addition, she bravely went from house to house collecting signatures and even organizing a car-boot sale, to which she gave many favourite toys and several of her mother's best dresses.

Paris, pretending not to be interested, read every paper and watched every bulletin. If Larks closed, Janna would leave the area and he'd never see her again. She looked so thin, pale and tense in her photographs. He ached to comfort her.

Ashton and Cindy were getting increasingly rattled. If only the Americans could bomb Larks, but with their track record, they'd probably miss and take out Cavendish Plaza and the Close instead.

As a counter measure, S and C deliberately held their first public meeting to debate Larks's fate on the far side of town on a night when Larkminster Rovers were playing at home. As a result hardly any Larks supporters showed up and instead of pleading her case quietly and reasonably, as she'd intended, a riled Janna lost her cool and a lot of support as she heckled the speakers. A dreadfully dismissive report in the *Gazette* followed.

Meanwhile, Wally with a son, Emlyn with a hoped-for future wife and Hengist and Sally with a daughter were increasingly worried that Bush and Blair would raise two fingers to the UN and plunge into war.

'It's all oil. They don't want the Russians and the French to get their hands on it,' said Hengist.

Wandering across the dry cracked pitches to the Family Tree, he fingered Oriana's carved initials on its trunk. Was she going to be taken from him like Mungo? He longed to ring Janna and find solace in her freckled arms, but he was nervous that any transgression might invoke the anger of the gods, so he walked home to Sally.

Before the second public meeting, which was to take place in late March, Hengist met Rupert and Jupiter at Jupiter's flat in Duke Street, St James's, which had a lovely view over the park lit up by white daffodils and young green willows. A pink moon on its side like a rugby ball hung above Big Ben and the Houses of Parliament. Would they suffer the same fate as the Twin Towers if Britain got into bed with the Americans? wondered Hengist.

The charming flat had once belonged to Jupiter's father, Raymond, a highly successful art dealer. Consequently, the walls were covered with wonderful pictures. On a side table was a photograph of Jupiter, his beautiful sweet-natured wife Hanna and their adorable two-and-a-half-year-old son Viridian.

'That should come in useful when we're electioneering,' said Hengist.

Jupiter, who was as pale as Rupert and Hengist were dark brown from skiing, smiled coolly.

'When are we going to war?' asked Hengist.

'Any minute, pushed as much by the unqualified encouragement of IDS as by Blair's ambition.' Jupiter glanced at his watch. 'I've got to be back in the House in an hour. Would you like a drink?'

'I'd like several,' said Hengist. 'Christ, what a day.'

Rupert looked up from the sofa and the racing pages of the *Evening Standard*. 'Oriana's fantastic on the box.'

'Isn't she? I see her face on every bulletin – so

frustrating to touch the screen not her.' For a second Hengist betrayed his desolation, then, reverting to his usual flippancy: 'I was so depressed by my own company, I made the mistake of taking Randal Stancombe for a walk down the pitches this afternoon. He showed an unhealthy interest in Badger's Retreat, but failed to notice leaves leaping out of the wild cherry, breathtaking against a navy blue sky, or the sweeps of primroses and violets. Only sees land as a way of making money.'

'I wouldn't argue with that,' said Rupert.

'Can we skip the nature notes and get on with the meeting?' said Jupiter, pouring Hengist a large whisky.

Hengist turned back from the window where he could see cranes like malignant vultures preying on the city, destroying and rebuilding everywhere.

'We've got to save Larks Comp.'

'Whatever for?' Jupiter looked amazed. 'We can't anyway, once a school's targeted for closure, it's doomed. Only point of public meetings is for the county council and S and C to pretend they've listened to people's views. Anyway,' he went on, shooting soda into his own glass, 'do we really want to antagonize Stancombe, who's good for a massive donation, in order to save a small, pretty awful school? We've also got to work with S and C.'

'You have no heart,' drawled Rupert, getting out a pen to do the quick crossword. 'Janna Curtis was rather pretty, I remember.'

'I can afford to antagonize Stancombe even less,' admitted Hengist, 'he's giving me a six-million-pound science block. But you could take him on, Rupert.'

'I don't mind. His daughter's foul to both Xav and Bianca. What's he got against Larks?'

'He wants it and the entire Shakespeare Estate razed to the ground so they don't lower the tone of his absurdly overpriced Cavendish Plaza.'

'It's the Casey Andrews sculpture in the forecourt

that should be razed,' Rupert said. 'Who was the brother of Romulus, five letters?'

'Remus,' said Hengist. 'I suspect Randal's after Larks's land. Whoever buys it, S and C and the county council will make a killing. So this meeting's the ideal opportunity to discredit both Lib Dem and Labour and make them look like heartless, unprincipled shits.'

'I like a good fight,' mused Rupert. 'Taggie and I got together when we were rushing round Gloucestershire, pitching for the Venturer franchise.'

'And Janna Curtis has been very shabbily treated,' pleaded Hengist.

Rupert glanced up, white teeth lighting his dark brown face.

'So you did get into her knickers.'

'Certainly not,' snapped Hengist. 'Caesar has to be above suspicion as well as his wife these days.'

76

The gods appeared to be on S and C's side. On the night of the second public meeting, which was held in a WI hall five miles south of Larkminster, the weeks of dry weather ended in a torrential rainstorm, which halted windscreen wipers in their tracks and turned country lanes into raging rivers.

'Larks parents and teachers'll never turn out in this,' gloated Ashton. '*EastEnders* and the war in its twelfth day will keep them safe in front of the TV. It'll be a walkover.'

He was therefore appalled on arrival to discover chairs being frantically unstacked to accommodate the crowd, a foyer reeking of drying macs and anoraks, and steaming umbrellas huddled together like coloured mushrooms at the back of the hall. The bar was already crowded out.

Emlyn and Wally, desperate to be distracted from the war, had all evening been bussing in parents from the Shakespeare Estate, bribing them with beer, wine, Dawn's hot sausage rolls on the way, and the prospect of a lift home, so they could drink themselves insensible. Stormin' Norman and Pearl's boxer dad were already well away.

They were soon joined by friends and fellow tipplers from the protest marches; Lily, the Brigadier, Ian and Patience Cartwright, whose daughter,

Sophy, would be out of work if Larks were shut down.

The Brigadier was rather shyly autographing anti-closure leaflets.

'Love your programme, Brig.'

'All that matters is that every student achieves his or her potential,' intoned Cindy Payne as she hung up her soaking wet cape. One had to have nerves of steel to close down a school.

Having heard rumours that both Randal Stancombe and Rupert Campbell-Black were expected, Cavendish Plaza wives, with streaked hair, gold jewellery and beauty department make-up, were out in force. They'd all vote for closure, as would their drenched husbands, who'd nervously left their Mercs and Porsches in the car park before scuttling through the downpour, as would a bristling posse from the Close and the older Larkminster houses.

But there was a dangerously large anti-closure contingent from Bagley: including Dora and Dicky, Bianca, Amber and Milly and the Chinless Wanderers, who, changing allegiance on another front, had become thoroughly excited at the prospect of war in Iraq and kept marching about saluting each other.

'Why aren't you in school doing your prep?' asked Cindy disapprovingly.

'Part of our citizenship course is understanding how local government works,' said Amber piously. 'Mr Brett-Taylor was very anxious we should be present.'

Fuck Hengist, thought Alex, who never swore, even mentally, except in extremis and who had just rolled up with Chally and Poppet, plus her latest baby.

Alex was stressed. Over the weekend Poppet had insisted he look after the kids while she lay outside RAF Fairford protesting against the war. Tonight she had insisted on bringing Little Gandhi and would later breastfeed him. Nothing wrong with that, but this simple act of motherhood seemed to engender such misogyny in his Bagley colleagues.

In the foyer and his father's astrakhan coat, Cosmo examined notices about singing workshops and evenings of circle dancing, as he played 'The Lark Ascending' on his violin. Not missing a trick, he watched the Great and not-so-Good: Ashton, Cindy, Russell, Chally and now Alex and Rod and their wives, drinking cheap red or white in an ante-room. Talk about a witches's coven. And what had happened to Ashton's Sancho Pansy, Crispin?

Cosmo had exchanged a soulful eye-meet with Ashton when he arrived. In front of him, on the floor, he had also placed a dark blue butcher-boy's cap to swell the fund to save Larks. He had already raised two hundred pounds, half of which he intended to keep. His mother, despite her millions, was tight with money.

Inside the hall, Cambola was cheering everyone up playing golden oldies on the tinny upright piano.

' "Night And Day",' sang the Brigadier, sweeping Lily into a quickstep.

'Who's chairing this meeting?' she asked.

'Col Peters.'

'That's totally loaded against Larks for a start; you ought to chair it, Christian. Talk of the devil.'

A hiss went round the hall as Col Peters, more toad-like than ever, put his crinkly black hair and bulging eyes round the door, then retreated to the ante-room.

Dora, meanwhile, was in her element talking on three mobiles.

'Great turnout. I'll ring you the moment it's over, Mr Dacre.'

The rain was growing more frantic, scrabbling against the windows, begging to be let in out of the storm. A shudder and hiss went through those present from the Shakespeare Estate as Uncle Harley walked in in a black fur-lined suede jacket and more jewellery than all the Cav Plaza wives put together.

'Useful if there's a power cut,' giggled Amber.

Having clocked who was present, Uncle Harley took

up his position against a side wall where he could watch both platform, hall and gallery, which was also nearly full up.

There was an equal hiss from Cav Plaza, remembering too many broken windows and missing car radios, as Feral slid in bouncing his football. He was absolutely soaked, his black curls flattened, raindrops leaping off his black lashes and running down his shining face. He had just exchanged a damp high five with Lily and the Brigadier, when Bianca, who'd specially worn a new crimson ra-ra skirt and a shocking pink fake-fur coat, leapt up and waved. It was a year since they'd danced together in *Romeo and Juliet.*

'Over here, Feral, I've kept a seat for you.'

Feral had no option; nor did he want one. Padding up the aisle, drenching people as he wriggled along the row, he dropped into the chair next to heaven.

'You're frozen,' wailed Bianca and, putting his ball under her seat, she whipped off her pink coat and wrapped it round him and everyone whooped and whistled. 'No, keep it on,' she cried, doing up the buttons.

Feral beamed.

'Suits you. Wolf in sheep's clothing,' shouted Johnnie Fowler.

Feral rolled his eyes, flung back his head and howled three times. Then he turned to Bianca. 'How yer doin'?' And he couldn't say any more, she was so adorable and gazing at him with such joy, her little shoulders hunched in ecstasy.

'When are we going to dance again?'

'Soon,' said Feral, tapping his feet as Cambola broke into a jazzed-up version of 'Hark, Hark! the Lark', because Janna was trying to slink in unobserved, aware she looked rough, ducking to avoid the exploding of flashes. Larks was about to break up for the Easter holidays and there'd been so many loose ends to tie up with children and teachers leaving, she'd had no time

633

to wash her hair, which, lank and out of condition, she'd pulled back off her pale, pinched, face. She was wearing a silk dress the colour of faded bracken and an amber necklace, both of which Hengist had given her.

But he's not coming, she thought, glancing round the hall in despair and shame that she could think of him when her school was falling round her ears.

'No comment, for the moment,' she told the reporters.

'Miss! Miss!' Pearl shot out and, dragging Janna into the Ladies, applied coral lipstick and blusher to her blanched cheeks. 'That fluorescent light really drains you.'

'It's my Jane Eyre look.'

'Triffic turnout,' said Pearl proudly. 'My boxer dad's come; he's getting pissed with Lily and the Brig.'

'Thank you, dear Pearl.' Hitching up her smile two minutes later, Janna braved the hall, moving from parents to teacher to pupil thanking, cheering, encouraging, only accepting a Perrier water so she didn't lose her rag as she had at the last meeting, before taking her seat in the second row, between Mags and Sophy Belvedon.

As the clock struck half past seven Col Peters, reluctant to wait any longer, trooped onto the platform followed by Cindy, Ashton, Russell Lambert, leading Labour and Lib Dem councillors, and the Bishop of Larkminster, whose window Feral's football had cracked. To accommodate them all, the Prussian-blue curtains on either side of the platform had to be drawn back even further.

Col was then prevented from starting by an avalanche of latecomers, starting off with Sally Brett-Taylor, who ran in wafting Jardin des Bagatelles and looking absolutely stunning in a dark blue velvet cloak over a lilac silk dress and with a rakish lilac sequinned butterfly in her gold hair.

'Looking good, Mrs B-T,' yelled Jack Waterlane to howls of laughter.

Sally smiled, then called up to Col Peters:

'So sorry for being late. Hengist'll be here in a moment.'

'Doesn't Sally look smart? Ah good, here comes Randal,' agreed the Cav Plaza wives in excitement.

They had been admired through Randal's telescope when they sunbathed topless in their gardens. Some of them had been summoned to romp in his Jacuzzi. Randal didn't want that dreadful school nearby; he'd fight their corner.

Here's Stancombe, thought the Shakespeare Estate, better not get too pissed or we might deck him.

Both factions waved sycophantically as Stancombe sauntered in flanked by heavies. He was wearing a dark brown leather jacket, black polo shirt and black cords and looked more attractive than usual, Janna decided. The flash jewellery had gone and his hair had been more becomingly cut with ragged gypsy tendrils softening his predatory face. Was this Mrs Walton's influence? Janna blushed as he caught her staring, particularly when he smiled and waved.

'Don't frat with the enemy,' hissed Mags.

'Daddy, Daddy,' shouted Jade, clambering over the seats to sit with him.

'Hi, princess.' Stancombe kissed her on the mouth.

'Yuk,' said Dora.

Col Peters had just tapped the microphone, hammer poised, when another batch of Larks parents, dug out by Emlyn and Wally, poured into the hall and were reluctantly split up into the remaining single seats.

'There's my da, hope he's sober,' prayed Graffi.

'And my mum,' said Pearl, 'hope she doesn't deck my dad, and Chantal with Kylie and Cameron an' Aysha's mum in a headscarf.'

'That's brave,' murmured Janna to Mags, 'with so much anti-Muslim feeling about.'

Hall and gallery were completely packed out; people were standing among the umbrellas at the back.

'Feral's so vain, we're going to have to gaze at his profile all evening,' Amber, who was sitting just behind him, said acidly.

For Feral was gone. He couldn't take his eyes off Bianca. As if it had a mind of its own, his hand slid into hers; he tried to retrieve it in case he was being forward, but she hung on, gripping it with a surprising strength, gently stroking his palm with little, pink-nailed fingers.

I'm dreaming, he thought, sent reeling by the sweetness of her breath, the faint tang of lily of the valley, the huge, laughing eyes with lashes even longer than his, her pink coat caressing his chin.

'I'm out of luck there,' sighed Amber. 'I'll have to revert to my unrequited passion for Attila.'

Boffin was ostentatiously reading a biography of Marie Curie.

Randal was on his mobile. He'd love to have had Ruth on his arm, but he concentrated better without her. One never knew from where trouble was coming. Rising in his seat, he located Dora taking a photograph of the Bishop. Good, she still had her untidy plaits. He couldn't see if her breasts had begun to bud, but his cock stiffened beneath the *Evening Standard.* He must ask her mother out to dinner next time Ruth was in town. Bloody hell, he'd never expected such a turnout.

Nor had Col Peters, who was prepared to wait no longer. He needed a report of the meeting in tomorrow's *Gazette*, which would be picked up by the nationals.

But in the foyer, Cosmo had launched into 'Hello, Dolly!' as Taggie Campbell-Black ran in, wide-eyed, long-legged as a colt. The fuchsia-pink cashmere shawl she'd flung over her black sequinned dress was already drenched.

That's one woman I'd like even better than Bianca, decided Cosmo.

'Thank you,' he purred as Taggie fumbled in her bag for a fiver. He'd frame it. If he landed Bianca, he could have Taggie as well.

Seeing her husband, not his greatest fan, and Hengist approaching, both in dinner jackets, Cosmo slid into a side kitchen. 'To adjust the temperature in the hall,' he read, 'turn the boiler on or off at the control panel.'

Take more than a switch to control this lot.

Rupert and Hengist were followed by Jupiter. Why's he here? wondered Cosmo. He jumped as Hengist tapped him on the shoulder and handed him a tenner. 'Can you get Mr Campbell-Black a very large whisky?'

Everyone was excited by the latest arrivals, particularly by Jupiter: that really put the evening up a rung. Whose side would he be on? He was already proving a very effective MP.

Furiously, Col Peters raised his hammer, but Hengist was lingering in the doorway, talking intently to the press, asking, no doubt, for any news on Iraq. Janna was shocked how tired he looked. But as he wandered into the hall, he seemed to shrug off his concerns and his face broke into a wicked smile.

'So sorry to hold you up, Col, Ashton, Cindy, Russell, my lord Bishop.' Mockingly Hengist nodded to each in turn. 'Evil night. Fleet's about to burst its banks and sweep S and C away. Hope you've brought your lifebelt, Ashton, you're going to need it before the evening's out. Do kick on, Col,' and, turning his broad, dinner-jacketed back, he edged along the row, shaking hands, hailing Bagley and Larks children, blowing kisses to friends, stopping to grin at Janna – 'Lovely dress, darling' – spying Poppet – 'How's little Gandhi, hope you're resting enough?' – then in a stage whisper to Jupiter, who was following him: 'She's had plenty of rest, lying down in the road to stop the B52s leaving.'

'For Christ sake, sit down,' hissed Jupiter, 'why must you deliberately wind people up?'

Bringing up the rear was Rupert, who stopped to congratulate the Brigadier on the pilot of *Buffers*: 'We got bloody good ratings. I'll ring you tomorrow.'

'Col Peters is going to have a coronary,' observed Mags.

'With any luck,' said Janna. 'Isn't it wonderful Hengist and Co. have showed up?'

Christ, that Campbell-Black/Brett-Taylor/Belvedon faction was hell, thought Emlyn. Only way to shut them up was to cut off their heads – preferably with a guillotine. Hengist was insufferable in this apparatchik-baiting mood. Bloody Hoorays, aren't we wonderful, we all know each other.

Actually the most hip Hooray was Rupert, Emlyn decided, not just because of the beauty of his still, cold toff's face or the casual elegance of his lounging body, but his total indifference to the impact he had on everyone in the room as he devoured printouts, a large whisky in one hand, the other idly caressing his wife's sweet face as they compared notes on the day. Taggie had removed her soaked shawl and was wearing his dinner jacket round her shoulders.

Even if Oriana came home safely from Baghdad, wondered Emlyn wistfully, would she ever look up at him with a quarter of Taggie's tenderness, or in the adoring way their daughter was gazing at young Feral, still wrapped in her pink fur coat.

Brought up to loathe the Tories, it confused Emlyn that, for some ulterior motive, it was Tories who were coming to Janna's aid and New Labour in their sharp suits, quite unrecognizable from his dad's beloved cloth-cap party, who'd palled up with the beige, open-toed-sandalled Lib Dems to grind the faces of the poor.

Oh God, here was Vicky, putting down her flower-festooned umbrella, rushing towards the platform:

'Col, I am so sorry, I couldn't find anywhere to park. Emlyn dear, could you find me a chair? Oh, Poppet's kept a seat for me.' As she ran along the gap between platform and audience, pausing in front of Janna: 'Jannie, I am *so* sorry it's come to this. Hello, Magsy, hello Cambola, you poor dears', Vicky was beginning to sound just like Sally. 'I'm so guilty I haven't called,' then, lowering her voice only a fraction: 'And so guilty getting out in time. What a blow too, losing darling Chally. I must find her later.'

'Bitch,' exploded Sophy Belvedon, 'thank God she left before I arrived.'

'What an appalling number of beards,' grumbled Rupert, and jumped out of his skin as Poppet Bruce suddenly cried out, 'Rupert, Roopert.' Thrusting up baby Gandhi, she made him wave: 'Hello, Uncle Rupert.' As Rupert cringed behind Ian Cartwright, Poppet went on: 'And there's Auntie Taggie. Hello, Auntie Taggie.'

Taggie, who'd been hopefully looking round for Xav, waved weakly. As if reading her mind, Poppet yelled out, 'Xav's got another detention, so we couldn't let him out. Sorry. Let's have a word later.'

Seeing her mother red-faced and furious, Bianca whispered to Feral, 'Xav's been caught drinking again. He seems to be pissed all the time.'

'I thought he was mates with Paris,' murmured Feral. Somehow with Bianca's hand in his it didn't hurt so much.

'They used to be really close, but Paris is so taken up with his rugby friends and his extra lessons with Theo, he hardly notices Xav exists any more. Why didn't you ring me?' she asked.

'I wanted to. It's complicated.'

If only Paris held my hand like that, thought Dora.

'Don't worry,' Ashton whispered to Col, 'let them mess around for as long as they like, it'll give them less time to air their non-existent grievances.'

77

At last everyone was settled and Col Peters bashed the table so hard, he spilt all the glasses of water.

'Good evening,' he said. He had a thick, oily voice that seemed drenched in chicken fat. 'Good evening, everyone. We're running behind schedule and as some of you' – he glared at Rupert and Hengist – 'clearly have other engagements, we'd better kick on. We have come together to discuss the proposed closure of Larkminster Comprehensive' – loud boos and cheers – 'and we know you've all got lots to say. We want as many people as possible to air their views, so it'll be easier if you don't interrupt.'

'Save our school,' yelled Johnnie Fowler.

'And show some manners,' snapped Col. 'Not the best way to convince people that your school is worth saving, Master Fowler. I shall now hand over to our county councillor in charge of education, Miss Cindy Payne.'

Hearty cheers from Bruces, Hydes, the Close and Cavendish Plaza.

Cindy, anxious to project a cosy, earth-mother image, had for once abandoned her red trouser suit for a flowing dark brown caftan. Above this her round, ruddy, determinedly smiling face, from which rayed out her light brown hair, bobbed like a setting sun on the horizon.

640

'I have prayed and prayed for guidance on this issue,' she began, 'and must admit that closing a school is a very painful process.'

'Not for them what's going to make a fat profit,' yelled Pearl's boxer dad to roars of applause. Stancombe's heavies squared their shoulders.

'I didn't hear that,' twinkled Cindy. 'Our aim is to give first-class education to each and every secondary student, which I am afraid Larks Comprehensive is not providing.'

'Who says so?' yelled Monster Norman. 'We isn't complaining.'

'Well said, son,' bellowed Stormin'.

'Closing a school is a painful experience,' Cindy ploughed on, her twinkle becoming fixed, 'but we are convinced this is a democratic decision because the vast majority of local parents have made it quite clear they don't want their children to go to Larks in that they have voted with their feet.' Then, as if taking a run at a fence, she added quickly, 'We've had many, many letters supporting closure, but during this formal consultation period, I'm so sorry, we've only received fifty letters of protest.'

'That's because Larks parents and pupils can't write,' yelled Brute Stevens, the rugger bugger from St Jimmy's.

'Hush, that's unkind,' reproved Cindy fondly.

'It's also fucking out of order,' shouted Johnnie Fowler, jumping on Brute and pummelling the hell out of him. As Johnnie was smaller than Pearl's boxer dad, Stancombe's guards were about to move in when Emlyn pre-empted them.

'Pack it in, for God's sake,' he snarled, peeling Johnnie off like a Polaroid.

'Thank you, Mr Davies,' said Cindy archly. 'Only fifty letters of protest,' she repeated, 'which included ten from a Miss Dora Belvedon, who doesn't even live in the area.'

Screams of laughter and bellows of 'Good on yer, Dora' were interspersed with shouts of 'Shame' and 'Cheat'.

An oblivious Dora was muttering into a tape recorder.

Mags Gablecross then leapt to her feet and introduced herself in a quiet, clear voice. Seeing her approaching the platform clutching a bulging box file, the platform recoiled in horror as if she were a suicide bomber.

'I thought people might be interested in the five hundred and fifty letters we received that were against Larks closing down and our petition signed by more than fifteen thousand people. I didn't want to hand these over before the meeting,' she added politely as she gave the box to a boot-faced Col, 'in case the figures were doctored as they were in your Review of Secondary Schools.' She smiled sweetly at Ashton. 'Please note I've taken a photostat of the petition, Mr Douglas.'

'That is a gwatuitously offensive remark,' snapped Ashton.

'We too have had overwhelming support for closure,' chipped in Cindy. 'Take this excellent letter from a Mr Bernard Brooks.' She waved a piece of paper: '"Having observed both teachers and pupils at Larks Comp over the last eighteen months, I can honestly say it's the worst school I've ever encountered. I recommend closure instantly."'

There was a roar from the gallery as Graffi stopped snogging Milly and dropped into the hall, slithering across the umbrellas.

'That's Boffin Brooks, you snotty bastard.' Racing up the aisle, Graffi reached into the row, seizing Boffin by his Alex Bruce house tie. 'Don't you dare slag off our school.' Egged on by a roar of Larks approval, he was about to ram his fist into Boffin's face when Johnnie Fowler tugged him off.

'Let me do the honours.'

'Don't touch me,' screamed Boffin.

'Put Boffin in a coffin, boom, boom, boom,' yelled Bagley and Larks in delighted unison.

As Johnnie raised his fist, Emlyn once more shot across the room, prising Johnnie and Graffi off by their collars.

'Stop it,' he bellowed, then, lowering his voice: 'You're not helping Larks.'

'Nor's Boffin, dissing us like that.'

Trying to wriggle free, Graffi made another lunge, but Emlyn hung on, tightening his grip.

'Stop it, both of you.'

'You's choking me.'

Fortunately a nasty scrap was averted by Amber Lloyd-Foxe crying out, 'Oh, why don't you manhandle us, Mr Davies, it's so sexist to pick on boys every time.'

'Why are we being discriminated against?' chorused Kitten, Milly and even Primrose from the gallery. 'We all want to be manhandled by Mr Davies.'

The hall rumbled with laughter.

Blushing furiously, Emlyn dragged Johnnie and Graffi outside and shoved their heads under the kitchen tap.

A scented, blond jangle of jewellery had meanwhile risen to her feet.

'That kaind of behaviour says it all, reely.'

'Oh shut up,' said Pearl, glancing up from the dress she was designing.

'I won't shut up,' said the blonde shrilly. 'As a resident of Cavendish Plaza, Larks kids make our lives a misery. They graffiti our walls, key our cars, carpet our pavements with chewing gum, beat up and spit at our kids. Why should we fork out for security guards to protect us? This isn't the inner city.'

'Larks should be closed down,' shouted a Cavendish Plaza husband in broad pinstripe. 'It's a breeding ground for thugs and drugs. If you live in a pleasant private estate, you don't expect a sink school that is almost a pupil referral unit on the doorstep.'

The platform was nodding in delight as an old biddy knitting in the front took up the cudgel.

'I don't have the privilege of security guards,' squawked Miss Miserden, 'I live next to Larks and I never feel safe in my bed.'

'You'd be quite safe in anyone else's bed, darling,' yelled Graffi, who'd somehow found his way back to the gallery, 'no one's going to jump on you.'

This was followed by more cheers and cries of 'Shame' and 'Disgusting, insulting a pensioner'.

'Who's she?' asked Dora, who was furiously making notes.

'She's the one who brings letters of complaint in every day,' said Junior, who'd been doing work experience on the Gazette. 'She's called Name and Address Supplied.'

And so the slanging went on, with the closure brigade attacking Larks and its record and Larks supporters defending it.

When a rather flushed Milly Walton shouted from the gallery:

'We at Bagley love meeting young people from a different background and Larks kids are great, we've had so much fun together,' Randal Stancombe made a note to alert Ruth, who didn't at all approve of her daughter's liaison with Graffi.

Sophy Belvedon then made an impassioned plea for the children and particularly Year Ten, who mustn't be abandoned in mid GCSE course.

'Year Ten will be accommodated and taught much better in other schools,' said Ashton, rising to his feet. It was time this meeting was wrapped up. 'My name's Ashton Douglas,' he told the assembled company smoothly, 'S and C Services Diwector of Opewations.'

'Operations performed without the use of anaesthetics,' shouted Hengist. 'No wonder your collaborator is called Payne. As she keeps informing us: "Closing a school is a Payne-full experience."'

As the audience cheered, Ashton's soft, bland features set into a cement of hatred.

'It is also an unnecessary and dishonest operation,' went on Hengist, rising to his feet, his deep, husky, bitchy voice carrying to every corner. Again he seemed to have shaken off his tiredness and worry. 'This discussion is about surplus places. The education department, we have been told, are very worried about the one thousand six hundred surplus places in Larkshire schools, which will evidently double by two thousand and ten.

'Why then,' he asked coolly, 'if our child population is ebbing away, does the housing department predict that two thousand five hundred extra houses will be built – no doubt roughshod over Larkshire's loveliest green belt – in the next three years? Will all these houses be inhabited by childless couples?' He paused for effect. 'Clearly not, and even more interestingly, that one-off contributions from developers will be put towards new and temporary classrooms to accommodate extra pupils.

'Tut, tut, Ashton, Cindy and Russell, have you enlisted the health department to doctor your figures?

He paused again to allow a roar of approval from Larks supporters.

'It seems that S and C and the county council use figures selectively – just as they rigged the Review of Secondary Schools and, when challenged, blamed the falsely poor figures for Larkminster Comprehensive on typing errors. But did anyone have the decency to admit this publicly?'

'No,' roared at least half the hall.

'I don't know what you're talking about,' spluttered Cindy.

'As a Larkminster county councillor, you don't seem

to know what *anyone's* talking about,' cracked back Hengist to more cheers. His dark eyes had recaptured all their old sparkle. 'It's absolutely typical of a Lab/Lib Dim council to have no idea what other departments are up to, or to pretend they don't to achieve their ends. This is a corrupt hung council which ought to be hung out to dry because the only thing that matters to them is selling off Larks's ten acres of prime land and putting millions of pounds into their own and S and C Services' pockets.'

'Save our school!' Stamp, stamp, stamp went a thunder of feet on the parquet as Emlyn grinned across at a flabbergasted Janna.

'Can you tell us' – Rupert had taken up the baton, his light, clipped, contemptuous drawl carrying just as easily round the hall – 'why Randal Stancombe is putting up a large building for Rod Hyde to accommodate extra pupils? This building was commissioned in autumn 2002, at exactly the same time as the Review of Secondary Schools, with rigged figures, was sent out and a report, targeting Larks as the proposed choice for closure, leaked to the *Gazette.*'

'I must protest,' spluttered Rod Hyde.

'Feel free,' said Rupert sarcastically, 'but first, tell us why Larks, particularly after such a good Ofsted report, was chosen to be closed down.'

'Because it's the pits,' yelled Brute Stevens.

As Emlyn grabbed Johnnie Fowler's collar, Cindy saw a chance to dive in:

'As I keep saying, because the people of Larkshire preferred to send their children to other local schools or, failing that, go private or out of county, rather than Larks.'

'Rubbish,' snapped Rupert. 'Plenty of schools in Larkshire have empty desks. The difference is that Larks is sitting on twenty-two million pounds' worth of prime land, with Gap and Borders and Waitrose nearby. S and C have had a catastrophic year; shares in all their other companies have fallen. Selling off Larks would put them nicely in the black.'

Randal Stancombe was by now looking even less amused than Queen Victoria's portrait, which hung on the wall at the end of his row.

'How dare you make these slandewous accusations,' squawked Ashton.

'Because they're true. You've targeted not the most failing school but the one that would bring in the most money. Janna Curtis has been dealt a marked card,' said Rupert chillingly. 'Her only crime was to succeed too well against all the odds, so her character and her school had to be repeatedly blackened by reports in your papers, Col, demoralizing pupils and staff and, in particular, changing the minds of parents intending to send their children there.'

'Oh, well done, Rupert. Col the toad will soon explode,' giggled Dora. 'I am a poet and I do not know it.'

'This is disgraceful,' thundered Russell.

'Disgraceful for Janna and Larks,' shouted the Brigadier.

Janna's face was in her hands, she couldn't believe such incredible support.

Feral gazed at Bianca.

'What are they going on about?'

'I've no idea.'

'This is totally out of order.' Col Peters crashed down his hammer. 'I hope Hengist Brett-Taylor can substantiate these accusations.'

'Only too easily.' Most of the platform, despite the heat, lost colour as, out of his inside pocket, Hengist produced a sheet of paper covered in writing and waved it at the audience. 'This is a list of people likely to profit from the sale of Larks. The wages of Cindy, for example, will be considerably enhanced.'

'How dare you?' squawked Cindy Payne.

'Shall I read it out?'

647

'Mr Fussy doesn't look too happy either,' whispered Amber.

'Perhaps little Gandhi needs changing,' whispered back Dora.

'Save our school!' Stamp, stamp, stamp, thundered Larks supporters.

'Well?' taunted Hengist.

The big hand of the hall clock was pointing directly upwards: nine o'clock. Saved by the hour and just managing to contain his fury, Col Peters gathered up his papers.

'I'm afraid we've run out of time,' he said.

'Cop out, cop out, read the list, read the list,' roared the hall.

'I have a paper to get to bed with a report of this meeting,' Col said firmly, 'and we mustn't keep Sally and Hengist or Mr and Mrs Campbell-Black from their dinner party.'

'Read out the list,' shouted the *Western Daily Press*.

Hengist laughed and shook his head.

'Not yet. Unlike the editor of the *Gazette*, I feel it more honourable to substantiate rumours before spreading them.'

'Where are you off to?' asked the *Stroud News* as Sally and Taggie hurried towards the exit.

'Highgrove,' piped up Bianca proudly. 'Have a lovely time, Mummy.' Turning to Feral, she handed him three pieces of paper. 'Here's my number, put it in both pockets and in the pocket of your jacket, then there's no excuse.'

Danijela meanwhile had risen trembling to her feet.

'Before we go, I am an asylum-seeker from Bosnia, we love going to Miss Curtis's school, it is our home and best of England.'

Janna's eyes filled with tears.

'Exactly,' called out Jupiter who, having let Rupert and Hengist do his dirty work, totally distancing himself all evening, now moved in for the kill. 'If Larks closes, all its children will have to find new schools, the teachers, cleaners and support staff new jobs. What will happen to the Shakespeare Estate without their school? Larkshire's other schools and several greedy individuals will profit. That's how private business works: targets must be met, so you sell off your best asset.' The whole room had gone silent. 'And so a whole community will be destroyed.'

There was a long pause.

'Save our school,' croaked Rocky.

'Janna Curtis has been dealt a marked card,' murmured Dora to the *Independent*.

'Let's have a quick show of hands,' said Cindy hastily.

'Those in favour of closure?' called out Col Peters, glancing round the hall as a lot of Rolexes and braceleted hands were held up and a County Hall minion did some cursory counting. 'And those in favour of retaining Larks?' Then as a forest of hands sprung up: 'I think that gives closure a clear majority. I will convey the feeling of the hall to the appropriate authorities,' he added and fled the hall to deafening boos.

The place was in uproar. Hengist fighting his way towards the door met Emlyn coming back in.

'Any news?'

'Definitely not Oriana,' said Emlyn, 'it was a British soldier in a car crash, poor sod.'

'Thank Christ.' Throwing back his head, Hengist took in a great breath of relief. 'And for you too. But, oh God, the poor man and his family. I must go and reassure Sally. See you in the morning. Thanks for everything.'

Running through the deluge, Janna caught up with Hengist on the edge of the car park.

'Thank you all ever so much,' she stammered, 'you were wonderful. I must have made you so late for dinner. Where did you get all that amazing info?' Then, when Hengist laughed: 'At least let me see that list of names.'

'You can have it.' He handed her the piece of paper. 'It's Dora Belvedon's essay on why fox hunting shouldn't be abolished. She got an A star.'

'There were no names?'

'Not before I began counting the people who turned green this evening. Rather a good bluff, don't you think? I must go, darling. Just coming,' he called to the others, waiting in Rupert's revving up BMW.

Desire made Janna ungracious. 'You know how I disapprove of hunting,' she said furiously.

'Don't look gift hunters in the mouth, you chippy child. I'll come and see you over the weekend.'

78

Seeing a drenched Janna returning to the hall, Emlyn assumed her air of desolation stemmed from the likely loss of her school and suggested they go and have supper.

He swept away Janna's protests that she had so many people to thank.

'I've got to ferry several busloads of parents back to the Shakespeare Estate. I'll meet you in the Dog and Duck at ten. And put something warm on.'

The pub was packed when Janna arrived. Emlyn had already found a corner table and ordered a bottle of red and two and a half steaks for himself, Janna and Partner.

At the next table sat a group of students from the local agricultural college and their pretty, Sloaney girl-friends, who all had long, clean streaked hair, endless jean-clad legs and were equally excited by Emlyn and Partner. 'What a sweet little dog.'

The men hardly gave Janna a second glance. She must make more effort. She hadn't even bothered to comb her hair.

'So exciting, this war,' cried one of the Sloanes as the pub television was turned up for *News at Ten*, 'one needn't bother to get out a video any more.'

'I feel so sorry for those poor Baghdad dogs,' said a second, 'that terrible howl going up just before the bombing started.'

'Pretty amazing,' said her boyfriend, 'the way you can see the B52s leaving Fairford on television and, unlike British Rail, arriving on time in Baghdad.'

'You feel so guilty sitting in a warm pub when all this is going on,' shivered the first Sloane. 'I'm crazy about Rageh Omar.'

'Not nearly as crazy as I am about Oriana Taylor,' said her boyfriend.

Janna glanced at Emlyn, who put a finger to his lips.

According to Breaking News, as it was now known, the Americans were pushing on towards Baghdad and a British soldier had been killed in a car crash. His parents, the sadness already carved into their faces, showed great fortitude.

'He was such a wonderful young man,' said the mother, 'he'd been ten years in the army and knew it would never happen to him because he was invincible.'

There were clips of the soldier's divine baby and lovely blonde wife, now a widow, but so brave.

Janna blew her nose noisily; even the Sloanes were hushed. Then it was Oriana reporting from Baghdad, her face growing thinner, paler, more shadowed by the minute and looking so beautiful – as if the stars and rockets and coloured smoke behind her were purely backdrop to enhance her fragility and the suffering and outrage in the same dark eyes as Hengist's. Predictably her sympathies were entirely with the beleaguered Iraqis.

'She's awfully left wing,' protested a Sloane.

Emlyn never took his eyes off Oriana's face.

'You must be so proud,' whispered Janna.

Their steaks had arrived. Janna cut up Partner's on a side plate and put it on the floor.

'Oh how sweet,' said the Sloanes, smiling at Emlyn.

Janna, who hadn't eaten all day, found she was starving.

Emlyn, for once, poured his heart out, expressing his

doubts that Oriana would ever settle down. 'It'd be like caging a song bird.'

' "We think caged birds sing, when indeed they cry," ' quoted Janna. Seeing Emlyn wince, she asked quickly, 'How did you become an item?'

'More an out-of-sightem, these days,' said Emlyn bitterly. 'I used to glimpse her from afar at Oxford. She broke men's hearts like Zuleika and had the added lustre of having a legendary rugby player as a father. Then, some years later, we actually met at a party, the night Tony Blair won his first election. Both euphoric; suddenly there was hope. We got hammered and ended up in bed. I couldn't believe my luck. The first months were miraculous, but in retrospect I always made the running.'

Janna let him bang on but finally, fed up with hearing about Oriana and having nearly finished her steak because Emlyn was doing the talking, she said, 'That meeting was wonderful,' and, having thanked Emlyn profusely for all his hard work, added, 'And Hengist and Rupert really turned things round.'

When Emlyn didn't say anything, she glanced up and to her horror saw only pity in his eyes.

'You don't think I'm going to save Larks?'

'I don't guess so, lovely.'

'But Hengist ripped them to pieces.'

'Hengist is a fox, he kills for the hell of it. Tonight he got what he wanted: publicly discrediting the Lib Dems and Labour.'

'You think he was only making political capital?' Janna's voice was rising.

'No, no, he's fond of Larks and devoted to you. But at the moment, he's out of it. He lost Mungo, and he's overwhelmed with terror he's going to lose Oriana.'

'But he proved S and C are crooks and in bed with the county council.'

'I know, but despite the bribes they'll dole out and the cut they'll take for themselves, they'll still hand over such a hefty whack to Larkshire's schools. By not saving your school, they'll help everyone else's.'

'Torture the one to save the half-million? Why in hell did you waste your time ferrying all those parents over?' Realizing she was shouting she lowered her voice. 'I'm sorry.'

'Because I couldn't live with myself if we hadn't tried every avenue. I'm truly sorry. I just think S and C's minds are made up and all the protests, placards and petitions are piffle in the wind. They're not going to change anything.'

'I can't give up.' Janna thumped the table in real anguish. 'I'll sell my house or get a second mortgage. At least I must save Year Ten.'

'Hush, hush.' Emlyn came round and sat down beside her, engulfing her with a huge arm. 'I may be wrong.'

'Don't humour me. I only need a hundred and twenty thousand to pay for a handful of staff and for a building to teach them in, just for a year. Jubilee Cottage is too tiny. Just to give them a chance of getting some GCSEs.'

'Don't be unrealistic, lovely. Have another drink.'

'To hell with you, you're so bloody defeatist!' All Janna's Yorkshire vowels spilt out so loudly and angrily that Partner shot off to observe battle from the knees of one of the Sloanes, who were all listening, shocked and fascinated, to every word. 'I'm going to save Year Ten.' Janna wriggled out from under Emlyn's arm and, slapping thirty pounds on the table, gathered up Partner and fled into the night.

The rain had stopped. Climbing the sky was a sad orange half-moon. With a headscarf of black cloud lining her face, she looked like an Iraqi.

'Don't bug me either,' shouted Janna, 'I've got my own war to fight.'

Tomorrow she would seek out Randal Stancombe, who had smiled at her this evening, and ask him for help.

She was so shattered, she didn't check her messages until morning. The first of many was from Mags. Feral had been arrested for pulling a gun on Brute Stevens and, when grabbed by a Stancombe heavy, had misfired, taking an eye out of Queen Victoria's portrait.

As Feral was only fifteen he was later bailed by the Brigadier and the case adjourned.

'How could you, Feral?' stormed Janna. 'Everything was going Larks's way.'

'Brute stole my football and he dissed Bianca,' said Feral. 'He called her a posh black bitch. He showed no respect.'

'None of that'll emerge till the case comes up, which'll be too late for Larks.'

Brigadier Woodford wasn't pleased either.

'If you don't pull yourself together, Feral, and stop carrying guns, you'll be in and out of prison for the rest of your life.'

Feral chucked his jacket and jeans into the washing machine at the launderette deliberately blurring all Bianca's numbers.

The *Gazette* predictably ignored any reference to skulduggery and led on Feral being arrested in front of the Bishop and Ashton Douglas, confirming everyone's worst fears of Larks. They also reported a show of hands in favour of closure and drew attention to Larks's normally vocal headmistress, Janna Curtis, having no words to say in her school's defence.

79

It was not until well into the holidays that Janna screwed up courage to ring Randal Stancombe, who couldn't have been more charming.

'Come and have a drink this evening, any time after seven. I'll warn the guy on the gate.'

How did one dress for a man whom one wanted to convince one was worth a loan or, better still, a gift of £120,000? Peanuts to Stancombe, but the rich got rich by watching the pennies. A hundred and twenty thousand might buy another Ferrari, or a diamond necklace for Mrs Walton, both of which could be sold. You couldn't sell Year Ten.

At least she'd got some sleep and soaked her hair in coconut oil for twenty-four hours so it gleamed glossier than the coat of any Crufts red setter.

She wore a brown velvet pencil skirt and a cotton jersey twin set in the same soft apricot pink as the glow which ringed the horizon as she drove towards Cavendish Plaza.

'One, two, three, four, five, once I caught a big fish alive,' sang Janna.

Despite the deluge on the day of the public meeting, drought and late frosts, as if in sympathy with the war, had bleached the fields khaki. Hungry horses had stripped trees blown down in the gales of their dark bark, leaving pale bone below.

On the car radio she learnt that five Americans taken prisoner had been paraded on television and that, after bashing hell out of the Iraqis for nearly three weeks, the Americans were having the temerity to bang on about the Geneva Convention. She was so ashamed it was Labour who'd taken Britain to war. Great unpatriotic cheers had gone up in the staffroom every time the Iraqis were reported as fighting back bravely.

Stancombe, on the other hand, who was rumoured to be, among other things, an arms dealer, would probably be madly pro-war. She must keep her trap shut.

Janna didn't know which was more beautiful: Larkminster, gold in the setting sun, seen through Stancombe's telescope, which was so powerful she could pick out primroses on Smokers' and even the crumbs Wally, to distract himself from the war, was putting on the bird table, or Stancombe's apartment itself, which was a soothing symphony of sands and terracottas with soft suede sofas, fake fur cushions and fluffy rugs. Two walls of the vast lounge were window, the other two were crammed with wonderful pictures: Rothko, Chagall, Tracey Emin, Sam Taylor-Wood, CDs largely classical and admittedly many of them still in their cellophane wrappings and surprisingly interesting books: biographies of Alan Sugar, Bill Gates and Philip Green rubbing shoulders with Louis de Bernières, Sebastian Faulks, Donna Tartt, a first edition of *Lolita* and even some poetry.

Chopin's Second Piano Concerto rippled through speakers as though Marcus Campbell-Black and the BBC Symphony Orchestra were actually in the room.

'Whatever my feelings for his toffee-nosed father, I cannot get enough of Marcus,' announced Stancombe as, like Venus hot from some exciting, foaming jacuzzi, he welcomed her. His hair was damp and curling on his strong, suntanned neck. He was wearing just a dark blue, crew-necked cashmere sweater and white chinos, which clung to his sleek, still damp body. He smelt of toothpaste and Lynx, his favourite aftershave, as he padded round in beautifully pedicured bare feet.

Janna was flattered he'd glammed up for her, even if he was probably going out later.

'What a gorgeous apartment.'

Stancombe smiled. 'I used to think books and CDs ruined the look, but I've mellowed.'

On a glass side table in an art deco frame was a beautiful photograph of Jade, taken by Lichfield.

'How pretty she is,' sighed Janna.

'Takes after her dad,' joked Stancombe, handing Janna a long, slim glass of champagne; then, suddenly serious: 'She's a bit lost actually. Bloody Cosmo Rannaldini's messed her about.'

Ushering Janna onto a pale brown leather sofa, so vast Janna's little feet only just reached the edge, he sat down beside her.

'Hard being first-generation public school. You pick up the posh accent and the clothes, even the education, but not the roots. People laugh at me because I'm flash and vulgar. They laugh at Jade when she doesn't know things or people or pronounces them wrong. It makes her flare up, easily on the defensive.'

'Like me,' sighed Janna. 'If only I could keep my temper and learn some tact.'

Stancombe clinked his glass against hers. 'To the flash and the vulgar, may we inherit the earth. Problem with education, you've only got one chance. I often think Jade would have been happier at a state school. Nice if she could have been taught by you. You'd have understood her.'

Janna had never felt so flattered or warm inside, particularly when he refilled her glass.

'People like Rupert, Hengist and Jupiter take your money, even ask you to their homes,' he went on bitterly, 'but they never really accept you and they laugh at us behind our backs – even Sally.'

'They were wonderful at the meeting,' protested

Janna. 'They came out on a vile night to save me.'

'With respect, they saw it as a chance to rattle the other parties.'

'Oh,' wailed Janna, 'Emlyn said the same thing.'

'Emlyn's one of us.'

'You truly don't think I can save Larks?'

Stancombe shook his head.

Wriggling off the edge of the sofa, which was like falling off the edge of the world, overwhelmed with despair, Janna was tempted to walk straight through the big glass window and splatter on Casey Andrews's sculpture in the forecourt miles below.

On a side table was a *Telegraph* colour magazine open at an interview with Stancombe, photographed in this same flat with Mrs Walton.

'Lovely picture,' she said dully.

'Even with Ruth,' she realized Stancombe was saying a minute later, 'I have to watch myself. She gives me a lot of advice. I thought "mangy" was pronounced like "man".'

'Isn't it? She's so beautiful.'

'Works hard enough at it.'

'And succeeds.'

'She'd get an A star in leisure and tourism. She's in Rome with Milly as we speak.'

Janna could see La Perdrix d'Or, where she and Hengist had had their first lunch, and Larks, appearing at a distance innocent and unscathed with the green blur of spring on its trees – as if for a last time.

'I like a woman who works,' said Stancombe joining her, then, glancing sideways: 'Why are you crying?'

'For Larks.' A great shuddering breath racked Janna's small frame. 'If I can't save it, would you help me to save Year Ten? Only about forty of them. Imagine if your Jade had to leave halfway through her GCSE course. Rod Hyde loathes my children; he'd bully them into the ground. Rutminster Comp's a jungle; they'd just give up.

659

'I only need a hundred and twenty thousand for some teachers and a new building or to rebuild Appletree. Would you lend me it? You can have my house as security.'

'How much did you pay for it?'

'One hundred and seventy-five thousand; three-quarters of that mortgage. I could sell it.' She wiped her eyes with her sleeve.

'How would you pay your staff?'

'That's why I need a hundred and twenty. Please, please help me.'

Stancombe retreated to get the bottle.

Janna put her hand over her glass. 'I'm driving.'

'A very hard bargain. I need time to think. I'll do all I can. I'll lean on Ashton to keep the school open a bit longer.'

Janna was overwhelmed with weariness. 'I think it'd be too difficult to rebuild now. So many teachers and children have left.'

'If I get you the money . . .' Stretching out a hand, Stancombe caressed the back of her neck . . . 'you've got to promise to sleep with me.'

Janna opened her mouth and shut it again, feeling herself growing very hot and wet as if she were fantasizing about something of which she was ashamed.

Stancombe laughed. 'OK, you need time to think, like me.'

'I must go.' As she jumped away, his hand closed on the scruff of her twinset.

'Why must you?'

'I just ought.'

'The first time I saw you, through this telescope on your first day, you were so bonny with your flaming red hair, like a beacon waiting to light up the town. Next time at Hengist and Sally's, you were so upset, because you'd found that little dog blown up, I still thought you were very tasty, but I'd just met Ruth – the road not taken.'

'I love that poem,' said Janna in surprise.

'Now you're patronizing me and my yob culture, too busy scrabbling his way to the top to read poetry. Then I saw you at the public meeting, I thought how tired and diminished you looked and how cheap your clothes were.'

Janna longed to protest that the dress was pure silk and from Hengist.

'And I wanted to take you under my wing and make your life happier and easier.' Stancombe dropped a kiss on the top of her head and let a leisurely hand move down over her bottom, exciting her unbearably.

'I must go, I've got the same little dog in the car,' she stammered. 'Thank you for seeing me.'

'It's good to talk,' said Stancombe, almost spoiling things.

As she ran to the lift in utter confusion, he caught up with her and pressed the button.

'D'you know the sexiest thing in the world?'

'What?'

'Courage – and you've got it in spades. I'd like to help with your school and I'd like you to help me with Jade, she's so unhappy. Ruth's not the ideal prospective stepmother.'

As he drew her towards him, she felt his wonderfully fit body burning through the blue cashmere, his rock-hard cock practically raping her belly button. So much taller, he had to bend his head to kiss her. Janna gasped and resisted, then her mouth melted beneath his mouth as he sucked and his tongue caressed her lips with such tenderness and delicacy. He was so sexy.

'I want you to look bonny and happy again,' he whispered. 'I want to take those dark circles away and put them back for a different reason, "the lineaments of gratified desire".'

Recognizing the quote, Janna thought: This is ridiculous, he's appealing to my intellectual snobbery.

As the lift opened directly into the flat, she leapt into it.

'That was lovely, thanks ever so much.'

All the way down, she expected him to press a button from above and imprison her deep down in the hellish bowels of the building, for treating with the devil of whom Hengist, Mags and Emlyn so disapproved and yet who had just been so disturbingly adorable.

'One, two, three, four, five, once I caught a big fish alive,' sang Janna to Partner all the way home.

80

'One of the privileges of the great', wrote Giraudoux, 'is to witness catastrophes from a terrace', or, in Randal Stancombe's case, from the air. Flying off to the Far East, he never got back in touch, leaving Janna to her fate. Nor, after their Titanic support at the public meeting, did Hengist, Jupiter or Rupert return to fight her corner.

The war in Iraq, therefore, ended much less decisively than Larkminster Comprehensive when in the middle of May, the School's Organization Committee voted unanimously and conclusively to close it down.

This, although expected, came as a devastating death blow. On the steps of County Hall, a stunned Janna defiantly announced that even if the guillotine had fallen, she would still battle on to save her school. Inside, she knew this was impossible. There was no more money in the kitty.

The following morning, however, she was sitting in the kitchen drinking very strong tea and wondering how to stagger mortally wounded through the rest of her life, when she heard Partner barking at his very good friend the postman. Next moment he had rushed in carrying a blue envelope in his mouth, leaping onto Janna's knee to deliver it. The letter inside was on plain blue paper.

'Dear Janna,' she read, 'I'm sorry about your school. I thought you might need this in your battle to save Year Ten. A banker's draft for £120,000 should now be in your account. Best of luck.'

Janna gave a gasp of disbelief; it must be some cruel joke. There was no address, no signature, only a Royal Mail postmark; nothing to identify who'd given it her. But when she rang her bank in Larkminster, the manager, markedly more friendly and deferential, confirmed the money was indeed in her account, but that the donor had insisted on remaining anonymous.

It couldn't be Hengist, thought Janna, nor Rupert, nor Jupiter, unless Emlyn had told them of her desperate concerns about Year Ten. So she rang Stancombe, gibbering her thanks. After several moments of evasion, there was such a long pause that she thought he had hung up, then he said ruefully:

'I wanted it to be a secret.'

'I cannot believe such kindness. I'll pay you back somehow, I promise.'

'No, no, it's a gift. Lovely ladies deserve a leg-up.' Stancombe laughed softly. 'Just remember our bargain.'

And again Janna felt the warm quiver between her legs.

'I'm off to the States with Ruth on Monday,' Stancombe went on. 'I'll be back in June and we'll find you a building to accommodate your tearaways and get some decent funding from Ashton.'

'I won't accept a penny from him.'

'Don't be stupid. You'll need his help. See you in June.'

'He hasn't failed me, he hasn't failed me.' Gathering up Partner, Janna waltzed him round the room. 'You'll have another year with your friends, darling.'

Then she collapsed back on her chair, unable to comprehend such golden benison after the darkness of yesterday, reeling at the prospect of how much battling would still be needed to get the project off the ground. After she'd worked out the figures, she also realized she would need a lot more money to pay salaries, feed the children and heat and light the building, not to mention exam fees.

Janna remembered very little of the remaining summer term. As dogs moult in hot weather, Larks shed teachers and pupils. Many of the latter returned tearfully from their new schools: 'They called us Larks scum, miss, and put chewing gum in our hair.'

Ashton showed no desire to help Janna find a home for Year Ten. Instead, in early June, he offered her a headship turning round a failing Larkshire school.

'It's a challenge, Janna, restore your sense of self-worth.'

Janna refused; she'd no desire to kill off another school. She continued to refuse jobs and endured the humiliation of all the other schools in the area descending like vultures and slapping different coloured stickers on desks, books, computers and laboratory equipment, which they would collect after Larks finally closed down on 12 July. Enid, who'd built up the library over six years, was in perpetual floods. The choir school was the greediest and earmarked the most.

'The nearer the pulpit, the further from God,' observed Cambola sourly.

Janna felt particularly guilty about teachers like Sophy Belvedon, who'd refused to abandon ship and so heroically carried on helping Year Eleven through their GCSEs that Janna was amazed the vultures didn't slap a coloured sticker on them as well.

Jupiter and Rupert returned to the attack and continued to hassle S and C and the county council, not just on the dodgy ethics of 'closing down' Larks, but also accusing them of diverting the education budget to other areas. Who, for example, had paid for Ashton's Hockney?

S and C and the county council denied everything, but they were rattled, particularly when, after Russell Lambert's resignation as chairman of Larks governors, Brigadier Woodford took over as temporary chairman and asked for the minutes of meetings over the past five years.

They were also fed up to the back teeth with Janna ringing every day demanding a building for Year Ten. Who would rid them of this turbulent priestess? Despite falling S and C shares, even if it would mean a year's delay before getting the big money from the sale of Larks, they decided it might be prudent, and in the end cheaper, to allow Janna to remain on site.

'We must snatch the moral high ground from the Tories,' insisted Cindy Payne. 'Let's go and look at Larks.'

There had been a hosepipe ban and all the little saplings planted by Wally in the autumn had died in the drought. Leaves were falling out of the trees, even though it was only June, as Ashton and Cindy arrived. Janna utterly jolted them by taking them first over the main building. Like an elephant left to die in the jungle, all the flesh had fallen off its bones. Apart from the damp and the boarded-up windows, not a ceiling or a roof tile was in place. Doors had been ripped from their hinges, plugs and lavatory chains torn out, every classroom trashed. Wally had lost heart.

'I wouldn't educate a dog in here,' said Ashton faintly. 'How could this have happened?'

'The children did it. They were so hurt and angry you closed their school.'

Through gritted teeth and because the main building was beyond redemption, Ashton and Cindy agreed two weeks later to rebuild the annexe, Appletree. They then revealed to Janna that Randal had very, very generously offered to do the job at cost. After all, he was donating a science block to Bagley and a so-called vocational studies unit to St Jimmy's. Appletree would be another example of his wonderful philanthropy.

In the first week in July, therefore, S and C and the county council called a press conference.

'In view of the closure of Larks Compwehensive,' Ashton, in a new mauve striped shirt, told his large audience, 'it has been decided not to diswupt Year Ten in the middle of their GCSE course. S and C Services have therefore decided to pwovide a building in which they can be taught and to put funds towards their education for a further year, until June 2004.'

These funds were of course hugely bolstered by the £120,000 Randal had given to Janna – but he wished this donation to remain anonymous. Ashton, however, did go on to say the rebuilding of Appletree would be supervised by Janna Curtis and carried out, on very generous terms, by Randal Stancombe Properties. Janna was to be given an extended contract until the end of August 2004, to close the school down finally.

'Mercy has a human face,' announced the *Gazette*, alongside a soppy picture of Ashton, which everyone graffitied.

Stormin' Norman appeared on television punching the air instead of anyone else and shouting 'Yes' when the news broke.

'Why isn't Janna Curtis more grateful?' grumbled Cindy Payne.

This was because saving Year Ten was small comfort compared with the anguish of saying goodbye to the other years.

'Why didn't you save us as well?' sobbed the little ones.

'Why didn't you march for us on Drowning Street?'

It was like working in a slaughterhouse, or a vivisection clinic, making their last moments as comfortable as possible. Janna tried heroically to remain cheerful, but on the last day, when the media poured in to photograph the death of a school, she lost it and screamed at them all to booger off.

'Why couldn't I have saved them?' she sobbed to Mags and Cambola as her children set off on their last journey down the drive to St Jimmy's or Searston Abbey or pupil referral units or to uncertain futures and no likelihood of a decent job, unless, in Year Eleven's case, they had notched up a few GCSEs.

Janna felt more and more grateful to Stancombe who was planning to extend Appletree to include a dining room, a big hall, a gym and new labs.

'I'd like to rename it Stancombe House,' she told him when he dropped in with a bottle of champagne after the first day of work.

Stancombe shook his head. 'That'll tell everyone who funded it. It was a gift, remember?'

Although they were alone in the roofless, windowless building and could see a new moon scything its way through the soft blue twilight, Stancombe made no attempt to extract payment. At first Janna thought he was sensitively appreciating her mood of utter desolation, then he shyly confided that he and Ruth were off to Italy and that he was thinking very seriously of asking her to marry him.

When Janna hugged him in delight and urged him to go for it, he assured her that Teddy Murray, his foreman, would keep an eye on everything and told her to ring him on his mobile if she needed help.

Janna was heartbroken to lose Lance and Lydia, who both needed to work full time. She was, however, touched by the teachers who wanted to stay on: Mags, Cambola, Mr Mates, even Basket and Skunk, who she prayed would rise to the challenge. They were all taking early retirement, but were allowed to work two and a half days a week which was all that would be needed to cover the new Year Eleven's GCSE syllabus.

This suited Mags who had been only doing two and a half days a week anyway.

Among the younger teachers, sweet Sophy Belvedon had opted to stay. Wally and Debbie would both remain full time and, to the delight of the children, the Brigadier and Lily, who'd both been cleared by the Criminal Records Bureau, would respectively teach history and help Mags out with French, Spanish and German.

One of the nicest compliments came from Rowan who, having signed on for an advanced course in the summer holidays, offered to come in and teach IT.

'I know we've had our differences,' she told Janna, 'but I want to see Larks through to the end and, frankly, anything's better than looking after children full time.'

Gloria was staying on to take PE, so apart from maths and food technology, everything was sorted.

Everyone was being so kind; Janna couldn't think why she couldn't stop crying. There was the afternoon at Appletree when she was dickering over what colour to paint the new hall, when Partner shot off into the park. Janna only just had time to hide her swollen eyes behind dark glasses before he proudly led in Cadbury and Dora.

Dora was delivering a card which said: 'Sorry about your school, good luck, Paris', which nearly set Janna off again.

Dora was also in low spirits. She'd had to spend a lot of time recently counselling her brother, Dicky, because his hero David Beckham had moved to Real Madrid. She had continued to put sweets in Paris's locker but he hardly noticed her. He had been so gorgeous as Jack Tanner in the end-of-term play, *Man and Superman*, it had fanned the flames of her hopeless love for him. But life must go on. Dora cleared her throat.

'I feel one must put something back into the

community,' she told Janna gravely, 'so I'd like to offer my services teaching media studies at Larks next term.'

Janna started to laugh and found she couldn't stop. Dora got quite huffy until Janna began to cry, whereupon Dora rushed off to the Ghost and Castle and bought her a quadruple vodka and tonic. When she assured the landlord: 'I'm not a binge drinker, it's for Miss Curtis, whose school has closed down,' he quite understood.

81

Bianca Campbell-Black was so dazzled that Feral had defended her with a real gun at the public meeting, she sent him a new violet and Day-Glo yellow football, a diamond cross and ear studs, did no work through the summer term dreaming of him and throughout the holidays bombarded him with cards inviting him home.

Feral longed to accept. Time and again he hitched a lift or 'borrowed' a car to drive over to Penscombe. On his first visit, he mistook the dear little lodge at the bottom of the drive for Bianca's home and thought how cosily he and she could live there. But when he knocked and was told by an ancient retainer that Bianca lived in the big house at the end of an avenue of chestnuts, whose trunk shadows striped the drive like an endless old-school tie, he turned round and went home.

On subsequent visits through the baking summer, he had borrowed Lily's binoculars and paused on the road out of Penscombe village. Here he had gazed longingly across the valley at fields filled with horses and the long lake squirming in the sunshine beneath Rupert's big, golden house, in the hope of catching a glimpse of Bianca, but knowing there was no way of him ever affording her, particularly as he had a court case pending, and if it was held in September he would be sixteen and named in the paper.

Nor had life in the big golden house during the holidays been peaceful. Xavier had got an even worse report than Bianca, indicating that he hadn't a hope of a single GCSE unless he did four or five hours' work every day in the holidays.

Shut away in his bedroom, ostensibly wrestling with *Macbeth* and the Russian Revolution one stifling mid-August afternoon, Xav looked up at the posters of Colombian beauty spots and fine-looking Colombian Indians, which his mother had had specially framed to make him proud of his origins.

Xav was very aware of the blood of his Indian ancestors flowing through his veins, blood tainted by an excess of drink and drugs, both of which he was now illicitly indulging in. Drunk or stoned, he felt capable of anything; the sadness and terror ebbed away. He forgot he was thick, friendless and had grown fat and spotty by stuffing himself with cake and chocolate when he was coming down.

On the wall hung a little wooden Madonna hollowed out inside to smuggle cocaine. These had been on sale in the Bogotá convent from which he and Bianca had been adopted by Rupert and Taggie. Rupert had nicked one as a souvenir and later given it to Xav, little realizing that Xav was putting it to its original use and, because Rupert himself indulged so rarely, that Xav had been regularly helping himself to his father's stash of cocaine.

At first, Xav had assumed people disliked him at Bagley because he was black, but seeing everyone swooning over Bianca when she arrived, he realized it was just him they didn't like. This was reinforced when Feral, who was much blacker than Bianca, had rolled up, so agile, beautiful and larky that girls fell for him in droves, so Xav could no longer blame his colour for his not getting a girlfriend.

Formerly his great passion and bond with Rupert

had been horses, but after a horrible hunting fall in the Easter holidays, when he had smashed his elbow, he had lost his nerve and the one way he could always win his father's respect. If he mounted a horse now, he trembled and poured with sweat. After a few abortive attempts to take him out on a lead rein, Rupert had given up and left him at home.

Finally, Xav's beloved, endlessly wagging, black Labrador, Bogotá, was on his rickety last legs. Rupert had never had any problem with adopting black children. Xav and Bianca were his son and daughter and that was that. Chided in the nineties by a social worker that Xav wasn't making enough black friends, Rupert had insolently bought the boy a black Labrador puppy and called it Bogotá, after Xav's birthplace. The puppy had ironically grown up into the best and truest friend Xav had ever had. Now Bogotá, temporarily oblivious of the arthritis that plagued him, lay snoring at Xavier's feet.

Rupert had been frantically busy all summer running the yard, politicking with Jupiter and Hengist and fighting off takeover bids for Venturer, the television company which he ran with his father-in-law, Declan O'Hara. Venturer was still very successful, but like all independent TV stations, was having an increasing battle attracting advertising.

Nor did the bloodstock market ever sleep, as emails poured in from Tokyo, Dubai and Kentucky. Despite his legendary energy, chronic lack of sleep was making Rupert increasingly ratty and preoccupied, otherwise he might have attributed his son's mood swings to more than adolescent angst.

Hearing a terrific bang and the frenzied barking of dogs, Xav raced out onto the landing with Bogotá hobbling after him. Down the stairwell he could see his mother running white-faced out of the kitchen to be confronted by an outraged Bianca:

'Daddy's shot the television because Mr Blair's on it.

I'll just have to go and watch Sky with the lads,' and stormed off.

Taggie clutched her head. She was desperately low both about Xav's deteriorating relationship with the entire family and because she was quite incapable of helping either child with its holiday work. Her agonizing was interrupted by the telephone.

'Helloo, helloo.'

Recognizing the strangulated Adam's apple whine of Alex Bruce, which instantly recalled her own disastrous school days, Taggie started to shake.

'Just checking you're on for our fundraiser for the new science block next week.'

Oh God, she'd forgotten.

'What date is it?'

'Twenty-first of August.'

Taggie went cold. That was Xav's birthday; he went berserk if it weren't celebrated in style. Alex Bruce had caught her on the hop when, back in June, he'd issued the invitation, implying that Xavier's behaviour wouldn't be so 'challenging' or his learning difficulties so excessive if the parental back-up were more committed.

Riddled with shame and guilt, Taggie had weakly accepted but failed to tell Rupert, who was allergic to being gazed at by mothers and forced to put one's hand in one's pocket, when one was already bankrupted by bloody fees.

'Helloo, helloo?' Alex was still on the line. Taggie shuddered at the thought of his pursed red lips framed by beard pressed against the receiver.

'We'll be there,' she bleated.

'Randal Stancombe's agreed to host our promises auction. How about your spouse donating a helicopter trip to the Arc, complete with hospitality, or a peep behind the scenes at Venturer Television? Some of our parents might bid quite high for a chance to appear on *Buffers*.'

'You'll have to ask Rupert,' gasped Taggie and rang off.

Rupert, as she predicted, was insane with rage.

'I'll be in France – there's no way I can get there before nine.'

Taggie said she'd go on ahead, which made Rupert even crosser. He loathed his beautiful wife being out on the toot without him: predators were everywhere.

But his rage was nothing to the sullen fury of Xav that they were abandoning him on his birthday.

'I'm so sorry, darling, I muddled the dates.'

'You should have known it was my birthday from the date. Not that it's my real birthday – that's why you don't care.'

'Don't be bloody to Mummy,' protested Bianca, thinking how unattractively white-tongued and covered in zits her brother looked.

'You can fuck off,' spat Xav, then, swinging back to Taggie: 'Can I have a party at home that night?'

Taggie quailed. 'Of course you can, darling.'

What the hell was Rupert going to say? Mrs Bodkin, their ancient housekeeper, was far too doddery to keep order.

'Will you ask Feral?' pleaded Bianca. 'And Paris? If you ask Paris, Feral might easily come. Oh per-lease.'

'I might.' Xav stormed upstairs, slamming his bed-room door.

Talk about an own goal. Pushing aside a rug and rais-ing a floor board, he lifted out a half-empty bottle of vodka and having filled a tooth mug, hid it again.

He had been so endlessly sulky and difficult at Bagley he had no friends to ask. Girls were repelled by him. Sweet Aysha would never be allowed out by her bullying father. The only reason boys might turn up was to have a crack at Bianca or because the mothers delivering the girls wanted to gawp at the house and his father. He could try the children of his parents' friends: Junior, Amber, Lando and Jack Waterlane. Milly, Dicky and Dora might come. As a brown-nosing gesture, he could ask the hateful Cosmo, but they were probably all away.

Why did his father increasingly hate leaving his dogs and horses and not take them on holidays abroad, so they could row in the Caribbean or Mauritius like everyone else's families? Then he wouldn't have to have a party.

Xav took a slug of vodka, then jumped out of his skin as the door opened, but it was only Bogotá, entirely white face smiling, pink tongue hanging down like a tie, black legs going everywhere.

'You can be guest of honour,' said Xav, giving him a piece of KitKat.

He'd better text people with invitations. He was too shy to telephone. If only Paris were still his friend, then everyone would have come.

Over the next week no one accepted.

'No one answers invitations these days,' Bianca consoled him. Not wanting her brother to be humiliated, she wrote to Feral: 'Xav is having a party on Thursday. Please come, he has asked Paris who would love to see you, so would I. Love, Bianca'.

As the party approached, the spats grew worse.

'How many yobs from Larks are coming?' demanded a departing Rupert.

'I'm not sure,' stammered Taggie.

'They'll chuck all your quiches at each other. For Christ's sake, lock up the silver and bolt all the yard doors.'

Taggie had racked her brains what to give Xav. Before his fall, it had been anything horsey, even on occasion a horse, or a drawing by Lionel Edwards or Munnings. Soon, but not yet, it might be a puppy. Xav didn't want clothes until he'd lost weight. Desperate to placate him, she spent far too much on DVD portables and computer games and mobiles which became cameras. As Rupert was abroad on the day of his birthday, Xav felt free to play up and hardly opened anything, which resulted in a blazing row when Bianca accused him of being an ungrateful pig.

'Mummy's spent days making yummy food and mixing this gorgeous drink.' Bianca pointed to the Pimm's cup floating with exotic fruit in the big blue bowl on the terrace table.

'I wanted people to have Snakebite or Black Russians, not piddling fruit salad,' snapped Xav, who'd been smoking and drinking all day to cushion himself against the nightmare ahead.

At least it was a beautiful evening, with air balloons drifting up the valley out of a soft rose glow in the west and flocks of birds returning home from scavenging in the fields. Beyond the stables, turning poplars soared like paintbrushes dipped in gold.

Taggie had tied scarlet and blue balloons saying 'Happy Birthday, Xav' on the gate and the balustrade running along the terrace, on which panted Rupert's pack of dogs, grateful that the cruel heat of the day was subsiding.

Rupert's horses were still inside to protect them from the flies and because he didn't want them galloping about, laming themselves on the rock-hard ground. From the rim of brown rush on the water's edge, the lake could be seen to have dropped a couple of feet. Eminem on the CD player battled with the roar of combines.

People had been invited for eight. At five minutes to, Taggie hurtled downstairs. Insufficiently dried, her dark hair fluffed out like Struwwelpeter. Her big, silver-grey eyes were red and tired. Never had her and Rupert's huge four-poster seemed more inviting.

'You look lovely,' lied Bianca, her hands shaking as she fastened a double row of pearls round her mother's slender neck.

'And you look heavenly,' said Taggie, very aware that her daughter was showing too much flesh in a pale pink crop-top and ice-blue shorts and wearing far too much make-up. Bianca had ironed her black curls straight, so a long lock fell over one eye. Jewelled flip-flops showed off ruby toenails and Taggie recognized her own Arpège on Bianca's hot, excited body and her own rubies in Bianca's ears. Rupert would have gone ballistic.

Xav was smouldering in the doorway to the terrace.

'Have a lovely evening.' Taggie tried to kiss him, but Xav, humiliated that, in her high heels, his mother was about seven inches taller than he, shoved her away. Although longing to bury his face in her lovely, scented bosom and beg her to make the party disappear, he couldn't thaw out.

'Don't expect we'll be late, Daddy'll have had a long day.' Then when Xav mumbled about olds not spoiling the fun: 'Don't worry, we'll creep in.'

The moment his mother had left, Xav chucked a bottle of gin into the Pimm's cup.

82

Over at Bagley, the Mansion, square-walled and square-windowed like a great doll's house, was softened by floodlights. Someone had tied pink balloons to the bay trees on either side of the front door and left an empty champagne bottle in one of the dark blue tubs. From the open ground-floor windows came the yelping roar of suntanned parents being force-fed drink to elicit more generous promises later in the evening.

On the way in Taggie bumped into dear Patience Cartwright, who, when he'd kept a pony at Bagley, had been one of the few people Xav had liked and talked to.

'Summer has been rather wearying,' Patience now confessed in her raucous voice.

Ian had let the school to a football academy, who'd trashed the kitchens on their last night, and a youth orchestra rehearsing for a prom, which had entailed non-stop Stockhausen and Hindemith. 'If only it'd been a nice Haydn symphony.'

'How's Paris getting on?' asked Taggie, wincing at her gaunt reflection in the hall mirror.

'All right.' Patience touched wood, then, lowering her voice: 'Could we have lunch and compare notes sometime?'

'Oh, do let's.'

'Paris has been a bit up and down. We love him,'

Patience went on firmly, 'but we're not quite sure how much he loves us.'

'I know the feeling,' sighed Taggie. Crossing her fingers, she asked: 'Is he coming to Xav's party?'

'Oh dear, didn't he answer? I'm so sorry. He's going to Jack Waterlane's. A whole crowd: Amber, Milly, Junior, Lando, Kylie, Pearl and Graffi have hired a minibus and taken sleeping bags. That's why David Waterlane isn't coming tonight. He won't pay fees, let alone for promises, and he wants to keep an eye on the Canalettos.'

Oh God, thought Taggie in horror. That lot were the core of Xav's party.

The next moment Daisy France-Lynch had hugged her. 'I've got a message from Lando. Will you apologize profusely to Xav, but he'd already accepted Jack's party which is only a couple of miles down the road. Cosmo and Jade are going there too.'

Next moment Dora was offering Taggie a trayful of brimming champagne glasses. 'Can you tell Bianca and Xav I'm terribly sorry I had to work. Mummy gives me no pocket money. Anyway, if Feral turns up, Bianca won't have eyes for anyone else. Paris has gone to Jack Waterlane's,' Dora added wistfully.

Taggie grabbed a drink, gulping down half of it. Poor, deserted Xav. She wanted to rush home to Penscombe but she had to wait for Rupert.

Creeping into the General Bagley Room, which had just been repainted in a glowing scarlet called Firestone, appropriately since so many of the mothers had acquired spare tyres cooking three meals a day for their offspring and visiting friends all summer. Most of them hid these bulges beneath floating flower prints or white caftans to show off suntanned breasts and shoulders.

Led by the frightful Anthea Belvedon, one mother after another charged up saying: 'No Rupert?' in aggrieved tones, as though Taggie'd pushed him over a cliff. Fleeing to avoid No-Joke Joan, who was obviously going to lecture her on Bianca's lack of application, Taggie went slap into Poppet Bruce, beaming like a lighthouse and clutching a hideous baby sucking on a pink dummy.

'Just off to give the babe his supper. Do let's exchange views,' cried Poppet and next moment Taggie found herself perched on a sofa in a side room as Poppet plunged a dishcloth-grey boob into goldfish-mouthing Gandhi.

Oh God, she hoped someone had arrived at Xav's party.

As if reading her thoughts, Poppet said, 'We must encourage Xavier in social skills, he's very troubled.'

'He's very shy,' protested Taggie.

'Last term his behaviour was distinctly challenging. I know parents of adopted children often blame them-selves for disasters that happen in any normal families, but you and Rupert lead such full lives, I sometimes wonder if anyone is listening to Xavier.'

'I haven't left the house all summer,' squeaked Taggie, 'and it's difficult listening to someone who won't talk.'

Poppet's bright, cheery eyes were boring into her like diamond cutters. 'Are you able to help him with his maths?'

'I can't do them at all,' gasped Taggie. If only she could ram a dummy into Poppet's mouth.

'Then I advise you to have some coaching. We have a good friend, Mike Pitts, who could come to the house three or four times a week.'

'I don't have the time,' stammered Taggie, which was quite the wrong answer, as Poppet frowned and suggested Taggie made time.

'Nor do I feel Rupert is a supportive father.'

'He absolutely adores Xav.'

'Maybe, but the lad must miss his birth parents. The wound never heals.' Smugly Poppet unplugged baby

Gandhi and hooked him onto another dishcloth-grey tit. 'I cannot advise you too strongly' – her tone grew more bullying – 'to take Xav to birth-mother groups. He could then witness grieving mothers coming to terms with giving up their babes and might achieve closure. Have you told Xav everything about his background?'

'I couldn't,' yelped Taggie.

'Have you wondered if your longing for your own children makes you reject Xav in some way?'

'No, no.'

Out of the window, Taggie could see General Bagley gleaming in the moonlight and longed to climb onto the back of his charger so he could gallop her home to Penscombe.

Rescue instead appeared as Hengist, resplendent in a dark blue velvet smoking jacket, appeared in the doorway.

'Taggie, darling, I've been looking for you. Your drink's empty, unlike little Gandhi's.' He and Poppet exchanged smiles of radiant insincerity. 'Come and talk to me.' He pulled Taggie to her feet, sliding his arm round her narrow waist and stubbing his thumb on her protruding ribs. 'You're losing too much weight. Has that bloody Milk Marketing Board been hassling you? I fear the geeks when they come baring breasts.'

Taggie didn't laugh. She was adorable but not very bright. Not that Rupert was the Brain of Britain.

As the gong went, Taggie pulled herself together. 'It was so sweet of Sally and you to send Xav a birthday card.'

'Sweet of Sally – she remembers everyone. She's the light of my life, as you are of Rupert's. I'm terribly sorry Alex has dragged you along to this grisly jaunt in the holidays. It was also Alex's grisly idea for parents to sit at their children's housemasters' tables. Afraid you're lumbered with Poppet and Alex again.'

Next moment Janey Lloyd-Foxe had buttonholed Taggie. 'How are you, darling? I can't wait for Amber and Junior to go back. We'll starve if I don't get some work done soon.'

Janey unnerved Taggie. She was married to Rupert's best friend, Billy Lloyd-Foxe, and was a well-known journalist who always seemed to know more and worse about you than you did yourself.

'Billy always complains he never gets any sex in the summer holidays because I'm so exhausted,' Janey went on. 'Amber and Junior's friends have been pouring through the house all summer.'

Which was more than Xav's had. Retreating to the Ladies, Taggie rang home. 'Are you OK?'

'Fine,' said Bianca. Dropping her voice: 'No one's arrived yet. Hang on, there's the doorbell. We're OK, bye.'

As she belted in from the terrace, Bianca passed Xav downing another mug of fruit cup and Mrs Bodkin in the study, sleeping peacefully through *The Two Ronnies*.

Followed by two striped lurchers, three Labradors and a couple of Jack Russells, Bianca opened the front door. There was no one outside, but the dogs carried on barking.

'Who's there? They're noisy but harmless,' shouted Bianca.

Very slowly, blacker than the shadows from which he emerged, long, lean and relaxed in a soft leather jacket, with the peak of his Arsenal baseball cap over one ear, a diamond cross gleaming at the neck of his black shirt, black jeans glued to his long legs, was Feral.

'Oh Feral!' Joy spread over Bianca's face like the glow in the west returning. 'You found us.'

'I did.' Feral couldn't believe how pretty she looked – and older, with her sleek, black hair and pale pink lipstick and dark liner emphasizing her ravishing mouth and eyes. He no longer felt avuncular, just lustful. 'Not sure about those dogs.'

'They're as dopey as anything.' Terrified he might run away, Bianca grabbed Feral's hand and led him into the hall, which was hung with pictures of horses and more dogs, and past rooms filled with beautiful battered furniture and splendid portraits.

'Who's that old git?'

'Our grandfather. He's been married five times.'

'Must like wedding cake. Looks familiar.'

'He's in *Buffers*.'

'So he is, friend of the Brig.' Then, peering into the library: 'Who reads those books?'

'No one. Mummy can't read; Daddy only reads Dick Francis and the racing pages.'

Out on the terrace, they found Xav, eyes crossed and slumped against the balustrade, just sober enough to say 'Hi' to Feral.

'This cup is cool,' said Bianca, 'I've eaten most of the fruit out of it. I'll get you a glass.'

As she went off to find one, Xav, who admired and envied Feral, offered him a line of coke.

Feral shook his head. 'Don't do drugs. Don't drink much.'

'This'll kick-start you.' Xav plunged the ladle into the Pimm's, picked up Bianca's glass and missed it.

Behind them the house reared up watchfully, ordering them to behave. A lawn to the right was almost as big as a football pitch.

'Paris coming?' asked Feral.

'Not yet,' mumbled Xav, 'evening's young.'

Bianca came back with a glass and filled it. Feral took a cautious sip, then a gulp.

'It is cool, man.' He took another gulp, then, putting down the glass, edged a box out of his tight jeans and handed it to Xav. 'Happy birthday.'

'Thanks.' Xav put it on the table.

'Open it,' nagged Bianca, 'Feral brought it all this way.'

It was a bracelet, consisting of two black straps

attached, instead of to a watch, to two silver skull and crossbones flanking the word FUCK in diamanté letters.

Xav's face lifted, showing for a second how good-looking he could be. 'That is wicked, man, really wicked.' He was worried he'd got too fat, but it did up easily.

'Thank Feral,' chided Bianca.

'I was about to, you stupid bitch.'

Feral, who'd been admiring the lake in the moon-light, swung round to defend Bianca, but she shook her head and his fists unclenched.

'It's great,' mumbled Xav. 'Can't wait to wave it at Poppet and Alex,' and he wheeled off into the house.

Justin Timberlake, fortissimo and blaring out over the valley, obliterated the need to talk.

'Don't people complain about the noise?' asked Feral, thinking of the fuss Miss Miserden made at Larks.

'Not really, Daddy owns the land,' said Bianca simply. 'What have you been doing all summer?'

'Working here and there, mostly for Lily and the Brig. He's been doing a series of *Buffers*; I've helped him dress – cufflinks and fings.'

'Daddy says it's going to be a huge hit, the network's taking it. Grandpa's booked for the next series. So naughty, he forgets I'm his granddaughter sometimes and pinches my bottom.'

'Not surprised in those shorts.' Feral drained his glass.

'They ought to do a programme about me called *Duffers*,' said Bianca, filling it up.

'And me.' Feral collapsed on a bench. He wanted to kiss Bianca's ruby toenails in those jewelled flip-flops. 'Can your mum really not read?'

'Hardly at all, she's dyslexic. Suits me, she can't read my diary. Dora's mother's always reading hers.'

'What does yours say?'

'Feral didn't come and see me today. Boo hoo.'
Bianca was on the bench beside him, edging up like a
kitten. She had no wiles, no defence mechanism; he
knew she was dying to be in his arms just as he was to
be in hers.

'Are you hungry?' asked Bianca.

'Kind of.' It wasn't cool to say he'd been too nervous
to eat all day. 'This drink's strong. Perhaps I should.'

'It'd be nice if you could. Mummy's worked so hard.
Poor Xav, I don't think anyone else is coming.'

'Bad for him, suits us.'

There is a limit to the inroads three people, two of
them dottily in love, can make on supper for twenty.
Feral ate some chicken pie and some chocolate
roulade and Bianca toyed with a piece of quiche. Xav
had another line of cocaine and another glass
of Pimm's and passed out on the sofa.

'Shall we go upstairs?' murmured Bianca, taking
Feral's hand, 'Daddy and Mummy have gone to some
dinner.'

Drunk with love and fruit cup, Feral had to cling on
to the crimson cord to pull himself up the splendid oak
staircase.

He would never have followed Bianca upstairs, or
even turned up, if he hadn't been boosted by the
prospect of a trial with the Rovers on Monday. A
contributory factor had also been that this week
(earlier than expected) his court case had come up.
The Brigadier had accompanied him to court and
vouched for his good character. Luckily the magistrates
were all fans of *Buffers* and had let him off, and because
he was still just fifteen, none of this had been reported
in the papers.

Inside Bianca's bedroom, someone appeared to have
shredded a rainbow, as clothes she'd rejected littered
bed, chair and carpet. As she gathered them up, chucking them on a blue and white striped sofa, Feral
admired the daffodil-yellow curtains and the pink and

violet quilt on the little four-poster. On the powder-blue walls, framed photographs of Colombian beauty spots – sweeps of orchids, giant water lilies, the lake where the legendary El Dorado was hidden – rubbed shoulders with posters of Michael Owen and Justin Timberlake, which he wanted to tear down. When he was striker for Larkminster Rovers, he'd have his own posters.

'This used to be the nicest spare room, but Daddy hates having people to stay so much, he let me have it.'

Feral leapt for the wardrobe in terror as he heard what he imagined as frantic hammering on the door, but it was only the hooves of Rupert's horses being let out into the fields in the cool of the evening.

'It's like a zoo here,' he grumbled, peering out of the window. 'Graffi'd be in heaven with all these horses and pictures.'

'Bring him tomorrow,' begged Bianca.

Feral had had so many girls, taking what he wanted without compunction, but none had touched him like Bianca, nor been as beautiful. Her clear, pale, coffee-coloured complexion was flushed with rose, her slim, supple body quivering to be entwined with his. He longed to bury his lips in her belly button and progress downward, to caress the delectable curve of buttock emerging from her blue shorts, to feel against his thighs the fluttering caress of her sooty eyelashes. Grown-up things.

But this was a child's room. On the shelves Harry Potter and Jacqueline Wilson fought for space with Barbie dolls, rows and rows of lipsticks and coloured nail polish. She was only thirteen – where the hell could it lead?

Above the bookcase hung a glass plate engraved with the words: 'Welcome to Penscombe, Bianca Maud Campbell-Black. May 1990'.

'I don't remember arriving here, I was only three months old, but Xav does and there were flags and balloons all the way up the drive. Mummy and Daddy crossed the world to find us,' Bianca added proudly. 'They were sad they couldn't have children but so pleased to have us. Our mother is the sweetest woman in the world.'

Feral edged towards her. 'Makes two of you.'

Bianca shrugged. 'Daddy's tricky, I used to be jealous of how much he adored Xav, but now they fight all the time.' She crossed the room, peering out at the empty terrace and the stars nearing their full brightness. 'I'm really sorry, it doesn't look as though Paris is coming.'

'Don't matter.' On her return from the window, Feral reached out for her, realizing she was trembling as much as he was.

'Why didn't you ring me? I gave you my number on three pieces of paper.'

'They ran in the washing machine. I tried once and got your Dad and bottled out. I watched your house across the valley for hours like a stalker.'

'Promise?'

'Promise, promise.'

Grabbing her tiny waist, encountering goose flesh, he caressed the edges of her springy, surprisingly full breasts, then he bent his head to kiss her arched-back throat, then her closed eyelids, the tip of her tiny nose, behind each ear, breathing in the deliciously heady Arpège. Finally he kissed her soft, sweet, pink lips, which parted shyly, her darting tongue touching his, flickering then retreating like a dancer, drawing him into heaven.

As her little hands closed on his head, his hair felt so thick, vigorous and right, compared with the floppy silken tresses of other boys she had snogged, that she clung on. Their first, magic kiss seemed to last for ever.

'Oh Bee-unca,' murmured Feral, collapsing back onto the bed, 'I have dreamt of you.'

'Why, uncle, it isn't a shame at all,' giggled Bianca, collapsing beside him. 'Xav's passed out, Mrs Bodkin's asleep and Mummy won't be back for centuries.'

83

Mrs Axford and her fleet of waitresses were clearing away the main course of chicken supreme with tagliatelle and wild mushrooms when Rupert stalked in. He could have murdered a quadruple whisky, but couldn't drink as he had to fly home. A ripple of excitement ran through the hall as mothers readjusted their cleavages and checked their reflections in little gold compacts. The only man in the room not in a dinner jacket (except Alex Bruce, who'd refused to wear one on principle), Rupert in a crumpled off-white suit and cornflower-blue shirt suddenly made everyone else look overdressed.

Hengist leapt to his feet. 'You've made it, well done, you're over here.'

Rupert had already clocked his wife looking utterly dejected between the appalling Alex Bruce and the just as appalling old queen Biffo Rudge. Serve her right for dragging him along to such a ghastly evening.

'OK?' he asked as he kissed her rigid cheek.

'No one's come to Xav's party,' whispered Taggie in anguish, 'they've all gone to Jack Waterlane's.'

'Might teach him to be nicer to people,' snapped Rupert.

Nemesis descended swiftly with a jangle of ethnic bracelets as a voice cried, 'Rupert, Rupert, you're here,' and Poppet Bruce patted the chair beside her.

'You've got Joan Johnson on your left, so we can enjoy an exchange of views about Xavier and Bianca. You know Alex and Biffo, of course, and Boffin's parents Gordon and Susan Brooks, and Anthea Belvedon.'

'Oh, Rupert and I are old friends,' said Anthea, delighted with an opportunity to captivate. She'd always thought Rupert was gorgeous and wasted on Taggie. How infuriating Dora, watching her every move, was waiting at table and had now rushed over and dumped a large piece of venison pâté in front of Rupert.

'Poor thing, you must be starving. Toast's on the way. How's Penscombe Peterkin?' That was Rupert's star horse, much fancied in the St Leger.

'Awesome, but we need rain, he loathes hard going.'

'Then he wouldn't like sitting between Joan and Poppet,' whispered Dora.

Seeing amusement in Rupert's eyes, Anthea said icily, 'You're supposed to be working, Dora. Had a good day's horse racing, lots of winners?' she called across the table.

'None,' said Rupert.

'Are Meridian going to take over Venturer?' asked Gordon Brooks.

'Not if I can help it.'

Out of the corner of his eye, Rupert caught sight of Hengist, Ruth Walton and his friend Billy Lloyd-Foxe at the next table, laughing their heads off at his plight.

'Trapped between Silly and Charybdis,' sighed Hengist, 'poor Rupert.'

As compensation, Rupert had a direct view of Mrs Walton, golden brown and replete in a beautiful Lindka Cierach dress in old rose silk, with a tiny pink cardigan knotted under her glorious boobs. She smiled lazily at Rupert, who smiled back, an exchange instantly registered by Randal Stancombe. At least he was at the head's table and not Rupert, who made no effort and called him Randolph (if he deigned to recognize him).

Gordon Brooks was now discussing some chemical formula with Joan, so Rupert turned to Poppet. 'How's the new baby?'

'Flourishing, flourishing. His siblings are so supportive. They relish developing their parenting skills. Parenting could be a good GCSE for Bianca.'

'Bit premature, she's only thirteen. Might qualify her for a free house, I suppose.'

'Now you're deliberately misunderstanding me.' Poppet laughed merrily. 'And we need to discuss Xav.'

'He's fine.'

'He has very few friends.' Poppet sipped her cranberry juice reflectively. 'If it's any consolation, Charisma, our eldest daughter, was dreadfully bullied for being severely gifted.'

'Not Xav's problem.'

'They accused Charisma of being "posh".'

'Posh? Your daughter?' said Rupert in genuine amazement.

'Because she always gets A stars. Charisma, of course, is a workaholic.'

'Neither of my children's problem,' snapped Rupert. 'Thanks, darling,' as a grinning Dora exchanged his venison plate for a plate of chicken.

'I've given you lots of mushrooms, they're really good.'

Greedily shovelling up butterscotch ice cream, Poppet trundled on: 'Xav yearns for acceptance by his peers.'

'Peers live in the House of Lords,' said Rupert coldly, 'or they did before Blair gelded the place.'

He glanced across at Taggie. Accustomed to being married to the prettiest woman in the room, he noticed her red, swollen eyes and unbecoming, unruly hair and felt outraged that Alex Bruce was wrapped in conversation with Boffin's mother and Biffo had gone off table-hopping, leaving her stranded. A second later, Biffo's seat had been taken by Sally B-T.

'How's Xav's birthday going? Such a super chap.'

'Are you sure we're talking about the same child?' Rupert answered for Taggie. 'Six weeks into the school holidays, he's emerging as the devil incarnate.'

'Rupert,' gasped Taggie in horror.

Rupert crashed his knife and fork together, chicken hardly touched, fingers drumming, and turning to No-Joke Joan for heavy relief, learnt she'd been giving a paper on the evolution of the potato.

'Does Bianca lack social skills?' he asked finally.

'Quite the contrary. She and Dora Belvedon never stop chattering. I shudder to think of their phone bills. I'm afraid there's little likelihood of Bianca getting any GCSEs unless she buckles down.'

'It's a first step of the most evil tyrants,' Alex Bruce was droning on to Boffin's mother, 'destroying the teaching profession. In the seventies, teachers and academics arrested by Idi Amin never re-emerged because he tortured, then murdered them.'

'What a sensible man.' Rupert took a swig out of a nearby Perrier bottle.

As Alex went purple and stormed off, Poppet renewed her attack.

'There's a wonderful government initiative called Dads and Lads, Rupert. Fathers reading with their sons and helping them with their homework. I'm sure you could give your Colombian lad a lift.'

'Dads and Lads?' said Rupert softly.

'If you and Taggie struggle with the homework,' joined in Joan, 'I think Bianca's only salvation is to board.'

'She will not,' said Rupert, so sharply everyone looked round and Randal Stancombe decided to join the table, taking Alex's chair. He made a great show of kissing first Taggie's, then Anthea's hands, before expressing hope that they were all going to make promises he could auction later in the evening.

'What's on offer already?' asked Poppet.

'Lord Waterlane's offered lunch at the House of Lords,' said Stancombe consulting his clipboard. 'Ricky France-Lynch has pledged polo lessons; Daisy his wife has offered to do a free pastel of the person of your choice. Billy Lloyd-Foxe' – he raised his voice so Billy and everyone at the next table stopped talking and laughing – 'has promised a tour round Television Centre, lunch in the canteen and tickets to his programme *Sport and Starboard*.'

'Good old Billy!' everyone cheered.

'What have you offered us, Randal?' simpered Anthea.

'Two weeks in a Caribbean villa and a free flight,' said Randal modestly to more cheers. 'Dame Hermione—' he began.

'Christ, is she here?' Rupert was about to dive under the table.

'Dame Hermione is at a gig this evening,' reproved Joan. 'She has pledged tickets for Covent Garden and supper afterwards. We're still looking for more bumper prizes.'

'How about a night at the Ritz with Rupert Campbell-Black?' yelled Billy.

'Yes, Rupert,' asked Poppet archly, 'what are you going to pledge?'

'A day at the Arc in your private box?' suggested Stancombe. 'And a ride back and forth in your chopper?'

'Or on your chopper,' shouted Janey Lloyd-Foxe to shouts of laughter.

'That would be an exciting pledge,' dimpled Anthea.

'For whom?' snapped Rupert.

'Oh, come on, Rupert, that's not going to break the bank,' chided Stancombe.

'Racing's work. I can't concentrate if I have to spend the day being charming.'

'You'll just have to try harder,' teased Poppet.

'Poor Rupert,' murmured Mrs Walton, 'he does look

fed up. Is he ever unfaithful to that sweet, stupid wife?'

'Certainly not,' said Billy with rare sharpness, 'and she's not stupid, Penscombe would crumble without her holding it together.'

'Let's go and cheer him up,' whispered Mrs Walton to Hengist.

Leaving Billy, filling up everyone's glasses with a fresh bottle of red and pulling up two chairs beside Rupert, Hengist muttered:

'Are you OK?'

'Not until you find me a red-hot poker to ram up Mrs Bruce's ass.'

'Hush,' giggled Mrs Walton.

'Those emeralds are stunning,' said Rupert, unthawing slightly, 'and they couldn't have a better setting.'

'Randal brought them back for me from Bogotá.'

What was Stancombe doing there? wondered Rupert. Drug centre of the world; Xav's birthplace. Remembering the happiness and excitement when they'd brought him and Bianca home, he vowed to make things better.

Glancing across at Taggie he saw she was shaking with terror. Toothy Susan Brooks, whose favourite subject was Boffin, had got on to GCSEs and whether it would be too taxing for her G and T son to take fourteen.

'How many did you take, Poppet?'

'Ten, but they were O' levels.'

'And you, Anthea?'

'Nine.'

'And you, Ruth?'

'Eight.'

'And you, Hengist?'

'About twenty-five. That's enough of that.' Hengist, who'd also noticed Taggie's twitching face, drained his glass and announced it was time for a pee break before the auction.

But Poppet refused to leave it. 'How many GCSEs did you get, Taggie?' she asked loudly.

'None,' whispered Taggie, colour suffusing her grey cheeks.

'Really?' said Anthea in amazement. 'None at all?'

'I didn't get any either,' said Rupert quickly. 'Never took any.'

'How the hell did you get into the Blues?' asked Hengist.

'I took a civil service exam, which was the equivalent, then went before a selection board at Westbury. I was only in for a year or two before going back to showjumping.'

'No O' levels between either you or Taggie,' mocked Poppet.

'One wonders if you could achieve a GCSE today?' Alex quizzed Rupert as he returned to the table.

'Course I could. They're so bloody easy. You can take in calculators and history notes and poetry books. I'd walk it.'

'What a wonderful idea.' Poppet clapped her hands with another mad jangle of bracelets. 'You and Xav must take a GCSE together. English literature. You can read the books he's working on and exchange views at mealtimes.'

'Don't be fucking stupid, I haven't got the time,' snarled Rupert.

'You mean you haven't got the bottle,' taunted Stancombe. 'You wouldn't risk it, knowing you'd fail.'

'I bloody wouldn't.' Rupert had risen to his feet, shaking with rage, about to leap across the bottles and glasses and strangle him.

'Kindly don't swear in front of our spouses,' said Alex querulously.

'Oh fuck off.' Rupert turned back to Stancombe. 'I have got the bottle.'

'Prove it,' taunted Stancombe softly. 'I bet you a hundred grand, which I'll pledge to the Bagley Fund, you can't pass Eng. lit.'

'I'll sponsor you for ten thousand, Rupert,' said

Gordon Brooks, 'but only if you get a C grade or above.'

'My newspaper would sponsor you for at least fifty thousand, Rupe,' shouted Janey Lloyd-Foxe leaping up and down in excitement, 'as long as we can have the story. Make a fantastic diary: Rupert takes a GCSE.' She was now scribbling on her wrist.

Offers of sponsorship were coming in from eager mothers all over the room.

'I'll give you twenty-three pounds,' said Dora.

'We'll have paid for the new science block in one night,' murmured Theo Graham.

'Then it's a done deal.' Stancombe jumped onto a chair, shouting, 'Rupert Campbell-Black has agreed to take an English lit. GCSE and has already been sponsored to the tune of two hundred and fifty thousand pounds if he gets a C grade or above.'

Rage no longer robbed Rupert of speech.

'I fucking haven't,' he howled. 'I've got a yard and a television station to run and there is no way I'm taking any exam,' and he stalked out of the hall.

Table Ten were very slow in getting coffee, petits fours and their ordered liqueurs, because Dora, their waitress, had retreated to the sixth-form common room.

'Wicked!' she was whispering into her mobile. 'Rupert Campbell-Black is going to take a GCSE. Yes? I swear. At a promises auction at Bagley. Parents have sponsored him to over a quarter of a million already. It happened after a row with horrible Randal Stancombe, who was taunting Taggie and Rupert for not having any O' levels. English lit., I think, although according to his daughter Bianca, Rupert only reads Dick Francis and the racing pages.'

There was no way Dora was going to let that old tart Janey Lloyd-Foxe pip her to the post.

84

Taggie raced after Rupert as he strode towards his helicopter.

'I'm so sorry, I'm so sorry. You were so kind to defend me, it was all my fault.'

As he waited for clearance to fly, Rupert rang Lysander, his assistant, who said everything was as quiet as a mouse.

'Most of the horses are out, except Peterkin and the ones racing on Monday. No sound from the house, hardly any lights on and no music for ages. Party must be over, frankly I didn't see anyone arrive.'

Flying into Penscombe, Rupert looked down at the empire he had created without a single O' level. There was the ancient blond house with its billowing woods and venerable oaks skirting a fast-emptying lake, more than a hundred horses out in the fields, all weather gallops, indoor school, tennis court, swimming pool, animals' graveyard, and the moonlit ribbon of the Frogsmoor stream, like a white parting down the valley. An empire built up by his own hard work. There was no way he was going to take any fucking GCSE.

He was so angry he ignored the fact his wife was crying. On landing, he went straight to the yard. Penscombe Peterkin whickered at his master's approach, hopeful of being let out to join his friends. The son of Rupert's Derby winner, Peppy Koala,

Peterkin had been born and brought up at Penscombe, where everyone loved him. When one of Rupert's jockeys used a whip on him in a race for the first time, the little colt was so outraged, he stopped in his tracks and was never whipped again. Since then, he'd never lost a race. A huge amount was already on him for the St Leger. Rupert patted and gave him a handful of pony nuts and wandered back to the house to find chaos and his wife frantically wiping up pools of sick in the hall.

The dogs had obviously raided Taggie's supper. Stalker, Rupert's favourite Jack Russell, was polishing off a chicken pie abandoned on the terrace table, from time to time dropping pieces onto the flagstones for a patiently waiting Bogotá to hoover up.

Mrs Bodkin was still asleep in front of some X-rated film. Xav's presents were still unopened, little beast.

'I told you not to give him a party,' growled Rupert, avoiding another pile of sick, then catching sight of a black leather jacket over the banister.

Feral had had so many girls before, but this was the real one. The problem was keeping Bianca's love in check. She was so anxious to give him everything. He had removed her bra and stroked her sweet, tip-tilted breasts; he had buried his face in her scented shoulders, stroked her hair and kissed her on and on. They were too preoccupied with one another to hear anyone arriving.

Suddenly the door burst open.

'What the fuck d'you think you're doing? Get away from her, you black bastard,' howled Rupert.

Only when Feral reared up, shaking off the duvet, did Rupert realize Bianca was only naked to the waist and Feral still wearing his black jeans. Standing, he was almost as tall as Rupert.

'I ain't no black bastard, man,' he said with quiet

dignity. 'Back in the dark ages, my dad was married to my mum.'

Next moment he had leapt onto the blue striped sofa and jumped out of the window, falling on a yew hedge. But as he dropped down onto the lawn, landing awkwardly, a sharp pain gripped the right ankle of his shooting foot. He gave a groan as he limped away, keeping to the shadows.

'Daddy, how could you?' screamed Bianca. 'We were just snogging. How dare you call Feral a black bastard? I made all the running.'

'You shouldn't bloody be in bed with him,' said Rupert, slightly shaken. 'I suppose your brother's passed out?'

But Xav, sobering up and lurking on the landing, had overheard the row.

'Black bastard?' he yelled. 'Black fucking bastard? I'm black and I'm a bastard. Now I know what you really think of me.'

'Oh, for Christ's sake, it's just a figure of speech.'

'How dare you insult Feral?' sobbed Bianca. 'We were only kissing.'

'Go to bed,' shouted Rupert.

But Xav was fired up.

'My birthday was the day I was wrenched from my mother and chucked out on the streets to die. If only I had died. I've always had shit birthdays.'

'Xav,' pleaded Taggie, running up the stairs, 'that's not true.'

Xav turned on her. 'Shut up! I never wanted you as a mother, I hate you, *hate* you. You never loved me either, because I'm fat, ugly and useless.'

He ran sobbing out of the house, slamming the door in poor limping Bogotá's white face, heading out for the yard. Peterkin was delighted to see Xav, who had been the first person on his back and had often slept in his box. Both horse and boy had moped when Xav went away to Bagley. Xav led Peterkin into the yard by his head collar, jumped onto his back and set off across the fields, flat out towards the main road. Moonlight, more silvery light than day, sculpted dark grey trees and pale grey walls.

'Black bastard, black bastard,' yelled Xav in time to Peterkin's galloping hooves. Cocaine and booze had cushioned him against fear. He wasn't frightened of anything, not even his father. I hate him, I hate him, I hate him.

Rupert had poured himself a quadruple whisky and was just telling himself Xav would come home as soon as he sobered up, when the best horse he'd ever owned and trained passed the window, hurtling towards the main road on rock-hard ground. Rushing out to the yard, Rupert leapt on a mare who was racing on Monday. He'd have to head Xav off.

Xav by this time had turned Peterkin round and, rejoicing he'd got his nerve back, was riding quietly home across the fields, when Rupert thundered up and whacked Xav across the face, yelling:

'Get off that horse, you can bloody well walk home.'

As Xav slid to the ground, he felt all his fuses blow. He watched Rupert pull off his tie and slot it through Peterkin's head collar, then began almost conversationally:

'I know all about you.'

As Rupert paused, he went on:

'I know how much you drugged and boozed. I know you beat up your horses and your first wife. I know you bullied Jake Lovell witless on the showjumping circuit. You're an utterly crap role model. I don't belong to you any more, I want a divorce.' Xav's quiet voice had risen to a scream of pain.

'I dug out my secret files in the cellar. I know I was battered and left for dead as a baby because they thought my birthmark was the sign of the devil. Well, now I'm older, your fingermarks on my face are worse than any birthmark. They're the sign of a devil.' He spat at his appalled father's feet. 'The curse of being your son and a Campbell-Black.'

Hearing screams and shouts, fearful it might be Rupert after him, Feral hobbled faster. Glancing back, he saw Rupert's drive stretched out in the moonlight like a bandage to bind up his broken heart or his totally fucked ankle. No trial, no Bianca.

Next morning, Peterkin was as crippled lame as Feral. All the late editions of the papers picked up the *Independent*'s story about Rupert taking a GCSE.

85

For the first time in her life, Bianca Campbell-Black was utterly miserable. She had always been so proud of her parents, but now her father had revealed himself as a foul racist – and after all her coaxing, Feral had shot back into the jungle again. She kept imagining his cat's eyes shining out of the beech wood behind the house.

The Saturday after Xav's party, she and Dora went into Larkminster to see *I Capture the Castle*, a film Dora loved because she identified with the diary-writing heroine and her large eccentric family. Afterwards, she and Bianca went on to a Chinese restaurant where, as they rolled duck, sliced cucumber and dark sweet crimson sauce in pancakes and harpooned sweet and sour prawns, Bianca relayed the events of the last few days and Dora's eyes grew bigger and bigger.

'Your father was horribly hassled before he left Bagley,' she said in mitigation. 'He'd been trapped by Joan, Mrs Fussy and my mother all evening, then he was manoeuvred into that GCSE which he's been forced to agree to take.'

'That was shocking. Someone must have leaked it to the papers that very night.'

'Shocking,' agreed Dora. 'Some people have no principles.' Then, hastily changing the subject – after all, dinner tonight was being paid for by the *Independent*'s cheque: 'Do you think Feral would be caught in bed with me if I paid him? How ballistic would Mummy go? OK, OK, only joking.'

Dora vowed on this occasion not to ring any newspapers, Bianca was so desolate. She'd eaten nothing. Dora had to finish the spring rolls and prawns and bag up Bianca's duck for Cadbury. Unable to bear seeing her happy friend cast down, she suggested they call on Feral.

It was getting dark. The Shakespeare Estate was only 750 yards away, but they might have been plunging thousands of miles into the depths of hell. Rasta music fortissimo, football commentary, shouts and screams poured out of graffitied buildings. Jeering gangs of youths roamed the streets. Tarts screamed abuse. Addicts, like corpses dug up from the grave, hung stinking and unwashed over broken fences.

'If only Cadbury was here to defend us,' quavered Dora as a snarling Dobermann hurled itself against a gate. 'Shall we try another day?'

'We'll be safe when we find him,' pleaded Bianca. 'Here we are. Macbeth Street, number twelve.'

All Feral's windows were boarded up, as though he no longer allowed himself to look out on the world. The garden was full of burnt-out cars, fridges and wheelless bikes. Running up the path, Bianca hammered on the front door, which was answered by a fat man in a filthy vest, clearly off his face with drugs. Leering, swaying, he beckoned them inside, where Uncle Harley, immaculate as ever in black leather, Feral's diamond cross gleaming at his neck, was watching a revolting film in which a man and a woman were clearly enjoying sex with a little girl.

'Not something you'd show the vicar,' mocked the fat man.

Nearly asphyxiated by a stench of sweat, puke and fags, ready to bolt, but hearing the front door bang behind them, Dora bravely announced they'd come to see Feral.

The fat man jerked his head. 'Next door.'

In the kitchen they found glasses and plates piled high in the sink and a woman, presumably Feral's mother, lying moaning on the floor in a drug-induced stupor, surrounded by playing children.

Then Bianca gasped as she caught sight of Feral, stripped to the waist, shiningly beautiful in this midden of squalor, masculinity in no way diminished by the fact he was working his way through a pile of ironing and trying to feed a yelling baby in a high chair.

Bianca was still speechless, but over the lecherous cajoling of the man in the porn film, Dora yelled:

'It's us, Feral.'

Feral looked up in horror. Hissing like a cornered wild cat, he screamed at them to get the fuck out.

'I wanted to say sorry for Daddy,' sobbed Bianca, 'and see if you were all right.' Then, when Feral said nothing: 'I love you.'

'Well, I don't love you. Get out.' As he hobbled towards them, brandishing the iron in their faces like a riot shield, Dora caught sight of a bandage on his ankle.

Next moment, Uncle Harley had lurched into the room and made a grab at Bianca who, catching him off balance, shoved him crashing against the sink, smashing several glasses. Dora meanwhile had clouted the fat man with her bag and unchained the door, enabling them to flee out of hell. Seeing their terrified faces, a prostitute screeched, 'Taught you a lesson, did it? Don't mess with Uncle Harley.'

Dora and Bianca didn't stop until they reached the bridge. Leaning against it, gasping for breath, Dora couldn't stop shaking.

'What an utterly disgusting, revolting place.'

Bianca couldn't stop crying; her only emotion was sympathy for Feral living with those crackheads.

'That's why he's so poor,' she wailed, 'and why he wouldn't go on the geography field trip, or take up that games scholarship at Bagley. There'd be no one to look after those children. What are we going to do? I daren't tell Mummy and Daddy where I've been.'

'I'll just call Dicky and check Cadbury's OK. I expect they're both watching disgusting porn on the internet too. Then let's take a taxi to Janna's.' Dora put an arm round Bianca. 'Don't cry. She'll know what to do.'

Music louder than any on the Shakespeare Estate poured out of Jubilee Cottage. The Brigadier had been sent a crate of red by a fan and he and Lily were teaching Janna and Emlyn the Charleston. They were all hammered.

'I'm terribly sorry, we haven't got enough for the taxi,' were Dora's first words.

After Emlyn had paid it, Bianca gazed into space shuddering whilst Dora, one hand on her hip, the other gesticulating wildly, described their adventures.

'Poor Feral,' she said indignantly. 'Rupert called him a "black bastard" and chucked him out of Penscombe, although he and Bianca were only snogging, or as Mummy calls it "heavy petting". Mind you, there are plenty of pets at Penscombe.'

Meeting the Brigadier's eye, Lily tried not to laugh.

No one was laughing by the time Dora had finished.

'Oh poor, poor Feral,' whispered Janna.

'We must rescue him,' wept Bianca.

'I think we've all drunk too much to do anything tonight,' said Emlyn. 'Janna and I'll go round in the morning and sort it out.'

'Feral's got a soccer trial on Monday. Should cheer him up,' volunteered the Brigadier.

'I don't think so,' sighed Dora, 'he was lame as a cat.'

'That's from escaping out of my bedroom window,' wailed Bianca. 'It's all bloody Daddy's fault.'

'Better stay the night,' Lily told Dora and Bianca to the Brigadier's regret.

* * *

'Shall I come with you?' asked the Brigadier next morning, as he tried to keep down a Fernet-Branca.

'Fewer of us the better, less ostentatious,' answered Emlyn as he coiled his long length into Janna's green Polo.

'Something rotten in the state of Larkminster,' he observed as Janna drove past smashed-up playgrounds, shuttered shops, shells of houses, front gardens full of junk instead of flowers, and parked at the end of Macbeth Street. Emlyn edged her inwards so he could walk on the outside of the pavement.

'Although this is the sort of hell-hole where I should walk on both sides of you.'

At first Feral wouldn't open the door.

'If you're from the social,' observed an old biddy scuttling past, 'they've gone.'

Hearing a baby crying, Emlyn continued thumping.

When Feral finally let them in, they found him alone with three young children and the howling baby, whose nappy he'd just changed. From the mop in a bucket of suds, he'd obviously been cleaning up the floor. There was no fridge. Flies were everywhere.

After a lot of coaxing and a cigarette from Emlyn, he admitted that Uncle Harley and his mother had pushed off abroad to punish him. Gradually, eyes cast down, stammering out the sentences, occasionally returning to his former hauteur, he explained how he'd stolen to feed his brothers and sisters and carried a gun to protect them.

'Harley used my mother as a tom, kept her short of money and drugs, to make her reliant and desperate. Anyfing I earn from Lily and the Brig, she takes to feed her habit. Even if I hide it in the toes of my trainers, she finds it. Does my head in. What'll happen to her? She's not beautiful any more; Harley'll kill her.'

As Feral got up to wave away a swarm of flies settling on a plate of beefburgers, Emlyn noticed him hobbling.

'So you're no good for the trial on Monday?'

'Fanks to Mr Rupert Fancy-Black, I've gotta let the Brig down.'

'Does Harley give you a hard time?'

Feral nodded bleakly. 'He went ballistic I wouldn't deal when I got access to all those rich Bagley kids. Nearly buried me when I turned down that boarding place.'

Now the howling baby was sleeping in her arms, Janna wanted to howl herself. Feral had been so proud, so brave, his constant lack of funds the only giveaway. Emlyn was being wonderful too. With one child on each muscular thigh, and the third watching, he was singing nursery rhymes to them.

'They're not going into care!' Feral became almost hysterical. 'They'll never come back.'

'Only for a bit, while we sort ourselves out,' promised Janna. 'Everyone needs a leg-up occasionally. I accepted money from Randal Stancombe to keep Larks going.'

With trepidation she called Nadine who, fired up by a new scheme to unite social services and the education and health departments, turned out to be an absolute star.

The Brigadier, who had just been cleared by the Criminal Records Bureau to teach history at Larks, had grown so fond of Feral, he asked him to stay until things got straight. Janna would be up the road with Lily next door, so Feral wouldn't be lonely, and he could do the odd job round the house. Nadine then arranged for the children and the baby to be taken into temporary care with a good, kind family in the next village, so Feral could pop in and see them whenever he wanted. Feral listlessly agreed to everything because he saw no other way out. He loved Bianca, but like Juliet she was not yet fourteen; Rupert would always show him the door.

'Rupert called me a "black bastard",' he kept telling the Brigadier.

Feral moved in, but like a feral cat, he couldn't bear being trapped and begged the Brigadier not to lock the doors at night. 'I'll be your guard dog, man.'

86

Janna had worked flat out throughout the summer holidays supervising the rebuilding of Appletree, because the moment she stopped being busy, she was wiped out by guilt, sadness and despair. These feelings were reinforced by record temperatures, dire news of global warming and melting icebergs. Would there be a world at all for the children to inherit?

Despite gallant work by the remaining teachers, there had been so much disruption during the summer term that in the end only eight per cent of Larks children achieved the Magic Five. Ashton was on the telephone in seconds.

'Dear, dear, dear,' he gloated, 'how lucky for you we OK'd Appletwee first. If we'd had a sight of these wesults, you'd never have got your building. I do pray you do better with Year Ten.'

The *Times Educational Supplement* had reported that the proportion of U grades was the highest ever.

'Most of them from Larks,' observed Ashton bitchily.

Janna had also observed a faint neglect of late. Throughout July, Hengist had frequently rolled up at Appletree around dusk to admire work in progress, before making love to her in the long, pale, dry grass of Smokers' with the stars emerging as voyeurs overhead.

'Do you know it's illegal to have sex out of doors?'

709

Janna had teased him on his last visit. 'I'm sure Miss Miserden's got a periscope.'

'It's called outreach, because I reach out for you,' said Hengist.

Above them on the right of an apricot-pink harvest moon, Mars, like an angry red-gold lion tossing his mane, dominated the evening sky.

'This year's belonged to Mars,' said Hengist, as he zipped up his trousers, 'that's why you won your battle over Year Ten, but you must watch Ashton. I don't know what he can still do to hurt you, but I don't trust him. Two thousand and four, thank God, will be Venus's year. She'll shine so brightly, I'll fall in love with you all over again.'

As he smiled down, he noticed, like scratches on a scraper board, new lines on her face.

'Darling, you must get a break. Why not come and crash out for a few days in the house we rent in Tuscany? I'll call you.'

But after that visit in late July she had heard nothing for nearly five weeks. She knew he was back because she'd read in the *Independent* about the fundraising evening and Rupert's GCSE, which he'd only finally agreed to take because all the papers claimed he'd never pass. Janna had been tempted to drop him a line and ask him if he'd like a place at Larks. That would solve any woman-teacher recruitment problem.

Throughout the summer, her thoughts had flickered too often to Emlyn. She was so grateful to him for helping sort out Feral that she called him to say the Welsh National Opera were doing *Turandot* at the Bristol Hippodrome. If she got two tickets, would he like to come?

'And I'll buy you dinner afterwards.'

'I can't, lovely; I've got a lot on.'

And Janna felt snubbed.

'When I suggested another night,' she told Lily, 'he said he was going to see his mother. He hasn't flown anywhere to see Oriana this summer. Do you think' – Janna loathed the thought – 'he's got someone else?'

Lily shook her head.

'I'm sure he's still crazy about Oriana and thinks that somehow, if he's faithful, God will reward him.'

'How complicated,' sighed Janna. 'What's she like?'

'Bit chilly and critical. Ambitious like her father, but she lacks Hengist's warmth and *joie de vivre*.'

87

Hengist was full of joy as he changed for dinner at St Matthew's, his old Cambridge college. He and Sally had had such a magic evening last night, listening to Mahler Three at the Proms and watching a rainbow soaring out of the turning trees, which after rain were all glittering gold in the setting sunlight. They had then rushed up to bed and made such warm, passionate love that they had forgotten their mobiles, lying like lovers side by side on the terrace table, both still working perfectly in the morning, despite a further shower of rain – like our marriage, thought Hengist.

He was still battling not to be too triumphalist over Bagley's leap in the league tables; they were only a place below Fleetley. What matter if, to Alex's fury, St Jimmy's were only five places behind Bagley?

Dear Theo had, once again, got everyone through everything. He must put him forward for a Teaching Award, it would so annoy Alex.

The evening at St Matthew's was all Hengist could have wished for: exquisite food and wine and, although he loved women, as a man who had always charmed his own sex, he found there was something so wonderfully uncorseted about an all alpha-male evening. He loved keeping the table in a roar. He adored the wheeling and dealing, the superior gossip, learning of a brilliant undergraduate who, after he came down, might like to spend a year or ten teaching at Bagley, and dropping in turn hints about a brilliant Bagley boy.

'We plucked him out of the state system and a children's home. Theo's been coaching him.'

There was a lot of chuntering about admissions tutors being forced to accept lower grades from poorer students and a great deal of laughter over Rupert Campbell-Black's GCSE.

'You know him well, Hengist.'

'Love him – but he'd rather die than fail.'

'His son is a rare pianist, I never thought the Grieg could reduce me to tears.'

Over the port, people started table-hopping and the Master drew Hengist into a window seat, and in a voice as soft as the bloom on the black grapes asked him if he'd be interested in Fleetley.

'Hatchet Hawkley's retiring in two thousand and five.'

'The end of a great era,' said Hengist lightly.

'May we put your name forward, Hengist?'

Hengist looked at the wise, knowing face:

'I don't know how delighted Hatchet would be. I used to be one of his junior masters ... Our son Mungo ...'

Hengist didn't add that his passionate affaire with Hatchet's wife, Pippa, had only been discovered by Hatchet after her death.

'I know you have painful memories,' said the Master.

'Sally more.' Through the dusk Hengist could see the first yellow leaves falling on yellowing lawns.

'Hatchet has always been laid back about recruitment,' urged the Master, 'you could raise it to new heights.'

'I'll think about it very seriously,' said Hengist with that smile that could melt icebergs.

After a college restoration meeting the next morning, followed by a light, excellent lunch and a trip to buy a

713

lovely oil of a greyhound for Sally, Hengist was in celebratory mood, and picked up his mobile:

'Darling, I'll be with you around eight and don't wear any knickers.'

As he left, he noticed a mower cutting to pieces any fairy rings on the college lawn.

In Hamburg, negotiating the building of a hypermarket, Randal Stancombe rang Ruth Walton between meetings. Their relationship had recently suffered a setback. Lorraine, his estranged wife, had not been amused when reports on Randal, goading Rupert into taking a GCSE, had referred to Ruth as 'the utterly gorgeous new love of his life'. Nor had Milly; outraged at being banned from seeing Graffi, she had promptly accused Randal of groping her. Ruth had staunchly dismissed this as fantasy on Milly's part, but did suggest it might be better if she and Randal cooled it until next week, when Milly was safely back at Bagley.

Randal now rang in the hope that the coast might be clear. Sadly it wasn't.

'We've got to do Milly's trunk. She's put on seven pounds in the holidays, most of it round the bust.'

Like her mother, thought Stancombe. He must keep his hands off Milly.

'And I've got a Bagley's governors' meeting early evening. After that Milly and I are getting a takeaway; she says we never talk these days.' Ruth added more hot water to a jacuzzi as big as the Bagley lake. 'But once term starts, I'm all yours.'

'What a lovely "all",' purred Stancombe.

Ten minutes later, racked with lust, he decided to kill the meeting and fly home for the night. He bought Milly a bottle of Obsession at the hotel shop and he would sweep her and Ruth out to the La Perdrix d'Or. Somehow he must persuade Ruth to marry him. To hell with Lorraine taking him to the cleaners; he could afford it. Ruth made him feel like a god in and out of bed and after all the surgery he'd paid for, he felt he owned most of her anyway.

As he let himself into the Cavendish Plaza flat he allowed her to live in for nothing, he was touched at first to find candles on a table. Ruth, like the good mother she was, was taking her bonding session with Milly very seriously. Two bottles of his Krug, lobster and strawberries in the fridge were pushing it a bit, as was the Château d'Yquem. There was even a rocket and asparagus salad and, most caring of all, home-made mayonnaise.

On the triple bed, on the other hand, was a Janet Reger carrier bag with a suspender belt, tutu and negligee spilling out, too good even for Milly's trunk, and sweet-scented roses and lilies everywhere.

Stancombe flicked on the machine. The deep, lazy, patrician tones were unmistakable.

'Darling, I'll be with you around eight and don't wear any knickers.'

Clearly this governors' meeting was only for two people. Quivering with clumsy rage, Stancombe removed flowers, food, bottles, underwear – all Ruth's seduction kit – from the flat. He wanted to kill them both so badly, he nearly ran his Ferrari into the Casey Andrews sculpture adorning the exit to Cavendish Plaza. The bastard, the bitch, the bitch, the bastard. His brain was a red fuzz. He'd cancel the Stancombe block at Bagley, but it was already a quarter up, which was more than he was. Desperate for a pretty shoulder to cry on, he drove straight round to Janna's.

Janna had been anticipating a quiet evening. She was delighted to see Lily off on a date with the Brigadier, which would include watching a recording of *Buffers*. Emlyn had swept Feral off to see a Welsh rugby sports doctor about his ankle and spend the night with Emlyn's mother in Wales.

The birds in Janna's garden had stopped singing, too

exhausted by caring for their young at the end of the summer holidays. She had just opened a tin of Pedigree Chum for Partner when she heard a car outside.

At first, when she saw the bottles of Krug in Randal's hand, she thought he'd come to exact payment in kind for financing the rebuilding of Appletree. When he plonked them on the kitchen table, along with a bottle of Château d'Yquem and a carrier bag spilling over with pink underwear, she asked him if he'd won the lottery.

She was just hastily washing Pedigree Chum off her hands, when he returned with armfuls of flowers and a carrier bag containing two lobsters, strawberries and a bowl of mayonnaise and told her to put them and the Krug in the fridge.

'How lovely,' squeaked Janna. 'Would you like some of your own drink, or shall I put these in water first?'

Then she noticed Stancombe was wearing a suit and tie, as though he'd just come from the office, that he was shuddering and there was a green tinge to his permatan.

'Whatever's the matter?'

Stancombe slumped down at the kitchen table and started to cry.

'Oh, my poor love.' Running round, Janna put her arms round him. 'Is it Jade? What's happened?'

'Ruth,' sobbed Stancombe.

'Oh my God, is she OK?'

'She's OK, the fucking bitch. She's seeing someone else.'

'Are you sure? She always seems mad about you!'

Ashamed of breaking down, Stancombe blew his nose on a piece of kitchen roll and proceeded to pace up and down the tiny kitchen like a tiger penned in a travelling crate.

Janna took down a vase and as the roses were beginning to droop, found a rolling pin to bash the stems.

716

'God I loved her, the bitch,' said Stancombe despairingly.

'She was just probably being friendly with whoever.'

'Like hell. I decided to surprise her and she had dinner prepared and my flat decked out for your friend Hengist.'

'Ouch!' The rolling pin crushing her fingers and the rose thorn plunging into her thumb were nothing to the pain. 'Hengist? It can't be. He and Sally . . .'

'Fucking hypocrite. "My darling Sally", indeed.'

'How long's it been going on?' asked Janna numbly.

'Dunno. A bit – he left a message on her machine telling her not to wear any panties.'

Ouch, thought Janna. Why can't men get a new script?

'He's always treated me like shit,' went on Stancombe, getting the Krug out of the fridge. 'No wonder he wouldn't make me a governor – interrupt their little footsy footsy under the boardroom table. It's the lies I hate, pretending Milly needed some quality time with her mother, when she only wants to be shagged by Mr B-T.'

They went outside and Stancombe and (mostly) Janna drank the first bottle of Krug. Janna had the sprinkler on, defying the hosepipe ban, and kept drenching herself as she moved it round the parched lawn, or leapt up to liberate a Japanese anemone or late delphinium bent double by bindweed. Occasionally an apple thudded to the ground.

Partner, sensing her desolation, stayed very close as Stancombe ranted on and on about expensive trips, surgery, designer clothes for both Ruth and Milly and Milly's school fees.

'Ruth'll be begging for a place at Larks. She won't be able to afford Bagley any more.'

In the middle, Janna rushed next door to Lily's to feed the General and found, instead of cat food, she had emptied a tin of pineapple chunks into his bowl.

On her return with the second bottle of Krug, Stancombe was still cataloguing grievances.

'And I'm getting those emeralds back. I really loved Ruth.'

And I really, really loved Hengist, thought Janna. In the dark Stancombe couldn't see the tears pouring down her cheeks.

'I'm so sorry,' she muttered. 'Shall we open this?'

'I've got a better idea.' Seizing her hand, Stancombe dragged her upstairs. 'Nice little property, this.'

'"What gat ye to your dinner, Lord Randal, my son?"' cried Janna wildly. '"Make my bed soon, For I'm weary wi' hunting and fain wald lie down."'

'Say again?' asked Stancombe.

'Only an old lay – rather like me,' muttered Janna. Was she going mad? Aware what a pathetic figure she must cut, compared with radiant, bosomy Ruth, she dawdled over undressing, tripping as she tried to escape from her knickers. Stancombe, by comparison, was resplendent, far sleeker than Hengist.

'Why should she cheat on me?' He flexed his muscles in the mirror, then added curtly: 'Put on her underwear.'

'It won't fit.'

Janna's much smaller breasts went straight through the cut-outs for nipples of Ruth's pink lace bra. To stay up, the suspender belt had to be tied behind. The black fishnet hold-ups had to be folded over like long socks.

'God. She knew how to please men,' groaned Stancombe. As he lay back on ivory satin sheets bought to please Hengist, his cock was almost a kingpost supporting the beam. Without any foreplay, Janna was dry as the fields outside and screamed as he tried to force his way in.

'Get that fucking dog out,' yelled Stancombe as Partner rushed yapping to the rescue.

Terrified he might mistake Stancombe's cock for a

particularly splendid stick, Janna shoved Partner outside and cautiously rejoined Stancombe on the bed, wondering what to do next. Stancombe had no doubts. Waving his penis like a torch, he said:

'Suck it, you bitch, it won't suck itself.'

So Janna went down on him, hands going like pistons, licking, sucking, flickering, to an accompaniment of whining and scratching from an incensed and banished Partner. Thinking of Mrs Walton's leisurely expertise as she despatched Hengist to heaven, Janna gave a despairing sob.

'Keep going, darling.' Stancombe's hand clutched the back of her head. 'Keep going. Aaah.' And he shot into her mouth.

Stancombe was showered and dressed in five minutes. On the way out he said:

'Sorry. I dumped on you in every way.'

Seeing the misery on his face, she said:

'I'm sure she'll come back.'

'No one cheats on Randal Stancombe.' And he was gone.

Janna felt dirty and utterly desolate. Unable to stop crying, she gulped down the second bottle of Krug to take away the taste of Stancombe.

'Forgo your dream, poor fool of love.'

The pain was so excruciating, she couldn't go on.

Ripping some October pages out of her diary, much aided by Chateau d'Yquem, she settled down to write a suicide note. Lily was away; no one would find her until it was too late.

'My heart has been utterly broken by Hengist Brett-Taylor,' she began. 'My life is no longer worth living.'

When she'd finished, she couldn't find the bottle of paracetamol. As she tried to climb upstairs to look for it, she fell in a crumpled heap on the bottom step and passed out.

* * *

Driving back from Wales early next morning, marvelling at the white biblical rays of sunlight falling through the thinning tree ceiling, Emlyn fretted that he'd snubbed Janna over the Welsh National Opera and *Turandot*. He was so fond of her and in such a muddle about Oriana. He'd almost sensed Oriana's relief when he'd announced he wouldn't be flying out to see her this summer, but it had in no way diminished his longing. Lily, the Brigadier and Sally kept encouraging him to take Janna out. But although he wanted her friendship and her body, he knew if Oriana walked through the door, he'd be as hopelessly hooked as ever, so his muddle was unsorted.

The trip to Wales had at least been a success; the Welsh expert on rugby injuries said Feral's ankle needed only rest. Emlyn's mother had spoilt them both rotten. As he'd just dropped Feral off to visit his brothers and sisters in the next village, Emlyn decided to call on Janna.

Partner was ecstatic to see him and promptly led him to his mistress, who had somehow got herself onto the sitting-room sofa. As she was still asleep (and, he noticed, wearing some very saucy underwear beneath her dressing gown), Emlyn wandered off to the kitchen, taking in the empty bottles, the flowers, the fridge door open, the lobsters inside and blood from Janna's rose-pricked fingers everywhere.

'I wish you could talk, boyo,' he told Partner as he fed him and filled up his water bowl.

Then he picked up an envelope on which was scrawled: 'To whom it may concern – no one probably'.

Inside was Janna's suicide note, scrawled on pages from Yom Kippur to Halloween. Whistling as he read it, Emlyn felt amazement, sadness and fury. Bastard Hengist, bastard Stancombe.

Having fixed himself a cup of very sweet black coffee and a plate of lobster and home-made mayonnaise, he proceeded to mark the suicide note: F for grammar –

'two split infinitives and tenses all to pieces'; G for spelling; U for handwriting – 'almost indecipherable towards the end'; C for imagination; E for narrative skill – 'confused and repetitive'; D for vocabulary – 'somewhat repetitive'. Only for melodrama did he award her A star.

Janna came round at midday to find Emlyn polishing off the strawberries.

'How long has Hengist been shagging you?'

'Don't be ridiculous.' Then, slowly registering the suicide note in his hand: 'About a year and a bit.'

'And Stancombe?'

'Oh, not at all, at all.'

Again Emlyn waved the note.

'Well, maybe last night.' Janna frowned, trying to remember. 'Only to stop the pain.'

'Which must be even worse now judging by the booze you've shipped.'

When she reread the suicide note, complete with Emlyn's marking, Janna started to giggle helplessly.

'You shouldn't make horrible jokes when my heart is broken. Why do I get so hurt?'

'Shouldn't sleep with married men.' Emlyn handed her a glass of Alka-Seltzer. 'If they cheat on their wives, they'll cheat on you.'

'According to this, I didn't sleep with Stancombe.' Janna shuddered.

Emlyn had caught the sun yesterday, his face was tawny brown rather than ruddy, but the expression on it was unreadable. Janna longed to collapse sobbing into his arms. She put a cushion over her face. 'I can't go on. I love Hengist so much.'

'Don't be wet,' said Emlyn briskly, 'you've got forty kids to get through GCSEs. Mrs Walton's the one in trouble. Who's going to bankroll her now? Hengist certainly won't leave Sally.'

'You won't tell anyone about Hengist and me?'

pleaded Janna. 'Stancombe hasn't a clue' – she shivered – 'but he's out to bury Hengist.'

'Ruthless in both senses of the word,' sighed Emlyn.

Hengist was in fact extremely twitchy. Not since David Hawkley went through the effects of his late wife Pippa had he been caught out. At first he and Ruth thought the flat had been burgled, then they saw a copy of the Hamburg evening paper. Hengist had made himself scarce. Only later, after Randal had come round and had it out with her, did Ruth ring him at home in hysterics. Sally, thankfully, was staying with her mother.

'Randal heard the message about me not wearing knickers' – Hengist went cold – 'and he's keeping the tape as evidence. He didn't beat me up, but he's chucking me out in the morning and he's stopped all my credit cards and taken back the Merc.'

'God, I'm sorry.'

'It's all your fault,' screamed Ruth. 'Where am I going to live and what about the school fees? You'll have to give Milly a bursary.'

As Milly was definitely C/D borderline, Alex wouldn't be at all amused. Oh dear, how rash he'd been.

'Where did Stancombe go when he found out?'

'Straight round to Janna Curtis.' Then, bitchily: 'You're always saying how good she is with difficult children.'

'Christ.' Hengist had gone even colder. 'What did she say?'

'Evidently they talked for hours, and probably ended up in bed. What the hell am I going to do – sue him for palimony?'

Hengist even in extremis couldn't resist a joke.

'You could get a flat in the catchment area of St Jimmy's. Everybody's doing it for A' levels, then the universities couldn't discriminate against Milly for being at a public school.'

'Oh, for Christ's sake, be serious. There's no way Milly's going to a state school. My life is ruined.'

So will mine be if the news reaches Sally, thought Hengist.

In the middle of Friday afternoon, more flowers arrived at Jubilee Cottage. For a moment Janna's heart leapt, hoping that they might be Hengist apologizing, but the card said, 'Thank you for listening, Randal Stancombe'.

Stancombe had already decided to make a play for Anthea Belvedon. It would infuriate Ruth, who disliked her intensely, and it would mean access at last to Little Dora.

88

Hengist did not officially announce that he would be leaving Bagley at the end of summer 2005, because neither the job as Jupiter's Minister of Education nor as head of Fleetley had been firmed up. But from the start of the autumn term 2003 he began dropping hints, setting in train a hunt to find his successor, who must be both a giant and a genius at recruitment. The procedure was to appoint someone at the end of the penultimate year of the departing head, which in Hengist's case would be summer 2004. A small sub-committee of governors would be elected to look for a new head.

Alex Bruce, already hell-bent on getting the job, was consequently even more determined to improve his own house's results by chucking out potential failures like Xavier Campbell-Black. Poppet was already meddling in the leadership struggle by trying to get herself elected to the sub-committee and urging it to monitor applicants to maintain a gender balance. She then encouraged Joan Johnson to put herself forward as a suitable candidate, to which Hengist exploded that after his predecessor, Sabine Bottomley, he wasn't having 'another bloody dyke at the helm'.

A shocked Poppet reproached Hengist for homophobia.

She's probably right, reflected Hengist ruefully.

He had never stopped regretting that he had passed up Artie Deverell as deputy head in favour of the robotic Alex. He had done this not just because he'd wanted Alex to take over all the tasks he detested, but because he'd felt that having a self-confessed homosexual in the job might deter parents. He had been quite wrong. The parents adored Artie, who in his sweetness had never once reproached Hengist for such a betrayal.

Now Hengist was paying for it. Alex, the tortoise to his hare, was slowly imposing his stranglehold. Last term Alex had tried to sack Rufus because missing coursework had been discovered by a cleaner under his bed. Now, on the first Friday of term, the school photograph was being taken and Alex in a frenzy of bossiness was making sure everyone was wearing correct uniform, their hair was brushed and their heights similar. A diversion had been created by Dicky Belvedon, one of the smallest boys in the school; in a desperate attempt to make himself look taller, he had coaxed his hair upwards with pineapple gel, which on a warm, windless September afternoon had attracted a swarm of wasps.

It was only after a blushing, mortified Dicky had returned from washing out the gel, and Alex had finally got everyone settled, that Dicky's sister Dora pointed out that all the Upper Fifths taking GCSEs with Mr Graham were missing, including two star pupils: Cosmo and Paris.

The glorious thing about Theo Graham's classes was that he was not only inspiring on his own subject – the ancient world being populated with people he seemed to know intimately – but also easily diverted onto others.

On Wednesday, the Upper Fifth had discussed in what kind of ship Ulysses would have returned to Ithaca. Today, Theo had produced a cutting about Sutton Hoo, where a lot of Anglo-Saxon remains had been unearthed. They'd even dug up an entire eighty-nine-foot-long ship with its warrior captain buried inside it. Another warrior had been found buried with his horse.

'Imagine your father being buried beside Penscombe Peterkin,' mocked Jade.

Not a road Xav wanted to go down. Peterkin had been scratched from the St Leger. He doubted if his father would ever speak to him again.

'Siegfried was carried down the Rhine on a funeral ship,' murmured Cosmo with an evil smile, 'but he was already dead. Black shit no-hopers like Xavier Campbell-Black ought to be buried alive.'

Theo was about to rebuke Cosmo savagely when Alex Bruce burst in, purple with rage:

'You have forgotten the school photograph, Theo, how dare you keep everyone waiting. You were reminded of this yesterday – very black mark indeed.' Then, as the class poured out of the room: 'And why aren't you using the whiteboard?'

Arriving at the last moment as usual, Hengist ran his eyes over the rows. Xavier looked dreadful, covered in spots, narrowed, dark eyes sliding in his squashed flat face. Hengist was off to London this evening, but tomorrow he'd have the poor boy in for a drink.

He also noticed how grey Theo was looking and hoped Alex wasn't bullying him. And there was Dora's twin, Dicky, cringing behind a couple of bruisers from the first fifteen. Pulling Dicky to the front, because his awful mother would raise hell if he weren't in the picture, Hengist took his place in the middle of the front row beside Sally. God, he hoped Stancombe hadn't shopped him to Alex, who would tell Poppet, who would certainly feel it her duty to tell Sally all about Ruth. Hengist felt extremely exposed.

After the utter humiliation of the school photograph, Dicky Belvedon was still curling up with embarrassment on Friday evening. Dicky was so pretty he had even received a Valentine from Tarquin Courtney. At thirteen, his voice was only just beginning to break, he had little pubic hair and it was a nightmare being called Dick and only having a tiny one, particularly with Cosmo Rannaldini poncing around in the showers brandishing a cock a kilometre long.

Dicky had a passion for Bianca Campbell-Black, but appreciated the competition was too stiff. He was confused because he'd had a wet dream about Paris the other night. He also idolized David Beckham and back in February had written a letter to Beckham commiserating with him for being hit by Alex Ferguson's boot. Beckham hadn't replied.

Dicky had been even more devastated than Dora by the death of his father but, unlike Dora, loved his mother. He tried to overlook her deficiencies and prayed for her in chapel:

'Make my mother marry again, but someone very kind and very rich, who likes me and Dora.'

Like Dora, however, Dicky was a pragmatist, and lion-hearted. Running his own shop at Bagley, he did a roaring trade in drink and fags. Wearing one of his mother's wigs, he would make sorties into Bagley village, returning in a buckling taxi, which the more louche and lustful house prefects helped him unload.

Anthea, noting so many pupils hailing Dicky on Speech Days, was always boasting that her son got on with all ages. Little did she realize most of them were customers. One of Bagley's punishments for bad behaviour was having to run ten or twenty times the two hundred yards down to the boathouse and back. Dicky hid a stash of booze in the boathouse. It kept both vodka and white wine cool.

Because his housemaster Alex Bruce was devoted to Anthea, he tended to leave Dicky alone. Not so Xavier, whom Alex had asked Boffin to spy on and who, that Friday evening, was in an explosive mood, fuelled by fast-diminishing supplies of drink and drugs. How dare Cosmo call him a no-hoper and black shit in front of the class?

It was only a week into term and Xav had run out of money. He couldn't help himself to Rupert's cellar or his cocaine stash any more. He was heavily overdrawn at the bank and had gone back to school in such a rage that he'd forgotten to ask for a top-up. He already owed Dicky Belvedon a hundred pounds from last term. Dicky was too frightened of Xav to press for it, but when Xav came storming into his dormitory after supper that Friday night and demanded a bottle of vodka, Dicky stalled.

'You owe me a hundred.'

'So fucking what? D'you want to make an issue of it?'

Dicky didn't. There was something so mad, Neanderthal and truculent about Xav. Dicky extracted a half-bottle of gin from under his mattress. 'You can have this, but it's the last you're having till you've paid up.'

'We'll see about that.' Xavier lurched off.

Dicky sighed. He'd promised the gin to Amber for a midnight feast. He'd better sneak down to the boathouse and get some more. Unfortunately Mr Fussy and Poppet were in the garden celebrating yet another ghastly brat on the way with a supper party, to which Boffin, as Charisma's boyfriend, had been invited, so Dicky didn't manage to escape until after eleven.

It was very dark; only a sliver of moon was mirrored in the depths of the lake as Dicky ran past. The boathouse formed a covered link between the lake and the river. Boats, which could be pushed out into either, floated in rows: long ones known as eights in which the school eights competed at Henley; Biffo's dinghy; and little rowing boats in which juniors occasionally paddled round the lake and where, under a tarpaulin, Dicky hid his booze.

It was spooky inside, just the slap of the water against

the boats' sides and a snatch of distant song from the Junior Common Room.

As Dicky emerged with a bottle of gin under his pyjama top and tweed jacket, three figures emerged from out of the curtains of a willow tree and grabbed him. 'Come here, you little bastard.'

Dicky's blood froze. It was Cosmo.

Earlier in the evening, as part of a fiendish plan, Cosmo had pretended to make friends with Xavier.

'I've got some crack,' he lied. 'It'll take your mind apart. And some Charlie – we'll have a party to make up for calling you "black shit" earlier. I was only joking.'

Xav, who had already demolished the half-bottle of gin or he might have been more suspicious, was absurdly flattered.

'Why don't you get some booze from Dicky Belvedon?' suggested Cosmo.

'He refused me any more earlier,' grumbled Xav, 'but we'll see about that.'

'We certainly will. High time Master Belvedon was done over. He's in your house, Xav, you'll have to lure him out.'

Dicky wasn't in his dormitory and Poppet, Alex, Charisma and Boffin were still squawking away singing madrigals, so Xav had crept out of the house again and he, Cosmo and Lubemir, after a line, had walked in the direction of the boathouse. Meeting Dicky creeping back along the edge of the lake, they had relieved him of his bottle.

'We've other plans for you,' said Cosmo softly. 'We're going to stage your funeral and send you down the river, Dicky.'

'No, please,' begged Dicky, frightened witless, gibbering with horror as they tugged off his clothes and tied his hands behind his back. 'You can have all my booze, it's stored in the last boat under the tarpaulin.'

'We'll have it anyway,' said Lubemir, roping together

Dicky's frantically kicking feet, before tying two scarves tightly over his mouth and his eyes. 'This is to punish you for cheeking Xav earlier and refusing to give him any more credit.'

Xav was confused. None of this was quite right, but he was so flattered to be in league with Lubemir and Cosmo.

'Come on, Dicky, into the boat,' said Cosmo. 'Great warriors were buried in eighty-nine-foot ships. Wimps like you don't need anything that long.'

As he identified seats, slides and shoe fastenings beneath his naked back and felt the boat rocking in the water, Dicky realized he was in one of the eights and wriggled and bucked in terror.

'Look at his tiny little dick,' mocked Cosmo, giving it a vicious tweak. 'You don't deserve to live with a cock that tiny, Little Dick. You're in the river now; off you go.'

Panic-stricken, totally disorientated, drenched in icy sweat, Dicky felt the eight give and sway as it slid into open water and moved away.

'Bon voyage,' murmured Cosmo, 'or rather, farewell.'

Then there was silence.

Dicky tried to scream through the scarf as the cold wet fingers of a weeping willow stroked his bare body. In a few minutes the boat would reach the whirlpools and the weir. With his hands and feet bound, he couldn't swim. He couldn't breathe. I'm going to die, thought Dicky, I mustn't shit myself.

89

Charisma Bruce had fallen in love with Boffin after he caringly held her long mousy hair out of the way whilst she threw up into a flower bed during a teenage party.

Now, humming madrigals, she and Boffin walked hand in hand round the lake.

'"A maid and her wight Come whispering by",' quoted Boffin sententiously. '"War's annals will cloud into night Ere their story die."'

Charisma was wearing a new floaty dress. Her long face looked rather lovely in the moonlight. She and Boffin could hear the croak of frogs and compared notes on the dissecting of other frogs and on future A' levels.

'I enjoy *Cracker*,' confessed Charisma. 'It's popular television, of course, but, like Mother, I'm a people person, so I'm going to take psychiatry as one subject.'

When Boffin kissed her, she tasted of cider and her mother's prune and fig sorbet. As a black cloud, indistinguishable from the ebony trees, edged over the moon, Boffin turned on his torch and in its beam, caught sight of one of the eights in the middle of the lake. On closer inspection, he found it contained a wriggling, moaning, naked body.

Charisma, who'd obtained all her life-saving medals, flung aside her shawl and plunged into the water in her floaty dress, which Boffin, diving after her, found floated up most excitingly. Together they towed the boat to the shore.

'Why, it's Dick Belvedon,' said Boffin as Charisma untied the black scarves and wrapped her own shawl round Dicky's frozen, shuddering body.

'Poor little boy, who could have done this wicked thing?'

Cosmo and Lubemir, lurking inside the weeping willow, made a successful run for it, but Xav, off his face with drink and drugs, tripped over a log and went flying.

'Stop,' cried Charisma. As Xavier, trying to struggle to his feet, was caught in the light of Boffin's torch, she picked up her mobile. 'Dad, Dad, come down to the lake and alert the sick bay, Xavier Campbell-Black's tried to murder Dicky Belvedon.'

Rupert and Taggie were in Provence. As neither of their children were speaking to them, they had decided to get away for the weekend and had just enjoyed a most delicious dinner, for once not cooked by Taggie, and reeled upstairs drunk and happy.

Only when Rupert undressed his wife did he realize quite how much weight she'd lost over the summer, particularly on her breasts, which had not dropped because she'd never fed the babies she'd so desperately longed for. Instead she and Rupert had derived incredible happiness from adopting Xavier and Bianca, aware that both had lost parents, vowing to do everything in the world to make them feel happy and safe.

'We will again,' Rupert had promised Taggie over dinner. He found it much easier to forgive Xav now because Peterkin was nearly sound.

Rupert had ordered that on no account should they be disturbed, so the manager had to come upstairs and bang on the door.

'Monsieur Campbell-Black, telephone, it's urgent.'

'Fuck off.'

'It might be one of the children,' said Taggie, wriggling out from under him. Rupert reached for the telephone.

'It's Alex Bruce here, I'm afraid I've had to exclude Xavier. He's not only drunk and stoned but, desperate for a fix, he raided Dick Belvedon's store of booze, then tried to murder him.'

'How?'

'Tied him up, stripped him naked and blindfolded him.'

'All by himself?'

'So it would appear, then put him in one of the eights' boats and, telling him it was the river, sent him out on the lake.'

Rupert went cold.

'Probably just a prank. Is Dicky OK?'

'Far from it. He was in the middle of the lake hyperventilating. Luckily Bernard Brooks and our daughter Charisma were out for a midnight stroll and managed to rescue the lad. Trying to escape the scene of his crime, Xavier fell over a log, so drunk he couldn't get up.'

'If he was that drunk, he couldn't have done all that on his own.'

'Our daughter and Bernard saw no one else. Xav's too inebriated to testify; we've locked him in the sick bay and will have to wait for him to sober up.'

'Fifteen-year-olds don't talk. Where the fuck's Hengist?'

'Our Senior Team Leader's away.' Alex nearly added, As usual.

Hengist was incandescent with rage when he got back next morning. Why the hell hadn't Alex tried to sort it out internally? But by this time, Dora, equally furious with Xav for trying to kill her brother, had leaked the entire story to the *Mail on Sunday*.

Alex, who'd longed to kick Xav out for years, was in

heaven, particularly over the publicity. At last, he was man of the hour who'd made the tough decision to rout out bullying. His photograph appeared in all the papers alongside G and T Charisma, Dicky's courageous saviour.

The press, who loved any story about Rupert, proceeded to dig up all his past misdemeanours: drinking and drugging and particularly bullying fellow showjumper Jake Lovell on the circuit.

'Chip off the old Campbell-Black', said the headlines, accompanying a particularly evil photograph of Xavier, with monotonous regularity.

Almost the worst part was being in emotional debt to Anthea Belvedon, who was really milking it.

'Thank God Sir Raymond is no longer alaive. My Dicky is such a plucky little fellow, he'll bounce back. Of course I won't hold it against you, Rupert, but I do feel, at the very least, we should take a holistic approach and get round the table for family counselling. I and Dicky wouldn't want Xavier excluded. If we discover what happened and why, Dicky and Xav can achieve closure.'

Xavier, who was utterly mortified when he realized what he'd done, had written a letter of apology to Dicky, but he never shopped Cosmo or Lubemir.

Dicky was allowed a few days at home. On the Monday after his terrible boat trip, his mother, having tucked him up in bed, indulged in a little daydream. If Dicky had passed away, heaven forbid, she would have set up 'Dicky's Fund' and campaigned to stop bullying in schools. She would have fundraised tirelessly and lectured in schools and to Government ministers.

'Lady Belvedon talks such good sense and always looks so lovely.'

She could just imagine herself getting an OBE from the Queen, or, with a huge blow-up of Dicky at his most blue-eyed, blond and adorable behind her, talking to Dermot and Natasha on breakfast television.

Heaven forbid, she wouldn't want darling Dicky to die. Dora was a different matter. Anthea had opened an envelope addressed to Dora from the *Scorpion* containing a cheque for three thousand pounds the other day. Dora could jolly well pay her own school fees in future. Perhaps Rupert could pay them for a bit – to make up to her for not suing. Rupert was so attractive – pity about Taggie.

Anthea's musings were interrupted by the telephone and by such an exciting, intimate voice.

'Lady Belvedon, sorry about little Dick, is he OK? Nasty piece of work that Xav Campbell-Black, takes after his dad more than you would think.'

It was Stancombe. Anthea thought of his handsome, sensual face, his dark devouring eyes and his billions.

'Wondered if we could go out for a meal this week.'

'I must be there for my Dicky, but he should be back at Bagley by Wednesday. What about Wednesday evening?'

'Perfect. To avoid the tabloids, as you're such a high profile lady, why not come to my place?'

Life was full of surprises. Lady Belvedon gave Stancombe the best blow job he'd ever had.

Things were also looking up for Dicky. He received a signed football shirt and a get-well card from David Beckham, who was a friend of Rupert, and if Dicky and a friend would like to watch a Real Madrid match one Saturday, Rupert's helicopter was also at their disposal. Dicky definitely thought he'd live.

Xav, who'd gone into rehab, wasn't sure.

'Perhaps he'll meet Feral's mother in there,' said Bianca wistfully.

Such bad publicity for Rupert and Bagley was not good for Jupiter's New Reform Party and he had the temerity to tell Rupert so.

'You're chairman of his governors, why don't you tell Hengist to spend more time there?' Rupert had howled back and wandered off to Venturer to watch a recording of *Buffers*.

Here he had found his father, as one of this week's panel, downing large whiskies in the green room.

General Broadstairs, the Lord Lieutenant and a governor of Bagley, was also on the programme, which resulted in lots of apoplexy and cries of: 'I couldn't agree less.'

Fortunately the contestants were too old to storm very fast off the set and the Brigadier kept the whole thing under excellent control.

Afterwards Rupert had a drink in the bar with the Brigadier, who said he was thinking of asking Ian Cartwright on the programme, what did Rupert think?

'Bit young, isn't he?'

'Sound tank man, read a few books.' Then, after a pause: 'Might get him to bring young Paris with him. I might bring young Feral too. Fun for them to see the inside of a studio, still fascinated by it myself. Think the two boys miss each other.'

The Brigadier longed to tackle Rupert about calling Feral a 'black bastard'. Feral was still so miserable about Bianca, but Rupert was after all the Brigadier's boss, paying him a splendid salary, so he turned to the more neutral subject of Ian Cartwright and then realized Rupert hadn't taken in a word.

'Sorry about Xavier. Couldn't have been the only one. Dicky's small but he's a wiry little chap. Strong mentally too, refusing to shop anyone, like your Xav won't. Where's Xav now?'

'In rehab. Terrible that one doesn't see what's going on under one's nose. Christ knows what we do with him once he's dried out.'

Rupert's despondency was as unusual as it was touching.

'Why not send him to Larks?' suggested the Brigadier. 'Janna Curtis is a genius with disturbed children. The classes are going to be tiny, might get some GCSEs.'

'God in heaven,' cried Rupert in horror, 'it'd make him ten times worse.'

'Christian Woodford suggested we send Xav to Larks,' he told Taggie when he got home. 'Of all the bloody silly ideas. "Do you want to finish him off completely?" I said.'

90

Meanwhile, over at Larks, Janna was heroically forcing herself not to betray her heartbreak over Hengist and having a mad scramble to get Appletree ready in time. She was still searching for a maths master when Mike Pitts called and, having asked for a meeting, rolled up clear-skinned, bright-eyed, with no wine and food stains all over his clothes and asked if he could have his old job back.

'I haven't touched a drop for two months. I so much admire what you've done and I'd like to see my students through to the end.'

Janna leapt up and hugged him, realizing how much paunch and flab he'd lost and how his shakes were from nerves rather than booze – and what courage had been needed to approach her.

'Come back immediately. That is the best news in months,' she cried and, glancing at her watch, added, 'It's nearly six, let's have a vast drink to celebrate.' Then, realizing what she'd said, she screamed with horrified laughter. 'Oh God, sorry, at least we can have a cup of tea and a piece of lardy-cake my auntie sent me from Yorkshire.

'I'm desperate for a maths teacher, and I so need your experience,' she went on, pointing to a rough timetable on the wall as she switched on the kettle. 'I hope it'll work. With only forty-odd children, no one need do more than two and a half days a week. So many of your friends are still here: Skunk, Mr Mates, Basket, Cambola, Mags, darling Sophy Belvedon and Gloria. Lily Hamilton, who speaks masses of languages, is helping out Mags. Brigadier Woodford, who's madly in love with Lily and taught at the Staff College, is tackling history. Wally's going to lend a hand in D and T.'

'What about IT?' asked Mike, mouth watering as Janna cut off two big slices of lardy-cake and drenched them in ruby-red plum jam.

'Rowan's very sweetly staying on to teach it and look after me; she also confided that anything was better than staying at home full time looking after Meagan and Scarlet.'

Mike knew the feeling. For a second, like a butterfly on his upper lip, his ebony moustache quivered. What he didn't tell Janna was the utter nightmare of the last months. No one had wanted to employ him, except Poppet for maths coaching which had come to nothing. His wife had never stopped complaining about having him under her feet, as though he were lying permanently on the kitchen floor singing and waving a whisky bottle, which had not been far from the truth until he forced himself onto the wagon. He felt giddy with relief.

'The place looks superb,' he said, looking round. 'I like all these fawns and sand colours – very soothing.'

'We thought we'd give primary colours a miss, make the children feel it was more like a college.' Janna poured out Mike's tea, remembering the two sugars. 'The only exception is the hall which doubles up as a theatre. Graffi's painted the ceiling sky blue, and covered it in stars, suns and angels, who all have faces like Milly Walton.'

Janna winced, thinking of Milly's mother.

'I'm right glad to see you, Mike.'

'You've cut your hair,' said Mike looking at her for the first time. 'It – er – suits you.'

'Chally would say it's much neater,' said Janna acidly. 'It takes minutes rather than hours to wash in the morning.'

In a gesture of defiance and despair after she'd found out about Hengist and Ruth, she'd rushed into Larkminster and had her shaggy red mane cut off. Now it fell from the crown in a straight hard fringe to an inch above her eyebrows and to an inch above the collar at the back – typical middle-aged head teacher hair: hideous, or rather headious. But Hengist had gone. It was her farewell to love.

Sally Brett-Taylor had popped in several times, replacing many of the dead saplings with new ones from the Bagley plantation, creating a herb garden with Wally and planting plenty of bulbs, so 'we'll have lots to cheer us up in the Hilary Term.'

Each time she arrived, Janna felt glad she and Hengist were over but it didn't lessen her helpless longing.

With Mike on board, everything seemed to be falling into place. Wally hated the sand colours: too much like Iraq where his son was still serving, but he'd applied them with his usual expertise. Only the blue board outside the school had been left empty so the children could think up their own name. Thank God, now Janna was her own mistress, she could call the shots and start term when she chose – several days after bloody Bagley.

Thank God too for Debbie, who would love working in such a shiny new modern kitchen and who had already been freezing curries and pies.

But just a few days before term began, Debbie had sidled into Janna's office with a piece of shortbread for Partner, who immediately leapt onto her knee. Then, eyes cast down, she muttered, 'I'm so sorry, but I won't be staying on at Larks after all.'

'Why ever not?'

'I'm going to work for S and C – or more precisely for Ashton Douglas.'

'You can't. He's a monster!'

Debbie's face went dead.

'I take as I find. He's always been very courteous and pleasant. It'll be nice cooking for one gentleman, dinner parties and things.' Her face softened. 'I've loved working for you, Janna, and little Partner.' She stroked his ginger forehead. 'But there's been a lot of sadness and I'm tired. Forty kids and their teachers is a lot with just me, Moll and Marge. Mr Douglas has got such a lovely quiet house in the Close with a nice top floor for me, Wayne and Brad. And he's promised to get them into the choir school, just two minutes away.'

Wow, thought Janna, Ashton has pulled out the stops.

She felt like the final runner in the relay race, who reaches out for the baton and finds it bashing her over the head.

'I can't bear it,' she wailed. 'I don't mean to rubbish Ashton, but he's been no friend to Larks. I'll try and put up your wages.'

'Thanks all the same, but my mind's made up.'

Where do I find Larks's answer to Nigella Lawson in twenty-four hours, thought Janna.

Bloody Debbie to walk out without notice. Even bloodier Ashton. Then she flipped and sent him an email.

'How dare you poach my cook, you conniving shit. Poaching means dropping into boiling water, so don't you dare hurt or bully Debbie, or I'll cut off your goolies. Janna Curtis'.

The bastard, it was the dirtiest trick he could have played. No army could march on unfilled stomachs.

'Who's going to keep back the best bits of chicken for you?' she asked Partner.

It was dark outside; the wind had risen. The trees were doing aerobics, swaying and tossing their branches from side to side. It was too late to start ringing catering agencies. Then she saw lights. Was it

Ashton come to fire her? But Partner, having jumped on the sofa to check the window, first wagged his tail then snuffled madly under the door. Definitely not Ashton. Next moment, Emlyn barged in. He was sweating and wearing a dark blue tracksuit.

'Ashton's poached Debbie,' cried Janna.

'I know.' Emlyn waved an email at her. 'You pressed the wrong button.'

'Ashton deserved it, the bastard. He bribed her with a massive salary and places in the choir school for Brad and Wayne, who both sing like crows with laryngitis. Lemme get at that computer.' Plonking herself down, Janna was about to fire off her rocket to the intended target.

'Pack it in,' snapped Emlyn, 'or you'll get sued for libel and suspended before term begins. Debbie'll come back when she realizes what a shit he is. I'm sorry, lovely.' Then he stopped in his tracks. 'Kerist, what have you done to your lovely hair?'

'I know, it's horrible,' said Janna despairingly. 'But as I'm clearly not a sex object any more, I'm putting all my energies into looking like a head.'

Emlyn smiled ruefully. 'You haven't got the big ass and dinner-lady arms to go with it, angel.'

In the past, Janna had been able to soften and hide the effects of her exhaustion behind long hair and a floppy fringe, but the hard new style exposed the dark circles and the added lines, leaving her with the face of a novice monk unsure of his vocation.

Crossing the room, Emlyn took her in his arms, his big hands ruffling the short crop, then coming to rest on an expanse of bare neck, which reminded him agonizingly of Oriana. But the cut that enhanced Oriana's flawless features did nothing for Janna.

'It'll be easier to keep,' she mumbled into his warm, comforting chest. 'Keep men away, I mean. My love life is over.'

'Bollocks. Ask Sally for some Gro-more. It'll be rippling over your shoulders in a month or two. Mind you' – he squinted down at her – 'you'll appeal to a completely different market now, and have Artie, Theo, Biffo and Joan after you – even Ashton might start pressing his pale grey suit.'

'Yuk,' shuddered Janna, but she started laughing.

It was nice holding her in his arms, reflected Emlyn. Reluctantly, he released her.

'I must go, I'm supposed to be in a staff meeting. It all looks great.' He admired the big collage Janna had made from photographs of every member of the new year Eleven and their teachers.

'I'll have to remove Debbie's photo,' sighed Janna. 'Where the hell am I going to find another cook, and how do I know if any of the children will turn up on the first day?'

'Turn it into a party,' said Emlyn.

And so Janna did – dispatching every child an invitation to 'A launching party at Appletree House to welcome Larks Year Eleven. Buffet 12.30 onwards, no uniform to be worn.'

On the following Monday, the staff settled in, rejoicing over the labs, the IT suite, the light airy classrooms, the big windows that didn't rattle, and the roof which didn't leak despite a downpour outside. They particularly liked the new staffroom, with its circle of comfortable chairs, coffee percolator, fridge, bar, dishwasher and a television with Sky. Randal had done them proud.

On the Tuesday from midday onwards, the children began to drift in. Making the most of the warm September sunshine, many of the girls showed off bare shoulders and midriffs, their flares sweeping the floor. Both sexes, however, looked edgy. Were they going to be the centre of too much teacher attention, drawn into an exam factory and sweatshop?

'It's weird,' grumbled Johnnie Fowler, 'there's no one above us and no one beneaf us.'

But gradually their fears vanished as they were welcomed by a hug from Janna and a glass of Buck's Fizz from Mags, and Bob Marley over the loudspeaker. Everything was certainly going to be all right as they raced round Appletree, admiring the whiteboards and the big windowed dining room, designed with a bar like a Wild West saloon. They were soon swinging on ropes in the gym and screaming with excitement over the boys' lavatory, where as you peed into a shiny steel trough, turquoise and indigo water gushed out and swept it away.

They also loved the hall, with the sky-blue ceiling full of angels looking like Milly Walton. Most of all, they loved the sand colours and beiges.

'Wicked, wicked, wicked, miss, it don't look like a school any more,' shouted Pearl. 'Oh look, TV's arrived. Anyone want mike-up?'

Partner was in heaven to see all his friends again. Janna was particularly pleased to see Aysha. The Brigadier's great coup had been to make a special journey to see Mr Khan, who only dealt with men and whose own father had been in a Punjab regiment. Invited on the set of *Buffers*, flattered to have his brains picked on the Punjabs' courage when the Japs invaded Burma, Mr Khan had finally agreed to let Aysha return to Larks. She looked so pretty in her apricot-pink headscarf and was knocked out by the new labs.

'Kylie Rose has put on a lot of weight,' whispered Cambola. 'Hope it's not what I'm thinking.'

'This drink is yummy,' said Kitten Meadows, 'can I have another one?'

'If you mop it up with some food,' said Mags, running in with a huge shepherd's pie from the Ghost and Castle. Lily, who'd offered to help out in the kitchen, had made several plum tarts and blackberry and apple crumbles.

'We'll start hellfy eating tomorrow,' said Rocky, who'd already had two showers in the changing rooms.

'Like your hair, miss, it's cool,' said kind Kylie.

'It's gross,' said Pearl. 'You'd better let me cut it next time.'

Outside, where the ground had been levelled for a small pitch with goalposts, Feral was playing football with Graffi, Johnnie, Monster and a frantically yapping Partner.

After everyone had had lunch, Janna called them into the hall for a group photograph and Pearl went round taking the shine off everyone's noses.

'I saw Chally in Tesco's this morning,' moaned Basket. 'She was so unkind.'

Janna put her hands over her ears. 'I don't want to hear it.'

'She said, "None of those no-hopers could ever get a job, that's why they're hanging on at Larks for another year."'

'Bitch. We'll show her,' said Janna, clapping her hands for silence. 'I'd like to thank Brigadier Woodford so much for providing the champagne. Is everyone's glass filled up?'

As Sophy and Gloria rushed round with bottles, Cambola played the theme tune from 'Band of Brothers' on the piano, then, as the music faded away, Janna smiled round.

'"We few, we happy few, we band of brothers",' she said softly. 'Today is for welcome and celebration. The purpose of the year ahead is to get some grades and have a ball. You're students now. This is a college. You may have noticed that Wally hasn't painted anything on the board outside because we thought you could kick off by naming your school yourselves.'

'What about Curtis College?' shouted Pearl.

'What about Cool School?'

'What about Shakespeare School?'

The suggestions came from all sides.

'What about Larkminster High School?' Aysha said.

'Because larks fly high, and we're aiming for the

745

stars.' Graffi pointed up at the sky-blue ceiling. 'Bloody good.'

Everyone cheered.

'Larks High it shall be,' went on Janna. 'We've also decided to dispense with a few rules. What causes most rows in schools?'

'Uniform and short skirts,' shouted Pearl, 'and jewellery.'

'Smoking,' said Johnnie, throwing his cigarette into a fire bucket, 'and chewing gum.'

'Mobiles,' said Kylie, as hers rang. 'Hi, Jack, ay can't talk to you right now.'

Everyone roared with laughter.

'Right,' said Janna, 'in future you can smoke, but not in the classrooms, and as long as you don't stub your fags out on our lovely new floors. Ditto chewing gum. You can use your mobiles as long as you ask permission and go out of the classroom to take calls. You can also wear what clothes you like and any jewellery, but be sensible: no hoop earrings and tie back your hair in the labs.

'You've all seen how beautiful your new building is. So please cover the walls with examples of good work, not graffiti. And as we're a band of brothers, please don't bring in any guns or knives. PC Cuthbert' – loud cheers from the girls – 'will be popping in and out. You can also call us by our Christian names if you like.'

'We do, Janna,' yelled Johnnie to more cheers.

'The only sad news,' went on Janna, consulting her notes, 'is that Debbie has left us, so I'm putting up a rota of people who'll help clear away after lunch and load the new dishwasher.'

'Terrific,' interrupted Rocky, 'as long as it's only the women,' which caused a howl of protest from the girls.

'We'd also like two of you to take it in turns to sit in reception doing homework and welcoming guests to the school and offering them tea, coffee or hot chocolate from our wonderful new machine. And please remember to fill up Partner's water bowl.'

'She's very good,' murmured Lily to the Brigadier.

'That's all.' Again Janna smiled round at them. 'Don't hurry home, look around and enjoy yourselves. We may have been called "no-hopers" in the past, but we're going to prove everyone wrong.'

Rocky, who'd been gazing into space, suddenly shouted hoarsely, 'God bless Larks High and all who sail in her. Three cheers for Miss Curtis, I mean Janna.'

'Janna,' shouted everyone, draining empty glasses.

'We few, we crappy few,' sang Graffi happily.

'That went really well,' said Mags as she and Basket loaded up the dishwasher. 'Johnnie must be drunk, I've just seen him doing a high five with Monster.'

'I don't mind doing this today,' Janna said as she shared the last bottle of the champagne between their three glasses, 'but I've got to find a cook. The one I interviewed yesterday was a battleaxe who wanted six hundred pounds a week. Taggie Campbell-Black's coming to see me at three-thirty, I wonder what she wants.'

91

Pupils were still hanging around gossiping when Taggie arrived. Kylie Rose, recognizing her from *Hello!* and most of the papers and determined to be the hostess with the mostess, rushed forward to welcome her, offering her hot chocolate.

'I'm sure there are some biscuits in the kitchen, Mrs Campbell-Black, I'll bring them in.' She ushered Taggie along the corridor, passing Monster and Johnnie, who, having suspended peace talks, were having a fight, then Pearl, in a micro skirt, smoking and shouting, 'You can fuck off,' into her mobile.

As Taggie entered Janna's office, she was shaking worse than Mike Pitts. She was also so tall, long-legged, huge-eyed and vulnerable, Janna felt they were taking part in some Aesop fable about a red squirrel and a giraffe. Partner immediately curled up on Taggie's knee to make her feel at home.

'What a sweet dog.' Taggie had a surprisingly deep, gruff voice. 'Reminds me of my little mongrel, Gertrude. I've got a lurcher now, who's adorable, but you can't cuddle them on your knee. They fall off. All dogs are best dogs, but Gertrude was my best, best dog. What a lovely office.'

Taggie was rattling now and when Kylie Rose arrived with hot chocolate and some Bourbon biscuits, the cup

Taggie took from her rattled in accompaniment like a woodpecker.

'Can I get you a tea, miss, I mean, Janna?' asked Kylie, dying to find out why such a star had descended to earth.

'I'm fine thanks. Shut the door behind you, Kylie. How can I help you?' Janna smiled at Taggie.

'I'm looking for a school for Xav when he comes out of rehab next month.'

Janna nearly fell off her chair.

'He was just going into Year Eleven, like your children,' stammered Taggie, 'and Christian Woodford says you're a genius with d-d-d-difficult, unhappy children.'

Janna brightened. 'He did?'

'You can hardly have failed to notice how Xav was expelled from Bagley. Such a public humiliation for both him and Rupert, who's hardly bullied anyone since he left school. Poor Xav's been so difficult since he went to Bagley, I feel terrible not realizing he was drinking and drugging.'

'Tell me about this summer.'

Feeling horribly disloyal, Taggie did so.

'Marcus and Tabitha have done so well,' she said finally, 'and Bianca just floats through life. Xav feels so hopeless. I was the same, the really thick one, between a brilliant brother and sister. Alex Bruce always thought Xav was stupid and was waiting for an excuse to sack him.'

'We have to prove him wrong then.'

Taggie glanced up, not daring to hope. 'D'you mean . . .?'

'I certainly do. We'd love to have Xav. He was so kind to Paris on the geography field trip and he worked terribly hard during *Romeo and Juliet*. Aysha, who got on very well with him, is staying on at Larks, so he'll have a buddy to look after him.'

Taggie's stammering ecstatic gratitude was cut short by the telephone. The call was equally short.

'Bugger, bugger, bugger.' Janna switched off the handset. 'A cook I interviewed yesterday has decided not to take the job after all. Our wonderful Debbie has been poached by Ashton Douglas.'

Taggie's silver eyes widened like rain rings in a pond.

'Not that horrible smoothie at the public meeting?'

'That's the one.'

'What does the job involve?' asked Taggie.

'Well, basically, dinner every day for about forty. The staff and lots of the children will only be working a two- or three-day week and many of them just have baguettes or salads and rush off and play in the grounds. I've got a very good temp for September starting tomorrow, but after that . . .' Janna splayed out her fingers in despair.

'I know someone who might be able to help you,' said Taggie, colour suffusing her pale face. 'Before I married Rupert I used to cook for dinner parties. I could give it a try until you found someone.'

Taggie had been so desperately low about herself both as a wife and mother that the sun really came out when Janna jumped to her feet in delight and pumped Taggie's hand.

'I can't think of anything more wonderful for Larks's street cred. The children will be so chuffed to have two Campbell-Blacks here.'

'You don't think it'll embarrass Xav?'

'Some mothers, yes, but not you. And I think, as he'll have just come out of rehab, we'll have to keep an eye on him.'

Taggie loved the new kitchens, 'much more modern than ours at Penscombe'.

'I'd like to start a breakfast club,' said Janna as she walked Taggie to the front door, 'even if it's only orange juice and a bacon sandwich. So many of our children face a wall of indifference and hostility beyond the school gates. Xav will find himself one of the very lucky ones. Some of them lead such deprived lives. This is one of the worst cases,' she whispered as, on cue, bouncing his violet and yellow football along the corridor, came Feral. He had lost his sheen like a conker forgotten in a coat pocket. Poised for flight, he looked at Taggie warily as if awaiting blows.

'Hello, Feral, I'm so sorry about the other evening,' she stammered.

'Xavier's coming to Larks,' said Janna.

'Wicked,' said Feral and skittered past them into the dusk.

Back at Penscombe, Rupert was in a foul temper. Where in hell was Taggie? There was no sign of dinner. He'd taken advantage of her absence to have a look at one of his GCSE set books, which he'd found in the library next door: a first edition of *Pride and Prejudice* with the pages uncut, which he'd scribbled notes all over. He hadn't been able to make head nor tail of *Macbeth* and even less of the Ted Hughes poem he'd tackled yesterday. Why had he ever let himself be bullied into taking this bloody exam? If by some miracle he passed, he wouldn't give a penny to Alex Bruce's science block after the way he'd treated Xav.

Hearing a car and joyous barking as dogs bounded down the stairs and along from the kitchen, and old Bogotá looked up hopefully through his sightless eyes praying it might be Xavier, Rupert shoved *Pride and Prejudice* under a cushion. As Taggie ran in, eyes shining, colour back in her cheeks for the first time in days, he thought she'd never looked prettier. How enticingly that white T-shirt clung to her. Dinner could wait; he took her hand: 'Let's go to bed.'

'Something wonderful happened,' gasped Taggie, 'I must just tell you.'

'Are you out of your mind?' asked Rupert two minutes later, in the soft bitchy voice that always made Taggie want to bolt like a hunted hare. 'Xav is totally unstable, and you're throwing him to the wolves: the flower of the Shakespeare Estate who'll force-feed him glue, steroids and crack cocaine; brutes like Feral Jackson who whip out guns at public meetings, nick cars and beat up old ladies.'

Rupert's icy rage could halt global warming, but Taggie stood her ground.

'Christian Woodford's teaching there, and Lily. They love Feral. You liked Janna. You went out of your way to try and save Larks.'

'For other people's children. You're committing Xav to a crap bunch of teachers and geriatrics, only clinging on because they can't find work anywhere else.'

'Most of them are your age.' Taggie was appalled at her own bitchiness. 'They've just led more stressful lives. Xav's going; I've signed a form.'

'Which you couldn't even read,' said Rupert brutally.

'Janna read it to me. I'm going to give it a try.'

'Shouldn't you have involved Xav "in the decision-making process" as Mrs Bruce would say?'

Taggie lost her temper. 'You haven't tried to find him anywhere. Why are you being so bloody negative?'

'I'm going out.' Rupert snatched up his car keys and stormed off, slamming the door.

Returning at two in the morning, he couldn't have insomnia in the spare room, because he'd given it over to Bianca, so he had to go and freeze in a musty deserted bedroom and let in all the dogs to keep him warm.

'I miss him as much as you,' he mumbled as he hoisted poor blind Bogotá up beside him.

Bianca, next day, was angrier than Rupert.

'I can't tell people you're going to be a cook like Mrs Axford. Who's going to take me to school? You'll have to drop me off at eight in the morning if you're going to get Xav to Larks by eight-thirty. I might as well board, I'm not going to be a latchkey kid.'

Running upstairs, Bianca threw herself down on the pink and lilac quilt and sobbed her heart out. She'd never believed anything could hurt so much. Only this afternoon, as one of the grooms was driving her home, she'd mistaken a rain-soaked trunk halfway down the chestnut avenue for Feral and, leaping out of the car, raced towards him.

If her mother went to Larks, Feral would fall in love with her like everyone else did, she thought despairingly.

What enraged Rupert was the ribbing from Jupiter and Hengist.

'Why don't you take your GCSE at Larks, and make it a full house?' suggested Jupiter. 'Estelle Morris is always ticking off ministers for not sending their children to maintained schools. Think of the brownie points if you sent yourself.'

'Did Taggie say how Janna was?' asked Hengist.

'From that picture in the *Gazette*, she's acquired an Eton crop and completely lost her looks,' said Jupiter.

Hengist missed Janna terribly. He felt so sad and so guilty about her, as if he'd plucked a bunch of wild flowers on a walk and found them dead in the porch three days later because he'd forgotten to put them in water.

92

It was arguable who was more terrified, Xav or Taggie, when they arrived at Larks in late September. Xav had just emerged from rehab, utterly mortified he had nearly killed Dicky and written off Rupert's best horse.

Learning his destination, he panicked: 'I can't go to Larks, they'd skin me alive. They'll have read what I did to Dicky. They'll think I'm some pervy Hooray. Have you seen the hulking brutes like Monster Norman and Johnnie Fowler?'

'Give it a try,' pleaded Taggie, 'I so need your help to read recipes and tell me everyone's names.'

'You do?' Xav looked dubious. 'What'll you do if the other guys slag me off?'

'I'll thump them,' said Taggie.

Xav smiled slightly.

'And there's a sweet girl called Aysha looking forward to seeing you.'

Xav's face brightened. 'I thought she'd gone to Searston Abbey.'

'Brigadier Woodford talked her father round.'

Inside, Taggie was quailing. What if Xav hadn't stopped drinking? She had been comforted by her father, Declan, who was passionately opposed to private education, particularly boarding schools. 'Xav'll get to know all the local children,' he told Rupert.

'Hardly, at thirty miles away,' said Rupert sourly.

'We're to roll up after assembly around ten o'clock so it won't be too public,' Taggie reassured Xav. 'And you don't have to bother with uniform, although you've lost so much weight, we'd better go and buy you some jeans.'

'They'll look too new,' grumbled Xav.

There was a row as they were leaving. How could they possibly abandon Bogotá? He'd get so confused.

'He'll have all the other dogs and the stable lads,' begged Taggie.

'But he's used to having you or me.' Xav was nearly hysterical, particularly when Bogotá tried to jump into the car, missed, fell and, tail drooping, unseeing eyes bewildered, was lifted back into the house.

'Poor old boy,' said Rupert, who'd been deliberately keeping his distance, 'abandoned like everyone else.'

More frightened of his father's icy disapproval, Xav shot into the car. God he could use a drink, or a line. How could he possibly slide unobtrusively into Larks with Taggie in tow, looking utterly gorgeous in a pale pink polo shirt and black jeans?

Dora, who had not forgiven Xav, had also been at work and they arrived to find the school gates swarming with press and television cameras.

Xav grabbed the door handle. 'I'm going home.'

'We can't let Janna down.'

A blond woman thrust her tape recorder through the window. 'Why are you sending Xav to Larks?'

'I've heard wonderful things about it,' stammered Taggie.

'Oh, come on,' said a repulsively familiar toad face with olive-green teeth: Col Peters had turned up in person. 'Larks has just been closed down.'

'Janna Curtis has very kindly offered Xav a place. He's into his second year's GSE' – mumbled Taggie, who could never master initials. 'GECS course. Xav knows a lot of the children and the staff.'

'After the way Xav nearly totalled Dicky Belvedon, he won't have any difficulty holding his own,' sneered Col.

'Is Rupert going to take his GCSE at Larks?' asked a man from the BBC.

'Find his own intellectual level if he did,' quipped Col.

'And Rupert knows all about bullying, doesn't he, Taggie?' The crowd of press were making it impossible for Taggie to push through. Out of the corner of her eye, she could see Wally and PC Cuthbert belting down the drive, but Xav was too quick for them. Leaping out of the car, he grabbed Col's lapels.

'You're one to talk when it comes to bullying,' he yelled. 'Leave my mother alone, you great asshole.'

To his amazement, he was then given a round of applause by the rest of the press.

Next moment, PC Cuthbert had moved in:

'That's enough. Morning, Mrs Campbell-Black, morning, Xav.' He directed them to the car park, then on to reception, where a huge banner said: 'Welcome to Larks High, Taggie and Xavier'.

Cambola played 'The Campbell-Blacks are coming, hurrah, hurrah' on her trumpet, and Kylie stepped forward and presented a bunch of orange freesias to Taggie to a chorus of wolf whistles. No one seemed to be at lessons. Janna came out and hugged them both.

'That your sister, Xav?' shouted Johnnie.

'We're doing media studies, Xav,' giggled Kitten, 'and we just sit round reading the tabloids and about you and your farver all day.'

'Thank goodness you're here, Taggie, we're starving,' shouted Graffi. 'And who's going to win the big race this afternoon, Xavier?'

'Probably Hellespont,' muttered Xav, and a score of mobiles were switched on.

The warmth of his and Taggie's reception was due first to their novelty factor in arriving a fortnight after the beginning of term on a beautiful day, and secondly because Janna's no-hopers were having the time of their lives. In small classes of half a dozen, they were really blossoming, and the teachers who'd stayed on, her 'Golden Oldies' (except for Sophy, Gloria and Rowan) as Janna called them, were regaining their skills, their confidence, and at last having time to teach and prepare their lessons.

After initial doubts about the Brigadier – 'He looks old enough to have been in the First World War,' grumbled Johnnie Fowler – both sexes had been utterly captivated by his lessons, playing war games all over the park, moving pepper pots round polished tables.

An additional advantage was an excellent press, except from the *Gazette*, on Xavier's first day, with several references to his challenging Col Peters for cheeking his mother. His street cred rose even higher when Hellespont won by five lengths.

Xav arrived a scarred, angry, screwed-up ex-junkie, terrified he was going to be beaten up for being posh, thick and black. Instead, he found he was brighter and further ahead in most subjects, particularly in Spanish.

Gradually, as the acceptance of the other children won him over, he began, as Janna had predicted, to appreciate the horror of so many of their lives.

It was Taggie who, because people talked to her, learnt that Johnnie Fowler supported the BNP because his mother had been nearly beaten to death by a black lover and that Monster's dad had arrived last weekend after an absence of five years and left again after a blazing drunken row. Feral's mother had also vanished like smoke, but any moment she and Uncle Harley might roll up and ruin everything. Feral was getting on all right with the Brigadier. His brother and sisters were thriving with the foster parents, but kept escaping to the amusement arcades in Larkminster. Feral had bought the two eldest mobiles, so he could keep track of them, but they kept running up bills. All this Taggie explained to Xav.

Rocky, who was madly in love with Taggie, was building a dog kennel for Bogotá in D and T.

Fearful fights still broke out, particularly between the boys who were so in need of a father figure. Christian Woodford was much admired but a bit old, as were Skunk, Pittsy and Mr Mates. Janna thought longingly of Emlyn, who instantly diffused rows whenever he appeared.

For the first time, Xav found himself looking forward to PE with the glamorous Gloria. He could now get into size 32 trousers; his spots had gone; his hawk-like South American-Indian features were emerging, and suddenly he discovered he was attractive to girls. Pearl and Kitten were both giving him the eye, but Xav still only had eyes for Aysha. Sad, beautiful and timid as the deer that sometimes invaded his father's woods, she was working on her first science module, which had to be finished by Christmas.

'Ask her out,' urged Feral.

'Her dad wouldn't let me near her,' sighed Xav.

Feral knew the feeling. Bianca was boarding at Bagley now and it crucified him to think of her at the mercy of Cosmo, Anatole and the predators of the lower and upper sixths.

During Ramadan, on top of all her school work and helping out at home, Aysha was expected to fast from sunrise to sunset. One afternoon she fainted in the corridor. Xav, who found her, was demented. As he loosened her headscarf and her top button, he couldn't resist kissing her pale lips. Aysha had fluttered open her lashes, smiled as if she'd gone to Mecca, then realized this was earth, cried out in terror, staggered to her feet and fled.

Another of Xav's momentous encounters was with Mike Pitts. Returning to Mike's classroom to collect some forgotten maths homework, Xav found Mike about to take a slug of whisky from a bottle. He had had a gruelling afternoon, with Monster and Johnnie refusing to understand quadratic equations. Xav took a deep breath.

'If you're anything like me, sir, you don't really want to drink that.'

Mike had nearly jumped through the roof, but he lowered the bottle.

'Shall I take it, sir?' Xav felt an awful prig as he emptied it out of the window. 'I'm desperate for a drink whenever I get stressed,' he confessed, 'but if I can somehow get over the moment . . .'

'Thank you.' Mike wanted to beg Xav not to tell anyone. 'Shall we make a pact? If you feel like having a drink, you call me.'

'And if you feel like it,' said Xav, 'you call me – any hour of the night,' he added gravely.

He could feel the dampness of Mike's hand as they shook on it. Xav told no one, but was gratified that he and Mike exchanged three or four calls a week.

Xav was almost proudest that Taggie's cooking had encouraged all the children to switch to school dinners and of how Taggie enslaved them with her gentleness and sweetness when she started helping them with their food technology GCSE. Part of the coursework was to provide a menu and food for Larkminster Rovers Football Club. Taggie was determined to put in a good word for Feral.

As the weather grew colder, more and more children started rolling up to her breakfast club to eat bacon and eggs or croissants with apple jelly from the Penscombe orchard. In addition they joined an after-school club where they could do their homework, undisturbed by yelling families.

The children also saw Xav with his arm round Taggie's shoulders as he deciphered memos and recipes for her, and told him how lucky he was.

'Christ, I wish I was adopted,' sighed Graffi. 'Paris's

foster muvver looks like a horse. Yours is like a gazelle, she's beautiful.' Graffi had done some lovely drawings of Taggie, which Xav would have shown to his father if Rupert had been in a better mood.

Sally Brett-Taylor, who often popped in to tend the garden, always sought Xav out to see how he was and give him the gossip, to which Janna was unable to stop herself listening.

Oriana was due home at Christmas for a long stint. Hengist was utterly obsessed with the rugby World Cup.

'If there's any possibility of England reaching the final, he's been asked by Venturer to fly out and cover it. So exciting,' confided Sally. 'He's also been terribly busy writing speeches for Jupiter for the Tory Party conference.'

Once Larks was up and running, Janna was distracted by a constant stream of visitors. Wendy Wallace wrote a lovely piece for the *Times Educational Supplement*. The BBC in Bristol came over to interview the children and told the viewers how well the experiment was working.

Ashton Douglas was not happy with this publicity, particularly if it established a precedent and failing schools all over the country started clamouring for buildings and funding to enable them to keep going for another year for the sake of a few Year Tens.

Meanwhile Rupert was keeping his distance. He'd enjoyed *The Mayor of Casterbridge*, and in his present mood, was very tempted to auction Taggie at Sotheby's. He'd struggled to the end of act one of *Macbeth*. He only thawed fractionally when Taggie brought him a bottle of Jack Daniel's and a foot of Toblerone with her first pay packet. He yawned like Jonah's whale when Xav and Taggie gossiped about Larks.

'Is Janna interviewing cooks? I thought this was a temporary job?'

'She's trying, but she's got so much to do,' mumbled

Taggie, who also had so much to do and was as distressed by Rupert's rage as by Bianca's refusal to come home at weekends.

Bianca, who was too proud to tell her parents how much she loathed boarding, was also furious Xav was having such a good time.

'He gets away at four and often doesn't have homework even in the subjects he's taking. I have to work until six o'clock and have two hours' homework after that.' And she stormed into Miss Painswick's office to ring Childline.

In the second week of October, when the gutters were filling up with leaves and conkers crashing down, Cosmo, Anatole and Lubemir, armed with a huge bottle of vodka for Janna, rolled up at Larks, uninvited, to see what sort of cock-up Xavier was making of his life.

In the corridor they bumped into Xav himself, who started to shake. Fortunately, he was flanked by Johnnie, Monster, Feral and Graffi.

Any skirmish was averted by Janna coming out of her office and offering the Cosmonaughties a cup of tea and lardy-cake and expressing profound gratitude for the vodka.

The trio returned to Bagley absolutely furious.

Why couldn't they smoke, use their mobiles in class, not wear uniform, call the teachers by their Christian names and have cosy lessons on sofas?

'It's great at Larks,' Anatole admitted to the rest of a madly curious Upper Fifth. 'Xav is doing really vell and getting A stars.'

'Boffin Black,' mocked Cosmo, 'born in a Bogotá gutter, he's found his own level. How could Mr Fussy have let such a genius slip through his fingers?'

'Oh, cool it, Cosmo,' snapped Lubemir, who was profoundly grateful to Xav for not shopping him over Dicky Belvedon's boat trip. 'Xav looked really good, he's lost so much weight, and Pearl, Feral, Graffi, Kylie and Johnnie – all of them – sent their best to you,' he added.

'That's nice,' said Amber.

'To me?' asked Paris, looking up.

'No, how funny,' drawled Cosmo, 'no one mentioned you at all, not even Janna, who's had the most awful haircut. They've all forgotten you.'

93

Paris was faring patchily at Bagley. Work, particularly in English, Latin and Greek, was miraculous. He had caught up with and overtaken the class. Playing regularly for the third fifteen had given him a rugger bugger swagger and the friendship of Lando, Junior and Jack Waterlane, who all found his help with both homework and coursework invaluable. In turn they protected him from Cosmo and Boffin, who were furious he had so often supplanted them as teacher's pet.

Things were going less happily at home, where Paris kept on drinking Ian's drink, staying out late, and being sullen and uncommunicative when Ian and Patience's friends dropped in.

Ian was already uptight because of a fee-fixing scandal, which had just broken. As a comparatively new bursar, he had received emails and telephone calls from other independent school bursars round the country, and assumed it was standard practice to compare notes on fees. Now two major public schools had turned supergrass and the independents were being accused of forming a cartel and denying parents the chance to seek cheaper options.

Alex Bruce, predictably, had gone into a frenzy of disapproval, demanding total access to Ian's files and accusing him of sharp practice.

As Alizarin Belvedon, Sophy's husband, was working flat out for a major exhibition in New York and London, and Sophy was working at least three days a week at Larks, Patience frequently looked after their three-year-old daughter Dulcie, which, as well as the yard, meant a lot of work. Dulcie, with blonde curls and huge dark blue eyes, was utterly adorable and very self-willed. She adored Paris and, accompanied by Northcliffe, trailed constantly round the house after him, interrupting his homework.

The afternoon Cosmo returned from Larks and taunted Paris that no one had asked after him, Paris had stormed out of the classroom and Lando had run after him, trying to comfort him.

'Don't rise, man, Cosmo's just winding you up because he's jealous. I'll walk back to the Coach House with you, I need to check Barbary. He was lame yesterday, and on the way you can tell me the plot of *The Mayor of Casterbridge*.'

But as they shuffled through a burning fiery furnace of leaves, Paris snapped, 'Look it up in the *Oxford Companion to English Literature*, you idle sod. I'm pissed off doing your donkey work,' and ran ahead into the gloom.

Reaching the yard, he found Patience giving the horses haynets and Dulcie, in pale blue denim dungarees and a blue and white shirt, trying to sweep up straw with a fork. Both called out to Paris, but he belted upstairs and slammed his bedroom door.

How could Janna not ask after him? How could Graffi, Pearl and Feral forget him?

' "I am – yet what I am, none cares or knows",' he quoted bitterly. ' "My friends forsake me like a memory lost." ' Glancing round the room, he flipped.

Whoosh went the fixtures, cards and photographs on the mantelpiece. Whoosh off the shelf by the window went the china Labrador head bookends containing his poetry books; crash went pots of felt tips, marker pens and biros, and piles of files and videos, as he tipped over his work table and upended chairs.

'Fuck, fuck, fucking Cosmo.'

'Pawis, Pawis,' said a voice, accompanied by banging on the door. 'Pawis, let me in.' It was Dulcie.

'Fuck off,' screamed Paris, hurling a stapler on the floor so its innards spilled out.

Dulcie looked round in delight. 'Whatyerdoin', Pawis?'

'Trashing this room, now sod off.'

The radio hit the wall with a sickening crunch. A vase of winter jasmine, picked and arranged by Patience, crashed to the floor.

'Let's play twashing,' screamed an enchanted Dulcie, picking up a video of *Macbeth*.

'No,' yelled Paris as she chucked it against a skirting board, following it with a bust of Homer, which lost its nose.

'All fall down.'

'Not that either,' howled Paris as she grabbed a leather-bound copy of the Greek *Epigrams* given him by Theo, and dropped it in the winter jasmine water, before smashing Paris's alarm clock on the floor.

'Twashing, twashing,' crowed Dulcie, pulling books out of shelves.

Only when she grabbed the snow fountain containing the Eiffel Tower, given him by his mother, did Paris finally come to his senses. Catching it just in time and returning it to the window sill, he burst out laughing, and gathering up Dulcie, tossed her in the air until she screamed with even more delight. It was thus how Patience found them.

'We'd better tidy things up before Grandpa gets home.'

Ian was less amused and rang Theo to ask him over for a drink and to seek advice about Paris.

Putting down the telephone, before taking up his

translation of Sophocles, Theo looked out of his study window onto the playing fields and woods of the school he loved so dearly. Maybe he'd last another year? He was in terrible pain, but he must cling on to finish Sophocles and to set Paris on course. One felt the ecstasy of teaching and opening up such a receptive mind half a dozen times only in a career.

Hearing a thud, Theo noticed Hindsight, his vast ginger tom cat, had landed on a table by the window, endangering a bust of Socrates, and in greedy pursuit of a peacock butterfly clinging to one of the brown curtains. Groaning, Theo crossed the room and cupped the butterfly in his hands, pulling down the window handle with his little finger. He hated chucking butterflies out in winter but today was perhaps mild enough for it to survive. He laid it on a wisteria stem. Next moment it had taken off into the dusk. Perhaps he could do the same for Paris.

Ignoring Hindsight's filthy thwarted look, he pressed three emerald-green Anadin Ultra out of their silver wrapping and washed them down with neat whisky from the bottle.

Later, he limped over to the Old Coach House, admiring a huge fox-fur ring round the moon – a presage of storms to come.

He liked Cartwright, who poured a good mahogany whisky. He was a little inflexible for Paris perhaps, but kinder and more down to earth than some silly, sandalled, muesli-munching liberal. Noticing a yellow brick road of Wisdens along the bookshelf, Theo was touched when Ian shyly produced Theo's own translation of *The Bacchae* and asked him to sign it. They then got on to their favourite topic, bitching about Alex Bruce.

'The archives are definitely for the chop,' grumbled Ian. 'What does it matter to Alex if Bagley old boys won six VCs or that one got the Templar Prize for a biography of Auchinleck?'

'He's got an even more sinister plan for reports,' growled Theo. 'A computer program limited to a choice of a hundred and forty different phrases to describe a pupil and his work. Christ, when one considers the infinite riches of the English language. "Think of the time you'll save," said Alex. "You've only got a handful of pupils anyway, Theo Graham, and they'll drift away as the classics lose their relevance."'

'"He loves no plays, As thou dost, Antony,"' sighed Ian, ' "he hears no music."'

'I hear the scratching of new brooms,' shivered Theo, 'scratch, scratch, scratch along floorboard and carpet, sinister as the dry snake scales crawling up the roof in Rikki Tikki Tavi. I'm sure Hengist is going to Fleetley.'

'God, I hope not,' said Ian in horror as he topped up both their glasses. 'We'll all be for the high jump. Hengist is spending too much time away, not even doing anything worthy like fundraising. He must watch his back. D'you think a word with Sally?'

But the door had burst open and in ran Dulcie, wearing a blue dressing gown and mouse slippers.

Ian's angry face softened. 'Come to say goodnight, darling?'

'Let's play twashing,' cried Dulcie, picking up a photograph of her Aunt Emerald and smashing it on the floor, followed by a cranberry red glass bowl, which Ian, once a fine slip, leapt forward and caught.

'That's enough, Dulcie,' he said sharply, as *The Bacchae* flew across the room.

'Twashing,' cried Dulcie, beaming at her grandfather and briskly upending Theo's overflowing ashtray on the carpet, followed by a Staffordshire milkmaid. 'Pawis and I played twashing this afternoon.'

She took a swig of Theo's whisky and spat it out.

'Ugh, poison.'

'Very possibly,' agreed Theo.

After Patience had bustled in and whisked Dulcie off

to bed, Ian said, 'Paris's influence, I'm afraid. He's being tricky at the moment.'

'Testing you,' said Theo. 'He's terrified of losing you and the comfort and security you've given him. I'm photostatting a very good poem called "Yearning Difficulties" he wrote this week. Don't let him know I've shown it to you.'

Upstairs, as Patience read *Jemima Puddleduck* to Dulcie, she was aware of Paris stealing down the landing. He loved listening in, particularly when Patience was teaching Dulcie nursery rhymes. He also loved playing with Ian's old train set, showing Dulcie how to work it with infinite patience because he was enjoying himself so much. It broke Patience's heart that he'd missed out on a childhood.

Pretending they were presents from Dulcie, she'd brought him a teddy bear, a duck for his bath and a CD of nursery rhymes. She'd also rooted out Emerald and Sophy's old copies of *The Just So Stories*, *The Jungle Book* and Hans Andersen.

Dora insisted Paris was like Little Kay in *The Snow Queen*. 'His heart must be melted before it freezes over completely.'

Paris had filled out from rugby, was nearly six foot and so beautiful, Patience couldn't take her eyes off him. She felt so sorry for poor besotted Dora, who put sweets in his locker, and who was having a horrid time at home.

Randal Stancombe was in hot pursuit of her mother, piling on the presents, inviting Anthea on thrilling trips. He was clearly very taken. Anthea was pretty, clear-sighted, excellent at running a home – Ruth had been a slut and very lazy – and wonderful in bed.

Anthea, in her turn, was captivated by Randal's money, but found him difficult to control; and she'd rather wait until he got his K, so she could move seamlessly from Lady Belvedon to Lady Stancombe. She was touched by the way he wanted to win over her children, but she wished he wouldn't try quite so hard with Dora. So did Dora who, when she was at Foxglove Cottage, slept with Dicky's camel-hair dressing gown buttoned up to her neck and Cadbury, who loathed Stancombe, across her legs.

'I'm going to make myself a chastity belt in D and T,' she told Bianca.

Anthea had made a huge fuss about Stancombe's birthday one Sunday in late November, giving him a beautiful glass engraved with his initials and buying a card to which she insisted Dicky and Dora added their names.

'I don't ever wish him to return happily,' stormed Dora.

Randal was charmed by his present. Then, having said the only thing he'd rather drink from the glass was Anthea herself, spoilt it all by murmuring that:

'Of course, the most precious gift a woman can give a man is her daughter.'

Anthea had gone bright red.

'Don't make disgusting jokes. Dora hasn't had her first period yet and she's not remotely interested in boys except for that gormless Paris Alvaston.'

While Anthea was cooking his birthday lunch next door, an unrepentant Randal had stroked Dora's cheek.

'I'll have to put you down for a few years, then you'll mature like the finest wine.'

Revolted, Dora had stormed off to tell Paris and Dicky as they queued in the drizzle to go into chapel that evening.

'Randal Stancombe is desiccating our father's bed.'

'And we've got to spend Christmas with that poisonous Jade,' sighed Dicky.

'Jade had the gall to complain to Joan she was a victim of peer abuse because Amber chose to go to the cinema with Milly rather than her,' said Dora scornfully. 'Joan took Jade's side. That woman's getting such a hold on Bagley. She's finally got permission for her all-female window in the chapel. She's chosen Elizabeth Fry, Florence Nightingale and Marie Curie, I ask you!'

'Who's Elizabeth Fry?' asked Dicky.

'She was a penis reformer,' said Dora.

'I wish she would do something about mine,' said Dicky gloomily.

Worst of all for Dora, Cadbury was in jeopardy again. He'd been banished from the kennels for gobbling up all the beagles' food, and was back in the air-freshened, floral-print femininity of Foxglove Cottage with Anthea. 'Mummy forgot to get him any Butcher's Tripe, so she fed him on cat food. No wonder he farted throughout their romantic candlelit dinner, just like the bombardment in Iraq. Any minute you'd expect Oriana Brett-Taylor to pop up announcing Breaking Wind.'

Paris laughed. He loved Dora in this mood.

'Now Mummy's threatening to have him castrated because he growls at Stancombe. She's longing to give him away,' exploded Dora, 'so I must go home again next weekend and sort it. I feel so guilty deserting Bianca. She's too proud to go home and I won't be around to protect her from Cosmo.'

I'd protect her, thought Dicky wistfully.

'Poor Bianca's jealous because Taggie and that murderous brute Xavier are getting on so well with Feral.' Grabbing hymn and prayer books, Dora handed them to Paris and Dicky. 'Bianca loves Feral so much and he never rings or texts her.'

Not by a flicker of expression did Paris betray how interested he was.

94

Bianca was indeed miserable. Joan continually hassled her to work harder and she desperately missed Rupert and Taggie and the cosseting at Penscombe. In the past, she had flirted with everyone but escaped in the evenings; now there was nobody to shield her from Jade's bitchiness or Cosmo's lust. So many parents were splitting up. If Taggie and Rupert weren't getting on they might be next. Cruellest of all, Feral had never got in touch.

The following Friday, smelling baked cod which she detested, Bianca decided to skip lunch and wander down the pitches. She had been slightly cheered by an excellent dancing lesson and intimations that she might land the part of Cinderella in the Christmas ballet. Most of the trees were bare now, but the beeches still hung on to a few orange leaves, reminding her of the towering wood behind the house at Penscombe. Feeling the familiar crunch of beech husks beneath her feet, overwhelmed by homesickness, Bianca decided to bury her pride and go home tomorrow. Turning two cartwheels, she started practising dance steps.

Paris, who'd been stalking her like a deer-hunter for days, never revealing his presence, had watched her setting out with that dancer's strut, feet in flat pumps turned out. She was the one everyone wanted:

how satisfying to snatch the prize – particularly from Cosmo.

As she reached Badger's Retreat, where smaller trees were protected by larger ones, leaves were still falling. Laughing, shrieking, dark hair escaping, Bianca bounded about trying to catch them like some rite of autumn. Swinging round to catch a red, wild cherry leaf, Bianca caught sight of Paris.

Smiling, she showed no fear.

'What are you doing?' he asked.

'Every time you catch a leaf, it gives you a happy day.' Reaching out, grabbing a dark brown ash frond, she thrust it into his breast pocket. 'Seven leaves. That'll give you a happy week.'

Paris just stared with those light, utterly focused eyes, exciting and unnerving her, lean jaw moving as he chewed gum.

'My father fell in love with my mother when he saw her racing around catching happy days for him.' Bianca snatched a falling yellow hazel leaf and shoved it in his side pocket. 'Daddy kept all the leaves, but felt he was too old and wicked for Mummy. He'd had billions of women before her, like you've had' – she peeped up at Paris from under a thicket of black lashes – 'but Mummy persisted and they've been happy for almost eighteen years – at least they would be if she hadn't taken this stupid job and Daddy wasn't taking this stupid GCSE. So stupid of Feral to say I was out of his league.'

She kicked a red spotted toadstool, did a pas de chat and fell into Paris's arms. Glancing down he saw the despair in her eyes.

'I'm not out of your league, am I?'

'Totally' – Paris spat out his chewing gum – 'but I don't care.'

Once he'd kissed her, she was lost. Scrabbling to remove his school tie, tugging at the short end, she nearly throttled him.

'Lemme do it.' Paris yanked off his own, then hers, then unbuttoned her shirt, pulling her down on a dry, crackling bed of yellow sycamore leaves, black-spotted like leopard skin.

Like both Feral and her father, he had laid so many girls – in the open air, in parks at dusk or on banks in the gardens of care homes – but none as delicately desirable as Bianca as she beamed up at him in ecstasy, her face the same soft shiny umber as the ash frond she had given him.

As he peeled off her tights and knickers, he could smell her body, already hot and excited from dancing and even more so from him.

'D'you really want it?'

'Oh yes, definitely yes.'

Her tiny clitoris was hard as a ball bearing; below lay a buttery sticky cavern, measureless to man and terrifyingly narrow.

'I don't want to hurt you.'

'You won't, you won't.' Then as Paris produced a condom, 'We don't need that, my period's due tomorrow.'

'Better be safe.'

'Well, I'm not going to be sorry.' Unzipping his trousers, she released a cock hard and white as ivory.

'Why isn't it green like one of Mrs Sweetie's courgettes?'

Paris gave a gasp of laughter. 'Shut up.'

'Please, please go on,' begged Bianca, writhing against his lovingly stroking hand as it travelled down her belly, up the insides of her thighs, sliding into her pubes, fingering, stoking, slowly bringing her to ecstasy. 'Oh pleeeeese.'

For a second his cock buckled at the entrance, then straightened.

'Ouch, ouch,' cried Bianca, 'oh bloody ouch.'

Blokes were supposed to recite something boring to stop themselves coming. Paris had been learning the

Latin verb *vastare*, to lay waste, but he only reached the future perfect third person singular when Bianca's sleekness and tightness overcame him; three more stabs and it was over.

'I am so sorry,' he muttered.

'Thought you didn't do "sorry".'

Paris slowly opened his eyes to find her laughing up at him.

'I was dying to lose it. Goodbye, virginity.'

Paris wriggled free, falling back on the leaves, ashamed of having come so quickly.

'I'll do it properly next time.' A year ago he'd have said 'proper'.

'When did you get that tattoo?' said Bianca, fingering the Eiffel Tower on his shoulder.

'When I was ten. Saved up my pocket money for a year, sneaked out of the home. Once it was done, nothing they could do.'

Bianca leant up on her elbow, pushing the straight blond hair out of those pale unblinking eyes. 'Do I look like a mature woman of experience?'

'You look beautiful.'

But as the light filtering through the remaining leaves fell on her warm brown skin, her thick dark lashes (such a lovely contrast to her white teeth and the whites of her eyes), Paris was suddenly and agonizingly reminded of Feral, whose great love he had just stolen.

Sitting up, Bianca examined herself.

'I don't seem to be bleeding much. Dora reckons she's ridden such a lot she hasn't got a hymen any more.' Bianca giggled, then squeaked, 'Oh my God, Dora!'

'What about her?' Paris dried Bianca with a handful of leaves.

'She loves you so much.'

'Well, I don't love her. I like her when she's outrageous and funny, but when she hangs around like a kicked spaniel, she does my head in. I don't need a dog, I've got Northcliffe . . .'

He could see the athletics team pounding towards the all-weather track.

'Will your dad horsewhip me?'

'He mustn't know.' Bianca looked aghast. 'I don't want anyone to know – not Feral. Although he probably wouldn't give a stuff. I've just slept with the best-looking guy in the school, and I don't want Jade or Amber scratching my eyes out, or Dora ringing the *News of the World*.'

'Or Cosmo challenging me to a duel,' agreed Paris, tugging on his trousers and buckling the leather belt Dora had given him. '"Twere profanation of our joys To tell the laity our love."'

'What's that?'

'Some poem.'

'You'll have to help me with my homework, now Dora won't – well, may not want to any more.'

Dora, Bianca reflected, had listened and listened when she'd been miserable about Feral and her mother and boarding. Dora had helped her endlessly with homework, acting out poems so Bianca would remember them. Last week it was one called 'Death the Leveller', and Dora had thrown her riding hat and Bianca's baseball cap down the Boudicca's stairs to illustrate:

> Sceptre and crown
> Must tumble down,
> And in the dust be equal made.

'I feel a pig. What an extraordinary tree' – Bianca patted the trunk – 'all writhing together like dancers.'

'Hengist calls it the Family Tree,' said Paris. 'Look, he, Sally and Oriana have carved their initials on the bark, symbolizing a family clinging together against winter and tempest,' he added bitterly. 'Oriana's supposed to be coming home for Christmas, so Emlyn will be happy again.'

'Talking of families,' said Bianca, testing the water, 'I was going to ring Mummy and ask if I could go back to being a day girl.'

'Don't!' snarled Paris, taking her face between his hands, for a second betraying his need for her. 'Just don't.'

'I'm not going to.' Bianca flung her arms round his neck, kissing him, until her heart was beating louder than the pounding footsteps of the athletics team.

'You're my boyfriend now, aren't you, but above all, we mustn't hurt Dora.'

95

Christmas approached. The erection of Stancombe's Science Emporium seemed to be taking for ever. General Bagley and Denmark, their view of the Long Walk impeded, rose out of a sea of mud. Dulcie spent a lot of time with the builders, who brought her a little wheelbarrow so she could help them. Progress, however, was repeatedly held up by the Lower Fourth doing moonies at the builders from the fire escape.

'Rubble, rubble, toil and trouble,' sighed Hengist.

Poppet Bruce, who was pregnant again, said there was no way she would curtsey to the Queen if she opened the emporium.

'I wish Rupert wasn't taking this GCSE,' grumbled Jupiter. 'He's always working and he's getting even more left wing than Mrs Bruce.'

'He's so seriously stuck into *Macbeth*,' warned Hengist, 'he'll knife you in your bed and take over the Tory Party.'

Nothing could dim Hengist's high spirits. The end of term was nigh and so was his darling Oriana, who was due to arrive at Bagley in time for Christmas and stay at least a week.

Janna's end of term had been a great success, with trips to the pantomime and a carol service at the cathedral, where Kylie Rose had sung 'Mary's Boy Child'. On the last day, the food technology candidates helped cook a glorious Christmas lunch, ending up with more carols, mulled wine, mince pies and every boy in the school trying to manoeuvre Taggie under the mistletoe hanging in reception.

Driving home through the twilight, seeing a fuzzy newish moon like a little pilot light, Janna turned on the car radio to find a voice of exceptional beauty singing 'See Amid the Winter Snow' and burst into tears. She'd thrown herself so wholeheartedly into Larks High, she hadn't given herself time to mourn the loss of Larks Comp or of Hengist, or even her sweet mother, whom she always missed most at Christmas. It was probably exhaustion and still not having a man in her life and wild jealousy of Oriana, because Hengist and Emlyn were so excited about her return.

Among her post on the doormat, however, was a letter from Sally. 'Darling Janna, If you're not busy we'd simply love you to join us for Christmas dinner. Oriana's home and we need some bright attractive young to amuse her. Black tie for the chaps so do dress up. So hope you can make it. Love, Sally'.

Hardly pausing to open a tin for Partner, Janna shot next door to find Lily making fudge and salted almonds.

'Sally B-T's asked me to Christmas dinner.'

'Well, that's very nice, you must go.'

'But I was coming to you.'

'Never mind, you can come on Boxing Day. It'll be fascinating for you to meet Oriana.'

Relieved to see Janna, who'd been very near the edge recently, looking ecstatic, no doubt at the prospect of seeing Hengist again, Lily was too kind to say she and Christian had already refused Sally's invitation to Christmas dinner because they didn't want to desert Janna and Feral.

'Sally said dress up.' Janna glanced at herself in Lily's kitchen mirror, hardly able to see her reflection for photographs of General slotted into the frame. At least her fringe covered her eyebrows now, and Rowan had had a whip-round and the staff had bought her a day of pampering at the local health spa. What could she wear to win Hengist back? But she mustn't think like that, it was so kind of Sally to ask her.

'Naughty Dora's given me a Christmas hamper full of pâté, plum cake and some lovely red,' announced Lily. 'Shall we have a glass now? The end-of-term party was fun, wasn't it?'

'Lovely. Amazing how the Golden Oldies have mellowed; Skunk's so loyal to Larks High he even snogged Basket in the store cupboard.'

'The nicest sight was Xav dancing with Aysha,' said Lily, who was rootling around for a corkscrew, 'so happy, both of them. You'll never guess what Christian has got Feral for Christmas: two tickets for an Arsenal match.'

'Lovely,' said Janna, who wasn't listening. 'Do you really think I should go?'

'You will anyway,' said Lily.

Sally had in fact invited Janna because, a week before Christmas, Oriana had rung and dropped the bombshell that she'd be bringing her producer Charlie Delgado with her for Christmas.

Sally couldn't help being thrilled as she asked Alison Cox, their housekeeper, to make up the bed in the spare room. She'd always known that Emlyn wasn't the answer for Oriana – too chippy and the wrong class; things like that grated in the end. Emlyn also seemed to have been seeing a bit of Janna recently, so with any luck he wouldn't be too upset about Charlie Delgado.

What a shame Christian and Lily couldn't join them. Christian, she knew, was anxious to have Oriana as a guest on *Buffers* and was longing to hear about the war in Iraq. It was a tragedy too that Artie Deverell couldn't make it. Artie and Oriana loved each other, and he had

779

such a wonderfully emollient effect on both her and Emlyn and could discourse on any subject. But Artie and Theo had decided they needed some sun and taken off to Greece together. Nor could Ian and Patience, who had both daughters staying, make it, so in the end it would be a cosy family party: Janna and Emlyn, Charlie and Oriana, herself and Hengist.

Sally went to the present drawer and found Charlie some cufflinks, English Fern aftershave (which was liked even by men who regarded scent as sissy), David Hawkley's lovely translation of Catullus in paperback, and a jokey yellow silk tie decorated with pink elephants from Elaine.

Sally had been feeling tired, what with all the presents and parties to organize and over a thousand cards now slotted into the drawing-room books in a huge patchwork of glitter and colour, but the prospect of Charlie Delgado had given her a second wind. Not that she was a snob, but Oriana Delgado had a nice ring to it. Although, knowing Oriana, she'd keep her maiden name.

Emlyn, who'd been told in a very casual way that Oriana was bringing some workmate, was getting increasingly twitchy and poured his heart out to Artie on the eve of his and Theo's trip.

'I don't know what she feels any more. She's always been a workaholic, but in the old days she always found time for me and we had fun together. Now I see her on TV growing harder and more glittering. She never answers my emails and puts herself out of communication – as though she and her mobile are both switched off. I'm sure she's got someone else.'

'Only Mungo and the desire to compensate for his death. If he'd lived, she could have shown how much in everything she excelled him. What's she like in bed?'

'Like playing Rachmaninov Three on a soundless piano. Pouring out love and emotion to no effect somehow. I teach lovesick schoolboys; I don't want to act like one.'

'Sorry to desert you, dear boy, but Theo needs to get away – he wants to see Attica.'

'For a last time?'

'Probably. Poor Paris. He loves Theo and Theo's so desperate not to abandon him. When are you going to Wales?'

'Tomorrow and driving back on Christmas Day.'

On Christmas morning it started to snow, just a few flakes drifting down; by five o'clock it had settled, but Hengist couldn't. He was playing *Charpentier's Oratorio de Noël*, which had reached the jolly jiggy tune of the shepherds on their way to the stable. The house looked ravishing, filled with crimson roses, flame-red amaryllis and white candles everywhere. Holly and pine branches were banked in corners. The whole house smelled divinely of jasmine, pine, orange zest, beeswax and the heady sweet scent of Sally's indoor hyacinths, waxy white and pink flowers rising out of their mossy earth. In the hall, the blond head of the fairy on the top of the Christmas tree touched the vaulted ceiling.

Hengist and Sally had opened their presents earlier. They had so many, and they didn't want to embarrass Charlie Delgado who would have so few. So many of the cards had congratulated Hengist on his wonderful reporting of the World Cup. He still had a dark tan and had not come down to earth. He had managed to get a signed photograph of Jonny Wilkinson for Dora.

He had already received ten copies of Martin Johnson's autobiography and five copies of Lynne Truss's book on punctuation and a digital camera, on which he had just photographed Elaine in an emerald-green paper hat watching a squirrel raiding the bird table, whose roof was already covered with snow three inches thick.

Newspapers kept ringing up for his reaction to

Saddam's arrest – pity, strangely – and for his New Year's resolution. To get stuck into his biography of Thomas and Matthew Arnold, vowed Hengist.

Sally had given him an 1867 first edition of Matthew's poems, which included 'Dover Beach', 'Rugby Chapel' and 'Thyrsis'. 'Ah, love, let us be true To one another!' read Hengist. 'And we are here as on a darkling plain ... where ignorant armies clash by night.'

Sally should have been washing her hair but, ever conscientious, was scrabbling round in old address books to reply to a card from a cook who had left ten years ago. Hengist was therefore delighted to welcome Dora, who'd turned up to waitress, and gave her a glass of champagne.

Dora then told him about lunch at Randal's. 'Dicky got drunk, kept mistaking Randal's furry cushions for cats and apologizing to them. Mummy and Randal are now at home, offering most surprisingly to dogsit. Probably because they want a good bonk.'

After taking a frantically over-excited, capering Elaine for a run in the snow and failing to teach her to catch snowballs, Dora retreated to the kitchen to help Mrs Cox. She had great hopes of tonight. Oriana was a huge star since Iraq. Several newspapers were interested in any titbit about her. Dora couldn't believe her luck when Mrs Cox, who had never really warmed to Oriana and who was utterly devoted to Emlyn, let slip in her indignation that Oriana was rolling up with a new man.

Concentrating on washing up saucepans, Dora didn't reveal how fascinated she was, particularly when Sally breezed in, wet hair in a towel, to check the goose was browning and to remind Coxie that the roast potatoes in their goose dripping should go in at seven-thirty.

'That smoked salmon pâté is delicious, Mrs B-T.'

'I'm glad, Dora. There's plenty of food in the fridge

if you're hungry,' suggested Sally, noticing that the parsnip purée and the bread sauce, as well as the salmon pâté, were pitted with Dora's finger marks.

To distract her, Dora said she'd dropped in on Patience and Ian on the way. 'Dulcie's so sweet, she asked me if I was going cattle singing.'

'I'd like a grandchild just like Dulcie,' said Sally.

'I'd like a mother just like you or Mrs Cartwright.'

Sally had written people's names on little cards decorated with holly and mistletoe.

'Shall I put them round the table?' offered Dora. 'You'll catch cold if you don't dry your hair.'

'That's kind. Janna on Mr B-T's right, Emlyn on my right,' said Sally.

'Hengist, Sally, Janna, Oriana, Emlyn, Charlie,' read Dora.

In the shadows of Hengist's study, she switched on her mobile. 'Oriana's got a new boyfriend coming called Charlie,' she murmured. 'I'll keep you posted. So pants for Mr Davies.'

Out of the window, the snow was still falling, transforming the laurels into an army of lop-eared white rabbits.

'She's here, she's here!'

The crunch on the gravel was softened by the snow. Oriana wriggled out of the dark green Peugeot, gathering up parcels and pashminas, a bunch of red freesias between her teeth like Carmen.

'Hi, Mum.'

Oriana had never been a cuddly child, arching her back to wriggle out of every embrace. Now she rested first in Sally's, then in Hengist's arms, pressing her smiling red lips to their cheeks. Softened and glowing as never before, she took Hengist's breath away.

'Hi there, Coxie.' She hugged a startled Mrs Cox before handing her a squashy, scarlet-wrapped present.

'Here's yours, Mum and Dad, Charlie'll be here

around eight-thirty. The house looks glorious – I'm so used to New York minimalism and neutral colours . . . and that's new, and that too!' She paused in front of a John Nash of weeping ashes, then a William Nicholson of a child and a dog asleep in a haycock. 'Lovely, both of them.' Then, peering into the dining room: 'That green wallpaper's great.'

'Show's how long you've been away,' said Sally.

From a dark corner of the hall, Dora took pictures on her mobile.

'Who's coming tonight?' asked Oriana.

'Just a very small party. You are staying for a bit, aren't you, darling?'

'Well, at least till the New Year, if that's OK. I want to show Charlie the West Country,' said Oriana, running upstairs to her old bedroom.

'Oh, how lovely you haven't changed anything, except for that sweet little blue chair.' Fingering the Christmas roses and snowdrops in a vase on the dressing table, she said, 'You do know how to make things pretty, Mum.'

She must be in love to be so complimentary, thought Sally.

Hengist gasped when Oriana came down a good hour later. Her slenderness was enhanced by a sleeveless dark brown velvet dress, split to the thigh to show off long greyhound legs and very high heels. Her short spiky hair was softened by pearl drop earrings and, for Oriana, a lot of eye make-up, blusher and scarlet lipstick. She reeked of familiar scent.

'You look absolutely gorgeous, darling.'

She must be bats about this Charlie. Where the hell did that put poor Emlyn?

'Can I take a photograph of you and Mr Brett-Taylor?' asked Dora, sliding in with a champagne cocktail on a silver tray.

Before long, Oriana reverted to being as spiky as her hair.

'You've obviously been fundraising,' she told Hengist. 'Place looks more like a country club than ever, I nearly got lost on the way in. What are you teaching at the moment?'

'First year,' said Hengist, unstoppering the whisky decanter. He intended to get gloriously drunk this evening.

'Hardly extending yourself.'

'It's a very good way of acquainting oneself with a new intake, and, quite frankly, teaching is something I do in my spare time these days.'

Then he tried to tell Oriana about Paris and the brilliant poem he'd written about England winning the World Cup, because for once David (Jonny Wilkinson) and Goliath (Martin Johnson) were on the same side. But he soon realized Oriana was interested neither in Paris nor the World Cup: 'It wasn't reported in the States; it was irrelevant on a global scale!' nor in him fulminating about the dumbing down of the GCSE history syllabus, which now included the restoration of historic houses and the producing of television documentaries.

'The aim is to make it more vocational, Jesus! They're even talking of combining history and geography as one subject. It's madness.'

Noting Oriana yawning, probably jet-lagged, Hengist put another log on the fire and switched to Iraq.

'Seeing Saddam's statue pulled down reminded me of Ozymandias, "round the decay Of that colossal wreck". But I felt unaccountably sorry for the poor sod when he was arrested. Looked as though he'd been sleeping rough outside the Savoy. What's going to happen about Iran?'

'Oh, please don't interrogate me, Dad. We've got all next week, I just need to unwind.'

'Sorry.' Hengist patted her rigid shoulder. 'I'm just so proud of you. Wonderful if you could talk to the school about Iraq, you've got such a fan club here.'

But Oriana was rearranging her spikes in the mirror, a muscle rippling her flawless jawline. She's hellishly nervous, thought Hengist, as he put on a CD of carols sung by his old college choir.

96

Sally knew Oriana was home because her bedroom had been ransacked for tights, shampoo, dental floss; Beautiful had been left unstoppered, Hengist's after-shave ditto. Toothpaste lay like patches of snow in the basin, towels all over the floor. The hairdrier, still plugged in, was on the carpet. Favourite pearl drop earrings were missing from her jewel case.

Sally smiled and put on sapphire earrings instead.

'It came upon a midnight clear . . .' floated up the stairs as she pulled on a midnight-blue skirt and a turquoise frilled silk shirt. A dash of lipstick, a touch of mascara. Thank God for a good skin. Sally hoped Charlie Delgado would think her pretty. She imagined him dark-eyed and slightly Latin; perhaps he'd kiss her hand.

A second champagne cocktail hadn't cured Oriana's nerves; she glanced yet again at the clock and tried to ring someone on the remote control, then, cursing, punched out the number on her mobile.

Emlyn was the first to arrive as the grandfather clock in the hall chimed eight. He'd had a gruelling time with his mother, who was missing his father dreadfully and hinting that the only thing that would cheer her up was grandchildren. Nervous about the evening ahead, he'd done little justice to the Christmas lunch she'd spent so much time preparing. She had cried when he left. He longed to sweep her up and bring her to Bagley, but the contrast between their tiny over-crowded terrace house and the Brett-Taylors' splendour, with all the candles, crimson roses, great glittering tree and the fire leaping in the lounge, would have been hideous.

Aware his dinner suit was crumpled and his face red from lurking outside in the cold, he felt horribly bucolic compared with Hengist, whose cream shirt open at the neck showed off his tan and whose dark green smoking jacket, another present from Sally, emphasized his merry dark green eyes.

'Come in, dear boy. Happy Christmas.'

Emlyn's spirits drooped even further as Oriana ducked her head when he tried to kiss her.

'You look fantastic,' he said, addressing her lowered grey and brown streaked eyelids, then handed her a small square parcel. 'Happy Christmas.'

'Thanks, I'll open it later.'

Was she scared it was a ring?

Dora had no such inhibitions as she swept in with more champagne cocktails.

'Hello Mr Davies. Merry Christmas. What's that, a ring? Randal Stancombe gave my mother a lovely brooch, green enamel mistletoe with pearls as the berries. "Either wear it or put it in a safe," he told Mummy. Then, so she'd find out how much it cost, told her to insure it at once. So pants! Do open it.' She edged forward.

'Come on, Dora.' A grinning Hengist dragged her out of the room. 'Give Oriana and Emlyn a moment together.'

After a long pause, during which Emlyn longed to enfold and kiss the life out of her, he asked, 'How was the flight?'

'OK, except I can't get used to being recognized and pestered for autographs everywhere. It's impossible to be an observer when you're constantly observed.'

'Hasn't hurt John Simpson or Kate Adie,' said Emlyn, more sharply than he meant. 'You're a super-star now, and you look like one. Lovely dress.'

The snow had stopped and the clouds parted to reveal Orion in his glittering glory. Janna wished she could pluck him down from the skies as her escort this evening. She hadn't seen Hengist since before Stancombe caught out him and Mrs Walton. How would she feel about her great lost love? She was so nervous, she couldn't understand why her car wouldn't start until she realized she was trying to jam her seat-belt buckle into the ignition keyhole.

Her lovely day at the health spa yesterday had only made her realize, as hands massaged her face and body, how desperately she needed love in her life.

The snow was falling quietly and steadily again, blotting out caution. Hearing a scrunch on the gravel, Oriana raced to the window. It was not Charlie, but a surprisingly pretty redhead running up the steps as an icy wind blew aside a pashmina the colour of faded bracken to reveal a clinging dress in leopardskin print.

'Darling, darling, "a pardlike Spirit, beautiful and swift".' Opening the front door, Hengist drew Janna into a muscular, lemon-scented embrace. Then, when she glanced up, he kissed her on the mouth, holding her steady as she swayed in amazement and wonder. 'So nice to see you again,' he murmured. 'Have you forgiven me?'

Janna's heart leapt in hope. Did he still care for her? Then he swept her into the lounge, grabbed her a drink and introduced her to Oriana, who had Sally's delicate features but Hengist's colouring, and who, because of her courage and left-wing views, had long been a heroine of Janna's, but who was now looking at her with hostility. Particularly when Elaine, who'd hardly budged when Oriana arrived, now jumped down sleepy-eyed from the sofa to nudge and chatter her teeth in welcome.

'So pleased to meet you. I'm such a fan,' said Janna, taking Oriana's damp hand; then, turning to Emlyn: 'How are you, how was Christmas and your mum?' which made Oriana even frostier. Perhaps she'd heard Emlyn and Janna were friends.

'How's Larks?' Hengist laced her champagne with a slug of brandy. 'You've got to fill me in on everything – and how's Xavier getting on?

'Good,' he said when Janna finished telling him. 'I felt we let him down really badly. And how's the divine Taggie? Is Rupert unfreezing at all?'

It was clear Hengist was on automatic pilot, firing questions, not listening to a word, because he was trying to overhear what Emlyn was saying to Oriana. Not a lot, it seemed. Oriana, equally clearly, was trying to find out what Janna was saying to Hengist.

'How's Xav getting on?' repeated Hengist, and Janna was overwhelmed with sadness.

'Since nothing all my love avails, Since all, my life seemed meant for, fails . . .'

Emlyn looked as though he'd been turned to stone, or rather red brick.

Hengist was deploring universal ignorance again.

'Ninety per cent of secondary-school children interviewed couldn't name a single composer, and seventy per cent of them thought Churchill was the dog in those insurance ads, which is quite funny if it weren't so dreadful. Mind you, teachers aren't much better. Forty-seven per cent, according to the *TES*, couldn't name Charles Clarke as the Education Secretary.'

'They're too busy to read newspapers,' protested Janna.

'Or too out of touch to teach children,' mocked Oriana.

'Janna's head of Larks,' said Hengist.

'I thought it was about to close.'

'It did,' said Janna.

'Not entirely,' said Emlyn evenly, 'it's called Larks High now. I'm going to switch to Scotch, if that's OK, Hengist?'

The restless Oriana had just put on *L'Enfance du Christ* when Sally rushed in.

'Sorry, everyone. Mini crisis with the goose. Janna darling, how lovely you look, such a saucy dress. Emlyn dear, how nice. Hengist, look what Dora's given us, it's an American greyhound calendar, with different photographs of greyhounds for every month.'

Armed with her camera and following Sally into the room, Dora said, 'February's has such a look of Elaine, and April's the spitting image of my father's dog, Grenville, who lives with my sister now, and November's just like Maud who— Smile please, Janna and Mr Davies, and er, Miss Brett-Taylor.'

Headlights shone into the room. There was another crunch on gravel.

'Can you answer the door, Dora?' said Hengist to shut her up, but Oriana had already flown from the room, past the banks of holly and pine, past the white candles and the crimson roses, letting in a blast of icy air before falling into Charlie Delgado's arms.

'Oh, thank God you're here.'

'How's it going?'

'Hairy, but I'm safe now.'

'You are. Now I'm here.'

'So good you've already changed. Let's get your stuff out of the car.'

Two minutes later, with shouts of laughter and excitement, they came back into the house. Charlie's arms were now full of presents and, carrying coals of fire to Newcastle, a huge bunch of crimson roses. Oriana dropped Charlie's very smart suitcase in the hall.

'Come and meet everyone.'

Dora emerged from the shadows and shot back in

again in a state of profound shock. For Charlie Delgado was around five foot eleven, lean, raven-haired, lynx-eyed, handsome, wearing an exquisitely cut dinner jacket and very, very female.

'My God.' Hengist's hand flew to straighten his tie and smooth his hair.

Next, thought Janna wearily.

'Oh dear,' said Sally gaily, 'I've screwed up the numbers. Give Charlie a drink, darling, and take her up to the spare room.'

'Oh no, Charlie'll be sleeping with me,' announced Oriana.

97

It was as though a suicide bomber had blown the conviviality of the party to smithereens. An evening of excruciating embarrassment followed.

Dora put her head back round the door, eyes on stalks, and belted off to tell Coxie.

Oriana filled up a glass for Charlie, and was just about to take her upstairs when Hengist said, 'Mummy'll take her,' and dragged Oriana into his study, where neither of them noticed Dora's charging mobile.

Like some outer Mongolian warlord, Ghengist Khan no less, Hengist's eyes had narrowed to slits in his furious brown face.

'What the fuck are you playing at?'

All the radiance had drained out of Oriana. Unfazed by snipers or Scud missiles, she now looked white and utterly terrified.

'I didn't know how to tell you.'

'You could have bloody well tried.'

'I'm gay, Dad. I'm sorry I can't marry Emlyn and provide you with the son who'll play for England.'

'Don't be fatuous. Have you told Emlyn?'

'Not yet. I've never really fancied men.' She was trembling violently. 'I've been so unhappy about it.'

'For Christ's sake, it's just a phase. Scores of people are bisexual.'

'Not me. You and Mum wanted me to be a boy so I guess I tried to please you.' When Hengist opened his mouth to protest: 'No, let me finish. I walked into the Palestine Hotel in Baghdad in April; Charlie was at the bar. Another journalist introduced us. Charlie just stared at me, then said in that glorious deep voice of hers, "Why are you so late?" "What d'you mean?" I stammered. "I've been waiting all my life for you," she said. "I knew the moment you walked into the room." '

Oriana collapsed on the red leather fender seat.

'It was the *coup de foudre* for both of us; we've been living together ever since. I wanted to tell you, Dad.'

'You could have found a better time to do it. Poor Emlyn.'

'I know. But don't think it's been fun.' Having reeled on the ropes, Oriana was beginning the fight back. 'Usually when people announce they've met Mr Right, the champagne comes out and everyone starts ringing round the family. We don't get any of that. No engagement in *The Times*, only being brushed under the carpet and an awareness of murdering one's parents' happiness. I can't help my sexual orientation.'

Through the open curtains, the snow was covering the past, stifling feelings.

Hearing voices, Hengist said, 'We better go back and cause as little hurt as possible.'

Oriana scuttled upstairs.

Next door, Emlyn had turned grey, megalithic, anguish carved on his face. Janna tried to comfort him, but it was like offering junior aspirin to an elephant with a spear through its heart.

Sally, having returned from upstairs, looked equally stunned.

'I'm so sorry.' Janna found herself hugging her. 'I'd better go.'

'No, please don't, we need you,' begged Sally, then lowering her voice: 'It isn't so big a thing.'

Next moment Hengist walked in, also pale, but

totally in control, and he put an arm round Sally's shoulders.

'More drinks all round, I guess,' and he poured champagne for Sally and Janna and much darker whiskies for himself and Emlyn.

'I'm afraid our daughter's "come out".'

'Poor Emlyn,' gasped Janna.

'Poor Sally,' snapped Hengist.

They were then joined by Charlie and Oriana, with all her lipstick kissed off.

'Mrs Brett-Taylor, you are so kind,' cried Charlie. 'I've just opened my gifts. These cufflinks are so neat, look' – she shot out her silken ivory cuffs – 'and I'm wearing the perfume, it's delightful.' She held out a wrist for Sally to smell. 'And this is so appropriate.' She waved the pink elephant tie. 'From what Oriana tells me about Brett-Taylor hospitality, I'll be seeing pink elephants of my own in a day or two, and finally Catullus is one of my favourite poets, and translated by Lord Hawkley. He came and lectured us at Smith.'

' "Let's live and love, my Lesbia," ' muttered Janna, who was starting to get drunk and lippy. ' "Heed not the disapproval of censorious old men," ' and received a filthy look from Oriana.

'I've brought you some bottles of fine wine,' went on Charlie.

Dora, snapping away on her telephone camera, was livid when Hengist gave her twenty pounds and told her to buzz off.

'How are you going to manage? Coxie can't wait on her own, she was hoping to put her feet up with a plate of goose and *The Wizard of Oz*.'

'Go on, hop it.'

Dora rushed off across the snow to the Old Coach House.

'Guess what, Oriana's a lesbian; she's turned up with a tall woman called Charlie. They're sharing a bed, imagine them licking each other, it's so pants.'

Ian and Patience, who'd had several drinks after a gruelling day with Paris, had great difficulty not laughing.

'Shall I go and cheer him up?' asked Dora wistfully. 'Oh well, I'd better toboggan home.'

Charlie proceeded to dominate the conversation. She had spent six years teaching English at Smith before going into television on the news side. She had been everywhere and knew everyone. She was also a know-all, decided Janna, although it might have been to impress the Brett-Taylors.

She immediately recognized *L'Enfance du Christ* on the record player but, on picking up the CD cover, said she preferred Sir Colin Davis's version with Janet Baker singing Mary.

The mistletoe hanging in the hall on the way into dinner was an excuse for a little lecture on druids gathering it by moonlight.

'Mistletoe was alleged to cure infertility,' continued Charlie, 'ill humour and offer protection from lightning.' Then, tucking her arm through Oriana's: 'There should have been some hanging in the Palestine Hotel the night we met.

'Omigod.' She clapped her hands as she entered the dining room. 'How glorious.' Yet the scarlet napkins, crimson roses and army of white candles lighting the room and casting a sheen on the frozen snow outside seemed less suited to the mood of the evening than the dark jungle wallpaper.

Glancing at the place cards, Sally wondered if Charlie ought now to be on Hengist's right rather than hers, particularly as Emlyn was on her left, glowering like some huge cliff face across at Charlie, who was unfolding her red napkin like a matador and banging on about the New York apartment.

'Oriana and I have kept things neutral. Then we can vary the look by adding cushions and throws.'

'We've done the same at my school,' piped up Janna. 'Alas the boys do most of the throwing.'

But Charlie had been sidetracked by a lovely Nevinson of Battersea Power Station, opal smoke drifting in the morning sun, which had been recently hung on the wall opposite.

'Although I prefer the gritty realism of Nevinson's war oeuvre. Oriana, like him, is a war artist. The tautness and poetry of your daughter's reportage, Hengist and Sally, will become TV classics.'

'Oh Charlie.' Oriana blew her a kiss.

They're bitches. Poor Emlyn, thought Janna furiously. How could they chatter away as though everything was normal?

Hengist, who never squandered an opportunity to work a room, was quizzing Charlie about the American political scene, which he and Jupiter were busy cracking. Who were the movers and shakers? Charlie dismissed most of the ones he knew as right-wing bigots.

The first course of smoked salmon mousse and poached scallops was delicious but the latter were definitely undercooked, like eating chunks of female flesh.

Emlyn gagged and put his knife and fork together, suddenly overwhelmed with longing for his wise kindly father, who'd so disapproved of any link with the Brett-Taylors. What was he to do? He could hardly challenge Charlie to a duel. And how did you compete for a woman with another woman, who was so self-assured, so smart and who looked so much better in a dinner suit and her own skin than you did yourself? Emlyn drained his glass of Pouilly-Fumé and poured another one.

Charlie was a slow eater, because she talked so much, which was a good thing, because Coxie was so incensed to be abandoned that she refused to do much waiting.

Oriana and Sally helped her in with the goose,

parsnip purée, roast potatoes, sprouts and bread sauce. As Hengist began carving, Elaine sidled round the table, dark eyes bright and loving in anticipation of goodies. On learning her name, Charlie launched into Tennyson:

'"Elaine the fair, Elaine the loveable, Elaine, the lily maid of Astolat."'

'Oh, fuck off,' muttered Emlyn.

'Pardon me?' asked Charlie, then demanded what aspect of American history Emlyn was teaching. Learning it was the Wild West, she hoped Emlyn was stressing the victimization of the Native Americans.

'No one more than Emlyn,' snapped Janna.

'Here you are, Emlyn.' A sympathetic Coxie shoved a huge plate of goose in front of him. 'I've given you the breast.'

And so it went on. Glasses were filled several times as candlelight etched the deepening crisis on each face. On the surface, people contradicted each other, some with passion, some with dogged authority, while everyone watched. Was Charlie revving up to ask Hengist for Oriana's nailbitten hand? wondered Janna. She had been worried about which fork to use. This lot would hardly have noticed if she'd rammed one into Charlie's arm.

The crimson roses were shedding petals on the polished table like drops of blood. Janna shivered, remembering Cara Sharpe and the scarlet anemones.

Oriana, in truth, was irritated Emlyn was behaving so angrily and gauchely. She could see Charlie was wondering how Oriana could have attached herself for so long to such a boor. Emlyn could be so funny and sharp, but every time Charlie threw him a question, he ignored it like a great vegan sea lion rejecting fish. She also wished her father were less right wing, and her mother less like a crystal lustre, tinkle, tinkle, filling in silences with inane chat.

Janna she couldn't read. She'd been convinced she

was her father's latest, but from the way Janna was sticking up for Emlyn, Oriana wasn't sure.

The food was sublime. Never were sprouts more crunchy, potatoes more golden crisp and creamily soft inside, or goose more tender without being fatty. Charlie, who hadn't had any lunch, was particularly taken with the parsnip purée and had a second helping.

'It's Taggie Campbell-Black's recipe,' said Sally, who was now gazing into space.

As Charlie proceeded to annihilate the Bush administration, and make disapproving comments on 'not forgetting the starving worldwide' as more food seemed to go back on everyone else's plates than was put on them in the first place, Elaine was having a field day.

Sally, who'd been fingering the cut-glass ridges of her water glass, suddenly filled it up from the gravy boat without realizing it.

'It's my turn to clear away.' Janna leapt to her feet, stacking up the plates and grabbing Sally's glass.

In the kitchen, she found Coxie in tears and attacking the brandy.

'My dinner's ruined and poor Mr Davies.'

'It was a wonderful dinner. Everyone's upset, that's all.' Janna put an arm round Coxie's heaving shoulders as Emlyn walked in with the goose.

When she and Emlyn came back to the kitchen with vegetables and sauce boats, Janna murmured that Charlie and Oriana were fearfully anti-Bush.

'Except each other's,' snarled Emlyn.

Janna screamed with laughter, then stifled it, stammering how desperately sorry she was about everything.

Returning to the dining room with hot plates, Christmas pudding and brandy butter, they caught Oriana and Charlie in a clinch in the hall.

'Christ!' exploded Emlyn. 'Shall we unjoin the ladies?'

Ignoring him, as a further act of solidarity, Charlie and Oriana moved their chairs together, pulling crackers, putting on paper hats and giggling over riddles. Inside Charlie's cracker was a yellow whistle which she kept blowing.

Janna put the Christmas pudding on the sideboard; Hengist defiantly emptied half a bottle of brandy over it. As he set fire to it, blue flame nearly scorched the ceiling. Emlyn felt similar anger flaring up inside him: Oriana should have levelled with him. Even if there was a certain relief that it wasn't him specifically she didn't fancy, just blokes in general, her lack of response had constantly humiliated him, eroding his masculinity. He'd felt so heavy and ham-fisted, like a rhino trying to shag a gazelle.

'D'you remember how you used to put silver 5ps in the Christmas pudding, Mum?' asked Oriana.

'It was bachelor's buttons in my day,' said Hengist, scooping Christmas pudding into silver bowls, which Janna handed round.

'I wonder who'd qualify for that,' said Sally in a high voice.

Seeing she was shivering, Janna took Emlyn's seat next to her, praising the brandy butter, saying what joy her indoor bulbs had brought the children.

'How nice.' Sally attacked her Christmas pudding, then, putting her spoon down, said:

'D'you remember the time you got Elaine a doggy bag from La Perdrix d'Or, pork chops wrapped in silver foil, and forgot and put it under the tree? By the time you opened it on Christmas night, it had gone orf and stank like hell.' Sally started to laugh shrilly on and on. Janna put a hand on her arm.

'It's OK,' she murmured, 'you're doing fine.'

'I haven't had much practice.'

Hengist, who'd been trying to get some sense out of Emlyn about rugger, glanced across at his wife with such concern.

She's the one he loves, thought Janna. Me, Ruth Walton, even Oriana aren't in the frame compared with her.

'Don't know why everyone goes on about Taggie's cooking,' said Hengist, 'my wife's is just as good. Let's all drink to her.'

After they'd drained their glasses, Hengist filled them up again and proposed a toast to absent friends.

'Mum,' said Janna.

'Mungo,' said Oriana bitterly.

'Dad,' muttered Emlyn with a break in his voice.

He was looking so sad, Janna poked him in the ribs with a cracker. Inside was a key ring attached to a perky little black dog with pricked ears.

'How darling,' said Charlie covetously, 'an Aberdeen terrier. My mother has one.'

'We call them Scotties in England,' said Janna tartly, 'and Emlyn's going to have it.' She dropped it into his dinner jacket pocket.

'Where are Artie and Theo?' said Oriana fretfully.

'Gone to Athens,' said Hengist, 'staying in the Grande Bretagne, lucky things. Artie's hiring a car and they're going on day trips to Corinth and Sparta.'

'Such a shame, I so wanted Charlie to meet them.'

'They're both such dear persons,' said Sally.

'Why are male couples "dear persons" and not women?' said Oriana, who was getting punchy. 'Dad's always slagging off Joan Johnson and Sabine Bottomley, but if they're men, it's fine.'

Hengist and Janna escaped with the pudding bowls.

'Save it for the birds,' he cried as Janna started to tip rejected pudding into the bin. 'Christ, what a bloody awful evening. Is that appalling Charlie going to stay behind and drink port with me and Emlyn?'

But as they returned to the dining room, the grandfather clock struck ten-thirty and Charlie, looking at Oriana with sleepy suggestive eyes, announced she was exhausted.

'Thank you so much, Sally and Hengist, for letting me invade your evening and for your wonderful gifts. If it's OK, I'll give you mine tomorrow after I've unpacked. A very merry Christmas.'

Then she kissed Sally, shook hands with Hengist and Janna and told Emlyn it was good to meet him, and turned towards the door.

'I'm coming with you.' Oriana leapt to her feet.

'No, you're not.' Emlyn grabbed her arm. 'We've got to talk.'

'Tomorrow.' Oriana winced at the exerted pressure, then, thinking her arm would snap like a wishbone: 'Oh, OK then.'

They went back into the drawing room, where neither could be bothered to bank up the dying embers.

Out of nerves, Oriana put a Christmas compilation on the CD player, hastily turning down the sound when the first track was 'O Come, All Ye Faithful'.

Emlyn watched as she idly flipped through the white invitation cards on the chimney piece, then wandered to the window, gazing out at the snow, which, growing too heavy, was sliding off branches and had bowed down her mother's beloved ceanothus to breaking point.

Snow might have fallen on the stretch of white neck between Oriana's dark hair and her brown velvet neckline. This can't be happening, thought Emlyn.

'I'm so desperately sorry.' Her voice was so low he had to move closer. 'I hadn't the guts to tell you. I thought you might have guessed. I'll always love you in my head, but not between my legs.'

'Thanks.' Emlyn helped himself to several fingers of Hengist's whisky. 'How long's it been going on?'

'About eight months. War forces people to take chances, but I just knew it was right.'

She ought to be more contrite, thought Emlyn. She has all the self-righteousness of the infatuated.

'Couldn't we be friends?' she begged.

'I doubt it, not when one's shot down by friendly fire.' As a log fell into the grate in a shower of sparks he went on, 'Hengist won't get his rugby Blue grandson now.' Emlyn removed Hengist's pale blue tasselled Cambridge cap from a bust of Brahms.

'He could.' Oriana swung round. 'Can I ask you a favour? It's a compliment really. Charlie and I want a baby.'

Emlyn caught his breath. Fuck, he'd pulled the tassel off the cap.

'Unto us a boy is born,' sang the CD player.

'Not unto us, it ain't,' said Emlyn flatly.

'It could be. I can't think of anyone in the world I'd rather have as father of my child. You're brave, loyal, funny and such a wonderful athlete.'

'And thick,' said Emlyn. 'You'd provide the brains presumably.'

'Oh, Emlyn.' If he could joke, the worst was over.

She reached out and took his hand, irresistible in her hopeful beauty. 'Daddy'd be so pleased too, he's so fond of you. Will you sleep with me while I'm here, Charlie truly won't mind, but if you can't face that, at least be the donor?' Then when he didn't answer: 'You could have access,' she added.

'You fucking bitch,' said Emlyn softly. 'I joined this school because of you, and sold my principles down the River Fleet. You ruthless bloody bitch. Using your rough trade to provide hybrid vigour. No fucking thank you.'

'No need to be obnoxious,' said Oriana huffily, as though he'd refused to give her a lift to the station. 'I could easily have married you and had women on the side, taken the easy route. But Charlie and I thought about this long and hard.'

'Hardly the operative adjectives.' Emlyn's voice grew in fury. 'There is absolutely no way a child of mine is going to be brought up by a couple of lesbians.'

'Pity,' sighed Oriana, 'our gay male friends have been very supportive and are very happy to oblige. They see the bigger picture.'

'Or bugger picture – we are talking about a child.'

'Charlie would actually prefer IVF to make sure of a girl, but she knows I so want to give Dad a grandson.'

'You've had it all planned,' said Emlyn softly. 'I never, never want to see you again,' and, fumbling with the French windows, tripping over the door ledge, he stumbled off into the blizzard.

Hearing doors slamming and shouting, Hengist, who'd just seen Janna, who should not have been driving, into her car, marched into the drawing room.

Towering over Oriana, terrible as an army with banners, he roared, 'Your mother's devastated. I can't think of a crasser way of hurting her. I'm amazed you didn't announce it on television. Heartbreaking News. And what the hell have you said to poor Emlyn?'

When Oriana told him, adding that she hoped it would be some compensation to Emlyn to feel he was involved, Hengist flipped.

'How can you be so fucking insensitive?'

'You wanted a son, a grandson; I'm doing my best.'

'Not one brought up by two dykes.'

Oriana winced. 'Why are you and Emlyn so homophobic?'

'Children need a father.'

'Charlie and I love each other,' said Oriana. 'You've always surrounded yourself with children who you love more than me. You loved Mungo more than me. I'm just trying to give you another Mungo,' she sobbed.

'Don't drag Mungo into it. Get out, GET OUT, I never want to see you or Charlie again.'

Charging upstairs to her bedroom, Oriana discovered the long, lean, olive-skinned nakedness of Charlie, stretched out across the four-poster. Her high breasts and sleek flat belly would never have need of surgery.

Arms on the pillow behind her head showed off armpit hair as glossy as her dark brown Brazilian. On the bedside table awaited oil for fingers that went everywhere, releasing Oriana utterly, driving her to heaven.

'Come to bed, my darling,' called out Charlie softly, then, seeing the anguish on Oriana's face, asked anxiously, 'Whatever's the matter?'

'It's a good thing you haven't unpacked yet,' sobbed Oriana, 'there's no room at this inn.'

Out on the pitches, it was as light as day. In contrast to her master's anguish, Elaine skipped and cavorted, white on white, snorting excitedly, tunnelling her nose along the snow. Hengist, who had no treads on his black evening shoes, fell over twice and heaved himself up. Reaching Badger's Retreat, he found a tall big ash had been blown over in yesterday's gale, knocking most of the branches off the east side of the Family Tree, smashing every sapling springing up around it.

Like Charlie, invading our Christmas, destroying us, he thought. A few remaining branches swung loose like broken limbs. Others were bandaged in snow. Hengist gave a howl and flung his arms round the trunk trying to hold the family together.

From now on, his sights would be set on Paris.

By the time he got home, Oriana and Charlie had departed and he was greeted by a tearful Sally, furious with him for chucking Oriana out.

'It was the way she was born, poor child.'

'Bloody wasn't. How could she treat poor Emlyn like that?'

'She loves Charlie, who was sweet when they left. She apologized and hoped she hadn't come on too strong at dinner, but she didn't know how to handle Emlyn and she was so nervous about meeting us.'

'Bollocks,' raged Hengist, 'she's as nervous as a basking shark.'

98

Dora, of course, leaked the entire story to the press, who came roaring down to Bagley, wildly interested in the coming out of Oriana.

'Of course we support Oriana,' Sally told the *Telegraph*. 'Hengist and I are naturally disappointed as we've always longed for grandchildren and feel life is easier if you have a conventional marriage.'

'If your daughter does something reprehensible,' Hengist was quoted as saying, 'you take it on the chin.'

Rupert put down *Lord of the Flies*, which he was rather enjoying, to ring Hengist to commiserate.

'Same thing happened to us with Marcus. Hell of a shock at the time. But he's very happy with his boyfriend and it didn't do his career any harm.'

Bianca was absolutely fed up with Rupert staying at home to read his set books during the holidays, which meant she couldn't slope off and see Paris. Why the hell couldn't he take up blood sports again?

Although most of the staff at Bagley were very sympathetic towards Hengist, Sally and Emlyn, there was a faction, headed by Poppet Bruce, who felt the Brett-Taylors had been a little too smug about Oriana's achievements.

Janna tried to comfort a monosyllabic, devastated Emlyn, who was outwardly stoical, thinking more of Hengist and Sally. Inwardly he identified with the

Brett-Taylors' Christmas tree, which had held up the lights, the tinsel, the fairy and the coloured balls, with everyone oohing and aahing. Now the decorations had gone back into their box until next year, but the tree had been chucked out on the terrace on Twelfth Night, destined for the bonfire. That's how he felt Oriana had treated him.

Somehow he had survived the beginning of term, welcoming back boys, taking lessons and rugby practice, drinking only a little more than usual, refusing to talk to the press, who nevertheless quoted him as saying: 'I feel a proper Charlie, although that's probably Oriana's role now.'

On the other hand, history mocks were never marked down more savagely. Even Boffin Brooks only got a D, while one boy ordered to run ten times down to the boathouse on frozen ground was carted off to the sick bay with a broken ankle. Emlyn was again taking no prisoners. He coped until the second week of term when he and Sally were wandering towards the lake discussing the situation.

The snow had nearly thawed. The brightest thing in the landscape was the warm brown keys of the ashes and Elaine in her red tartan coat, bounding ahead. A soft grey mist was coming down. The press, thank God, had retreated.

'I'm so worried about Oriana's career and her relationship with Hengist,' Sally was saying as she tightened her dark blue silk scarf under her chin. 'He so adores her. When you and she were together, you always made room for him, but Charlie seems to be all-consuming. I doubt, even if he came round, she'd let him back in again.

'I like lesbians,' she added firmly, 'Joan's a dear. But I just feel their chances of happiness are limited and it's more difficult to gain social acceptance because the world is so ignorant and the press is so cruel.'

Emlyn gathered up a remaining patch of snow and

hurled it into the lake. 'Guys get excited by the idea, but only if it's two lush blondes on a bed and they can watch or join in. They're threatened by the reality.'

He and Sally were so engrossed they didn't notice Poppet Bruce waiting like Horatius as they stepped onto the Japanese bridge which crossed a narrow stretch of the lake. Poppet looked very cheery in a woolly hat, muffler and gumboots all in orange and, because she was pregnant, she had added a blue and orange wool cloak. She was full of her own Christmas.

'We enjoyed goat's cheese quiche for the festive meal and instead of exchanging Christmas gifts, we donated a goat to a family in Africa. I'm very excited by my latest project: swimming for Asian women.' Then, eyes sparkling with malevolent enthusiasm, she went on, 'I'm so pleased to bump into you, Sally, because I so rejoice for you.'

'Whatever for?' Searching for carp in the grey water, Sally braced herself.

'That Oriana's gay. What a thrill for you and Hengist. What a new and fascinating take it will give you on life, with particular resonance for Hengist who's so homo-phobic. I would urge him to have immediate counselling. As a professional, I'd be happy to oblige.'

Reading their silence as approval, Poppet turned and walked back across the bridge with them. 'What is more, I much look forward to meeting Charlie Delgado. I so admire her oeuvre. Might Oriana be pre-vailed on to address the Talks Society, not just about the war, but about coming out? She and Charlie could do a fascinating double act.'

They had reached the other side.

Sally, quite unable to speak, was gazing in horror at Poppet. Not so Emlyn, who was so angry, he gathered up his deputy headmaster's wife and threw her into the lake.

'It's not just Asian women who go swimming. If you were a bloke,' he roared, 'I'd smack you round the face, you insensitive bitch. And you're *not* going to rescue her.' He seized Sally's arm.

As he hurried her away, Sally reflected on life's ironies. She had been so delighted when she thought Oriana had a new man, but now, how lovingly and gratefully she'd have accepted Emlyn as a son-in-law. Furiously spitting out pond weed, Poppet swam to the bank.

Emlyn had hardly got back to his flat and poured himself a vast whisky when Alex Bruce, glasses steaming up in righteous indignation, barged in.

'How dare you chuck Poppet in the lake? You could have killed her and our babe.'

'Witches deserve drowning,' yelled Emlyn. 'My only mistake was not to do it sooner. If you come down to the lake, I'll be happy to hold you under.'

Such was Emlyn's fury, Alex backed hastily away, knocking over a chair overloaded with unopened Christmas presents.

'You're only resorting to vulgar abuse, taking it out on your colleagues, because you can't handle rejection. Oriana is clearly seeking closure.'

'Shut up about Oriana!' Emlyn drained his glass of whisky and got to his feet, his massive frame blotting out any light from the window. Next moment, he had grabbed Alex's lapels, dislodging his spectacles. 'You little weasel.'

'You'll get fired for this.'

'Good,' said Emlyn, 'I couldn't work under the same roof as you and that vindictive cow a moment longer,' and his fist propelled Alex through the air onto a rickety sofa, sending flying piles of rugby shirts and unmarked mocks papers and face-down photographs of Oriana.

Despite a possibly cracked cheekbone and his terror of this vast, fire-breathing Welsh dragon, Alex felt a surge of satisfaction. Emlyn, with his working-class, state-school background, was an ace in the

Hengist-Artie-Theo pack, because he saw good in their traditions, whereas Alex only saw evil. Emlyn was also young, left wing and progressive and so loved by parents and pupils alike that Alex feared him as an outside candidate for headmaster. His loss to the old guard would be immeasurable.

'Can I accept this as your resignation?' he spluttered.

'You certainly can, now get out.'

That day Emlyn walked straight to Janna, who took care of him. For twenty-four hours he was delirious, ranting and raving in the pits of drunken despair. It was hard to tell if the bitch he was inveighing against was Poppet, Charlie or Oriana.

Janna, therefore, hid a letter she had been amazed to receive from Oriana, which apologized for being rude.

'I'm protective towards my mother and I mistakenly thought you were after Dad. Will you keep an eye on her and on Emlyn? I really do care for him and I bungled the whole thing. Charlie sends her best. We hope to see you when we're next in England.'

Janna felt oddly comforted.

'What are you going to do?' she asked Emlyn when he finally sobered up.

'I've been screwed by the Brett-Taylors.' Emlyn gazed moodily into a cup of black coffee. 'Until Charlie rolled up, they had no real desire for me to marry Oriana. To that lot, being working class is worse than being lesbian. Fucking upper classes, fucking independent schools.'

He rubbed his stubble reflectively. 'I might go back to the maintained system; I might go and work for the Welsh Rugby Union. I dropped in on them when I was home at Christmas. They said there was always a job going. I'd like to be part of building up a team to bury England at Twickenham. But for the next two terms, I'd like to help you out at Larks, if you'll have me?'

Janna gazed at him, eyes and mouth opening wider and wider. '*Have* you?' She frantically wiped her eyes. 'It's the best news ever. Are you sure? God, we need you. They love the Brig and Pittsy and tolerate Skunk and Mates, but they worship you. The Brigadier's awesome on Nazi Germany, but he's rusty on the Russian Revolution and it'd be wonderful to have someone to referee fights and see off Ashton Douglas and just have you around.'

Hengist, by contrast, was devastated. He'd lost a marvellous master, a soulmate and a favoured heir apparent. He tried to persuade Emlyn to reconsider.

'We could always claim Poppet provoked you. None of your class has completed its coursework. Their parents are going to be livid. You can't let them down. Look at the way Janna stood by her no-hopers. What the hell are you going to do?'

'Go to Larks to help out Janna,' which didn't please Hengist one bit.

'Well, don't break her heart then. And what about our rugger teams?'

'Denzil will have to get up in the afternoon for a change.'

'Where are you going to live?'

'I've got temporary digs in Wilmington High Street, opposite Brigadier Woodford,' which pleased Hengist even less.

The pupils were equally enraged at Emlyn's departure. Posters and graffiti everywhere demanded his return. Alex was shouted down and booed in chapel and he wrongly blamed Theo when someone painted 'Ite domum' on the roof of his house.

Nor did having Boffin caringly applying rump steak to one's black eye compensate for being called 'Alex Bruise'. Alex festered as he corrected the proofs of his *Guide to Red Tape*, which was due out in June.

Poppet, on the other hand, was nauseatingly

forgiving. 'Emlyn was hurting,' she told everyone, 'it came out as anger.'

Artie and Theo walked to chapel past the lake, on whose banks, as a result of the gales, twigs, branches and even ivy-mantled trees were strewn like an antler factory. The wind of change blowing out dead wood, thought Theo, with a shiver.

'How's Emlyn?' he asked.

'Resigned,' replied Artie sadly.

'Is that a verb or an adjective?'

'Both.'

'We have lost our Hector,' said Theo mournfully.

Dora leaked the story to the papers, who all came roaring back to Bagley: 'Top rugby school loses star coach'.

99

The despair of Bagley at losing their star coach was only equalled by Larks's joy at inheriting him. By blacking one of the detested Mr Fussy's eyes, Emlyn had achieved cult status and it rocketed morale to have such an attractive man round the place. Even though it was winter, the gap suddenly increased between jeans and crop tops, skirts climbed, Rowan's dark bob was highlighted for the first time, even Miss Basket, sparked up by snogging Skunk at the Christmas party, drenched herself in lavender water.

'Lovely for the boys to have a role model,' said Mags.

'I'm a roly-poly model,' sighed Sophy, who'd put on seven pounds over Christmas and now joined the netball team in the lunch hour.

Weatherwise, Emlyn's first morning was unpromising, with lowering skies and a bitter east wind sending leaves scuttling like mice across the playground. Inside, all was warmth. Graffi had designed a banner for reception showing a red dragon being greeted by a lot of larks. Pupils wandered in and out of a staffroom thick with cigarette smoke when they wanted to talk to a teacher. The purple and cyclamen-pink ball dresses worn by Pittsy and Skunk as Ugly Sisters in the staff pantomime still hung on a rail with everyone's coats. The noticeboard was thick with cuttings about Larks and a mocks timetable with a red line through it.

Thought for the week was: 'Chewing gum: we're gumming down.'

Sophy had brought in her daughter, Dulcie, who was playing with Kylie Rose's Cameron and being monitored by several pupils taking GCSE child care.

Miss Cambola rushed up and kissed Emlyn on both cheeks.

'At last, we have a baritone. We aim to sing the German Requiem in the cathedral.'

At break, Taggie Campbell-Black brought in a rainbow cake she was trying out for coursework and gave Emlyn the biggest slice.

After break he gave his first lesson on the Russian Revolution: a great success, particularly when Rocky retreated once more to the cupboard at the back of the room and kept the class in fits of laughter.

Emlyn told them about the first general strike in Moscow when there was no electricity and Tsar Nicholas, in his amber room, had to read and write his letters by candlelight.

'What was he experiencing for a first time?' asked Emlyn.

'People power,' boomed the voice from the cupboard.

'Excellent, Rocky. Well done.'

Knowing their attention span was short, Emlyn moved on to the Monk with the burning eyes who had such a hold on Queen Alexandra.

'Can anyone tell me his name?'

'Omar Sharif,' intoned the cupboard.

Rocky, who liked talking to adults, wandered into the staffroom during the lunch hour.

'Get out before I kill you,' bellowed the Brigadier in mock fury as Rocky helped himself to Lily's last cheroot.

Both Brigadier and Lily, Emlyn noticed, were in fine fettle, the Brigadier arranging his teaching days to coincide with Lily's so he could give her a lift in and out.

In the afternoon, Janna went through the children's mocks papers with the Brigadier and Emlyn, expressing doubts whether any of them would manage a decent grade in history.

'If they'd been marked down as ruthlessly as they're supposed to be, they'd have been in minus figures,' she added dolefully.

'If it's any comfort' – the Brigadier patted her hand – 'Rupert Campbell-Black asked me to mark his English lit. mocks papers for him. I'm afraid I had to fail him too. In an exam, one really cannot say: "Sylvia Plath's the most fucking awful woman I've ever come across," or, "Mrs Bennet's exactly like Anthea Belvedon."'

Emlyn grinned.'He got that bit right.'

Emlyn was keen to improve Larks's history marks but, filled with underlying rage against the whole arrogant, elitist public-school system, his ambition was to thrash them at the game at which they considered themselves invincible: rugby football. The boys at Larks were already fired up by the World Cup, so Emlyn had no difficulty in forming a rugby team, who grew markedly less enthusiastic when they had to run through the frozen water meadows before sunrise and train after school in the dark evenings. Admittedly, Emlyn jogged with them and shed twenty pounds and his gut. With his soft Welsh lilt becoming a sergeant major's roar, he had no difficulty keeping the roughest, toughest boys in order, particularly when he dropped them from the team if they didn't shape up.

Johnnie Fowler was kicked out for two weeks because he rolled up in a dirty shirt.

'You're meant to be covered in mud at the end of a game, not the beginning.'

'The washing machine's broke.'

'Go to the launderette.'

'Haven't got no money.'

'Wash it by bloody hand then.'

Emlyn's genius was to draw the most out of players, so they achieved way beyond their own and everyone else's dreams. He knew which boys, like Johnnie and Monster, to slap down and which, like Xav and Rocky, to build up. He was an expert at pinpointing a player's weakness and finding a solution, adapting teaching to the individual. Rugby, above all, taught boys teamwork and to keep their temper. As a result, flare-ups and loutish behaviour within the school dramatically decreased.

Emlyn increasingly appreciated the difficulties in getting these children through GCSE. Not that they were thick, but they were flowers planted in stony, dry, infertile soil, buffeted by winds.

'Try and speak French with your family at home,' he heard Lily urging, '*c'est très bon.*'

'Our family don't even speak in English,' said Johnnie. 'They just throw fings at each other.'

But as the weeks went by, the children gradually mastered the basics of volcanoes, earthquakes, heredity, the rise of Hitler, the Cuban missile crisis, the effect of tourism on world debt, the splitting of the atom, the circulation of the blood, the reflexes of the eye, electricity, dissecting sheep's hearts and learnt how to book a ticket in French or to go shopping in Spanish.

They had fun with geography coursework, deciding where to locate a factory.

'In Miss Miserden's front garden,' said Pearl.

'That won't mean a lot to the examiner,' said Basket.

'Well, Baldie Hyde's back garden then.'

In his coursework, Graffi wrote eloquently about how roadworks in Shakespeare Lane, which ran into the Shakespeare Estate, inconvenienced people. 'Makes me late for school. Mum can't get to Tesco's. Dad can't get to the pub. Cavendish Plaza can't get to their hairdressers. Randal Stancombe takes a helicopter, so the rich get inconvenienced less than the poor.'

Emlyn found the teaching much tougher than Bagley; it was like having to crank up an old Ford for the shortest journey when one had been driving a Lamborghini, but the rewards were greater, seeing understanding dawning on children's faces. Increasingly too he admired Janna, how she exhausted herself worrying about Wally's son in Iraq, Mags's premature grandchild, Mr Mates's arthritis.

She was outwardly cheerful, but he realized how near cracking up she was when, one late February morning, she wandered wailing into his history class.

'Look, look, Sally Brett-Taylor gave me these hyacinth bulbs back in October, I put them in a black dustbin bag at the back of the stockroom and forgot about them.'

Thus imprisoned in darkness, the white leaves and stems, from which sprouted tiny, colourless, misshapen flowers, had struggled to a hopelessly etiolated twenty-four inches, hanging pathetically down over the edge of their blue china bowl. Their whiskery roots had completely clogged the bulb fibre.

'They were so desperate to reach the light and flower like the children in the Shakespeare Estate,' she sobbed. 'I left them in the dark; I failed to give them water and light.'

Jerking his head towards the door to tell Feral and Co to scarper, Emlyn put the bowl on his desk and took Janna in his arms.

'It's all right, lovely, it's all right.'

'I killed them.'

'You didn't – it's only this year's hyacinths. The bulbs themselves are fine, they'll flower again next year. Look, already the leaves are turning green in the light, like your kids'll blossom because you've given them love and hope.'

To cheer her up, he took her to the new James Bond film that evening and she slept right through it.

The children at Larks had been so furious when

horrible Rod Hyde won a Teaching Award in October that when a small ad appeared in the *Gazette* asking for nominations for next autumn's awards, they decided to enter Janna.

'Miss is such a good filler-in of forms, but we can't expect her to fill in her own,' said Kylie. 'Let's ask Emlyn.'

Gradually Janna became calmer and happier. It was so great to have someone to kick ass so she could concentrate on cherishing.

Emlyn was still gutted about Oriana; he missed Artie and Theo and the pupils at Bagley, but he loved the Brigadier and Wally and even grew fond of Skunk, Pittsy and Mr Mates – and they of him, because he treated them as equals, even regarding them as young enough to be roped into refereeing.

Gradually, as the almond scattered its pink blossom, crocuses purpled the emerald-green spring grass and the days grew longer, Xav's remaining fat turned to hard muscle, Monster, Johnnie and Rocky formed an impenetrable back row, Graffi, talking Welsh to Emlyn to annoy the others, and Danny, a Belfast boy, known as 'Danny the Irish', grew fleet as forwards. Feral, to crown it, was a natural, with the wisdom, the speed, the ability to pass, kick and dodge of a potential international. Like a feral cat, his eyes swivelled the whole time, assessing danger, checking where everyone else was on the field and where they were going to be in five seconds' time.

Emlyn longed to keep him for rugby, but he had made a Faustian bargain. If Feral gave him one term and a sporting chance of beating Bagley, he would put Feral onto the football map. At heart, he hoped Feral might become sufficiently enamoured of rugby to convert.

With Stormin' Norman on the sidelines yelling the heroes on, Larks was gradually transformed into a 'lean, mean, killing machine'.

100

Hengist meanwhile, aware that Bagley needed to do more to bond with the community, challenged Larks to a fun charity rugby match on the last Sunday of term.

Randal Stancombe, as Larks's increasingly self-confessed backer, immediately donated a rugby ball in gold plate, on which the name of the winning team would be engraved.

'And when you move on to your next school,' he told Janna, 'you must carry on the fixture,' murmuring that he had great plans for a new school on the water meadows below the Cathedral, 'a city academy, which you would run.'

Janna couldn't fail to be flattered and although Randal gave her the creeps since their hideous sexual encounter back in September, she had to recognize that with the £120,000, the rebuilding of Appletree and the minibus, which could now take half the school to matches or outings, he had provided fantastic support. So she smiled over gritted teeth when he popped in to show off her brave experiment to high-powered friends, hinting she'd never have pulled it off without his six figure leg-up.

Emlyn detested Randal sauntering in as though he owned the place. As if he could possibly build a school on the water meadows, when they were well below the flood plain. Randal was far more likely to flatten the Shakespeare Estate.

Nor did Randal miss an opportunity to drop in on Taggie's classes. Lady Belvedon might be the blow-job queen, but Mrs Campbell-Black was the stuff of dreams and far too sweet to patronize or put him down as Anthea often did.

'How's your hubby's GCSE going?'

'He's working very hard,' sighed Taggie.

Taggie had another admirer, Pete Wainwright, the new Larks Rovers under-manager, a bluff, tough Lancastrian, with whom she'd been liaising over her class's coursework. As well as lunch in the director's boxes, this included a pre-match meal for the players and snacks for the crowd.

Pete Wainwright was so impressed, he was thinking of adopting Taggie's menus for the club. Taggie, in turn, was determined 'to screw her courage' (a phrase that came from one of Rupert's set books) to ask Pete to give Feral a trial.

Despite Taggie's success at work, things were not easy at home. Rupert, displaying the same competitive streak that took him to the top as a showjumper and an owner-trainer, was hell bent on winning his bet. Having ploughed his mocks, he had given up drink for Lent and incessantly mugged up his set books as hounds checked between coverts or his helicopter flew him to race meetings round Europe.

Xav seemed much happier, although in despair that Aysha, having completed her coursework in record time, had reluctantly gone back to Pakistan to meet her future husband. Xav was also panicking about the proposed match against Bagley. Would they flay him alive?

Taggie was more worried about Bianca who, on the occasions she came home, was moody and detached: the dancing sunbeam permanently hidden behind dark clouds. Over half-term she'd shut herself away in her room. On the Sunday afternoon, Taggie was wearily clearing away lunch and planning her lesson for tomorrow: 'a cake for a celebration: christening, birthday or wedding', when Bianca rushed in in tears.

'Darling! Whatever's the matter?'

'I don't want to go back to Bagley tomorrow.'

'Oh, angel.' Taggie's heart leapt guiltily: how blissful if Bianca had decided to go back to being a day girl. 'Whyever not?'

'Because I want to go back tonight,' sobbed Bianca, 'but bloody Daddy's so busy writing an essay on *Pride and Prejudice* he'll only take me first thing tomorrow morning. He says I'm obsessed with boys, like Lydia Bennet.'

With the lighter evenings, Bianca had made plans on her return to drug Jade Stancombe's cocoa, climb out of her dormitory window and run to Middle Field, straight into Paris's arms. The effort required for the two of them to be alone added frisson to their affaire. They had made love in Plover's loose box, behind the bicycle shed, in the science lab and the boathouse and had somehow escaped discovery.

Bianca adored Paris; she was reduced to jelly when their eyes met in chapel, or their hands clasped in the corridor. But she found him very difficult to talk to. He was wonderful at making love, his touch so sure and tender, but he was undemonstrative; he told her that she was beautiful, but never that he loved her. There was a detachment and cool about him that fascinated while intimidating her. He was so clever: he sent her witty text messages, wrote her poems she didn't understand and he was always reading. Bianca, who never read, liked chatting, dancing and shopping. It was also impossible to escape Dora who, like a dog suspecting its owners are about to go out, clung ever closer.

Paris had been devastated by Emlyn's departure. Rugby, such a release of aggression, had lost much of its charm. He could always talk to Emlyn, who understood the demons and anger lurking beneath the surface.

Hengist, stung by Oriana's accusations that he'd given up teaching, was now taking the Upper Fifth's history set abandoned by Emlyn. This was a revelation to the pupils because he made the subject so vivid and amusing. On one occasion, they acted out the Munich Conference. Boffin, with his supercilious, toothy face, made the perfect Chamberlain, Lubemir was Mussolini, and the nasty German diplomat demanding more and more of Czechoslovakia was naturally Cosmo.

Lessons went in a flash. Paris wanted to tape every word. You could hear the tramp of jackboots, smell the gas of the concentration camps as Hengist built up the nightmare menace of Nazi Germany.

Hengist, desperately missing Oriana, found great solace in teaching Paris. So did Theo, whose back grew increasingly painful as he laboured to finish Sophocles, but was somehow soothed as he and Paris talked long into the night, devouring the great classical writers.

Obsessed with work, Paris had less time for either Bianca or Dora, but he still went back to the Old Coach House on Sundays, shutting himself in his room to read and work and never too busy to admit Dulcie and Northcliffe, who both loved nothing better than to curl up on his bed.

Paris's over-active imagination was invariably triggered off by things he read. When a Sunday tabloid, early in March, claimed that badly abused children often torture animals and abuse smaller children, he grew utterly distraught, banishing a tearful Dulcie, pushing away a bewildered Northcliffe, terrified of harming them, before trashing his room.

Ian, under continuing pressure from Alex Bruce, was fed up with Paris and increasingly muttering about returning him to care. Only last week, when he had merely removed a leaf from the boy's hair, Paris had clenched his fists and nearly thumped him.

This terrified Patience. As Paris was doing *Macbeth* for GCSE coursework, in a desperate attempt to cheer him up and provide him with inspiration, she drove him, on the third Saturday in March, to see a Royal Shakespeare performance. Paris, who'd wanted to slope off and see Bianca, hardly spoke and listened to a tape of *Lord of the Flies* all the way there.

Poor Patience, no intellectual, was desperately tired and, despite the thunderclaps and battle din, fought sleep throughout the play. She was worried Paris minded being seen in public with such an old scarecrow and tried to keep her raucous voice down. When they went to the bar in the interval, lots of people gazed at the white beauty of Paris in his severe dark grey school suit and then at her, pondering the connection. She had ordered half a bottle of white and some smoked salmon sandwiches, cobwebbed in cellophane, and thought what a ghastly middle-class, middle-aged thing to do.

'"Screw your courage", "Is this a dagger"? We always intoned, "Out, damned spot!" when we had spots at school. *Macbeth*'s so full of quotations,' she gabbled, desperate to keep the conversation going.

Paris answered in monosyllables. Patience longed to get tanked up, but she had to drive home. Conscious of Paris's set, white face beside her on the return journey, she was filled with despair. Ian was right. It wasn't working. He clearly loathed living with them. A small voice inside her also said: He might be more grateful.

It was after midnight when they reached home, greeted by a grinning, sleepy-eyed, singing Northcliffe.

'I do hope the play didn't upset you too much,' said Patience. 'It is very harrowing and so sad at the end.'

As Paris went towards the door, she asked if there was anything about it he'd particularly liked.

'The bogs in the theatre were nice,' muttered Paris and shot upstairs.

Patience went out to check the horses, who at least whickered and were pleased to see her, even when she sobbed into Plover's dappled grey shoulder. When she finally came to bed, she found Ian in a martyred heap. 'Of course I haven't slept, I've been worried stiff about you on those roads.'

Next day was Mothering Sunday – a traditional day for children in care to go berserk because they were made so aware of not having a mother around. Remembering last year's hysterical scenes, when Paris had broken up his room yet again, screaming how he missed his mother and that Ian hated him and anyway, Ian and Patience were so old, they'd die soon and he'd be sent to another foster home, Patience steeled herself.

She'd fed the horses and, as it was a mild day, turned them out in their rugs. She was simultaneously frying bacon, grilling sausages and mushrooms and emptying the bins when Paris walked in. Grabbing the black bin bag and taking it to the dustbins outside, he dropped an envelope on the kitchen table.

He's leaving, thought Patience in panic, oh please God no, but, opening the letter with trembling hands, she found a Mother's Day card of shocking pink roses, with the words 'To a Wonderful Mother' on the front.

'Dear Patience,' Paris had written inside. 'Thank you for *Macbeth*. It was so awesome I couldn't speak afterwards. Love, Paris'.

She had to read it three times before the words swam before her eyes, then she broke into noisy sobs.

'I'm sorry.' An appalled Paris, returning, snatched the card from her. 'I didn't mean to—'

'No, no.' With one large, red hand, Patience reached for the kitchen roll, with the other she snatched back her card.

'It's the most wonderful thing that ever happened.

It's just unexpected, that's all. I was worried we were old and boring and you didn't like living here.'

Paris shrugged. 'Well, I do.'

'We want you to stay with us more than anything,' muttered Patience. 'We've tried to act cool because we didn't want to frighten you or make you feel claustrophobic.'

Paris said nothing, but his normally ashen face was flooded with colour.

They were brought back to earth by the smell of burning sausages. Next moment Dulcie marched in with the little wheelbarrow given her by the builders working on the Randal Stancombe science block. Today it was full of sand.

'Those men better get their arses into gear,' announced Dulcie, 'or the building won't be fucking ready in time.'

Patience turned to retrieve the sausages and Paris rescued the bacon on the Aga, both trying to hide their laughter, which diffused the situation.

101

The match between Larks and Bagley's third fifteen took place a week later, on an unexpectedly mild evening. Unbeaten all term, Bagley regarded victory as so certain that the entire team had raging hangovers from a tarts and vicars party the night before. For those in need of succour, Cosmo, still in his dog collar, was circulating with a big brown jug frothing with Alka-Seltzer.

'Attila the Hunk can't work miracles,' he said bitchily, 'even if he does have scores to settle.'

'It'll be more than fifty–nil,' said Lando, who hadn't bothered to wash off his tart's eyeliner and scarlet lipstick. 'I've had a bet.'

Over at Larks, Xav was refusing to get on the bus.

'Please don't make me go back to Bagley,' he begged Emlyn. 'They'll lynch me for bullying Dicky.'

'Not if I'm around. You're the only player with big match experience, who knows the capabilities of the Bagley team.'

As a V-sign to Alex Bruce, who'd sacked them both, Emlyn had made Xav captain. It had been worth it to see the terror and delight on Xav's broad, normally impassive face.

Now terror predominated.

'Cosmo and Lubemir are in the team, they'll bury me.'

'Feral's the one they'll try and bury. You've got to be there for him, to stop him losing his rag. He didn't sleep last night.'

'Nor did I,' grumbled Xav.

Feral ricocheted between longing and panic. Pete Wainwright from Larkminster Rovers was coming to the match and, if impressed, might offer Feral a trial. He might also see Bianca again. Agonizing rumours had filtered through that she and Paris were an item. How could he not murder Paris?

Under his cheerful air of imperturbability, Emlyn was churning worse than his team at the prospect of returning to Bagley, 'the land of lost content', where he'd been so happy and hopeful and so hurt and humiliated by Oriana's coming out. Hengist wouldn't miss an opportunity to emphasize the good he was doing for the community, so the press would be out in force – raking things up.

Hengist, who'd combined a governors' meeting over lunch, had laid on a bar and buffet in the pavilion and buses to transport Larks supporters to the game. He had also invited local bigwigs: the Mayor and the Bishop. Ashton and Cindy who, like Randal, loved to pretend they'd been responsible for saving Larks, had also rolled up.

Ashton, eyeing up the Bagley boys, who were certainly pretty, was in fact feeling bleak. The business pages that morning had launched blistering attacks on S and C and other private companies that had specialized in education. Not only were LEAs they'd taken over not meeting their targets, but the buildings they'd imposed on schools had turned out to be shoddy, poky, taking too long to build and not able to withstand the wear and tear of children. S and C badly needed a hit.

Still, it was hard to be bleak on such a lovely evening. Crowds already thronged the touchline and, although the daffodils were nearly over, primroses starred the banks and a pale haze of green leaf softened many trees, while others were pinky roan from buds about to burst. Heavy rain earlier enhanced the jade green of the pitch.

It was even mild enough for Randal Stancombe to descend from his chopper in a new, exquisitely cut off-white suit. Still smarting from being cuckolded by Hengist, he had rolled up with Anthea Belvedon, radiant in Parma violet, with a calf-length mink flung round her shoulders and a huge sapphire ring on her right hand.

'What a ravishing fur,' sighed Vicky Fairchild.

'A gift from Randal,' said Anthea, loudly enough to be heard by Ruth Walton, who'd just arrived, flushed from lunch, in last year's Lindka Cierach. 'I didn't realize it was going to be so warm – hello, Ruth – Randal and I feel for Dicky, Dora and Jade's sake it's so important to show one's face at such functions.'

'And I'm reporting you to animal rights,' hissed Dora, feeding roast beef sandwiches to Cadbury. 'That coat is so pants.'

Alex Bruce was fuming. How dare Hengist schedule a rugby match on the same day as a GCSE science revision workshop, which no one would now attend. Even Boffin had defected and, already miked up with a silver whistle round his scrawny neck, was poised to referee the game. And how dare Hengist invite back Emlyn, who had nearly drowned Poppet?

'Ten Downing Street is deceptively large once you get inside,' Poppet, several months pregnant, was now boasting to Anthea.

Noticing Mrs Walton looking a shade disconsolate, Cosmo thrust a large vodka and tonic into her hand.

'Ever considered a toyboy?' he murmured.

Hengist, not confident of shaven-headed Denzil, who preferred any game to rugger, was himself revving up the rest of the Bagley third fifteen. 'Never take any team coached by Emlyn for granted. He'll have told them to attack and attack and that nothing matters except getting points on the board.'

'It's still going to be three hundred to nil,' grumbled Lando. 'Christ, my head hurts.'

'Here they are, here they are,' went up the shout as Randal's crimson minibus rumbled up the drive.

'Larks wouldn't still exist without Daddy,' boasted Jade. 'He's given them so much financial support.'

'Oh shut up,' muttered Dora.

Bagley, incensed by the loss of Emlyn, watched Larks emerge with mixed feelings.

'There's Graffi, still lush,' sighed Milly.

Graffi, still grinning although black under the eyes, was reeling with relief because he'd completed his ten-hour art exam earlier in the week and was happy with what he had produced.

'My God,' said Amber, cutting off her conversation with the Master of Beagles at Radley, 'is that really Xavier? He must have lost a couple of stone and grown a foot. Looks quite attractive.'

'Very attractive if one remembers his trust fund,' agreed Milly.

'Hi, Xav.'

'Hello there, Xav,' purred Jade.

'Welcome back, Xav,' shouted Amber.

'Booo!' shouted Dora, who'd been at Dicky's hipflask. 'Have you forgotten he tried to kill my brother?'

'Shut up,' hissed a discomfited Dicky, as an equally discomfited Xav belted across the grass to the visitors' changing room.

'And here comes the Larks Lothario,' shouted Amber.

A pair of black-jeaned legs, as long and pliable as liquorice, were finally followed down the bus steps by a Nike scarlet jacket and a haughty black face.

'God he's awesome,' sighed Milly.

Glancing coldly round, reluctant to take a first step on enemy territory, Feral caught sight of Bianca standing on top of a car, in a bright orange poncho, her dark hair lifting in the breeze; he started violently as they gazed and gazed and gazed at each other.

'Move it, for fuck's sake.'

From behind, Johnnie, Monster and Rocky ejected Feral onto the gravel.

Oh God, thought Bianca in panic, I still love him.

Thank God, thought Feral in ecstasy, she still loves me.

In a daze he glanced up to see if she was real, then, smiling, shaking his head, waving his hands, he reeled after Xav.

Paris, who'd witnessed this eye-meet from the home changing room, felt punched in the gut. Then he saw Janna jumping out of Emlyn's muddy Renault. At first he was shocked how tired, pale and old she looked, but when both Larks and Bagley pupils ran forward to welcome her, and her face was illuminated by that tender, joyful smile, he realized how her new, short, curly hair became her, and how protectively Emlyn was towering over her, sheltering her from the mob as it surged around them.

'Mr Davies, Mr Davies, look, it's Mr Davies back.'

Paris wanted to join the throng and beg Janna's forgiveness and friendship. He wanted to bolt back to the Old Coach House and hide. He couldn't play rugby with so many cross-currents.

'Janna, darling.' It was Hengist, hugging her and then shaking hands with Emlyn. 'Marvellous to see you both. Sally sent her apologies, she's had to go and see her mother.'

Like hell, thought Janna. Normally such a trooper, Sally had taken Oriana's coming out very badly, particularly the press delving around and raising the ghost of Mungo. Today, with Emlyn's return, they would be out in force, and she hadn't been able to face it.

'Tell her her bulbs are being miraculous,' said Janna. 'Sheets of daffodils and hyacinths, even fritillaries; they've cheered everyone up so much.'

'I will; she'll be so pleased. Come and have a drink.'

'Janna can,' said Emlyn. 'I'm going to crank up my team.'

Emlyn found his Larks players strangely silent as with clumsily shaking hands they tried to find the necks of their crimson and yellow striped shirts and zip up shorts less white than most of their faces.

'Ouch,' yelled Johnnie Fowler, as he bit the inside of his cheek instead of his chewing gum.

Emlyn smiled round, steadying them, then placed a rugby ball on the floor in front of them.

'This is your best friend, so don't give him away. He has one destiny, over the line or between the posts. Don't let them bait you, don't swear at the ref, don't spit, or bite, kill the ball, or collapse in the scrum. However much you want to, it'll only put points on the board for the other side, not for us. Watch, watch the whole time.'

Larks parents were out in force. Cigarettes slotted into their lower lips, fathers with tattoos, earrings and T-shirts, they looked so young compared with the tiny sprinkling of Bagley parents.

'S'pose you have to grow old before you're rich enough to afford fees here,' observed Graffi's father, Dafydd, who was getting tanked up with Stormin' Norman.

Pearl's boxer dad had a whole quiche in one hand and a pint of red in the other.

Pearl and Kitten, in crop tops showing off grabbable waists, their purple flares sweeping the damp grass, tossed their shining, straightened manes as they paraded up and down, giggling and being eyed up by the Bagley boys.

Randal moved around pressing the flesh, getting himself and his beautiful suit photographed as much as possible, distributing largesse to the inhabitants of the Shakespeare Estate.

'So pleased Larks is doing well; what subject is your youngster taking in GCSE?'

'Sex and violence,' quipped Dafydd cheekily and regretted it when Stancombe's face blackened and he made a note on his pocket computer.

Through the cobweb-festooned window, Xav could see everyone nudging and staring as his parents arrived. Bianca, full of chat, dragged Taggie off to the bar. Rupert, who had no desire to socialize, stayed in the car with a bottle of brandy and *Opening Lines*, the OCR poetry set book, which, after repeated slugs, he was finding increasingly difficult to understand. He'd never met such a bunch of whingers moaning on about their dreadful childhoods. He could relate to Philip Larkin or Simon Armitage stealing from his mother's handbag and punching an irritating wife, but what the fuck was this guy Stevie Smith going on about?

> To carry a child into adult life,
> Is good, I say it is not.
> To carry the child into adult life
> Is to be handicapped.

In his wild youth, Rupert had had a Rolls-Royce with black windows. He could have done with it now, to stop so many ghastly mothers waving and gazing in. Nor could he avoid seeing Taggie being welcomed by all her dreadful new friends: Pittsy and fearful stinking, whiskery Skunk and that ghastly football manager, Pete Wainwright, who'd clearly got the raging hots for her, not to mention that fat Welshman who seemed to have bewitched Xav.

Rupert knew he was in the wrong. Since he'd decided to take this wretched exam and Taggie had proved such a hit at Larks, he'd been vile to her and ratty with the children.

Christ, she was even allowing the caretaker Wally to peck her on the cheek. Rupert was finding it as hard to climb out of his mega sulk as to break out of Broadmoor. Bloody hell, Stancombe, looking an absolute prat in his white suit, was now kissing Taggie – pity a snow plough couldn't run him over. Rupert was going to win this bet if it killed him. He took another slug.

Knowing they would expect great things, Paris observed that Ian and Patience had formed a merry party with Artie, Theo, the Brigadier and Lily.

'Larks look alarmingly fit,' grumbled Jack Waterlane as Monster, Johnnie and Danny the Irish thundered past chucking a ball to each other.

'Only because they stayed in last night,' said Anatole.

Bagley's shirts, sea blue with white collars, gave them a look of deceptive innocence. The sun, darting in and out of big white clouds, spotlit the Mansion one moment, an acid-green lime in Badger's Retreat another, Mrs Walton's laughing face as a passing Cosmo waved to her the next.

It was Larks's first glimpse of Paris for eighteen months. He had shot up and filled out, his jewellery had gone, his white blond hair, no longer gelled upwards, was longer with a side parting and, like Rupert Brooke's, poetically brushed back from his forehead. He was as dead pan as ever, but he had a new confidence. Nodding to his old classmates, but not stopping to say hello, he turned to Junior Lloyd-Foxe, yelling at him to pass the ball.

'Parse, parse,' mocked Monster.

'Lord, la-di-da,' shouted Johnnie, 'listen to the Prince of Posh "parsing" the "bawl". He's too grand for his old friends now.'

Paris ignored them, but a flush crept up his cheek.

Bagley won the toss, and chose the Mansion end, with the soft west wind behind them.

'Bagley to kick off.'

'OK, boys,' quietly Xav echoed Martin Johnson, 'let's take this game.'

'Very plucky of your lads to take on Bagley,' Poppet was saying patronizingly to Janna.

'Have you ever seen anything so gross as Boffin's bum in those shorts?' hissed Dora as Boffin blew a shrill plaintive note on his whistle.

Lando booted the ball over the heads of the Larks forwards. Next moment Feral moved into its path, caught it and set off for goal, dodging round Anatole and Lubemir, flashing his teeth at them, charging straight for the Hon. Jack, aiming for his right side, luring him onto his right foot, then bolting past on his left.

'Tackle him,' bellowed Lando, but Lubemir, hurling himself at Feral, only caught air as Feral skipped out of the way, streaking over the line, burying the ball under the posts to ecstatic, flabbergasted cheers.

'That gorilla won't kick it ten yards,' drawled Cosmo, as Rocky, having laboriously readjusted the plastic stand, finally managed to balance the ball on top of it.

'Our Farver,' mumbled Rocky and belted it over the bar to even more flabbergasted cheers.

'Very plucky of you to take on Larks,' Janna told Poppet.

'I ain't no gorilla.' Rocky marched up to Cosmo, shoving a huge fist in his terrified face.

'Rocky, no!' howled Xav.

Reluctantly Rocky lowered his fist.

'If you do that again, Rocky,' Boffin's miked voice echoed round the field, 'I shall send you to the sin bin.'

Three minutes later, Rocky leapt miles in the air in the line-out and catching the ball, passed to Xav, who passed to Graffi, who trundled down the field like a little Welsh pony, black hair tossing, slap into the Bagley defence, powering his way through them and crashing face down in the mud over the line, but with the ball staying firm between his palm and the pitch. Again Rocky converted.

'Rocky by name, Rocky by nature,' yelled the increasingly intoxicated crowd of Larks supporters.

'Steady, steady,' pleaded Emlyn, a great golden bear prowling the touchline. 'Oh Christ, well done,' as Xav kicked eighty yards up the field into touch.

Bagley rallied. Lubemir, winning the scrum, passed to Anatole, who passed to Jack, who found himself running into a solid Berlin wall of defence: Monster, Rocky and Johnnie Fowler, who brought him crashing down. Xav took the ball off him and kicked it up field, where it was gathered up by Feral, who with Ferrari acceleration charged up to the Bagley defence, their gumshields glaring, waiting to flatten him, and popped over a glorious left-footed drop goal.

As he sauntered back, festooned with cheering, thumping, ecstatic Larks players, Miss Cambola, who'd been practising with Kylie Rose and the choir, started to sing 'Swing Low, Sweet Chariot', as, from all sides, crimson Larks banners were waving.

'That's our tune,' snorted Biffo Rudge.

Bagley were now displaying all the symptoms of nerves, losing in the line-out, high tackling, killing the ball, sledging, biting, resorting to every dirty trick. What was also plain to everyone was that Paris was out of it, passing to the wrong people or the other side, kicking in empty spaces, and when Boffin blew the whistle, first on Monster for high tackling, and then on Johnnie for swearing and spitting at Cosmo, Paris missed two easy penalties.

'Lord Posh, Lord Posh,' barracked the Larks crowd.

'Lord, la-di-da, nose in the air,' bellowed Stormin' Norman to the edification of the entire field, 'you're as useless as tits on a bull.'

Pete Wainwright laughed happily because he was gaining intense pleasure watching Feral. You could see the boy thinking, glancing around each time he had the ball, using his brain. The others mostly kicked and hoped. Xavier was playing beautifully too. It was gratifying to see two black boys working so well together, cleaning up in the white heartland of an English public school. Pete was so pleased to see the delighted pride on Xav's sweet mother's face.

'The directors loved your lunch – it was a great success,' he told Taggie.

Johnnie Fowler's mother, Shelley, swayed up to Rupert's car. 'Your Xav's playing like a little king, Lord Black.' Then, when Rupert lowered the window a millimetre: 'My Johnnie's the good-looking one, didn't go into Larks much in the old days, had a lot of days off, but since Emlyn, Taggie and the Brig's taken over, he's hardly missed a day.' Noticing how handsome Rupert was, she added, 'Would you like me to get you a drink?'

'If you're going that way.'

Seeing Rupert looking more friendly, Poppet Bruce rushed over. 'Rupert, Rupert, how's your GCSE Eng. lit. going?'

'Fine,' snapped Rupert.

'Oh! You're reading *Opening Lines*. Charisma's finding it so enriching. Each poem yielding its meaning.'

'Not to me, they don't. I can't make head nor tail of this chap Stevie Smith.'

'Oh, how priceless.' Poppet went off into peals of laughter. 'Smith's a woman, Rupert.'

'Explains why the poem's such crap.'

'Don't be so sexist. You'll never pass your GCSE that way. Why not join our workshop in the Easter holidays?'

Fortunately relief arrived in the form of Shelley Fowler and a large brandy and ginger.

'Get in,' hissed Rupert, winding up the window.

'Johnnie's got that book too,' said Shelley, picking up *Opening Lines*. 'Didn't understand a word till Janna explained it.'

*   *   *

Half-time. The sides gathered in two groups, towelling
away sweat, swigging bottled water, pouring it over their
heads. Hengist strode onto the pitch.

'What the hell are you playing at?'

'They're as tough as shit,' protested Jack Waterlane.
'I think I've cracked a rib.'

'They really vant to vin,' grumbled Anatole.

'I've fucked my ankle, sir,' lied Cosmo.

'Well, you better go off for the second half.'

Larks were down to fourteen men: Danny the Irish had
cramp. Wally was working on his instep.

Emlyn was talking in a low voice to his team, praising
them to the now pink and blue flecked sky, isolating
individual triumphs.

'But the second half's going to be tougher; you'll be
getting tired. If I sub any of you, it's a compliment,
means you've played your hearts out. Rocky, you've
been awesome, and Monster and Johnnie.' Emlyn's
square face glowed. 'I can't tell you how great it's been,
good as scoring for Wales.'

Janna, watching Emlyn's joy, felt conflicting
emotions. How glorious to see Larks ascending, but she
felt so sorry for Paris.

Dora's despair, on the other hand, was total. She
could see Hengist giving the team hell. Poor Paris,
head hanging, face concealed by a damp curtain of
blond hair, must be feeling suicidal, not just about his
dud performance, but about Feral and Bianca as well.

'Stop bullying him,' she shouted. 'It's so unfair.'

Cadbury, who'd been stuffing his face all afternoon,
wandered off to drink from Middle Field Pond.
Following him, Dora decided she must save Paris.

102

As the pep talk ended and the teams changed ends and took up their positions, they were distracted by howls of laughter and wolf whistles as a streaker came running out of Middle Field and raced across the pitch skipping and dancing, arms outstretched. Her high breasts and bottom were too small to wobble. The waist, in between, as yet lacked definition, the racing legs were still a little plump. A pale blonde triangle was just discernible between her thighs. Her face was hidden by a pulled-down baseball cap.

'Who is it? Who is it?' yelled the delighted and cheering crowd. Then, as the streaker did a cartwheel and two handstands, her baseball cap fell off, her blonde plaits tumbled out and a chocolate Labrador bounded onto the pitch after her.

'My God, it's Dora,' said Lando. 'Look, sir, a streaker.'

Hengist swung round and laughed.

'Good heavens, so there is.'

'Gone away,' brayed Jack Waterlane as Siegfried's horn call rang out joyfully on Miss Cambola's trumpet.

Binoculars and little oblong silver cameras were being raised all round the pitch as the cheers escalated. The press raced along the touchline.

'Go for it, Dora,' yelled both teams, momentarily distracted from despair and elation.

' "Like an unbodied joy whose race has just begun",' murmured Theo.

'Lovely little bottom,' sighed Artie.

Northcliffe growled at the sight of a passing Cadbury. Boffin clamped his hands over his eyes in horror. Anthea, who had been upstaging Poppet, turned back to the pitch.

'Oh look, a streaker, how common. We should never have allowed this bonding with Larks!' Then she gave an almighty squawk: 'My God, it's Dora. Dicky! Randal! Do something!'

Randal, only too happy to show how fit he was, set off in pursuit.

' "The Assyrian came down like the wolf on the fold," ' murmured Ian Cartwright.

Hot on Randal's heels came Joan. 'Dora Belvedon,' she bellowed, 'come here at once.'

'Sit!' howled Cosmo to roars of laughter. 'Stay!'

Evading capture, circling, Dora galloped up to Paris.

'Get your stupid finger out,' she panted, breasts quivering, face red from running, eyes flashing, hair escaping from her plaits. 'You've got to loosen up and win this game. You can't let Feral beat you.'

As she slid to her knees in the mud, pretending to shake an imaginary football shirt at the crowd, Paris started to laugh. Then he heard footsteps and caught a whiff of aftershave; Randal was thundering in from the left, Joan, like the Paddington–Larkminster Intercity, from the right.

'Come here,' yelled Randal.

'Come here,' bellowed Joan.

The crowd were in uproar. Both Hengist and Emlyn tried to contain their laughter as Dora gave her pursuers the slip again.

Scenting danger, detesting Randal, Paris tugged off his sea-blue shirt to more wolf whistles and belted after Dora, grabbing her and forcing the shirt over her head, but having to loosen his grip as he tried to shove both her arms in. Next moment Dora had scuttled off giggling – slap into Randal.

Alas, in the slippery patch near the goalposts, Randal's Guccis had no grip, and he slid past her flat on his back, covering his lovely new suit in mud. The press went berserk.

'This is the way the gentlemen ride,' shouted Amber, 'gallopy, gallopy, gallopy and *down* in the mud.'

'That ain't no gentleman,' said Cosmo, topping up Mrs Walton's glass.

Dora, running away, turned to laugh, and promptly hit the buffers of Primrose Duddon's vast bosom.

'I've got her, JJ.'

Thundering up, Joan flung her duffel coat round a frantically wriggling Dora.

'How dare you bring Boudicca into disrepute?'

'I had to jolt Paris out of his despair.'

'This way, Dora, to me, Dora,' yelled the photographers, as, clapping and punching the air, Dora allowed herself to be frogmarched up to Anthea.

'Take your daughter home, Lady Belvedon.'

'You little slut,' hissed Anthea, and the next minute had slapped Dora viciously across the face, then again with the back of her hand, catching Dora's pink cheek with Randal's huge sapphire, so blood spurted down Joan's duffel coat and Paris's blue rugby shirt underneath.

'Stop that.' Outraged, Janna shot forward. But Cadbury was quicker. Leaping to the defence of his mistress, he threatened Anthea's tiny ankle with his big white teeth, making her scream her head off.

'Get away, you brute.' Randal, racing up, aimed a vicious kick at Cadbury.

'Don't you hurt my dog,' squealed Dora, kicking Randal in the ankle, spurting blood all over the part of his white suit that wasn't coated in mud, before grabbing Cadbury by the collar.

On cue, Partner, who'd been chatting up his old

friend Elaine, rushed up to Cadbury, jumping up and down, licking his ears in congratulation.

'My leg,' shrieked Anthea, pretending to faint into Alex Bruce's skinny arms, as a tiny drop of blood seeped through her flesh-coloured hold-ups. 'I must have a tetanus jab.'

'And a tourniquet,' murmured Amber.

Randal was howling abuse at Cadbury and Dora. It took Hengist to restore order.

'Neither you nor Dora are allowed back onto the field with blood injuries,' he told Anthea. 'You all right, Dora, darling?' Whipping out a blue spotted hand-kerchief, he mopped Dora's cheek. 'Looks nasty. We better get on with the game. I'm sure First Aid'll sort you out, Anthea. The ambulance is over there. Meanwhile we'd better find Paris another shirt and you take Dora to the sick bay, Joan.' Then, when Joan looked mutinous: 'Now.'

There was no way he was going to abandon Dora to the untender mercies of Randal and Anthea.

'She can't bring that dog,' announced Joan. 'Hand him over to your mother, Dora.'

'I can't.' Tears, near the surface, spilled over, mingling with the blood on Dora's cheeks. 'Randal will put him down. He and Mummy hate Cadbury.'

'I'll take him.' Ian Cartwright took off his tie for a lead but Northcliffe's golden hackles were up, his teeth bared.

'I'll take him,' said Dicky, borrowing Ian's tie.

As the second half began, Paris, in a no. 16 shirt, could hardly bear to see Dora being dragged off, defiantly yelling: 'Come on Bagley,' to deafening applause from both sides. Joan looked absolutely furious.

Amber shook her head. 'How can that woman, who has no heart, teach us about the heart in biology?'

The heat of the day had subsided; the horizon was ringed with rose; through still bare trees a moon to match the yellow stripe in Larks's shirts was rising to aid the floodlighting switched on for the second half.

'What a dreadful waste of electricity,' chuntered Poppet. 'Why couldn't Hengist schedule this match earlier in the day?'

Johnnie and Graffi, who'd played their hearts out, had been subbed, which gave Graffi the chance to chat up Milly, and Johnnie a chance to chat to the media.

'Emlyn's cool,' he was telling the BBC. 'I always got sent off at football because I had scraps. Emlyn's helped me wiv my anger management.'

'He could give Lady Belvedon a few lessons,' said the interviewer.

Primrose and Pearl were discussing their respective revision of the Russian Revolution.

'We've been watching a video of *Doctor Zhivago*,' volunteered Pearl proudly.

'Hengist is taking us to St Petersburg for a long week-end after Easter,' said Primrose.

The roaring and cheering were continuous now. Bagley had come back with a vengeance and two tries from Paris who, feeling he owed it to Dora, was playing like a man possessed. Rupert had abandoned his sulks and Stevie Smith, and was yelling his handsome head off. 'Come on Xav, come on Larks.'

' "You'll Never Walk Alone",' sang Kylie, her sweet voice ringing out to the accompaniment of Cambola's trumpet, and all the Larks parents, children and teachers joined in.

Janna wiped her eyes. It was wonderful seeing Skunk and Pittsy really cheering, and she was so proud of Emlyn.

Probably the only people not concentrating were Cosmo and Mrs Walton.

'I've always wanted you,' murmured Cosmo. 'Will you come back to my cell?'

'I thought you were injured,' teased a once more radiant Ruth.

842

'I've sprained my ankle, not my cock. You must give me lessons. One cannot be too good in bed.'

Five minutes to go. Bagley was playing catch-up. They were six points behind Larks. A try and a conversion would do it. Somehow Larks hung on with heroic tackling and covering work, but gradually their defence was driven back.

Only a minute to go. Janna couldn't bear to look. Please dear God, for Emlyn's and the children's sake.

Paris had the ball and was scorching down the pitch.

'Come on,' yelled Theo, Artie and the Cartwrights. He was through, but with Aston Martin acceleration, Feral stormed in from the right, tackling him five yards from the line, his arms clamping round Paris's hips, bringing him crashing to the ground. The line was a foot away – beyond it, the heavenly city. Wriggling forward, Paris lost control of the ball, which fell forward over the line.

'Let go of me, you fucker,' he howled, trying to struggle forwards in the mud to touch it down. But Feral clung on. A second later, Rocky had pounded up and kicked the ball into the crowd as the whistle went.

Feral and Paris lay on the ground, hearts thumping, both winded, checking they weren't hurt. Then they turned to look at each other, both faces caked in mud, Paris's as brown as Feral's. For a second, panting and exhausted, they scowled.

Then, as if in a dream, their hands stretched out and, as they grinned, their hands met in a grounded high five.

'You was wicked, man,' gasped Paris.

'We've won, we've beaten Bagley.' All restraint gone, screaming her head off, Janna raced onto the pitch, running from exhausted Larks player to player, kissing their dirty faces before falling into an equally ecstatic Emlyn's arms:

'We did it, we did it.'

Tipping her head right back, Janna smiled up into his rugged, ruddy, overjoyed face, feeling his hot sweating body and his heart pounding against hers. They were brought back to earth by the jeering of Johnnie Fowler.

'Cheer up, you fat commie. At least you came second.'

'Take zat back, you smug little vanker,' howled Anatole.

It was only Emlyn's lightning reaction, dropping Janna, swinging round and catching Anatole's arm before his fist smashed into Johnnie's face, that prevented a riot.

'Break it up, you two,' he roared, in addition grabbing Johnnie's shirt collar, 'or I'll bang your thick skulls together. It's only a game.'

'That's not what you told us in the dressing room beforehand,' panted Johnnie, aiming a kick at Anatole. Then seeing Emlyn's face blacken: 'Sir!'

'That's enough, Anatole,' said Hengist, taking him from Emlyn. 'Be more gracious, you were outplayed.'

103

Ashton, Cindy and Randal, having had a good stretch of their legs to take in Badger's Retreat, were now claiming credit for Larks's victory to *The Times*.

'We felt it crucial to give these disadvantaged youngsters a second chance,' Cindy was saying. 'Yes, "Payne" with a "Y".'

'We're keeping a close watch, of course,' purred Ashton. Catching sight of Hengist, he added, 'Bad luck, you must be very disappointed and surprised.'

'Not when you consider Emlyn's been coaching them,' said Hengist lightly. 'After those rather worrying reports in your Sunday paper today' – he smiled at *The Times*'s reporter – 'about S and C's catastrophic involvement in the educational field, they must regard Larks High, particularly after today's triumph, as the jewel in their crown.' Then, nodding at a scowling Ashton and Cindy: 'Do grab a drink before the presentation.'

Captain Xavier went up to shake hands with Randal in his muddy suit and to collect the gold-plated rugby ball to deafening applause from his parents and those from the Shakespeare Estate, who were already legless.

Xav was followed by his players who, in the floodlighting, cast giant shadows in two directions. But Randal, on the podium (provided by himself), cast the biggest, blackest shadow of all.

Feral was Man of the Match.

845

'Well played,' said Pete Wainwright, handing him his card. 'For once your supporters didn't exaggerate. Football isn't that different to rugby. Give me a bell and I'll fix a date for a trial.'

'That's wicked, man,' muttered Feral.

Maybe, maybe Bianca soon wouldn't be so out of reach after all. 'Give me time, baby.'

Inside, Hengist was seething, but he'd learnt to be magnanimous in defeat.

'Fantastic victory, Emlyn, terrific entertainment for the spectators.'

Emlyn grinned. 'I think Dora should have won Man of the Match rather than Feral.'

'That bitch of a mother,' exploded Janna.

'Hush, darling,' Hengist took Janna's arm. 'Come and have a drink. You'll want to be with your boys, Emlyn.' It was an order. 'Join Janna and me later. You must be so proud,' he told her as they set off towards the pavilion.

The first pale stars were coming out, as if the deepening blue sky wanted to boast it had primroses too.

'So pleased about Feral's trial,' said Hengist. 'If he needs any advice about converting to soccer . . . ?'

How generous and sweet you are, thought Janna.

'Paris played really well in the end,' she said. Then, as they were out of earshot: 'Do you think he's still hung up about us?'

'Not at all, he's working incredibly hard. Well played!' Hengist ruffled a passing Xav's black hair. 'Really good to see you back. Your parents must be ecstatic.'

As they moved on through a copse of young wild cherry trees, he murmured, 'Are *you* still hung up about us, darling?'

Janna started. Hengist turned her to face him, gazing down at her, laughing eyes for once serious. 'I truly didn't mean to hurt you.'

'But you love Sally,' finished Janna. 'I know – and it

doesn't hurt any more,' she added, realizing in amazement it was true. 'It's just lovely we can be friends. I do love you.'

'And I, you,' and he dropped a long kiss on her forehead.

Emlyn, still euphoric, accepting congratulations from Artie and Theo, about to round up his team for the plunge bath, reflected that he hadn't thought about Oriana since he arrived. Irked by being dismissed by Hengist, he glanced idly towards the pavilion, then saw Hengist and Janna had not even reached it but were lurking in the wild cherry copse, talking intimately, smiling at each other; now Hengist was stealing a kiss. Emlyn felt his great blaze of euphoria turn to ashes.

Then soft dark hair brushed against his cheek, and a childish little voice said:

'Well done, Emlyn, I couldn't help cheering like mad for my old school.'

It was Vicky, pretty as ever in a turquoise blazer, with a schoolboy's turquoise and olive-green scarf round her neck, looking as young as any of her pupils.

'I'm having a party at my flat here tonight. Why don't you come? Lots of Bagley people will be there. You can always stop over in the spare room, if you don't want to drive.'

'I've got to take the team home,' said Emlyn, noticing Hengist and Janna were still gazing into each other's eyes. 'But thanks, I might well look in later.'

Paris wandered towards Badger's Retreat in total confusion. He cringed at the memory of the missed penalties. He'd played atrociously, only redeemed by those tries in the second half, when Dora's streak had shaken him out of his despondency. As if he were coming round after an operation, not knowing how much it would hurt, he hadn't worked out how he felt about Feral and Bianca. Like Philip Larkin in their poetry set book, he'd probably been 'too selfish, withdrawn And easily bored' to love Bianca.

Now he was haunted by the thought of Anthea cutting up Dora's round, sweet face. Randal had ruined his suit; Lady Belvedon had ruined her image as a 'lady' – the vicious bitch. Neither would forgive Dora.

After half an hour, when Emlyn hadn't joined the uproarious party spilling out of the pavilion, happily remembering how lovely his arms had felt round her earlier, Janna went in search of him. She found him among the crowd waving off the still stunned Larks fifteen.

'Are you coming back to the Dog and Duck to celebrate?' Janna tucked her arm through his. 'Lily and Christian and Cambola are just leaving.'

'I'll give it a miss tonight,' said Emlyn brusquely. 'Some of the Bagley teachers are having a party; I said I'd join them.' Not meeting Janna's eyes, he didn't see the hurt and disappointment. 'Can you get a lift with the Brig?'

'Of course,' said Janna in a small voice. 'Thank you for all you did for Larks today.'

But Emlyn had stalked off towards the car park.

As Graffi's father and Stormin' Norman were decanted onto the last bus and went home singing "Ark, 'Ark! the Lark', Hengist reflected that being a host without Sally was very hard work.

How sweet Janna had looked; he'd have loved to whisk her upstairs to bed. All the same, he felt unusually tired – must be the end of term.

Back in his study in the Mansion, he poured himself a large whisky, put on a CD of Fischer-Dieskau singing *Winterreise* and, picking up his note-laden copy of Matthew Arnold's poems, settled down on the sofa with a weary Elaine's head on his lap. Headmasters' dogs get tired too, trailing after them, her gusty sigh seemed to say.

These holidays, vowed Hengist, he was going to write his book rather than politicking. Jupiter was too bloody demanding.

There was a knock on the door. Elaine, a good judge of character, didn't wag. It was Alex.

'A word, headmaster.'

The bloody man would only accept Perrier and sat bolt upright, as though it would be an act of decadence to collapse into the bear hug of one of Hengist's armchairs.

'That was a catastrophe.'

'Losing to Larks, I agree.'

'No, Dora Belvedon's disgusting display. How should we address the problem?'

'Having that bitch of a mother, not to mention the odious Stancombe as a possible stepfather, should be punishment enough.'

Alex looked pained and cracked his knuckles, his Adam's apple wobbling as he swallowed. 'Anthea and Randal are supportive friends.'

'Not to poor Dora, they aren't.'

'She must be excluded for the rest of the term if not permanently.'

'Don't be fatuous, there are only a few days left. It was just high spirits.' Hengist drained his drink. 'At least she shook Paris out of his doldrums and brightened a dire afternoon.'

'Tomorrow's press will be disastrous.'

Hengist's anger boiled over.

'If you hadn't engineered the departure of the best bloody rugger coach Bagley has ever had, we'd have walked it today.'

'Too much emphasis is placed on competitive sports.'

'Bollocks,' roared Hengist. 'It's crucial for strengthening character, fostering qualities of leadership and channelling aggression. Look how Xavier Campbell-Black blossomed. He looks great and played a terrific match. But you had to kick him out without any kind of investigation. We failed him – and we've made an enemy of Rupert. How d'you think it feels having Campbell-Blacks yelling for Larks? Well, you're not getting rid of Dora. Now get out and wreck someone else's evening.'

Janna gave herself a talking-to as she made herself a cup of tea the following morning.

'You prayed and prayed that Larks wouldn't be humiliated by Bagley, so for heaven's sake be grateful for very large mercies, and don't go slipping in any prayers about Emlyn. I'm lucky to have you,' she told Partner, who wagged his tail in agreement. Emlyn was amiable enough, but had big feet for treading on paws.

Janna left early to buy a big celebratory cake from the baker's and to drape banners across the gate and reception. She felt the fifteen should tour Larkminster in an open-top bus like the World Cup players.

It was an exquisite morning, with only her and the sun in the quiet street, and celandines opening like more little suns on the banks.

She slowed down as the postman approached.

'Saw you on TV last night, Janna. Great result. That Feral played a blinder. *Scorpion*'s got a cartoon of a Red Dragon carrying lots of larks on his back.'

Janna was enchanted. She must get it framed for Emlyn. Why shouldn't he whoop it up with his Bagley mates. His car wasn't outside his digs. He probably never came home.

As she drove down Wilmington High Street, however, she was flagged down by a scarlet windmill – it was Vicky in a red rugger shirt nearly reaching to her knees, about to get into her pale blue Golf. She wore no make-up; her hair was drawn back and falling in a Jane Austen cascade, pretty as always.

'Jannie, how are you? So sorry to miss you yesterday.'

'What are you doing here?' Janna made no attempt to look friendly.

'Emlyn celebrated victory so full-bloodedly last night,' simpered Vicky, 'I had to bring him home. I'm coaching Jack and Lando at eight o'clock – not that they'll be in any fit state, after drowning their sorrows – so I borrowed one of Emlyn's rugby shirts. Rather fetching.'

I'm not hearing this, thought Janna.

'Emlyn is so gorgeous.' Vicky stretched voluptuously. 'Oriana needs her head – or rather the lower parts of her anatomy' – Vicky giggled coarsely – 'examined. You must come to kitchen sups in my little flat in the hols. Shall I ask Ashton to make up a four, or don't you two still get on? Anyway, must fly.'

'Fuck, fuck, fuck,' said Emlyn looking down from his first-floor window. That had not been the way to get over Oriana.

Dora's streak ensured that Larks's victory over Bagley was headlined in most of the papers.

'Welsh dragon turns heat on old school', said *The Times*.

'Full back', was the *Scorpion*'s caption on a charming, naked rear view of Dora, which she agreed was one way of reminding all her press contacts what she looked like.

104

Larks High's pupils were on such a high on the morning after the match, they failed to notice that both Janna and Emlyn were very subdued. Over at Bagley, an equally ecstatic Cosmo was spending a free period stretched out on the fur-covered triple bed in his study. As token coursework, he was making notes on Andrew Marvell's 'To His Coy Mistress', and thinking about Ruth Walton, who wasn't at all coy and might very soon become his mistress. What a coup. Cosmo was so elated, he had no need of his elevenses spliff.

As it was nearly Easter, he was also playing a CD of his father's recording of the Good Friday music from *Parsifal*. Hearing distraught sobbing and finding Dora and a worried Cadbury outside, he pulled them into the room and slammed the door.

'Whatever's the matter?'

'The music,' wailed Dora. 'It was Daddy's favourite. They played it at his funeral. I miss him so much.'

Cosmo let her cry, tempted to comfort her in the only way he knew. She'd looked extremely fetching streaking round the pitch yesterday.

'Daddy would have saved Cadbury. He liked dogs almost more than people. Hengist's Elaine is the great-niece of Daddy's greyhound Maud. Mummy's so furious about me streaking and Cadbury threatening her, she's insisting he's got to be put down, or

852

castrated, or go to the nearest rescue kennels. I can't let him go. He's my only friend except for Mrs Cartwright,' she added, as Cadbury put a large paw on her knee in agreement.

'Bianca was a best friend, but after she took up with Paris, she got too embarrassed to talk to me. And having sworn she couldn't help herself because he was the great love of her life, she's now bats about Feral again and I so don't want to hear how dreadful she feels about breaking Paris's heart.'

'No, I can see that.' Cosmo handed her a hand-kerchief and a glass of orange juice.

'Thanks,' sniffed Dora. 'I daren't keep Cadbury at Boudicca, because if Joan finds him she'll shunt him straight back to Mummy and the gas chamber. Mummy's terrified I'll be expelled and she and Randal won't be able to have revolting sex all the time. I think Randal's a paedofeel. He groped my non-existent boobs last time I fell off my skateboard.'

'Hum,' said Cosmo.

'I've got a double period of English. Can Cadbury stay here for a couple of hours?' pleaded Dora.

'Sure.' Cosmo looked at his watch. 'I've got maths, but he'll be OK on his own.'

'Can I use this for water?' said Dora, emptying some alabaster eggs out of a Lalique bowl.

'Yeah,' said Cosmo, 'it's insured.'

Left to his own devices, Cadbury whined for a bit, scratched at Cosmo's door, jumped onto the bed, peered out of the window, growled at Theo's cat Hindsight, then started to sniff round the room. Finding an open packet of biscuits, he devoured them, then smelt something much more exciting under the mattress. Pink nostrils flaring, snorting wildly, tail frantically waving, Cadbury began burrowing.

Double English with Miss Wormley droning on about

The Tempest seemed to go on for hours. Wheedling a Pyrex bowl of shepherd's pie out of Coxie, Dora rushed over to Cosmo's study to find Cadbury sitting on Cosmo's bed, swaying from side to side, yellow eyes glazed, an inane grin on his panting cocoa-brown face.

'Whatever's the matter with you?' wailed Dora.

Concern turned to panic when Cadbury refused the shepherd's pie. Labradors have to be dying not to eat. Hearing a step in the corridor, Dora leapt to close the door and leant against it. Cosmo, however, shoved his way in.

'Cadbury,' gasped Dora. 'He's been poisoned.'

'Don't be silly, there's nothing poisonous in here; he's probably stuffed his face with too many biscuits.' Cosmo picked up the remains of the packet.

'He's never been ill before – look at him,' sobbed Dora as Cadbury, pink tongue lolling, swaying like a windscreen wiper, beamed up at Cosmo.

'Looks more like the village idiot than ever.'

'He does not. The vet's too far away' – Dora's voice was rising hysterically – 'You must help me get him to the sick bay.'

'I must not,' snapped Cosmo, who was expecting a call from Ruth Walton. 'I'll get thrown out for harbouring an illegal immigrant.'

Dora didn't care. Rushing outside, she found one of the builder's trolleys which had been nicked last night to wheel home a drunken Anatole.

'Help me,' she begged Cosmo.

'I'm bloody well carrying the front end then. Christ, he's heavy. I'll rupture myself,' grumbled Cosmo as they heaved Cadbury onto the trolley. 'You're on your own now.'

Stumbling, swearing, diving into alleyways and behind trees to avoid Poppet Bruce, who as eco-chief was furiously fingerprinting dropped empties, Dora trundled him round the back of the school.

'Please don't die,' she pleaded. 'Don't give up on

me. Please God, save Cadbury, don't make Matron shunt him back to Mummy.'

Luck, however, was on Dora's side. Only two pupils were in the waiting room: a boy with athlete's foot and a girl from Boudicca wanting the morning-after pill.

'It's an emergency,' panted Dora. 'Can I go in first?'

Even better, as she dragged Cadbury through the door, a deep, expensive voice exclaimed, 'Why, Dora, darling, how lovely to see you.'

'Dr Benson. It's even nicer to see you.'

James Benson was the raffishly handsome, ultra-charming private GP who for the last thirty years had looked after her family, the Campbell-Blacks and the France-Lynches.

'Whatever are you doing here?'

'A locum. Rather like working in a sweet shop with so many gorgeous girls around, and talking of gorgeous, you've grown really pretty, Dora.' James Benson smoothed his black and silver hair. 'And so like your father, such a sweet man.'

'Thanks so much.' Dora had no time for pleasantries. 'It's Cadbury I'm worried about, I think he's been poisoned or having some kind of fit. I haven't got time to get him to the vet. Please help.'

Cadbury, dopier than ever, collapsed on the rug, pupils vast, beaming inanely and swaying rather more slowly from left to right.

'He's going to die.' Dora burst into noisy sobs. 'I bet it's Mr Fussy or Poppet who's poisoned him.'

James Benson shot his very white cuffs and looked at Cadbury's eyes, his tongue, listened to his heart, then proceeded to laugh a great deal.

'It's not funny,' exploded Dora.

'I think he'll live.' Dr Benson wiped his eyes. 'If I were you, Dora, darling, I'd take him home, turn down the lights and put on a Bob Marley record.'

'I don't know what you mean,' said Dora huffily.

'I don't know where your dog's been, but he's completely stoned.'

Even Cosmo found this amusing. In fact he was in such a good mood after hearing from Mrs Walton, he forgave Cadbury for tunnelling between two mattresses and locating and swallowing a whole eighth of skunk wrapped in cellophane, and agreed that Cadbury could sleep off his excesses on the fur-covered bed.

'He could have a brilliant career as a sniffer dog,' said Dora in excitement. 'According to the *Daily Mail*, dogs get paid five hundred pounds a morning searching for drugs in state schools.'

'He can start by sniffing out all the drugs at Bagley,' said Cosmo evilly, 'and then we can confiscate them.'

Returning for the summer term, Bagley discovered that Poppet Bruce as eco-chief was becoming more and more of a bully, waddling very pregnant round the corridors, charging vast fines for lights left on or doors not closed to preserve heat.

On a late-night patrol on the first Friday of term, Poppet discerned noises coming from the art department. Hammering on the door, she found it locked and, hearing a crash, fumbled for her master key. 'Let me in, let me in.'

Switching on the light, she was confronted by the excesses of the Upper Fifth's coursework, which included a six-foot straw donkey, a robot Christ on a steel cross, and Lando's sin bin: a flame-red tent painted with demons. Hearing a cough, her gaze was drawn to a naked member of the Upper Fifth, who was clutching a palette in an abortive attempt to hide a very large penis.

'Cosmo Rannaldini,' squawked Poppet, 'what are you doing?'

'You're not going to believe this,' mumbled Cosmo, 'but I come here to be near you.'

'How d'you mean?' asked Poppet, thinking how beautifully the lad was constructed.

'Your p-p-p-picture,' stammered Cosmo, pointing a trembling finger at Boffin's half-finished but already absurdly flattering portrait of Poppet breastfeeding little thirteen-month-old Gandhi.

'What a caring interpretation,' cried a delighted Poppet.

'Indeed. This is seriously embarrassing,' went on Cosmo, 'but I'm so obsessed with you, Mrs Bruce. I come here sometimes to, er, jerk off in front of your portrait. I have such strong sexual urges, which I don't want to impose on my fellow students. It helps me to destress. Please don't be angry with me.' Cosmo hung his dark, curly head, a tear glittering like a diamond on his cheekbone.

Poppet was deeply moved and very understanding. She appreciated the pain of young love. Cosmo mustn't feel guilty about masturbation. He would get over her and find some lovely young woman of his own.

'Never,' swore Cosmo, 'I think of you constantly. At least let me have hope.'

'Alex and I have a very strong partnership.' Poppet perched on a fibreglass wildebeest. 'Not that I haven't had my admirers.'

'I bet you have.'

Cosmo's penis was pushing most excitingly through the hole in the palette. Alex was rather meanly endowed, although Poppet knew size had nothing to do with pleasure. A snort from the direction of the sin bin made them both jump.

'What was that?'

'Probably a rat. Lando keeps leaving half-eaten Cornish pasties around.'

Poppet noticed Cosmo was shivering. 'You mustn't catch cold.'

'Could you bear to leave me to get dressed?' begged

Cosmo adoringly. 'And have a moment of quiet reflection on your words of wisdom?'

'Of course, I'll lock up in a quarter of an hour,' said Poppet. 'Good night, Cosmo.'

'Good night, sweet princess,' said Cosmo soulfully, then, ten seconds later, 'All clear,' and a naked Ruth Walton, who'd been stuffing Cosmo's shirt into her mouth to stop her laughter, emerged from the sin bin into his arms.

'Thank you for saving me.'

'We've got ten minutes.'

'No, we haven't, it's not safe – well, perhaps it is,' gasped Ruth as Cosmo pushed her down on Primrose Duddon's ethnic quilt and plunged his cock into her. 'Oh God, what heaven!'

They escaped down the corridor just in time.

'You are the biggest thing in my life,' confessed Cosmo, kissing her in the shadows of the car park.

'And your thing is the biggest I've ever had in my life,' teased Mrs Walton to hide how enamoured she was.

Cosmo was chuffed to bits. He and Ruth couldn't get enough of each other and the pillow talk was as exciting as the sex. He was learning so much about the governing body and the sexual and social habits of Randal Stancombe. The only blot was that Poppet Bruce, unable to keep a secret, revealed Cosmo's passion to Alex, who was casting even blacker looks in Cosmo's direction.

A fortnight later, Poppet had her baby, another girl, Cranberry Germaine, a little Taurus, whom Poppet breastfed in public at every opportunity, particularly in front of Cosmo: 'To domesticate his passion and help him see my breasts in a different light.' She also bombarded him with leaflets from SHAG: the Sexual Health Action Group.

105

Over at Larks, Feral's football trial, a midweek friendly at Larkminster Rovers, approached. Good as his word, Emlyn spent hours helping Feral transfer back to football, increasingly conscious that he was dealing with genius.

When the trial day arrived, Feral in turn felt more positive than ever before. Emlyn had given him such confidence. If he could get a place with the Rovers, who looked like they'd be going up to the first division next season, he'd soon be on serious money, then he'd be in a position to look after his mother, his brothers and sisters and even ask Bianca out. Suddenly he had hope.

It was a perfect day for football, warm but slightly overcast. The Brigadier, Lily, Janna, Emlyn and, to Rupert's intense irritation, Taggie were all going to the ground to cheer him on. As it was midweek, Bianca couldn't get out of school. Feral was relieved. He needed nothing to distract him.

Feral and Xav, who'd come along to give moral support, made their way to the football ground through the Wednesday market. Xav had already handed Feral a good-luck card of a sleek black velvet cat. Inside it said, 'Stay cool, thinking of you, all love, Bianca'.

Feral was nervous but terribly excited. He was wearing the same socks which brought him luck against Bagley and, doing scout steps, running twenty paces, then walking twenty, dreamt of becoming the next Thierry Henry. No footballer's wife would be lovelier than Bianca; she would light up any stand.

Oh please, God of footballers, this is my one chance to break in.

They were early and as they passed the cheese stall, then breathed in the smell of beefburgers and rotating golden brown chickens, Xav asked Feral if he were hungry. Feral shook his head. He couldn't have kept down a potato crisp as he skipped to left and right practising moves. They stopped to admire some leather jackets. Xav tried on a black one.

'How does it look?'

'Cool,' said Feral absent-mindedly.

'My father, stupid twat, thinks leather coats are common, so I'm going to buy one. My mother always sides with my father. "Why can't you wear that nice denim jacket?" Parents get on my tits.'

Xav, who was very antsy about the GCSEs ahead, tried on a brown jacket, then decided the black one was nicer.

'Blacks look good in black,' agreed Feral.

'I'll have it.' Xav produced a Coutts cheque book, a sheaf of identification and wrote a cheque for £160.

'Parents are never off your back,' he went on irritably as he pocketed the receipt. 'My father never gave a stuff about my working hard until he started this stupid GCSE. My mother's over the moon because Larkminster Rovers are so excited by her coursework ideas. If you land this job, you'll probably live on Steak Taggie for the rest of your life.'

'Shut up, you spoilt bastard,' snapped Feral. 'You don't deserve no respect, man. Every kid in the school wants to be you, living in a palace wiv horses, buying coats wiv what would keep most families for a monf.

You've a beautiful sister, your mother's a lovely woman – your dad's a shit, admittedly, but he's always been there for you. You're fucking smuvvered wiv love, and you can't stop dissing them. For Chrissake, stop whingeing.'

A gust of wind blowing blossom out of the trees scattered pink petals over them, as they scowled at each other, fists clenched. Then Feral said:

'Sorry, man. I'm uptight about the trial, didn't sleep last night.'

They did a high five. Feral glanced at Xav's Rolex; there was still time to buy Janna some flowers.

'She's always been there for me.'

Just as he was paying for a bunch of red carnations, he felt a faint scratch on his back. Swinging round, he saw a corpse – almost a skeleton – with a white scabby face, thinning hair, unseeing bloodshot eyes: a nightmare life in death against the technicoloured riot of the flower stall.

She had bruises and cuts all over her arms, was wrapped in stinking rags and trembled uncontrollably in what Feral instantly recognized as an advanced state of heroin withdrawal.

'Have you got a pound for a cup of tea?' she mumbled.

'Mum,' whispered Feral in horror.

Xav took Feral firmly by the arm.

'You've got a trial, it's your big chance. You've got to walk away from her.'

'Fifty pence for a cup of tea,' whined Feral's swaying mother.

Xav gave her a fiver and frogmarched Feral towards the football ground. They could see the flags and the stands ahead, but as they reached the High Street, Feral turned and bolted back, disappearing into the crowd. Janna's red carnations fell from his hand and were trampled underfoot.

* * *

Xav searched for Feral everywhere, but fruitlessly. By the time he turned up at the match, play had been going on for half an hour and everyone had washed their hands of him.

Pete Wainwright, who'd set the whole thing up, was apoplectic with rage. 'Made me look a complete prat. It's obvious the lad's got no commitment.'

Lily, Janna and Taggie in the stands were devastated; the Brigadier and Emlyn hopping mad with fury. How could Feral have bottled out of the thing he wanted most in the world?

'It isn't as though any of the trial players are a quarter as good as him. He'd have walked it,' exploded the Brigadier.

Rupert who, not trusting Taggie with flash football managers, had at the last moment rolled up as well, said the whole thing was 'absolutely typical'.

Seeing Xav, they all charged down the stands.

'What the hell's happened?'

As Xav finished explaining, Rupert launched into blistering invective. 'It's not worth investing a bloody penny in him.'

'It was his mother, for Christ's sake,' shouted back Xav. 'You wouldn't leave someone like that.'

'I'll come and help you look for him,' said Janna.

'So will I,' said Emlyn.

Having combed the market and the main streets, they tried the Shakespeare Estate. Janna ran up the path past the burnt-out car and the stinking dustbins. A pretty black girl, reeking of sex and booze, her great body shown off by tight orange vest and rucked-up yellow mini, answered the door.

'We're looking for Feral,' begged Janna, then flinched as the girl was joined by a leering Uncle Harley, clearly off his face and zipping up his trousers.

'Nice to see you, Miss Curtis.'

'Have you seen Feral?'

'He's not here. He in trouble again?'

'Feral obviously daren't go home,' Janna told Emlyn as she jumped back into his car.

A distraught Xav didn't get back till late evening. There had been no sign of Feral or his mother, so Emlyn had called the police.

'I'm sorry,' Xav told Rupert defiantly, 'but I admire Feral more than anyone I've ever met.'

Next day the police found Feral hiding out under the railway bridge. His mother beside him, drifting in and out of consciousness, was rushed to hospital. The police had been searching for her anyway on three drug-related offences. The following day, she just avoided a prison sentence by promising to go into rehab and was admitted to a local drying-out clinic.

'I'm jolly well going to pay for six weeks of it,' said Taggie.

'Don't be bloody stupid,' snapped Rupert, particularly when Taggie threatened to sell her diamonds.

Feral, suicidally aware he'd let everyone down, ashamed that he'd been too frightened of her getting arrested to take his mother to hospital, was amazed that the Brigadier allowed him back. Lily was there when, head drooping, a picture of dejection, he walked through the door.

'Come and sit down.' Lily patted the sofa.

Collapsing beside her, Feral broke into the most piteous sobs.

'So sorry, Lily, so sorry, man.'

It broke the Brigadier's heart.

'Poor fellow, poor fellow,' he said, patting Feral's heaving shoulders. 'So pleased you're home. Missed you around the place very much. Tried my hand at cooking corn beef hash for tonight, but have a dry Martini first.'

106

All round Larks, as the summer term began, Wally had nailed up signs saying: 'Get your finger out and your coursework in. All your hard work will be worthless unless you write tidily.'

The teachers stood over the children, reading, redrafting, adding, criticizing handwriting, improving spelling and grammar and finally marking each piece of coursework.

Staff teaching the same subject, like Skunk and Mates, or Janna and Sophy, would then read coursework by each other's pupils, to see if they felt the grades given were fair.

'I do feel this mark's a little too generous for Feral,' sighed Janna.

'A little,' agreed Sophy, 'but marking him up seemed the only way of helping him get a grade.'

There was a drama over the food technology coursework, which included lunch for the hospitality boxes at Larkminster Rovers. The chicken and vegetable jalousie, which consisted of chicken legs wrapped in ham with pepper and tomato sauce, smelt so delicious that Rocky wandered in and scoffed four of the entries. As the external examiner was due in an hour, Taggie felt justified in remaking them herself, just in time.

Other members of staff felt it was like Christmas all over again, as they packed up coursework and despatched it to the examining board. They needed a pantechnicon to accommodate the contribution from design and technology, which included Danijela the Bosnian girl's beautiful blue and green embroidered wedding dress and Rocky's six-foot dog kennel. On the side he had written in pokerwork: 'Dog house I will live in if you do not pass me'.

Other packages included geography projects on traffic-calming and the shaping of industrial development and RE dissertations on death and dying, which seemed a welcome option to the exams ahead, which began on 14 May with Urdu listening.

In Xav's view, Aysha had been listening to a great deal too much Urdu claptrap from her bullying father.

He and Aysha had revised together in the Larks garden, she helping him with science, he her with Spanish and French, occasionally getting electric shocks when their hands touched.

'You must get an A star in Urdu to beat my vile ex-housemaster's wife,' said Xav. 'She and her awful daughter Charisma are taking the subject to show off.'

'How's your dad getting on with English lit.?' asked Aysha. Her little diamond nose stud glinted in the sun-light. Her face and hands were the soft brown of Penscombe Peterkin's glossy coat. As she raised big, brown, almond-shaped eyes to him, Xav's heart shook his body like an overloaded washing machine.

'My dad is very short-fused and not concentrating enough on the yard,' he replied gloomily. 'Hasn't had as many winners as last year. I tried to give him a few tips I'd learnt in business studies, but he told me to get stuffed. Got a good horse called Fast running on the twenty-eighth.'

' "Do not adultery commit; Advantage rarely came of it",' intoned Rupert.

What a ridiculous syllabus! Of all the sins teenagers

committed, adultery must be bottom of the list. Half the poems on the other hand seem to be cooing over new babies, the last thing one wanted to encourage in the young. A poem by some woman called Pilkington (who'd only lived thirty-eight years, so God had struck her down) claimed the only way to get on in politics was to tell lies, which didn't dispose Rupert to join Jupiter and Hengist in their proposed coup.

The whole anthology was deeply silly.

Fed up with poetry, Rupert slotted *Pride and Prejudice* into his Walkman. Not a bad book, quite funny, and he completely identified with Darcy: sound fellow, looked after his friends and his tenants, ran his estate well, couldn't be bothered with riff-raff like Mrs Bennet.

Rupert was still spitting because he'd received a letter from Aysha's father, Raschid Khan, who owned a curry house in Larkminster, asking him to stop Xav pestering Aysha. Damned cheek. Both children were black. Xav was clearly desperately in love. Rupert's daughter, Tabitha, had been besotted by a tractor driver called Ashley and got over him, thank God, but he hated to see Xav so unhappy about Aysha's arranged marriage.

As soon as the summer term began, the press, nudged by Dora, had started ringing Bagley for reports on Larks's Golden Boy, only to be told by Hengist that he was confident that not only Paris, but all the school's candidates, would excel in their forthcoming exams. They were all working extremely hard.

This was not strictly true. Boffin and Primrose Duddon had been working steadily all their school careers. Paris had worked hard since he'd been at Bagley. The rest of the year had been cramming know-ledge into their heads, aided by caffeine and speed, but only for three weeks. Even the promise of an oil well and his own six-bedroom dacha hadn't motivated Anatole. Even the promise of a Ferrari if he achieved straight As had not halted Cosmo's nightly visits to Mrs Walton, whom he had installed in a cottage on the far side of Bagley village.

Disapproving of all work and no play, Poppet urged her RE students to keep up their voluntary work and 'enrichment activities', which enraged Lubemir, Anatole and Cosmo. How could they enrich themselves by flogging exam papers, when Alex Bruce had once more changed the combination on the school safe? Why should generations of Bagley pupils profit from their enterprise and not they?

Primrose Duddon was overwhelmed how popular she'd suddenly become, enjoying heady weekends staying with the Lloyd-Foxes, helping Amber and Junior with English revision, and at Robinsgrove where, with his dark, sleek head resting on her splendid breasts, she had initiated Lando France-Lynch into the mysteries of the double helix and the circulation of the blood.

Paris's first exam was Latin on the afternoon of 18 May. The night before, Hengist, just off a plane after a big speech in Washington, summoned Paris to his study in the Mansion to check things were all right.

Still in crumpled off-white trousers and a purple shirt, Hengist had hung his jacket and tie over Darwin, the ancient stuffed gorilla, which Alex and Joan had recently sacked from the biology lab on the grounds that he would be too scruffy for Randal's Science Emporium. In an excess of Bruce-baiting, Hengist had rescued Darwin from the skip, placing him beside the stuffed bear and topping him with his own mortar board. Elaine, enchanted to have her master home, was following Hengist round, nudging him in friendship, sweeping off with her long tail the pile of faxes, emails and letters Hengist couldn't be bothered to look at.

Switching off his telephone, Hengist hung a 'Do Not

Disturb' notice on the door, tore the gold paper off a bottle of Moët and prepared to give Paris his full attention.

It was a perfect evening. Cricket games were in their last overs. Cow parsley foamed along the rough meadow between pitches and golf course; buttercups streaked the fields beyond. An overpoweringly sweet scent of lilac drifted in through the big open windows.

'Don't be silly,' Hengist murmured fondly as Elaine jumped then trembled as the champagne cork flew out. 'You've heard enough of those in your time.'

Perched on the dark red Paisley window seat, Paris could just see the lake. Here Artie Deverell lounged in a panama hat and a deckchair, with several bottles of Sancerre cooling in the water among the forget-me-nots, reading his favourite poems in his gentle bell-like voice to his favourite GCSE candidates.

'I bet he's chosen Lamartine's "Lake" or Baudelaire's "Voyage to Cythera".' Hengist handed Paris an excitingly large glass. 'Poetry that no longer appears on any exam syllabus. Great literature, as William Rees-Mogg was saying recently in *The Times*, teaches us to understand human nature. People still sulk like Achilles, get mad with jealousy like Othello, loathe their stepfather like Hamlet, have happy marriages like Hector and Andromache.' For a second Hengist's finger caressed Sally's sweet face in the photograph on his desk. 'Literature, Rees-Mogg rightly claims, is the road to the general understanding of the heart and the head. History's the same. If you study William's conquest of England in ten sixty-six, you can appreciate how the Iraqis feel today.'

'Mr Bruce doesn't feel like that.' Paris rose to his feet, gazing at Hengist's books with a longing most boys would reserve for Sienna Miller. 'He's hell-bent on chucking out the classical library and Theo's archives.'

'Not while I'm running this joint. This bloody Government is already destroying public libraries.

Wants them to replenish their entire stock in five years, in the name of multiculturism and vibrancy. Jesus! I can accommodate Darwin' – he patted the gorilla on the shoulder – 'not sure there's room in here for the archives.'

'You will protect Theo. He's such a cool teacher,' Paris stammered and blushed. 'He read us Plato's description of the death of Socrates the other evening, tears pouring down his cheeks the whole time. It was awesome, but I think he's very near the edge.'

'I'll make a note of it,' said Hengist gravely, noting how exhausted Paris looked. His bloodshot eyes glowed like rubies in the intense white face.

'I know how hard you've been working, but this time in a month, you won't remember a single equation or date you've forced into your tired brain.'

'I have to say, sir' – Paris took a gulp of champagne, and moved to sit down on what was left of the sofa by a stretched-out Elaine – 'I was gutted when Mr Davies left, but your classes are wicked, just as interesting as Mr Graham's. I can relate now to Lenin, Khrushchev, the Tsar, even to Hitler and Stalin. You don't make us take sides. Emlyn was always pushing for the underdog, the peasants, the Jews or the communists, but you show us tyrants don't start off wrong, they're often convinced they were doing right. Like in Euripides. I suddenly find I'm right behind Medea. You're like Euripides, sir.'

'Why, thank you, Paris. I've been called a lot of things. Which English set book did you like best?'

'*Macbeth*. Wish I'd been able to take it in the exam, rather than just as coursework.'

'Rupert Campbell-Black has very strong views on Macbeth.' Hengist shook his head. 'I so hope he's going to pass. I toned down some of his ideas in which he described Malcolm as a "heartless shit" for being so bracing with Macduff just after his wife and children had been butchered. The Prince of Wales would have handled it far more sympathetically, according to Rupert.'

'That's right,' said Paris.

Down below, he could see Dora scouring the ground with her eyes one moment, looking round for him the next, with Cadbury bounding after her. He'd had a disturbing dream last night: Dora had rescued him from a particularly horrible children's home, and held him safe and kissed him. It had been lovely, but Dora was only a child, sexually light years behind Bianca. He must stamp on any feelings.

'Dora's been great,' he added to Hengist. 'She's helped me to revise, testing me on everything. Pity she's not taking her GCSEs. She knows the textbooks backwards.'

'I'm devoted to Dora,' said Hengist. 'I'll never forget inviting her in for a glass of champagne on her birthday her first term and asking her with what adjective would she best like her friends to describe her. She said, "There." I said, "That's not an adjective." And Dora said, "I'd like my friends to say I was there for them."'

'And she is,' said Paris.

'How are you getting on with Ian and Patience?' he asked.

'OK. Patience took me to *Macbeth*. Brilliant production, except the weird sisters were sleek, young and glamorous, which is garbage: Shakespeare categorically states they had beards and were ugly. And they can't have been in Macbeth's imagination, because Banquo saw them too.'

'Rupert explained it as Macbeth and Banquo being off their faces with drugs,' volunteered Hengist, 'like the entire US Army in Iraq.'

'Magic mushrooms, perhaps,' suggested Paris.

'"The instruments of darkness tell us truths",' murmured Hengist, then, regretfully: 'I must go and change. We're dining with the Lord Lieutenant – such a sweet, boring man, I'll never stay awake. Look, you'll walk these exams. Try and write legibly and read through if you've got time. Examiners are awfully keen on inessentials like punctuation and spelling. Easy to ignore if you're writing at the gallop.'

Paris finished his glass of champagne. If he hadn't been a bit drunk, he would never have tried on Hengist's mortar board. With it tipped over his long nose, and shielding his red eyes, his blond hair floating, he looked so ravishing, Hengist caught his breath.

'Certainly suits you better than Darwin. You must go to my old college, and get the first Matthew Arnold and I, upsetting our fathers so dreadfully, didn't get.'

As Hengist showered, watching the black hairs flowing down in deltas over his strong muscular chest and thighs, he was gripped with excitement. What a transformation in two years! Paris was able to relax, joke, put forward opinions, even exchange compliments. Hengist imagined his first book of poems, dedicated to 'Hengist Brett-Taylor, without whom . . .'

Ian, Patience and Theo, too, must be doing a good job. All the same, the boy would have fared even better with him and Sally. If he took the job at Fleetley, could he take Paris with him? If he went into politics, a beautiful adopted son would be great for his image. Christ, he mustn't think like that. He missed Oriana so much. Even in Washington he hadn't rung her. Not a word had been exchanged. Was Sally speaking to her secretly?

Wrapped in a big red towel, wandering to the window, Hengist saw Paris sprinting down to the lake to join Artie and his friends.

In the Bruces' back garden he could see Boffin, his nose in his revision folder, and Alex smugly rereading a proof of his *Guide to Red Tape*. He must get on with Tom and Matt. Please God, prayed Hengist, make Paris do better than Boffin.

107

'Before the GCSEs, you can expect panic attacks, moodiness, tears and temper tantrums,' Janna sighed to Taggie, 'and that's just the parents.'

The staff weren't behaving much better. Despite the outwardly convivial atmosphere, Pittsy was desperate his maths candidates should do much better than Skunk's scientists. Basket wanted better grades than Sophy and Cambola. Even sweet, calm Mags and jaunty Lily got snappy with Emlyn and the Brigadier over hijacked marker pens. There was so much at stake.

Discounting art and Urdu, which Graffi and Aysha had already taken, exams started in earnest with business studies on the morning of 21 May. The evening before, Janna took refuge among the cow parsley on Smokers', breathing in a heady mingling of wild garlic and balsam, watching the last scarlet streaks of the sunset jazzing up the black silhouette of the cathedral and listening to the exquisite singing of the nightingales in the laurels. Partner, who'd been rabbiting, was drinking out of the pond, avoiding the tadpoles the children had been too busy revising to collect in jam jars.

Like Orpheus visiting the underworld, Janna was still shaking from dropping off good-luck cards to houses in the Shakespeare Estate. If her children scraped just a few GCSEs, they could escape from that hell-hole.

Johnnie, Rocky, Monster, Danny the Irish, whose father had just been arrested for punching a particularly irritating female social worker, were all light-fingered and, with no job prospects, would revert to crime and the streets.

Aysha would be beaten within an inch of her life if she didn't get the Magic Five. Kylie was expecting a second child any minute and her voice would need to take off like Charlotte Church's to support them both. Feral had the back-up of the Brigadier and Lily, but although he'd tried hard, she doubted if he'd get any grades except PE. At least Rocky was ensured a good D and T grade with his massive dog kennel.

Graffi worried her the most. Ever since his da Dafydd had been sacked for cheeking Stancombe at the rugby match, he'd been blacked by other firms and drunkenly out of work. Dafydd's mood had not been improved by his dotty mother, known as Cardiff Nan, moving in with them. Graffi, stacking shelves all night in Tesco to make ends meet, was constantly hijacked during the day to mind both his little handicapped sister Caitlin and Cardiff Nan in their enclosed worlds.

Graffi was clever. He'd already got a starred A for art and could easily notch up the Magic Five if he could get some sleep and somewhere quiet to revise. Earlier, she had found him fallen asleep in reception, brush in his hand dripping black gloss onto the floor, in the middle of painting a lucky black cat ringed with gold horseshoes.

The sun and the nightingales had disappeared into the darkness. Going indoors, Janna checked the gym, where in the half-light, like a chessboard, each white square table a metre apart, awaited exam papers. Partner's claws clattered on the floorboards as he sniffed around.

Going into her office, Janna jumped as her mobile rang. Emlyn? she thought ever hopefully, but the number was unfamiliar. The sinister, lisping, stammering voice was not.

'Pwepared for tomorrow, Janna? After all our effort, support and financial commitment, I hope you're not going to let us down. Wemember how you hassled us to give your kids a chance to get some gwades? Now it's your turn to deliver; the world is watching, you owe us spectacular wesults.'

'You've got the wrong number, this is not Sadists Anonymous and I'm taping this conversation, so bugger off.'

Janna slammed down the receiver. How dare Ashton wind her up when she needed to be at her most calm and cheerful? She longed to unlock the safe and photocopy every paper. Not that it would help the children unless she wrote the answers for them. By the time Rocky, Feral and Danijela had struggled to the end of the business studies case histories and worked out what questions needed answering, time would be up. Oh God, had she pushed them beyond their capabilities?

If only she could call Emlyn, but since the rugby match their stand-off had continued. But whatever his sadness over Oriana, Emlyn had gallantly thrown himself into the Larks GCSEs, even to the unprecedented step of getting himself to the breakfast club most mornings and conducting question-and-answer sessions until the history candidates were date perfect. Often the Brigadier had joined him, performing a splendid double act.

Over at Bagley, Alex Bruce tiptoed along the landing after lights out. Hearing murmuring coming from the junior dormitory, he drew closer, then smiled as he heard Boffin's voice: 'Please remember in your prayers that over the next four weeks I'll be taking my GCSEs.'

It was nearly midnight at Penscombe, but still stiflingly

hot. The shrill neigh of a horse trembled on the night. Earlier, Xav had bravely delivered a good-luck card to Aysha's house and been sent packing.

Now he looked out on a tossing silver sea of cow parsley and ebony woods menacing as an approaching tidal wave on the horizon. Bogotá panted at his feet. *Understanding Business*, black with notes, lay open on his bed.

Xav had never more wanted a drink to take the edge off his nerves and his sadness. He had shouted at his poor mother for asking for the hundredth time if he were all right, and threatened to punch Bianca for pestering him for the millionth time not to forget to pass on Feral's good-luck card, which she'd put in his school bag. There was a knock on the door.

'Bugger off,' hissed Xav.

It was Rupert, bearing a cup of cocoa.

'Thought this might help you sleep. Know what you're going through. I'm shit scared already and I'm doing only one subject; you're doing loads.'

'Thanks.' Xav took the cup. 'Not so much money on me. You've got to wipe that smug smirk off Stancombe's face.'

The cup of cocoa, the first and last Rupert would ever make, was absolutely disgusting. The cocoa was still in powdery lumps, sugar hadn't been added and, by not sieving the milk, Rupert had left a thickening layer of skin on the top. Xav was so touched by his father's concern, he drank the lot, managing not to gag.

'Those marketing ideas aren't bad,' admitted Rupert, 'although I doubt if direct mailing the Shakespeare Estate would find us any new owners.'

To Xav's amazement, the cocoa sent him to sleep.

'"Nessun dorma!"' sang Miss Cambola, but pianissimo so that it wouldn't wake her fellow lodgers.

When she'd taken O' levels, far too many years ago,

her English had been so poor, she'd failed everything except music. Her set pieces had been Brandenburg Four, the Egmont Overture and the 'Waldstein'; she could still remember every note. The last year had been such a joy; Cambola absolutely dreaded the future. Kylie had such an exquisite voice, but would she ever be able to use it?

Over at Wilmington, the Brigadier couldn't sleep. All his unrelaxed bones were aching. Had he simplified the Great War enough? Would they ever remember the essentials? Feral had received a lot of good-luck cards – even one from his mother in rehab, whom he'd promised to ring after every exam. Business studies this morning, however, had been considered beyond him, so, getting up at five, the Brigadier left him to sleep.

Out in the deserted street, every car had a cat stretched out on the bonnet or underneath, like a union meeting. Lily's cat, General, obviously the shop steward, lay in the middle of the road, and strolled off huffily as the Brigadier started up his car. Noticing ominous pewter-grey clouds over Larkminster, he prayed the forecast rain would hold off. As had been proved in elections, the working classes tended not to come out in bad weather. He and Emlyn would have to jump into Stancombe's minibus and round up the defectors.

The cuckoo was singing in a nearby wood as he reached the next village. In the churchyard, the graves, like swimmers in a marathon, nearly disappeared in a white sea of cow parsley and wild garlic flowers. The yellow roses he'd put on his wife's grave on Ascension Day were shedding their petals. He wondered if she'd rest in peace if she knew he was plucking up courage to propose to Lily.

The church door creaked as he went in, followed by another creak as Lily, kneeling in a front pew, struggled to her feet.

'Don't believe prayers work unless one kneels down,' she confessed. 'Couldn't sleep, just popped down here to wish them luck.'

Without rouge and lipstick, Lily looked pale; pink moisturizer ringed her nostrils; her face was as rumpled as the bed in which she'd tossed and turned. There was a white hair on her upper lip and a big bunch of dark and light purple lilac, with stems bashed, on the pew beside her.

'I so want them and Janna not to be humiliated.'

The Brigadier's heart expanded with love.

108

Over at Larks, from eight o'clock onwards, Partner, sporting a smart crimson bow tie, welcomed everyone with joyful barks. Across one whole wall of reception, defiantly defacing Ashton's property, Graffi's grinning black cat juggled gold horseshoes and lashed a tail at a lark ascending into gold clouds. In black letters, Graffi had also named each candidate and wished them all luck.

The heady smell of Sally and Lily's flowers, however, couldn't disguise a reek of cheap scent, sweat and terror. No one could face Taggie's cornflakes and croissants; they could hardly keep down a cup of tea.

With their hair drawn back and twisted up into knots, their smocks with shoelace straps showing off bare shoulders, and their jeans flopping round their ankles, the girls looked like extras in a BBC Jane Austen ball scene above the waist, and the technicians making the film below it.

But their pale faces, seamed with strain and weariness, came straight out of a Dickens slum scene. Every so often, one of the girls would break into terrified sobs and trigger off the others.

'Got the runs, miss.' 'Toilet's blocked, miss.' 'Stink makes you frow up.' 'Fink I've come on.' 'Miss, I'm goin' 'ome.'

'No, you're not,' said Janna firmly.

After quick prayers in assembly – 'May an angel ride on your shoulders' – Cambola played them out with 'Hark, Hark! the Lark' on the trumpet.

Now at the far end of the gym, Mags Gablecross sat calmly smiling, ticking off candidates as she called out their names in alphabetical order.

Xav being Campbell-Black was one of the first in. Taggie gave him a huge hug.

'Can I have a hug too?' asked Rocky.

Danijela's little teeth were chattering frantically.

'Even my buttyflies have buttyflies.'

Danny the Irish, who'd only come in because she had, held her hand.

'I'm so exhausted I can't remember my candidate number,' moaned Pearl.

'Can I have a hug?' Monster begged Taggie, his lower lip trembling like a little boy's.

Inside the gym, the windows were too high to reveal anything except ever-darkening purple sky.

'At least we can hang ourself on the ropes,' sighed Kylie, whose bulge was so big she could hardly get at her desk.

'That's not a metre between your desks, Danny and Danijela,' called out Mags as she checked everyone had written their names and numbers properly. 'If you want to hold hands, do it after the exam.'

Aysha, a bruise darkening her cheek, cast down her eyes, terrified of looking at an anguished Xav.

As Janna watched the tail-enders forlornly filing to their doom, she wanted to ask if they'd packed their pencil boxes themselves.

'Perhaps we should strip search you for mobiles,' she joked.

'Yes, please,' giggled Kitten, 'but only if Emlyn does it.'

'Kitten Meadows, you've never worn a long skirt in your life, what have you got hidden?' shouted Pearl.

'Shut up, all of you,' yelled Cambola.

Turning, Janna noticed Emlyn leaning against the wall watching her. He had just rounded up and brought in Johnnie Fowler. 'Worse than getting a mustang into a lorry.'

'I feel like Gérard Houllier,' confessed Janna, watching through the door as Mags handed out the papers. 'Once they're on the field you can only pray, we can't even substitute Boffin or Cosmo.'

'Don't expect too much, they've crammed a two-year course into one year, but it's been such a fantastic year. It'll stand them in good stead for ever,' said Emlyn. As his big, warm hand gathered up hers and squeezed it, she let it lie there.

'Everyone here?' demanded Mags, consulting her list. 'No Feral?'

'He's not taking business studies, miss.'

Mags looked round the room. 'Graffi's not here either.'

At that moment, a schoolmaster bringing back the birch, the rain lashed the window panes.

'I'll go and find him,' said Emlyn, letting go of Janna's hand.

Torrential rain scrabbled and clawed at his windscreen; rotting fruit, veg, fag ends and needles flowed into the cul-de-sacs of the Shakespeare Estate. Emlyn found Graffi wandering down Hamlet Street. It was hard to tell if his face was soaked by tears or rain; his black curls hung in rat's tails.

'Cardiff Nan's fucked off.'

'Hop in and leave her.'

'Can't, she's left all her clothes at home.'

'A Welsh undresser.'

'She'll catch her death.'

'I'll find her after I've dropped you at Larks.'

'Can't do the exam now, it's too late. My hands are frozen.' Graffi was shaking uncontrollably. 'I can't write.'

'You can have a go.'

Five minutes later, having swapped his drenched

T-shirt for Emlyn's jersey, which reached his knees, Graffi slid into the gym to giggles and cheers from his supporters.

'I've got the shakes, I can't do this.' He picked up the paper and read: 'Greenstreet PLC are planning to build their fifth supermarket on the edge of an ancient and much-loved country town. Question one: How should they set about winning local acceptance and planning permission?'

Familiar territory, Mr Randal Greenstreet, thought Graffi.

'Well, maybe I can.' He picked up his pen.

The silence of the exams was interrupted only by occasional expletives, rain grapeshotting the windows, sweet papers rustling, tummies rumbling, the click of Mags's knitting needles and the pacing of Cambola, the invigilator, up and down the rows, to be replaced after thirty minutes by the clattering of Gloria's high heels.

Gloria, dreaming of PC Cuthbert, didn't notice Kitten's denim skirt falling open to reveal useful business terms and formulas written on her succulent thighs. Distracted by the sight, Monster lost his train of thought. Pearl opened her KitKat, turning it over thoughtfully. On the back, with a compass, she had also scratched terms and formulas.

Sweating when they came in, the bare-shouldered girls were now shivering.

I'm three-quarters through. I can do it, thought Xav joyfully. Looking across, he met Aysha's eyes. He wanted to kiss her purple bruise better.

Even Rocky, vast in his tiny desk, like Bultitude Senior in *Vice Versa*, was writing slowly but steadily.

'Got my period,' announced Pearl. 'Got to go to the toilet.'

Out she went, returning in a spitting rage.

'Who removed *Understanding Business* out of the toilet cistern?'

Over at Bagley, Stancombe's Science Emporium was being built for the Queen's visit in the first week in November and the builders continued to make an unconscionable din: bang, bang, drill, drill, setting the children's teeth on edge, so the GCSE exams were being taken in the newish sports hall.

Well into business studies, Primrose was writing steadily. Paris was thinking, then scribbling frantically, wishing he could instead write a short story about the idealistic young couple in Question Three, who were trying to make their garden centre break even by taking in another director.

Amber was writing to her boyfriend at Harrow. Boffin was filling pages and pages, between smirking and cracking his knuckles. Cosmo had polished off his paper in half an hour and was writing to Mrs Walton. He did hope Milly wouldn't want to come home and veg for a week at half-term.

Plugged into Jade Stancombe's ear, and hidden by a curtain of tortoiseshell hair, was a little mobile, the latest technical device from the Philippines, which as she tapped in the number, gave her the answers to each question as slowly or as fast as she chose. For this relief, she had almost forgiven Daddy for shacking up with Anthea Belvedon, particularly as he'd promised her a thousand pounds for every A grade.

Gloria had been replaced as invigilator by Basket, whose spangled flip-flops, daringly acquired in Skunk's honour, flapped as she padded up and down, doing everyone's heads in.

'Turn down the fucking volume,' snarled Monster.

The rain was easing, the windows framing grey clouds topped with white rather than purple.

Mags put down the shawl she was knitting for Kylie's baby.

'You've got five minutes left.'

Danijela burst into tears, gazing helplessly at her hardly touched pages. Others scribbled final answers or tried to reach into the depths of their memories, as one might rootle in a bag for a taxi fare, and find nothing.

'Put down your pens, please.'

Dazed, like miners coming up into the light, they spilt out into the drizzle. They had an hour and three-quarters to eat and drink something before PE theory that afternoon. Feral, bouncing his football, had just arrived; Partner, barking round his feet, hoped for a game.

'Howdya do?' Feral asked Xav.

'Not bad, once I got going. I've got a card for you.'

Pearl the drama queen was making her usual fuss.

'I've failed, I've failed. Couldn't do any of it. We wasn't taught the syllabus.'

'Yes we was,' said Kitten. 'I thought it were easy.'

Janna rushed round encouraging and consoling.

'First one's always difficult. Sure this afternoon'll be much easier. Just make certain you have a proper dinner.'

It had been hard to settle to anything this morning, all she could think was that Emlyn had held her hand.

PE theory lasted two hours. Feral had got top marks in the practical exam, but he couldn't make head nor tail of this paper. So he slowly deciphered Bianca's card.

It was her parents' last-year's Christmas card, with a picture of Penscombe Peterkin gambolling in the snow with Rupert's Jack Russells.

Inside were printed the words 'Merry Christmas and a Happy New Year' and at the bottom 'Rupert and Taggie Campbell-Black'. There was no way Rupert would ever wish him any happiness, thought Feral wearily.

'Dearest Feral,' Bianca had written. 'This card is the right one because I want to know you next Christmas and the next and the next, for ever. Good luck, I miss you, please ring me. All love.'

With a groan of despair Feral shoved the card in his pocket and gazed at the blank pages of the booklet in which he was supposed to write down his answers. The princess and pauper: how could he ever give Bianca the life she deserved?

When Graffi got home from his night shift at Tesco, the dawn was already breaking and his father roaring drunk and raging mad.

'How dare you let out Cardiff Nan? Day centre brought her back and fucking charged me for the loan of a dressing gown,' and he hit Graffi across the lounge.

109

PE theory was followed by information technology, German listening and religious studies, leading up to the big one, English lit., on the Friday morning before half-term. For Rupert, the Thursday had been punctuated by telephone calls from skittish Bagley mothers, including the fearful Dame Hermione, saying that as they'd pledged large sums of money, they did hope to be rewarded with a party if he got a good grade. The final call at midnight had been from ghastly Stancombe, saying he hoped Rupert was going to honour his promise and roll up at Cotchester College tomorrow.

'There's a lot at stake.'

'The stake should be through your fucking heart,' howled Rupert and hung up.

Randal turned gleefully to Anthea, stretched out naked on his bed beside him. 'Pressure getting to his Highness.'

'Good,' said Anthea. 'Ay hope he gets a U. He's always been far too big for his raiding boots.'

Rupert was so livid, he'd never sleep now. In the old days of showjumping, or when he was Minister for Sport, he could always ease the tension by pulling a groom or a groupie. Now he was mocked by an entire library of books, which he'd never read, and by *Lord of the Flies* reminding him how horribly he was bullying darling Taggie at the moment, by being so sulky and resentful. Thank God term would be over in a few weeks and she'd be back home with him again. But would she be bored? Had Larks whetted her appetite for more company and excitement: for bloody Pete Wainwright or that fat Welshman?

Rupert wished he could have taken the exam at Larks instead of Cotchester College, which would be swarming with press. But when he'd dropped into Jubilee Cottage to ask Janna, she had very sweetly said his presence in the exam room would be far too distracting.

'The girls would all gaze at you, and the invigilators too, enabling all the lads to cheat like mad and no one would notice. You're still the most attractive man in the world,' she added, blushing furiously.

'Huh – doesn't get me anywhere.' Rupert had stalked off into the sitting room and been blown away by Graffi's mural.

'That's so bloody good. Christ! There's Rod Hyde and ghastly Ashton in one of his poncy mauve shirts and that asshole Bishop. What's he called, Graffi? He must come and do one of the hunt before bloody Blair closes it down.'

Rupert's mood didn't improve on the morning of the exam. Taggie and Xav had left for Larks and weren't even there to wave him off. The forecourt of Cotchester College was swarming with press, including a grinning Venturer camera crew.

'To me, Rupert', 'Look this way, Rupe', 'Over here', they shouted, as Rupert deliberately parked his dark blue BMW in the space reserved for the Dean of the College, and, gathering up *Lord of the Flies*, *Death of a Salesman*, and *Opening Lines*, leapt out like a snarling tiger.

'God, he's lush,' sighed a presenter from Sky.

'What have you learnt from your studies of English lit.?' asked the *Guardian*.

'That the term "mature student" is an oxymoron.'

'Randal Stancombe says you haven't got a hope in hell,' taunted the *Scorpion*.

'Stancombe's an expert on hell,' snarled Rupert. 'Now, get out of my way.'

He was about to pick the *Scorpion* reporter up by his lapels when he was distracted by a vast fluffy black pantomime cat padding up to him, purring loudly and rubbing itself against his thighs.

'What the fuck?' Rupert was about to punch or kick the cat away, when a deep gasping familiar voice spoke.

'I've just come to bring you luck.'

Rupert's scowl widened into a huge smile, his voice cracked: 'Oh Tag, darling, oh Tag,' as he pulled the cat to its feet and into his arms.

'Purrrr, purrrr,' giggled the cat, tickling his face with its whiskers.

Rupert was still laughing as he sat down. Oblivious of his fellow candidates, he got out a blue fountain pen and wrote his name and number. Then, opening the paper, he read the first question on *Lord of the Flies*: 'Describe the importance of Jack in this novel.'

' "This is a good island",' wrote Rupert, with a sigh of relief. ' "We'll have fun." '

Finishing his answer on *Death of a Salesman*, he had half an hour left for poetry and to explain the ways Seamus Heaney and Dannie Abse wrote about the father/son relationship in two poems, which he'd enjoyed and identified with. Heaney was sound on ploughing and he liked the Abse line about his son playing pop music and 'dreaming of some school Juliet I don't know'. He'd never get a chance to meet Aysha if Raschid Khan had his way.

Thank God there wasn't a question on that whining bitch Sylvia Plath.

Having finished the paper, Rupert felt very flat. Cursing himself for things he should have put in, he shook off the press, and drove straight to Larks to collect Xav. Taggie would already have left to collect Bianca from Bagley.

As he hurtled down the back roads, he noticed the cow parsley turning green and going over and the chestnut candles scattering their creamy petals. He'd been too busy to appreciate them and now he'd have to wait until next year. The baton had been taken over by hawthorn, exploding everywhere in white-hot fountains, its soapy bath-day smell competing with the reek of wild garlic, much stronger now the leaves were yellowing and decaying.

Thank God he'd be able to concentrate full time on racing once more. A new dark brown filly called Fast was running in the first race at York. Pulling into the Larks car park, where, judging by the 'Please Be Quiet' sign, Eng. lit. was still going on, he switched on the little television on his dashboard.

Next second, a white van with Star of Lahore Curry House printed on its side drew up, driven presumably by Raschid Khan. Rupert had been about to take a large swig of brandy out of his hipflask, but Khan looked the sort of evil bugger who'd report him to the police.

Fast was dancing round the paddock looking almost too well. The bookies had her at twelve to one. Rupert was about to ring Ladbrokes, when he noticed Mr Khan, despite his air of extreme disapproval, sneaking a look at the television.

'Hi,' said Rupert.

'Good afternoon,' replied Mr Khan stiffly.

'I know who you are,' drawled Rupert. 'You have an exceptionally clever daughter. In my experience, the more you tell teenagers not to see each other, the more they want to.'

Mr Khan was about to close his window, when Rupert added:

'The attachment is as abhorrent to me as it obviously is to you.' Then, when Mr Khan looked astounded: 'Do

888

you honestly think I want Xavier, with all he is likely to inherit, to chuck himself away on a total nobody?'

'A nobody?' Quivering with fury, Mr Khan inflated like a turkey cock.

'By comparison,' said Rupert coldly.

'That's a racist remark.'

'You're the racist,' snapped back Rupert, 'being foul about my son, who's much blacker than your daughter, who I gather is utterly enchanting. My wife Taggie is almost more devoted to her than Xav is.'

'There is nothing more to be said. Aysha is engaged to be married.'

'Right. If you'll forgive me,' said Rupert, punching out Ladbrokes' number, 'I've got a potentially very good horse in this race. If you want to take a chance and have a bet, the odds are excellent.'

There was a long pause. In the dust of the car park, two robins were quarrelling over a feather. Mr Khan, unable to resist a flutter, extracted a tenner from a paperclip full of notes in his breast pocket and handed it over. 'I will have a bet.'

Matters dipped when Fast, no doubt excited to be carrying Rupert's dark blue and emerald green colours for the first time, took off at the start and ran halfway round the course, before her jockey could pull her up. She then lined up with the starters, set off at a cracking pace, and with Mr Khan and Rupert both yelling their heads off, lived up to her name by flying down the straight to win by six lengths.

'You've made a hundred and twenty pounds,' said Rupert jubilantly, 'and I've just bought one fantastic horse.'

When Xav and Aysha wandered wearily out of English lit., deliberately keeping their distance, utterly dejected at the prospect of not seeing each other for ten days, they were flabbergasted to see Rupert and Raschid Khan leaning against Rupert's car, deep in conversation.

'Xav tried to introduce marketing to my yard.'

'Aysha tried to introduce food technology to my restaurant, which I would be honoured if you would visit one evening.'

'How did you get on, Dad?' asked Xav nervously.

'Not bad, might have scraped a G. How about you?'

'Not great, I've never understood that Heaney poem. Is his father senile, or is he haunted by his memory?'

'Senile, if he's anything like me. Have you met Mr Khan? Fast just won by six lengths.' Rupert turned back to Raschid: 'Why don't you, your wife and Aysha come to Epsom one day next week?'

'How could you schmooze up to that terrible guy?' exploded Xav as Rupert drove over the bridge towards Penscombe. 'He blacked Aysha's eye last week.'

'No, he didn't, Aysha's younger sister did that. Aysha wanted to revise and turned off *EastEnders*. Raschid told me,' said Rupert smugly.

Winding down his window, narrowly missing a jogger, Rupert chucked Sylvia Plath into the River Fleet.

110

Half-term wasn't helpful. The candidates felt they deserved a break, but guilty if they eased off and lost momentum, particularly on the Monday after, when faced with two heavyweights: geography and double science. As a result of being in a confined space, everyone had colds or tummy bugs and the heat wave had kicked in. At nine-thirty it was already like an oven in the gym. Sophy was invigilating and unless she walked in the straight line required of sobriety tests, her splendid bulk sent papers flying and candidates into fits of nervous giggles.

They were just about to start geography when Johnnie Fowler was found to be missing. Then Janna ran in saying Johnnie's sister had rung to say at the prospect of two such gruelling exams, Johnnie had gone 'on the booze, then on the rob' and been arrested.

'Go and bail him,' Skunk Littlewood begged Emlyn, 'he's got double science this afternoon. He could get a B.'

Emlyn found Johnnie in a cell, cross-eyed with hangover.

'What happened?'

'I got hammered, mugged an old lady for anuvver round, but I was so drunk I didn't realize it was Graffi's Cardiff Nan, what had escaped. It's not funny,' he grumbled. 'Anyway, I don't want bailing. Can't I stay here and miss science, maffs, French, D and T, English, anuvver bleeding geography and German and history and more science?'

'Come on,' said Emlyn.

Outside, he fed Johnnie black coffee and later chicken soup and dry toast and got him back in time for science.

'Don't,' groaned Johnnie, clutching his head as the other candidates gave him a round of applause.

Monster had had baked beans for lunch; consequently, his farts were worse than Skunk's heat-wave armpits.

'I'm going to faint,' said Johnnie, even more so a minute later when he opened the paper, which was a brute. 'And to fink I could be kipping in some nice cell.'

'Holy shit.' Feral screwed up his paper and walked out, bouncing his football.

'Don't give up,' the Brigadier, who was hovering in the corridor, begged him, 'you've got plenty of time and an extra half-hour for being dyslexic.'

'If I stared at that paper for a hundred years, I couldn't do a word of it, so don't get yer hopes up, Brig, I'm going to play football.'

Pearl unfurled another KitKat weighed down with equations. Within twenty minutes the room was almost empty; only Graffi, Aysha, Xav (because it gave him the chance to gaze at Aysha), Kitten and Pearl were left.

'Bloody hell,' said Graffi, 'I need a fag and a piss.'

'Hush,' said Basket in horror.

'And for you to take off those fucking, squeaking shoes.'

'Nuffink on circulation, nuffink on the heart, nuffink on the solar system, or electricity or radiation,' raged Pearl as they came blinking and utterly dispirited into the sunlight.

'I thought it were easy,' said Kitten and got punched in the face by Pearl.

* * *

Over at Bagley earlier, Mr Fussy hung round the sports hall, hurrying in his students, 'Don't be late, don't be late,' hell-bent on smashing Theo's record of getting everyone through.

Milly, practising a yoga relaxation technique Poppet had urged on her, was nearly asleep. Jade made another mental note not to thrust her fingers through her hair and reveal the tiny transmitter in her ear.

Lando was at the back, murmuring, 'Define a quark, define a quark. It's the sound that an upper-class duck makes,' and laughing at his own joke so much, he was furiously hushed by Boffin. From where Lando was sitting, he could admire the splendid swell of Primrose's left breast. Cosmo, having finished his paper, was reading *The Secret History*.

When it came to the two-hour maths exam the following day, Xav was determined not to let Pittsy down. Ex-alkies should stick together.

'If Mrs Rock borrowed £2,000 at ten per cent compound interest and paid it back together with total interest after two years, what would be her total repayment?' read Xav.

'£2,420', he wrote a minute later.

Over at Bagley, the Philippine gremlin whispered £2,420 in Jade's ear, in answer to the same question. Jack Waterlane, utterly defeated by the same paper, was relieved to receive a text message on his smuggled-in mobile, saying Kylie Rose had gone into labour.

When in doubt, take the easier option. As Jack ran out of the exam hall, Biffo, who was invigilating, leapt down from his chair and chased after him. The best way of stopping Biffo following him, decided Jack, was to take Biffo's car. Although he was only sixteen, Jack had been driving tractors round his father's estate since he was ten and, leaving a furiously windmilling

Biffo, set off at ninety miles an hour for the hospital.

Kylie Rose's face when he walked into the maternity ward made everything worthwhile.

'I thought you' – groan – 'was in the middle of a maffs paper,' progressed to, 'Oh' – groan – 'of course I'll marry you.'

Chantal spent the rest of the labour crying with joy.

Lord Waterlane, when he rolled up some hours later, was in a towering rage. On the other hand, Jack's mother, Sharon, who insisted on referring to herself as Lady Shar, had once been a nightclub hostess and a hell of a goer. David had always suffered from *nostalgie de la boue* and found Chantal, who was only thirty, extremely pretty and, after all, Kylie had given birth to a boy.

'We're going to call him Ganymede David,' she told her future father-in-law proudly.

The first English paper, which also contained literature questions, was on 10 June. Dora, knowing this was a crucially important subject to Paris, had finally tracked down five four-leafed clovers and, with Patience's help, had glued them on a card. 'Dear Paris,' she had written inside, 'Good luck in English and all your other exams, you'll do brilliantly. Love, Dora'.

Her timing, admittedly, was lousy. A thoroughly strung-up Paris, flanked by Junior, Lando and Jack, was just going into the exam when Dora had rushed up, thrusting the card into his hand. Paris glanced down.

'What the fuck?'

'Please open it.'

Paris gazed at her in disbelief.

'Just fuck off, can't you see I'm busy? Get out of my life and leave me alone.'

Dora cried great rasping sobs all round the pitches, missing French. Artie Deverell, who'd picked up on the exchange, dispatched Bianca, not the ideal person, who found Dora sitting on a log sobbing into Cadbury's shoulder.

'Good thing Labradors like water,' observed Bianca.
Dora went on crying.

'Paris is heartless, Dor. Even when he was crazy about me, he couldn't show it. It's his upbringing; he doesn't know how to express love, he hasn't had any practice. He's got a slice of ice in his heart.'

'Put not your trust in Arctic Princes,' sobbed Dora.

Jade Stancombe, in the evening, was more brutal. 'You were like an autograph-hunter interrupting Tiger Woods as he teed up at the eighteenth hole. Paris just tore up your card and chucked it in the bin. Stop making a fool of yourself; he's out of your league.'

In the sports hall earlier, Paris dispatched Housman and Hood's rosy view of childhood: 'Lands of Lost Content'. Poets all seemed to have had wondrous childhoods and gloomy, insecure old ages.

I've had a gloomy, insecure childhood, thought Paris; God help me if the rest of my life is even worse. I remember, I remember the children's homes where I wasn't born.

He turned to the next question: 'Describe a place you hate.'

I hate my own heart [wrote Paris] because it is cruel and hard. My best friend, Dora, is honourable and good like Piggy in *Lord of the Flies*. She has helped me revise all my exams: where the world moves and sits in space, Martial's recipe for happiness, drumlins, the Battle of Arginusae and the trials of the Generals. She gave me a beautiful good-luck card decorated with four-leaf clovers, but I tore it up and told her to piss off, because I was uptight. I would like to apologize to Dora on behalf of all my sex. Where women are concerned, we always get things wrong and I most of all. Dora is well named because she is adorable.
I hate my heart because it lets me down; its beat

quickens when I hear beautiful music or poetry, but when a friend tries to get close, it freezes over. To twist Catullus: whenever I love, I seem to hate or resent as well. We dissected a pig's heart in biology, but if you dissected my heart, it would pump not blood but poison.

'A place I hate,' wrote Boffin Brooks, 'is the head-quarters of the Tory Party.'

The place I hate is my deputy headmaster's drawing room. He calls it a lounge, which is a complete misnomer because no one could lounge in such an uncomfortable place [wrote Lando]. The chairs are ramrod hard; the sofas murder your coccyx. No parents stay more than five minutes because he offers such tiny glasses of indifferent sherry and doesn't want anyone to linger. There are no pictures, no books except the very odd scientific manual. When you enter, you always get a lecture on bad behaviour.

'The place I hate is a vivisectionist's laboratory where the animals' vocal cords are cut on arrival so their screams cannot upset the staff or visitors,' wrote Amber and made herself cry even more cataloguing other iniquities.

Glancing round, Primrose Duddon smiled sympathetically and shoved a box of Kleenex in her direction.

I like Primrose, decided Amber, I like her much better than Milly or Jade. Primrose had helped her with revision beyond the call of duty. Amber resolved to buy her a cashmere jersey as a thank-you present. On the other hand, it would take a lot of cashmere to accommodate Primrose's splendid bosom and might be rather expensive. Better to give her scent instead.

111

The sun had long since set, but it was still so hot that, despite wearing only shorts, a cotton shirt and loafers, Theo had left his study windows wide open. In the past month, he had been soothed by the 'liquid siftings' of the nightingales in the laurels. Tonight they had all departed – like pupils at the end of term. Would he still be alive next year to hear them?

He had been wrestling with a difficult letter in answer to a telephone call telling him one of his favourite old boys, Jamie Pardow, had been killed in Iraq.

'We knew you were fond of each other,' Jamie's father had said, 'in fact in his very last letter home, he said: "If you see Theo, tell him I'm still not tucking my shirt in."' The father's voice had cracked then and he'd had to ring off.

Such a lovely boy. Theo shook his head. He should be writing reports. He should be working on Sophocles. Instead, he poured another large Scotch to wash down a couple more painkillers. A bottle of morphine, illegally prescribed by James Benson, was hidden behind the books, for when things became unendurable.

Would he could take something to ease the ache in his heart that after the end of term he wouldn't see Paris for eight weeks. In a way it would be a relief. He needed to be alone to calm his fever, to think about the boy. He knew Ian Cartwright, Cosmo and even Dora were jealous of their friendship. He must try not to favour him next term.

On a positive side, he was delighted Paris was on course for A stars in Greek and Latin. Hengist, who had a key to the school safe and, against all the rules, often looked at finished papers, had reported exquisite translations of Homer and Virgil, wise, witty, lyrical comments on Ovid and Horace and Iphigenia's pleading for Orestes and flawless unseens in the language papers. How Socrates would have loved him.

Paris, according to Hengist, had also submitted brilliant papers in other subjects, including a matchless first history paper. 'He writes so entertainingly.'

Paris had science tomorrow morning and a second history paper in the afternoon, covering the Russian Revolution and Nazi Germany, which had both fascinated and haunted him. Then it was all over.

Although it was after eleven, golden Jupiter was the only star visible in a palely luminous blue sky. The trees on the edge of the golf course, olive green in the half light, seemed to have faces, hollow-eyed, too, after a month of exams. The mingled stench of rank elder-flower and decaying wild garlic was overwhelming.

As Hindsight padded in, leaping onto the table, Theo grabbed his glass – there was enough whisky spilt over the reports and his translation of Sophocles already – and guided the cat's fluffy orange tail away from the halogen lamp. A mosquito was whining around his bald head looking for a late supper; Theo lit yet another cigarette to deter it.

He smiled briefly as he caught sight of a poster on the wall Paris had had framed for him for his birthday, which showed a woman with a balloon coming out of her mouth saying: 'I'm voting for Martial, he's not clever, he's not honest, but he's handsome.' Alex had banished it from Theo's classroom as being too sexist.

Theo had seen a lot of Paris in the last ten days. Not entirely, he was realistic enough to recognize, because Paris relished his company. The boy, it appeared, had been so gratuitously cruel to poor little Dora that that dear, kind, soul Patience Cartwright had ticked him off roundly. This had so shocked Paris, he had since shunned the Cartwrights' and spent his evenings working in the library or talking to Theo. Theo suspected and genuinely hoped Paris was much fonder of Dora than he let on. He could do worse. Dora was brave, resourceful and good-hearted.

The evenings together had been an exquisite pleasure. They had listened to music and discussed books and Paris's choice of AS levels: Greek, Latin, theatre studies and English. Paris also brought Theo the latest gossip. How Lando had been caught listening to the Empire test match on his walkman during science, how Anatole had mistaken downers for uppers and slept peacefully through French, and how Boffin, 'stupid twat', was already immersed in one of next year's set books: *The Handmaid's Tale*.

Hengist was in Washington, due back this evening, but grounded by a strike. He had nevertheless rung in to wish Paris luck in his final history paper tomorrow.

Theo emptied the bottle into his glass. On his desk lay an advance copy of Alex's *Guide to Red Tape* (or *Tape* as it was now known), which the self-regarding idiot had presented to Theo to illustrate that he, Alex, despite being busier than anyone, was capable, unlike Theo and Hengist, of meeting deadlines.

Theo, instead, turned to Aeschylus, whose *Philoctetes*, covered in drink and coffee rings, he'd been reading earlier. Philoctetes, driven crazy by a snake bite, as he was by his ransacked spine. How admirable was Maurice Bowra's translation:

Oh Healer death, spurn not to come to me.
For you alone, of woes incurable, are doctor,
And a dead man feels no pain.

Theo hoped this were true. Awful to reach the other side and immediately find oneself bound on a wheel of fire, like Ixion.

Back in his cell, Cosmo peeled off his mother's blond wig, which she'd worn for *Norma* and in which he had disguised himself in his walk down to Bagley village to pleasure Ruth Walton.

He had finished *The Secret History*, the best book he had ever read, in which young people had totally waived morality and taken justice into their own hands. He had put on Matthias Goerne, a voice of unearthly beauty, singing Bach cantatas and was flipping through scores for the end-of-term concert. But he was not happy.

He had spent half an hour earlier mending Theo's DVD machine, but Theo's eyes still didn't rest on him with as much tenderness as they rested on Paris. No matter that he was going to get straight A stars and one for shagging from Ruth Walton, Cosmo wanted to be loved best by all the people by whom he wanted to be loved best. Even Hengist had rung from Washington to wish Paris luck.

He never rang me, thought Cosmo bitterly.

Cannoning off the walls on his way to bed around midnight, Theo saw a light on in Paris's room and went in. On the Thomas the Tank Engine duvet lay the boy's dark green history revision folder. In his sleeping hand was clutched the Greek Epigrams which Theo had given him for his sixteenth birthday. Theo was touched.

Paris looked so adorable with the lamplight falling on his long blond lashes and silky, flaxen hair. Playing cricket without a cap had brought a sprinkling of freckles and a touch of colour to his pale face. In sleep, the wolf cub relaxed and one could appreciate the beauty and casual grace of his body. Theo removed the Greek *Epigrams.*

Cosmo, skulking on the landing on the lookout for trouble, froze at the sight of Theo's battered copy of Philoctetes and his late-night whisky outside Paris's bedroom.

Suddenly terrible screams ripped the night apart, followed by anguished sobbing, which slowly subsided. Five minutes later, Cosmo, lurking in the shadows, saw Theo, a faint smile on his cadaverous features, coming out of Paris's room and going through the green baize door into his own apartment.

Cosmo retired to his cell and, setting aside the end-of-term concert scores, lit a fag, poured himself a large brandy and reflected. Alex Bruce wasn't his greatest fan, particularly since the Poppet art department incident. Poppet had even asked Cosmo to address the Talks Society on the morality of onanism. It wouldn't hurt to win some brownie points.

After a preliminary rootle round Theo's study, Cosmo let himself out of the front door, dropped his empty brandy bottle in Poppet's bottle bank and knocked on the Bruces' door. Alex, awake, much enjoying a third read of *Tape*, was soon reassuring Cosmo that he had done exactly the right thing.

Telling each other it was for Paris's sake, they let themselves into the house and to Theo's study, which thankfully looked out over an entirely deserted golf course. Judging by the bottles in the waste-paper basket, Theo was unlikely to wake up.

Alex's lips pursed at the overflowing ashtrays and the pile of reports unmarked, except by whisky stains. From Theo's desk drawer, Cosmo unearthed some love poems to Paris in Greek.

'Who was it said Greek letters on a blank page look like bird's footprints in the snow?' asked Cosmo, then when Alex clearly didn't know the answer, added, 'These are pretty explicit, sir, and those letters here, here, here and here, spell Paris, although it could be the Paris who triggered off the Trojan War.'

'I doubt it.' The gleam of triumph in Alex's eyes was obscene, particularly when, from under Theo's desk drawer lining paper, Cosmo pulled ravishing nude photographs of Paris, with the Eiffel Tower tattoo on his right shoulder, as well as a DVD in a plain brown wrapper.

Hearing a crash, they both jumped out of their skins, but it was only Hindsight arriving through the window.

'I'm amazed that cat hasn't died from passive smoking,' said Alex, shoving him out again. Breathing more heavily than a French bulldog on the job, Alex then fastidiously parked his bottom on Theo's rickety chair and put the DVD into the machine, which came up with a film of ravishing naked youths re-enacting classical myths with men sporting curly hair and ringleted beards.

'That's Narcissus and that must be Ganymede,' volunteered Cosmo.

'Don't look.' Alex clapped a sweating hand over Cosmo's eyes.

'All part of my development,' said Cosmo, tugging the hand away.

The mosquito, earlier deterred by Theo's cigarettes, whined, circled and plunged her teeth into Alex's arm.

'I thought Mr Fussy was going to pounce,' Cosmo told Anatole next morning. 'I couldn't tell if he was more turned on by the porn or the chance to nail Theo. The Martial voting poster on the wall and *Red Tape* chucked in the bin were the *dernière paille*.'

112

Arriving at the police station in the early hours of the morning, Theo was locked in a windowless cell measuring five foot by eight foot and strip-searched. This included a policeman getting out a latex glove and telling him to bend over. He was then moved to another cell, by which time, deprived of whisky, cigarettes and morphine, he was crawling up the walls. Every so often, officers lifted the flap in the door to look at him.

He realized he had entered the twisted world of the morally repulsive when he saw the stony contempt on the faces of the two interrogating officers, one man, one woman, who obviously wanted to find out if he were part of a wider paedophile ring.

'I'm innocent.'

'Those photographs and that DVD weren't innocent, sir.'

'They were planted. Look, I need to make a telephone call, I'm worried about my cat.'

'Cat's least of your worries, sir.'

The policewoman clearly found him distasteful. He'd grabbed a maroon polo neck knitted for him by an aunt, but was still in his shorts, knees continually knocking together. Stinking of booze, fags and sweat, grey stubble thickening, he must cut a repugnant figure. They had removed his shoelaces and his belt, so his shorts kept falling down.

As the night wore on, they kept trying to make him confess.

'I'm innocent, I never laid a finger on the boy.'

'What about those nude photographs?'

'Never saw them before in my life; you won't find any of my fingerprints; must have been taken years ago – Paris has got a completely different haircut.'

'And the images of an obscene nature on the DVD machine?'

'The sixth form gave it to me as a Christmas present. I can't work the damn thing.'

'And the poems?'

'Certainly, I wrote those.' Theo groaned; his back was excruciating. 'Nothing obscene about them. I've been framed.'

'They all say that. You're in denial, Theo. Admit your guilt, you'll feel so much better. Then you can be put on a course for sex offenders.'

'And never teach again.'

'You were carried away, you'd had a bit too much to drink. Do you always entertain young boys alone? D'you sit close to them? D'you always make a habit of going into their rooms at night?'

Sadness overwhelmed Theo. Paris must have shopped him.

'If you confess,' the policewoman was now saying cosily, 'you might easily get off. Crown won't want a lengthy trial; happens a lot.'

The only reason he might confess, thought Theo, as the sky turned from electric blue to the rose pink of sunrise, was to get some more morphine.

In the morning, he came up before the magistrates and was given police bail, on condition that he didn't get in touch with anyone from the school.

'You must not speak to any members of staff,' he was told, 'or discuss the incident with anyone. You're to have no contact with the boy or any of the pupils.

904

You must give an address well away from the school.'

Theo gave them the name of a dilapidated cottage on Windermere, left him by the aunt who'd knitted the maroon polo neck.

The case would now be adjourned for a pre-judicial review, which might take three weeks. Theo would come up in court three weeks after that. If the magistrates decided there was a case, it would be tried in a Crown court, probably not before Christmas.

Outside the court, Theo found Biffo, who had been selected by Alex as a safe bet to pack up his belongings. Biffo had also driven over in Theo's ancient Golf, which was loaded up with books, clothes, bottles of pills. He had also packed Theo's credit cards and cheque books, the seven plays of Sophocles, the manuscript in progress and Theo's notebooks.

'Where's my cat?' demanded Theo.

'I couldn't find him.' Biffo couldn't meet his eyes. 'All the police cars and disturbance must have scared him.'

'You must find him!' Theo was nearly in tears. 'I've had him since he was a kitten.'

'You often left him in the summer holidays.'

Biffo, Theo felt, at last had a legitimate excuse for detesting him.

'You've got to help me, Biffo, I must talk to Paris and Hengist.'

'You can't talk to anyone. Hengist is still away, anyway. You can ring me, here's my number, but only about things unconnected with the case.'

'I'm not resigning, I'm innocent.'

'I can't discuss it.'

Theo gave Biffo the address and telephone number of his cottage in Windermere. 'At least give it to Artie.'

'I can't promise anything. I've filled your car up with petrol.'

'Please try and find Hindsight, I'll pay for someone to come and collect him.'

Theo was still missing when Paris returned from his history exam. Barging into his housemaster's sealed-off study, he found whole shelves of books and Theo's manuscript gone, and Biffo nosing around.

'Is Theo back?'

'Gone away.'

'Where?'

'I'm not at liberty to say.'

'Don't be fucking stupid. I need to phone him. He never said goodbye; what's he supposed to have done?' Paris was nearly hysterical, particularly when Hindsight jumped in through the window and, mewing piteously, started weaving round his legs. 'Theo must have been pushed; he'd never leave without Hindsight. Tell me.'

Biffo backed away as, from a miniature Greek urn on Theo's desk, Paris grabbed a pair of scissors.

'I'll have those,' said Dora, grabbing the scissors as she marched in with a plate of cod from the kitchens and the *Larkminster Gazette*, which she handed to Paris.

'Page three,' she added as she started to cut up the cod for Hindsight.

'Bagley master arrested over sex abuse claim', Paris read the headline, then, with dawning disbelief, the copy: 'Theo Graham, aged 59, a housemaster who frequently took groups of boys on trips to Ancient Greece, was arrested last night for harbouring images of an obscene nature, but was released on police bail this morning.'

Paris turned on Dora. 'You didn't flog this story?'

'Certainly not. Poor Mr Graham's been victimcised.'

'Who's he supposed to have jumped on?'

'Why, you, of course.'

The temperature had dropped; a mean east wind was systematically stripping the petals off Sally's shrub roses. The A' Level candidates were still wrestling with law and French papers and police cars were parked outside the Mansion when Hengist finally got back to Bagley.

Marching into Alex's office, he found his deputy head in a high state of almost sexual excitement, forehead white, eyes gleaming more than the gold rims of his spectacles, whole body shivering with self-righteous disapproval, damp patches under the arms of his shirt, whose sleeves were held up by frightful garters.

'What the hell's going on?'

'Very grave news, S.T.L. Theo Graham's been arrested.'

'Whatever for?'

'Sexually abusing Paris Alvaston.'

'Don't be ridiculous, Theo'd never jeopardize a boy's exams like that.'

'His baser nature overcame him,' said Alex heavily.

'Is Paris OK?' demanded Hengist. 'Did he take his history paper?' Then realizing how self-interested that sounded: 'What's he got to say?'

'He became hysterical and leapt at both Biffo and the policeman when asked the simplest question, which pre-supposes . . .'

'Bloody nothing,' roared Hengist.

'Theo entered Paris's room last night. Bloodcurdling screams were followed by desperate sobbing.'

'Probably a nightmare. Too much *Macbeth*, or mugging up Stalin's purges and the death camps, for Christ's sake. The boy's always been highly strung. Who reported this?'

'One of his peers, Cosmo Rannaldini.'

'Whoever believed a word Cosmo says?' said Hengist contemptuously. 'He'll have rung up the *Scorpion* by now.'

'I think not.' Alex put steepled fingers to pursed lips. 'Concerned for a fellow student, Cosmo behaved caringly and approached me late last night. I phoned the police instantly. They arrested Theo in the early hours.'

907

'For Christ's sake, Alex, why didn't you talk to Theo or ring me?'

'Your mobile was switched off. I consulted with Biffo, Joan and the bursar who, as the foster father, was very concerned.'

'You always wanted Theo out because he resisted your bloody modernizing.'

'We are accountable for our students' safety. In Theo's drawers were found naked photographs of Paris' – let Hengist think the police discovered them – 'poems dedicated to Paris of a homo-erotic nature and an obscene DVD of child pornography.'

Hengist looked out of the window at a blackbird splashing in the bird bath: such an innocent joyful pleasure. He felt a great sadness and said with less certainty, 'Theo's been framed.'

'I'm sorry, S.T.L.' Alex pinched the bridge of his nose. 'I know you were fond of the old boy. I was fond of him too. The whole thing has been most distressing.'

And you want me to feel sorry for you, thought Hengist.

'When did Paris find out?'

'We didn't apprize him this morning. I didn't want to stress him before a science paper.'

'Your subject, natch,' snarled Hengist. He wanted to hurl Alex to his death through the window.

'By lunchtime, Paris was searching for Theo. Rumours were circulating. The story had broken on Radio Larkminster. So Poppet broke the news to Paris, saying Mr Graham was helping the police with their enquiries.'

'Poppet? How did Paris take that?'

'Hard to tell, he never says much.'

'Jesus, if he's screwed up history, deputy heads will roll. I'm telling you, Alex, it's a set-up. Cosmo was clearly jealous of Theo's closeness to Paris.'

'Even if Paris does deny everything,' said Alex smugly, 'the photos and the pornography are enough to suspend him. I emailed the parents first thing. Better they knew before it hit the press. I've already received several back, and many supportive phone calls.' Alex handed Hengist a sheaf of paper. On top was a fax from Randal Stancombe: 'Hope that bloody nonce goes down and gets the thrashing he deserves. He's always sidelined my Jade.'

The second came from Boffin's mother: 'I don't want my Bernard at risk.'

'With an arse that size, he'd hardly be in jeopardy,' said Hengist contemptuously.

'That was uncalled for. I've arranged for Jason Fenton, who knows a little Latin, to take Theo's classes. Fortunately, the classics don't attract many students. Goodness knows who's going to write Theo's reports.'

Alex paused as Miss Painswick, who'd never been berserk about Theo either, rushed in in a state of high excitement.

'Oh, you're back, headmaster. Thank God, there are so many messages.' Then, turning to Alex: 'The police want to talk to you, Mr Bruce, and afterwards, the press would like a word.'

Quivering with self-importance, Alex bustled off.

'The *TES* want that piece on the advantages of the baccalaureate by tomorrow,' Painswick added to Hengist.

Finding the general office empty, Hengist unlocked the safe and took the GCSE history papers, which had just been handed in, upstairs to his office and groaned when he saw Paris's booklet. The boy had scrawled his name: Alvaston, Paris; his candidate number; and signed his name at the bottom. The rest was gibberish, the work of a fast unravelling mind. What did they expect with yet another father figure snatched from him?

Hengist was demented; his great scheme fucked. He turned to Boffin's booklet. In his greed to get at the paper, the little beast had forgotten to put his name at the top, only his candidate number which ended with a three which could easily be curved and billowed out into an eight.

Hengist glanced through the questions.

'The main reason for the collapse of the provisional Government in 1917 was the work of Lenin and the Bolsheviks. Discuss.'

That was a doddle.

'Do you agree that the increased Nazi support in the period 1930–32 was due to the personal appeal of Hitler?'

Hengist suddenly had a better plan. Picking up the telephone, he rang Painswick.

'I better get shot of that TES piece before anything else blows up, Miss P. Won't take more than an hour. I don't want to be disturbed.'

Alex was relishing his interview.

'Mr Graham was a scholar of the old school, officer. He had that rather Greek thing of cultivating friendships with boys, never girls, and insisted on working one to one with vulnerable youngsters like Paris Alvaston. He liked to flout convention.

'Believing in transparency, officer, I installed glass panels in classroom doors so one could monitor practice. Theo Graham deliberately hung his coat over the panel. He could be very subversive.'

An hour later, Hengist was just deciding how best to handle the Theo debacle when his office door was pushed open and Elaine flew in, throwing herself on him, chattering her teeth in delight, circling and sending all the urgent messages flying. She was followed by Sally, who'd clearly been crying.

'Darling, why didn't you tell me you were back? This is so terrible.' Quickly she kissed Hengist. 'Thank God you're here. Poor Theo could never have done this. We've got to rescue him.'

'I'm just off to nail Alex, come with me.'

In Alex's office, they found Poppet dropping some herbal painkiller made from drops of valerian into a glass of water, which Alex gulped down noisily, his Adam's apple heaving. Hengist couldn't bear to look at him and went to the window, from which he could see pupils, aware of some great crisis, milling about, talking, glancing worriedly up, then looking away.

'What did the police say?'

'They're taking it very seriously.'

'So am I. They've hijacked my best teacher,' snapped Hengist.

'And granted him bail,' said Poppet, who was now massaging her husband's shoulders. Alex closed his eyes.

On a side table, copies of *A Guide to Red Tape* rose to the ceiling.

'I've signed you a copy, S.T.L.'

Then, when Hengist didn't answer, Poppet said accusingly, 'Alex didn't get any sleep last night.'

'Didn't bloody deserve to.'

'Alex has a duty of care for young people,' reproached Poppet.

'Theo's name should never have been released to the media before there was any proof of guilt,' said Sally furiously. 'Why couldn't it have been dealt with internally, Alex?'

'Things are so much better handled in the maintained system,' piped up Poppet. 'Theo could have sought help from the union. We could have called an emergency meeting of the governors. The union rep would have then rolled up with the offending member.'

'If they can persuade the offending member to withdraw,' added Alex – for a second Hengist's eyes met Sally's – 'i.e. resign at once, things can be hushed up.'

'Why should Theo resign?' shouted Sally. 'He's innocent.'

Theo drove north until he found a church that was open, such was his need of sanctuary. How would he cope without James Benson's morphine? But the pain in his heart was far crueller.

Gasping for breath, he collapsed in a front pew, resting for a long time . . . When he looked down, he saw a pool of tears on the stone floor of the church.

Over at Larks, insulated against the outside world, the Brigadier and Emlyn heaved sighs of relief to find the history paper had included a question about the number of people killed on the Somme.

'On the other hand,' said Emlyn, 'Rocky's just informed me he was so pleased he remembered to tell the examiner we'd never have won World War I if Hitler hadn't attacked the Russians. How d'you get on?' he asked Feral.

'Bad as usual.' Feral shot outside to join his friends, who, euphoric the last exam was over, were playing football. Partner raced about yapping encouragement, particularly to Feral, who seemed to have wings on his heels. No one could stop him as he found goal again and again.

But what was the use? I'm thick, thick, thick, he told himself as he psyched himself up to ring his mother to let her know he'd screwed up yet again.

Pete Wainwright had just rolled up with a crate of wine to say thank you for the suggestions Taggie and her class had put forward for the Rovers' next season's menus. Bottles were therefore being opened in the staffroom to celebrate the end of the GCSEs when Emlyn walked in looking wintry.

'Afraid I can't stay.'

'Whyever not?' asked the Brigadier, who was mixing a pink gin for Lily.

'I've got to go over to Bagley. Artie's just phoned.

Theo was arrested last night for possession of child porn and sexual abuse.'

'Paris?' whispered Janna.

'So it seems.'

'I don't believe it.'

Oh God, she thought, we should never have let him go to Bagley.

113

The last exam at Larks was followed two nights later by the end-of-term prom. Janna and her staff had such a frantic scramble getting everything ready that they had scant time to agonize about Paris and Theo – particularly as they were full of their own regrets that the year of grace was almost over.

Lily spent the day of the prom at home making sausage rolls and mushroom vol-au-vents for the buffet supper and trying not to cry. She was going to miss her Larks friends horribly, particularly seeing so much of the Brigadier. They'd planned a dance routine of Fred Astaire songs as a cabaret. Christian, rather smug he could still fit into them, was going to wear tails, and Lily had been forced to sell a last piece of Georgian silver to pay for a blue silk ball dress and pretty silver shoes in which to perform. Her cottage was achieving fashionable minimalism faster than she would have liked.

Lily was nervous of making an idiot of herself. If she drank enough to give herself courage she'd probably fall over. One of the numbers was 'Stepping Out with My Baby', and how could she pass as a 'baby' when she was over eighty with hair drawn into a dreary bun? If only she could afford to go back to Sadie, her darling Larkminster hairdresser, who'd cut her hair so beautifully.

As she packed bottles of elderberry wine into a

cardboard box, she wondered who would feed the birds at Larks or the silver carp gliding, like Concorde, through the pond. She mustn't cry. Weeping at her age so devastated one's face. Sometimes she thought Christian loved her, but she was terrified her bridge might dislodge if he kissed her, leaving a great red toothless gap, and her body undressed was not a pretty sight, and with her too-long grey hair down, she looked like a witch.

Despite being poor, Lily had never stinted on General, who, too fat for the cat door, was mewing to go out. Wiping her eyes with a drying-up cloth, she opened the front door to find Pearl on the doorstep, weighed down by make-up kit.

'You've been so kind to me Lily, I fort I'd give you a make-over.' Then, at Lily's look of alarm: 'You've got such pretty hair, I'd love to cut it, and there's a new blue rinse called Sapphire Siren to bring out your blue eyes.'

'It's very kind. I'm not sure.'

'You'll look great.' Pearl marched into the house, dumping her cases in the kitchen. 'You've got such lovely skin. Christian says you're wearing blue tonight for the cabaret.'

'It's a secret,' squeaked Lily. 'We may not do it, depends how the evening pans out.'

'Everyone's looking forward to it,' said Pearl. As she unpacked her bottles, six tenners from the Brigadier crackled comfortingly in her breast pocket.

'I think I'll cut your hair before I wash it. Have you heard about Paris? Do you think Mr Graham's really been giving him it up the bum?'

'I'm sure not,' said Lily faintly.

'I often wondered whether Paris wasn't a woofter. Never made a pass at me,' said Pearl.

The rest of the staff kept trying to send Janna home early to make herself beautiful. Twenty years wouldn't be enough, she thought wearily; she'd need her jaw wired up in a permanent smile to get her through the evening.

She had been trying to complete the children's year books and certificates of achievement, when Sally had popped in with 'a bit of blotting paper': namely a mountain of smoked salmon wrapped in cling film and 'some nice white wine for you and Emlyn to drink behind the bus shelter'.

Janna thanked her profusely and, thinking for the first time Sally looked her age, begged her to stop for a cup of tea.

'My dear, I'd have loved to – look how well those oriental poppies are doing – but we're all in a bit of a state over Theo and Paris. Paris hurled a brick through Alex's window last night, because no one will give him Theo's address. Emlyn's been wonderful with him, but the poor boy's hysterical, says he'll only talk to the police if he's allowed to talk to Theo first, which the police say is impossible. Nadine and Cindy Payne are putting their oars in; press everywhere.'

The sympathy in Janna's eyes prompted Sally to further revelations. 'Emlyn's also had a bit of a shock, poor boy. Oriana's expecting a baby – I'm not sure who the father is – due in November.' For a second Sally's face crumpled. 'I'm sure I'll love it once it's born, but Hengist doesn't want anything to do with it or Oriana. He's terribly cut up about Theo. Oh Janna, I do hope you don't feel we've failed Paris.'

Janna was reassuring Sally she didn't and was kissing her goodbye when Randal Stancombe came on the line. God, how she now hated his oily, over-intimate, threatening voice.

'Hi, Jan, can I be frank? Feel rather let down; I didn't get an invite for tonight's end-of-term do. Didn't think our friendship was that shallow.'

'Oh, it isn't, it isn't.' Janna curled up in embarrassment. 'It's only small, just staff and children.'

'Don't weaken,' mouthed Rowan from the doorway.

'But do drop in,' mumbled Janna.

'I'm actually taking Jade out for a meal, but we'll look in on the way. You asked any media?'

'No. Doesn't mean the bastards won't turn up.'

'Gosh, you're brave,' said Bianca, 'I should so die of embarrassment if Mummy was tempted onto the dance floor.'

'Unlikely,' said Xav as he tied his black tie. 'Dad's ordered me to shoot anyone who comes near her.'

He was delighted that the waistband of his DJ trousers had had to be taken in six inches and the legs let down.

Downstairs, Rupert helped his wife, ravishing in a scarlet halterneck, load chocolate torte and bowls of strawberries into the car.

'Keep an eye on her,' he said to Xav. 'You both look marvellous.'

He wouldn't have admitted to a soul, that he couldn't wait to get back and finish *Emma*. Mrs Elton was even more like Anthea Belvedon than Mrs Bennet.

'I'll be down in a minute, pour yourself a drink,' Lily shouted down the stairs as Christian Woodford put the elderberry wine, the crumbles and the sausage rolls into the car.

The Brigadier choked on his drink as Lily came down the stairs. Her short silver-blue hair softly caressed her cheekbones, brought out the intense blue of her eyes and matched a dress short enough to reveal the most charming ankles. She had pawned all her jewellery except her sapphire engagement ring and her pearls, which she asked him to do up.

' "My precious Lily! My imperial kitten!" ' sighed the Brigadier, letting his fingers linger on her neck.

With his white tie and tails setting off his golfing tan, his fine square features and his thick silver hair, the

Brigadier looked infinitely handsomer than Fred Astaire and Lily told him so.

'Could you also zip up my dress, which is beyond my arthritic fingers?'

'Much rather unhook it,' said the Brigadier, who had this afternoon signed a two-year Venturer contract to make another series of *Buffers*, along with some poetry drama documentaries kicking off with 'Horatius' and 'Morte d'Arthur'.

' "Steppin' Out With My Baby",' sang the Brigadier, smiling at Lily as they reached the outskirts of Larkminster. For a moment, he thought he was back in the last war, as, like submarines gliding stealthily through the blue evening, stretch limos with black windows kept overtaking them. Then out of these limos onto the Appletree forecourt, like a conjuror's coloured handkerchief, spilled the children, the boys in hired tuxedos with red, blue, green and tartan bow ties, the girls in pink or mauve satin trouser suits or ball dresses showing off pearly shoulders and pretty legs, enhanced by jewelled high heels and sparkling ankle bracelets.

With their hair descending in ringleted waterfalls and secured with combs decorated with flowers, their faces glittering with excitement, they could have been re-enacting the Netherfield ball from their set book. Intoxicated by their new beauty, they tore around Appletree, taking photographs, shrieking how wicked each other looked. Judging by the giggling, they'd already been at the booze.

The boys were fingering the Brigadier's tailcoat.

'That retro shawl collar's dead cool, Brig, did you get it from Matalan or the internet?'

'It's my own,' confessed Christian, 'I used to wear it night after night to dances. I like your gym shoes, Graffi.'

'Fort I'd treat myself.' Graffi waved a dark blue and pale blue trainer with a two-inch heel in the air. 'They cost a hundred and ten quid. What d'you think of Beckham's new hair?'

'Not as good as mine,' said Rocky, patting four-inch-high vermilion-gelled spikes. 'And you look even gooder, Lily.'

As the others laughed and agreed, Lily told them they all looked wonderful too.

The hall had been utterly transformed. Mags had blocked out any light from the big windows with full-length black curtains, which she and the other teachers had covered in silver and gold paper stars. On the stage below a huge glittering blue sign saying 'Larkminster High School Prom 2004', a group of suntanned men in black, known as the Butchers (as in 'I'm butcher than you'), were belting out 'American Pie'.

From the ceiling, concealing Graffi's angels, who all looked like Milly Walton, hung hundreds of coloured balloons like an inverted bubble bath. The floor was carpeted with dancers, gyrating under the flickering lights, clapping their hands above their heads. Many of the boys wore luminous rings in blue, emerald or red round foreheads or necks. The air was a dense fog of cigarette smoke.

Chairs for spectators had been grouped along one wall on either side of a trestle table, offering Coca-Cola, lemonade and Fanta. Officially, because Ashton or Cindy might gatecrash, the evening was dry.

I could murder a proper drink, thought Lily.

As if reading her mind, Janna glided out of the dancers. She had at long last had a chance to wear her slinky black velvet dress, off one freckled shoulder and split to the thigh on one side. With the front of her hair coaxed upward in smaller russet spikes than Rocky's, her huge eyes ringed with raw sienna, her big trembling mouth painted scarlet, she looked as young suddenly as any of her pupils.

'You look stunning! Isn't Pearl a genius,' she and Lily shouted to each other over 'American Pie'.

919

'Keep this for yourself,' added Janna, filling a glass with Sally's white, then handing bottle and glass to Lily.

'What's that?' Lily noticed Janna was drinking straight from a Fanta bottle.

'Teachers' lemonade, taught me by a primary head. No one can tell it's half filled with vodka. Will you crown the Prom King and Queen for us?'

'As long as I don't have to make a speech. Who's won it?'

'Wait and see. But it's a grand result.'

Next moment Pearl had rushed up.

'I want a group photograph of my favourite teachers,' she said bossily. 'That's you, Pittsy, you, Janna, you, Taggie and the Brig and Lily.'

Flattered, the five lined up as Pearl spent ages getting them in the right position. 'You go behind Janna, Taggie, and Lily in front of Pittsy, or we can't see you. Where's Emlyn? I'd like him as well.'

'Oh, get on,' grumbled the Brigadier, 'Lily and Taggie need top-ups.'

Dutifully they all waited as Pearl peered into her viewfinder, then, suddenly saying: 'Oh, I'm bored with this,' she wandered off to photograph someone else.

'Little madam,' exploded the Brigadier as Janna and Lily got the giggles.

'It's the first time I've seen Aysha's hair in four years. She looks absolutely gorgeous,' said Pittsy as Aysha timidly followed Xav onto the floor to join the big circle of dancers.

Aysha had only been allowed to attend the prom if she was chaperoned. As a result, Mrs Khan sat in the darkness watching her daughter, knowing how sad Aysha would be tomorrow. At least tonight, as she swayed in flowing turquoise chiffon before Xav, she could forget her heartache.

'Get Mother Khan some teachers' lemonade,' suggested Wally.

'Where's Emlyn?' asked Janna for the hundredth time.

'He was here shifting furniture until the last moment,' said Cambola, who kept dragging boys onto the floor to dance; they lasted thirty seconds before belting back to their mates.

Outside, the sky was pale grey, the lace mats of elder-flower caressing the window panes. Thinking Basket looked rather fetching in her tobacco-brown crimplene, Skunk led her off for a stroll.

They were passed as they went out by Feral wandering in, late because he'd been playing football. Unable to afford a tuxedo, he still looked a million dollars in black jeans and polo neck.

' "Here's mettle more attractive",' cried Cambola, bearing him off to dance to loud cheers.

114

Janna was dancing with the children again, singing along to Katie Melua as she rotated two pink luminous flowers above her head, surrendering herself to the music.

'One forgets how young she is,' Lily murmured to the Brigadier, adding doubtfully, 'You don't think our cabaret's too old for them?'

The Brigadier squeezed her hand.

'To use a mendacious expression of Randal Stancombe's: "Trust me."'

'Talk of the devil,' complained Lily as Randal, resplendent in a dinner jacket, pink carnation in his buttonhole, appeared in the doorway.

I'd like to be his arm candy, thought Kitten, running her hand through her hair and sticking out her breasts. Oh hell, he'd brought a woman. No, it was that bitch Jade.

Graffi, drunk and furious with Stancombe for sacking his father, reeled over and handed him his glass, which Stancombe was about to drink out of, then realized it was empty.

'Get me a Bacardi and Coke,' Graffi ordered him airily, then, at Stancombe's look of fury: 'Oh, I fort you was a waiter.'

'Graffi!' Anticipating punch-ups, Janna ran off the dance floor. 'Hello, Randal, let me get you a drink.'

'Evening, Janna, looks as if you're enjoying yourself.' Stancombe then dragged her into the corridor, pointing to walls on which Graffi had caricatured every child in the school. 'Made a bit of a mess of the property.'

'Nothing a lick of paint won't cure,' answered Janna defensively. 'One day, Graffi's murals'll be worth more than this place put together.'

'Your geese are always swans,' sneered Stancombe.

Suddenly photographers seemed to be everywhere.

'Go away, this is a private party,' Janna told them furiously.

'Just a few piccies,' insisted Stancombe, 'with the kids beside the minibus,' which had suddenly appeared, parked in the forecourt.

'I can't drag them off the dance floor.'

Jade, Kitten and Pearl were insincerely congratulating each other on their dresses. Jade in Versace was miffed they were looking so good. She was used to being the belle of the ball. Feral, Graffi, Johnnie, Danny the Irish, even Xav, all looked gorgeous. Why weren't any of them asking her to dance?

'Come and dance,' Rocky asked her a minute later.

'Thanks, but I'm not stopping. Daddy's about to make a statement to the press,' answered Jade as the music died away.

'As one who has enriched these youngsters' lives,' Stancombe told the reporters, 'I've been haunted by the statistics that it's six times as difficult for kids from poor homes to go to uni.'

'You did it without a degree, Mr Stancombe,' said a blonde from the *Scorpion* admiringly.

'I was lucky,' admitted Stancombe modestly. 'I only hope my not insubstantial financial contribution to Larks High has paid off and the students get some good grades.'

'Oh, shut up,' muttered Janna.

'Can we have a photograph of you dancing with the kids?' asked the *Gazette.*

'You'd better do it,' Janna urged the children, as the band started up again, 'then he'll push off.'

Stancombe, however, had turned back to Janna.

'Terrible news about Theo Graham. I'd castrate all paedophiles.'

'Hengist is convinced he's innocent.'

Stancombe was about to argue, when he noticed Xav, euphoric after another dance with Aysha, bopping off the floor and demanded, 'How did your dad get on in his Eng. lit. exam?'

'Very well,' replied Xav coldly, then as Stancombe's eyebrows shot up, 'my dad does everything well. He's got a horse running on Saturday called Poodle. I'd have a big bet if I were you. It's the only way you'll pay the money you owe the Bagley Fund when the results come out.'

Scenting trouble, it was Xav's mother this time who rushed over.

'Ah, the lovely Taggie – a quick dance?' Randal seized her hand.

'I don't think so.' Xav stepped in front of his mother, scowling up at Stancombe. 'My father asked me to look after Mum – he wouldn't like it one bit if she danced with you.'

Stancombe, who now much regretted leaving his guards behind, said furiously:

'I can only assume you've been drinking.'

'I don't drink,' said Xav.

'I'll get even with you and your arrogant bastard of a father.' Hurrying Jade towards the door, Stancombe went slap into Emlyn.

'I was just saying,' he yelled over the band, 'Theo Graham ought to be castrated and not allowed near vulnerable youngsters.'

'Get out,' growled Emlyn, holding open the door.

Jade suddenly longed to stay. As she watched Xav rushing back to Aysha, she decided he'd become very attractive, not least in the way he'd stood up to her father. She'd love to join the great ring of dancers. She wished she had friends like that. It was all her parents' fault for not sending her to a comprehensive.

'Come on, princess,' shouted Randal.

'You OK?' Janna asked Emlyn, noticing how tired he looked, but his answer was blotted out by a roll of drums. It was time for the awards.

'At least it might mean the music is a bit less loud,' the Brigadier murmured to Lily.

Janna grabbed the mike and announced she was now going to give each pupil his or her year book and certificate of achievement.

'I'd rather have some money,' shouted Rocky to roars of applause, which continued as each child went up and Emlyn took photograph after photograph, because everyone wanted a record of themselves beside Janna.

When it was Johnnie's turn, he grabbed Janna, kissing her on and on to whoops and catcalls until Emlyn tapped him sharply on the shoulder: 'That's enough.'

'Your turn now, Mr Davies,' chorused the children, screaming with laughter as Emlyn handed a blushing Janna his handkerchief to wipe off her smudged lipstick.

Who would have dreamt a year ago, I could have had a ball at a ball without a drop of booze? thought Pittsy.

Janna then thanked all the children for making the year so memorable and rewarding.

'I'd also like to say on behalf of all the weird staff who came to teach you, that we've never had it so good.'

'Hear, hear,' shouted Skunk, squeezing Basket's spare tyres.

'And I'd like to thank all the teachers, wondercooks' – Janna smiled at Taggie – 'terrific dinner ladies, Rowan and, most of all, Wally, who's taken care of us all, and made this evening possible.'

'Don't forget Mistah Davies,' shouted Graffi.

'And of course, Emlyn, thank you all.'

Pittsy then seized the mike and admitted:

'In twenty-nine years of teaching, this is the best year I've ever had because of that woman over there.' He pointed to Janna, to deafening applause. 'She's the best boss I've ever had—' His voice cracked. 'She's been dead good.'

Are they talking about me, wondered Janna in bewilderment, particularly when a big screen to the right of the band lit up and there was Kylie, clutching her new baby and singing: 'To Miss . . .' instead of 'To Sir, With Love'.

'Oh hell,' grumbled Pearl. 'There goes my make-up again,' as Janna's tears swept away a flotsam of mascara and glitter, particularly when Kitten curtsied and presented her with a gold pen engraved 'To a great head'.

'Thank you ever so much and I'll write to you all with this pen.' Janna mopped her eyes with Emlyn's hand-kerchief. Then, desperate to get the praise onto someone else: 'And now Lily is going to crown the Prom King and Queen, voted by their peers.'

'I first have to read the citations,' said Lily, putting on her spectacles and joining Janna in the middle of the floor.

' "We thought you was very snooty when you joined Larks," ' she read, ' "but we realized you was just shy and now you're a good friend to all of us." Very nice too.' Opening the envelope: 'And our Prom Queen is none other than Aysha Khan.'

Aysha gasped and clapped her hands over her eyes: 'I don't believe it.'

As Xav proudly led her up, Mrs Khan stood up and cheered, then shushed herself in horror. Lily placed a gold cardboard crown, inset with red, blue and green jewels, on Aysha's dark head, and the room erupted.

'She looks absolutely gorgeous,' sighed Pittsy.

'She certainly does,' agreed a grinning Xav as he slid back into the crowd, but not for long, as Lily read out the next citation.

'"We was worried when you came to us, but you mixed in really well, and you was never posh."' Hands trembling with excitement, Lily ripped open the envelope. 'And the Prom King is Xavier Campbell-Black.'

More deafening roars of applause followed as Lily had difficulty getting the crown over Xav's Afro.

'Thank you so much,' shouted Xav, 'I can't believe this.'

'Nor can we,' yelled Graffi. 'Never had a poof on the frone since James I.'

'Give your queen a kiss,' shouted Pearl, and Xav turned and kissed Aysha on the lips for the first time since Ramadan, and Aysha, after a terrified glance at her tearful, ecstatic mother, who had nearly finished her bottle of teachers' lemonade, kissed Xav back to a thunder of stamped feet.

'Look at Taggie,' whispered Lily as Xav's mother wiped her eyes with her crimson pashmina.

Xav and Aysha reopened the ball, never taking their eyes off each other. A second later, Emlyn led a laughing, protesting Taggie onto the floor.

'It's so refreshing,' beamed Mrs Khan as Janna replaced her Fanta bottle.

Supper followed and the starving hordes fell on tuna and cucumber sandwiches, bridge rolls filled with egg mayonnaise, Lily's sausage rolls and vol-au-vents, Sally's smoked salmon sandwiches, strawberries, blackberry crumbles and chocolate torte.

The girls were back on the floor dancing together, flashing lights picking up glossy tossing curls and gleaming bare shoulders. Janna was among them, swaying like a maenad, waving a glittering blue butterfly in figures of eight.

Why haven't I asked her to dance? wondered Emlyn. What am I afraid of?

Out in the limos, groups were drinking Cava and smoking weed. Others were signing each other's T-shirts, certificates and year books. There was a second roll of drums. 'It's now time for your cabaret,' shouted the lead singer, 'performed by Brigadier Christian Woodford and Mrs Lily Hamilton.'

Clapping and whooping, the dancers retreated to be joined round the edge of the floor by others running in from the cars.

Lily fled to the Ladies, shaking with terror. If only she'd had a little more to drink. Pearl was waiting when she came out of the loo.

'Just let me fix your face.'

Getting out a brush, she added blusher to Lily's blanched cheeks, used another brush to repaint her trembling lips and another to fluff up her hair, before spraying on some rather bold scent.

'You look great, Lily. Let's hide that bra strap, and straighten your dress, off you go. Good luck.'

The children had begun to stamp their feet and slow handclap. Christian, waiting with a mike in his hand, was looking anxious, but his smile was beautiful, even when Lily muttered, 'You got me into this bloody thing,' as he led her onto the floor.

'Doo di doo, doo di doo di, doo di . . .' sang the Brigadier in a delightful baritone, then, brandishing both mike and a large green umbrella, launched into 'Singing in the Rain', ending up with a little tap dance round Lily, before sweeping her into 'Stepping Out With My Baby'.

For a second, Lily stumbled; the Brigadier held her tightly and they were off. It was such a beautiful tune.

After that Lily was fine. In no time, Christian was singing 'Cheek To Cheek', as with faces pressed together, they glided round the floor.

Lily would never in a thousand years have accused

the Brigadier of showing off, but she was not displeased when he too stumbled, and this time it was she who had to hold him up.

The pupils, utterly entranced, bellowed their approval.

'Good on yer, Brig. Wicked, Lily. Come on, Fred and Ginger, give us an encore.'

'I'm out,' said Lily firmly, so the Brigadier, gazing into her eyes, sang 'Our Love Is Here To Stay'.

Seizing Basket's hand, Skunk stole off into the moonlight.

'I love you, Xav,' whispered Aysha.

'Hic,' said Mrs Khan.

How much longer can I go on staying cheerful, wondered Feral as, in the middle of the floor, the Brigadier beamed down at Lily.

'Oh, cut to the chase, Brig,' shouted Graffi, 'you know you love her.'

'I believe I do,' said Christian, kissing Lily on the forehead.

As the band broke into 'YMCA', the hall filled up again. Monster was dancing with Mrs Khan, Rowan with Pittsy, Wally with Janna, Sophy with Graffi, and Rocky with Gloria.

Aware that his wits might be needed if fights broke out, Emlyn, unlike Mrs Khan, had stayed off the drink. Watching the high jinks on the floor, he thought: They're all so pixillated by the transformation of the school and themselves, they've forgotten the dark to come.

Tonight for him had been a cut-off point. Before, despite everything, he'd had the faint hope that Oriana might realize Charlie was a dreadful mistake. Now she was pregnant, it was over.

' "You're The One That I Want",' sang the bronzed lead singer.

115

It was the last dance; Johnnie hand in hand with Kitten, Pearl with Graffi, Feral with Janna, Danny with Danijela, all formed a great circle. The dope-smokers, who'd got the munchies and been raiding the buffet, came racing onto the floor, sandwiches in their hands, as the balloons came down. Yellow, emerald, blue, pink, scarlet and orange, a technicolour snowstorm cascaded into the flickering lights until the ground was one great technicolour bubble bath.

Then the boys waded in, as if this was what their huge trainers had been awaiting all evening, symbolically stamping on the balloons, bang, bang, bang, followed by the girls leaping in with their stilettos, pop, pop, pop, as though war had broken out.

Instinctively, Janna had dropped Feral and Graffi's hands looking round for the tranquillizers for Partner, then remembered he was safe at home.

'Summer Days' sang the band, as dancing went on over an ocean of shredded rubber. Some of the balloons had been saved. Kitten had six, Danijela had one and burst into tears when Rocky popped it with a cigarette. Feral kept back an orange one, in case Bianca was in the car collecting Xav.

It was stiflingly hot in the smoke-filled hall. Everyone was glad to surge out into the cool of the night.

A glittering full moon, like a halo searching for its

lost saint, clearly felt upstaged by the splendid explosion of fireworks which followed. Golden fountains overflowed, surging silver snakes belched forth great flurries of blue sparks, rose-pink Roman candles and hissing orange Chinese dragons were followed by a series of colossal bangs, producing screams from the spectators.

Bounding round, setting alight Catherine wheels, avoiding squibs, launching off rockets, Emlyn was glad he'd stayed sober, particularly when Rocky lurched forward.

'Want to light a rocket, want to light a rocket,' and fell flat on his face, lit cigarette narrowly missing the remaining fireworks in the box.

Heaving him up, Emlyn allowed him to light one, which, with a sound like Velcro being ripped apart, soared gloriously upwards, before tossing its emerald and royal blue stars over the Shakespeare Estate.

At the end, more blazing white-hot stars spelt out the words 'Goodbye Larks High', then faded, bringing everyone back to reality with a bump.

Suddenly Mags was reassuring sobbing pupils: 'This school is a launching pad not a crashing down to earth.'

As Pearl in her pretty periwinkle-blue dress wept on her shoulder, Janna could feel her desperate thinness.

'I'm going to miss you, miss.'

Janna was quickly drenched as child after tearful child came up.

'Thank you, miss, for everything.'

'You're the bravest girl I know.' Mags was comforting an inconsolable Aysha.

Cambola, clinging to her trumpet, was also in floods. She had no family, no husband, no job; her pupils were all.

'Do drop in for a cup of tea whenever you're passing,' she begged as each one came up.

'Never been kissed by so many pretty women,' said Pittsy.

Even Skunk was getting his fair share of hugs and shrieks, as cheeks were tickled by his bristly beard and moustache. The girls far more enjoyed weeping on Emlyn's chest. Kitten was clinging to him, leaving frosted-pink lipstick all over his shirt, when he glanced across at Janna, seeing her tears glittering in the moonlight. Setting Kitten gently aside, he crossed the grass, gathering up Janna's soaked body, and she let herself go.

It was such a haven, amid such desolation, to feel his arms round her; he was so big, solid and warm. She knew he was still carrying a torch for Oriana, but she wished he'd go on hugging her for ever.

Emlyn, meanwhile, thought: My heart is in smithereens over Oriana, but it feels nice with my arms round Janna; I'd like to keep them there.

'Can I give you a lift home?' he murmured into her spiked hair.

Janna's heart leapt. 'Oh yes, please.'

'At last,' said Lily, turning in satisfaction to the Brigadier.

Gradually the limos glided away. Most of the teachers had retreated to the staffroom, where the pink and purple ball dresses still hung from the Christmas pantomime and the cuttings from the rugby match against Bagley: 'Comp thrashes Posh', curled on the noticeboard. Mags had pinned up Monster's definition of a mentor: 'Someone you can talk to, an adult what ain't your parents, but is a friend.'

'Once they realized we weren't on supply, they began to trust us,' said Pittsy.

The telephone rang.

'I've been phoning all evening,' screeched Miss Miserden. 'Never heard such a noise. A rocket landed on my patio. Scamp shot up the pear tree. I'm about to call the police.'

'When we have another party,' said Pittsy sarcastically,

'we'll give you a warning,' but as he replaced the receiver, his face crumpled. 'But there never will be. Best boss I ever had.'

Putting off the evil day, to cheer up her staff, Janna had organized some jaunts for later in the week. The list, also pinned up, included the Barbican and Kensington Palace to see Princess Diana's clothes collection one day, a clay and archery shoot on another, with a buffet at school to include partners on another, then a fun supper just for Larks staff the next.

None of this cheered up Cambola, sobbing in the corner: it was like the end of an opera tour. Tomorrow, we rest.

As Janna waved the band off with profuse thanks, Rupert and Bianca arrived to collect Taggie and Xav, who was clutching his crown.

'He was voted most popular boy in the school,' cried Taggie.

Rupert put a hand on Xav's shoulder. 'That's better than grades, well done.'

'Is it all right if we drop Aysha and Mrs Khan off on the way?' whispered Xav. 'I think someone's spiked her drink.'

Bianca had jumped out of the BMW, big dark eyes searching everywhere for Feral. Reading her mind, Xav said, 'I'm sorry, he's gone home, I tried to keep him.'

Bianca shrugged and huddled into the back. Feral, hidden behind the big swamp cypress, watched the BMW roll down the drive, before fleeing into the night.

Emlyn was desperate to leave, suffering the edginess of not drinking, jangling his car keys attached to a black plastic Scottie with a tartan collar. He found Janna in the IT room gazing abstractedly at a computer screen, where Larks High School, like a house in a twister, rolled hopelessly over and over into a bright blue eternity.

'I saved you this.' Emlyn handed her a red balloon, splaying his fingers over hers. 'Let's go.'

'I'll just say goodbye to the others.'

Outside the staffroom, however, they found Danijela in tears.

'This school is my home.'

Emlyn gritted his teeth as Janna, the eternal hostess, put Basket's beige cardigan round Danijela's thin shoulders. Janna was just making her a cup of tea when Monster wandered in.

'My mum's not answering.'

'Where is she?'

'Moved house if she's got any sense,' quipped Rocky.

'She's asleep. Probably can't hear the doorbell,' whined Monster.

'Pissed,' mouthed Wally from behind his back.

'My bruvvers and sisters are asleep, no one won't let me in,' he whined.

'So you walked back here, poor Martin.' Janna poured boiling water over Danijela's tea bag.

'I got nowhere to go.' Monster looked round pathetically.

There was a long pause. Pittsy looked at his feet, so did Cambola, so even did Mags and Emlyn. Janna counted to ten.

'You better come home with me, Martin. We'll put a note through your mum's door: "I'm in Miss Curtis's house." You'll have to sleep on the sofa.'

Then she caught sight of Emlyn, his face a death mask.

'I'm off. Night, everybody.' He gathered up his car keys and was gone.

Janna caught up with him in reception. Graffi's black good-luck cat grinned down at her unsympathetically.

'Come in for a drink on the way home,' she pleaded. 'We can put Monster to bed.'

'Where?' snapped Emlyn.

'In the lounge. We can talk in the kitchen.'

'Talking wasn't what I had in mind.'

Janna's heart started to thump in excitement, then faltered as Emlyn said, 'And I'm not coming to any of those jaunts next week, I've got interviews.'

'You what?' Janna fought back tears of disappointment. Every trip had been planned with him in mind. 'Who with?' she asked, following him through the front door.

'The Welsh Rugby Union, among others.'

Out in the warmth of Midsummer Night's Eve, the bitter acid tang of elder and the overwhelming sweetness of the white philadelphus mingled to symbolize the bitter sweetness of the evening.

'You're lovely, Janna; all things to all children,' said Emlyn bleakly, 'but you're not going to change. I'm fed up with women who want to save the world.'

As he strode towards his car, Janna ran after him. 'I'm sorry about Oriana's baby. I know you're upset: please talk to me about it.'

'I don't need any counselling. Poppet Bruce had a go earlier.' And he was in his car, storming down the drive, not even bothering with lights or a seatbelt.

Janna couldn't bawl her heart out because of Monster.

'So much food left,' she said, returning to the staffroom. 'If we put it in the fridge, the children can have it tomorrow.'

'There isn't going to be a tomorrow,' sobbed Rowan.

Cambola, however, switched off her mobile, tears drying on her beaming face.

'Jack and Kylie have just asked me to be godmother to little Ganymede.'

Both the Brigadier and Lily had been drinking, so they left the car at Larks and took a taxi to Elmsley church, where the Brigadier put a balloon on his wife's grave. Then they walked hand in hand down the tree tunnel with shafts of moonlight piercing the leaf ceiling lighting on Lily's pearls and the Brigadier's diamond shirt studs.

Pearl had forced a fish-paste sandwich on Lily, made by her mum, to keep up her strength, so Lily had to do something to sweeten her breath. Pearl's proffered Juicy Fruit chewing gum might have pulled her bridge out. Fortunately, she always kept three boiled sweets in her bag, one for the walk there, one for the walk home and one just in case. The just in case was blackcurrant, which she was sucking furiously.

Despite his outward sangfroid, the Brigadier was more nervous than he had ever been under fire.

Just outside Wilmington, they paused to rest against a five-bar gate. The Brigadier took a deep breath. Lily looked so beautiful with her silvery hair and her face bathed in moonlight.

'Darling Lily, I fell in love with you on the second of October two thousand, the day you moved into Wilmington.'

There was a crunch of boiled sweet as he took her in his arms, kissing her gently then passionately, and both their teeth stayed put.

'Oh, Christian, my Brigadearest,' sighed Lily.

'If I go down on one knee, will you help me up afterwards?'

'Of course.'

'Sweetest Lily, will you do me the great honour of marrying me?'

'Oh yes, yes I will.'

Anxious to kiss his betrothed, Christian held out a hand, Lily gave it a tug, but he was too heavy for her, and next moment had pulled her down on the grass beside him. The only way they could clamber up, some time later, still laughing helplessly, was gate bar by gate bar.

Back at Larks, Graffi and Johnnie, who'd been indulging in a hilarious spot of dogging, observing Basket's plump white bottom bobbing up and down in

Skunk's heaving Vauxhall, had returned to the staffroom to mob up Janna.

'Not sure Monster wants to come home with you, miss. Finks you're going to jump on him.'

'There's a perfectly good lock to the lounge door,' snarled Janna. 'Come on, Martin, I can't abandon Partner any longer.'

Having once bound a firework to Partner's tail, Monster showed even more reluctance to spend the night under the same roof.

'He'll get me in the night, miss.'

Janna drove home very slowly, tempted to knock on Emlyn's door, but there was no car outside. She had great difficulty not strangling Monster, particularly when the hulking great beast announced he was starving, then complained the scrambled eggs Janna made him were too sloppy.

Partner growled so much at such ingratitude, Janna let Monster sleep in her bedroom, and heard the key turn in the lock.

Outside, it was getting light, the longest day dawning after the longest saddest night. Except for the jaunts, which were meaningless without Emlyn, Larks was over. She must face up to the fact that she was totally, hopelessly in love with him and had utterly blown it by not being there when he needed her. Having sobbed herself to sleep, her first lie-in for weeks was interrupted by pounding on the door at six o'clock.

'Can you run me into Larkminster, miss? It's my paper round.'

116

'Teachers should never go on holiday for at least a fortnight after the end of the summer term,' Pittsy was
always saying. 'One needs two weeks at home unwind-
ing and invariably contracting some bug, then fourteen
days abroad in the sun, before a fortnight psyching
oneself up for the rigours of the autumn term.'

Janna had no such luxury. She had to work out her
contract with S and C until the end of August, leaving
Appletree immaculate for the new incumbents, whoever they might be, and supervising the removal of
property by neighbouring schools, who were so
avaricious, she was tempted to put a 'do not remove'
label on Partner's collar.

To depress her further, it rained throughout July and
August as estate agents and developers splashed
through the school grounds, skips filled with water and
rubble, windows were boarded up, machinery dis-
mantled and cork and whiteboards ripped down, until
only Janna's office remained operational.

In it, apart from her personal belongings, were a
framed photograph of the staff and children of Larks
High in happier days and the computer and printer,
out of which the GCSE results would thunder.

Still on the wall was the cupboard Emlyn had put up
by nonchalantly hammering in the screws. Janna never
dreamt she would miss him so dreadfully. Her constant

companion as a child had been a vast English sheep-dog, whose huge reassuring presence she kept imagining round the house for months after he died. So it was with Emlyn. He had landed his grand job with the Welsh Rugby Union, but, according to the Brigadier, he was hoping to get back to Larks for Results Day on 26 August. The children so longed to see him.

Even after term was ended, they hadn't been able to accept the dream was over and still piled in every day: 'Let's play bingo, miss,' or offering to help her clean the building and littering it with Coke cans and crisp packets.

As Results Day approached, they grew increasingly jittery about not getting enough grades to qualify for sixth-form places in colleges or other schools, or for a good job, or to satisfy their parents, or to not feel a fool in front of their friends.

None of them aspired to the miracle of the Magic Five, which would give Larks a point in the league tables.

In the evenings, Janna had visited every parent on the Shakespeare Estate, trying to explain that further education didn't just mean top-up fees and the loss of a family breadwinner.

She was most worried about Feral, who'd left the sanctuary of the Brigadier's cottage and moved with his mother into a two-bedroom flat so poky there was hardly room for his football. If his mother stayed off drugs until Christmas, her other children might be returned to her. But she was so listless and easily cast down, Feral was terrified she'd lapse, particularly if Uncle Harley rolled up again. He hated leaving her, even to stack shelves with Graffi every night.

As Janna was shredding confidential papers referring to the staff at Larks, she had come across one of Feral's essays which young Lydia had kept. He must have dictated it to Paris.

My dream [he had begun] is to leave home when I'm nineteen and be married by the time I'm twenty to the girl I stay with for the rest of my life and have two children. I'm going to buy a house in a nice area for my children to grow up decently. I will buy a car for my wife. She can go to work or look after the children. I'm going to give her a big posh kitchen worth £1,000 and go on holiday three times a year, twice abroad and once to Skegness.

'Well done, Feral,' Lydia had written, 'work hard and chase your dream.'

It was dated March 2002, just after he had met Bianca. Oh, poor Feral, Janna nearly wept, the desire of the moth for the star.

At least this year the incessant rain had kept alive the saplings Wally had planted last autumn; perhaps they might symbolize the survival of her children.

Against all this, she longed constantly for Emlyn and could have done without Basket popping in, flashing Skunk's diamond and saying, 'I know you'll find a Skunk of your own when you least expect it,' until Janna nearly kicked her teeth in.

Janna shared Wednesday 25 August with Mags and Pittsy, closeted together in her office, sworn to secrecy until the official release time which was eight o'clock on the morning of the twenty-sixth.

The results arrived by email and, as they were downloaded, were logged onto a big wall chart with a list of candidates' names in alphabetical order down the left-hand side, and the subjects starting with history along the top. It was surprising Miss Miserden didn't ring up and complain about the shrieks and yells of excitement as the trio caught sight of and analysed each result.

'We're going to need several king-size boxes of tissues tomorrow,' confessed Mags, 'but, bearing in mind how far behind they were at the beginning of the year, haven't some of our no-hopers done well?'

Pittsy was delighted he'd got more candidates through than Skunk or Basket. Serve them right for being so smug. The Brigadier and Emlyn had done very well in history, Mags and Lily in languages, Janna and Sophy in English.

Over at Bagley, the mood was less rowdy, but just as feverish, as, in scenes resembling Wall Street, department heads reached for their calculators to check if they'd beaten other departments, or set in train computer programmes to work out the crucial percentage of children who'd got the Magic Five. Could they have overtaken Fleetley, St Paul's or Wycombe Abbey, or shaken Rod Hyde off their heels?

Miss Painswick was flapping around so that the moment the official results came in tomorrow and were checked for inconsistencies, they would be faxed or emailed immediately to candidates on yacht, grouse moor, Aegean isle or, in Paris's case, the Old Coach House.

At six o'clock on the morning of 26 August, Janna dressed herself in a clinging new yellow and white striped T-shirt and tight sexy white jeans, in case Emlyn showed up. She then drove to the central post office in Larkminster to pick up the envelopes with coral labels containing official result slips for each candidate.

After yesterday's downpour it was a beautiful day: very hot with a bright blue sky flecked with little cirrus clouds and larger grey cumulus clouds, behind which the sun kept disappearing, as if to illustrate the miseries or splendours of each candidate.

The press awaited Janna at Larks.

'How's Rupert Campbell-Black done?'

'No idea.'

'And his son, Xav, the thick one?'

'I'm not going to tell you.'

941

She then rushed into her office and spent the next hour with the other staff, shoving the results into envelopes for each child, checking them against yesterday's emails. Aysha had got an A star, not an A, for maths, Kitten an E rather than a D for English lit.

'I nearly wore *my* white jeans,' said Rowan, 'but I thought it was too casual for such an important day. Oh look, here's an email from Emlyn. Oh no! He's had to fly out on some pre-season rugby tour. He sends huge love to us all and good luck. The kids will be gutted.'

Et moi aussi, thought Janna, Oh Emlyn! But she must hide her despair; it was the children's day.

Most schools just pin up the envelopes on the wall for pupils to collect. Janna, however, sat in her office determined to go through every result with every child as they lined up in the corridor, frantically chewing gum, faces dead, pacing up and down.

'I'm going to get all Gs.'

'I'm going to get straight Us.'

Pearl, shaking and sobbing, had to be carried by Mags and Cambola into Janna's office – Pearl the former truant and disaster area. Janna jumped up and hugged her.

'Oh Pearl, this is one of the best results in the school. B in English, C in history, C in home economics, C in maths, C in science. D in business studies. Well done.'

Pearl was turned to stone like Niobe, when, like the fountain, her tears gushed out.

'I don't believe it, miss. I done brilliant.'

'You certainly have.'

'I got the Magic Five,' shrieked Pearl, racing round the playground hugging everyone. Then she rang her mother and then the factory where her boxer dad worked, asking them to broadcast the results over the tannoy, then rushed off to the toilets to redo her face before she faced the press.

Back in Janna's office, there were more yells of

excitement and cries of 'Good lad, well done', 'Good girl, you've got a B in RE and a C in geography and a C in home economics', as stunned candidates reeled out of the room. Graffi, despite stacking shelves, had got four Cs and an A star for art and was calling his parents. Danny the Irish had managed a B and two Cs, Kitten was over the moon to get four Cs and a D in English, until she heard Pearl's grades were even better and blamed it on a social life so much more active than Pearl's.

Johnnie, against all the odds, had notched up two Bs and four Cs.

'I worked, like, hard,' he told the press, 'but I'd have screwed up, like, if it hadn't been for Emlyn and the Brigadier getting me here.'

Janna was so good at comforting the sad ones. Danijela was inconsolable. She'd only got an A in D and T for her blue and green wedding dress and a C in food technology.

'But that's brilliant. You spoke no English when you came here, you can always retake the others.'

Janna was also euphoric about Rocky, who'd been special needs level three and on the at-risk register, but had still got a B for his D and T dog kennel, a C for history and a D for business studies.

'He must have learnt more in that cupboard than we thought,' laughed Pittsy.

Kylie had notched up three Ds, a B in child care and an A star in music, which enchanted Cambola. Chantal had arrived with Cambola's little godson, Ganymede, who looked just like Jack Waterlane, and, thoroughly carried away, was now telling the press: 'My Kylie Rose is destined for music college. She done superior to her hubby, the Honourable Jack, who may well stay home and mind Cameron and Ganymede.'

'Jack'd love that,' muttered Graffi. 'He'll be able to drink and watch racing on TV all day.'

Graffi couldn't believe those results. The Magic Five.

His father had just rolled up with Cardiff Nan and was looking at him with new respect.

'Good luck,' called out everyone, as, trembling and terrified, Aysha crept into Janna's office.

'I don't want to let down my dad.'

'No fear of that.' Janna clasped her hands. 'You got an A star for science, an A star for Urdu, Bs for history and English, an A star for maths and Cs for French and Spanish. Best result in the school, Aysha. Your parents will be so thrilled.'

Aysha gazed at the results slip for a moment; a storm of relieved weeping followed.

'Do you think Dad will let me see Xav now?'

'I'm sure he will.' Janna plied her with Kleenex. 'Get out,' she screamed as a cameraman shoved a lens in through the window.

Summoned by mobile and text, excited parents were soon storming the playground, bearing flowers in cellophane, cards in coloured envelopes, and accepting paper cups of wine handed out by Wally, who was beaming from ear to ear. He'd helped out all year with D and T and his pupils had done really well.

Pearl's boxer dad, who'd been allowed the rest of the day off, was hugging Pearl's mother. Pearl, thoroughly above herself, was telling the television cameras: 'The world is my lobster. I was planning to go into hairdressing, but getting the Magic Five, I've gotta refink my options.'

A dazed Aysha had already been offered places at four schools, but would she be allowed to take up any of them?

The press were now photographing pupils jumping for joy, tossing their papers in the air, the eternal cliché only before afforded to St Jimmy's and Searston Abbey.

'Where's Emlyn? What can have happened to Feral?' asked everyone. 'Where's Xav?'

117

Over at Penscombe, none of the Campbell-Blacks had slept. The plan was to go into Larks to collect Xav and Taggie's results, making a slight detour on the way to Cotchester College to discover Rupert's English lit. grade. Both Rupert and Xav would have preferred to learn their fate in solitude.

The fact that Rupert had just flown in from the Athens Olympics, where his daughter Tabitha and her horse had been in the medals, had, on the one hand, made him incredibly proud. On the other, he was now even more anxious that Xav would be utterly demoralized if, by contrast, he didn't notch up a single GCSE.

To steady his nerves, Rupert was riding around the estate, followed by his pack of dogs. He admired two yearlings, Macduff and Thane of Fife, known as Fifey, checked fences and noted the casualties of summer: rusty branches hanging like broken limbs from the sycamore, field maples eaten to bits by the squirrels. The dawn redwood, prematurely russet, looked a goner too. Despite the rain, it had been an incredibly fecund year, elders already crimson black with berries, brambles covered in gorging wasps.

The sun was coming through the clouds to highlight a triangle of jade field one moment, and touch the shoulder of a beech tree – Shall we dance? – the next.

Since he had read English lit., he appreciated nature and character so much more.

It was bliss having Taggie home again, but they had all found it difficult to settle this summer, worrying about three different sets of results.

This is a good horse, thought Rupert: dark bay, strong, confident, too slow to race, the perfect hunter, but hunting would be banned soon. Democracy was gradually being eroded, but did he really mind enough to go back into politics?

There had been so much rain, the fields had only just been topped. Buzzards screamed overhead searching for carrion; a fox had caught a pigeon, its dark grey and light feathers all over the stubble – not a good omen. Nor was the single magpie rising squawking out of the wood.

'Morning, Mr Magpie, how's your wife? How many A to C grades did your children get? You piebald smartass,' snapped Rupert.

Dear God, he prayed, if Tag gets some children through food technology and Xav just one or two decent grades, he'd gladly give up his English lit. pass. Everyone knew he was a philistine. Helen, his first wife, had told him often enough.

Xav huddled in his room, hugging smelly, old, comforting Bogotá, who was too old to join the pack on the ride.

What if he got no grades at all? Mr Khan and Alex Bruce would gloat and say I told you so. He couldn't bear the humiliation, but he couldn't miss a chance of seeing Aysha one last time. Bianca, equally desperate for a last chance to see Feral, banged on his door.

'We ought to go, it's nearly eleven.'

She was wearing red shorts, red boots and a sleeveless crimson T-shirt.

'You look cool,' said Xav.

Taggie was in the kitchen praying and unloading the

dishwasher, when the telephone rang. It was Mags.

'My dears, are you coming in? Good, but I thought you might like Xav's results in advance.'

Taggie, a potato masher in one hand and two mugs hanging on the end fingers of the hand holding the telephone, sat down on the window seat, just missing Bianca's kitten.

'Can you read them again?' she gasped a minute later.

'And again?' a minute after that, then a minute later. 'And again.'

Afterwards there was a long pause.

'Are you all right?' asked Mags anxiously. 'I thought you'd like to hear the food technology results as well.'

'Yes, no.' All Margaret could hear was sobbing. 'I'll ring you back.' Taggie slotted back the telephone.

Walking back from the yard, noticing dew-spangled spiders all over the lawn, Rupert caught sight of Taggie running out onto the terrace, the same sun lighting up the tears pouring down her face.

'It's all right, darling.' Rupert raced up the lawn, folding his wife in his arms, struggling to hide his disappointment. 'He was Prom King and he's got friends; that's much more important. He worked really hard too.'

But he so wanted to pass, said a voice inside Rupert, we should have fought harder to keep him at Bagley.

Taggie was still sobbing.

'It's all right.' Rupert gritted his jaw. 'We'll look after him. I could never take exams.'

'No, no,' Taggie gulped and gasped. 'He passed. He got four Cs and a B for Spanish. The Magic Five, and D grades in all his other subjects.'

Rupert shut his eyes. Back went his head as he breathed in deeply and incredulously.

'You did it,' he muttered. 'You had the courage to send him to Larks.'

'Shall we go?' Xav walked out, saw his mother

947

crying and knew all was lost. 'Sorry,' he mumbled.

His parents pulled him into a sodden hug.

'You got it,' said Rupert. 'They've just rung. You got the Magic Five.'

'That is really wicked,' said Xav.

Rupert put a crate of Veuve Clicquot in the car. Taggie was so happy she couldn't stop giggling. Glancing at the back, she noticed Bianca gazing out of the window, her painted scarlet lips moving: 'Please God, give me Feral,' and put a hand back on her daughter's knee.

In Cotchester, the roads were blocked with mothers frantic to collect their children's results from various schools. The forecourt of Cotchester College was swarming with mature students comparing results and with even more press, who raised their cameras and tape recorders as Rupert approached, but warily. In his time, the Golden Beast had broken more than a few photographers' jaws. Today he didn't look in a party mood. Rupert had withdrawn his bargain with God. He'd mind like hell if he failed.

Pushing through the swing doors, he entered the exam room, waving his student card.

'Can I have my GCSE result?'

'Oh, it's you, Mr Campbell-Black,' said the woman at the table reverently. 'We hoped you'd come in.' She coughed loudly.

As secretaries suddenly appeared, peering excitedly through the glass panel behind her, she handed him a sealed envelope, her kind round face full of concern.

'Summer 2004,' read Rupert, 'Campbell-Black, Rupert Edward. English Literature GCSE, Grade B.' He gasped. 'There's no mistake?'

'None. Many congratulations.'

'My God.' Rupert leant over the table and kissed her on both cheeks.

Out in the sunshine he sauntered over to the assembled press.

'How d'yer do, Rupert?'

'B for bloody brilliant.' He brandished the slip of paper. 'And two fingers to Randal Stancombe, who now owes the Bagley Fund a lot of money, and my first wife, Helen, now Lady Hawkley, who always told me I was thick.'

Taggie was so excited she nearly ran over an old man wheeling a tartan bag across a zebra crossing.

Back at Larks, Monster was moaning he'd only got Cs for English and business studies, after working like stink.

'That's terrific, well done,' said Janna, making Monster feel so good that he decided to ring Stormin', who was on nights and asleep at home.

If you can wake her, thought Janna bitterly, you horrible gooseberry, who ruined my last chance with Emlyn.

Only Feral had bombed totally. Not a single grade, nothing above a G – darkness at noon. He was now on his mobile, huddled in misery.

'Didn't do enough revision, I guess, sorry, Brig, sorry, Lily. See you both later.'

As he rang his mother, Graffi and Kylie were hovering to comfort him.

'There's good news and bad news, Mum. First the bad news, I failed all my exams. Yes, all of them. But the really good news to cheer you all up, is everyone else in the school passed somefing.'

Heroically brave, he deserved an A star for courage. Janna bit her lip as she remembered the essay of hope about the girl to whom he stayed married for the rest of his life and took on holiday to Skegness.

Kylie put an arm round his shoulders. 'How was your mum?'

'OK,' lied Feral. 'Not now, perhaps later,' he added to Partner, who was nudging him to play football. Oh God, he prayed, don't let the bad news start Mum off again.

Everyone – children, parents and press – was knocking back the bottles of white and red. Graffi's dad was getting legless with Pearl's boxer dad and mum and Stormin' Norman, who'd just arrived. Even Raschid Khan, sipping apple juice, was looking quite mellow.

'I agree, Raschid,' Dafydd Williams was saying. 'None of my family's ever been to uni, we work in factories or on the building, we don't go on to better things.'

Janna climbed onto Appletree steps and clapped her hands. 'I'd just like to thank and congratulate all the children who worked so hard and made such fantastic progress. These are a terrific set of results. The greatest thing in life is an ability to pick yourself up from the floor and you all did this, and I'd like to thank your parents for all their support.'

A second later Feral had grabbed the microphone from her, clutching his battered violet and yellow football like a hot-water bottle with the other. In his deep hoarse voice, gallant in defeat, he thanked particularly Janna and the teachers.

'For being so brilliant, and giving us the best year of our lives. They've taken a year out to look after us and no one's worked harder than they have.'

What on earth's he going to do now? thought Janna despairingly.

'Oh, look,' cried Chantal, as the press went berserk, photographing a new arrival.

For a horrible moment, Janna thought it might be Stancombe, then she realized it was Pete Wainwright, grinning on the edge of the crowd. Last week, he'd been appointed manager of Larkminster Rovers and was now a god in Larkshire.

Shaking off the press, he came over and shook Janna's hand. 'How did Taggie's class do?'

'Fantastic,' said Janna.

'She coming?'

'I hope so.'

Pete Wainwright glanced across the euphoric,

teeming playground at Feral, a picture of desolation slumped against the fence, listlessly tapping his football back and forth to Partner, dark head on Graffi's shoulder as Graffi patted him on the back.

'Ain't the end of the world, man.'

'Certainly isn't,' said Pete Wainwright, joining them. 'Here's something to cheer you up, lad.' He handed Feral a typed envelope.

Feral stared at it stupidly.

'Well, open it and read it,' ordered Pete.

'You ought to know, man, I didn't get no English.'

'I'll read it,' said Graffi. 'Wow!' he said after a quarter of a minute. 'Fuckin' hell, fuckin' wicked!' and went into a series of Tarzan howls. 'Mr Wainwright's offering you a job, man, as a junior player at Larkminster Rovers, starting next week.'

Feral swung round in bewilderment.

'I ducked out of that trial.'

'I know, and I know why you did. I saw you playing one evening after exams. Emlyn showed me some tapes. You'll have to clean a few boots to start with, spend a bit of time observing on the bench. But you're good and so was that speech you just made. I like generosity in my players.'

Feral tried to read the letter.

'It ain't no wind-up?'

Janna by this time had rushed up, hugging Feral, telling everyone the good news. 'Oh Pete, this is really wicked.'

After that Feral, like Pearl, got thoroughly above himself.

'I'm going to be the next Thierry Henry,' he yelled, punching the air, 'and I'll be so fucking rich, I'll be able to take out that bastard Rupert Campbell-Black – in fact he'll be crawling to have me marrying his daughter.'

'He probably will,' said a dry voice behind him.

It was Rupert, who'd just arrived with Taggie and Xav.

'Feral's got a job,' cried Janna as the press surged forward, 'with Larkminster Rovers. And well done, fantastic results!' She hugged Xav. 'And well done, Taggie.'

'Taggie, Taggie!' The children surged round her: 'I got a B.' 'I got a C.' 'I got an A.' 'I got a C.'

'I can't believe it.' Taggie tried to hug them all.

Meanwhile, Rupert had turned to Feral.

'I've brought you a congratulatory present,' he drawled.

And Bianca erupted out of the car and, stopping, gazed at Feral, who gazed at her in wonder.

Slowly, they moved towards each other. Seizing her hand, chucking his ball to Partner, Feral led her off into the garden.

'I thought your father didn't approve of Feral,' whispered Kylie.

'He's just got a B in English lit.,' whispered back Xav, 'I think he'd even accept Tony Blair as a son-in-law.'

Having congratulated Taggie on her food technology triumph, Janna was now hugging Rupert – such a pleasure as he was so handsome.

'Randal is going to be furious about your B.'

'Good,' said Rupert. 'I should be congratulating you and apologizing for doubting that you and Larks would be the best thing for Xav. He's found himself.'

Across the playground, Xav was surrounded by friends, thumping him on the back.

'I've bought a few bottles, they're in the car,' added Rupert. 'Which one's Graffi? I want a mural in the long gallery.'

Feral, wiping off crimson lipstick and grinning like the Cheshire cat, later talked, somewhat warily, to Rupert, who said,

'Sorry I called you a black bastard.'

'It's OK, man. If I caught my daughter in bed with

some no-good nigger, I guess I'd call him the same thing.'

They looked at each other, dislike melting away.

'Thank you for looking after Xav.'

'Thank you for beating Stancombe. He's a bastard, really evil, and I know, man.'

'You do interest me. Why don't you come out to lunch with us?'

'I'd like to, man' – Feral looked longingly at Bianca, who was dancing by herself, as lightly as the thistle-down drifting in from the long grass – 'but actually I'm lunching wiv Lily and the Brig. I'm going to be a witness at their wedding,' he added proudly.

'Hmmmm, that sounds a party that'll go on,' said Rupert. 'You'd better come to lunch tomorrow.'

Grinning, very tentatively they exchanged a high five.

Round the back of the building, Rupert tracked down Graffi spraying in large purple letters: 'Graffi Williams for the Tate, Feral Jackson for Wembley, Randal Stancombe for the High Jump.'

'Excellent sentiments.' Rupert handed Graffi a paper cup of champagne. 'But I want something marginally more figurative for Penscombe. Are you anti blood sports?'

'Not if you pay me well enough,' said Graffi.

'Then I'd like you to do the hunt.'

Feral and Bianca were dancing in the hall.

Graffi's board saying 'Larkminster High School Prom 2004' had been thrown in the bin, but the silver moon and stars still curled on the long black curtains.

'And I will take Feral and cut him out in little stars, and he will make the face of heaven so fine,' said Bianca softly.

Feral picked up a fragment of balloon.

'Since Romeo and Juliet, I haven't fort of anyone or anyfing but you. I couldn't ask you to be my girlfriend when I had nothing to offer. Now I have.'

'I'll come and watch you every week.'

'Every goal will have your name on it.'

'You will come to lunch tomorrow, won't you, or it'd break my heart.'

Feral drew her into his arms. Both of them had to hold each other up, as he kissed her.

Later Bianca was approached by a man from the *Daily Express*. 'Your family's done so well today. Your mum's candidates all got through, Rupert got a B and Xav the Magic Five.'

'I've done best.' Bianca did a joyful handstand, peering back and up from between her arms and black waterfall of hair. 'They got Bs and Cs, but I got Feral Jackson.'

118

Over at Bagley, the celebrations were no less euphoric, as faxes and emails spread over the globe to Lando France-Lynch playing polo in Deauville, Lubemir in a casino, Anatole on a yacht and Cosmo on top of Mrs Walton.

'In my case, my angel,' boasted Cosmo, 'GCSE stands for Great Cock Satisfaction Ensured.'

There was as much press interest in Bagley as there had been at Larks, particularly when a jubilant Hengist announced that not only Cosmo Rannaldini and Primrose Duddon, but Paris Alvaston had achieved straight As and A stars, and Bagley appeared to have gone above Fleetley in the league tables.

Paris who, as it was still holidays, was one of the only boys in school, was bewildered by his results and ran straight over to Hengist's study.

'I couldn't have got an A star in history, sir,' he panted, 'I trashed my second paper.'

'You're imagining things,' Hengist said firmly. 'You'd been working too hard and were understandably upset about Theo. You didn't know if it was Christmas or Easter when you took that last paper. I saw it. It was fine.'

'I wrote gibberish,' insisted Paris.

'Strange things have happened this year. A boy at Fleetley evidently got an A star in English lit. and missed an entire P3 module. Your first history paper must have been exceptional. Ian and Patience will be delighted.'

They were. Ian had opened a bank account and put in £25 for each brilliant grade, totalling £250, but Paris wasn't happy.

'I want to ring Theo.'

'You can't, I'm afraid.' Hengist went to the fridge and got out a bottle of white. 'Let's have a drink to celebrate.'

'I want to ring Theo.'

'You can't. How many times do I have to tell you the police have expressively forbidden any contact.' Hengist ran his hand through his hair. 'Imagine how I'd like to ring him, but I don't want to prejudice his case.'

'How can it, if I just thank him and give him my grades?'

'Biffo'll tell him.' Hengist was rootling round for a corkscrew.

'Who?' asked Paris quickly.

'Someone will,' said Hengist quickly. 'Oh look, Rupert and Xav are on the box, turn the sound up.' But Paris had shot out of the room.

Hengist shook his head. He must calm Paris down.

After some lovely film of Penscombe, the lunchtime news cut to Sian Williams in the studio. What a pretty thing she was; Hengist turned up the volume.

Xavier Campbell-Black, she told the viewers, who'd been excluded from Bagley Hall for bullying last September, had just notched up five A–C grades at his new school: Larkminster High. A maintained school had thus succeeded where a prestigious independent had failed.

Xav used to be such a fat slob, thought Hengist, now he was clear-eyed, smiling, good-looking and confident.

'I made so many friends at Larks,' he was now saying,

'I didn't need to bully anyone. I found teachers who believed in me and helped me to understand. It helped that my mother joined the staff as a teaching assistant. Everyone she taught food technology to passed.'

'Did you find the teaching better at Larks?'

'Much,' said Xav, who'd been at the Veuve Clicquot, 'and Alex Bruce, my housemaster at Bagley, was a twat.'

Hengist choked on his drink as the interviewer hastily asked Xav about Rupert's B.

'He's laid back, my dad, but he worked incredibly hard and we're all really proud of him.'

Now it was Rupert's turn. Age cannot wither him, thought Hengist, particularly when he's happy, mouth and long eyes lifting.

'I'm knocked out by my wife Taggie's results,' admitted Rupert, 'and Xav's and my own.'

'Who taught you?'

'Well, Miss Jennings at Cotchester College gave me some very good coaching, but mostly I read and wrestled on my own. Couldn't understand a word of it at first. Lucky to have Xav's headmistress, Janna Curtis, and Bianca's headmaster, Hengist Brett-Taylor, to tell me when my ideas were crap.'

'And by passing you won your bet with Randal Stancombe, for an undisclosed sum.'

'Not at all undisclosed, it was a hundred thousand pounds, which is not going to worry Stancombe. He spends that in a day on aftershave and greasing palms.'

'Bastard,' howled Stancombe, who was watching the same news, 'and he got that treacherous bitch, Janna Curtis, and that shit, Hengist, to help him. No wonder he got a B. They've obviously been cramming him. After all I've done for Hengist. Building the Science Emporium and his taking Ruth off me. My God, I'll bury all three of them.'

Alex Bruce, also watching, was even more outraged. How dare that insolent brat call him a twat, and how could he have got the Magic Five? Janna Curtis must have shown him the papers. Even more distressingly, Lando and Jack had ploughed science, so Alex still hadn't equalled Theo's record of getting everyone through.

Worst of all, his star pupil Boffin Brooks had not achieved straight As. He had just had Sir Gordon Brooks in a towering rage from his villa in Portugal.

'There's no way Bernard could only have got a B in history. It's one of his strongest subjects. That's why I donated five thousand for a history prize, which will now go to some other student.'

'Rest assured, Gordon, I shall approach our Senior Team Leader and appeal. May I have a word with Charisma?' She was staying with the Brookses.

'I can't understand, Dad, I only got a B for Urdu,' whined his G and T daughter.

The last parents and children had drifted away; only Mr Khan lingered.

'You have a brilliant daughter,' pleaded Janna, 'won't you just consider her going on to sixth-form college?'

'She has a husband waiting for her in Pakistan. He has been very patient. He is a good man and will take care of her.'

'But she's so young— Excuse me, that's my mobile.'

It was Hengist. 'Darling, I've just seen the one o'clock news. Well done, Xav, how brilliant and what a smack in the face for stupid Alex for letting him go. How did the others do?'

After Janna had told him, and about Feral's fantastic new job, she asked after Paris.

'Wonderful.' What purring content in Hengist's voice. 'Straight As and A stars for Greek, Latin, both Englishes and history. Absolutely wonderful.'

Janna was ecstatic.

'Ian and Patience must be so thrilled.'

'Relieved, as well. Little Amber did surprisingly well, too.'

'How's Paris in himself?'

'Withdrawn. We had a bit of a set-to just now. He wanted to ring Theo and tell him about the A stars to give him some comfort. But he mustn't get in touch. All the press are hanging round. They all know it's Paris, but he can't be named because the so-called "offence" began when he was fourteen.'

'Oh God, poor Theo. Will he get off?'

'Christ, I hope so. The evidence is pretty damning. Case comes up later in the year, bound to coincide with the Queen's visit. The press'll make a meal out of two old queens. One shouldn't laugh.'

Janna had taken refuge in her office; glasses and discarded envelopes were everywhere.

'Jade only scraped five Cs, which won't please Stancombe,' Hengist was now telling her, 'and, by the way, I've just seen Rupert on the box saying how much we helped him and slagging off Stancombe. It's going to be a long time before dear Randal forgives either of us.'

'I don't care.'

'I do miss you. Let's have a drunken celebration before term starts.'

Dear Hengist, Janna smiled as she switched off her mobile.

Outside the playground was empty; Mr Khan had gone. Tomorrow, she thought wearily, she'd continue the battle to stop the parents chucking it all away. Lily's wedding was at two-thirty; she'd better step on it. Hastily, she toned down her flushed cheeks and shrugged on her white jacket. What did it matter how she looked, if Emlyn wasn't going to be there?

'Next week,' she told Partner as she tied a white silk bow round his neck, 'you and I will look for a job and probably somewhere to live. Today all that matters is those fantastic results.'

But as she splashed Diorissimo on her wrists, Ashton rang.

'I can see why you haven't phoned, Janna, these wesults are dweadfully disappointing.'

'Disappointing?' cried Janna in outrage. 'They're brilliant. You should focus on where those children came from. No one expected them to get any grades at all. You forget there are four pass grades below C. They may not all have got brilliant grades but they got grades. It's a miracle.'

'Janna, Janna,' sighed Ashton, 'exonerating yourself as usual. It's going to be tewwibly difficult justifying all the extwa funding you've had from the DfES. We expected far better.'

'My kids really worked, so did my teachers,' yelled Janna. 'What d'you know about work, sitting in your ivory tower surrounded by hundreds of apparatchiks doing fuck all on vast salaries? Don't talk to me about wasting money.'

'No need to be offensive. You've failed, that's all, but there's no point in talking to you in this mood.' Ashton rang off.

Like a slow puncture, Janna's pride and delight ebbed out of her.

'These are the children that God forgot,' she whispered in horror as she gazed up at the happy, optimistic group photograph on the wall. 'I'm not going to change anything for them; I just suffered from hubris, putting them through exams because I wanted to prove to the world that I was a brilliant head.'

119

To ward off her desolation over Emlyn's absence and Ashton's vile remarks, Janna got dreadfully drunk at Lily's wedding and danced most of the night away with a euphoric Feral and Lily's whacky, charming family, who included Dicky and Dora. Lily, in the same blue dress she'd worn to the prom, had no need of Pearl's make-up. Never was a bridegroom prouder than her Brigadearest.

Next morning, groaning with hangover, Janna went over to Larks. She had only three days left to leave the place shipshape. Wally had lent her a van to clear out her belongings. At first, as she drove up the drive, she thought a television crew had rolled up, then she realized the place was swarming with workmen; one of them, in a bulldozer, had just smashed down half a dozen of Wally's saplings. Drawing closer, she recognized Teddy Murray, Stancombe's foreman, who'd supervised the rebuilding of Appletree.

'What the hell are you doing?'

'Taking over,' said Teddy curtly.

'On whose authority?'

'Stancombe's, of course.'

'Stancombe?' said Janna in horror as another bull-dozer crushed Sally's oriental poppies. 'What's he got to do with it?'

'Owns the property. Just paid twenty-five million.'

'Don't be ridiculous.'

'See for yourself.' Teddy waved a heavily tattooed hand towards the bottom of the drive and the hayfield of a lawn outside the ruins of the main buildings, where two big crimson signs announced 'Randal Stancombe Properties'.

'What's he planning to do?'

'Search me. Slap luxury houses all over it. Flog it to some supermarket giant. Flatten the Shakespeare Estate and move in some decent customers. All part of his caring "clean up Larkminster" campaign.' Just for a second sarcasm predominated over indifference in Teddy's voice. 'Now, if you'll excuse me, Janna . . .' Revving up he smashed down two willows.

'Stop it,' screamed Janna, but he had wound up his window, so she ran into Appletree, to find all her stuff had been dumped outside her office.

She was on to Stancombe in a flash.

'Have you bought Larks?'

'I have indeed.'

'You never said anything.'

'You never let on you were coaching Rupert Campbell-Black, you treacherous bitch.'

'I didn't help him,' protested Janna. 'Rupert showed me one essay, from which I deleted a few swear words.'

'After all the support I gave you,' howled Randal, 'I don't feel predisposed to help you ever again.'

Janna gave a gasp of horror as, outside the window, she noticed a JCB gouging out the pond. What would be the fate of Concorde, the carp, and the natterjack toads?

'Anyway,' went on Stancombe, 'I put up the money for Appletree, so I own it anyway,' and he hung up.

120

Boffin Brooks's sense of grievance was aggravated on his return to Bagley to find both Cosmo and Paris had better grades.

'I couldn't have got a B in history,' he spluttered to Alex. 'I remember every word I wrote, I could only have got an A star.'

Urged by Charisma, Boffin had started wearing blue tinted contact lenses, which gave him a glazed, almost defenceless look – definitely Alex's blue-eyed boy.

'I have already contacted the exam board,' Alex reassured him, 'to request a clerical check that your history marks were added up correctly. If need be, there are good friends I can phone in the exam world, but I don't want to be accused of pulling strings.'

Together they tackled Hengist, who was bogged down writing beginning-of-term speeches and welcoming new pupils and masters. He was not in a co-operative mood, telling Boffin not to be a bad loser and employing a lot of uncharacteristically hearty clichés like 'biting the bullet' and 'taking it on the chin'.

'We were also warned,' he added sourly, 'that only a limited number of candidates in each subject, irrespective of how well they did, were going to be allowed A stars. You were just one of the unlucky ones. The goalposts have been changed by this bloody Government.'

Boffin and Alex winced collectively.

'It's tough,' concluded Hengist, then begged to be excused because the Queen's Private Secretary and the Lord Lieutenant, General Broadstairs, who was also a Bagley governor, were coming to see him about the royal visit. 'You cannot imagine the red tape. You should give them a copy of your book, Alex.'

Alex's smile creaked.

Getting up, Hengist opened the door. 'We've got just under eight weeks. I hope everything's going to be ready in time.'

Retreating down the stairs, Alex swelled with rage; after all the spadework he'd put in on the royal visit, as usual, Hengist swanned in when it suited him.

'I'm going to appeal,' whined Boffin. 'There's no way I got a B. Mr Brett-Taylor never encourages me.'

Alex was equally determined not to let his star pupil down.

'I shall request the return of your answer paper and have the marks checked, then we'll ask for a total remark. It costs around sixty pounds; Bagley can foot the bill.'

'What a beautiful school,' said the Private Secretary as Elaine left white hairs all over his dark suit, 'and what a beautiful dog.'

'Isn't she?' said Hengist happily. 'People think she's snarling, but she's really smiling.'

'We have Labradors, they smile too,' said the Lord Lieutenant, producing a file already as big as the Larkshire telephone book.

'I want Her Majesty to have a really nice time,' said Hengist, pouring Pouilly-Fumé into three glasses. 'I know she's got to open the Science Emporium, but I thought she might like to watch some polo if the weather's fine and meet the school beagles? One of our star pupils, Paris Alvaston, might read out one of his beautiful poems and, of course, Cosmo Rannaldini, another star pupil, will be conducting the school orchestra and his mother, Dame Hermione Harefield, in a welcoming fanfare.'

'That sounds a good start,' said the Lord Lieutenant.

'Recently, we bonded with a comprehensive,' Hengist told the Private Secretary, 'who did very well in their GCSEs. It would be a miracle for them if Her Majesty could hand out the certificates.'

Later, with an entourage of press officers and detectives, they walked a possible course. Approaching the Science Emporium, still a pile of rubble, they passed General Bagley's statue.

'That's a fine beast.' The Private Secretary patted Denmark's gleaming black shoulder.

'Isn't he?' agreed Hengist. 'And his rider, our founder, General Bagley, is, I think, a distant relation of Her Majesty's mother.'

'How interesting.' The Private Secretary made a note. 'Her Majesty might like to refer to that in her speech. We'll need potted biogs, in advance, of all the people she's going to meet.'

No one was more excited about Paris's results than Dora.

'Ha, ha, ha, hee, hee, hee,' she sang to her friend Peter on the *Mail on Sunday* a few days later. 'Boffin Brooks has got a B.'

'Any more news of Theo Graham?'

'None, poor thing, he can't get in touch with us or we with him, until after his court case. Paris has been transferred to Artie Deverell's house. Artie's really nice, but Paris can't forgive him for not being Theo and Paris nearly strangled Cosmo yesterday for suggesting Hengist was stupid to put Paris into the house of yet another shirt-lifter.'

'How's the Queen's visit?'

'Chaos. Mrs Fussy's refusing to curtsey and wants a dust sheet put over General Bagley. No one can decide

965

on the right shade of red carpet. But guess what, I've bought a man's wig and a white coat which I've splattered with paint so I can pose as a workman and listen in on meetings, so expect some good copy.'

'Good girl.'

'Randal Stancombe, my mum's grotesque boyfriend, is flooding the place with workmen to get his Science Emporium up in time. It's even got a space centre, so hopefully once it's finished we can land Poppet and Alex on Mars for good.'

'And your handsome headmaster?'

'Utterly euphoric we've gone above Fleetley in the league tables and off next month to Bournemouth to the Tory Party conference with my brother Jupiter.'

Awaiting Rupert's helicopter to fly him to Bournemouth, Hengist took Elaine for a quick walk down to Badger's Retreat. In one hand, he had a piece of toast and marmalade, in the other, a private and confidential letter from David 'Hatchet' Hawkley, now Lord Hawkley, the head of Fleetley.

Dear Hengist [he read],
This is a difficult letter to write. This week you will be offered the job of headmaster of Fleetley, a school I have loved and cherished for twenty-five years. I have long deliberated over whether you are the right person to succeed me. You are a genius at recruitment and getting the best out of both masters and pupils, you are hugely enter-taining, charismatic, with a foot in the old world and the new, and generally filled with the milk of human kindness.

In the past we have fallen out . . .

This was a massive understatement. Hengist righted himself after nearly falling down a rabbit hole. He had feared David Hawkley would block his candidacy, but in his fairness, he had not. The letter ended: 'Look after my school, I trust you.'

Hengist was touched. It was a huge olive branch. Looking down, he saw Elaine had nicked his toast and marmalade. But would Fleetley remind Sally too much of Mungo and Pippa, David's then wife, and would it turn out to be a grander, more rigid version of Bagley?

Here he could offer Paris the odd glass of champagne and the run of his books; here he could refuse to disband the school beagles and allow Dora to keep her chocolate Labrador. Could he cope with the lack of freedom? Hengist sighed. Jupiter had just offered him Shadow Education, which would be a complete change of career and an adventure.

Sally would make the perfect minister's wife and Hengist had written Jupiter such a cracking conference speech that by next year he might have seized power. Hengist was flying down to make a fringe speech on education, before flying up to St Andrews in time for dinner at the Headmasters' Conference.

He glanced back at David's letter. He couldn't take on both Fleetley and Education. David, who was a great friend of Theo's, had added a PS: 'To sadder matters, how can we rescue Theo? I am convinced of his innocence. We must battle to clear his name and enable him to finish Sophocles. You have the greater clout.'

Hengist had reached Badger's Retreat. A robin sang in a hawthorn bush, its orange breast clashing with the crimson haws. Like a unicorn, Elaine bounded through the trees he had planted and nurtured. The ground was littered with conkers, which always gave Hengist a stab, remembering how he'd collected them for Mungo.

The Family Tree, its keys turning coral, had lost much of its charm since he'd thrown Oriana out, but, still clinging together, the three trunks and many branches had survived the onslaught of the fallen ash. Perhaps he and Oriana might be friends one day.

Bagley was a far more beautiful school than Fleetley, which, although fed by the same River Fleet, was a squat, grey, Georgian pile surrounded by very flat country. Hengist believed he would miss Badger's Retreat most of all.

Heavens! He must hurry. There was Rupert's dark blue helicopter, in which it would be so cool to arrive at the Headmasters' Conference this evening.

He would earn far more money in politics than at Fleetley. The paths of glory lead but to the gravy train, reflected Hengist.

121

Jupiter's speech was a wow, constructive and marvellously bitchy about the Opposition. Then word got around about Hengist's fringe speech and the main hall had emptied, particularly of young MPs, who had crowded in to hear his good tub-thumping stuff about the real England and freedom from the stranglehold of the curriculum and Brussels.

'Let them be our allies but not dictate our way of life.'

So many interviews and congratulations followed, he only just reached St Andrews in time for dinner. The conference was being held in a lovely hotel, the St Andrews Bay, overlooking the golf course, which was being buffeted by an angry, grey North Sea.

Fiddling to get Radio 3 and the television working, emptying a miniature Bell's into a glass, Hengist called Sally.

'I'm in the most enormous suite, I wish you were here to share it. The guest speaker, some lady novelist, will address us in the Robert Burns Room.'

Sally loved Burns and had, when they first met, compared Hengist with John Anderson, my jo of the bonnie brow and the raven locks. Hengist, in turn, had recited 'My love is like a red, red rose', to her at their wedding.

'Jupiter's speech was marvellous,' cried Sally, 'terrific

jokes and he seemed so warm and sort of sincere.'

'That must be a first. I'm moving towards accepting his offer, if you can cope with the incessant ripping apart by the press.'

'As long as we're together.'

'That's the only certainty. Can I fuck you the moment I get home?'

'The Bishop's coming to lunch . . .'

'I'll get there early then. I love you so much and a pat for Elaine.'

Hengist always enjoyed the Headmasters' Conference and never more so than tonight, when Bagley had finally gone above Fleetley. Whilst changing for dinner, many of the heads had seen clips of his and Jupiter's speeches, or his helicopter landing, and he was subjected to a lot of rather envious joshing.

'You going into politics, Hengist?'

'As a head, is one ever out of them?'

'Did you write all Rupert's coursework?'

Then, in lowered voices: 'Sorry about poor old Theo Graham.'

Listening to the cheerful roar of 250 like minds, anticipating a very good dinner, Hengist thought what a good bunch of chaps they were. Personable was the word. There were intellectuals, like David Hawkley or Anthony Seldon at Brighton College, who'd written a biography of Blair, or Martin Stephen, who'd just taken over St Paul's, who wrote excellent historical novels. These men had read hugely and could pick up any literary allusion. A new breed, more interested in management and marketing, had hardly read a book.

Except for a sprinkling of headmistresses, the membership was all men. Milling around they could be mistaken for army officers out of uniform, showing half an inch of clean, pink neck between hair and collar, wearing trousers that when they sat down rose to sock level above highly polished shoes.

'The *Guardian* described us as "grey men in grey

suits",' grumbled old Freddie Wills of St Barnabas. 'Not true: we're in navy blue, mostly pinstripe.' With cheerfulness breaking in with flamboyant ties, thought Hengist: technicolour checks or swarming with elephants or dolphins.

They had listened all day to seminars.

'Jenni Murray was excellent on gender,' Freddie Wills told Hengist, 'but Andrew Adonis predictably told us "the Labour Party loves us", because they want to bleed us white propping up city academies. Don't seem to realize most of us have a hell of a struggle making ends meet.'

Then, a few feet away, standing in front of a mural of a 1930s' golf match, with players in pancake caps and plus fours showing off well-turned ankles, was David 'Hatchet' Hawkley, appropriately hawklike, immensely distinguished, his shyness so often coming across as brusqueness.

Hengist waved in greeting. 'Thank you for your letter.'

'You got it? Good. Better get into dinner. You're at my table.'

Hengist, already high on a successful Bournemouth and three large whiskies, found himself seated between the jolly lady novelist guest speaker and David's second wife, Helen.

As her previous husbands had included such unashamed Lotharios as Rupert Campbell-Black and Cosmo's late father, Roberto Rannaldini, it was hardly surprising Lady Hawkley insisted on accompanying handsome David everywhere. A redhead with big, yellow eyes and the nervous breediness of a fallow deer, she was easily the most beautiful woman in the room.

Hengist would far rather have been seated with his chums, fellow junior masters in earlier schools, particularly as, through a vase of yellow carnations, Hatchet Hawkley was watching his every move. Would Helen follow Pippa and fall under Hengist's spell?

In fact, Hengist found Helen earnest and a dreadful intellectual snob. Having clocked him landing in Rupert's helicopter, she immediately tackled him on Rupert's B grade.

'Do we need any more proof that GCSEs are getting easier?'

'Rupert worked very hard,' protested Hengist, who hadn't eaten all day and was buttering his roll, 'and he's discovered he rather likes English lit. There's a copy of *Henry Esmond* in the helicopter and he's mellowed since the old days, when he was Lord of the Unzipped Flies. He's so delighted Taggie did so well and Xav got the Magic Five, he's thinking of turning Penscombe into a second Bloomsbury.'

Oh God. Hengist realized he'd goofed. Helen was clearly so scarred by her marriage to Rupert, she loathed any reference to the success of his second marriage. She had now put her knife and fork together, rather like her legs, leaving her divine russet slab of pâté untouched. Hengist was tempted to ask if he could have it, but this would probably be construed as too intimate a gesture by David, who was still peering at them through the carnations.

Hengist still hadn't decided one hundred per cent between Fleetley or politics.

'We're putting your ravishing Tabitha and her horse on the front of the *Old Bagleian*,' he told Helen, 'although no one could look less like an Old Bag. We're all so proud of her silver!' Then he realized he'd goofed again. He'd forgotten how jealous Helen was of Tabitha, whom he supposed looked too like Rupert.

'You look absolutely stunning,' he murmured. 'Most heads' wives resemble overgrown tomboys, short pepper and salt hair, slim figures: senior, senior prefects. It's not homosexual, just that most heads feel easier with boys. How are you looking forward to David retiring?' he went on. Christ, he hoped they didn't move into a cottage on the Fleetley Estate.

'We've got a house in Umbria,' said Helen, 'and we're looking for somewhere in Dorset. We're both going to write. David's doing Aeschylus and I'm working on a literary memoir.'

Hengist was about to say Helen's inside story of marriage to Rupert and Rannaldini would sell much better than any translation of Aeschylus, but just stopped himself. 'We'd better get another bottle.' He tipped back his chair.

At the next-door table, two of his dearest friends, Tim Hastie-Smith, head of Dean Close, and Pete Johnson, head of Millfield, were discussing Colin Montgomerie's triumph in the Ryder Cup. As waitresses and waiters in grey silk cheongsams rushed in with the main course – large squares of roast lamb and shiny brown parsnips – Hengist turned to the lady novelist, who said she was writing about two schools and asked him to tell her about being a headmaster.

'Big egos and like this' – Hengist plunged his knife into his lamb to reveal its pink interior – 'very square but tender inside.'

'I must remember that,' laughed the lady novelist. 'What else makes a great head?'

'Ability to fill the school and pick first-class staff.'

'Energy and charm?'

'Certainly.' Hengist filled up her glass.

'Intellect?'

Hengist shook his head. 'Huge self-belief is much more important.'

'Have you ever won anything at the Teaching Awards?'

'No, that's a state-school affair, even though Lord Hawkley's one of the judges. They think we have it too easy.' He noticed she was looking down at some speech notes on her lap.

'Don't be scared, we'll be a terrific audience, so used to laughing at parents' weak jokes.'

'I'm going to end by quoting from "Rugby Chapel",

about heads as heroic great souls leading and inspiring others on to the city of God.'

' "Ye, like angels, appear, radiant with ardour divine!" ' quoted back Hengist. 'They'll love that.'

The lady novelist was thrilled Hengist was writing a biography of Thomas and Matthew Arnold.

'Will you send me a review copy?'

'How bad was that school, Larks something, you joined up with?' shouted old Freddie Wills across the table.

'Well, they had a geography mistress who'd never been to London,' said Hengist, howling with laughter, so everyone else joined in.

Anyone could charm the birds off the trees, reflected David enviously, with a packet of Swoop, but Hengist could charm the birds away from a loaded bird table on the coldest of winter days, because it was so much more fun to be in his presence.

He, Freddie and the lady novelist, who'd probably end up in bed with him later, were discussing a collective noun for heads.

'You've got a pride of lions, a gaggle of geese,' said Freddie.

'How about a hurrah of heads?' suggested the lady novelist.

'Or a "Hail, fellow, well met" of heads?' volunteered Hengist.

Aware that Hengist was having far more fun with the plump lady novelist with the loud laugh and shiny face, Helen knew she had been crabby. She had always found him disturbingly attractive. With his sallow skin, laughing slit eyes, dark curls rising from his smooth forehead and spilling over the collar of his dinner jacket, he looked like some Renaissance grandee. His height, strength, merriment and overwhelming vitality made one long to be in bed with him.

'How's my ex-stepson, Cosmo?' she asked. 'As obnoxious as ever?'

'Probably,' said Hengist, 'but he's very clever. I'm afraid he makes me laugh.'

With no Sally to drag him home, Hengist had a lovely end to the evening, drinking the minibar dry in his suite and playing bears round the furniture with his friends.

'Are you going into politics, Hengist?'

'No, no, I could never leave teaching.'

122

Next morning, Hengist had a frightful hangover and didn't get away as early as he'd hoped. This was the way to travel though, flying over magenta ploughed fields flecked with gulls, like waves on a wine-dark sea. Down below was St Andrews, with its ancient university and town hall built of big, proud, yellow stone, the colour of the turning trees. What a lovely place for Sally and him to retire to. A seat of learning, where he could at last write his books. Perhaps he didn't want Fleetley *or* politics.

At midday, the helicopter dropped him at Bagley, sending the leaves flying upwards, then whizzed off to take Rupert racing.

Dropping little bottles of shampoo and body lotion on Miss Painswick's desk, although her body was not somewhere he wished to go, Hengist asked if anything interesting had happened.

'Only these.' She handed him two letters marked 'private and confidential', one presumably offering him Shadow Education, the other asking him to take over Fleetley in the Michaelmas Term of 2005. Hengist pocketed them.

'How was the trip? asked Miss Painswick. 'You were awfully good at Bournemouth.'

'And awfully bad at St Andrews. Could you get me a vast Fernet-Branca?'

'Mr Bruce is in your office, by the way, says it's urgent.'

Bounding up the stairs, Hengist was amazed to find Alex sitting in his archbishop's chair, flipping disapprovingly through his mountainous in-tray. Alex's blackcurrant eyes glittered behind his spectacles with the same air of excitement as when Theo was arrested.

Feeling even more in need of a hair of the dog, Hengist edged towards the whisky decanter, then, dropping a St Andrews Bay Hotel bath cap on the big oak table in front of Alex:

'I've brought you a present. I know how you like transparency.'

Alex didn't smile.

'You'd better sit down. Something very serious has occurred.'

Not Sally? Hengist felt a lurch of terror, but Painswick wouldn't have been looking so cheerful.

'"Lay on, Macduff,"' he said lightly.

'I'd like you to explain this.' Alex chucked an exam script down on the table. 'This was handed in as Paris Alvaston's second history paper.'

Hengist picked it up and went cold to his bones. His heart stopped, then began to crash out of control. 'So what?'

'That is not Paris's writing. Only four people knew the combination to the safe: the exam officer, Ian Cartwright – who as Paris's foster father was not a disinterested party – Miss Painswick and yourself.'

'Course it's not Cartwright. I can't imagine Painswick achieving an A star either.'

'We've checked with a graphologist' – although he'd have recognized anywhere that arrogant, flamboyant scrawl seen so often on praise postcards – 'it was your writing, headmaster.'

There was a crash of cut glass on glass as Hengist poured himself a large whisky. For Paris's sake, he mustn't give in without a fight and prepare a defence, which of course was non-existent.

In a flash, he realized he would lose his school, Shadow Education and Fleetley, and Paris would lose his A star. It might have been better if Sally had died. She was so straight and true, the disgrace that would submerge him would kill her anyway.

It was a few moments before he realized Alex was saying, 'I suppose you couldn't bear your little guinea pig to fail.'

Then he backed away as Hengist turned on him, like a raging lion:

'It was your bloody fault. If you hadn't shopped Theo in the middle of GCSEs, Paris would never have screwed up. He was knocked sideways by Theo leaving.'

Hearing a thud, they both jumped.

'We're busy,' called out Alex.

The door flew open and in bounded Elaine, hurling herself on her master with joyful squeaks, then racing round the room knocking over a side table, a waste-paper basket and a vase of scarlet dahlias with her thwacking tail, before jumping on the window seat to indulge in some scrabbling running on the spot.

'Get that beast out of here,' screamed Alex. In no way could he more have asserted his new ascendancy.

Elaine was followed by Sally. Devastated by the Oriana saga, she had been looking tired and drained for some time. Now, with highlighted, newly washed hair softening her sweet face and a pale blue cashmere jersey caressing her breasts, she looked utterly ravishing.

'Darling, when did you get back? How lovely. The Bishop's caught up in traffic, but he'll be here in half an hour.' Time for sex, her eyes smiled. 'And some prospective parents have turned up.' Then, noticing a muscle bounding in Hengist's jaw and Alex's face longer than a tomb stone: 'What on earth's going on?'

'I regret our Senior Team Leader has been caught cheating,' said Alex heavily.

In the distance, Hengist could see spirals of mist, the

ghost of his career, curling up from Badger's Retreat. '"O! the fierce wretchedness that glory brings,"' he said bleakly.

'Hengist wouldn't cheat,' cried Sally in outrage. 'He's the most honourable man.'

Hengist turned back, stroking Elaine, who, wagging her tail gently and joyfully, was gazing up from the ripped window seat.

'I'm afraid it's true.' He tried to meet Sally's eyes. 'Paris found out Theo'd been arrested and made such a cock-up of his paper, I wrote it instead.'

'Oh, Hengist,' Sally clung on to the back of the sofa, 'how could you? Poor Paris could have retaken it! He'll be mortified, the press will crucify him after all the crowing about A stars.'

'Paris Alvaston, in fact, suspected foul play,' intoned Alex. 'Joan Johnson overheard him saying he couldn't possibly have got an A star, as he'd trashed his second history paper.'

Loathing herself, Sally turned to Alex: 'Does this have to get out?'

'My duty is to the other students,' said Alex primly, 'and I must immediately inform the chair of governors.'

There goes politics and Fleetley, thought Hengist. His heart was thumping relentlessly, his knees shuddering together.

'As I'm not prepared to be an accessory to a crime' – Alex cracked his knuckles – 'I have also alerted the police.'

'Oh dear,' sighed Hengist, draining his whisky, 'such a bad effect on recruitment. To have one master arrested looks like misfortune, but two, definitely carelessness.'

'Don't be so bloody flippant,' yelled Sally.

Elaine vanished under the sofa.

'Theo's was a lapse, motivated by lust,' said Alex sanctimoniously. 'This is a far greater crime. Who knows how many papers Hengist tampered with? Our entire year's GCSE marks could be declared null and void. I'm sure Fleetley will appeal.'

A smell of moussaka was drifting from the kitchens. In two neighbouring practice rooms, pupils could be heard hammering out pieces for the Queen's visit.

Alex sat back in Hengist's chair. Perceptibly, he was shrugging on the mantle of power. I hope he gets it better cut than his suits, thought Hengist irrationally.

As Sally slumped on the sofa, he could see the line of her suspender belt through her grey skirt and that she was wearing sheer black stockings and high heels.

'It's a sad way to end your career, Hengist, but I have to think of Bagley,' sighed Alex. Then, seeing a Panda car emerging from the Memorial Arch: 'Here come the police.'

As he opened the door, Miss Painswick nearly fell into the room.

'The new parents will be old parents if they're kept waiting much longer,' she said tartly, 'and the Bishop's arrived.'

Alex smoothed his beard. 'I will entertain his lordship.'

'Mrs Cox has made celeriac purée,' said Sally in a high voice, 'the Bishop liked it so much last time.' Turning to Alex, she stammered, 'Hengist only did it for Paris's sake.'

'No, I didn't, I did it for myself,' said Hengist. 'I'd invested so much in Paris, I couldn't bear him to fail.'

'You have brought independent schools and the entire exam system into disrepute,' said Alex, no longer feeling the need to conceal the extent of his loathing. 'You could get five years.'

What a dreadful combination, thought Hengist, Alex and ruin staring one in the face.

After lunch, in a frenzy of righteousness, Alex rang his chair of governors, not only to tell him about the cheating, but that Hengist had been knocking off a member of the governing body.

'Good God, not the Bishop of Larkminster?' said Jupiter in alarm.

'No, and a parent too, I'm talking about Ruth Walton.'

Jupiter said, 'Good God,' a second time. He'd always fancied Mrs Walton. One of his favourite sayings was: 'That man's the true conservative Who lops the moulder'd branch away.' There was no way Hengist was going to get Education now.

Putting down the telephone, Jupiter was about to dial Fleetley, then, remembering Lord Hawkley would be still at the Headmasters' Conference, he called the St Andrews Bay Hotel.

123

Hengist was arrested, taken down to the station for questioning and kept overnight. Dora, dying to find out what was going on, in overalls, wig and the guise of smartening up the general office for the Queen's visit, was so shocked as she assimilated the terrible truth that she managed to paint Miss Painswick's coat, as well as an entire wall, vicarage green.

Sally retreated to Head House, sat on the bed in which she'd been looking forward to Hengist making love to her, and cried. She'd never dumped on others. She'd been too busy listening to other people's problems and, unlike the clubbable Hengist, had always kept her distance. So she was now intensely alone.

What would happen to them? Hengist would never get another job in teaching. Nor would the New Reform Party look at him and – apart from the terrible disgrace – what would they live on? They had always spent a fortune on entertaining, on pictures, books and the garden, but never bothered to buy a house or save any money. When he had gone abroad on school or political business, Hengist had invariably picked up the bill. And how would such a free spirit ever survive in prison?

Randal Stancombe, who loved hospital cases, decided as night fell to call on Sally. The humiliating amount of coverage over Rupert getting his GCSE, abetted by Hengist and Janna, had increased his detestation of all three. He'd zapped Janna by moving the bulldozers in on Larks; now he was overjoyed to learn, from a very over-excited Poppet Bruce, of Hengist's arrest.

'How's Sally?'

'In shock. I took round some organic hot cross buns and offered her counselling, but she insisted on being on her own. I'm sure she's hurting.'

Randal had always fancied Sally. What sweet revenge to take her off Hengist. Champagne might be too celebratory a gesture, so he settled for a huge bunch of bronze chrysanths.

He didn't tell Anthea of his plan, even though she'd been delighted by the turn of events. Sally and Hengist had always shown their preference for Anthea's late husband, Sir Raymond, and constantly displayed favouritism towards Dicky and particularly Dora. Anthea didn't feel Sally deserved any sympathy, so Randal decided to make a mission of mercy on his own.

Showering in his penthouse at Cavendish Plaza, he drenched himself and the blue spotted handkerchief with which he had so often wiped away ladies' tears in lavender water rather than Lynx. Lynx would come later. If there were people with Sally, he'd just leave the flowers with a caring message: 'Thinking of you, Randal', which would soften her up for a later pounce.

Nice property, Head House, thought Randal as he pressed the doorbell. How long would Alex let her stay on?

Sally had clearly been crying a great deal; her face was blotchy and swollen, bloodshot veins intensifying the blue of her eyes. Upset by her mistress's tears, Elaine rushed to the door hoping Randal might be Hengist to make her better.

At first Sally didn't recognize Stancombe. With his mahogany tan and huge circular shield of bronze chrysanthemums, he resembled a Zulu warrior.

'I only popped in, Sal, to offer my condolences,' and he was over the threshold.

He could tell she was in a state. She was shuddering uncontrollably, the fire had not been lit, none of the sidelights had been turned on and she had obviously been trying to persuade that bloody dog to eat. An untouched bowl of chicken curled and dried on the carpet.

'You shouldn't be on your own.'

'It's awfully kind, but I'm better that way. Rupert thinks Hengist will be bailed first thing tomorrow, unless he comes up before Anthea Belvedon. Oh, I'm sorry, Randal, it's Rupert's way of joking.'

'I know,' said Randal bleakly, 'only too well.'

Sally started frantically plumping cushions. 'I don't mind for me, but Hengist was so excited about the future. He would never have touched Paris's paper if Paris hadn't been so devastated by Theo's arrest. Hengist wasn't there to reassure him and came back to find Paris had put in a completely dud paper, just signed his name and a few incomprehensible sentences. So Hengist answered the paper for him.'

'No wonder Paris got an A star,' said Randal coldly. 'I don't approve of cheating, Sally.'

'Neither do I, but Hengist has lost everything.' She started to cry. 'Please go.'

'I'm not leaving you like this.'

Randal had changed his hair, Sally noticed mindlessly, it was shorter and gelled upwards like an oiled, black pincushion. Turned upside down, he could be used to spike up the leaves littering the lawns outside. He was now telling her she was a fine woman.

'Look at that dog, Sal, asleep on its back, taking up nine-tenths of the settee, leaving you no space. Hengist is the same, taking up nine-tenths of your life. You've devoted yourself to a taker who wasn't worth it.'

'That's not true.'

'Hengist broke my heart.'

'Your heart?' Sally stopped plumping a silver wedding cushion in which the embroidered initials H and S had been entwined.

'I cared very deeply for Ruth, then discovered she and Hengist were having a relationship.'

'Ruth's a great friend of both of us!'

'Hengist is a persuasive guy. He also had a relationship with Janna Curtis. Sorry to be brutal, Sal, but you're too straight and sincere not to know the truth.'

Sally gazed at him bewildered. 'But Janna's such a dear.'

'Stands to reason.' Randal paced the room turning on radiators. 'If ladies are sweet to you, you'll invite them to your posh dos and they'll have a chance to pop upstairs for a quickie with Hengist.'

'Don't be revolting. How dare you? Hengist is such a super chap and so kind, mothers, pupils, school-mistresses are always falling in love with him.'

Stancombe produced a trump card. 'Here's a love letter he wrote Ruth and a picture of them in Paris. She left it under the lining paper in my penthouse apartment.'

Sally glanced at a very loving photograph in some nightclub and a letter which began: 'Ah love, let us be true To one another!' in Hengist's writing, and threw it aside. Randal had his blue spotted handkerchief at the ready.

'Get out, you revolting sneak,' yelled Sally.

'I could make you happy' – a squirt of Gold Spot – 'I can't bear to see you so alone,' and Randal had grabbed her, tugging her towards him, burying his full, cruel lips in hers, pressing his muscular body against her.

'You b-b-bastard,' screamed Sally.

'My, you're a foxy lady,' panted Stancombe as under her discreet cashmere jumper, he'd discovered splendid breasts, supported by a pale blue lacy bra. Putting his other hand up her tweed skirt, he encountered stockings and suspenders but no panties; remembering Hengist on the answerphone to Ruth: 'Darling, don't wear any knickers,' he added, 'You know you want it, Sally.' He would have taken her on the sofa if it hadn't been for Elaine.

'I don't,' shouted Sally. 'If you don't get out I'll call the police,' and gathering up Volume One of the *Shorter Oxford Dictionary*, she clipped him round the ears, sending him reeling backwards, splintering an occasional table.

'Why, you vicious cow . . .'

Rushing to her mistress's defence, Elaine nipped Randal on the back of his thigh, then darted off as the doorbell rang.

'GET OUT,' sobbed Sally.

Randal, in his haste, had not shut the front door properly. Next minute Paris, clutching a half-bottle of Ian's brandy, marched in. 'I wanted to see you were OK. Oh, sorry.'

Elaine accompanied Paris, snaking her long nose into his hand, whacking his jeans with her tail.

'Randal was leaving,' gasped Sally, hastily reloading her bra and pulling down her jersey.

'Good,' said Paris, noticing a trickle of blood flowing from Randal's forehead.

'You'll regret it, Mrs Brett-Taylor. I came offering support,' shouted Randal, banging the front door behind him.

Paris went to the kitchen and poured Sally a large brandy, which she choked on but which warmed her.

'What did he want?'

'To gloat. He brought some hideous flowers.'

'Bin them.'

'Not the flowers' fault, must give them the chance of a few more days of life.'

Sally slumped, shivering, on the sofa. Both Ruth and Janna . . . Oh, Hengist. And he'd sworn after Pippa: never again. Wretchedness was sinking in as his laughing, open, reassuring face looked down at her from Daisy France-Lynch's charming little portrait on the right of the fireplace ... Paris, having topped up her glass, was meanwhile consumed with his own concerns.

'I'm sorry, but no one will tell me the truth. Did Mr Brett-Taylor switch my and Boffin's papers?'

'No, he wrote yours. It was a very wrong thing to do. But he knew how brilliant you were and couldn't bear you not to produce the goods.'

'So Boffin really did only get a B.'

Paris's satisfaction, however, was short-lived.

'According to Dora, who's been hanging around Painswick's office, Hengist will be fired if he doesn't resign, so both Theo and Hengist lost their jobs because of me.'

Paris was deathly white now, trembling in horror.

'It's not your fault.'

'And if Hengist goes, Artie will be next and Ian and Patience will be turfed out.'

'Theo may well get off.'

'But Hengist's career's ruined.'

'No, no, there are thousands of things he can do – write his books ... Oh, God.' Tears were pouring down Sally's face; shock was taking over as she knelt by the fire, sweeping up non-existent ashes.

'What did Stancombe really want?'

'To badmouth Hengist. Oh, Paris ...' Sally wiped her eyes with a sooty hand, 'I shouldn't be telling you, but Randal said Hengist had been ... been ... having an affaire with Ruth Walton. I didn't want to believe it, but he produced such a happy photo of Hengist and Janna in Paris.' She clutched her head. 'I mean Ruth.'

'Janna?' said Paris unthinkingly. 'That was in Wales.'

'Then it's true.' Picking up the lovely little Staffordshire dog, which had fallen off the occasional table during Randal's descent, Sally promptly dropped it on the fender where it smashed in a dozen pieces.

'Oh no, watch out for Elaine's paws, that was a wedding present.'

'I'm sorry.' Clumsily Paris swept up the pieces. 'I never told anyone. I caught them on the geography field trip. He was at her bedroom window.'

'So that was why you never came and saw us?'

'Sort of. Fuck, I never meant to tell you.' He tipped the fragments into the waste-paper basket.

Sally couldn't stop crying. Paris wasn't embarrassed; people had always been crying in the children's home. He put his arms round her. 'I'll look after you. I'm sure they were one-night stands and one thing is certain: Mr Brett-Taylor adores you. Like Brutus, you are his true and honourable wife, as dear to him as the ruddy drops that visit his sad heart.'

'Oh P-p-p-p-paris.'

He was stroking her hair; Elaine snuggled up on the other end of the sofa, so he stroked her too.

'You ought to go,' gulped Sally.

'Have you got a best friend I can ring?'

'Not really, Hengist was my best friend.'

Paris felt so sorry for her. He gave her another top-up of brandy, then kissed her juddering mouth very tentatively.

'Hush, please don't cry.'

Sally struggled like a captured bird, then went still.

Paris was amazed by the voluptuousness of her body. Sliding his hand up her silken black legs, he encountered shaved pubes, or did women her age go bald down there? It felt smooth, then sticky. Her legs were long and slim and there was only a tiny roll of fat round her waist.

Sally gave a moan as his hand slipped between her legs and slowly, caressingly, moved upwards. The other hand unhooked her bra; out tumbled beautiful, high breasts, still darkened by the Tuscany sun.

'I always dress up for Hengist when he's been away,' she muttered.

For thirty years, only Hengist in his heavyweight strength had made love to her. Paris was Narcissus, Adonis, Endymion, a slender Greek youth with a body and a cock as hard and white as marble. He didn't give her time to think, because it was the only way he knew of lessening both their anguish. It was quick and, because of his kindness, extraordinarily cathartic.

Afterwards, as if she were Little Dulcie, he removed the rest of her clothes, dressed her in a white cotton nightgown and put her to bed.

'Got to do my teeth.'

'Do them in the morning, they won't fall out.'

Then he filled up a hot-water bottle and found her a sleeping pill in the bathroom cupboard.

'I don't take them,' protested Sally. 'Hengist tries to cram too much in and has bouts of insomnia.'

'Take one now.'

Sitting on the bed, Paris stroked her face.

'Elaine,' she mumbled.

'I'll take her out and see she gets something to eat.'

'And the poor, hideous flowers.'

'Yeah, yeah. Don't feel guilty in the morning. I reckon Hengist owed us.'

She was woken from heavy sleep by the telephone. It was Oriana.

'Mum, it's just come over the internet. "Toff school head arrested for cheating". Is it true?'

Sally shook herself into consciousness.

'I'm afraid so.'

'What happened? How could Dad?'

Clutching the telephone, Sally wandered groggily downstairs. Paris had put Stancombe's chrysanthe-mums in the mauve bucket with which Mrs Cox cleaned the kitchen floor. There was a bowl of untouched cold roast beef beside Elaine.

'You're beautiful,' Paris had written on the hall mirror in marker pen, 'all the guys fancy you.'

Oriana was still talking: 'Dad threw up his entire career for one GCSE?'

'I guess so,' said Sally, 'and we're getting a divorce.'

'That's not like you, Mum.'

'I can cope with cheating but not being cheated on.'

Echoing her father last Christmas, Oriana told the press that 'when one of your family does something reprehensible, you take it on the chin.'

124

Once Sally demanded a divorce, Hengist seemed to lose any interest in fighting his case. Despite Rupert bringing down an ace barrister to defend him, he refused to offer any excuse. His actions had been unforgivable. He apologized unreservedly for the distress he had caused a great school and particularly his wife and Paris Alvaston. He appeared unmoved when he was subsequently sent down for three months. Life without Sally was such hell anyway, it didn't much matter whether he was locked up or not. He insisted on no visitors.

Bagley was devastated. Hengist had been hugely popular. He had raised the school's profile at the same time as his own, and any liberty he had taken with his globe-trotting he had returned in glamour, vision, kindness and fun.

' "There hath passed away a glory from the earth," ' sighed Cosmo.

Bagley also loved Sally. They knew how tirelessly she had shored up Hengist, how kind she had been, particularly to the non-teaching staff, how many miserably homesick children she'd comforted, how diligently she'd rammed coronation chicken into square plastic boxes and raced up motorways to organize fundraising dinners.

Now the dream was over. She and Hengist had split

up and were to be chucked out of their ravishing house because Poppet and Alex, as acting head, wanted to move 'their brood' in before Christmas. Ideally, they would have liked Sally, who'd met Her Majesty on numerous occasions, to be out before the Queen's visit, but were loath publicly to appear uncaring. Then there was the little hurdle of the next governors' meeting when, hopefully, Alex would be confirmed as head with a salary of £150,000 a year.

Poppet kept dropping in on Sally to measure up rooms and windows and offer counselling. 'I'm sure once you leave Bagley, you'll find it easier to achieve closure.'

'Should we organize a leaving present?' she asked Alex. 'After all, Sally is leaving Hengist and Bagley. Perhaps a small refrigerator or a Dyson; I expect she and Hengist have only one between them.'

'And who will have custody of Elaine?' sobbed Dora, who would no longer be able to boost her pocket money and pick up stories waiting at Hengist and Sally's dinner parties.

'At least Alex and Poppet won't need Pickfords to move their lack of furniture,' drawled Amber. 'They could probably get it all into Van Dyke. Joan is definitely flavour of the month. Lando's got her at ten to one to get deputy head rather than Biffo.'

Rumour and suspicion were swirling round like autumn mist. Alex was determined to scrap the school beagles before February 2005, when hunting was bound to become illegal, and close the stables, which pandered to an elitist few and was the centre of subversive activity. He had also introduced a tagging system to ensure pupils were always in the right lesson and safe in their houses by eight o'clock.

'There'll be no more shagging in Middle Field,' sighed Milly as they waited to go into chapel, 'and Theo won't be allowed back even if he's proved innocent. Stancombe's builders are pulling down the classical library and the archives as we speak. Look what I've just found in the skip: Theo's translation of Medea.'

Paris snatched it. 'I'll have that.'

The press had a field day. Ashton Douglas was interviewed at length about his 'great wegret' that, against his better judgement, he had allowed Paris Alvaston to be plucked from the security of a care home and thrust into the hothouse atmosphere of a rich decadent public school, where he had had to suffer the humiliation of being cheated for when an exam was beyond his capabilities.

Col Peters's hatchet job in the *Larkminster Gazette*: 'The Head that wasn't there', picked up by all the nationals, listed Hengist's away days, leaked by Alex. Alex, photographed very flatteringly, was quoted as saying his goal was to put Bagley back on the rails and engage with the wider community.

In the same *Gazette* there was a profile of Ashton Douglas, entitled 'Schools Saviour', with a picture of him accepting a cheque from Randal Stancombe for £25,000,000 for the sale of Larks High School, which would go towards the education of Larkshire's children. Randal was quoted as saying he had very exciting plans for the area, including health and sports centres, playgrounds, a row of shops, even a police station for the Shakespeare Estate.

Nudged by Randal, Alex had immediately axed all Hengist's plans for the Queen's visit, liaising with the Lord Lieutenant and the royal household and guaranteeing Randal as much access to Her Majesty on the day as possible.

'Engaging with the community', Alex had also invited a lot of local movers and shakers to meet the Queen, but had pointedly left out Artie, Ian and Patience and, more seriously, Biffo, who was even more upset when he saw the agenda for the next governors' meeting and discovered he was not being put forward for deputy head.

'You promised me this, Alex, when I supported you over the Theo business.'

'That was before I analysed your maths results, which could have been better,' replied Alex coldly. 'You're nearly sixty, Biffo, and not cutting it any more. Of course I want you on side, but suggesting Sally Brett-Taylor be allowed to stay on was not helpful. I'd rather you didn't make suggestions like that.'

Alex speedily assumed the role of head. He'd been running the school for the last two years anyway. Now, like a second wife, he was determined to exorcise every trace of the Brett-Taylors; for a start, ordering the digging up of Sally's glowing, subtly coloured autumn borders and replacing them with regiments of clashing bedding plants.

Alex knew nothing of the art world, but had recently been putting out feelers for the right person to paint him. At some function, Poppet had met an interesting artist called Trafford, who, responsible for some ground-breakingly obscene installations, had been nominated for the Turner. Trafford, who was coming down for a recce next week, also had some challenging ideas, according to Poppet, about a sculpture to replace General Bagley and Denmark. Everyone knew of Arnold of Rugby, why not Bruce of Bagley? mused Alex.

He was gratified how many of the press were ringing him up for quotes, and now that he was appearing on the box a lot, he'd invested in contact lenses, like his icon Jack Straw, and a new wardrobe. Channel 4 was coming down for a programme entitled 'Whither Independents?' – or should it be 'Wither?' Alex had quipped to the researcher. They'd be filming outside, so Alex intended to wear a smart new raincoat in fashionable stone, belted to show off his good figure, which he'd acquired in celebratory mood the day after Hengist had been forced to resign.

The new raincoat was hanging in the general office when Dora, who was highly displeased with all Alex's pointless innovations, wandered in with cups of coffee for herself and Miss Painswick.

'Why is Tabitha Campbell-Black no longer on the front of the *Old Bagleian*?' she demanded. 'She's an icon.'

'Equestrianism is regarded as elitist,' explained Painswick sourly. 'Mr Bruce is replacing her with a picture of the Science Emporium.'

'How pants is that?' Dora was leaning forward to read the list of acceptances for the Queen's visit, which Painswick was typing out, when Alex walked in, causing her to jump and spill coffee all over his raincoat.

'Oh bugger, sorry, Mr Bruce.'

'Don't swear. Sorry isn't enough. You will take that raincoat to the dry-cleaner's, pay for it and return it by tomorrow when I need it. Why are you hanging round here anyway? You should be in . . .' He pressed a button on the tagging computer. '. . . French lit. Why hasn't Mr Deverell reported you?'

'Mr Deverell doesn't need the tagging system because we all love him. No one misses his lessons.' Dora glanced up at the clock. 'I'm only a minute late.' Grabbing the raincoat, she shot out of the office.

Later in the day, Dora returned sulkily to Boudicca. There was no way she was going to fork out for dry-cleaning, so she chucked Alex's mac into Joan's washing machine. Next morning, attaching safety pins and a couple of coloured tags to prove it had been dry-cleaned, Dora hung it back in the general office.

Alas, when Alex flung it on to go into the Long Walk with Channel 4, he was horrified to discover it had shrunk to mid-thigh, and wouldn't remotely button up. Alex was so thrown, he didn't get half his points across and forgot to plug *A Guide to Red Tape*. After the crew had gone, he summoned Dora in a fury.

'Those dry-cleaner's shrunk my raincoat.'

'They couldn't have. Perhaps you've put on weight.'

'Don't be ridiculous. I've weighed eleven stone two since I left Bristol.'

'You should have flung it round your shoulders like a matador.'

'Just shut up. Where's the receipt?'

'I chucked it away.'

'Well, find it then.'

'That Polly Toyboy on the phone for you, Mr Bruce,' called out Painswick.

Sidling out of the office, Dora remembered there had been a piece of paper with writing on in the mac pocket, which she'd left on her bedside table.

As Cosmo was as anxious as she was to depose Alex and bring back Hengist's very benevolent despotism, Dora showed Cosmo the piece of paper later in the day. 'It's in Mr Fussy's wincy little writing and it says: ' "BC Green Dolphin, six o'clock, August 27th", plus a mobile number.'

'What's BC?' pondered Cosmo.

'Before Christ – Mr Fussy's so old; and my God, that's Stancombe's number. Engraved on my heart. My mother's always ringing it.'

Next day, while Painswick was at lunch, Dora and Cosmo checked Alex's diary.

'He should have been at an "Against Gender Bias Workshop" in Birmingham at six o'clock on the twenty-seventh.' Cosmo clicked his tongue. 'Our Senior Team Leader has been moonlighting.'

Cosmo was a regular of the Green Dolphin, a trendy country pub, two miles from Bagley. Hanging on the walls beside fishing nets, tridents and leaping dolphins, was a mug engraved with his name.

As Lubemir had immediately cracked Alex's tagging system, Cosmo escaped that evening to the Green Dolphin to chat up his friend Susie the barmaid. Fortunately the place was virtually empty.

'Your usual?' asked Susie, getting down his mug and filling it up with a concoction made up of black vodka, Tia Maria and Coke, entitled Black Russian. He was a one, that Cosmo, with his soulful eyes and flopping curls.

Susie remembered 27 August well, because they were all there: 'Ashton Douglas, Alex Bruce, Rod Hyde, Col Peters (the revolting pig), Russell Lambert (the planning permission king, who allowed Stancombe's horrible expensive houses on the edge of the village here, blocking out the view from my mum and dad's cottage), Des Reynolds, smoothie pants, and his lordship, Randal Stancombe. They had a private room and drank buckets of Bolly, obviously celebrating something.'

'It's called "engaging with the wider community",' said Cosmo, making notes. 'Strange, or not so strange bedfellows: Randal, Alex and Rod perhaps, but what were Russell and Ashton doing there? I bet Stancombe handed out a few suitcases of greenbacks or Caribbean villas as going-home presents.'

As 27 August had been around the time Stancombe got his hands on the Larks land, Cosmo decided he must try and get into Stancombe's office. Difficult when he'd treated Jade in so cavalier a fashion – and when Stancombe had changed the locks after he split up with Ruth Walton. Alex Bruce had also put such a lock on his files recently, so Cosmo decided to try and gain access to those of another member of the party: Ashton Douglas at S and C.

There were advantages to having a famous mother. That very evening, Dame Hermione invited Ashton Douglas to a little supper party the following night in her beautiful house in neighbouring Rutshire. Ashton, an opera buff, was in heaven, kissing Hermione's white hands, almost too excited to eat his lobster pancakes.

Afterwards Dame Hermione sang to the guests, and during 'Where e'er you walk' gazed directly at Ashton.

Later, over a glass of Kummel, she told him:

'My son is obsessed with citizenship, Mr Douglas. He's taking it for AS level. He has such a feeling for his fellow citizens and the work of the Borough. It would be so wonderful' – Hermione opened her big brown eyes – 'if he could do a few days' work experience in your fascinating office to learn about education.'

'We'd be honoured, Dame Hermione,' said Ashton warmly, who had no idea of Cosmo's capacity for evil and thought he looked fetchingly like a Caravaggio catamite as, back home for the weekend, he sat quietly in the window seat engrossed in a book called *Know Your Town Hall*, which was actually a jacket wrapped round *L'Histoire d'O*.

'Bingo,' crowed Cosmo next day to Dora. 'I'll get access to Ashton's offices and find out exactly what's going on.'

Fortunately, most of the Lower Sixth were out on work experience and Alex was too obsessed with the Queen's visit to bother about Cosmo's destination.

'My interesting news is that my Aunt Lily and the Brigadier are planning to fight the development at Larks,' Dora told Cosmo, 'because the builders are endangering natterjack toads and loads of rare wild flowers, which aren't out at the moment, but which the Brigadier, who is a keen bottomist, recognizes by the leaves.'

'Ashton Douglas is also a keen bottomist,' said Cosmo. 'I'd better wear steel underpants. I might even write a musical called *Kiddy Fiddler on the Roof*.'

125

Paris was in despair, overwhelmed by the misfortune he'd brought on Bagley.

'You've created even more havoc than the Paris who started the Trojan Wars,' Boffin told him nastily as they came out of prep the following dank October evening. 'First Theo, then Hengist chucked out; both their careers ruined; Hengist's marriage wrecked. Artie, Biffo and your dear foster parents'll be next for the chop. Alex doesn't like fossils.'

Somehow Paris managed not to throttle Boffin. He'd caused enough trouble already. Bagley had completely lost its charm. Back at the Old Coach House, Ian was not sleeping and his temper grew shorter as Alex delved into every aspect of the school's finances. There was no Hengist or Emlyn for Paris to have fun with any more and every time he popped in to cheer up Sally, he found her unravelling with despair, and felt hideously responsible.

He loathed Dora and Cosmo having secrets and whispering in corners together. He liked the charming and emollient Artie, but didn't have the same bond with him that he had with Theo. Where the hell was Theo and how was his back and how was he getting on with Sophocles? And Paris had worries of his own. He'd be seventeen in January and if Patience and Ian didn't want or could no longer afford to keep him, he'd be out of care and onto the scrap heap, no doubt joining the criminal classes and the homeless, like so many care leavers.

Alone in the dusk, Paris punched the wall of the Mansion several times until his knuckles ran with blood, like Oedipus's beard after he'd pierced his eyeballs again and again with the brooch pins of his hanged wife and mother, Jocasta. A passage Theo had translated with such terrifying vividness. Paris shuddered. There was still one trail he hadn't followed up.

On his way back to Ian and Patience's for supper, having wrapped his hand in bog paper, he dropped in on Biffo to return a maths textbook. He found the old boy plastered in a thick fog of smoke, farts and drink fumes. The fire had gone out; Biffo was three-quarters down a bottle of red; another bottle lay in the waste-paper basket.

'Are you OK, sir?' Paris relit the fire, then played a sneaky trick. 'We're looking forward to you being deputy head.'

Like an old walrus confronted by an eskimo's harpoon, Biffo glowered at him. 'Not getting it.'

'Everyone thinks it's a done deal.'

'Huh, Alex says I'm not cutting it any more. Results not good enough.'

'You got me through maths, you must be a bloody genius.'

Paris waited for Biffo to nod off, then he grabbed his red leatherbound book filled with the addresses of old boys and other masters. Many entries had a diagonal through them and were marked RIP. There was only a handful of women's names.

He was half an hour late back at the Coach House. His steak pie had dried in the oven; Dulcie, expecting a goodnight kiss, had refused to go to bed. Ian and Patience were in their coats, waiting to go out.

'What's the point of a tagging system if you bloody

well ignore it?' yelled Ian. 'Alex has been on, demanding where you are. It's Patience and I who get it in the neck. Have you no consideration? What the hell have you been doing?'

'Looking for my real parents,' shouted Paris, running upstairs and slamming the door.

The following evening, Cosmo rang Dora in triumph. He had had a brilliant first day at S and C.

'I found several references to BC at the Green Dragon and other places. It must be some kind of club. The one on the twenty-seventh of August seems to be definitely celebrating Randal finally buying Larks. They had another get-together the day Hengist was arrested. They've obviously been trying to get their hands on the Larks land for ages. There was an email from Ashton to Rod Hyde way back in November 2002 saying – listen to this: "Despite all our efforts, Janna Curtis is not failing as expected. We must also watch our step, as she is accusing us of rigging figures and results and changing boundaries and bus stops."'

There was a pause.

'Have you heard a word I said, Dora?'

Dora, who'd been holding her breath like a baby, gave an almighty bellow.

'What in hell's the matter?'

'Paris has run away. He left an envelope with twenty-five pounds in to pay Ian back for not getting history. Then he said he was sorry for all the misery he'd caused and not to try and find him. And worst of all, there was no Hengist to give him a can of Coke and some sandwiches for the journey.' Dora bawled even louder.

'What an applause junky. Can't bear to be out of the limelight for a second,' sighed Cosmo, then, in a kinder voice: 'He'll come back when he's cold and hungry.'

* * *

Alex immediately alerted the police and the social services and, while blaming the whole experiment on Hengist, was desperate for Paris's return. The last thing he'd wanted was a crisis distracting either the governors when they met next week, or the media when they should be concentrating on the Queen's visit.

The police were very reassuring. Lads often ran away after a family row. At least he'd left a note; he'd probably be home in the morning.

But Paris did not come home. As the days crawled by, Ian and Patience sank into blacker despair. Patience wouldn't leave the house in case he returned. Dora kept bunking off classes and at night, combing the woods with Northcliffe and Cadbury.

'Where's Pawis?' cried Dulcie over and over again.

Ian couldn't concentrate on anything. How could he have shouted at Paris on that last evening? Taking a wireless into the bursar's office, he listened to every bulletin until Alex grew very sharp with him.

'It's only a foster child, after all.'

Pleading for help, Dora rang all her media contacts, who wanted to know if Paris was having woman trouble.

'Are you his girlfriend, Dora?'

'No, but I'd like to be. He's so beautiful, I'm sure he's been kidnapped.'

'We just want him home and safe,' Ian and Patience told the press.

'He might go to Feral or Emlyn,' suggested Dora. 'If he'd known where Theo was, he'd have gone to him.'

'We've checked Theo Graham,' said Chief Inspector Gablecross, 'but there's no sign.'

'And he can't go to Hengist,' sobbed Dora, 'because he's in prison.'

Sally felt desperately guilty. She never should have slept with Paris. They hadn't again, but he'd been so adorable, popping in most days, holding her in his arms and sending her praise postcards. Calling on the Old Coach House, Sally found Patience mucking out the horses, her mobile in the breast pocket of her tweed coat. Her face was utterly devastated by tears, her eyes huge purple craters.

'Oh Sally, we tried so hard not to crowd him; now we realize how desperately we love him. It's all our fault. Paris's last words to us were that he was going to find his real parents. Ian thought he was just trying to hurt us. We should have stayed in, but Poppet was holding some awful parenting workshop, and we felt we should go to gain brownie points.'

Patience collapsed sobbing on a hay bale.

Over at Wilmington, Janna had been equally devastated, not least by Hengist's arrest. Jubilee Cottage was on the market, the 'For Sale' sign creaking desolate in the east wind. As a hair shirt and to pay the mortgage, she was filling in for a head of English on maternity leave in the next county, which meant an hour's drive there and back every day, leaving poor bewildered Partner alone in the house, ripping up carpets, scrabbling at doors and biting the ankles of estate agents, who showed fewer and fewer people over the house.

Patience had called to tell her Paris had bolted.

'He so admired you, Janna. He might easily turn up.'

'Oh God, I probably won't be here, I'm working miles away and such long hours.'

'Poor Paris was devastated about Theo and Hengist. Alex is being such a brute turfing Sally out in November. She's just been here. Paris found out Ian and Artie were under threat too, poor boy. He must have felt all his security crumbling.'

As Janna switched off the telephone, she wondered if she ought to stay home, just in case Paris did turn up.

He loved me once, Atthis, long ago.

In need of comfort and the comfort of comforting, Janna rang Sally and thought she'd got the wrong number when the call was answered by a deep, lilting, utterly unforgettable voice that set her heart crashing.

'Emlyn. I must have misdialled. I wanted Sally.'

'I've just driven down to see her.'

There was an interminable pause.

Oh Christ, she'd craved the sound of that voice for the longest four months of her life, now she couldn't think of anything to say.

'How's the Welsh Rugby Union?'

'Fine.'

There was another long pause.

'Emlyn, I wrote to Sally about Hengist. How is she?'

'Not great.'

He was making no effort. He was still angry with her.

'Sally didn't write back and she's usually so punctilious. Is she OK?' Janna was so frantic to see Emlyn, she added, 'Shall I pop round?'

'I wouldn't. That bastard Randal told her Hengist was having an affaire with Ruth.'

'Oh no!'

'Randal was trying to pull Sally; then he told her about Hengist and you. Paris, caught off guard, confirmed it.'

Janna gave a wail of anguish.

'I can't bear it, poor Sally. Oh my God, I'm sorry. But it was over months ago.'

'Was it?' said Emlyn bleakly.

'Truly, truly, when I found out about him and Ruth, when you marked my stupid suicide note. Oh, please tell Sally she's the only person he's ever loved.'

'I'm sure she'll find it a great comfort,' said Emlyn acidly. 'I've gotta go.'

'Please, please don't.'

But he'd hung up.

Sobbing wildly, Janna drove over to Bagley and

parked in the hedgerow at the bottom of the drive.

After an hour, listening to the screech owls and watching the moon rise through the mist, she heard the familiar racket of Emlyn's Renault, careering and bumping down the drive. She prayed he'd turn left towards Wilmington, but she only caught a glimpse of his thick blond hair before, with a screech of tyres, he hurtled right towards Wales.

Patience and Ian sank deeper and deeper into despair. They had never known there were a hundred hours between each tick of the clock, and no sleep in the night, as a day became a week. There was no trace anywhere of Paris.

The police, by the increasing gravity of their demeanour, clearly felt something must have happened to him and suggested Ian and Patience appealed to the public for information at a press conference. This was absolutely packed out – the Arctic Prince being an on-going story.

The Cartwrights tried to be very stiff-upper-lipped, but they looked dreadful, hollow-eyed, trembling, their clothes falling off them and when Patience had to speak, she broke down.

'Honking away like a red-nosed reindeer,' shuddered Cosmo who was watching with Painswick and Jessica on the portable in the general office. 'Not much incentive to return.'

'We love him so much,' brayed Patience, her blotched face collapsing. 'We just want him to come home and know he's safe.'

'For God's sake, pull yourself together, woman,' hissed Ian.

'We were fostering him, but we wanted to adopt him,' struggled on Patience, 'if he'd have liked it, that is, but we never told him, we were so frightened of being pushy. We all miss him, particularly our little granddaughter Dulcie and Northcliffe our dog, who just sit waiting by the front door. Paris is such a super chap.'

'Cringe-making,' drawled Cosmo.

'Oh, shut up,' said Jessica and Painswick, who were both in tears.

After Ian and Patience, Nadine was interviewed and very indiscreetly confessed that she blamed herself: 'The placement was too middle class and Mr and Mrs Cartwright were too elderly to foster a teenage boy.'

126

When Hengist resigned so suddenly, Jupiter Belvedon, as chairman, had telephoned the rest of the governors and suggested they invite David Hawkley to attend the next meeting, to advise them on steadying the ship. This was agreed to be an excellent idea, particularly since Lord Hawkley was leaving Fleetley, and as he'd been touring schools with the Great and the Good looking for a Head of the Year for the Teaching Awards, he would have many fresh ideas.

It was also agreed that as the Queen's visit was so imminent, it would be better to have a holding meeting beforehand to discuss logistics and mull over possible candidates to take over as head, then schedule a second meeting shortly after Her Majesty's visit, when they could have a jolly post-mortem and probably confirm a shortlist for the new head.

The only person deeply displeased by this development was Alex, who wanted the matter sewn up. Gathering allies, he suggested that a previous winner of Head of the Year at the Teaching Awards, Rod Hyde of St Jimmy's, should be invited to join the meeting as an impartial adviser, as well as Joan Johnson, the favoured candidate for deputy head; also that to discuss arrangements for the Queen's visit Randal should be brought in at half-time.

As none of these three would be able to vote for

anything, Jupiter and the board agreed.

The governors had all loved Hengist and were very upset by his departure. Meetings in his day had been held in London over an excellent dinner at Boodle's, or at Bagley after a luscious lunch laid on by Sally with plenty to drink. Alex intended to scrap both these procedures. They were expensive, and people couldn't think straight if they were drunk.

Poppet, however, didn't want her hospitality to compare unfavourably with Sally's, and before the meeting, which was held at three o'clock on the fourth Friday in October, laid on a light buffet and soft drinks.

As a result, General Broadstairs, the Lord Lieutenant, who'd been up since five cub hunting and was absolutely starving, helped himself to most of Poppet's quiche, imagining it was a first course, which left cheese and cress sandwiches, plain yoghurts and figs for everyone else.

Jupiter retreated to a corner with David Hawkley:

'Any more thoughts on joining us on Education?'

'I'm sixty-five,' said David firmly, 'much too old for politics and about to retire.'

'Can you resist a chance to play God with the education of this country's children? Greek and Latin in every primary school?'

They were distracted by Poppet, bringing in and insisting on breastfeeding nineteen-month-old Gandhi.

'At least the lucky little sod's got a drink,' grumbled Jupiter as, hungry, resentful and very sober, the governors filed into the boardroom next door.

Here they were further distressed to find a less faded square on the magenta damask walls, between the portraits of General Bagley and Sabine Bottomley. This, at the last meeting, had been inhabited by Jonathan Belvedon's lovely, smiling portrait of Hengist, with his hand on Elaine's head and Sally's photograph on the bookshelf behind him.

'Beautiful picture. Hope it's been given to Sally,' chuntered the Lord Lieutenant.

Alex smiled thinly. Having learnt Jonathan's portraits went for over two hundred thousand pounds on the open market, a discreet sale could buy a lot more IT equipment.

Outside in the park, leaves were drifting downwards in free-fall. Jupiter sat at one end of the long polished table, with David Hawkley on his left and the Bishop on his right. Alex sat at the other end flanked by Joan and Rod Hyde, rigid with disapproval to be among the governing body of an independent school.

Miss Painswick, a box of Kleenex beside her, was taking the minutes and tearfully assuring Ruth Walton there was no news yet of Paris.

The Bishop kicked off with prayers, including one for Paris's safe return, then, when everyone was seated, added: 'I'd like to express the governors' universal regret at the departure of Hengist Brett-Taylor. We've all enjoyed Hengist's friendship and marvellous hospitality and felt privileged to be part of an exciting adventure in turning Bagley into a great school. The lapse that toppled him was regrettable, but understandable.'

'Hear, hear,' said everyone but Alex and Rod and Joan.

The first item on the agenda was the appointment of a new head.

'I'd like to stick my neck out,' said Joan bravely, 'and say that Alex has been virtually running the school for the past three years.'

Jupiter gave her a glare which said, 'You're a new girl so shut up,' and announced that it was essential to look at outside candidates.

'We always have. Several were being considered when it was rumoured that Hengist was taking over Fleetley on Lord Hawkley's retirement' – he smiled at David – 'and I think we should follow these through.

Not that I don't think Alex is doing an excellent job.'

'Then appoint him as head,' urged Rod Hyde. 'Schools should not be allowed to drift. A strong hand on the tiller.'

'I suggest we need more time before making a decision,' said the Lord Lieutenant, thinking what a damned attractive woman Ruth Walton was and the more meetings the better.

Ruth, in turn, was thinking that David Hawkley was utterly divine: strong, macho, brilliant and so gravely good-looking. Taking off her suit jacket, she breathed in deeply.

Alex then said he didn't wish to speak ill of the departed, but he did feel Bagley should be run more economically. So much of the land wasn't being utilized; so many bursaries had been offered to foreign pupils, particularly if the mother was, er, good-looking.

'And talking of good-looking women,' butted in the Lord Lieutenant, 'what about Sally Brett-Taylor, to whom we're all devoted? She should be allowed to stay in Head House till she finds somewhere suitable to live.'

'Hear, hear,' said all the governors, except Alex and his allies.

'Surely she could be lent one of the cottages off the campus,' suggested Rod Hyde, 'then Alex and Poppet, whom I see as the ideal couple to run Bagley Hall, could take over Head House immediately. It's hard even for acting heads to be constantly reminded of unfortunate past regimes. It divides loyalties.'

'I agree with Rod,' said Joan. 'Head House is a symbol of authority. The school needs strong management at once, particularly during the Queen's visit.'

Outside the window, Jupiter could see his sister Dora and Bianca Campbell-Black marching up and down brandishing placards saying: 'Bring back Hengist Brett-Taylor'.

Marching the other way, with a four-foot penis

destined for the body parts zone of the Science Emporium balanced on his shoulder like a musket, came a grinning Stancombe workman, reducing Bianca and even a tear-stained Dora to fits of giggles.

'Let's leave this decision until after the Queen's visit,' said Jupiter.

One of the school cooks then came in with tea and biscuits, on which everyone fell.

Stirring Sweetex into his cup, feeling he wasn't making sufficient headway, Alex said, 'Before Randal arrives to brief us, I would like to raise the matter of Theo Graham, whose case is due to come up next month.'

'I hoped the police were dropping the charges,' said David Hawkley quickly.

'The evidence is so overwhelming. It really pains me to do this,' lied Alex, 'but you should look at these.' Walking down the table, he placed copies of the poems and the photographs of Paris in front of Jupiter. 'The DVD of young boys of such a distressingly porno-graphic nature is still with the police.'

David Hawkley read one poem, then another and another, the hair lifting on the back of his neck. They were exquisite.

'Theo and I were at Cambridge together,' he said coldly. 'He is a man of utter integrity. I cannot believe he would ever touch a boy.'

'His base nature clearly overcame him,' intoned Rod.

'My problem' – Alex had returned to his seat – 'is whether to look for a new head of classics. A Mr Margolis is filling in for Theo, but my inclination would be to phase out the dead languages at Bagley.'

'You what?' thundered David Hawkley.

'Whatever the outcome of the case,' Alex battled on, 'if we let Theo back into school, the no-smoke-without-fire brigade would never let up. Theo's only two or three years off retirement. With a small pay-off, he could enjoy exit with dignity.'

'Theo is one of the greatest classical scholars of his age,' said an outraged David. 'If there's any further chance for your scholars to be taught by him, they should take it.'

'I agree with Alex,' butted in Rod Hyde, taking two more biscuits. 'Mud sticks. Bagley has had such appalling press recently, they must prove they're serious about rooting out corruption.'

'Almost all the boys in Theo's house have been dispersed, anyway,' Joan joined in the attack.

'Not quite all of them,' said a voice, and in walked Paris.

In one hand he was carrying a dark blue carrier bag patterned with gold Roman emperors, in the other a furiously leaping and mewing cat basket.

What a beautiful boy, thought David. Adonis bathed in moonlight. He'd never seen anyone so pale.

Miss Painswick dropped her shorthand notebook and burst into noisy sobs. 'Oh Paris, thank God you're safe.'

'Where the hell have you been?' Alex had gone as magenta as the wallpaper. 'The entire country's looking for you. How dare you vanish like that and then barge in here? Go to my office at once. I'll deal with you later.'

'You'll deal with me now,' said Paris coolly.

'Show some manners to your headmaster,' bellowed Rod Hyde.

'Deputy head,' countered Paris. 'I've come to talk about Theo.'

'This is not the time,' screeched Alex, 'and don't let that cat out.'

But Paris had opened the basket.

'He'll pee everywhere.' Jupiter snatched up his papers in alarm.

'No, he won't, I gave him a run five minutes ago.'

Everyone watched mesmerized as Hindsight landed on the table with a thud. The Bishop proceeded to pour some milk into a saucer and was delighted when Hindsight padded over and drank the lot.

'What a fine cat. Must have been thirsty.'

'Like most of us earlier,' giggled Ruth Walton. 'It's a lovely cat.'

Alex had had enough. Marching down the table, he grabbed Paris's arm. 'Get that cat and yourself out of here, at once.'

'I want to talk about Theo,' persisted Paris, prising off Alex's skinny fingers.

'As one person who has never given an account of that night,' said Jupiter, 'Paris is a crucial witness and should be heard.'

'Hear, hear,' piped up Miss Painswick, receiving a daggers look from Alex.

'This is Theo's cat,' said Paris, running his finger round and round Hindsight's plumey tail. 'He'd be an even better witness.' Then, out of the Roman-emperor-patterned bag, he produced an ivy-green leather folder filled with manuscript paper. 'Which one of you's Lord Hawkley?'

'I am.'

Paris flushed. 'Your translations of Catullus and Ovid are really cool.'

'Thank you.' David's hatchet face softened fractionally.

'Theo asked me to give you this with his love. It's Sophocles,' said Paris. 'Much better than your rotten *Guide to Red Tape*,' he added over his shoulder.

'Sophocles.' David was down the table in a flash, grabbing the folder, opening it, stopping to read bits in wonder, then flipping through to the end. 'My God, he finished it.'

'All seven plays, the night before last,' said Paris. 'I wrote out the final pages for him.'

'You were ordered not to contact Theo Graham.' Alex was spluttering, hysterical, impotent with rage. 'How dare you? This could compromise his trial.'

'Theo's dead,' said Paris flatly, seeing a flare of relief in Alex's eyes. 'He died yesterday in my arms.' Then, turning like a viper on Rod: 'Make something of that, you prurient bastard.'

The Bishop crossed himself. 'Took his own life.'

'Not at all, he had an inoperable tumour on his spine, claimed it came from being stabbed in the back so often.' There was only the slightest quiver in Paris's voice. 'He's been on morphine for weeks. Dr Benson's been looking after him. He drove up to Windermere this morning and signed the death certificate. He gave me a lift here.'

'I'm very sorry,' said a shaken Ruth Walton. 'Milly was devoted to Theo.'

David Hawkley put down Sophocles, a tear running down his cheek.

'How did you know where I was, Paris?'

'I rang Fleetley. They said you were here.'

'Why didn't the police find you at Windermere?' demanded Joan.

'They were evidently sniffing around last week. I only found him on Monday. At least we had three days together. Merciful death came at last,' he said carefully, 'and a dead man knows no pain.'

Hindsight, ready to witness more drama, settled himself, purring loudly, on the Bishop's knee. Paris strolled back to Alex and stood over him. 'You broke Theo's heart,' he said softly. 'He loved Bagley and his archives. They were his life, but he knew once Hengist had resigned, you'd never let him back.'

'You were told not to go near him,' repeated Alex, clearly jolted. 'Where did you get his address?'

'From Biffo's phone book. Poor old bugger was drunk with despair that even though he'd helped you get rid of Theo, you were still going to dump him: "Biffo, you're not cutting it any more." The sudden mimicry of Alex's reedy whine was so exact, the governors shivered.

'At least Biffo had the decency to make sure Hindsight was safely delivered to Theo's door in Windermere in July,' Paris told Alex contemptuously. 'You'd have put him down.'

'That is quite enough on the subject,' boomed Joan.

'I loved Theo,' said Paris softly and defiantly. '"Forty thousand brothers Could not, with all their quantity of love, Make up my sum."'

Glancing across the table at Alex, Rod nodded knowingly.

'I know about shirt-lifters and bum bandits!' Paris snarled at them. 'Since I was three, I've defended my ass in children's homes and foster homes all round the country.'

God he's wonderful, thought Mrs Walton as Hindsight, finding the Bishop's knees a trifle bony, settled on her bosom to get a better view all round.

'Theo never laid a finger on me.' Paris's voice trembled. 'The only thing he touched was my heart. He opened my mind; he shared things with me. Yes, I loved him, but not in the way you stinking pervs would understand. The night before the second history paper, I had a nightmare. I woke and found a man in my room, and screamed until I realized it was Theo; he was just turning off my bedside light and putting my books away. He calmed me down. I was so knackered cramming for history, in which I was so desperate to please Hengist, I fell back asleep at once.'

'What about the photographs?'

'They must have been taken on the geography field trip. Look at my hair now.' He shook his head so it flopped over his face.

'And the poems?' David handed them to Paris, who took a minute or so to translate the first one.

'I've never seen it before; it's beautiful.' For a moment he seemed about to lose it. 'It's a privilege to have inspired such love.'

No wonder Hengist cheated for him, thought David.

'Last night, after Theo'd died' – Paris had regained control of himself – 'I went outside. It had been grey and windy all day, but suddenly every star in heaven was out: Pegasus and Aldebaran, the Pole Star and the Great Bear, who Theo told me was once Callisto. They'd all come out to welcome a new star to heaven. I felt happy he'd got a lot of fans up there.'

Paris slumped against the wall, his face in his hands. Miss Painswick and the Bishop blew their noses. Everyone jumped at the sound of slow clapping as Cosmo sauntered in.

'Very good, Paris, you should really go on the stage.'

'Get out,' howled Alex.

'This is a private meeting,' said Jupiter icily.

Ignoring them both, Cosmo helped himself to a biscuit and, murmuring, 'Hello Hindsight,' stroked the cat and briefly the splendid bosom of Mrs Walton, who had earlier tipped him off that Theo's future was on the agenda.

'I shopped Theo,' he told the flabbergasted company, 'because I was jealous of Paris. Artie, Hengist, Theo, Sally, the bursar, even Emlyn were always fussing over him. I took and then put the nude photos under the lining paper of Theo's desk. I made out to Alex, who doesn't read Greek, that the poems were much dirtier. Theo asked me to get his DVD machine working, so I shoved in a pornographic DVD for a joke. When I heard screaming coming from Paris's bedroom and Theo came out, it seemed the perfect opportunity.'

'This is disgraceful,' thundered David Hawkley, who, being married to the widow of Cosmo's father, the late Roberto Rannaldini, was aware of Cosmo's capacity for transgression.

'It is,' agreed Cosmo soulfully. 'In fact, I was so ashamed when it all backfired, I confessed to Mr Bruce what I'd done and he simply wouldn't believe me, because he wanted Theo and Hengist out so badly.

He's keener on new blood than Dracula. There won't be a master left at Bagley, at this rate.' He smiled lovingly at Mrs Walton.

Alex was quivering with rage:

'How dare you tell such lies!'

The governors were clearly astounded. Even Jupiter looked shocked. And where does that put my deputy headship? wondered Joan.

'You can both get out,' said Jupiter.

At that moment, Miss Painswick's assistant, the comely Jessica, knocked on the door. 'Mr Stancombe's downstairs.'

Aware he'd put in a dud performance, Alex ordered Jessica to show Randal up at once, so they could regain the ascendancy, revealing the mysteries of the Science Emporium.

The governors, however, needed a few more minutes to decide whether Cosmo was telling the truth about Theo.

'Cosmo Rannaldini is a compulsive liar,' spluttered Alex. 'Any of my colleagues will bear this out. Theo is past history. Bagley must move on.'

'I think this whole affair'd better be set aside for reflection until after Her Majesty's visit,' said Jupiter.

Joan, who was watching Paris with difficulty shoving Hindsight back in the cat basket, decided to seize the initiative.

'Where are you going, Paris? Someone must alert the authorities that you're back. Have you any idea how much police time you've wasted? What the dickens d'you think you've been doing?'

'Finding my real parents,' snapped Paris.

On the Mansion steps, he and Cosmo faced each other.

'Plans are afoot to oust Mr Fussy,' said Cosmo. 'I'm doing work experience at S and C this week to get dirt on him.'

Then there was a long pause as a workman passed

them in the half-light, buckling under a huge gall bladder.

'Thank you for rescuing Theo's reputation,' said Paris softly, 'and that's for fucking it up in the first place,' and he hit Cosmo down the steps, before gathering up Hindsight and disappearing into the October gloom.

Over at the stables, Patience took the thousandth call from an increasingly frantic Dora.

'I'm so sorry, nothing I'm afraid. The police still think something might come out of our television interview. I'll ring you the moment we hear anything, and, darling, it's getting dark, don't go looking in the woods, it's not safe with just Cadbury.'

'Where's Paris?' wailed Dulcie, who was staying the night.

Patience had even greater cause for anguish. If the governors rubber-stamped Alex as head at today's meeting, she and Ian would be out of the Old Coach House by Christmas – so there would be nowhere for Paris to come home to.

A fatalistic Ian had left the office when Painswick went in to take the minutes and, in anticipation of their departure, was mindlessly sorting out drawers in the sitting room. He had discovered one of Paris's note-books. On the first page the boy had scribbled 'Paris Cartwright' over and over again, then the initials PC, then 'politically correct', then 'Mr Wright', 'Mr Wrong', 'Paris always Wrong'. Then 'Dora Cartwright', then 'Paris Alvaston Cartwright' over and over. Out of the middle pages fluttered a picture of Theo and a piece of paper with a blob, coloured olive green, turquoise, royal blue and shaped like a peacock's feather. Perhaps there had been something between him and Theo.

Overwhelmed with despair and longing, Ian gave a sob. If only he'd been more demonstrative towards the boy. Next moment, the notebook crashed to the floor as Paris walked in, ducking nervously as though expecting blows and recriminations.

Ian just took his hand and shut his eyes for a moment, then he mumbled, 'It's very, very good to see you, Paris.'

'You're out of logs, I'll get some.'

'Would you like a gin and tonic?'

'Yes, please.'

How sweet-faced the boy was, even though he looked as if he'd been sleeping rough, and had lost a hell of a lot of weight.

By the time Paris struggled back with the logs, Patience had been alerted and came galumphing downstairs.

'Oh Paris, how lovely to see you, we've missed you.'

She longed to hug him. Little Dulcie, who came rushing in in her blue pyjamas, had no such reserve and hurled herself into Paris's arms with screams of joy. Paris hugged her back, colour suffusing his shadowed face. A minute later Northcliffe bounded in, singing at the top of his voice, dragging one of Patience's huge bras like a mini Himalayas.

'The mountains have truly come to Mahomet,' observed Ian. 'I'll get some ice.'

Outside, he made a discreet telephone call.

'It's OK, Sally, he's home.' Then, not knowing the permutations: 'Could you let Janna know? And Feral too, if you get a moment.'

If only he could ring Hengist in prison.

After that, they didn't leave Paris for a second, fearful he'd vanish. Paris couldn't stop yawning.

'Your bed's made up,' stammered Patience, 'if you'd like to spend the night.'

'Please,' said Paris. 'There is just one problem.' Patience's heart stopped. 'I acquired a cat on my travels; he's outside.'

Patience laughed in relief.

'That's wonderful, we've got far too many mice and Northcliffe loves cats.'

They were just feeding Hindsight a tin of tuna when Dora rang.

'Bloody cow, bloody tagging system, Joan won't let me out. Is he really back?'

'Have a word,' said Patience, going off to fill a hot-water bottle. Paris was already in bed when she knocked on the door, an equally weary Hindsight curled into the back of his legs.

'I'm really sorry,' he said. 'Until I saw you and Ian on TV, I didn't realize.'

Patience sat down on the bed and took his hand.

'Doesn't matter; you're home. Ian is so pleased. He just loves having another chap around the house.' She tucked the hot-water bottle in beside him. 'Sorry there aren't any flowers.'

'That's OK – flowers are for guests. What really pissed me off was Nadine saying we were wrong for each other. You know I said that about running away to find my real mother and father?'

Patience nodded, quite unable to speak.

'Well' – Paris's hand tightened on hers – 'I guess being away taught me, if it's all right with you, that I did find them – that you and Ian are my real parents.'

Patience still couldn't speak, but she nodded frantically.

'I don't need to call you Mum and Dad, I'm just grateful I've found people I love, who, however horrible I am, seem to love me, so I can start again.'

'Oh, Paris.'

A tear splashed onto his hand.

Paris's eyelids were drooping.

'You're tired, shall I read to you?'

Paris nodded, but still clung to her hand.

Taking down Hans Andersen's fairy tales, Patience turned to 'The Snow Queen', and began: ' "Attend! We are now at the beginning. When we get to the end of our story, we shall know more than we do now," ' but by the time she'd finished the first paragraph, Paris was asleep.

128

It was time for the high noon of the school year, the National Teaching Awards, in which hundreds of teachers, including all the regional winners and their partners, are invited for a splendid weekend in London. Activities included a grand ball on Saturday night, seminars, and sightseeing. The climax, however, was the televising of the national winners receiving their awards at the Palace Theatre on Sunday afternoon, followed by a riotous party and no teaching the following week, because it was half-term.

The winners in the ten different categories had been originally nominated by two members of their school community. Their schools were then visited by regional judges and later by a team of national judges, amongst whom was Lord Hawkley.

'The Awards are an amazing celebration of teaching,' he told the Observer, 'although, of the six hundred people crammed into the Palace Theatre on Sunday, I will be one of the only public-school voices. No member of an independent has ever won an award.'

This year Alex Bruce, because of his clean-out at Bagley and his brilliant (except for Lando and Jack) science results and, of course, his *Guide to Red Tape*, was hoping to be the first. Rod Hyde, who'd formerly won Head of the Year, was hoping to score again.

A thousand years ago, it seemed, when Janna had been teaching English at Redfords, Stew Wilby had talked about putting her forward for an award. Now it would never happen. She no longer had a school to nominate her.

It was half-term Sunday, and she had reached rock bottom. The head of English on maternity leave for whom Janna was covering had brought in her adorable baby last week, and Janna had been overwhelmed with despair that she would never have Emlyn and his babies and the family life for which she so desperately longed.

In a bleak week, Stancombe, after a few hiccups – like the Brigadier pointing out the presence of fritillaries and natterjack toads in the grounds – had obtained a compulsory purchase order on both Larks buildings, to make way for – he'd finally come clean – a supermarket development.

The *Sunday Express* had rung for Janna's comments: 'Why don't you write us a piece about your battle to save Larks?'

'And call it Tesco of the D'Urbervilles,' screamed Janna.

She had been to the gym earlier, pounding out her hatred of Randal and Ashton on the machines. She ought to spend the rest of the day painting the kitchen some enticing pastel shade, as no buyer had yet come forward. Instead, she turned listlessly to the lonely hearts ads in the *TES*.

'Beautiful female,' she read, 'thirty, five foot seven, slim, brown hair, green eyes, enjoys long walks, reading, keeping fit, good wine.'

How bloody conceited to describe oneself as 'beautiful'.

'Eighteen-year-old woman, enjoys power boating, weightlifting, GSOH,' said the next ad, 'seeks female for friendship, possibly more.'

Janna supposed GSOH stood for good sense of humour – that was bloody conceited too.

How would she advertise herself? she wondered.

'Titchy carrot-haired loudmouth, failed head, near alkie, lousy SOH, seeks' – Oh God – 'Emlyn Davies for infinitely more than friendship.'

The Brigadier was revving up for his new series bringing epic poems to life. He and Lily were so dottily in love, Janna didn't want to be a dampener, and it was almost a relief they were in Rome recceing the first programme about Horatius keeping the bridge.

Still fatally drawn to Larks, Janna decided to go for a walk there and see the trees, probably for the last time. At least on a Sunday afternoon the bulldozers would be still.

Leaping out of the car, Partner immediately found a stick three times as big as himself and kept tripping over molehills as he lugged it round. The place looked desolate: great craters filled with rain, huge trees knocked over, bottles rammed into the tennis-court wire, the bird table still on its side in the playground. Catching sight of her, a robin shot forward hopefully.

The door to Appletree was open. As she wandered the corridors, she could hear the ghost voices of children. On the staff room wall, someone had scribbled: 'School's out for summer.' Underneath someone else had written: 'School's out for ever.'

'You will go through a time when everything hurts,' murmured Janna.

Still trying to negotiate his huge stick through the doorways, Partner dropped it and went into a flurry of barking, then scampered on ahead. Following him into the gym, Janna discovered the back view of a blond man in a navy blue jersey, so tall he could gaze out of the high window at the town. His hands were shoved deep into the pockets of his dark grey trousers, showing off a high, tight, beautiful bottom.

Janna lost her temper. 'Stop gloating, you bloody developer,' she shouted, then, as he turned round, she gasped, 'Emlyn!'

'I thought I'd find you here. Hello, boyo.' He stooped to gather up Partner, who, squeaking with delight, frantically licked his square blushing face, giving both humans a moment to collect themselves.

'I've got an invite for two for the Teaching Awards,' Emlyn said ultra-casually. 'Wondered if you'd like to come. We'd be home by ten. Artie, as well as Alex, has been nominated for an award. The first independent teachers ever.'

In panic, Janna grabbed back Partner. 'I can't leave him. He's terribly depressed. I have to abandon him during the day; Lily and the Brigadier are away.'

'They're back,' said Emlyn. 'They said they'd love to dogsit.'

Janna was confused. When they'd last spoken, Emlyn had been so antagonistic.

'I've got too much to do. I've got to paint the kitchen.'

'Paint the town red instead. It's a grand do.'

Then she noticed he was wearing a white frilled evening shirt under his blue jersey.

'This is a set-up.'

'Sure it is.' The warm, wide, unrepentant smile transformed his square, heavy face. 'Pearl's even waiting at home to do your make-up.'

After a lot of persuading, Janna went back and changed into the bronze-speckled Little Mermaid dress she'd worn to the geography field trip party in Wales. Full of chat, Pearl was determined to make Janna look beautiful rather than outlandish and straightened her hair so it fell in a sleek russet cascade to her collar bones.

'Knowing what a blubber you are, I'm not giving you any mascara on your lower lashes. Emlyn says it's a box-of-tissues evening, miss.' Then, as Janna pestered her for news of the children: 'Feral got two goals for the Rovers yesterday; Johnnie and Kitten have split up again; Kylie's up the duff again – no, maybe she ain't.'

The Brigadier and the new Mrs Woodford applauded when Janna came downstairs wrapped in her bracken-brown pashmina.

'What an incredibly pretty girl you are,' said Lily. 'Don't worry about Partner, he can have the extra piece of steak I'd bought in case you felt like having supper with us.'

'Here's a little something for the journey,' said the Brigadier, handing Janna a silver flask of vodka and tonic.

The sky was brilliant blue and the sun set behind them like a huge blood orange. Torrential rain nearly turned them back at Windsor. Emlyn wanted an update on the Larks children and regaled her with Bagley gossip gleaned from Artie. Poor Dora was evidently outraged because her bitch of a mother had had even poor Cadbury castrated. Cosmo, on the other hand, had been delighted to receive a red Ferrari for his GCSE results.

Emlyn's muddy Renault Estate as usual looked as though he lived in it. Books, newspapers, CDs, laptops were piled high and amid the chaos were a half-empty crate of beer, a midnight-blue velvet jacket in cellophane back from the cleaner's, clean shirts, new socks and underpants still in their packaging. The Christmas Scottie, she noticed, still bounced from his car keys – probably as a wistful reminder of Oriana.

Janna was even more confused. Why was Emlyn being so nice when he'd been so angry before? She ached to put a hand on his great chunky thigh or stroke his big strong hand on the wheel. He'd lost more weight, was muscled up and was clearly revelling in the new job.

'The boys are beginning to express themselves and play in their Welsh way, lots of attack and guile, and we've got a brilliant new centre called Gavin Henson.'

He even had cautious hopes of the Six Nations in 2005.

'What will it be like tonight?' asked Janna.

'Lots of on-message celebs handing out awards and attributing their entire success to some inspirational teacher; lots of winners attributing their success to everything from the school gerbil to the site manager; constant emphasis on the team effort rather than the individual, belied when rival heads are discovered throttling each other in the bog.' Emlyn's huge shoulders shook with laughter.

In London, the trees had hung on to their leaves; rain-soaked, shining gold, they softened every building.

'This city now doth like a garment wear the beauty of the afternoon,' sighed Janna, gazing in vodka-aided ecstasy at the gleaming river beneath glittering bridges and the London Eye, a silver halo tossed aside by some falling angel.

Teachers were decanting from buses and milling round outside the theatre as they arrived.

'Janna Curtis,' cried a pretty blonde, 'you did so well for your Year Elevens. Look, it's Janna, you know, from Larks High,' she called out to her friends, who all gathered round to praise Janna.

'You're much prettier than your picture.' 'Is that your partner?' 'Isn't he lush?' 'You put up such a good fight.'

'They've read every word about me,' squeaked Janna. 'So up yours, Ashton.'

As Emlyn, who'd been shrugging himself into the dark blue velvet jacket, shepherded her firmly through the crowd into the Green Room, large glasses of champagne were thrust into their hands.

'Oh look, there's Ted Wragg, he's so funny.' Janna took a huge gulp. 'And there's Lord Hawkley, and that redhead with him is Rupert's ex-wife. Taggie's much prettier,' she added defensively.

'Better have some blotting paper.' Emlyn beckoned a waitress bearing a basket full of chicken and prawns on long-pointed sticks.

'God, they look delicious' – Janna grabbed four – 'and those sticks are perfect for pricking bubbles as a "critical friend" – and talk of the devil, here come Rod and Alex.'

'What's going on in your neck of the woods?' a BBC minion was asking them solicitously.

'The Queen's opening our new Science Emporium on Wednesday week,' Alex was boasting.

'Goodness, it'll be Sir Alex soon,' said the minion admiringly. 'The other Sir Alex better look to his laurels.'

The smug smile was then wiped off Alex's face. 'What are you doing here, Janna Curtis? You can hardly qualify as a past winner or a nominee this evening.'

'Nominees up, Mother Brown,' sang Janna, doing a little dance. 'I came with Emlyn,' she announced happily, then, thrusting out her glass to a passing waitress, 'I'd love another one.'

The BBC minion, who had shiny dark hair streaked with scarlet and caramel, introduced herself as 'Bea from the Beeb' and said, 'Janna Curtis, I so admire your stand in Larkshire. We're so delighted you could make it.'

'Have you had a great weekend?' asked Janna.

'Amazing! Last night's dance was fabulous, and teachers are such lovely people, so modest and self-effacing; they hate being singled out from their colleagues for praise.'

'Alex and Rod are just like that,' enthused Janna.

Emlyn choked on his drink.

'Although one headmaster,' admitted Bea from the Beeb, 'who didn't win last year, was so furious he had a nervous breakdown.'

'There are the warning bells, we'd better go in,' said Rod frostily.

'Is that gorgeous guy your partner?' whispered Bea.

'I wish,' sighed Janna.

Not wanting to let her spirits droop a millimetre, she

managed to secrete a three-quarters-full bottle of champagne under her pashmina as she and Emlyn flowed with the laughing, excited tide into the auditorium.

It was a lovely little theatre, with cherry-red velvet seats and cherry-red boxes, like the drawers Janna hadn't pushed in before she left: those spilling over with rejected clothes, these with teachers, or with technicians manning a huge overhead camera like a pterodactyl to capture the Great and the Good in the audience.

'Oh hell,' said Janna, 'Rod Hyde and his admired wife and Alex and Poppet are just across the aisle.'

Poppet, in an extraordinary white broderie anglaise mob cap and a milkmaid's dress, was flushed with success from delivering her first TROT workshop.

'TROT stands for Total Recognition of Transpersons,' she was eagerly telling the Education Secretary. 'So enriching to exchange views with other caring professionals.'

'Silly bitch,' muttered Janna; then, as a female bruiser in the row in front swung round disapprovingly, 'You could use that one in your back row.'

'Hush, or we'll get thrown out,' warned Emlyn. He caught sight of Janna's bottle: 'What have you got there?'

'Petrol,' said Janna.

Emlyn tried and failed to look reproving.

They were in wonderful seats about ten rows from the front. Technicians, checking camera angles and locating possible winners, scuttled around in pairs, one carrying the camera, the other the wires, as though he was holding up the long tail of a mouse.

The beautiful set was hung with panels in Three Wise Men colours: glowing scarlet, amethyst, turquoise, and sapphire blue. A midnight-blue canopy overhead glittered with little stars. On the red and gold podium awaiting the first winner, was one of the awards. Named a Plato, it was a gold curved oblong with one end fashioned into the profile of a Greek god.

'He's got Rupert Campbell-Black's nose,' observed Janna. 'What a lovely party,' she added to Emlyn. 'There's David Miliband. He looks as though he's still in Year Ten.'

Emlyn had temporarily found room for his long legs in the gangway. 'You will tuck them inside when we begin?' begged a returning Bea admiringly.

Emlyn was so broad-shouldered, Janna also found it impossible not to brush against him as he leant in to avoid technicians racing past. There is not room in this theatre, nor in all the world, to contain my love for him, she thought helplessly as she took another slug of champagne.

A handsome organizer was now telling the audience they were here to celebrate excellence in education. 'To ensure maximum media exposure for the profession we all love, we want you to shout and clap as much as possible.'

'Hurrah,' yelled Janna, clapping like mad.

'I've been used and abused by the BBC,' grumbled an old trout in the row behind. 'I will not clap to order.'

There were so many shining bald heads and spectacles in the stalls reflecting the television lights that no other lighting was needed. Gales of hearty laughter, no doubt to show off their GSOH, greeted every joke from the warm-up man.

'All round the theatre, you'll find teachers seated in areas. There's Northern Ireland to the left in the dress circle and Wales over on the right.' Emlyn raised a hand to two young women teachers. 'And right over there are the Larkshire contingent. Look, they're waving at you.'

Janna waved back. 'Where's Yorkshire?'

'In the gallery.'

'Oh my God, there's Stew,' gasped Janna.

'Who?' Emlyn swung round sharply.

'My old boss.' He's put on weight, she thought.

She was brought back to earth by a roll of drums.

'Pray silence for your head boy of the evening,' said a voice, and on came Eamonn Holmes, who, despite a sombre dark suit and red spotted tie, looked, with his sweet little face and naughty grin, much more like the terror of Year Seven.

'Welcome to the Oscars of the teaching profession,' he said, looking round at the audience. 'Now you'll know what it's like to be in assembly.'

'He can't say that,' gasped a hovering BBC minion, 'it'll diminish them.'

'You're not allowed to make jokes about gowns and mortarboards, or about Whacko and canes,' whispered Emlyn.

There was another roll of drums, and actor Bill Nighy ambled somewhat nervously onto the stage to present the award to the Primary Teacher of the Year. As a photograph of him as a dear little boy appeared on the screen above the podium, he talked charmingly and deprecatingly about his school days, then announced the winner, who, from the gasp of joyful surprise, turned out to be a charming brunette sitting in the row opposite Emlyn.

As she ran down the aisle and mounted the steps to the platform, Janna cheered and cheered. The clips of her brilliant rapport with the children were so touching that the tears spilling down Janna's cheeks became a cascade when she glanced sideways and saw the winner's incredibly proud husband also crying his eyes out.

From then onwards, Janna worked her way through her box of tissues and her bottle. All the winners – from Best New Teacher, the Teacher Who Used IT Most Imaginatively, to the Teaching Assistant of the Year – were so brilliant, innovative and imaginative, and the children so sweet, and the celebrities so exciting. Janna loved Sanjeev Bhaskar and had always been a fan of Imogen Stubbs, beautiful, clever, posh, but also a true socialist.

129

Rupert arrived at the Palace Theatre alone and in a foul temper. The last time he could remember being in London on a Sunday, except for the Countryside March, was when he'd taken his ex-wife Helen out on a first date – and look what trouble that had got him into.

He'd only agreed to give away an award because Jupiter had insisted it would be good for his image and that of the New Reform Party to get in with the lefties. Except for Janna and Hengist, who'd both lost their schools, he loathed the teaching profession. They'd been so bloody patronizing about his GCSE and got so uptight if you mentioned their long holidays.

Now, still in his dark blue overcoat so he could make a quick get-away, Rupert stood in the Green Room drinking whisky, watching the whole thing on a monitor and thinking he'd never seen so many ghastly beards in his life, nor so many old boots built like semis in Croydon and with Tim Henman hair. Rupert loathed very short hair on women, even more than beards, particularly when it showed off hulking great necks. Talk about the planet of the napes. Rupert was so fed up, he couldn't be bothered to laugh at his own joke.

He'd been listening to the big match on the car wireless. Feral would shoot himself if Man U broke Arsenal's run of 49 wins. It was a measure of Rupert's increasing fondness for Bianca's boyfriend (whom he'd watched scoring two goals for the Rovers yesterday) that he'd started taking an interest in soccer as well as English literature – any minute he'd be taking up Morris dancing.

There in the audience was that stuffed shirt David Hawkley, married to Helen, stepfather to Tabitha and Marcus. How small the world was. Muttering about gravitas, Jupiter was determined to give Education to David in place of Hengist, who'd been so much more amusing. Rory Bremner had done over Jupiter last night – bloody funny.

'Isn't it a fun evening?' Bea from the Beeb broke into his thoughts with a plate of smoked salmon sandwiches. 'You should have seen all those major civil servants, not known for their frivolity, bopping on the dance floor last night.'

'Letting their lack of hair down,' said Rupert sourly. He loathed civil servants even more than teachers.

On the other hand, the blonde now accepting a Plato for school and community involvement was very pretty. He could happily have got involved with her. Lovely legs too; perhaps teachers weren't such boots.

Again and again the camera crews ran backwards down the gangway, as though they were filming royalty, and the little stars in the indigo firmament brightened as each winner, the real stars of the evening, mounted the stage.

'When's Artie going to get his award?' asked Janna.

'I'm afraid it's gone to that head of science, two categories back,' whispered Emlyn.

'Artie should have won,' protested Janna noisily, and was shushed. As her big gold programme kept sliding off her knees, rather than bury her head in Emlyn's lap when she retrieved it, she leant down to the left, which gave her the chance to take another slug from her bottle.

Emlyn was half laughing, but she wished he'd loosen

up and get into party mode. He still seemed tense and watchful as the lights turned his face glowing ruby, then sapphire, then aquamarine, then Lenten purple, each time more gorgeous. I love him, thought Janna helplessly. I just adore him.

'I know it's going to be Rod Hyde,' she cried in despair, then cheered and cheered, because the winner of the Lifetime Achievement Award wasn't Rod, but a darling old duck from a London primary who let the children run all over her office in the lunch hour.

'Please be quiet,' hissed the horrified Number Eight in the row in front.

Janna would have raised two fingers, if Emlyn hadn't held grimly onto her hands.

'You've got to behave yourself.'

'That's it for the evening,' said Janna, then nearly fell off her chair with excitement as a blow-up of a beautiful sulky little boy appeared on the screen, and a grinning Eamonn Holmes announced one last award to be presented by someone often described as 'the handsomest man in England', an owner/trainer, ex-showjumper and Minister for Sport, who'd called himself 'the most immature mature student' when he recently gained a 'B' in GCSE English literature.

And on stalked Rupert to a frenzy of wolf whistles and catcalls. He still had his overcoat on, but smiled slightly when Eamonn asked him the Arsenal/Man U result.

'Rooney scored in extra time,' replied Rupert. 'It's his birthday. He's a Scorpio like me.

''I was so useless at school,' he went on, in his clipped, flat drawl, 'that I normally don't like schoolmasters or -mistresses one bit, but I have to confess, watching the television in the Green Room, I have seen some fantastic examples of teaching that might have galvanized even myself.

'I'm here to hand out a special new award: the People's Prize, to the teacher whom the most pupils, parents, teachers and members of the public all round the country felt had done the best and most heroic job, and in the winner's case, pulled in five times as many votes as the rest put together.

'This was a head who fought against all odds for their school,' went on Rupert, 'and kept it open under remarkable circumstances, who inspired confidence in children who believed they were worthless, who inspired the staff into believing every teacher can teach and every child achieve, and who never gave up on a child.'

Tears rushing down Janna's cheeks took away the rest of Pearl's make-up. 'What a wonderful person she must be,' she murmured and, turning, seeing tears in Emlyn's eyes, added, 'Don't be sad.'

As she stroked his cheek, he trapped her hand.

The cameras were slowly creeping up the aisle.

'And the winner . . .' As, utterly deadpan, Rupert slowly opened the gold envelope, Alex Bruce, halfway out of his seat and deliriously punching the air, was sent flying by the overhead camera.

'The winner . . .' repeated Rupert with a triumphant smirk, 'is one of the few schoolmistresses I like: Janna Curtis of Larkminster High School.'

An explosion of cheering rocked the theatre, particularly from the South-West and from Yorkshire up in the gallery.

'I don't believe it,' gasped Janna, turning to a tearful, beaming Emlyn.

'Well done, lovely, you did it, just watch these clips.'

Among the television crews who'd been door-stepping Larks for the past year had been one from the BBC. Now they showed clips of Janna racing round hugging all the team when they beat Bagley at rugby; yelling, 'You're worse looters than the Iraqis,' at Searston Abbey staff when they arrived prematurely to remove earmarked books and computers; crawling across the park, waving branches of swamp cypress, bringing Birnam Wood to Dunsinane; and finally of her praising or comforting her children on Results Day.

Glowing testimonials followed from Stormin' Norman and Chantal Peck, who said Janna was just like a 'Citizen's Advaice Bureau', and the Mayor of Larkminster, who said she was a 'cracker'. Even the Bishop described her as a 'very live wire'.

Then there were clips from children all round the country who'd followed Larks's progress on the news.

'Janna seems so nice, we'd love to go to her school.'

Finally, Dora appeared saying how much they'd all liked her at Bagley.

'I cannot believe this,' muttered Janna as the film came to an end.

'Yes, you can.' Standing up to let her out, Emlyn steadied her, before setting her off on her tottering path.

Utterly shell-shocked and extremely drunk, she staggered up onto the stage, where Rupert caught her, enveloping her for a second inside the blue silk lining of his overcoat.

'Bloody marvellous, darling. Can you manage a few words?'

Turning, Janna reached out for and nearly missed the microphone. Freckles were the only colour in her face. As her speckled Little Mermaid dress, damp with champagne and tears, clung to her, people could see how thin she was.

'It's been a wonderful evening,' she began. 'I've never been so proud of my profession.' Then, pulling her thoughts together: 'I'd like to thank everyone who voted for me, and all the Larks teachers and children who worked so hard, and the parents, and particularly the anonymous donor who gave us a hundred and twenty thousand pounds so we could keep Larks open for another year, although S and C Services and the county council did eff-all to help us,' she added to equal laughter and gasps of disapproval.

'Rather a looshe cannon,' murmured a grinning Rupert, thinking there was something infinitely touching about Janna's little bitten nails clutching the mike.

'And we'd never have done it without the help of the staff and children from Bagley Hall,' she went on defiantly, adding, over a storm of booing, 'particularly without Hengist Brett-Taylor.'

'Hear, hear,' shouted Rupert.

'Cheat!' yelled the audience.

'Hear me out,' yelled back Janna. 'We must stop demonizing the independents as they demonize us. We've got to work together for all children. Hengist gave so many of our pupils a chance. He enabled Paris Alvaston, for example, to learn Latin and Greek. This is a Plato' – she brandished her award – 'but how many of you can quote a single line Plato wrote?'

There was a long pause.

'Plato said democracy leads to despotism, which is happening in this country today, when schools are closed down just because the powers-that-be want to make a fat profit selling off the land.'

The horror and alarm on the faces of the majority of the audience turned to sympathy as Janna burst into tears.

'But what does it matter? How can I be a great head if I lost my school? All I want is my children back.'

Emlyn was on his feet about to vault onto the stage. Rupert and Eamonn were moving forward when a dirty violet and yellow football rolled across the stage towards Janna's feet, followed by Cameron Peck, followed by his mother, carrying Ganymede.

'I'm training as a nursery nurse,' Kylie Rose told the audience, 'and taking singing lessons.'

She was followed by Aysha and Xavier, hand in hand, who were going to the same FE college. Graffi, waving a paintbrush, unrolled a scroll showing a draft of the mural he was painting for the long room at Penscombe. Kitten, looking breathtaking, was modelling and back in love with Johnnie, who was working in a racing car garage. Danijela was altering clothes at Harriet's Boutique. Monster had got a job working as a bouncer in a nightclub and, despite Rooney scoring in extra time, a beaming Feral came bouncing on, like Tigger, in Larkminster Rovers orange and black colours, leading a giggling Bianca, who was in turn leading Rocky, who was working on the Penscombe Estate as a chippy, until miraculously, every Larks High pupil was crowding the stage.

Pearl came last strutting around with her royal-blue rooster hair.

'I did Miss's make-up earlier,' she announced, then, turning to Janna: 'Looks as though you could do wiv a touchup, miss. Miss didn't have a clue we was all coming up, or she was getting an award. Mr Davies organized the whole fing. I'm working wiv Trinny and Susannah now, so I get paid for telling people they look gross. And if anyone wants my card . . .?'

The audience smiled fondly, particularly when Pearl took Janna's hand: 'Larks didn't die, miss. Honest. We just want to say it lives on in us and in all our memories, so thank you for everything you did.'

Great were the cheers and the rejoicing as they were all swept off the stage to make way for Lords Puttnam and Attenborough.

Afterwards it passed in a dream. Dazed and amazed, all Janna wanted to do was get stuck back into the champagne and talk to the children and find out about Graffi's dad and Feral's mum. But once Pearl had redone her face, everyone, particularly the press and the photographers, wanted a piece of her.

Overwhelmingly important at the back of her mind was what was Emlyn's part in it? Had he come over to Larks merely to lure her up to London? Had he persuaded all the children to vote for her because he cared for her or was it the altruism of a colleague wanting justice and recognition for a colleague?

She must ask him. She was just taking another slug of champagne to give herself courage, when Stew, her old head from Redfords, hove into sight and kissed her on both cheeks.

'Well done. I couldn't be more proud. Good, you stuck up for Hengist Brett-Taylor. Nice man, if misguided. I must have trained you jolly well. It's a crime you're doing supply,' he continued, lowering his normally loud commanding voice. 'How'd you like to be deputy head at a city academy I'm taking over in Lancashire?'

'Oh Stew, it's good to see you. You haven't met Emlyn Davies.'

The two men shook hands without enthusiasm.

'You must have been planning this for weeks,' said Stew, then, turning back to Janna: 'Mike Pitts has been telling me that everyone decided Emlyn would be the best person to hijack you, darling.'

Janna was hazily wondering why she loved Rupert calling her 'darling', but bitterly resented it from Stew. He was also too old for that trendy short hair at the front, as though a rat'd been nibbling it all night. Then she looked up at Emlyn, who didn't have a millimetre of meanness or weakness in his big kind face.

'What happened to Artie's award?'

Emlyn looked sheepish. 'I made that bit up.'

She was now seeing him through swirling black clouds.

Next moment Bea from the Beeb was asking, 'Could you bear to have your photograph taken with the rest of the winners?'

'All right, but don't go away,' Janna begged Emlyn. 'I want to ask you something. Oh look, there's David Puttnam, my hero. Oh dear, I don't feel very well.' She suddenly buckled, stumbled and flopped to the ground.

'She's fainted, give her some air,' shouted Stew.

'I think you'll find she's passed out,' said Emlyn. 'I'll take her home.'

Janna's children, quite used to bringing parents back from the pub, hoisted her aloft and carried her out of the theatre.

'"Go, bid the soldiers shoot",' said a grinning Rupert.

'Utterly deplorable,' chuntered the Bruces and Hydes.

'So unnecessary to bring up Hengist. She only won that award because of all the publicity,' grumbled Poppet.

'Shut up, you jealous old bitch,' shouted Aysha to everyone's utter amazement.

Emlyn wrapped Janna in her bracken-brown pashmina and his jacket and drove her back to Larkshire with the winter stars, Castor and Pollux and the big and little Dog Stars, accompanying him all the way home.

Janna was a winter star, he thought wistfully. The darker the night and things had got at Larks, the more brightly and cheerfully she had rallied everyone. She looked about fifteen; occasionally she muttered in her sleep, but as he took her little hand in his, she slept on.

She had been so reluctant to accompany him earlier and so defensive until she got pissed. Was she still keen on that asshole Stew, or on Hengist, whom she'd defended so fiercely this evening?

Using her keys to let himself into her cottage, he put her down in the hall while he switched off the burglar alarm. Next moment Partner hurtled in from next door, but even when he barked joyfully and rushed up and down hurling all his toys in the air, Janna didn't stir.

'I hoped I'd carry you over the threshold a different way,' Emlyn told her as he took off her shoes and put her to bed in her clothes, then, dropping a kiss on her lips and switching off her mobile, he left her Plato in her arms.

130

Janna was woken by *Newsnight* on the landline, congratulating her and asking her to come on the programme that evening. Clutching her head, wincing at white sky glaring through the window, noticing the time, she gave a screech of horror. She'd be fatally late for work.

'Can I call you back?'

But, as she started scrabbling for clean pants and tights, she caught sight of herself still in her bronze speckled party dress and then of the Plato gleaming in the dark folds of the bedspread, and, attempting to piece last night together, she remembered it was half-term.

Having splashed her face with cold water, scraped moss off her tongue and cleaned her teeth, she tottered downstairs. There was no note anywhere. What had been Emlyn's part in all this?

She was simultaneously reassuring Partner she'd feed him in a second and groping for Alka-Seltzer when a hammering on the door made her clutch her head again.

Outside Lily was looking distraught.

'You were wonderful last night, Christian and I were so proud, but, darling, I've done something dreadful.'

'You've never done anything dreadful.'

But Lily, it seemed, had been having a tidy-out, prior

to moving into a new house, and had discovered a recorded delivery she'd taken in for Janna two days after the Prom.

'I was so excited to be marrying Christian, I must have shoved it to one side and forgotten to give it to you.'

'Couldn't matter less. The only thing that matters at the moment is finding the Alka-Seltzer. It's probably a final reminder from the Gas Board . . .' Janna's voice trailed off. 'Goodness, it's Emlyn's writing.'

'Oh dear, that's even worse, I'm so sorry.' Janna hadn't seen Lily so upset since her mower broke down.

'Truly doesn't matter.'

'Come and have a drink at lunchtime and tell us all about the awards.'

'Sure, thanks.' Ripping open the envelope, Janna wandered back into the kitchen.

Darling Janna [she read incredulously]
I'm so sorry I was such a complete shit last night. I lost my temper because I wanted you to myself so badly and quite rightly you put the kids or rather Monster first. You probably won't want to but could we start again? You may be still crazy about Hengist and I had so much to work through with Oriana. But suddenly the prospect of not seeing you every day for the rest of my life fills me with such utter despair. I know you're busy winding up Larks, but why don't you come up to Wales next weekend? My mother longs to meet you, and there's a good head's job coming up in a school near here.

Janna couldn't read any more. She was blushing too much and reeled into the garden, collapsing onto the old garden bench surrounded by rotting apples, oblivious of guzzling wasps wooed out of hiding by such a warm windless day.

Emlyn had written this letter on the day after the prom, recording it to make sure it reached her, and she'd never replied. That's why he'd ducked out of Results Day, been so curt on the telephone when she'd rung him at Sally's and so tense and guarded yesterday.

'The prospect of not seeing you every day for the rest of my life fills me with such utter despair . . .' Oh Emlyn.

It broke her heart to think of him, waiting for the post and by the telephone, convincing himself she didn't care.

Then panic gripped her – perhaps he'd moved on, and found some Blodwyn to love. She didn't remember any emotions betrayed yesterday. He hadn't even bothered to leave a note. Looking up for guidance, she found the glaring white sky dalmatianed with liver spots. Midges shifted around like footballers adjusting before a corner.

She had to call Emlyn at once. Racing into the house, she switched on her mobile, which rang instantly, and she swooned with disappointment to hear a light, patrician, rather patronizing voice. It was Oriana, who'd seen the Teaching Awards.

'Well done getting a Plato, and thank you for sticking up for Dad.'

'Did I?' wondered Janna. The whole thing was such a haze.

'It was very brave of you,' continued Oriana, 'I'm so pleased they didn't edit it out.'

'I haven't watched the tape yet.' Janna sat down on a kitchen chair on top of a pair of trainers, feeling defensive.

Perhaps Oriana wanted Emlyn back.

'Was it really OK?'

'Fabulous. Charlie and I both cried.'

'How's the baby?' asked Janna, feeling more cheerful.

'Due in a month, thank God.'

Partner was pointedly shoving his empty bowl round the floor. As Janna reached for a tin of Butcher's Tripe, Oriana asked:

'Have you been to see Dad in prison?'

'He doesn't want any visitors,' sighed Janna.

'You're not still in love with him?'

'Oh goodness no,' stammered Janna.

'You deserved that award,' went on Oriana briskly, 'but frankly Emlyn orchestrated the whole thing. He got cramp writing all the kids' nominations and transcribing the tapes of the parents who couldn't write. Theoretically you shouldn't have won because you don't have a school any more, but Emlyn kept on at them.'

Oriana's awfully upfront, thought Janna, and how does she know so much about what Emlyn's been up to?

'Why did he make such an effort?' she asked sulkily, then felt utterly deflated at Oriana's reply.

'Because he has an innate sense of justice.'

'So did Pontius Pilate,' grumbled Janna.

'I'm now going to break a confidence,' announced Oriana.

Janna, who had been trying to rotate the tin-opener handle with the same hand that was holding her mobile, let go of the tin, which crashed to the floor as Oriana added:

'It's high time you realized it was Emlyn who gave you that hundred and twenty grand to save Larks.'

'Emlyn?' whispered Janna. 'Oh God, he couldn't have! And I spent so many hours banging on to him about Randal, and how Randal couldn't be all villain if he was capable of such generosity. I even speculated whether it could be Hengist or Rupert. Emlyn never said a word. Oh, how heroically kind of him—' Her voice broke. 'I never dreamt. Where did he get the money from?'

'He was saving up to buy himself and me a really nice house,' said Oriana reprovingly.

'This is terrible,' groaned Janna. 'That was why he was always so poor, not able to fly out to see you in Iraq, not flying out to watch England and Wales in the World Cup, refusing to go Dutch to the opera. Oh God, why didn't he tell me?' Her brain was reeling all over the place, as though its steering had packed up on a mountain road.

'And why me?'

'Because he loves you,' said Oriana.

'What did you say?' whispered Janna.

'Because he loves you. Look how he's given and given and given to you, ferrying your children and their parents to public meetings, organizing entire productions of *Romeo and Juliet*, even coming to teach at Larks, which must have been a helluva culture shock. Making sure of your career by getting you a Plato. What have you ever done for him?'

'Listened ad nauseam when he rabbited on and on about you,' snapped Janna. 'And you're one to talk after the revoltingly contemptuous way you treated him. I've never seen anything so horribly cruel and humiliating and in your face as you and Charlie last Christmas.'

To her amazement, Oriana laughed.

'Good – now I'm convinced you love him too. Well, it's payback time, so go and find him.'

'Are you sure he loves me? He didn't say anything last night.'

'You've got to make the first move.'

'Where is he?' gasped Janna.

'Training with the Welsh squad at the Vale Hotel in Glamorgan, just the other side of Cardiff,' rattled off Oriana. 'Exit thirty-four on the M4. Should take you an hour and a quarter. It's known as the Lucky Hotel, because entire teams hole up there before big matches and really bond and thrive – I'm sure you and Emlyn will do the same. And you can jolly well ask Charlie and me to your wedding.'

As she rang off, the purr of the telephone sounded like a great contented cat. Looking down, Janna saw Partner had the tin between his paws. 'Sorry, darling.' In a daze, she emptied the contents into his bowl. Then she wandered round the room, warming her hands on her burning face, trying to take in the enormity of Emlyn's colossal sacrifice. And bloody Randal had let her believe he'd given her the money, and let everyone else think so too. She'd murder him. But what did Randal matter? She must get to Emlyn.

All shaking fingers and thumbs, she tried to dial his mobile, but it was switched off. It was twenty to one now. He might only be training in the morning.

Gathering up Partner and her car keys, she ran out barefooted and still in her party dress to her green Polo. Never had the little car hurtled so fast, rattling poor Partner from side to side in the back. Respite came for him twice. First at the Severn Bridge, rising like huge palest green Aeolian harps over the shining levels of the Bristol Channel and needing a £4.60 toll. Janna, however, had forgotten to bring any money. In his booth, the toll-keeper, who had 'Carpe Diem' tattooed on his brawny arm, was utterly intransigent: no £4.60, no Wales. Fortunately a man in the fast-growing, hooting queue behind a sobbing, pleading Janna had last night seen the Teaching Awards and said it would be a privilege to pay her toll.

Gibbering her thanks, scribbling his address to return the money, Janna scorched on even faster. Partner's second respite came when his mistress was flagged down by a traffic cop as she was passing Cardiff. Fortunately the traffic cop had also seen the Teaching Awards and on learning Janna was trying to reach Emlyn Davies, who was a local hero, put on his blue flashing lights and gave her a police escort. This was a good thing, because she'd reached a state when she was muttering, 'M34, exit four', and would never have reached the Lucky Hotel without help.

But gradually the turning trees grew thicker, thronging the edge of the motorway like rugby crowds cheering her home. And there was the Vale Hotel in its lovely green valley, a beautiful Palladian house with red roses still flowering behind little box hedges and flags hanging limp in the windless air.

And there, even lovelier – she gave a shriek of joy and relief – was Emlyn's Renault, easily the dirtiest, scruffiest, most overloaded car in the place. Two women in white towelling dressing gowns, on their way to the spa, directed her to the Indoor Training Arena.

Tearing up a little hill to a big green building hidden by trees, Janna barged inside, past a big sepia photograph of Emlyn's hero, Gareth Edwards, through a glass door and found herself in a vast enclosed area, half the size of a rugby pitch and carpeted with artificial grass. It was so like a huge hangar, she half expected Kenneth More to roll up or a Hercules to taxi in after a hard night's work.

Instead, twenty odd members of the Welsh national squad, mostly pale-faced, black-haired, black-eyed and gloriously hunky, were running about practising back moves, set line-outs and tackling great red rubber bollards; and there, towering over them, shouting, encouraging, advising but not as sharp or focused as usual, in a grey tracksuit adorned with the three Welsh feathers, was her own golden-haired, ruddy-faced Hercules down from the skies.

'Emlyn,' screamed Janna, 'oh Emlyn.'

'Janna,' gasped Emlyn as, lovely as the Olympic torch approaching its final destination, still in her party dress, bare-armed and barefooted, she hurtled across the bouncy green grass towards him.

Six feet away, she halted, panting for breath, fighting back the tears.

'Oh Emlyn,' she gasped, 'I only got the letter you sent me back in June after the prom this morning. Lily

1049

signed for it, but she was so excited about Christian proposing, she shoved it in a drawer.'

Then seeing his face lighten in incredulous hope and bewilderment, she stumbled on:

'It's been the most miserable time of my life for me too. At first I blamed it on losing Larks, but now I realize I said goodbye to that months ago, and it was only you I was missing. I just love you to bits. I don't care where I live as long as it's with you.'

As she edged towards him, they were both oblivious of the flower of Welsh rugby also gathering round, transfixed with interest to see one of their normally roaringly articulate coaches utterly lost for words.

'And what is more' – Janna brushed away the tears – 'Oriana told me about the money. Emlyn, it was all your savings for her and your future and you never let on. I can't even begin to thank you and for all the other things you've done for me.'

'A lot of that money was left me by Dad,' mumbled Emlyn. 'Nothing would have pleased him more than it being spent on Larks. Oriana ought to be shot.'

'So ought Randal,' admitted Janna, but she was not to be deflected.

She was so close now she could feel the heat of his body and, looking up, see the dark underside of his blond curls, his massive torso heaving and his square jaw gritted in an attempt not to break down.

'D'you remember once asking me what I'd most like in the world?' she asked.

'You said a waiting list.'

'Well, I've changed my mind,' sobbed Janna. 'I want a wedding ring, and the chance to spend the rest of my life loving you and paying you back for all the kindness.'

When Emlyn just gazed at her and said nothing, she stammered, 'But only if you haven't changed your mind and still feel those wonderful things you said in your letter.'

It is difficult even in a fast lift to rise from darkest hell to heaven so quickly. Emlyn still couldn't bring the words out. Below him Janna's flaming red hair seemed to fan out as cheerfully as a bonfire on a grey winter day, and her love seemed as true and real as the grass beneath her little feet was artificial.

'If I still feel like that?' asked Emlyn slowly as, softly as a falling leaf, his hand touched her soaked cheek. 'Oh God, lovely, if only you knew.'

Wiping his eyes, pulling her into his arms, enfolding her in a great bear hug, looking down into her adorable face, where every freckle seemed to be declaring its love, he kissed her on and on and on until the ecstatic Welsh rugby squad gave them a standing ovation.

'With breath control like that, Emlyn,' shouted one of the forwards, 'you should be teaching underwater swimming.'

'Aren't you going to introduce the lady?' shouted a back.

The fast lift had clearly reached heaven. With a huge smile and an arm about a dazed but beaming Janna, Emlyn glanced round at the squad. 'I'd like you to welcome the future Mrs Davies to Wales,' he said proudly.

Instantly there was a patter of tiny feet as Partner, having wriggled out of the Polo window and conned his way to the training area, happily took up his position beside them.

131

Two days before the Queen's visit, Dora, utterly out-raged that Alex Bruce had banned all dogs from the campus and wearing a 'Ban the Ban' badge on each lapel, accompanied Artie Deverell and his two Jack Russells, Verlaine and Rimbaud, round Bagley village.

Dora loved Artie because in his languor, sensitivity, extreme kindness and slight air of helplessness, he reminded her so much of her late father, Raymond. Artie, in turn, was devoted to Dora. When his feckless, totally unsuitable chef boyfriend had finally walked out two years ago, it had been Dora who'd mounted a relief operation, which resulted in every member of the Upper Fourth bringing round their cod in cheese sauce, cooked in food technology, for his supper that evening.

Today she was in full flood. 'It's so pants of Alex changing everything,' she stormed. 'The eventing and polo teams and the beagles were going to meet the Queen at the gate and act as outriders up to the Mansion. You know how she loves horses and dogs. And Paris was going to recite a beautiful poem he'd written.

'Instead the poor dear's got to listen to an IT lesson, watch Poppet teach RE and then tour that stupid Science Emporium and witness Boffin perform some stupid experiment, splitting the atom or finding a cure

1052

for bird flu. Although Mr Fussy's flapping around so much, he'll give us bird flu anyway.'

Passing the charming cottage where Cosmo had installed Mrs Walton, reaching the White Lion, they wistfully breathed in the smell of lamb braising in red wine, parsley and garlic. School food had deteriorated depressingly since Poppet's lentil-loaded, salt-free regime had taken over.

'If we turn left here, down Stream Lane,' Dora told Artie, 'we can sneak the dogs back to your house undercover via Badger's Retreat and the golf course. I've done it often enough with Cadbury.'

It was a mild, windless day; gold leaves clogged the dark waters of the stream. Birds sang sweetly in the rain-soaked air. The path was strewn with tawny willow spears.

'"Yellow, and black and pale, and hectic red,"' quoted Artie, as the Jack Russells bounded ahead, stopping to fight and snuffle down rabbit holes.

'Hengist wanted the Queen to watch a history lesson,' said Dora crossly.

'Might have been tricky,' mused Artie, wondering nervously, as he lit a cigarette, how far Poppet's no smoking ban extended. 'The Upper Fifth are doing the Russian Revolution, the Middle Fifth, the English Civil War.'

'And we're doing the French Revolution,' giggled Dora, chucking a stick for the dogs. 'Might have been a bit tactless, all those kings and queens having their heads chopped off. But she'd have seen some terrific teaching. Hengist's lessons were wonderful. We were making a guillotine and tumbrels when he was arrested. The acting head of history Mr Fussy's roped in promptly put them on the skip. He keeps groping Bianca; we call him the Randy Republican.

'Emlyn was a terrific teacher too,' Dora sighed, as they crossed over a wooden bridge back onto Bagley land. 'Exciting about him and Janna getting married; I hope they ask me to the wedding. And wasn't it lovely her getting that Teaching Award and not Mr Fussy, and all the Larks pupils coming onto the stage. I think Paris was upset not to be part of it, he was very fond of Janna,' Dora added wistfully, 'and he's terribly upset about the bursar being booted out at Christmas. I do wish Hengist would come back.'

Oh, so do I, thought Artie.

Ahead, after a night of downpour, serpents of opal blue mist were writhing out of Badger's Retreat.

Artie let Dora run on. Since Hengist, his real, never-confessed love, had left, Bagley had lost its lustre. Artie had already had numerous approaches from other schools. Even Fleetley was putting out feelers. But he had loved Bagley so much and, like Theo, so longed to end his days here, he couldn't rouse himself to go to interviews.

In his breast pocket was a letter from Hengist.

'Dear Artie, I'm so sorry I let you down. If I'd made you deputy head as you deserved, none of this sorry business would have happened. Please look after Sally and the school if you can. Yours ever.'

Yours never, thought Artie sadly.

'Couldn't you be head?' Dora's shrill voice broke into his reverie.

'I don't think Mr Bruce would like that.'

'Everyone loathes him.'

'That's enough,' said Artie firmly, dodging to avoid a stick which Dora in her rage had thrown straight up in the air.

'My God,' he exploded as they reached Badger's Retreat, 'they've daubed red spots on everything, even Hengist's Family Tree.'

'Mr Fussy must be going to chop them down. He thinks woods are pointless. And he's banished Cadbury so the Queen won't meet him, which will be a great disappointment to her. Instead she'll have to listen to Alex's boring speech. Poor Painswick has to keep on retyping it when she's not ringing the Met. Office to check the weather: "Oh, it's you again, Miss Painswick, it's going to bloody chuck it down."

'And what's more . . .' Dora retrieved the stick, teasing the Jack Russells, who launched into a frenzy of yapping.

'For God's sake,' hissed Artie in alarm, 'they'll get arrested.'

'And what's more' – Dora chucked the stick – 'I was in the general office and quite by chance caught sight of the agenda for the next governors' meeting, and I promise you General Bagley and Denmark are for the chop. Because the General was an imperialist who kicked ass after the Black Hole of Calcutta, Poppet wants him toppled like Saddam Hussein and replaced, I would think, by some manky statue of Mr Fussy brandishing a test tube and a copy of *Red Tape*.'

Artie was appalled. 'They can't pull down General Bagley. It's a beautiful sculpture.'

'And Denmark's so realistic, I always want to give him an apple.'

'And the General was a most civilized old boy,' protested Artie, 'who took copies of Racine and the *Iliad* to India with him, kept springers, was an excellent watercolourist, then left all his land and his house to found this school.'

'Well, I do know' – Dora glanced furtively round – 'that Mr Fussy, who knows eff all about art, has asked an artist called Trafford to come up with alternative suggestions. I bet he doesn't realize Trafford, who is a best friend of my brother Jonathan, is wildly expensive and often charges twenty thousand for a maquette.'

Despite his horror at the threat to the General, Artie laughed. 'Trafford has certainly made a convert of Poppet,' he said. 'She much admired his latest installation: *Tranny by Gaslight: The Story of a Sex Change*.'

'Working title: *From Willy to Womb*. It's absolutely disgusting,' thundered Dora, 'and cost half a million pounds. And I bet she hasn't seen *Sister Hoodie*, Trafford's video of a teenage girl beating up an old woman.'

'How can Poppet accuse our beloved General of colonialism,' said Artie indignantly, 'when her new best friend Randal Stancombe is busy colonizing Larkshire?'

As they neared Bagley and Artie hid both Jack Russells under his coat, they passed Theo's old house, now the home of the Randy Republican, who'd put a picture of Trotsky in the window.

'I'm determined to plant an oak tree in Theo's memory,' said Artie, 'but Alex is resolutely against it.'

'He's also banned school fireworks tonight for the first time in twenty years,' raged Dora, 'because they leave even more mess than dogs.'

132

Twenty-four hours to go. To the excitement of the female pupils, Bagley swarmed with hunky security men and sniffer dogs checking everywhere for weapons and explosives.

The red carpet couldn't be laid yet because the white gloss on the corridor wainscots was still wet. The sea-blue curtain covering the plaque on the Science Emporium wall, which the Queen would unveil to commemorate her visit, had fallen off when Joan Johnson jerked it back in rehearsal, but was now firmly secured. The splendid lavatory, specially built for the royal visit and nicknamed the 'Roylet', had been equipped with pot pourri and Bluebell, allegedly the Queen's favourite soap and toilet water. The framed print of *The Laughing Cavalier* had been replaced by a more neutral field of poppies and relocated in the dressing room of Dame Hermione Harefield, who, with her demands for vintage champagne, four dozen yellow roses and her own private loo, was causing far more hassle than the dear Queen.

There was good news however. The forecast was fine, if chilly, and Alex's bible the New Scientist had accepted, alongside a huge turnout of press and television who didn't realize all the celebs, including the Russian Minister of Affaires and Rupert Campbell-Black, had cancelled out of loyalty to Hengist.

'What story do you want to tell the Queen about the school?' General Broadstairs, the Lord Lieutenant, who was a governor anyway, had asked Alex on their first meeting after Hengist's departure, and Alex had replied that he wished to 'showcase Bagley's scientific and technological achievements in an emporium which would be the envy of scientists the world over'.

What Alex really wanted was to nail the top job and for people to love him more than Hengist. He was furious Janna had won an award and had finally got together with that Welsh gorilla who'd tried to drown Poppet, but he supposed they deserved each other.

Alex didn't find diplomacy easy. He had failed to thwart Poppet's plan to serve vegetable curry for everyone after the Queen had gone. Randal Stancombe too, once he'd learnt Boffin was performing some ground-breaking experiment in front of the Queen, had insisted that his Jade must present the Queen with her bouquet. Alex didn't dare say he'd promised that role to Little Dulcie who, with her wheelbarrow, had laboured harder on the emporium than any of the workforce. He didn't need to appease Patience and Ian, quite the reverse, but he must buy Dulcie a teddy bear. Randal had also insisted that Dora, who, as Jade's potential stepsister, might be jealous, must present Her Majesty with some dog she'd made specially in pottery. Alex hated kow-towing to Randal and Poppet. Once he was head, he'd call the shots.

The Queen had several other engagements on the same day in Larkshire. It was essential none of them overran. She was due to reach Bagley at 11.30 and must, on pain of guillotine, leave by 12.30 to reach a hospital on the outskirts of Larkminster at 12.50.

After endless telephone calls and meetings with local police and members of the royal household protection team and the route being rewalked and the itinerary reworked to the final second, an increasingly uptight

Alex insisted on one more, school only, rehearsal after lunch.

Biffo, acutely aware his job was on the line, had been given a stopwatch and put in charge of operations. Searching for a stand-in for the Queen, he promptly roped in Trafford, the louche artist invited down by Alex and Poppet to provide an alternative to General Bagley, whom he found eating a doughnut and reading a porn mag in the staffroom.

'And since you're so good at acting,' Biffo added bossily to Paris, 'you can double up as Lord Lieutenant and headmaster until Alex gets here. Anyone involved in events the Queen is going to witness can take up their positions around the route.'

Dora should have been standing by General Bagley's statue waiting to hand over her pottery dog immediately after Jade had presented the Queen with her bouquet. Reluctant to miss anything, however, Dora had managed to lose herself among a group of Lower Fifths, including Bianca, whom Biffo had grabbed as they came out of the dining room to act as press. After all, no one is more qualified than me, rationalized Dora.

Trafford, meanwhile, attempting to appear more royal, had topped his shaved head, designer stubble and pig-like features with the large rose-trimmed mauve felt hat Miss Painswick had bought specially for the big day, reducing everyone to fits of giggles. Thus encouraged, Trafford pretended to jump out of a limo outside the Mansion steps, saying in a high voice:

'My husband and I, what a beautiful school, we haven't been here before.'

'Stop being silly, Trafford,' snapped Biffo, consulting his notes. 'Now, as Lord Lieutenant, Paris, you present Jupiter Belvedon as chair of governors and MP for Larkminster to Her Majesty.'

'Who will try and flog her a picture,' quipped Trafford, 'and take eighty per cent.'

'Shuddup,' said Biffo through gritted brown teeth. 'And now Paris presents Alex to Her Majesty and now you, Poppet.'

'And Poppet will give me a nice curtsey,' said Trafford.

'I will *not*,' squawked Poppet, 'I don't bend my knee to anyone.'

'Right,' said Trafford.

'Then, as headmaster, I present Mr Randal Stancombe, who's donated this wonderful building to Bagley for the furtherance of science,' said Paris, getting into the swing of things.

'And then his wife,' prompted Biffo.

'Mrs Hyacinth Bouquet,' muttered Dora.

'Who said that? That's not funny,' roared Biffo.

'Push orf,' announced Paris. 'One says that every five seconds to the press: "Push orf."'

'Then you present Mr Ashton Douglas,' said Biffo.

Everything went comparatively smoothly until they reached the Science Emporium.

'We're now touring these splendid zones.' Trafford was getting more regal by the second. 'My word, Mr Randal Stinkbomb, this is awesome, particularly this.' Trafford peeled a 'Bring back Hengist' sticker off a vast replica of the pancreas. 'How long have you been building this, Mr Stinkbomb? Push orf, press, although not if you're as ravishing as you are,' he added to Bianca.

Paris meanwhile was watching Dora, who was laughing so much she could hardly write in her reporter's notebook. He remembered her showing him how to make that peacock feather: 'Would you like to take part in an experiment?'

'How truly interesting,' trilled Trafford as the royal party entered the Zone of Chemical Investigative Science. 'My husband and I simply dote on chemistry.'

'Wake up, Paris,' snapped Alex, 'as headmaster you should be presenting Boffin.'

'As what?' drawled Paris sarcastically.

'Like this. I'm here, I'll do it,' said Alex, striding up. 'Your Majesty, may I present Bernard Brooks, the son of Sir Gordon and Lady Brooks, one of Bagley's most gifted and talented pupils, who's going to perform a ground-breaking experiment.'

Alex turned lovingly to Boffin who, dressed in white coat and goggles, his sparse light brown hair tied back, an expression on his shiny, spotty face of a priest preparing communion wine, was pestling silver and reddish powders together in a mortar.

'In this invention,' said Boffin pompously, 'I'm combining iron oxide and aluminium in order to weld railway tracks together.'

'You must patent it and sell it to British Rail,' gushed Trafford, pushing Painswick's hat to the back of his head, 'and our royal train will rattle more safely over it.'

'Boffin is so pants,' muttered Dora as Boffin carried on mixing, gazing round to see he had everyone's attention.

'Buck up, Boffin,' said Biffo curtly, 'we're ten seconds behind schedule.'

'Would anyone thus have hurried Archimedes?' reproached Poppet.

'Such procedures must not be rushed,' agreed Alex.

Next moment the Zone of Chemical Investigative Science was rocked by a mighty explosion that showered the floor with glass as the windows blew in and bottles and containers of chemicals flew off the shelves and everyone was blown six feet across the room.

'It's a bomb, it's a bomb.'

'Clear the building,' yelled Biffo as, amid shouting, screaming and sobbing, people fell over themselves to escape.

Paris, however, had only one thought. Grabbing Dora, he pulled her under the nearest table, shielding her with his body. As black smoke engulfed the room to a crescendo of choking and coughing, he became aware of delicious softness.

'Get out of here, everyone out!' bellowed Biffo.

Paris stayed put and, as the smoke cleared, he looked down and saw Dora, blond eyelashes mascaraed with soot, face blackened, but her eyes still duck-egg blue, widening as they gazed up at him. In them and in her sweet, pink, trembling mouth he saw no fear, only love.

Oblivious of the chaos around them, with a feeling of utter rightness and coming home, he dropped his head and kissed her, feeling her breastbone rise as she gasped in wonder, her mouth opening and her tongue creeping out tentatively to meet his. Paris put his hands on either side of her sooty face, stroking back her hair, smiling slowly, joyfully: 'It's happened,' he whispered, 'at last I can love you,' and he kissed her again.

'And I love you.' Dora choked slightly. 'I always have.'

'Paris Alvaston,' thundered Joan, whose red tie had been blown off, 'come out from under that table at once. You're unaccounted for outside. Watch out for broken glass. Who's that with you? Dora Belvedon, I might have guessed. What do you think you're doing?'

'Covering the visit for the school mag,' said Dora faintly.

Scrabbling up, pulling Dora to her feet, Paris brushed soot and glass off her blue jersey and pleated skirt as reverently as if he'd unearthed a hitherto unread play by Euripides. Unaware of everyone sobbing and shouting around them, he looked down at her in wonder:

'You and I were the chemical reaction that triggered off that explosion.'

'We were?' stammered Dora.

'What just happened to us could have blasted a man onto Venus, or broken the light barrier, or proved that God needn't exist because we do. Not even the universe began with a bigger bang, oh, darling Dora,' and he buried his lips in hers a second time.

'Paris!' thundered Joan.

'I cannot understand what happened,' Boffin's voice curled petulantly through the smoke. 'Perhaps too much aluminium?'

'What were you trying to achieve?' asked an ashen protection officer.

'A revolution in railway safety. It'll work next time. Ouch!' Boffin gave a furious squawk as Lando emptied a fire bucket into his face.

'You're an asshole, Boffin.'

'Thank God no one's been hurt.' Joan Johnson was comforting a shaken Poppet, who quavered that everyone was going to need counselling.

'Except those two,' giggled Bianca and everyone turned to see Dora, both feet off the ground in excitement, locked in Paris's arms.

133

The sight of Paris in a clinch with Dora proved the last straw for Stancombe, who'd just rolled up and taken stock of his ransacked emporium.

'You've got less than twenty-four hours to repair this building,' he howled at Teddy Murray. 'You can work all through the night. I want every man in Larkshire on the job.'

Such was his determination that even Graffi's father Dafydd was dragged out of the Ghost and Castle to help. Fortunately the damage was mostly confined to the one chemistry zone, which would need the windows mended, the walls replastered and repainted and all the flasks and containers replaced and refilled.

Boffin inevitably received an earful from Stancombe:

'Of all the fucking stupid, criminal things to do!'

To Boffin's fury, even Alex agreed with the royal household protection team and the local police that even if the building were declared safe in the morning, the Queen would open and tour the emporium and speak to the students but witness absolutely no experiments.

'Dad will not be pleased,' said Boffin ominously.

Despite unearthing splendid skulduggery at S and C Services, Cosmo and the rest of the Lower Sixth, returning from work experience, were gutted to have missed the fun. Cosmo was further irritated to find the ladder outside his room had yet again been removed by the protection officers. How could he ever escape to pleasure Mrs Walton? Replacing it, he leant a Randal Stancombe board across the bottom rung.

Although heavy frost was forecast, the lawn behind the Mansion, on which stood General Bagley and Denmark, was shielded from an icy north wind howling down the Long Walk by the vast, if temporarily damaged, bulk of the Science Emporium. Although the General was oblivious to cold, the pupils lugging four hundred chairs for the not so Great nor Good through the dusk and placing them under a blue striped awning were grateful for the shelter.

'Ha, ha, ha, my mother's twenty-two rows back, next to Rod Hyde,' crowed Dora, examining the seating plan. 'She will go ballistic.'

The pupils dispersed wearily to supper and prep, but Dora lingered and was discovered by Alex Bruce hosing down General Bagley and Denmark and chatting to security men and their dogs.

'So many pigeons have dumped on the poor old boy,' explained Dora, aiming the hose at the General's bristling moustache, 'we must wash it off. After all, he is our founder.'

Not for much longer, thought Alex, then ordered Dora to buck up and get back to Boudicca.

The moment he'd bustled off to urge on the frantic activity in the Zone of Chemical Investigative Science, a lurking Paris emerged from the shadows carrying gin and tonic in two paper cups. Balancing them on Denmark's quarters, he stood back to admire the big horse, gleaming like jet, in the lights from the emporium.

'Looks much better. Sure you're warm enough? I like winter, you can see so many more stars now the leaves have gone.' Running his hand in wonder over her little, cold face: '"and thou art fairer than the evening's air Clad in the beauty of a thousand stars".'

'Oh Paris,' said Dora, gruff with embarrassment and delight, 'that is so poetic.'

'Marlowe said it first,' Paris admitted; then, in bewilderment: 'I just feel a great Niagara of love has been released from inside me.'

'How heavenly is that?' Dropping the hose, Dora wriggled into his arms. 'How did it happen?' she asked, gasping for breath a minute later. 'I wanted it for so long.'

'I suddenly remembered you giving me the peacock feather. Bad things happened in the past, which made me bad at loving and at letting people get close.'

'Not any more.' Dora hugged him so tightly, he groaned. 'I'm here for you now,' and she kissed him again.

It was only when the abandoned hose started snaking around, soaking their legs, that she looked down and squeaked in excitement, 'I've got a brilliant plan.'

As Graffi's father Dafydd wandered past with a tool kit, she called out that they needed his help. Dafydd was only too happy. The entire workforce, he said, was on the verge of going on strike because Little Dulcie wasn't presenting the bouquet.

Much later, having downed two bottles of red to calm his nerves after the explosion, Biffo Rudge thought he'd seen a ghost, then realized it was Dora Belvedon astride Denmark, training a hose on the General's hat.

'What on earth are you doing?' he bellowed.

'I miss my pony so much' – Dora pretended to cry – 'Mr Bruce kindly allowed me to spruce up Denmark and the General. I'm just washing behind the General's ears.'

'Horse must have Arab blood' – Biffo patted Denmark – 'with those curved ears and wide eyes and that lovely dish face. Bagley was a good fellow too, not your usual military bonehead.'

'Isn't it tragic Mr and Mrs Bruce want to melt him down?' said Dora innocently.

'First I've heard of it,' exploded Biffo. 'Talk about the old order being ripped away.'

'Our founder flounders,' sighed Dora, 'and after he gave us our lovely school. But if he looks nice and clean tomorrow, more people will want to keep him. I've only got a bit more pigeon crap to get off, Mr Rudge, and then I'll race back to Boudicca.'

Fortunately, Alex Bruce was distracted during the evening by a crisis. The protection teams refused to allow in any more chemicals before the Queen's visit, so all the glass vessels being replaced in the Zone of Chemical Investigative Science had to be filled up with coloured water, by which time it was nearly ten o'clock.

'No longer Dirty Denmark,' said Dora, finally handing the hosepipe back to Dafydd. 'Do you want me to roll it up?'

'No, you get home, lovely. We'll be working all night. Shame Hengist's left, he wanted all the Larks kids to collect their GCSE certificates from the Queen, then bloody Bruce killed the idea. Chantal Peck had already bought her hat and been practising her curtsey all round the estate.'

'That's really sad,' said Dora. 'How's Graffi?'

'Triffic. He and Rupert are thick as thieves. Rupert's tickled pink with his muriel and I'm getting some triffic winners.'

Over in his minimalist living room, soon to be abandoned for the vast splendour of Head House, Alex was yet again going through his speech with Vicky Fairchild. The explosion in the emporium had removed his eyebrows so he could no longer raise them quizzically to make a point.

'Just a little more warmth in the words "Your

Majesty",' cooed Vicky. 'I know how shy you are, Alex, but let the caring persona shine through.'

Upstairs, Poppet slept soundly. Tomorrow's outfit, a crimson, yellow and green bandanna and a warm wool ketchup-red smock, was already folded on a chair. Little Cranberry Germaine was yelling her head off, but let Alex deal.

Alex plugged Cranberry onto Poppet's left breast and reflected that if tomorrow went well, he'd be voted head by the governors on Friday and could have mistresses like Hengist. He'd always admired Vicky Fairchild.

Sally Brett-Taylor turned over a sodden pillow. Tomorrow, so no one would be embarrassed and because she couldn't bear to look at the butchered school gardens, she'd make herself scarce. She must also pull herself together and find somewhere to live. In the old days, Elaine had slept, often on her back, on the chaise longue at the bottom of the bed. Now she kept vigil in the hall, painful for her bony legs and elbows, always facing the front door, pining, not eating, hoping Hengist would walk in. How do you explain to a dog that Master has gone to kennels?

Sally was pleased to learn from Patience, on the Bagley bush telegraph, that Paris and Dora had finally got it together and yet she was sad. Paris had comforted her during the bleakest time of her life. Like the Marschallin, she must let him go with both hands.

Post-Mrs Walton, Cosmo crept back into Bagley very happy. Work experience had been equally rewarding. He had found the initials BP in Ashton's diary for tomorrow night, after the Queen's visit. Amber, at work experience at the Gazette, had found BP on the same date in Col Peters's diary. Dora had found it in Mr Fussy's.

Cosmo had also discovered, when a card arrived in a

mauve envelope from the egregious Crispin Thomas, that it was Ashton's birthday tomorrow. Cosmo had therefore arranged for Dame Hermione, when she serenaded the Queen, to slip in a 'Happy Birthday to Ashton'.

Cosmo, who went every which way to gain what he wanted, even promising Ashton a blow job for his birthday, had introduced Lubemir into S and C's offices as a comely bit of rough trade.

Tomorrow, he and Ashton would spend all morning at Bagley, he to conduct his mother and the school orchestra, Ashton to be presented to the Queen. This would leave the office unguarded for Lubemir, who had already unearthed the shadow of an email from Alex to Ashton on 6 October: 'HB-T resigned. BR ours.'

What the hell was BR? Was it a typo for BC or BP? After a lot of thought, Cosmo decided it must be Badger's Retreat, so Stancombe could chop down Hengist's beloved trees, which had since been daubed with red plague spots, and, with Russell fiddling planning permission, slap desirable residences with a view all over the area.

Lubemir had also dug up so much shit on the bringing down of Janna and BC was looking increasingly like Birthday Club and BP like Birthday Party.

Russell had a planning office in County Hall and Milly Walton, working as a clerk in another department, had found a BP in his diary for tomorrow night. A good day's work.

On his way back to his cell, Cosmo called Milly's mother:

'Angel, can you do one thing for me? Suck up to Stancombe tomorrow, pretend it might be on again and see if you can wheedle your keys back. I desperately need to get into his files. I love you.'

Going upstairs Cosmo found Paris in his own cell, wrapped against the cold in a Black Watch tartan duvet, reading John Donne and looking happier than ever before.

' "She is all States, and all Princes, I, Nothing else is",' mocked Cosmo.

Paris flushed slightly. 'Whatever.'

Cosmo then debriefed him on the day's findings. 'Nasty little den of thieves going to that party tomorrow night,' he said finally. 'None of them has written down the address, so we may have to trail one of them.'

'Not in anything as obvious as your Ferrari,' chided Paris, but when Cosmo added that it was Ashton's birthday tomorrow, all the luminous happiness drained out of Paris's face.

'The third of November,' he said bleakly, 'that means he's forty-five tomorrow.'

'How d'you know?'

'Does he have a lisp, can't say his Rs, and have a big watch on the inside of his wrist and stink of asphyxiatingly sweet aftershave like poison gas?'

'That's the one.'

Paris shut his eyes, remembering the blindfolding, so every other sense was heightened, the holding down, the soft caressing hands, the laughter. The terrible pain and indignity going on and on, the grunting and heavy breathing: 'Shut up, you little wat or we'll weally hurt you.' The suffocating scent he could now smell on Cosmo.

As Paris glanced up, Cosmo was shocked by the depths of suffering in his face. He was shaking violently.

'How d'you know him?'

'I was the birthday present at his fortieth birthday party,' Paris said flatly. 'Not a bweeze, being gang waped.'

'My God, where was this?'

'In Oaktree Court, in a back room. I never saw any of them; they blindfolded me and tied my hands. God knows how many of them had me, I lost count. I don't know if Blenchley, the care manager, was one of them. Next day he told me I was imagining things. If I said anything, he'd move me on or have me taken out.'

Cosmo shook his head in bewildered admiration. 'And you never grassed?'

'I was only eleven, I was too ashamed, I felt so dirty. Who would have believed me? I was terrified of losing my friends. Ben Longstaff, who ran away from the home after threatening to grass them up, died in a very suspicious fire.'

If Paris had looked up, he would have found genuine compassion on Cosmo's face. 'I'm truly sorry. Was that why you screamed when Theo came into your room?'

'Yes.'

'Christ, I'm sorry,' repeated Cosmo. 'We'll nail them. Can you handle Ashton being here tomorrow?'

'It's OK.' Paris wandered towards the window. Through the newly bare trees he could see Dora's window in Boudicca. 'I can handle anything now.'

134

Bagley Hall was still in shock and in a growing state of mutiny over Hengist's departure. Both staff and pupils missed his warmth and genuine interest, his great laugh, even his bellows of rage. All they could think was how much he would have enjoyed welcoming the Queen, bounding down the Mansion steps, rubbing his big hands in joy, sweeping her off on a magical mystery tour of the school.

Instead they had to suffer Mr Fussy as powerless as Canute to keep back the great gold tidal wave of leaves unleashed by last night's frost, which now covered pitch, path and, mercifully, most of the hideously clashing flowerbeds. Mr Fussy was doing his nut and blaming every leaf on the bursar and his groundsmen.

Tension had also gripped Boudicca.

'Who's used all the hot water?' screamed Jade Stancombe. 'I'm handing the Queen her bouquet, I ought to have priority.'

Joan in a pinstripe suit was inspecting nails, hair, even breath for alcohol and that everyone was wearing the regulation on-the-knee sea-blue coat and beige skirt, with sufficiently polished shoes.

'And you're all to leave your mobiles behind.'

In the Science Emporium, the brightest pupils, their hair tied back, wearing white coats and goggles, nervously waited at their benches, ignoring the 'Bring back Hengist' stickers attached to the liver, the colon and the interactive whiteboards.

In the RE suite, the Lower Fifth played pass the parcel with a gurgling baby Cranberry and awaited Poppet to give them a lesson on birth as a rite of passage.

Outside, beneath a bright blue sky, crowds lining the route and gathered on the battlements shivered in the icy east wind. Inside the warmth of the Mansion, as the welcome party paced the black and white checked hall floor, Jupiter, Poppet and the Lord Lieutenant's wife, who'd arrived early because she'd driven down from London, were the only people not nervous.

Sweat crystalled Alex's forehead and was beading Ashton Douglas's discreet beige make-up. Stancombe's estranged wife, Lorraine, wheeled in for the occasion to present a united front, had disappeared yet again to powder her rebuilt nose. Stancombe constantly readjusted his gelled black spikes and his new, dark blue suit in the big gilt mirror. Jupiter was being gratifyingly friendly for once, and by chatting up Lorraine had freed Stancombe to rebond with Ruth Walton. Looking particularly sumptuous in an old rose velvet suit, Mrs Walton was clearly delighted to ignite an old flame.

Jupiter wanted Stancombe's billions for New Reform. But would this entail asking him to join the party executive, which might mean losing Rupert and Lord Hawkley, who had both formed an antipathy towards Stancombe? Bugger Hengist for letting them down.

'The Principal is within a quarter of a mile,' the Officer in Command, having received the message on his radio mike, told the welcome party and other relevant security units around the school grounds.

'I cannot think why you're all so nervous, she's only a senior citizen,' said Poppet as Ashton and Lorraine

1073

discreetly repowdered their noses. Even with a respray, Ashton's cloying aftershave was fighting a losing battle with the stench of vegetable curry drifting from the kitchens.

'Wise of the Queen to move on to lunch at Larkminster Hospital,' murmured Jupiter.

'Sally Brett-Taylor always provided the most delicious luncheon and the most beautiful flowers,' grumbled the Lord Lieutenant's wife, not known for her diplomacy. 'Garden's gorn off dreadfully, might be in a municipal park. Sweet thing, Sally. Is she here?'

'Sadly not invited.'

Nor were the bursar, Patience and Little Dulcie, as they forlornly lined the lower drive, waving flags alongside villagers and children from the local primary, only catching the briefest glimpse of the Queen as her car with its cavalcade of cars and motorbike outriders sailed past.

Oblivious of a demo of pupils waving 'Bring back Hengist' placards and Trafford and the Randy Republican on the battlements brandishing red flags and crying, 'Down with the Monarchy', the Queen stepped out of her car. Accompanying her were her personal protection officer, a lady-in-waiting, who had potted biographies of everyone the Queen was going to meet in her handbag, and the Lord Lieutenant in his splendid uniform with its epaulettes, medals and stars.

Anthea Belvedon, twenty-two rows back, swamped by the 399 dignitaries, was absolutely hopping that no one could see how lovely she looked. On a big screen, she could see the crowds ringing Mansion Lawn and Randal bending over Her Majesty like a street lamp and his ghastly common wife being presented as well. There was Ruth Walton, laughing away, when Randal had sworn it was over between them, and Poppet looking ridiculous in that fearful bandanna and ghastly red smock to disguise the fact she hadn't got her figure back. Now she was refusing to bob to the Queen. So rude.

I should be over there, thought Anthea darkly, I'm supposed to be a close friend of Randal and Poppet.

Beside Anthea, Rod Hyde and Gillian Grimston of Searston Abbey were equally unhappy. Why had they been confined to very hard seats under an awning with 398 nonentities and not been introduced to Her Majesty like Ashton and Russell Lambert?

Any deficiencies in Poppet's bob were more than made up for by Dame Hermione's curtsey, more regal than any queen, as she sank to the floor in her Parma violet Chanel suit, a saintly expression in her wide brown eyes.

This distribution of largesse was cut short when her son Cosmo leapt onto the rostrum, sharply tapped the lectern and swept the school orchestra into the National Anthem, involving his mother in an undignified scramble to her feet. All four verses were sung fortissimo, rattling the Mansion windows and dislodging more leaves, followed by 'Here's a Health Unto Your Majesty' and Randal's Largo, as it was now known.

Everyone was heaving a sigh of relief and preparing for the Queen to move on to the RE and IT suites, when Hermione clapped her hands and announced: 'Somebody here, Ashton Douglas, head of education in Larkshire, has a birthday today. I'm sure Your Majesty would like to join me in wishing Ashton many happy returns.'

Ashton looked as though he'd been kissed under the mistletoe. Paris, round the other side of the school, watching him on the same big screen as Anthea Belvedon, fingered his knife.

And Dame Hermione was off: 'Happy birthday to You-hoo!'

Randal, Alex and the Lord Lieutenant were as purple or red as the polyanthus clashing in a nearby flowerbed. Finally Hermione swept off.

'My mother's kind of hard to stop,' sighed Cosmo.

Her Majesty was just moving on when Hermione's dresser, who'd been bunged a tenner, cried out, 'Encore,' and, whisking out of her dressing room, Dame Hermione obliged.

Alex was about to have a coronary. There were still two students taking Duke of Edinburgh Awards to be presented and they now had only half an hour left and had to whiz through the lesson in the IT suite with no time to look at the pupils' work.

'We'll have to switch to plan B and cut the RE lesson,' said the Officer in Command.

Alex turned pale. 'We can't, my wife . . .'

Dora, waiting beside General Bagley's statue to make her presentation and also watching events on the big screen, put down her blue box and wrote in her notebook: 'Her Majesty is running behind in her tight schedule.'

Everyone was commenting on how tiny and pretty the Queen was. How kind her blue eyes; how genuinely warm and radiant her smile; how becoming her amethyst hat trimmed with palest green feathers and how even a colour as harsh as the purple of her coat couldn't diminish her flawless pink and white complexion.

On to the Randal Stancombe Science Emporium, where the royal party toured the different zones and exclaimed in wonder at the giant tree you could walk inside and the huge ear that could be taken apart and the echo chambers, giant fibre-optics and heavenly light displays. On to the Zone of Chemical Investigative Science, which, although miraculously restored with coloured water in all the containers, seemed rather dull after yesterday's excitement.

'The Queen has the ability to make everyone feel special. Even republicans become monarchists in her presence,' wrote Dora.

Not so Poppet Bruce, who, white-faced, tight-lipped, was determined to divert the Queen back in the direction of RE, rites of passage and little Cranberry.

'I am of course known as the Queen of Arts,' Dame Hermione was telling everyone, 'and why isn't my very good friend Rupert Campbell-Black here?'

Even without Rupert, however, the media were agreeing that the Randal Stancombe Science Emporium was a triumph, that Randal would be assured his handle and Alex Bruce the headship of Bagley.

As the Queen finally emerged from this futuristic Nirvana, it was at last the turn of Anthea and the 399 very cold other dignitaries on their hard seats to hear Alex's speech of welcome in front of General Bagley's statue with the Science Emporium towering in the background. Afterwards, Randal would say a few words about his part in the great endeavour. Jade and Dora had taken up their positions beside Denmark's hindquarters.

Paris was crowded together behind the barricade with the rest of the Lower Sixth to watch the ceremony. Gazing across at Dora clutching her blue box, wishing it was his hand rather than the east wind ruffling her pale blonde hair, Paris was overwhelmed with love. The knife was to protect Dora from harm as much as to stab Ashton. He hated to leave her to carry out their great plan, but her official position beside Denmark made it possible.

Having practised a little bob, Dora turned round and smiled at him. Witnessing this exchange, Randal Stancombe, even at his finest hour, felt a skewer dipped in acid plunged in his heart. His great speech, his knighthood, Ruth Walton were as nothing to his lust for Dora Belvedon. He could see the gap of pink flesh between her skirt and her rolled-over brown socks. He was brought back to earth by the Queen's gloved hand patting Denmark:

'What a splendid animal.'

Alex in turn patted the mike, cleared his throat,

raised his head self-importantly and began very, very warmly: 'Your Majesty, on behalf of students, teachers, parents, governors and supporters of Bagley Hall, I would like to thank you very much for visiting us today. It is a huge honour and marks an historical moment of our development.'

Nothing's going to stop him taking over now, thought a despairing Artie, gazing down from a staffroom window.

'On this momentous day for Bagley Hall and for science . . .' Alex was getting into his stride.

Goodness, the Queen's good at looking interested, thought Dora. As her eyes flickered towards Paris, he nodded. Imperceptibly, Dora's hand slipped between Denmark's back legs.

At first, people thought the heavens had opened; then, as there was no rattle of rain on the blue striped awning, they decided it must be a burst pipe. There was a gasp of consternation as the splatter continued and a great gush of water was located, splashing on General Bagley's plinth and spilling onto the grass.

Bewilderment, rage, horror, shock and broad grins could be seen on individual faces as it struck home that the torrent of very yellow liquid was pouring out of Denmark's cock.

'Quick, quick, he's staling,' yelled Amber. 'Stand up in your stirrups, General.'

There was a rumble of laughter. For a second, Her Majesty's face twitched. The photographers were going berserk, snapping Denmark and his gushing yellow cascade from all angles.

'The Empire Strikes Back,' murmured Artie in ecstasy.

For once, the Lord Lieutenant, the personal protection officer and the Officer in Command were at a loss.

'Stop it,' howled Randal. 'For Christ's sake, someone stop it.'

'Try one of Sweetie's condoms,' suggested Dora.

Then, to distance herself from blame, she rushed forward, trying to stem the flow with her notebook, but the torrent swept it aside like driftwood. A proffered bucket overflowed in a few seconds, a policeman's helmet met the same fate, as did the end of Miss Painswick's parasol rammed up as a catheter.

'Try a tourniquet,' said Dora.

But no one was around to solve the problem. Alex had not issued any invitations to the bursar's team of maintenance men. Randal was casting furiously about for one of his plumbers, but after twenty-four hours on, and having been ordered to 'bloody well hop it,' they had understandably done so. None of his workforce had been inclined to stay anyway after the snubbing of Little Dulcie.

'What a pity Graffi and Rocky were uninvited,' piped up Dora, 'they'd have stopped it.'

Like Don Giovanni's Commandatore, impervious to the Victoria Falls beneath him, General Bagley gazed fiercely at the Science Emporium: 'Serve you right, Mr Bruce, for trying to melt me down.'

'Can't stop it, sir,' a drenched security man muttered to the Lord Lieutenant. 'Better move on.'

Alex, meanwhile, had lost it, trying with rolling eyes to blurt out his last two crucial paragraphs about a breeding ground for the Hawkings and Einsteins of the future and thanking Randal for his historic contribution, but Denmark peed on.

The pupils and most of the audience were by now quite unable to contain their laughter. Rod Hyde and Gillian Grimston, even Ashton and Russell, were not displeased: Poppet and Alex had got a fraction above themselves recently.

Most of the school just thought: Hengist would have known how to handle it, turning the whole thing into an enormous joke. The gold hands of the school clock had edged round to 12.25. No time for Randal's speech.

'I would like to ask Your Majesty to mark your visit by unveiling a commemorative plaque,' mumbled Alex.

At least the sea-blue curtain didn't come away in Her Majesty's hand and the dark blue Parker pen worked when she signed the visitors' book. Joan, standing like a retired Guards officer in her pinstripe suit, tugged down Jade's skirt to just above her knees before she shimmied forward to present a big bunch of orange lilies and chrysanthemums, which the Queen passed on to her lady-in-waiting. Jade then managed to redress the balance a fraction by explaining it was her father, Randal Stancombe, who had bankrolled and master-minded the Science Emporium.

Then it was Dora's turn. Aware of so many of her media contacts watching, she once again turned and smiled quickly at an impossibly proud Paris, before executing a beautiful curtsey.

The Queen said she remembered Dora's father and how sorry she'd been when he died. Dora in turn said she was very sorry when the Queen had lost one of her corgis in a fight, but that she'd obtained a photograph of Pharos.

'You must miss her, so I've made you a model.'

Peering into the box at Pharos sitting on a royal blue satin bed, for a second the Queen bit her lip and Dora was afraid she was angry. Then she said Dora's version was lovely and very like Pharos and thanked her very much.

She was about to move on, the wind lifting the green feathers in her hat, when something in her kind face made Dora take a deep breath: 'As the most powerful person in the land, could Your Majesty possibly bring back our headmaster Hengist Brett-Taylor? We feel the heart has been torn out of our school since he left and we'd like him back.'

'That's enough,' exploded Alex as the Queen smiled and, handing the blue box to her lady-in-waiting, moved on. Alex was so livid, he forgot to present her with a copy of *A Guide to Red Tape*.

Many pupils and staff positioned on the other side of the Mansion didn't think they'd get a chance to see the Queen close up, but she left from a different side, passing Trafford high up in the battlements, who grabbed Miss Painswick's Union Jack and cheered his head off. On the way down the drive, Her Majesty was near the window and able to wave and smile at Little Dulcie.

135

Meanwhile, like the far-distant Oxus, a steady yellow stream of liquid still flowed out of Denmark's cock.

'Heads will roll,' screamed Alex. 'Who filled up that horse with water and how dare Dora Belvedon ask the Queen to bring back Hengist? It was probably her that filled up the horse, she was hanging round it long enough last night.'

The day couldn't have gone worse. He would now have to cope with Poppet's rage, because the Queen never reached RE. Not to mention Gordon Brooks, apoplectic because he'd driven all the way down from Manchester to find Boffin's experiment had ended up on the cutting-room floor. Stancombe was understandably angriest of all. All the press would concentrate on General Bagley's horse, no doubt already writing tomorrow's headlines about the Royal Wee, and hardly mention his heroic and historic contribution. And he'd just seen that white devil Paris Alvaston kissing Dora yet again.

Alex then had to host vegetable curry for nearly eight hundred, without any drink.

The day couldn't get worse, but it did when Dame Hermione slipped a bill for fifty thousand pounds into his top pocket.

'What is this?'

'My fee, Alex. I've given it to you at half-price for

Cosmo's sake and of course there'll be ten per cent off if you pay cash, which I know you can,' she added roguishly.

Alex was jolted. How could she know any such thing?

'There was no question of a fee,' he spluttered.

'Indeed there was. I never give my services for nothing, even if it's a fee for charity. A performance like today's takes so much preparation – like you, I am a true professional.'

How dare she? It was Cartwright's fault, he'd obviously agreed a fee with her. Cartwright could get out before Christmas.

The vegetable curry lunch in the great hall without any alcohol was not a prolonged affair, but it gave Ruth Walton time to commiserate with Randal Stancombe.

'The Science Emporium is awesome; posterity will always remember you for it.' Then, lowering her voice: 'I've missed you so much, Randal, why don't you pop round for supper tonight?'

'I'd like that, Ruth,' said Stancombe.

Rod Hyde, meanwhile, was sitting in a window seat with Anthea Belvedon, whom he regarded as a very pretty lady and an excellent JP.

'Why don't you pop round later for a jar?' he asked. 'I could show you over St Jimmy's. I'm sure our school could sort out your Dora. We're thinking of starting a boarding house for challenging students.'

'I'd like that,' said Anthea, who wanted to pay back Randal for bringing Lorraine and flirting with Ruth Walton. She was fascinated to hear about Rod's new villa in the Seychelles and thought he was rather excitingly masterful.

Poppet, determined to regain the ascendancy, insisted after lunch that Trafford unveil his ground-breaking maquette of a sculpture to replace General Bagley. The royal party had gone, but there were plenty of dignitaries and press still around. Trafford, creator of *Shagpile*, *Tranny by Gaslight* and *Sister Hoodie*, was always good copy.

Poppet, requesting quiet with a cymbal clash of bracelets, pointed to the maquette in front of her on the table, but hidden by a tarpaulin. She then introduced Trafford: 'One of our most exciting Young British Artists, who'd like to introduce his concept of a new work of art to replace General Bagley, whose image many of us strongly feel to be outdated.'

A great rumble of disapproval at her words turned to envy as the artist in question was seen to be holding a large glass of whisky.

'General Bagley's like, male, imperialistic, aggressive,' Trafford told his now very hostile audience. 'I wanted to create something like female, tender, loving and of the age.'

Poppet was in ecstasy, nodding in agreement as Trafford drained his whisky and whipped off the tarpaulin to reveal a maquette of two very stocky women going down on each other.

Alex turned green; his wife was made of sterner stuff.

'How apt – an act of reciprocal love,' she cried. 'Do we have a title?'

'It's called *Minge-drinking*,' said Trafford.

Hengist would have given everyone the rest of the day off. Alex, true to his puritan ethic, insisted afternoon lessons went on as usual. Stancombe then joined him in the head's office, where, judging by the shouting, the battle of Randal's Handle was joined. After twenty minutes, Randal stormed out and Alex went on the rampage.

He had never been so humiliated in his life. He was determined to track down the ringleaders responsible for the General Bagley fiasco. Denmark was still peeing merrily and to top it, some joker had leant a sign saying 'Flood Warning' against the General's plinth.

136

At dusk, a very tired Dora ran back to Boudicca to change out of her school suit. Trying to absorb the enormity of the last two days' events and the miracle of Paris loving her, she was suddenly racked with terror.

Up to now she had led a charmed life at Bagley. Hengist had adored her and after he'd gone to prison she'd been protected because her mother was a great friend of Alex and Poppet. But if Anthea had been relegated to row twenty-two under the awning, her mother had clearly lost caste and there would be nothing to stop Alex expelling her for begging the Queen to bring back Hengist.

If, in addition, she were expelled for the General Bagley escapade, Paris as her accomplice might get chucked out too and she'd never see him again, or Patience and Ian, who'd been so lovely, or Cosmo, Bianca or Artie or all her friends.

Paris had just texted her to ask where she was and she'd texted back to say she'd see him at supper. Cosmo, who'd managed to infiltrate himself into the unveiling of Trafford's sculpture, had also texted her that he'd overheard horrible Rod Hyde asking her mother for a drink at St Jimmy's later. Dora shivered as she remembered how well Anthea and Rod seemed to be getting on, on their hard seats. Her mother would love St Jimmy's because it was free. And how dare the old bitch not pop back to Foxglove Cottage to feed and let out Cadbury, then smack him if he made a puddle?

Dora had reached her dormitory and just taken off her suit jacket, when Joan barged in, bellowing:

'You were hanging round General Bagley's statue last night, Dora Belvedon, and you're no doubt behind that disgusting act of sabotage. Well, you're for the high jump. Mr Bruce wants to see you in his office at once.'

'OK, OK.' Dora raced out of Boudicca towards the Mansion, but the moment she was out of sight, she turned right instead of left, belted down the drive and didn't stop running until she reached Foxglove Cottage.

She was just being knocked sideways by an ecstatic Cadbury when her mobile rang. It was Stancombe. He'd tracked down an event horse called Kerfuffle, advertised in *Horse & Hound*, in which Dora had expressed an interest on her last leave-out.

'Lots of people are after him. Want to come and see him this evening?'

Looking at a horse was much better than being expelled and, out of the corner of her eye, Dora noticed Cadbury had chewed up one of Anthea's new silver sandals.

'Yes, please,' she said.

'Where are you?' asked Stancombe.

'At Foxglove Cottage.'

'Where's Mummy?'

'Having a drink with Rod Hyde.'

'Good. Don't tell her anything until we've bought the horse. She'll say I'm spoiling you. I'm tied up as we speak. I'll send a car to fetch you. See you in a bit.'

Dora was not pleased when creepy Uncle Harley rolled up ten minutes later. She'd only taken Cadbury into the garden, fed him and chucked the remains of her mother's sandals in next door's dustbin; she'd had no time to ring Paris to tell him where she was going or change out of school uniform into jodhpurs.

Uncle Harley was not pleased when Dora insisted on bringing Cadbury and sitting in the back with him.

'Who's going to guard your mum's house?'

'Who's going to guard me?' snapped Dora.

Outside, night had fallen like a shroud. No stars or moon pierced the sooty gloom as they left Bagley village and sped out of reach of street lamps, lighted windows or even chinks of light under doors, deep into thickly wooded country where trees writhed under the rising wind's lash, down by-roads carpeted with red and orange leaves, which danced in the headlights like the flames of hell. Even Uncle Harley's jewellery didn't lighten the dark. In horror Dora realized she'd forgotten her mobile.

'Can I borrow your telephone to ring my boyfriend?'

'There's no signal here.'

Dora clutched Cadbury tighter. Kerfuffle had better be good.

As Uncle Harley turned through pillars topped by winged monsters, with eagles' heads and lions' bodies, and drove up a long, pitted, bumpy drive, Dora couldn't see any horses beyond the rusty broken railings. As the car rattled over a sheep grid, she thought she must be careful of Cadbury's legs if they had to make a run for it. Ahead towered a house, shaggy with leafless creeper, which fell over the windows like too-long fringes.

'Where are we?' she asked nervously.

'Here,' said Uncle Harley.

Meanwhile, over the border in Rutshire, Mags Gablecross, avid to hear details of the Queen's visit to Bagley, was awaiting her husband the Chief Inspector's return for supper, when the telephone rang. It was Debbie, Larks's former cook, asking if Mags knew of Janna's whereabouts.

'She's in Wales with Emlyn. They're getting married, isn't it lovely?' Then, when Debbie didn't react: 'Are you OK, Debs?'

'Yes – no. I'm worried, Mags. I've handed in my notice here. Janna was right all along about Ashton. He's vile and he never stops watching my boys. I think he's put a two-way mirror in the shower.'

Mags shuddered. 'How horrible.'

'It may sound stupid, but I think something evil's going on. Russell Lambert had a birthday party here at Ashton's place back in August and instead of wanting me to help out, Ashton insisted I looked tired, and packed me and the boys off to the seaside for the weekend.

'Anyway, it's Ashton's birthday today. Stancombe called him first thing about some party this evening. I picked up the phone by mistake and got the impression' – Debbie's voice shook – 'Randal was lining up some little girl "for dessert" – those were his words – then Ashton laughed and said he'd be bringing something much more to his own taste.'

'You don't know where this party's going to be?'

'No idea.' Debbie started to cry. 'I thought I was imagining things but Brad went to his dad for the day, and when I got back from Tesco's this evening, there was no one home. When I phoned Brad's dad, he said he'd dropped Brad off an hour ago and Ashton had insisted on minding Brad until I got back.'

'There was no note?'

'Nothing. Oh Mags, I'm so worried Ashton has kidnapped him.'

'I'll get on to Tim at once,' said Mags.

Over at Bagley, Paris was equally demented. Dora hadn't returned to supper and she wasn't answering her mobile. There was no sign of her at Boudicca when he dropped in and when he raced down to Foxglove Cottage, the place was in darkness.

'Randal's always had the hots for her. I know the bastard's going to serve her up at Ashton's birthday party and dispose of her afterwards. I can't handle it, Cosmo. I love her so much.'

'Randal's safe with Ruth,' said Cosmo soothingly, 'she asked him over to supper.'

'Well, fucking ring and check if he's there.'

'Bit early. I don't want to rouse his suspicions. Oh, OK then.'

Mrs Walton answered immediately: 'Randal? Oh, it's you, Cosmo darling, any chance of you popping over later? I seem to have been stood up by Randal. Cosmo! Cosmo!'

But Cosmo had hung up.

137

Stancombe must have been looking out because the moment the car drew up, the heavy studded oak front door creaked open and he pulled Dora in out of the bitter cold. Inside it was tropical, which had given him the excuse to wear nothing but a very white, mostly unbuttoned shirt, black velvet trousers and a great deal of Lynx – hardly horse-buying kit, reflected Dora. The sort of soppy music her mother liked was belching out of speakers.

There was no furniture in the high vaulted hall, but Stancombe led her into a large drawing room with flames leaping in a big fireplace, walls lined with mirrors and leather sofas, fur cushions and a floor covered in thick, dark shagpile. In one corner, four-legged and big as a Welsh cob, stood a vast television. In another was a table covered in glasses and a trolley groaning with every kind of drink. In the centre of the room stood a strange padded leather table about three feet off the ground. Twigs and rose thorns clawed and scrabbled at the windows, like the buried-alive trying to escape from their coffins. At least the windows had handles in case she wanted to make a quick getaway.

Cadbury's hackles had gone straight up, his pink lip curled, his normally genial yellow eyes were hard and reptilian. He had no use for Stancombe, who in turn was furious Dora had brought a chaperon, but decided not to make a fuss. She looked so adorable in her school tie with her chubby little legs sticking out from underneath her beige pleated skirt and flesh visible in the gaps between the buttons of her white shirt.

Anthea was too mean to buy Dora new uniform until she was absolutely bursting out of it, and would have been appalled if she'd realized how additionally seductive this made her daughter look. Stancombe, who'd just taken the brake off any inhibitions with a vast line of coke, felt himself boiling over with lust.

As Dora plonked herself down on a brown leather sofa, Cadbury wandered off to explore, which suited Stancombe. It would enable him to shut the bloody dog away in another room.

'What would you like to drink?'

'A crème de menthe frappé,' said Dora airily, 'but shouldn't we see Kerfuffle? Another buyer might get there first.'

'He's in the stables, only five minutes from here.' Stancombe waved vaguely in the direction of the window behind her.

'I want to try him out.'

'Of course. They've got an indoor school.' Hell, he'd forgotten how to frappé ice. He was so on fire, he'd melt anything he touched.

'Wasn't the Queen lovely?' said Dora brightly. 'I thought it went so well.'

Stancombe picked up a steel hammer. 'It was a cock-up from start to finish. Whatever one's reservations about Hengist B-T, he'd have known how to run a show like that. Alex couldn't run a piss-up in a brewery.' Bash, bash, bash! The ice was going everywhere.

'It's awfully hot,' said Dora, 'can we open the window?'

'Take off your cardi, then I can admire your sexy figure. You get tastier every time I see you. Said I ought to put you down like a fine wine but I think you're grown-up enough for love now.' As he handed her her drink, his fingers caressed hers.

'I am too,' beamed Dora as he sat beside her. 'I've got a boyfriend. I've wanted him to be my boyfriend for nearly three years, since he played Romeo.' She took a gulp of crème de menthe. 'That's lovely, rather like mouthwash, but I don't want to be drunk in charge of an event horse. I've always fancied older men,' she went on dreamily. Stancombe preened, then scowled as she added, 'Paris is two years older than me.'

If I bang on about Paris, it'll put him off, thought Dora hopefully. He won't dare try anything if he's Mummy's boyfriend.

'Would you like a tour of the house?' murmured Stancombe.

Suddenly aware of his burning thigh pressed against hers, Dora jumped to her feet. 'I'd rather see Kerfuffle – and where's Cadbury? I bet he's found the kitchen.'

She ran out into the hall and, turning left, discovered herself in a room with a vast double bed and walls lined with more mirrors. On the bedside table was a pair of handcuffs, some manacles and an evil-looking black whip with a long lash, which was certainly not intended to be used on Kerfuffle.

Dora froze, increasingly aware she was in the presence of evil.

' "The Good Life",' sang Sacha Distel sforzando. No one would hear screams over that.

Next moment, Stancombe had grabbed her, hands going everywhere, like the sinewy tentacles of a mad, starved octopus. 'Little Dora,' he whispered, crashing his horrible, hot, full lips down on hers, ramming his great, hard, fat tongue between her teeth.

'Don't,' squealed Dora, 'let me go, you disgusting old man, or I'll bite your tongue off. I'll guillotine your willy. I trusted you because you're Mummy's boyfriend. She's a JP and I'm under age. She'll bang you up for this. Stop it. STOP it!' She tried to knee him in the groin as shirt buttons under siege were pinging everywhere.

'You know you want me,' taunted Stancombe, as wildly excited by her antagonism as by her plump, young flesh.

'I bloody don't, I've got a boyfriend.'

'That's where you're wrong.' Stancombe was tearing off her shirt, scrabbling for the hook of her pink gingham bra, about to rip it off in his frustration. 'You need a real man, not that little wimp.'

'I don't, he isn't, I love Paris.' Dora aimed a kick at Stancombe's shins.

'Stop it, you snotty little bitch.' As he pinned her against a mirrored wall, she was impaled by an erection big as a rounder's bat. 'Can't you get it into your fucking head, Paris is gay.'

'Don't be stupid,' panted Dora. 'He wasn't gay with my friend Bianca, or Amber, or your stuck-up daughter. You're just as green with jealousy as that crème de menthe.'

'Paris is a little tart,' hissed Stancombe. 'Look at the way he flashed his ass at Theo and Hengist and Artie and Biffo, all eating out of his hand.'

He was foaming at the mouth, veins like snakes writhing on his forehead. Dora had never seen anyone so angry and would have been scared witless if she hadn't been so furious.

'Come and look at this.' Grabbing her hand, Stancombe dragged her back into the living room where he pushed her down on the leather sofa. Then he took a video from the shelf and rammed it into the television.

Dora took a gulp of crème de menthe. She must get out and where the hell was Cadbury? Next moment, ridiculous, jiggy music flooded the room and despite everything, she burst out laughing at the sight of a lot of fat, naked old men dancing round, whooping and drinking out of champagne bottles. It was like the Elephants in 'Carnival of the Animals', except they had waggling willies instead of trunks.

'Oh yuk, yuk, yuk cubed,' cried Dora as they started groping each other, fondling and slapping each other's bottoms. Then she gave a gasp.

'My God, that fat one's Russell someone, Mummy knows him, he's the planning officer. And there's revolting Ashton Douglas who Dame Hermione sang happy birthday to. He's got his socks on too; expect he's frightened of getting verrucas. God, how gross – and there's Col Peters, vile pig and Rod Hyde' – Dora couldn't help giggling – 'with a wincy little willy.'

But when Stancombe fast-forwarded the tape, Dora shrieked in real anguish to see that Russell Someone was humping away – 'Oh God, no!' – on top of a thin, very young girl, lying on her front on the same leather table that was in the centre of the room, with her face concealed by flopping white-blonde hair. Although her hands were tightly tied together in front and Rod Hyde and Col Peters were laughing and holding her down, she was putting up a hell of a struggle.

'My God, poor little girl,' screamed Dora, 'he's raping her. How can you allow something so terrible? Turn it off, I can't look.'

'Yes, you can,' hissed Stancombe, yanking her head back towards the screen as the camera zoomed in. 'Look at the Eiffel Tower on his shoulder. That's your little rent boy.'

'My turn, my turn,' Ashton was now yelling, prising off Russell and taking over, to whoops of excitement from the others, and shafting away with unparalleled viciousness.

'Just watch,' gloated Stancombe as, in close-up again, the camera captured below the blindfold a long nose, lips curled back in agony, and teeth plunged into the black leather. The exquisite bone structure could only belong to Paris.

'You revolting pervert,' screamed Dora, hammering her fists against Stancombe's chest, 'you were raping him, that's what the Upper Sixth threatened to do to my brother Dicky. How dare you hurt Paris when he was a little boy in a children's home with no parents to protect him? That is the most disgusting, horrible thing I've ever seen.'

Rushing towards the television, Dora pressed the eject button, grabbed the video and, yanking open a window, hurled it out into the bushes.

'You stupid bitch,' howled Stancombe, 'you'll pay for it.'

'How could you film something so sick?' howled back Dora. 'So you could blackmail Ashton and Rod Hyde if they stepped out of line?'

'That's enough, it's your turn now, no one knows you're here.'

But as Stancombe lunged at her, they were both distracted by excited squeaking. Shoving Stancombe off balance with all her might, Dora ran to yet another room, a sort of study with a big desk. Here she found Cadbury, his pink nose deep in a wardrobe, his tail going like a windscreen wiper on speed.

'Drop!' yelled Stancombe, hurtling forward and kicking Cadbury viciously in the ribs.

'Don't hurt him,' screamed Dora, grabbing a steel lamp.

But Cadbury had been living at home with Anthea and shut in the kitchen and kicked in the ribs once too often. Next moment he'd thrown himself at Stancombe, knocking him to the floor, standing over him, growling furiously.

'Bastard dog.' Stancombe tried and failed to grab Cadbury by the balls.

'Ha, ha, ha,' panted Dora, 'serves you right for persuading Mummy to have him castrated. Pity she didn't have you done at the same time.'

When she first peered into the wardrobe, she thought she'd stumbled on a linen cupboard, then slowly realized Cadbury had sniffed out pillows and pillows of white powder.

'Good boy, good, clever Cadbury, keep him there.'
Dora rushed next door and seized the handcuffs.
Wrenching a terrified Stancombe's hands behind his
back, she clicked them shut. Then she bound
his ankles very tightly with her Boudicca house tie.

'That's a reef knot – only thing I learnt in the
Brownies. You won't get out of that, nor would Joan
approve of such disgusting language,' she added,
pulling his green silk handkerchief out of his pocket
and shoving it in his raging mouth.

'Let's see what else you've got in here.' Returning to
the wardrobe, Dora found several briefcases bulging
with notes and, at the back, a sleek, black gun, which
she laid on the desk.

'You evil man . . .' Then, horror and revulsion taking
over from a sense of achievement: 'How dare you do
that to my boyfriend?'

Picking up the house telephone she dialled 999.

'I want to speak to Chief Inspector Gablecross, it's
very urgent.' Then, after a pause during which
Stancombe wriggled like a netted tuna to free himself:
'Hello, Chief Inspector, this is Dora Belvedon, could
you come at once? I've just conducted a citizen's arrest
on Randal Stancombe. He's in big trouble. He's got a
lot of white stuff in his cupboard that doesn't look like
baby powder.

'My dog, Cadbury, deserves a medal, he's been so
brave. I've tied Stancombe up but he's not in carnival
mood, so please hurry. I've no idea where I am, but it's
quite grand with pillars at the bottom of the drive
topped with monsters . . . now I remember, Mr Brett-
Taylor's got one on his crest: they're griffins. The park
railings are all broken and could never keep a horse in
and it's a very shaggy old house with high ceilings.
There's the doorbell, it might be Uncle Harley back, so
please hurry.'

As the bell rang more insistently, Cadbury barked,
uncertain whether he ought to rush to the door or

guard Stancombe, who mumbled furiously through his handkerchief that Dora would now be for the high jump.

The doorbell rang again. Grabbing the gun, holding it behind her back, Dora tugged open the door to find Ashton Douglas, with his arm round a beautiful fair-haired little boy, cooing, 'Come on, Bwad, you'll love this wonderful house. Good evening,' he added with his thin smile. Then, clocking Dora's ripped, undone shirt, paused, unsure what game she might be playing. 'I've got an appointment with Mr Stancombe.'

'He's not here.'

There was a crash from next door.

'It's a man mending the boiler,' squeaked Dora.

Ignoring her, Ashton ushered Brad into the study.

'What the hell?'

Cadbury growled, but with more uncertainty. He needed another line of coke.

'Don't untie him, Mr Douglas,' ordered Dora, whipping out the gun, 'or I'll fill you full of lead. The police are on their way and this gun is loaded.'

'Don't be silly, little girl,' said Ashton, hastily shielding himself with a terrified Brad.

Oh help, thought Dora as the doorbell rang yet again.

'You wouldn't dare fire that gun, put it down.' Ashton, setting Brad aside, was about to untie Stancombe's feet.

'Oh yes I would.' Aiming above Brad, Dora shut her eyes and pulled the trigger. As a bullet shattered the mirror above his head, Ashton dropped Stancombe's ankles. 'And next time you go kiddy-fiddling,' she added furiously, 'take your socks off.'

'What are you talking about?' spluttered Ashton.

'A disgusting film of you gang-raping Paris.'

Ashton's face turned as green as his suddenly panic-stricken eyes. Next moment, Brad made a bolt for it. Catching him with her left hand, Dora drew him close: 'It's OK, you're safe now.'

Someone was leaning on the bell. Backing towards the front door, keeping her eyes on Ashton, Dora put on a deep voice and cried: 'Who's there?'

'Open up,' said a familiar, reedy voice.

'Mr Fussy,' exploded Dora as she opened the door.

Alex was disguised by a false beard, a deerstalker and dark glasses; his open-neck shirt, however, revealed his wobbling Adam's apple.

'Your friends are in there, you disgusting old man.'

Seeing the gun and Nemesis in the form of a Middle Fifth student with her clothes torn off, Alex turned and bolted slap into the arms of PC Cuthbert, who'd been working out with Gloria and who had no difficulty arresting Alex and slapping him into handcuffs.

PC Cuthbert was accompanied by a policewoman, into whose arms Dora thrust a sobbing Brad. Rushing back to Stancombe's telephone, punching out numbers, she was deep in conversation as Paris erupted into the room, fists clenched, eyes blazing, snarling like a snow leopard about to spring.

'Where's Dora, what the fuck's going on?'

Cadbury thumped his tail as Paris took in Stancombe flailing on the ground, Ashton cringing in the corner and Dora with all her buttons ripped off, putting back a receiver. Completely losing it, Paris leapt forward, enfolding her in his arms, clinging to her like a drowning man to driftwood, frantically kissing her over and over again.

'Are you OK? Omigod, what did that bastard do to you? Did he hurt you?'

'I'm fine, honest. I was just ringing Paul Dacre to ask him to hold the front page.'

For a moment Paris gazed down at her in disbelief, exasperation and then love.

'For fuck's sake, I've been through every hell in the world worrying about you. No one knew where you were. I thought I'd never see you again.' Paris's voice broke as, trembling violently, he clutched her tight.

'And don't watch, you bastard,' he added, giving Stancombe a big kick.

'I left my mobile behind, I wanted to ring you but I couldn't,' gasped Dora who, as reality reasserted itself, had started trembling far worse than Paris. 'I had to be brave for Cadbury and because I was so desperate to see you again.'

Tears were trickling down Paris's cheeks.

'I imagined such terrible things happening to you, I can't tell you . . . They're like . . . so terrible.' Having furiously wiped his eyes with his sleeve, still clutching Dora, he turned towards Ashton.

'Many happy weturns, Mr Douglas, wemember me?'

His voice was so filled with contempt and loathing that Dora shivered, Cadbury dropped his ears and Ashton backed terrified into the cupboard.

'We've never met,' he gibbered.

'Yeah, we did. On your fortieth birthday, remember, at a waif-swapping party at Oaktree Court,' spat Paris. 'I don't figure this birthday's going to end quite so well for you.'

For a second his fingers tightened convulsively on Dora's arms, then, as she said shakily, 'It's OK, I'm here for you, I love you,' police poured into the house.

'Break it up, you two,' said Cosmo, tapping them on the shoulder a few minutes later. 'Well done, Cadbury. Christ! Look at that Charlie.' He snorted a pinch from a claws-punctured bag. 'It's very good; I suppose we can't have the odd kilo for rounding up this gang of thieves?'

'How did you ever find me?' asked Dora, still keeping the firmest hold on Paris.

'We followed Mr Fussy,' said Cosmo, nodding at Alex who was remonstrating with PC Cuthbert.

'I can explain everything, officer.'

'And I can tell you, Alex, baby,' called out Cosmo chattily, 'that like Trafford's minge-drinkers, you're going down for a long, long time.'

While Col Peters, Russell Lambert, Des Res and Rod Hyde were being rounded up, all on their way to the party, Dora had a brief private word with Chief Inspector Gablecross.

'There was this hideous video in the machine which could send this lot to the electric chair. Could Paris possibly not see it? I chucked it out of that window into some bushes in the direction of the stables.'

'There aren't any stables,' said Chief Inspector Gablecross grimly. 'You've been very lucky; Stancombe's a very dangerous man. You must have been frightened.'

'I had Cadbury,' said Dora fondly, 'and, frankly, when a true writer gets onto a good story, they feel no fear.'

138

The police proceeded to fillet Stancombe's various properties and unearth every kind of skulduggery, more drugs and arms in other deserted warehouses and evidence that he had massively bribed Ashton, Rod Hyde, Alex Bruce, Russell, Desmond Reynolds and Col Peters with villas in hot countries and huge dollops of cash.

For these rewards, they had been instrumental in stitching up Janna and ousting Hengist from power, so Stancombe could get his hands on both the Larks land and Badger's Retreat, with, eventually, his eyes set on the water meadows and razing the Shakespeare Estate to the ground.

Stancombe and Uncle Harley were also convicted for importing and dealing in millions of pounds' worth of Class A drugs. In addition, Stancombe's inability to resist a chance to blackmail or keep in line the others by filming every birthday party had provided enough evidence to send the entire gang to prison for many years.

As there were at least a dozen other incriminating videos, Chief Inspector Gablecross managed to retrieve the one Dora had chucked in the bushes and never used it in evidence.

'Now Mr Fussy's gone, Hengist can have his job back,' said Dora happily.

Fussygate, however, was the third scandal to rock Bagley and, at the governors' meeting in mid November, it was unanimously decided, at Jupiter's instigation, to appoint Artie Deverell as headmaster.

Hengist wasn't due out till after Christmas and nobody knew if he'd even want to come back. Better to root out all corruption.

Ian and Patience were asked to stay on and Wally and Miss Cambola invited to join the staff. Artie would also have liked to have invited his friend Emlyn Davies back as deputy head, but Emlyn was finding both his marriage and his job with the Welsh Rugby Union far too exciting.

The photograph of Tabitha Campbell-Black and her horse was restored to the front of the *Old Bagleian* magazine. Aided by Artie, Lord Hawkley set about clearing Theo's name and overseeing the publication of his epic translation of Sophocles. A new classical library, large enough to contain the archives, was also commissioned. Randal Stancombe, it was noted, didn't tender for the job.

Other excitements included Dora and Cadbury getting their faces in all the national press and Cadbury getting his chance to meet the Queen after all, when he won an award for gallantry.

Just after Christmas, Artie Deverell was faced with his first challenge: a letter from Joan Johnson, saying in future she would like to be known as Mr John Johnson.

'She can take over Artie's old house,' observed Cosmo, 'and at least she won't be hassled to address the Talks Society.'

139

Hengist was released from prison in January, to the sorrow of his fellow inmates. He had written their letters, sorted out their financial and emotional problems and, when pressed, regaled them with hilarious anecdotes of the great and famous.

None of them felt he had committed a crime.

'When we took SATs at school, Henge, our 'ead gave us the answers.'

Despite his cheerful exterior, they were aware too of a heartbreak no prison doctor could cure.

Whilst inside, Hengist had kept up with the outside world, reading with pride of Jack Waterlane, Lando and Amber scuffling with the police over the hunting ban, with huge pleasure of Janna and Emlyn's marriage, noting without surprise the increasing closeness of Jupiter and David Hawkley, and, with amazement, the rounding-up of the Birthday Party club.

Being in prison, no one could ring him up for quotes.

'We'll sort out the nonces, Henge, if any of 'em end up 'ere,' promised his friends.

Artie Deverell was now at the helm, but in no hurry to desert his exquisite Regency house, so there was no longer any pressure on Sally to leave Head House. But she was so unhappy she wanted to escape as soon as possible. It was just the mental paralysis induced by having to dispose of twenty thousand books, innumerable works of art and beautiful cherished furniture; it was as harrowing as distributing beloved animals if you're forced to close down a zoo.

Since she'd demanded a divorce, Sally hadn't seen or spoken to Hengist. He had refused to allow her or anyone else to visit him in prison. Anxious not to embarrass pupils or staff, he returned to Bagley to pick up some books and clothes on the Sunday before the start of the spring term. Sally therefore said she'd make herself scarce.

Hengist arrived in a blue van lent him by Rupert and, before going into Head House, wandered up the pitches to Badger's Retreat. At least this had been saved from Randal's bulldozers. It was bitterly cold and had been trying to snow, but only with the coming of night was it starting to settle. Flakes swirling against a dark yew reminded him of a bottle-green polka-dotted dress with a full skirt that Sally had worn on their first date.

How he had missed his trees in prison, and his stars, only a few of which at a time could be seen through his cell window, and most of all, his white dog, whom he kept thinking he saw in the snow shadows.

The tall ash that had taken the huge side branch off the Family Tree when it fell the night Charlie visited Bagley and Oriana came out had been sawn into logs. These had been neatly stacked, as had the logs from the branches off the Family Tree. Two men were making a bonfire out of the brushwood. All our life tidied away, thought Hengist. On other trees, where branches had been sawn off, the circular scars had not closed up at the top, like horseshoes nailed to the trunk.

I could do with some luck, reflected Hengist.

Oriana coming out had been such a tiny thing compared to losing Bagley, Fleetley and Education. Although Education would have been a two-edged sword, now he fully appreciated the ruthlessness of Jupiter, who had scuppered any hope of his return to Bagley. It was some comfort that Rupert had resigned from the New Reform Party.

But none of this mattered a jot compared to losing Sally and the desolation of stretching out in bed and finding her no longer by his side and having no one to share and recapture the tragedies and triumphs and laughter of thirty years.

Above, the snow now lining the limbs of the trees was like the body lotion Sally had rubbed into her arms every day, always making herself soft and beautiful for him. He had thrown away a pearl far richer than his tribe.

The three figures of the Family Tree, although battered, were still locked together. This year's riveted olive-green buds were already formed; Hengist picked up one of the curling sepia leaves with its cherry-red stem and put it in his pocket.

' "I have lived long enough," ' he quoted wearily:

'And that which should accompany old age,
As honour, love, obedience, troops of friends,
I must not hope to have.'

Oh, he'd loved his troops of friends, but they were as nothing, again, compared with losing Sally. He had let her down, taken her for granted, betrayed her. For the first time in years, in prison, he'd had time to think.

He passed a young oak tree, planted 'In loving memory of that great scholar and schoolmaster, Theo Graham'. Hengist wished him well, free of pain in the Elysian Fields.

That must be Artie's work. The earth, although frozen, was newly dug. Artie would make a strong, wise and compassionate head.

Hengist had sent ahead a list of the books he particularly wanted and, arriving at the house, found them awaiting him in packing chests in the hall. On the hall table was a huge pile of post, including an emerald-green carrier bag with an envelope attached.

Recognizing the spiky handwriting, Hengist opened it:

> Dear Mr Brett-Taylor [Paris had written],
>
> I wanted to thank you for everything. I've just retaken history, and it was dead easy. I should get an A star, so a middle finger to Boffin Brooks. I'm staying on now that Mr Deverell's head and I'm going to work really hard to go to your old college at Cambridge. I won't have any problem with top-up fees as Theo left me everything.
>
> I'm sorry for all the trouble I caused you and Mrs B-T. Please don't take this wrong, but it meant a lot that you cared enough to cheat for me.
>
> Love from Paris
>
> PS Dora sends her love too.
>
> PPS These are for the journey.

Opening the carrier bag, Hengist found a can of Coke and some tomato sandwiches with the crusts cut off, and broke down and wept for the first time since he'd been arrested. Finally, deciding he must pull himself together, he opened a second letter, also recognizing the flashy, green scrawl.

'Dear Hengist,' Cosmo had written, 'I wonder if I could interview you for a programme I'm making for Channel 4 called *Cheating Heads*.'

And Hengist laughed until he cried, and this was how Sally found him as she tiptoed into the hall: once again the radiant, handsome, happy man she'd married. But when he turned, starting violently, she could see the deep lines of grief etching his face and that his thick, dark hair had gone completely grey.

'I didn't know you were going to be here,' he began.

'I wanted to see that everything was . . .' stammered Sally, clutching on to the front door handle for support.

Next moment the lights went out and the whole campus was plunged in darkness.

'Oh sugar, I lent the torch to Dora. She and Paris have taken Elaine for a walk.'

Jumping every time they bumped into each other, aching with longing, they found some candles in the kitchen and lit them from the gas cooker. Taking a lit candle into the drawing room to light more candles, Hengist could dimly see the snow outside tumbling down, blanketing everything in whiteness, making the ugliest shapes beautiful. Thinking sadly that he would never have cause to read it again, Hengist spread the pages of the *TES* on the remains of last night's fire. To his amazement, after few seconds, the pages leapt into flame. From the ashes, thought Hengist.

Sally brought down thick jerseys for them both. Hengist noticed her hair had been newly washed – probably not for him – and her faint, familiar scent of red roses made his senses reel as it mingled with the smell of white hyacinths in the peacock-blue bowl on the low centre table. Sally had always staggered her planting of bulbs so they brought joy throughout the dark winter.

Hengist poured them both large Armagnacs and they sat on the carpet in front of the fire, separately pondering on the impossibility of dividing up their possessions or their lives.

Take what you want, they had both written to each other. But as the firelight flickered over the room, Sally noticed the bronze greyhound Hengist had given her to celebrate Cheerful Reply's victory, which had sealed their engagement. Then all the wedding presents, the little Sickert from her father and mother, the green Victorian paperweight from David Hawkley, the Rockingham Dalmatian from Rupert Campbell-Black and his then wife, Helen. How could you cut Sickerts and greyhounds in half? Or that lovely photograph of Oriana on graduation day or of Mungo on his first day at prep school?

On the piano – had Sally been playing it? wondered Hengist – was the music for the entrance of the priests in The Magic Flute, which had been played at their wedding. Next to it was a wedding photograph of Sally looking ecstatically happy. After a second glass of Armagnac and with the warmth of the fire bringing colour to her blanched cheeks, she looked just as young and pretty as on their first date.

'I feel guilty about taking so long, when Artie must want to move in,' she said helplessly, 'but I just don't know how to divide things up.'

'I'll cut out my heart and give it to you, it's yours anyway,' said Hengist in a low voice. 'I never wanted to leave, but I'd destroyed our marriage. I'd let you down irrevocably. It was the only option. You were right to tell me to go.'

'What are you going to do?' asked Sally.

'Write, I suppose. There's Tom and Matt to finish and I might have a crack at the novel on the Fronde. I'm sure it would sell more than Alex's apparatchik lit. I got a nice letter from Transworld saying they'd be interested in my memoirs.' Then, with difficulty: 'How's Elaine?'

'She misses you appallingly, she really pined.' Sally's voice trembled. 'In her gentle way, she never complained, but I think she should go with you.'

Then the lights flickered and went on. Both Hengist and Sally scrambled to their feet, gazing at each other, both aged as though blasted by lightning, but frantic to reach out.

'Fuck, fuck, fuck,' howled Hengist as the doorbell rang.

There was a pause, followed by quick steps, then a dark head came round the door. The skin was so smooth, the big eyes so large, clear and purple-shadowed, Hengist thought at first it was a pupil returned early.

'Hello, Mum,' said Oriana, then her face lit up:

'Dad, I didn't know you were here.'

'Just going,' mumbled Hengist.

A wail from the hall made them all jump.

'I've brought Wilfred, if that's all right.'

Going out into the hall, Oriana returned with the most adorable baby, strong, deep-blue-eyed, chubby-faced, with already a down of dark hair. Sally took him in ecstasy.

'What a splendid little chap.' She gazed at him in amazement that something so wholesome and beautifully formed should emerge from such a strange, unpropitious union.

'Look at his sweet hands and his lovely skin, and I love that track suit, it must be American, they make such fun clothes. Oh Oriana, he's heavenly.'

After a minute she handed him on to Hengist.

'I hope you don't mind us giving him Hengist as a second name, Dad,' stammered Oriana.

'Not at all. Very gratifying; he's beautiful,' said Hengist in a choked voice as he gazed in wonder at his grandson.

'We chose a fantastic guy as a donor,' said Oriana, 'a baseball champion, a summa cum laude at Harvard, so Wilfie'll probably end up playing rugger for England after all.'

Profoundly relieved that her parents were taking it so well, Oriana then asked them if they'd like to come to New York for the christening next month.

'Charlie's parents are utterly spooked by the whole me and Charlie scenario,' she went on. 'You two would add a wonderful normality to the whole thing and be brilliant for my street cred.'

'Not me, surely,' said Hengist quickly.

'Hush,' said Oriana, reaching up to kiss his rigid cheek.

'Where is Charlie?' asked Sally.

'In the car.'

'She must be frozen, go and get her.'

'Only if you'll agree to come to the christening and stay on for a week or two. You both need a holiday.'

Sally didn't answer. The grandfather clock continued its jerky tick.

Outside Hengist could just make out Elaine hurtling home through the snow, kicking up a white spray like a downhill racer. But still, for him, the chasm loomed. Still Sally didn't speak; then her hand slipped into his.

'Yes, we will,' she cried joyfully, 'that would be grand, Daddy and I would simply love to be there.'

THE END

ACKNOWLEDGEMENTS

During the four years I have been writing *Wicked!*, so many people from both the maintained and independent sectors helped me, that a list of them all would be longer than the book. Most of them were insanely overworked, which made their generosity with their time and ideas all the kinder.

I should add that all were in some way experts in their field, but because *Wicked!* is a work of fiction I only took their advice in so far as it suited my plot. The end product is no reflection on their expertise.

I must start by thanking two inspired heads from the maintained sector: Virginia Frayer and Katherine Eckersley, to whom *Wicked!* is dedicated, because of their devotion to their pupils and the heroic attempts both made to save two wonderful schools, the Angel, Islington, and Village High School, Derby, from closing down.

Both Virginia and Katherine are happily now in other jobs, but at the time they talked to me for hours with great courage and allowed me access to their schools. I was also lucky to receive similar help from another inspiring head, Gill Pyatt of Barnwood Park, Gloucester. This school met a happier fate in 2005, when the Tories snatched control of Gloucestershire and with an hour to spare dramatically reversed an inexplicable decision by the County Council to close it down. To prove the point, Barnwood Park was later in the year declared the fourth most improved school in the country.

I was also made hugely welcome by two other brilliant local heads, Jo Grills of Stroud High and Vivienne Warren of Archway, who let me rove round their schools talking to pupils and witnessing inspirational teaching. Other great heads included Nigel Griffiths of John Kyrle School, Ross-on-Wye, Paul Eckersley of Selby High, Aydin Onac of Tewkesbury School, Jan Thompson of Cranham C. of E. Primary, Chris Steer of Sir Thomas Keble. I am also grateful for the shared wisdom of an awesome trio of former heads, Anthony Edkins, Jill Clough and Marie Stubbs.

The independent sector was equally helpful and I owe a massive debt of gratitude to two most humane and charming headmasters: Martin Stephen of St Paul's and Tim Hastie-Smith of Dean Close. They were always there when I needed help and gave me wise and witty advice on everything from royal visits to the endless speeches that bedevil a head at the beginning of term. In Tim's case, because Dean Close is indeed geographically close, I was allowed frequent access to his lovely school and enchanting staff and pupils.

I was also uniquely privileged to be able to pick the very considerable brains of two charismatic former heads, Dennis Silk of Radley and Ian Beer of Harrow, and to enjoy the beguiling company of Tom Weare of Bryanston, Peter Johnson of Millfield, Angus McPhail of Radley and Jennie Stephen of South Hampstead High School.

An incredibly valuable slant on school life was provided by headmasters' wives, who included Diana Silk, Angela Beer, Joanne Hastie-Smith, Joanna Seldon, by a headmistress's husband John Thompson and masters' wives Dee Brown and Emily Clark.

I would like to thank Hamish Aird, our son's Social Tutor and former Sub-Warden of Radley, for his wisdom over the years. Special gratitude is due to Colin Belford, Deputy Head of Archway, for his advice on everything and for being an absolute charmer, to Tony Marchand, Deputy Head (Academic) at Dean Close, for his help on exam procedure, and to Simon Smith, Deputy Head of Brighton College, who invited me down to his school to witness a most successful partnership scheme between the College and Falmer, a local comprehensive, which was crucial to the plot of *Wicked!* Martin Green from Brighton College, Norma Smith and Rose Styman from Falmer and both sets of pupils were also marvellously eloquent on the subject.

The teaching I witnessed on numerous occasions made me long to be back at school again. From Stroud High, Kathryn Loveridge was inspirational on the *Odes* of Horace, and Andy Webb on *Romeo and Juliet*, as was Guy Burge from the Angel, Islington, on English grammar, Steve and Ray Jones from Village High School on all aspects of GCSE history, Paul Davies from Dean Close on the Russian Revolution, Claire Matthews and John Evans from Archway respectively on *Macbeth* and football, while from Barnwood Park, Ursula Jeakins excelled in French, Gill Moseley on music and Beverley Atkinson, Head of Science, was particularly brilliant on explosions.

I also had most rewarding input from other wonderful teachers: Veronica Rock, Colin Dodds, Judith Drury, Di Medland, Dominic Hayne, Jose Hellet, Vanessa Macmillan, Anita Bradnum, Suzy Hearn, Sue Dean, who wrote a wonderful pantomime, Jill Barrow, Bob and Fran Peel, Andrew Cleary, Andrew Robinson, Vaughan Clark, Justin Nolan, Ailsa Chapman, Corinne Pierre, Trish Hillier, Carole Roome and Josephine Sutton.

In order to experience the terrors of teaching, I did give a two-hour lesson at Barnwood Park, in which I tried to explain to different groups the mysteries of writing a book and seeing it through to publication. As homework I set a task of designing a book jacket for *Wicked!* The results were fabulous and the children delightful. Nevertheless I needed to sleep for three days afterwards and was, as a result, even more overwhelmed with admiration as to how teachers can go so cheerfully through the same process day in, day out, thirty-nine weeks of the year – partly because they get such fantastic support from the non-teaching staff. On this front I'd like to thank Naomi McMahon, Marian Shergold, Margaret Turner, Clare Walsh, Brenda Dew, Ann Cave, Ali Sim and Jane Harrington for the support they in turn gave me.

I'm also grateful to those unsung heroes, the governors, who put in hours of unpaid work supporting their respective schools, and who were particularly patient in explaining the role they play. They include Peter Nesbitt, David Corbett, Deborah Priestley, Mark Westbrook and Mark Barty-King.

The true heroes of *Wicked!*, however, are the pupils. It is impossible for me to express my appreciation of those who helped me and the enthusiasm with which they entered into the whole adventure. Not a day passed without letters decorated with Pooh and Eeyore or Wallace and Gromit winging their way from Bryanston or Queen Anne's, Caversham, cataloguing the latest high jinks whilst stressing how hard everyone was working!

A stars must go to Tom Barber of Dean Close, for his marvellous run-down on life at a public school, to Carl Pearson, whose beautiful essay *My Dream* is reproduced on page 708, to Mabel McKeown and Anastasia Jennings for such entertaining dispatches from the front and to Karina Clutterbuck, who showed me how to turn an ink blob into a peacock feather.

Other pupils, who regaled me with riotous anecdotes and painstakingly initiated me into the mysteries of mocks and modules, include Henrietta Abel-Smith, Phoebe Adler, Jenny Frings, Alana Nash, Sam Muskett,

Georgia Morgan, Georgie Klein, Jessica Seldon, Kit Cooper, Frankie Hildick-Smith, Ned Wyndham, Max Morgan, Teddy Chadd, Theo Hodson, Freddie Miles, Robbie McColl, Sarah Kilmister, James Bowler, Harriet Manners, Georgie Clarkson-Webb, Leo Robson, James Merry, Michael Dhenin, Sam Rogerson, Dean Monahan, Charmaine Moss, Michelle Pickering, Lauren Doble, Harry Flinder, Natalie Torr, Carmelita Winslow, Anthony Scott and many others.

I cannot emphasize too strongly how genuinely bright and good-hearted these children were and would like to stress that although pupils, teachers, parents and supporting cast behave by turns heroically and simply dreadfully in *Wicked!*, no character is based on anyone living. Any coincidence is accidental, unless they are as eminent as Her Majesty the Queen or Lord Puttnam and appear as themselves.

I was lucky enough to be invited on four occasions by Lord Puttnam to one of the happiest events in the school calendar, the National Teaching Awards. Here I enjoyed great teaching, was beautifully looked after by Carolyn Taylor and Sarah Davey and revelled in the company of the Awards' irrepressible anchorman Eamonn Holmes and BBC producer, Kate Shiers. I hope I will be forgiven for inserting an extra category into the 2004 Awards.

A hugely enjoyable event in the independent calendar was the 2004 Headmasters' Conference in St Andrews, where I stayed at the lovely St Andrews Bay Hotel and found myself in the company of Titans. Here I would like to thank Martin Stephen for inviting me and Roger Peel and Chris Addy for their wonderful organization.

A large section of *Wicked!* is taken up with all aspects of GCSE, which I found unbelievably complicated, particularly when I introduced a mature student. I must thank Helen Claridge, Moira Gage, the exam officer of Stroud High, Cathie Shovlin of OCR, Madeleine

Fowler and Yvonne Hutchinson-Ruff of Stroud College. They were all heroic in their attempts to explain things. I hope the liberties I've taken aren't too flagrant.

Education has many luminaries supporting it from the outside, so I am equally grateful to Margaret Davies of Capita, who came in like Red Adair in a skirt to galvanize the LEA in Gloucestershire, to Andrew Flack, Director of Education at Derby City Council, to Dr Judy Coultars, Human Centre Technology Group, University of Sussex, to Jonquil Dodd, Senior Research Officer (Performance) Gloucestershire Education; and from Gloucestershire Social Services: Margaret Sheather, Executive Director, Alan Barton, Complaints Manager and Cathie Shea, Looked-After-Children Manager of Gloucestershire Social Services, Pat Gifford, Education Liaison Officer, Gloucestershire Children and Young People's Services, and to the staff of the former Causeway Care Home, Stroud. All nobly gave me their time.

I also had wonderful advice from Anne Clark, Lib Dem Councillor for Cotswold District Council and from Tory Councillors Jackie Hall and Andrew Gravells of Gloucestershire County Council who were both hugely instrumental in saving Barnwood Park School from closure in the nick of time.

My characters, both human and animal, sometimes fall ill and make miraculous recoveries, so I was lucky to be able to consult Dr Laurence Fielder and Dr Tim Crouch at Frithwood Surgery and John Hunter and his team at Bowbridge Veterinary Surgery. Carole Lee and Judy Zatonski from Greyhound Rescue, West of England and the Celia Cross Trust inspired me on Greyhounds.

I needed an exciting team-building activity in *Wicked!* to unite my two schools when they first meet. Hazel Heron of Roedean suggested I spoke to Ian Davies of Pinnacle Training, who in turn suggested a brilliant competition when groups of pupils compete to be the first to build and fly a hot air balloon.

There is a lot of rugger in *Wicked!* Here I got wonderful assistance from Matthew Evans of BBC Cardiff, David and Justine Pickering, Ralph Bucknell, Phil Butler and in particular from Stephanie Metson, Marketing Manager of the beautiful Vale Hotel, Glamorgan, known as the Lucky Hotel, because subsequently successful teams so often hole up there before big games. Stephanie showed me the vast indoor arena and entertained me royally.

On the sartorial front Robert Hartop of Grooms Formal Hire, Andoversford, initiated me into the latest fashion in men's evening wear, while Mariska Kay and Lindka Cierach advised me on lovely women's clothes. Duncan Armstrong, my bank manager at Coutts, and Stephen Foakes, my former bank manager, were brilliant on money. Dear Stephen Simpson of Hatchards is again to be hugely thanked for tenaciously tracking down any books I needed. Sounds Good of Cheltenham did the same for CDs. I am extremely grateful too to the resourceful and unflappable Phil Bradley of Cornerstones for driving me from school to school.

I am also indebted to Diane Law at Manchester United, Andrew Yeatman at the Met Office, Marc Stevens at the LSO for answering complicated queries and to Mike Zealey of ISIS, Lyn Sweeney and Sarah Hutchens for checking facts.

Gloucestershire police, as always, have been marvellous, answering my endless questions with patience, humour and imagination. I'd particularly like to thank Inspector Chris Hill for his advice on royal visits, Marie Watton, DC Liz Smith and Child Protection Officer DC Ian Bennett.

Last year saw the tragic, untimely death of Gil Martin, horse and lurcher lover and ex-super sleuth of Gloucestershire CID, who for fifteen years had advised me on all matters criminal. Gil was a brilliant, kind, enchanting man, whose loss to his family and legion of friends is immeasurable.

One of my heroes in *Wicked!* spends twelve years in care. On a train to Swindon, I was therefore very lucky to meet Josephine Cook, who told me most movingly about her experiences as a foster child. I am also grateful to Phil Frampton and Paolo Hewitt who each survived heartbreakingly harrowing childhoods in care to produce marvellous memoirs: *The Golly in the Cupboard* and *The Looked After Kid* respectively. Both books were an inspiration and both men, I'm proud to think, have become friends.

I am also beholden to the authors of the following books which provided both enlightenment and factual background: *Ahead of the Class* by Marie Stubbs, *Handsworth Revolution* by David Winkley, *But Headmaster!* by Ian Beer, *Why Schools Fail* by Jill Clough, *Special* by Bella Bathurst and the invaluable *Good Neighbours* by the Independent Schools Council.

Journalists do not automatically expect kindness from their own profession. Few, however, could have been more charming and helpful than Sarah Bayliss, editor of *The Times Educational Supplement*'s *Friday Magazine*, Rachel Johnson, Julie Henry, Amelia Hill, Geraldine Hackett, Quentin Letts, Chris Bunting, Will Woodward, Jo Scriven and Fay Millar of the Brighton *Argus*. I must also thank *The Times Educational Supplement*, who produce enough good stories every week to furnish a hundred novels, for keeping me up with events. Our local press were also an endless support. Ian Mean of *The Citizen*, Anita Syvret of the *Gloucestershire Echo*, Skip Walker, former editor, and Sue Smith, present editor of the *Stroud News & Journal*, so often paved the way for me with local schools.

Gold stars must especially go to *Guardian* writer Jonathan Freedland and Wendy Wallace of *Friday Magazine* whose moving pieces on the imminent closing of the Angel, Islington, and the rejuvenation of Village High School, Derby, sowed the seeds of so much of *Wicked!*

My friends, as usual, deserve straight As. Caterina Krucker, a lecturer in modern languages, was a shining example of the passion and effort that goes into preparing and delivering a great lesson. Edward Thring was magisterial on bursars, Marcus Clapham great on Greece, Pete Hendy on Ofsted and anything scientific, Andrew Parker Bowles on racing and Bill Holland on music. Peter Clarkson, Associate Lecturer on Art History at the Open University, lent me endless books and his marvellous thesis on the concept of chivalry and mediaevalism in Cheltenham public school architecture, and Paul Morrison was illuminating on developers. John and Anne Cooper valiantly tried to untangle the red tape of education law. Jo Xuereb-Brennan was dazzling on acronyms. My brother Timothy Sallitt and his wife Angela were funny as ever on everything. Other friends who came up with great ideas include Shona Williams, Jill Reay, David Fyfe-Jamieson, Derick Davin, Jane Workman, Peregrine Hodson, Marion Carver, Tim Griffiths, Susannah and Bill Franklyn, Sue Lauzier, Jane Farrow, Bill Holland, Liz and Michael Flint, Rosemary Nunneley, William and Caroline Nunneley, Marjorie Dent, Heather Ross, Anna Gibbs-Kennet, Rupert Miles, Roz Murray-Smith, Anna Wing, Janetta Lee, Joyce Ball and Karina Gabner.

I must also apologize to all the people who helped me who I have forgotten to include.

My marvellous publishers Transworld are a constant joy to deal with and I was particularly touched that Gail Rebuck, Larry Finlay and Patrick Janson-Smith kept in touch during the long haul, and never chided me for delivering late.

At the risk of adjectival overkill, I am convinced I have the sweetest, most encouraging editor in Linda

Evans, the nicest, most charismatic publicity directors in Nicky Henderson and Patsy Irwin and the kindest, wisest, most cheering-up agent in Vivienne Schuster of Curtis Brown. No author is so blessed. Nor should Laura Gammell, Anneliese Bridges and Stephanie Thwaites who assist them, be forgotten. Nor Richenda Todd, my brilliant copy-editor, and Deborah Adams, who gave splendid help at proof stage.

On the home front, it is hard to describe my gratitude to my PA Pam Dhenin for masterminding the production of such a vast ungainly manuscript. I thank her for her tolerance, huge encouragement and for never complaining about my appallingly indecipherable writing as draft after endless draft was followed by interminable corrections and checking. Great chunks of the manuscript were also typed equally brilliantly and heroically by Annette Xuereb-Brennan, Mandy Williams, Pippa Birch and Zoë Dhenin, who all deserved A stars for pitching in with suggestions, and producing the most beautiful typescript at phenomenal speed. Zoë Dhenin is also to be thanked for checking endless facts and tracking down everything from hotels in Baghdad to Croatian Christian names.

Other A stars should be awarded to my wonderful housekeeper Ann Mills and to dear Moira Hatherall, who restore order out of chaos, prevent the house disappearing under a tidal wave of paper and provide so much comfort and laughter.

Most of all I must thank my sweet family for putting up with force ten sighs and utter neglect for months on end. My husband Leo, our son Felix and his wife Edwina, our daughter Emily and her husband Adam Tarrant, our grandson Jago, and five excellent cats, all provide an essential mix of love, fantastic copy and endless good cheer.